Born in Melbourne, Patricia Shaw has worked as a teacher, a political journalist and an oral historian, but gave this up to pursue a literary career. Having won awards for her poetry and short stories, Patricia went on to write her first book, and *Brother Digger* was published in Australia in 1984. This was followed by *Pioneers of a Trackless Land*, *Valley of Lagoons*, *River of the Sun*, *The Feather and the Stone*, *Where the Willows Weep*, *Cry of the Rain Bird*, *Fires of Fortune*, *The Opal Seekers*, *The Glittering Fields*, *A Cross of Stars*, *Orchid Bay* and *Waiting for the Thunder*.

Patricia lives on the beautiful Gold Coast of Australia, enjoying the beaches and subtropical lifestyle. She has two children and two grandchildren and her other interests are reading and research, as well as being a devoted fan of native birds. She is a life member of the Animal Welfare Association.

D0881813

The
Dream Seekers

Patricia Shaw

headline

First published in 2001
by HEADLINE BOOK PUBLISHING

First published in paperback in 2002
by HEADLINE BOOK PUBLISHING

10 9 8 7 6 5 4 3 2

ISBN 0 7472 6850 9

Typeset by Avon Dataset Ltd, Bidford-on-Avon, Warks

Printed and bound in Great Britain by
Mackays of Chatham, Chatham, Kent

HEADLINE BOOK PUBLISHING
A division of Hodder Headline PLC
338 Euston Road
London NW1 3BH

www.headline.co.uk
www.hodderheadline.com

For John and Wendy Daniher,
Margaret and Lorraine,
In memory of Julia.

Part One

Chapter One

'Murder!'

The night seemed to reverberate with menace. A cleric, shivering from the cold, stayed in the nightwatchman's shed listening to the thump of boots on wet timbers as men ran past, their curiosity and anxiety causing them to call out through the fog as they neared the crowd milling about the dark, anonymous lane. It was almost as if they felt there was a crevasse ahead, a crevasse into which they might fall blindly if they didn't keep calling, lowing, feeling their way, for no one was bothering to answer them. Let them come, find out for themselves, no raised voices down here, only whispers in the grey gloom, as if not to wake or offend the dead. The men, the onlookers, grouped and regrouped, shuffling, spitting, waiting, pipe-smoking, warm breath blowing on cold hands, caps low on creased foreheads, eyes flicking about nervously, suspiciously.

The same questions reissued as newcomers folded into the groups and others drifted silently away, nothing more to see.

'A body! They found a body! Murdered. Down this here lane. In the old grain store.'

'What body? What happened to him? Who is . . . was he?'

'Got done in. Bashed something cruel. Throat slit too.'

'Never! My mate seen him. Never got his throat cut. 'Twas whacks about the head done it. Smashed his face and all.'

'Poor bloke, probably never knew what hit him. Where are you going?'

3

'To have a look.'

'No one goes down there now. The Inspector says keep out.'

'Who was he? The one got murdered.'

'I dunno. Not from round here. A sailor maybe.'

'No. I heard he was an actor.'

'Who says? An actor! Where'd you get that from? An actor! What next!'

'It's true. I heard them talking, the watchmen.'

'Did they catch the villains?'

'Not likely. Not round these parts. More footpads than true folk.'

'Who found the body?'

'A couple of whores looking for a snug corner. They fetched the watch. They fetched the Inspector and along comes a preacher.'

'In the nick of time?'

'Only if prayers for the dead work. The preacher, he knew the dead man. Identified him.'

'That'd be a shock.'

'Not to preachers. They get to see deaduns all the time. Nigh as many as soldiers.'

'And if they went to war they'd have seen more than anyone.'

'Ah, shut up, Bert. Go on home.'

'He's a turn, that Bert! What was a preacher doing hanging about the docks at this hour, anyway?'

'Boarding the ship, *Clovis*. She sails tonight. He's down there in the shed. Take your questions to him.'

That wasn't an option. The yellow lantern over the tavern door beckoned fuzzily from the opposite direction.

They heard a light cart clatter away from the other end of the lane, the morgue collection cart they supposed, so the excitement was over.

The last of the heavy figures melted into the fog as Inspector Backhaus strode out of the lane with his watchmen, glad that that was over. He would be home by nine, in time for a hot supper with the family before the fire in the stove died. There'd be no more wood left. The wood carters

4

had refused to deliver any more to his rooms until the bill was paid.

He gave a snort of anger, causing his two companions to smarten their steps, anxious to please lest he blame them for allowing yet another crime to be uncovered in his bailiwick. But what could they have done about this? Even the Inspector, seconded from the military to the Sector for the Protection of Citizens and Seafarers in the Vicinity of the Docks, as their new division was known, had admitted that the murder must have been committed elsewhere. The lantern search had not revealed any blood on the rotting floorboards, only drag marks in the dust.

They'd all stood and stared then, at the narrow gloomy streets and the rabbit warren of tenements, some five storeys high, that crouched above them, the haunt of felons, muggers and smugglers alike. Home too of the destitute and degenerate, all of them a danger to legitimate citizenry, including the inmates of inns and lodging houses waiting nervously for the call to board their ships. It was as if this sweep of humanity had come to a dead end here, by the deep swell of the harbour, and had simply sunk in, allowing only the fortunate few to escape.

Backhaus snarled at them: 'Someone must have brought him here! If you'd kept your eyes open you'd have seen someone acting suspiciously. Or don't you think humping a dead body around looks suspicious?'

They knew better than to point out that these cobbled lanes and underpasses leading to the wharves were a maze. Shadowy locales even in daylight. They couldn't patrol them all, all the time. Watchman Fritz had told the Inspector that a month ago, and had been sacked on the spot. Backhaus was a hard man. When poor Bruno Fischer was attacked by muggers who took his lantern, he'd had no sympathy for him either. The way the Inspector had carried on you'd have thought Bruno himself had committed a crime.

'Losing a lantern,' the Inspector had said, 'is akin to a soldier losing his weapon.'

The watchmen hadn't known what to make of that. Bewildered, they had discussed this revelation. Was it a crime for a soldier to lose his musket? They hadn't known that. Damn harsh, they thought. Anyone could lose a gun, misplace it, have it stolen, especially in what they imagined would be the chaos of war. But a lantern akin to a gun? The cosh maybe. Their only weapon.

No doubt this inspector was a bit mad. Nasty-tempered too. Best to keep on his good side. They almost sniggered, just then, when he slipped on the wet, warped timbers, but saved himself from falling on his arse by a flip worthy of an acrobat, so that his left hand took the weight and restored balance. His right hand couldn't have helped. It hung near to useless, the result of sabre slashes, wounds, they'd heard, that cut deeper than the flesh. Wounds that had severed him from the military and dumped him on the wharves, a sour, embittered man.

They were not to know that their boss had been promoted in the field only days before he was wounded, but the promotion had not appeared on his discharge papers. No matter his protests that he was in fact no longer a junior officer but an officer second class and therefore entitled to a pension, his cause was lost.

Backhaus himself hated this job but he dared not quit, with no other employment on offer. He couldn't support his family on the pittance he was paid, far less, he'd soon discovered, than the amount quoted to him by the clerk at the port offices. All he had, in fact, was a fine-sounding title for a role that equated with head watchman, and a bundle of debts, so he retaliated by bullying his men to give the impression of iron discipline; and by falsifying records.

Kristian Backhaus didn't care how many people were robbed, murdered or press-ganged in his sector, as long as his records showed that under his direction the crime rate was decreasing. On paper it was doing just that, at a very satisfactory pace, enough for him to be noticed by his superiors and mentioned for, perhaps, more senior responsibilities.

He stopped to light a cheroot. 'Where's this fellow?'

'The preacher, sir? He's up there in the shed. He wants to get going. Got to get aboard his ship.'

'He'll go when I say he can and not before. Bring him over to my office.

'Office,' he muttered to himself. 'More like a cell than an office.' He'd been spared a cold, dank room at the rear of the Customs House, large enough for his desk, a few chairs by the door and a honeycomb of shelving behind him containing district maps, some so old they pre-dated the Great Fire. The musty smell that exuded from the place was so overpowering that Backhaus was occasionally tempted to arrange an 'accidental' fire of his own.

He hurried across the road and on down the long flight of stone steps to this office, to settle himself at his desk before the fellow was delivered to him. This preacher. This interfering fool who'd come barging into the grain store at the behest of those screeching whores who had found the body, and then identified it. Damned bad luck that was. Requiring paperwork. If this preacher had kept out, the body in the morgue could have been just a number, forgotten. Nothing to do with his sector. Now, though . . . it was more complicated. That corpse, brought in from God knows where, didn't belong in these records at all. It could have been overlooked, should have been overlooked . . .

He was busy with quill and ink when the preacher edged in the door, dragging a bulging valise.

'Sir. I have told you all I know. I am deeply saddened by the death of that poor gentleman, but I must be on my way.' He clung to the valise as if it were an anchor, needed to steady him.

Backhaus waved the watchmen out and concentrated on the citizen. He was tall, about twenty-five years of age, with the spoiled white hands befitting his calling . . . fine features except for the sharpness of the nose. His hair and moustache, both in need of a decent cut, were reddish-brown. He was almost handsome, one might say, the Inspector mused, were it not for the weakness betrayed by his manner, since the fellow spoke with a cavernous, dirge-like voice and kept his eyes cast down. His calling again, the Inspector presumed, noting the bowed head and the knee ready to bend in supplication. But what could you expect? The

7

strong went into the military; the weak yielded to the Church.

He was cleanly dressed, though, in the accepted black hat and cassock and good buckled shoes, a size or more too big. Probably hand-me-downs.

'Name?' barked Backhaus, and the preacher jumped.

'Pastor Friedrich Ritter.'

'You may be seated. Occupation?'

'Sir, as you may note, I am a priest.'

'Denomination?'

'Lutheran. I have recently been ordained, having completed my studies at St John's Seminary here in Hamburg.'

'Yes. Yes. The name of the deceased?' Inspector Backhaus was taking notes on a sheet of paper that, for now, was lodged within an open journal. Too soon to commit them irreparably to the journal itself.

'Otto Haupt.'

'His occupation?'

'I do believe he was a person of the stage.'

'What? A mummer? A juggler? What?'

'A Thespian, I believe. I did not know him very well.'

The priest glanced about him in desperation, as if hoping for rescue, but the Inspector continued.

'I'm surprised you knew him at all. How did your paths cross?'

Ritter sighed. 'I was staying at a lodging house in Canal Street, an unpleasant place but all I could afford. I wanted to stay close to the wharves because my ship was due to sail, but they kept delaying departure for reasons best known to the Captain, though of no relevance here. I took my meals at a tavern further down Canal Street, and there I met Mr Haupt. He seemed a cut above the characters who inhabit the tavern so I was glad of his company . . . if only for safety's sake. Dear God, here I am thinking of myself, and poor Mr Haupt . . .'

'You were saying?'

'We had a good talk over supper, but when it came time to pay, I discovered that Mr Haupt had no money.'

It was the Inspector's turn to sigh.

'So I had to pay for both of us. As it turned out, Mr Haupt

had fallen on bad times. He was hoping to work his passage on a ship to London, where, he said, there are opportunities aplenty for stage people.'

'Did he come from around here?'

'No. He did not. I'm sure of that. I'm very nervous, sir, what with this terrible murder and the necessity for me to get to my ship. He may have said where he came from, I simply can't recall.'

'Where was he lodging?'

'He had no lodgings. He asked me for money but I could give him none. I saw him again the next day, and, taking pity on him, invited him to my room to share some bread and sausage and a warming glass of wine. It is a sad reflection of the times that Otto Haupt repaid me by stealing my cloak. It was a sturdy cloak too, excellent cloth, given to me as a farewell gift . . .'

'Probably what got him killed.' The Inspector shrugged. 'So your Mr Haupt was just a plain thief. Probably not an actor either. A villain preying on your naïveté. You should be more careful. Don't be so trusting in the future.'

'Excuse me, sir, but I really must take my leave. My ship is sailing for Australia. The fare is costly. I must board or I shall never—'

'What did you say? Where are you going?'

'Australia, sir. Aboard *Clovis* . . . she's a fine ship, a three-master. She will be getting under way soon.'

The Inspector's thin moustache twitched as if a fly had tried to settle under his nose, and his stern face gave way to a smile.

'Australia? My dear fellow. Why didn't you say so? You can't afford to miss that ship. Good God, no. You're voyaging to the other side of the world!'

He jumped up, and dashed about his desk to assist the gentle priest on his way. Rang the brass bell that hung outside his door. *Clang. Clang. Clang.* Which brought one of his watchmen running.

'Here! Take the Father to his ship. See that he gets safely on board. Carry that valise for him. I do apologise for having delayed you, Father. I pray you have a safe and pleasant voyage. Farewell to you now.'

9

The burly watchman whisked the preacher away into the darkness, and the Inspector waited patiently in the rectangle of light to make certain Ritter was indeed safely on his way to the Antipodes without knowing, or remembering, that it was usual for people, witnesses, to sign their statements. Then, well satisfied, Backhaus stepped back inside. No crime had been committed in his district as far as he was concerned, beyond the dumping of a corpse. There was no place in his records for this incident. The dead man was a common thief of no fixed address, identified by a fellow en route to the ends of the earth. A simple matter to forget them both.

He took his greatcoat from its hook, wondering why anyone would chance the great oceans to travel to a foreign continent like Australia. No matter. That was their problem. Things were hard enough here without venturing past the boundaries of civilisation. He tore up the notes he'd been taking. Time to go home.

Chapter Two

The eyes that gazed into the small mirror were grey-green, with flecks of gold, but dark-rimmed and steady. They were not the eyes of a weak man; they were too cold, too self-assured. They glinted into a grin as he swayed with the roll of the ship then plunged the few steps across the tiny cabin so that he could attach the mirror to a nail on the wall. Now he had to bend to see into it, but it would do. He addressed the face that confronted him.

'Well now, Pastor Ritter, here we are! Not much of a cabin, not even a porthole, but at least we've got it to ourselves. Fancy you travelling second class. The churches have got more money than the king. The least they could have done was send their apostle off in some comfort. But then I suppose comfort's for the bishops, and you're only small fry. Too mesmerised by their holinesses to kick up a fuss. It's a wonder you don't go in for flagellation as well. Or do you?

'Anyway, we got on board all right. No trouble at all. Easy as pie. So we might as well unpack.'

He dumped the valise on the narrow bunk and undid the straps to open it, lifting out a cloak that had been stuffed on top.

'I was freezing but I couldn't wear it,' he laughed, 'and I wasn't about to leave it behind. It *is* a fine cloak. A gift, you said. And stolen from you by that felon Haupt. A terrible man, desperately in need of God's forgiveness. But don't feel bad, Friedrich. You tried. You fed him. You prayed with him. You did your best. Only you should never have turned your back on him. Bad mistake. You just weren't up to the challenge, even though you'd spent years studying, to prepare you for the world.'

He turned to peer into the mirror again. 'Are you listening, Freddy? You don't mind me calling you Freddy, do you? "Pastor" seems too stilted now. You see, you have no real experience of the world. God knows how you would have fared in the Antipodes. Probably got eaten by a tiger in the first week. Or dumped into the sea by another Otto Haupt. You're altogether too trusting. And too enthusiastic as a brand-new, paid-up member of the Lutheran clergy. Bursting with goodness and light, believing everything you're told.

'And then you run into Otto. We'll call him that, though it's not his real name, nor his stage name.'

He began rifling through the valise, tossing out items of clothing.

'But some of what he said was true. He was an actor, a Thespian, and a damned good one too, though those clods of theatre managers couldn't tell the good from the bad. And true, he had fallen on hard times. He was in desperate straits. Desperate because he had escaped from your disgusting Hamburg prison . . . a small matter of robbery under arms . . . but that is of no relevance to us. He was trying to get to England, but you were so keen to tell him all about the new world that you were off to, that so many of our people were migrating to, that you talked him into it. You really did. Made it sound like the Garden of Eden.'

He threw aside slippers with socks tucked into them, and neat folds of cravats, shirts and underdrawers, and picked up some books to find a large cloth bag hidden underneath.

'Ah! What have we here?' As he untied the drawstring on the bag, his monologue continued.

'So. Otto thought, why not get the hell away altogether? Excuse my language. We'll have to watch that, won't we? But poor Otto didn't have the money for a feed, let alone a ticket to the other end of the world, the shiny new world you were bragging about. And the more he thought about it, the more he knew this was his destiny. You can understand that, can't you, Friedrich? You practically showed him the way. You put temptation before him. And right outside your door in that

12

dark alleyway was the fishmonger's barrow, left there until the early morn, just perfect for that swift run down to the grain store. Actually, that was where Otto had been sleeping nights because he couldn't afford lodgings.'

The bag contained two cheap leather pocketbooks. The first held only papers and the second letters and documents, but in the bottom of the bag was a purse.

'Hello! By the weight, I think we've struck gold. Ah, yes . . .' He counted the coins on to the bare straw mattress.

'We've got sixty marks here, Freddy and you claiming to be a poor man.' Could only spare Otto a feed! Shame on you. But now a question comes to mind. Where the hell . . . I mean, where on God's earth is this place you speak of? Across an ocean somewhere. But which ocean? And how long does it take to get to your dream land?'

There was a tap on the door, and he opened it to find two seamen with a wooden trunk.

'Yours, Pastor Ritter?'

'Indeed it is. Yes. There's the name on it, plain to see. Just push it in here.' He smiled broadly, a practised winning smile that caused his eyes to twinkle.

'Thank you, gentlemen, thank you kindly. By the way, Australia. What port do we land at?'

'Town of Maryborough, Father.'

'And how long will the voyage take?'

The older seaman elected to be spokesman. 'Now let's see. *Clovis*, she's a fast ship. She ought to make it, all being well, in three months, give or take a week or so. Yes, about that. February it'll be, Father.'

He closed the door behind them. 'Did you hear that?' he hissed. 'Are they mad? Am I on a ship of fools? Racing about the seas for months on end. That can't be right. And what's in this chest? What does a preacher need with a trunkful of clothes?'

But there wasn't much in the way of clothes, except for nightshirts and caps. It was mainly books . . . bibles, and tomes on spiritual guidance, Lutheran prayer books and hymn books and theological essays . . . packed and pushed in among household goods: bed linen, cutlery, plates, small lamps,

13

kitchen pans and even a decorated china pot. He grinned and set this last on the floor.

'You're travelling like a young bride, Freddy, but at least some of this stuff will make us comfortable. The bed linen for a start. I haven't seen clean sheets for an age.'

Still searching, he came up with some beautifully embroidered altar cloths, carefully packed with priestly vestments.

'I'll have to try them on. I think I like the white best. But we'll do that another time. I'd better repack this lot carefully; one always has to look after the costumes. But Jesus, Freddy! They could at least have given you some altar wine to take along.'

He closed the trunk and left it by the wall to act as a table, then he kicked at it.

'Christ! Months in this rocking box. A man could go stark staring mad stuck on this ship for that long. Clipper ships are supposed to be fast. Just our luck to be aboard the slowest of the bunch, with crazed sailors boasting of its speed.'

He heard the muffled notes of a foghorn and the sharp ring of ship's bells, and slumped on to the bunk with a groan. 'We're still sailing down river, we've hardly moved an inch if we're to measure this voyage in terms of time. Months! Maybe we should jump ship at the first port. I ought to get up top and find out what's happening. Yes, that's what I'll do.'

Carefully dressed again, with the cloak now folded regally about him, he rummaged about until he found the round velour hat – black, of course – that signified a man of God, then he stood at the door, in the wings you could say, preparing himself for the stage. He bowed his head, clasped his hands together, bent at the knees and stood with his toes turned in a little, as if he were pigeon-toed. His voice he lowered to a more genteel pitch, the accent more polished, and he added a singsong whine, as if from the pulpit.

'Good evening, madam, sir. How do you do? Ah, bless you, kind sir. A fine night indeed. A favourable wind, would you say?'

He rehearsed the lines over and over until he was satisfied, then he put on the black hat, pulling it down to meet his eyebrows for a serious and sanctimonious demeanour, and

14

ventured forth, a shy, humble pastor greatly in need of advice from seasoned travellers.

When he returned to his cabin he was flustered. 'We're not stopping anywhere. Not until we reach the Canary Islands. And do you know where they are? Off the coast of Africa. Africa! What sort of a crazy expedition is this? We have to pass a dozen ports to get right down there. French ports, Spanish ports, where I could have slipped ashore and disappeared into the night. But word is there's no stopping. Not even to restock the larders. There are a lot of people on board this ship, I can tell you that for a fact, so I hope there's enough food to go round.

'I got out there in time for dinner, which they serve in one long refectory, catch as catch can, with kids scrambling all over the place and their fathers shoving to get their greedy hands on every platter as it comes out of the kitchen and the women bustling around trying to make sense of it all. A real bunfight it was. But wait. Guess who got pride of place? Me! Yours truly. See . . . God favours the meek after all. Because I did loiter in the accepted holy manner. But then again, I think it was my priestly garb that did the trick.

'Room was made for the pastor. And how they all fussed! I haven't had such a nice time since my old man fell off his horse, skidded down a riverbank and got himself drowned. Being an orphan was good for a while. It didn't last, though, they soon forgot me and I was on the streets at ten, fending for myself. But listen, Friedrich, I'm damned sure this time the kindnesses will last. A lot of those passengers are scared out of their wits about this voyage, they won't be wanting to offend a priest, someone who will be able to talk to God direct, on their behalf.'

He laughed. 'I gave the situation a little push along when they asked me to say grace, reminding them of the mighty winds and seas, and the shipwrecks and drownings . . . one lady even swooned . . . that lay ahead if they didn't put their trust in the Lord. It was funny to watch. I really put a stop to the disorder, they all behaved like little mice after my prayers. The waiters, they call themselves stewards, could get on with

15

their jobs then. They were very grateful for my intervention. So . . . I had some soup, ham and tongue, sour bread and beer. Supper is on at nine, coffee and a packet of sandwiches each. I'll be there, not a penny to pay. This isn't such a bad life after all. I think I'll take a nap until then.'

The next morning he explored the ship thoroughly. The overcrowded steerage class reminded him of the many foul slums he'd endured over the years, and he turned away very quickly. He was amazed to find hen coops, sheep and cows in small pens, pantries heaped with vegetables and dried meat and vats of basic groceries.

'Like being on the bloody Ark,' he muttered sourly.

Then he began the climb aloft, ignoring the 'No Thoroughfare' signs and taking himself on into the first-class section; strolling the windy decks, prayer book in hand, admiring from under lowered lids all the beautiful people who passed him by, and appreciating the elegance of the deckchairs and tables, set out there under a canvas roof. Appreciation turned to envy when he went down a few steps to see the sheer luxury of the lounges and saloons that these people enjoyed. He peered into cabins by boldly opening doors, apologising, pretending mistakes, then wandered into a music room, past a polished piano, to study the books lining one wall, irritated beyond measure.

On a table he found a discarded menu that spoke of the previous night's dinner, and stood, shocked. It offered six courses, several choices, various wines and cheeses, a menu as splendid as one would find in a leading city restaurant. And these people could freely partake of such largesse, day in and day out! He went in search of the dining room, and sure enough the tables were all set aglitter in preparation for their lunch.

An officer approached him. 'Can I assist you, Reverend?'

'Yes. I appear to be lost.'

'I see. Then let me escort you to your cabin. You are in second class, I believe.'

'That is correct. But these passages are a maze. Could you tell me where we are now? The ship, I mean.'

16

'We're approaching the mouth of the Elbe, and soon we will be out in the North Sea.'

'Then what?'

'We head south into warmer climes, Father.'

'Ah yes. Of course.'

They were descending flights of steps to the lower orders, the Pastor noted, irritated. 'What language do they speak in Australia?' he asked.

'Mostly English. The natives have their own language.'

'No German?'

'Very little.'

'What a pity.'

'Once everyone has settled down, we arrange English lessons in each class. Twice a week. They are a great help to people.'

He drew himself up to retort: 'I am fairly proficient in English already, thank you.' Although he knew exactly where he was, he looked about him as if bewildered. 'Now where are we?'

The officer opened a door and, with a glance at the sign overhead, pointed ahead. 'Your cabin is down there, on this deck, Reverend. You really must not come past this door, it is forbidden to second-class passengers.'

'Goodness me, so it is.' He padded quietly away, the hand with the prayer book clutching the handrail, the other pressed to his chest as if to hold his cloak about him.

'Cabin!' he muttered, not for the first time. He knew now that it was only a partition, that above him were superb cabins, fit for a prince.

Still he marched in with a smile. 'Wait until you see what I've got here, Freddy!'

With a dramatic gesture he flung back his cloak to reveal a wine bottle shoved down the front of his waistcoat.

'Pinched it from a rack in the dining room, the upper-crust dining room, Friedrich. I'll bet you've never seen anything like it in your life. Poor chap. But Otto had. He'd dined in the best of them, fêted he was, by nobs, ladies and gents alike. Once you get a taste of that life, it's hard, damned hard, to sink back into poverty, so you have to start fighting, see. Nothing

17

to do with your sins and sinning and all that business about evil ways you peddle. Nothing at all. Times were hard, theatres closed, not much work even for a good actor, so Otto had to make his own luck.'

He rummaged in the trunk and came up with a corkscrew. Soon he was settled on the bunk, swigging from the bottle.

'A tasty brew, my friend. Bloody good! And to think it was just chosen at random, so to speak. But listen, did you know they don't speak German in that outlandish country? Only native and English. So . . .' He waved the bottle about knowingly. 'That puts me one up on you. I speak English rather well. I fell in with an English Shakespearean actor, and he taught me. We used to do scenes in English for the nobs at private soirées and house parties. They were very much in fashion for a while but never paid much, so he wandered off, back to England, I think.

'You don't believe me? Listen to this . . . "*But trust me gentlemen, I'll prove more true, Than those that have more cunning to be strange.*" Rather fitting, don't you think, Freddy? Really funny. Though somehow I don't believe you have much of a wit for comedy. Not even the bawdies. I rather enjoy ribaldry, it's great fun to perform, and those sort of audiences love it . . . the dirtier the better. But it's home for clowns, no place for the serious *artiste*, unless, like poor Otto . . . Well, never mind about him now. He's gone.

'Today, Freddy, *my good chap* . . . ignore that, I'm practising the English . . . we have work to do. I've been looking through these books of yours. Filing, you could say.

'First, I'm pleased to note that you have English grammars and a dictionary. So you did know we'd need English? Good man, they'll be very helpful. I'm not going to their lessons. We'll have our own lessons in here. Every day.

'Next . . . the tools of our trade. No shortage here. I suppose you had to study all of these books, from the Bible on? Sorry, but we're going to have to start all over again. I want to know what's in them. I have to know, don't I? Not that I give a shit, pardon me, about your religious theories, but it is obvious that I will have to lead prayers and propound

18

on the Lutheran ... I know ... nonconformist ideology. Sermonise, in fact.

'Now, Friedrich, you may know your catechism, but I'd beat you hands down from a pulpit.' He flung out his arms: ' *"All the world's a stage, And all the men and women merely players"* ... I just need the lines, and we'll find them in your good books.

'Next we come to all these bits and pieces you're carting about. Portraits of you with people ... keepsakes, how nice. But you won't need them any more.'

He tore them all up and threw the pieces into a bin.

'Letters of introduction, yes, we'll need them. Family letters, no.'

As he sifted through the papers, he finally came upon a directive from the dean of the Lutheran seminary setting out Pastor Ritter's appointment.

He was to proceed in the clipper ship *Clovis* to the port of Maryborough in the state of Queensland, Australia, and from there proceed via coastal steamer to the port of Bundaberg, estimated as two days' sail to the north. There he was to report to Father Hans Beitz, and serve his Lutheran community as a curate. Sixty marks in his possession was to be handed to Father Beitz immediately on arrival, this money being donations from kindly Hamburg parishioners.

'Oh-oh, Friedrich. Sorry about that.'

In a less formal letter, the Dean instructed the curate to do his utmost to assist Father Beitz in every way, since the gentleman was getting on in years and his friends were concerned for his health in that climate.

'Getting on in years? The boss? That's not a bad thing for us, Friedrich, that's if we hang about our parish for long. If we get there at all. We'll see how we feel by the time we get to the Canary Islands. We might bid this rocking horse farewell once and ashore.'

Before they disembarked, an officer called for 'them as is going ashore to this island' to assemble in the saloon, which doubled as a dining room.

Most of the second-class passengers answered the call,

19

eager for a chance to escape the ship and feel solid ground beneath their feet again. They were all in the jolliest of moods, applauding each snippet of advice given by the officer, even warnings of pickpockets, as if reward were required.

The Pastor stood at the rear, unimpressed to learn that the residents of this place spoke Spanish, a language of which he knew not a word.

'And some Portuguese,' the officer added, to yet another cheer.

But he was pleased to learn that one could change German money to English currency here, and do quite well. He patted a waistcoat pocket, to make sure the Dean's money was still intact, determining to make a bank the first port of call.

As they filed out of the saloon, each person was expected to sign his or her name, even with a cross if the art of writing had not been acquired, in a tall log book.

The Pastor looked at it disdainfully. 'What is this about?'

'Captain's orders, Reverend. As each person returns we ask him to sign on again beside his name.'

'What on earth for?'

'Stowaways, sir. The islands are where escaped convicts and slaves are hid, just waiting for a chance to sail away.'

'Surely I wouldn't be mistaken for an escaped convict, let alone a slave. I don't need to sign this.'

'It's also a count, Reverend. How many went ashore in the longboats and how many came back. We don't want to leave anyone behind.'

The Pastor was mulling over this. So if he took a mind to it and decided to jump ship here, unannounced, they would come searching for him, the damn fools. The only way he could quit the ship here, if he decided to do so, would be to inform the Captain, obviously. And that would draw attention to himself, and curiosity . . . He was holding up the queue.

A senior officer stepped forward. 'Be so kind as to sign your name, Reverend.'

He took the pen. He had never actually seen Friedrich's handwriting. Not his signature, anyway. Only a few notes here and there. All the other papers in the valise were to him or for him, not from him.

20

Suddenly he looked up and smiled at them, a beatific smile that took them by surprise, then signed his name with a flourish. *Pastor Friedrich Ritter*.

He almost laughed. What was there to be worried about? The return signature would be identical. What a silly sausage he'd been to let that bother him.

The port was hot and dusty, of no interest to the pastor at all. He brushed aside dark gypsy types selling baskets of trinkets and bolts of cloth, dodged passengers who invited him to stroll with them, hurried past a small sandstone church with a neat spire. In fact he hardly stopped until the large English banknotes were in his hands, gloating that his nest egg had now grown to eighty-one pounds. Not a bad day's work.

Then he disappeared into darker back streets until he found what he was looking for: a lonely little wine bar, too far from the seafront to count sailors as customers, where he settled himself into a worn and comfortable cane chair.

For the first time in a very long time – years, he thought – he was at ease, totally relaxed. Nothing to worry about. When the elderly waiter ambled over, he placed a pound note on the wobbly table and ordered a meal, and the best wine, in the house, and told the waiter to get him some good cigars.

'Excellent service,' he remarked to himself as he sat back, his feet on a chair, the ugly round hat and the white collar temporarily cast aside, drinking a robust red wine and smoking a marvellous cigar while the waiter, now cook, could be heard clattering about behind the high bar.

He remembered something else that the Dean had written to his fledgling missionary. The money, all those marks that were now miraculously transformed into pounds, was to be used as a foundation fund to build a school, a Lutheran school for German immigrants at their settlement in this town of Bundaberg. He'd insisted that a school would be a cornerstone for the secular and religious well-being of families so far from their own homeland.

'You're probably right, Dean, a good idea. But don't you think they ought to save up and build their own school? Much

21

better for them. And you've had Friedrich locked up far too long. I think he's entitled to a bit of fun now. You'll never miss that money.'

After the dreary fare aboard ship, this meal was splendid. Hot thick soup, rich with lumps of tomato and pork, tasty chicken and beans in a spicy sauce, fresh bread to mop up the juices, and another bottle of wine.

'Now you find me a woman, eh?'

The waiter shrugged and banged on the wall.

The Pastor waved away the woman who waddled in the back door with an expectant grin on her plump face, even as she heaved her corpulence around the end of the bar.

'I want a woman, not a cow!'

She glared at him, spat a few words that he thought might have been Spanish and, with a switch of her large wobbly rear, made her exit.

He was amused by the dramatic exit, wondering if they had anything better to offer.

And they did. 'God!' he muttered, drawing in a quick breath as a young girl was pushed forward by invisible hands, obviously those of the first contender. She looked about sixteen, a beauty. No doubt about that, with long hair almost to her waist and firm breasts pushing against a thin cotton blouse. Her skirt was only a coloured wrap, a short scrap of cloth covering slim, supple hips.

'Ah!' he said as she waited. And 'Ah!' again. Awed. Her face . . . high cheekbones, large brown eyes, and that mouth. He licked his own lips, staring at her, staring at her rich full mouth, lips like velvet. But she was black. Black-skinned. A Negress. He'd never been so close to a black person before . . . never given a thought to touching a black woman. He didn't know about this. Didn't know how he'd fare . . . if he'd be able to do it with her.

She moved closer to him. He could have reached over and flicked off that little skirt in an instant, just to see how she looked underneath. As if she recognised temptation, she swayed her hips a little and fiddled idly with the single cloth knot that held it in place, moving a bare foot forward to reveal more of that smooth black leg.

22

The decision made, fears overcome, he was on his feet, ready to follow her, but the waiter intervened.

'Pay first.'

The bill was totted up, counting plates, bottles, cigars and the girl, and he was charged one whole pound, exactly the amount he had put down on the table, which seemed rather a coincidence and gave no hint of how much he was paying for the *fräulein*, but by this time he didn't care. They could have charged him ten pounds, so eager was he to go down those back steps after her.

She had a bed in a cellar. It felt cool and dry in there, and light came only from a high barred window. He closed the door himself. And pushed the bolt on it. Normally he wasn't so shy, a fit, healthy lad in his prime, but this was different, more like an experiment, he told himself. And if it didn't work, it was only between him and the whore in a grubby corner of the world he'd never see again.

He lay on the bed, exhausted, exhilarated, as she washed the sweat from his naked body with a cool cloth.

'Never in my life . . .' he kept saying to himself. Never had he performed so well and never had he met a body, a woman like her; the whore was fantastic.

He grabbed her arm. 'Again. Come back, more. We have more.'

She giggled, dripping water on him. 'Cost more pound.'

'*Ja. Ja.* More pound. *Gut.*' He reached out to her gleaming black body and she moved quickly to straddle him.

'You like, Friedrich? You like dis?'

'Friedrich loves it,' he laughed. 'Friedrich's a very happy man.'

The whore was so sexy, so lusty, that for a fleeting while he considered jumping ship after all, and to hell with them. If they came searching he would simply announce his decision and instruct them to put his luggage ashore. He was under no obligation to offer explanations. He was his own man. He had his own money . . . but how long would it last? He hadn't noticed a plethora of theatres among the palm-lashed shanties, nor any faces that would be enraptured by his excellent rendition of Socrates' deathbed speech. He realised he'd met his own Lorelei . . . enticing, dangerous . . . for there really was nothing for him here. He'd have to leave eventually, go back to Germany and face capture, or to England to find some theatre work.

Now he strode back towards the wharf, his priestly demeanour restored as he fought off the new jauntiness in his step and the temptation to gloat to his fellow passengers. Who else among them had enjoyed one hell of a day like that? he mused with suppressed excitement. Who else of these dreary men, some poor and wan, others spruce and gentlemanly, had discovered the frantic passions of a Sabine, for that was her name, had ever been treated to a sexy adventure with a nubile whore with skin as black and smooth as velvet?

He sighed, allowing a faint nod of recognition at acquaintances from the ship, but keeping his progress to himself. He had to move on towards this new land, because he had a job. Or rather a role. Why go back searching for work to keep body and soul together when an easy path stretched before him? One that he had created himself, with his own efforts, drastic though they might have been. Drastic situations demanded drastic measures. That was a truism if ever there was one. And marvellously, in this role, far from the critics and managers, he could play the part any way he chose. Even when he'd struck that blow, he'd only seen the naïve preacher – his own size and age, with a modicum of resemblance – as an escape route. Now that he had taken a good look at the role, it was far more than that; it was the road to a life of ease. This time he was the boss, the critic, the manager, the author, if you liked. Even the audience. And best of all, the paymaster.

'I'm an important man,' he'd told Sabine.

But she'd shaken her head. 'No. Important men, they have beards and fat here under the belt,' she had teased.

The Pastor sat himself on a crate under a canvas awning as he waited for the longboat to come back for more passengers. He watched seagulls dipping into the blue waves of the harbour and looked further out at the ship. It was the first time he'd seen it from a distance, and he was impressed by its fine lines and its aura of confidence. That was how he felt this late afternoon.

'I think I'll grow a beard,' he said to himself.

Like so many other gentlemen from first class. Herr Hubert Hoepper was nattily dressed in a white duck suit that he hated. His daughter had insisted he buy two, because they were ideal for the tropics, though one could hardly say that this brisk and windy day was tropical. It provided sunniness, that was all, allowing some of the men to test this odd garb and the ladies to blossom forth with feeble parasols, not up to the job even today, and long white coats of serge or shantung.

Herr Hoepper might have been persuaded to wear this atrocious suit, but he would not relinquish his top hat, gloves and spats, not for anyone. He complained that the suit made him feel as if he were wearing heavy canvas, but his daughter, Adele, had assured him that the material would soften with washing, which, after all, was the point of the cloth.

'Men sweat a good deal in the tropics, Daddy. That is a known fact. Hence the necessity to wear washable apparel.'

Not to be outdone, he reminded her that their destination, the town of Bundaberg, was not in the tropics but south of Capricorn.

Her laugh filled his heart with joy, for the sound was so rare these days. He wished he could reciprocate; think of something humorous to say, but he seemed to have forgotten how.

'Really, Father, you are so funny. I expected you to be the seasoned traveller, since you have studied your geography for so long, but you don't seem to be able to interpret it. I'm guessing that since this town of Bundaberg is only about a hundred or so miles south of Capricorn it will be hot. It will be tropical!'

'We'll see,' he smiled. Hoping he was wrong. He wanted to be wrong, to please her. He'd do anything to make her happy, to keep her in this good mood.

Before he'd stepped ashore this morning he'd added a woollen scarf to his outfit, and now, late in the day, he found its presence comforting, if a little too warm. But it was a

25

reminder of the old world that he was abandoning, temporarily, for this sea voyage, on the advice of family and friends. For her health and his.

Not that he cared about his own health any more than was necessary to attend to his household and look after his daughter. He watched her buzz from the market stalls on the wharf over to the barrows of trinkets, in a last-minute shopping spree before they rejoined the ship. Adele was eighteen, he mused, marriageable age. She'd leave him one of these days. Instead of being saddened by this when it had dawned on him, Hubert had decided he should make the most of his daughter's company while he still could.

He really believed this to be a priority in his life. She was all he had left. They didn't always get on. She could be bold, headstrong. She would contradict him, argue, storm away from him, but that was Adele. She had always been highly strung, prone to bouts of the miseries and almost hysterical gaiety.

But she was, most times, kind and generous, a good daughter, so why shouldn't he plot his life around her well-being? Were it not for her . . . then what was left for him?

Oddly, this sea voyage had been suggested by her. By Adele, who had kicked up so much fuss when he'd first suggested Australia a couple of years ago. Sometimes he wondered if she thought that she was in some way responsible for his welfare, and though he couldn't bring himself to say this, not being much of a talker on emotional subjects, to say the least, he hoped she didn't. He had a duty to her and he wanted it all to himself.

She came flitting over, carrying a basket filled with oddments including a paper parasol, which he was sure would be a great help in a tropical downpour.

'They make sandals over there while you wait, Daddy. Why don't you go over and get some?'

'Because I don't need any.'

'But you will. You can't wear heavy shoes in the tropics.'

'Then I'll go barefoot.'

She twinkled. 'That I have to see. Don't forget to wear your top hat as well. Come with me, they have the cheapest pearl necklaces over here.'

He sighed. 'I've seen them. I had hoped to buy a rope for you. But they are of very poor quality. Look, dear, don't buy.'

As he settled himself on a bench outside a shop that was now closed, having despaired of selling tiny chickens in paper baskets to these unappreciative tourists, Hubert looked about him to cover the fact that he was surreptitiously tugging at the crotch of these damned trousers that were causing him quite some discomfort. He noticed a young priest seated comfortably on an empty crate as if it were a seat made and groomed for him, so elegant was the picture against the backdrop of the turbulent blue sea.

Hubert guessed this must be Father Ritter, often mentioned on board as a curate, also heading for the Lutheran community and mission in Bundaberg. He looked rather lonely, or maybe just meditative, sitting there, taking no interest in his surroundings, rather directing his gaze out to sea. He seemed a good stamp of a fellow, quiet and dignified, and Hubert had heard – made it his business to hear – that he was conducting himself as a Lutheran priest should. It was said he was a kindly man, though retiring, not given to socialising, and Hubert, a staunch Lutheran, appreciated that. Young priests, it was often said, could get themselves into difficulty on the romantic rounds of the great southern oceans, even finding themselves involved with women who were no better than they should be.

He decided to introduce himself to Father Ritter.

The curate was startled by the sudden interruption and Hubert apologised profusely. 'Forgive me. I'm dreadfully sorry if I intruded on you. It's just that I thought this was a good time for us to meet, since we are both bound for Bundaberg. Yes, it's true, my daughter and I are on our way to visit Father Beitz and all the others to see how they're getting along. They will have had a year to settle in by the time we get there, so it will be interesting, won't it?'

'Mmm. Yes, I'm sure,' Ritter responded vaguely, hardly bothering to turn away from his view of the sea, and Hubert was embarrassed, wondering what foolishness had possessed him to go barging up to the man in such an informal manner. He should have waited and had the Captain or one of the officers make the introductions in the proper way. But now Ritter seemed to have overcome his original displeasure.

'Since we haven't met before,' he said with a wry attempt at a smile, 'I presume you're travelling first class, Mr Hoepper?'

'That is so.'

'How very pleasant for you. In keeping with the Lord's teachings, I expected to be travelling steerage; indeed, I requested that privilege, but the Dean wouldn't have it. He insisted I voyage in second class, at least, to avoid the pitfalls of the dormitory accommodations in steerage.'

'I think the Dean was very wise. Have you enjoyed our little sojourn ashore, Father?'

'Ah, yes. I've been wandering around, merely stretching my legs. Have you noticed that the ground seems to sway underfoot now?'

Hubert smiled, relieved that the curate's attitude had thawed. 'It does. My word, it does. And it's the strangest experience. I thought I was the only one afflicted.'

He saw Adele approaching. 'This is my daughter, Father.'

The young priest turned and acknowledged Adele humbly, his eyes downcast, feet shuffling. Hubert hid a smile. Obviously the poor fellow hadn't met many women over the last few years, and certainly none as pretty as his Adele.

'How do you do, Miss Hoepper. I am pleased to make your acquaintance. But Mr Hoepper, would you be so kind as to address me as Pastor? The Dean felt that since I am very much junior to Father Beitz, it would not be correct for me to assume the title of Father. That is his prerogative.'

'By all means. Pastor it is then. We must go now, time we took to the ship again. Have you finished your shopping, Adele?'

'Yes. I have several bundles of things sitting over there. Will you help me carry them?'

'Allow me,' the Pastor said, and Hubert was happy to do just that. He didn't relish the indignity of carrying all of her colourful purchases, nor trying to step into the longboat with that stuff in hand. Let the cleric make himself useful.

* * *

He flung himself on the bunk. 'Well, Freddy, what a day I've had. What you missed! You probably died a virgin, to make matters worse. And today could have been the best in your life. Oh, I love this voyaging life. It's for me. But let me tell you . . . Sabine. Oh my good God! Sabine. A joy. A gift.' He burst out laughing. 'A gift from the Dean. He paid for her. Tonight I'll tell you all about her. Minute by minute, touch by touch. We'll have a good time. I might be able to filch a bottle of wine from somewhere if I'm careful, and we can celebrate. By the way, I met a passenger, Mr Hoepper . . . very posh. Rich I'd say. He's travelling first class, out to . . . guess where? Bundaberg. The place we're supposed to be off to. The end of the earth. And he knew you were on the ship, Freddy. So what does he do? Trots over and introduces himself. I nearly jumped out of my skin! I expected him to start shouting, once he got a good look at me. Start yelling, "This isn't Friedrich Ritter!" and me having to fall back on my other plan. Like, "You mean the *other* Father Ritter. I've heard of him . . . no relation . . . that sort of stuff.

'I tell you, Freddy, I was in a funk, I don't know if I'd have been able to get the lines out. Probably have bolted, more like it. But what does he do? Starts apologising for intruding on me. Apologises! Has a bit of a chat – about what, I've no idea, from sheer fright – then brings over the daughter. The daughter, Friedrich. Young, rich and beautiful. She's quite petite, but she's got a slim waist and good titties, and the silkiest blonde hair. I came back to the ship with them in the longboat and I had to battle to keep my eyes from her lovely face. And she's so sweet with it . . .

'I have to tell you, Freddy, I'm in love. I'm madly in love with her. I have to work out how to get closer to her. Probably the next port, if I can wait that long to see her again. There's something for you to do, Friedrich. Speak to the Lord. Entreat Him to deliver darling Adele to me and I'll be a saint for the rest of my life. Truly I will.'

Part Two

Chapter Three

Hubert Hoepper had always lived in Hamburg. Born and schooled there, he was apprenticed as a clerk to the firm of H. A. Hoepper & Co., merchants, founded by his grandfather. They said that Hubert at twenty was turning into the spitting image of old Hubert, with the same blue eyes, square jaw and straight dark hair with its neat hairline.

He was tall, too, broad-shouldered and barrel-chested, and, they said, when young Hubert fills out he truly will be old Hubert all over again, except . . . ah, yes. Except that old Hubert was a martinet. A hard, tough businessman, the jaw was jutting, belligerent, the grey-slashed hair clipped military style, while the grandson was a dreamer. No use arguing about that, he was a dreamer all right. He even looked the part, his hair long, swept back, his eyelashes thick and dark . . . as the girls said, he was 'dreamy'.

When old Hubert complained about him to his widowed daughter-in-law, who was also his housekeeper, she defended her son angrily, arguing that he was always punctual and did his work well, which was more than could be said of several of his supervisors. With Hubert, though, she was quieter, imploring him to pay more attention to the business, to let his grandfather know that he really was interested in everything.

'But I'm not,' he finally told her. 'I want to travel. I want to see the world. From the office window in the big warehouse I can see all those tall ships setting out to sea, and I'd love to sail in them.'

As if she didn't know that! As a boy he'd been drawn to wandering about the harbour, admiring those ships. His father had even bought him toy ships and replicas that were still displayed in his bedroom.

'You listen to me,' she said. 'You've got your head stuffed with all that travel nonsense. I ought to throw out those maps and things you've got in your room to make you pay attention. What do you think will happen to us if your grandfather leaves the business to your cousin Klaus? He's already the most senior employee in the firm, and only ten years older than you.'

Hubert smiled. 'That's reasonable. He has been there ten years longer than I have.'

'And who do you think is undermining you all the time? Whining about you to your grandfather?'

'Klaus? I don't think so. And anyway, what does it matter?'

'On your wage, could you support me and your two sisters? I don't think so. This house is owned by your grandfather. Can you be sure he'll will it to me, or to you? No, you can't! But why would you worry? You'll be gone, travelling to Italy or Egypt, not caring that we'll be thrown into the street. Surely you don't think your grandfather would leave the business to someone like you, who obviously isn't interested and who may not even be around? She was weeping. 'You don't care about anyone but yourself. That's your trouble The old man isn't stupid. He'll want to leave the business in good hands. That means Klaus, and I'll be beholden to him and his stupid wife for ever . . .'

Hubert put an arm about her, kissed her on the cheek. 'Please don't go on so, Mother. It's not that bad. Everything will be all right. You'll see.'

That night, though, he sat in his room, in his warm, comfortable room on the top floor, looking out over the rooftops, worrying this problem. He smiled, thinking of his mother's notion of a faraway land.

Italy? Egypt? Oh no. That was kids' stuff. She'd probably gained that impression from the old pictures of the Pyramids he'd had on his wall for years. No, Hubert had given a lot of thought to his travels. He'd studied maps, he even had his own globe on its wooden stand, and he'd read countless books, agreeing with one author who wrote about travel: 'Preparation is fascinating, but anticipation is exquisite.' He'd certainly found that to be correct, and over the years his tastes had matured. He'd realised it wasn't just the ships, he had to have a destination. That in itself was exciting . . .

By this time his mother was telling Grandfather that his hobby was geography, in order to explain the proliferation of geographical material stored in that top-floor room, but old Hubert still wasn't impressed.

Nowhere round the shores of Europe held interest for young Hubert; he could see himself on a tall ship nosing into huge heaving waves, out there in the wilds of the great oceans. But where? The obvious place was America. Straight across the Atlantic. That would be a great voyage, but what to do once he got there? Though it was a popular destination for travellers, that country didn't appeal to him because it looked too easy to approach, not much of a challenge. Besides, new world though it might be, it wasn't averse to wars, and Hubert was a pacifist.

A pacifist! His grandfather had almost thrown a fit at the dinner table.

'I've never heard of such a thing! My God, young man, were it not for the bravery of good soldiers like your father, God bless his soul, we wouldn't be here today, enjoying peace, enjoying a stable economy—'

'Peace, sir? For how long? More Napoleons? More "unity" struggles? More battles where thousands of peasants are dragged from their lands to fight the Austrians or the French? I ask you . . . why are grain and produce in short supply? Because they are needed to feed armies of men who should be labouring in the fields, where they belong. It's a vicious circle.'

'Have you no respect for your own father?' old Hubert thundered. 'He was not a peasant! He was an officer who died doing his duty! Get this wretch away from my table.'

'I wasn't criticising our dear father, sir. I wouldn't do that. You don't understand. I was—'

His mother had intervened, smoothing things over, telling Grandfather that Hubert's little sisters had prepared a concert for him; and that had worked, the quick change of subject. Grandfather liked nothing better than family concerts at the piano. He had a fine voice himself and loved to have the girls sing with him.

So . . . Hubert recalled. Best not to discuss the futility and cruelty of endless wars with him! You'd think that since he'd lost a son, his only son, not on a battlefield but in a cavalry charge, manoeuvres, playing at war, preparing, he'd be more amenable to his grandson's point of view. They'd taken his father; that was reason enough for a lad to be anti anything military. Why couldn't his grandfather see this?

Anyway, during the long winter nights, with Hamburg wrapped in snow, it was sheer delight for Hubert to continue his progress unhindered into exotic lands. He considered South America, and then Africa, the dark continent, full of mystery, and then all of a sudden it came to him that if he chose the newest world, the continent of Australia, he'd be able to see those other countries as well. At least get a glimpse of them en route, right around the world. That was a brilliant idea.

He turned his endeavours to discovering all he could about the Australian colonies, and became fascinated by this strange land so far away, so much so that he threw caution to the winds. He went to see his grandfather in his impressive inner sanctum that glowed with polished timbers and brass and leather and smelled of expensive tobacco.

Swept along by enthusiasm, Hubert was almost breathless as he began to tell the bearded eminence all about this great country lodged down between the Indian and Pacific oceans, about the sunny clime, the great expanse of land, barely explored, its new cities and strange fauna, but he was soon interrupted.

'What about it?'

'Well . . . I'd like to go there, sir. I've saved enough for my fare and a little extra, and I could probably get odd jobs to pay for excursions.'

'What about your job?'

'That's just it, sir. I was wondering if I could take some time off . . . a year, perhaps . . . then I'd come back to it.'

His grandfather tapped heavy knuckles on the desk in front of him, tapping very, very slowly, ominously.

'In other words, you think you're entitled to a holiday. Not a few days like everyone else, but a whole year. Do you think you've earned a holiday, boy? Answer me that! Do you think you've earned a holiday?'

'Not exactly. It would be, sort of, leave, you see. I would take a year's leave. Without pay, of course.'

'Without pay? That's kind of you, damned thoughtful, I'd say. You want to go to this ridiculous place, then go. I don't know why you're bothering to ask me. It's nothing to do with me, because if you leave your job for more than a day without good reason, I will replace you. Holidaying is not a good reason.'

Suddenly he sat up and leaned forward to thunder at Hubert: 'I'm a fair man. When you go out this door you can turn left or right. Turn right, you're out in the street for good. Turn left, you go back to your desk, where you'll pull your weight like everyone else. Got it?'

'Yes, sir.'

1872

Looking back on those years, Hubert, now sole owner of H. A. Hoepper & Co., knew his grandfather had been right. It had been foolish of him even to consider taking a year off, and very selfish. He was glad that he'd made the right decision. And having done that, he'd settled down to learn all he could about the business, making a considerable contribution rather than merely filling in time at his desk.

When his grandfather died, the estate was divided between Klaus and Hubert. To his mother's relief, they were able to keep the house on Nikolaifleet, and the business was jointly owned by the two cousins. They managed quite well, but eventually Hubert bought Klaus out because differences of opinion were upsetting them. Klaus preferred to carry on as their grandfather had, as importers, but Hubert could see a bigger market in less expensive local goods that even the gentry were beginning to accept. He encouraged local furniture and cabinetmakers and expanded into exporting German household goods.

The firm continued to prosper, and Hubert settled into comfortable middle age with his wife, his two fine sons, who were already working in his warehouses, and his daughter, Adele.

And then Hubert's fascination with faraway lands began to filter back into his consciousness. A voice kept needling him, whispering to him that he could now afford to fulfil that dream. He could afford to pack up his family and take them with him across the oceans, to flee winters in Europe and embark on a life of adventure. Before it was too late. Before he was too old. He would take them to Australia, to a place of sunshine and wide-open fields where families could have as much land as they liked. His sons needn't be locked into the penny-pinching world of profit and loss, sharing a dark office, day in and day out, as he and Klaus had done.

He walked over to the portrait of his grandfather to check his image in the darkened glass, observing, not for the first time, the grey at his own temples.

'I could do it,' he said aloud, for the first time. Erik and Ernst could live healthy lives with their families on their own estates out there. Hubert could already envisage their gabled farmhouses surrounded by oceans of golden wheat. Or maybe verdant countryside with some sheep and cows wandering about.

Though he couldn't as yet bring himself to mention this plan to anyone, family or friends, he began to make enquiries, discovering to his surprise that there was an agent right here in Hamburg recruiting folk to move to Australia.

Hubert was astonished. It seemed to him that this was meant to be, as he found himself in the office of a young gentleman called John Henderson, who was indeed working to encourage people to migrate to Australia, specifically to the north-eastern colony of Queensland.

Henderson was surprised that Hubert Hoepper was already so knowledgeable about the Antipodes.

'But what is this Antipodes?' Hoepper asked.

'The opposite end of the world to Britain,' he laughed. 'It's what we call Australia and New Zealand.'

38

Mr Hoepper frowned, unamused. 'Then to Australia and New Zealand, Britain is their Antipodes. Is this not correct?'

'I suppose so,' Henderson conceded. 'Perhaps you'd like to look at these maps so I could tell you about the various new towns that are seeking immigrants. Unless, of course, sir, being a businessman, you would prefer to make for this capital city of Brisbane?'

'I am more interested in finding farmland for my sons.'

'There is plentiful superb farmland around Brisbane.'

'And the further I go from the city centre, the cheaper the land.'

'Of course.'

'Is there any limit on the amount of land one might purchase?'

'Only by your purse. In fact the government is subsidising fares to Australia, to help populate the country.'

'Good heavens! How extraordinary!'

Henderson smiled broadly, certain he had a definite taker here, and a man with excellent credentials.

'How many would be in your party, Mr Hoepper?'

'Seven, including my servants,' he replied vaguely, as he sat making notes in a small diary.

Abruptly, though, he stood to leave. 'Good morning, Mr Henderson, thank you for seeing me. I shall need time to consider many aspects, so I shall call again.'

In fact Hubert almost ran from the office. He'd suddenly felt foolish, as if a fifty-year-old man should not be entertaining such radical ideas . . . as if, even, he was going a bit funny in the head. He could feel his face blanch behind his neatly cut beard. Would he really sell up everything? The family business? The fine formal house? To go off and live in the wilds? What was this nonsense? What would people say?

Did he think he was twenty again?

No, but my sons are. That stopped him in his tracks, turning him towards the harbour, where even bigger ships now lay at anchor.

It is my sons I should be thinking about, not my ego, nor even my comfort.

Then he smiled. But it would still be a great adventure.

When he arrived home they were all sitting grimly in the parlour, waiting for him.

'What's all this?' he asked. 'Cat got your tongues?'

Erik handed him the documents. 'We've been conscripted. Ernst and me. Both of us. We have to go into the army.'

'No you don't. I've arranged for exemptions.'

'They don't seem to have worked, Father.'

'Never mind,' Ernst said. 'It won't be that bad, I don't suppose. Can we get commissions?'

Hubert wasted no time. He sought an audience with the Minister for War but was fobbed off with excuses. He met with the colonel of the regiment, insisting that his sons were exempt from military service by reason of work duties, but the Colonel would have none of it. In desperation, Hubert began bargaining. He would pay for their release so that replacements could be trained, a veiled attempt at bribery which found fertile ground.

'I can't let them go altogether, Mr Hoepper. They'd have to do two years' service.'

'One.'

'What about eighteen months?'

'No. One year.'

'I'm sorry. Eighteen months is the best I can do. Let's say we add this amount to the price of their commissions, and uniforms and horses. They'd be better off in the cavalry.'

On principle, Hubert haggled over the final costs, though he would have paid double, and he left the barracks desperately upset, making straight for Henderson's office.

The agent was not in, but Hubert came across an elderly priest who was waiting patiently on a bench just inside the door.

'I fear our man is not at home just now. Are you a dreamer too?' asked the cleric.

'Oh, no. Hardly,' Hubert felt obliged to say. He was, after all, a successful businessman.

'Not interested in emigrating to Australia?'

Hubert was caught out. 'Possibly,' he allowed. 'Possibly, Father.'

'Aha. It is as well to be certain. A long way to go to change the mind. As for me, I made up my mind a long time ago.'

'You're migrating?'

The priest looked as old as Methuselah, with his long grey beard and shaggy hair. But suddenly his eyes twinkled.

'There's plenty of life in me yet, my son. My dream is twofold. Or maybe I should say I have two dreams. The first is to open a Lutheran mission . . . are you of our faith?'

'Yes, Father.'

'Good. I want to open a mission and bring the natives to our Lord. And the second is to gather together members of our flock who are migrating to a destination as yet undecided upon, in the colony of Queensland.' He stopped for breath, wheezing a little. 'Don't you think it would be truly wonderful to have them start up their own Lutheran community out there?'

'I imagine so,' Hubert said.

'They'd have the comfort of their own language . . .'

Language! Hubert spoke some English. No one else in his household did. He made a mental note to arrange lessons as soon as possible.

'. . . their own religion and traditions. An advantage, wouldn't you say?'

'Yes. I daresay it would be.'

'Then you'd not be averse to making an offering, a donation towards my enterprise.'

Hubert took out his purse and handed over two marks. 'Do you have many people in your flock, Father . . .?'

'Beitz. Father Beitz. About forty, sir. A good start, don't you think?'

Hubert nodded. Since Father Beitz kept seeking his approval, he thought the priest was probably unsure of himself and his grand plan, but he was wrong.

'I'm glad you agree with me, bless your soul. You'll be ideal. Are you bringing your family? I can't see you as a single, lone traveller. You must join us. You'd be most welcome. We'll be a happy, holy community, working together, you see.

I have made a promise to the Lord to carry His name far abroad, and there's no looking back now—'

A door banged behind him and Henderson bustled in from the rain and sleet, shaking water from his umbrella.

'Father Beitz! How good to see you again. And you have Mr Hoepper with you! Isn't that amazing? I was hoping to introduce you.'

'No need,' Beitz smiled. 'We're old friends. At least, our dreams are.'

Over the next few months, Hubert and Father Beitz became firm friends, and of course Hubert threw in his lot with the German contingent planning to migrate to Australia, as the old priest had known he would.

Beitz was a merry fellow, and extremely kind, but he was also rather impractical, so Hubert helped him when it came to planning. They ascertained that the poorer members of the group would obtain assisted passages in steerage so that the 'common purse' – their name for their migration fund – would only need to pay the balance. They worked on the principle that whoever could afford it would pay their own way, or whatever they could manage. Those who were migrating because of poverty were not expected to pay anything, and Hubert thought the scheme fair.

At long last the day came for Hubert to commit himself, and he made the first move by announcing the plan to his family, disappointed to find that none of them shared his enthusiasm. His sons, resplendent in blue uniforms, all tasselled and brass-buttoned, with their sharp peaked caps and high glossy boots, were well pleased with their new lives in the army, to their father's chagrin. They even confessed that they preferred the army to working in the family firm.

'With due respect, Father,' Erik told him, 'we appreciate that you've been good to us, but our jobs were boring.'

'Nondescript,' Ernst echoed. 'Really tedious. But the army is exciting, there's always so much going on and our new friends are really splendid chaps.'

'What madness is this?' Hubert cried, echoing his grandfather. 'The army isn't a charade, some sort of vaudevillian show put on for your amusement.'

'I know, Father,' Erik said, to soothe. 'We just wanted you to see that it isn't as bad as we expected. But this idea of yours, to migrate . . . I don't know what to think about that.'

They had a long talk and the lads came around to their father's point of view. They saw it as another great adventure with the promise of prosperity a bonus, and neither of them was sorry to hear the family business would be sold. A relief, in fact.

'You'll be out of those fancy uniforms as soon as I can arrange it,' Hubert told them. 'At this point you've got more than a year to go, but I'll need that time to make all the arrangements.'

'But what if Father Beitz and his people are ready to go and the boys are still in the army?' his wife asked anxiously.

'Then we'll just have to wait for them.'

She called Hubert aside, whispering, 'Can't you hurry things up? We ought to leave as soon as possible. I hate them being in the army, and I'm surprised at you for allowing it, now that there's trouble with the French again.'

'Gabi, there's nothing more I can do.'

'Yes there is. God knows, I'm not too happy about this wild scheme of yours, though they say ocean voyages are good for the constitution—'

'They are, Gabi. You've been poorly for a long time,' he said, eager to keep the flame of approval alight. 'It will do you the world of good.'

'That's not the point. I want you to book passages, get us aboard a ship as soon as possible. We'll take the boys with us. The Austrians might attack again, or the French. We have to get them away.'

Hubert was startled. His wife, usually a shy, retiring woman, sounded adamant.

'We can't do that. It's against the law.'

'Who cares? What can they do? By the time they find out, we'll be gone. They'll be on the high seas, well out of reach. Your idea of going to the other side of the world is perfect. No one will ever catch them out there.'

43

'But that's desertion!' Hubert stuttered. 'They can't do that.'

'They must! Who'd know in that place you're talking about? No one!'

'It's not a case of who would know, my dear. It's their honour.'

'Oh! I see. And what's so honourable about you trying to buy them out? Bribing senior officers?'

'That's for my conscience. I cannot and will not advise my sons to desert.'

'Then I will.'

Erik and Ernst would not contemplate desertion and they were cheered on by their younger sister, Adele, who was appalled at the very thought of leaving Hamburg, this beautiful city and their dear old house, not to mention all of her friends! For days she wept and sulked, and when the English teacher arrived, she flatly refused to attend the evening classes in the front parlour.

'Suit yourself,' Hubert said. 'A pity, though. Such a pretty girl as you to be known as the dummy, the one who can't make herself understood even to buy a jug of milk.'

Gradually Adele settled down to the inevitable – with bad grace, it had to be said – and began to attend the English classes, picking up the language much faster than anyone else.

Hubert introduced Father Beitz to the family, and they were all charmed by him, especially Gabi, who was greatly comforted to learn that he would be travelling with them. Then they began to meet other members of his future congregation, the first being farmers Jakob and Freda Meissner and their seventeen-year-old son, Karl. The appearance of this handsome lad cheered Adele immensely, and Hubert noticed that her grumblings became fainter.

Most of the group seemed to be farmers, strong, quiet men who took a keen interest in proceedings at the meetings but had little to say. Their women sat together at the back of the room, more interested in their own plots and plans than in the banks of questions that dominated every assembly. Also present on some occasions were various young men and women, peasants, uncertain of their rights or status and very much dependent on direction from Father Beitz, who went out of his way to encourage them and make them feel welcome. Then there was Lucas Fechner, whose occupation was as a groom, and his beautiful wife Hanni, a stunning blonde. They seemed to be very much in love, and Hubert guessed they were probably newly-weds. Other people came and went, some not to reappear, so to keep the continuity Father Beitz asked that everyone, wherever possible, attend Sunday mass at the Church of St John, and that was agreed upon.

Hubert didn't always agree with proposals put forward at these meetings, especially the suggestion that land should be bought in advance, sight unseen, from the common purse so that they'd have their own homeland, so to speak, from which to operate. Being a careful man, he spoke against this, but was voted down.

'We need it,' Father Beitz said. 'We are not going into cities but into the wilderness. We need our own ground to pitch our tents so that we are not beholden to others. From there, with the help of the Lord, we shall blossom forth and the land we own will be the site for our church. Glory be to God.'

Hubert's voice was lost in the claps and cheers. They only had to decide now exactly where to buy their common land, and John Henderson was delegated to look into the matter.

Hubert already felt himself slipping away from other family and friends, drawn more to the excitement of 'the travellers', as they now called themselves. Sunday mass was usually followed by picnics, weather permitting, when newcomers were brought along and encouraged to join them. Father Beitz was right, mused Hubert, we're all following our dreams, for all sorts of reasons, but not content with that, we can't help trying to sell them to others, so great is our enthusiasm for this grand plan. He even tried to persuade Klaus and his family to join them, but Klaus thought the whole idea was monstrous. To him, the wilderness meant isolation from civilisation, a rejection of culture.

'What is the use of culture when it is degraded by war and destruction?' Hubert asked him, but Klaus laughed.

'You really are naïve, with all this "back to nature" business,

Hubert. America is already degraded by shocking wars. Why do you think the Australian colonies will be any different?'

That sent Hubert in search of John Henderson. 'I have found the meetings very useful and am pleased with the cross-section of folk who are considering sailing with us, but now I need to know something very important. What is the military situation in the Australian colonies? Specifically in Queensland.'

Henderson blinked. 'What military situation?'

'Where sits the military in regard to the government? Who is the Minister for War?'

'You've lost me a bit here, Mr Hoepper. There is no military to speak of in any of the colonies. Just some leftover British troops.'

'Ah, but I note the Governor of Queensland also has the title of colonel. Is he also the Minister for War?'

'No. There are no war ministries in the whole country. There is no army.' Henderson grinned. 'No one to fight down there, cut off from the rest of the world. Except for the natives. The settlers and the blackfellows are bashing it out between themselves.'

'Are you sure? Perhaps the colonies have scores to settle between them, or land differences?'

'Why would they? They've all got more land than they know what to do with. Why do you think I'm here, sir? That country needs populating to survive economically, or else it will fall back into being a wilderness.'

'I see. One more thing, Mr Henderson. This is a delicate question, and several people have asked me to enquire for them. What about the convicts? Several of those colonies began life as prisons for deported felons . . .'

'And for folk starved into theft, yes, that's true.'

'Do we have to contend with convicts running wild in the country?'

'No. They serve their time and then they're given parole. If they re-offend, their lives are not worth living. They go to a hellhole called Norfolk Island. But on the whole, freed convicts have done quite well. Proves Father Beitz's theory of give a man a good start and he'll head for the winning post. As a matter of fact, both my grandparents were convicts.'

'Good God!' Hubert was embarrassed by his own shocked reaction, hardly the behaviour of a gentleman.

'That's all right,' Henderson said easily. 'My grandad was born in London. Dead poor. He stole a pair of boots and was sentenced to transportation to Sydney for seven years. Except no one mentioned how he and the rest of them were supposed to get home, so they stayed. Same thing happened to my grandma. She was Irish, and a feisty little lady she was too. Her mistress had her flogged for breaking a plate, so what did she do? After the flogging, blood still streaming, she marched back into the house and gave her mistress a whack in the ear. So off she went too. Transported to Sydney.'

'Oh dear. What a terrible thing to happen to a young woman.'

'Well, you might say that,' Henderson said grimly. 'She was raped aboard the transport ship by an officer. Bore the child, my father, in a cell in Sydney, and then she was sent out to a farm with the baby, to work as a milkmaid. There she met and married Grandpa, who was a shepherd.'

Hubert was fascinated. 'But you're an educated man. How did that come about?'

'Ah, Australia has her own rules. My grandparents did their time, gained their freedom and then travelled north into the back country, working for men who were opening up huge sheep farms for a pittance of lease money, paid to the government. So Grandpa and Grandma did the same thing . . . free as birds they were by this . . . got a bit of money together, went even further north in a dray, with my dad just a little kid, and selected a huge swatch of land all for themselves. Took them weeks to mark it out, with Aborigines breathing down their necks. And what do you think they did when they found they were the proud owners of ten square miles of good grazing country?'

'I've no idea,' Hubert said, fascinated.

'They lit a great bonfire to celebrate. And every year on the same date we have bonfires in memory of this. They named their station – or estate, you might call it – Tyrone

47

Station, after Grandma's home county, and they lived happily ever after. I was born there.'

'Where is this place?'

'On the Burnett River. A long way inland from a newly settled area called Bundaberg. I'm looking at that now as a possible "sitting-down place", as the Aborigines would call it, for your Lutheran community.'

'And where is the Burnett River?'

'Oh yes. I'm sorry. Well, let's see. It's almost three hundred miles north of the capital, Brisbane . . .'

He saw Hubert's sudden surprised intake of breath.

'Mr Hoepper, when contemplating that country, don't think in terms of distance. What matters is time. You either have the time to cover the miles out there, or you don't. Then again, you're travelling over new and interesting country where there are no clocks. And don't forget – the further you go from the major centres, the cheaper the land.

'But anyway. This settlement of Bundaberg is almost at the mouth of the Burnett River. It's about ten miles from the coast. It's becoming an important port for all of the inland stations surrounding it, because prior to this we had to overland everything to and from Brisbane.'

'It's not a town yet, though?'

'No, but it will be. You can bet your life on it.'

'I'm not a betting man, John. I doubt that site will interest me.'

'Fair enough. You have to please yourself where you go and be happy with your decision. I'm really only here for reference.'

Until now, Hubert had seen John Henderson as a clerk, no one of great interest beyond the information he was employed to supply. He'd thought Henderson was English, but now he'd discovered that the young man was actually Australian born – the first he'd ever met – and that put a different light on the matter. He should know what he was talking about. Hubert was still uncomfortable with his reaction to the information about Henderson's forebears and tried to make amends.

'I am sorry about your grandparents. I hope you don't think I was prying.'

'Not at all. And you needn't be worried about the convict

tag, Mr Hoepper. We have a saying that the English would have been better to migrate to Australia and leave their country to the convicts. In many ways, those transported prisoners were better off eventually than some plain English folk.'

Hubert nodded. 'I suppose that could be true if other convicts prospered as did your people, and they had the advantage of your salubrious climate. But I am wondering why you are here in Germany when you could be enjoying life on the family estate.'

John laughed. 'You should know the answer to that. It's called wanderlust.'

Hubert was relieved to be selling the business. He'd become reliant on his sons for the management of the bulk of the stores that passed through the warehouses. Erik and Ernst had indented and invoiced so efficiently he'd never had to give it much thought. Now he missed them. Their replacements were sloppy, careless lads who daily caused confusion and irritation.

As he walked home, looking every bit the respectable businessman in his neat frock coat and breeches, with his dark hat and silver-tipped cane, he felt a bit of a fraud, knowing he was about to throw off this persona and replace it with the sweet laxity of country life, after a long encounter with the great oceans. It was almost as if he were preparing to play truant, like a mischievous schoolboy, and the foolishness of such a concept made him smile, and put lightness in his step on this fine afternoon.

The front door to his house was open. The heavy front door with its large brass knocker lolled there unattended, and Hubert, mystified, peered in as if he were a stranger, stepping inside on to the tiles with a frown for the deserted lobby. The house was so silent the quarter-hour chime of a clock startled him, and he twisted about, to be almost tripped by the white cat as it scuttled past him.

Hubert closed the door, placed his hat and stick on the hall stand, strode past the staircase and pressed a bell to summon the housekeeper. When there was no response, he pressed the bell again, angrily tapping his foot. He would not call out in his own house, nor go searching about the kitchen, so he was about to stamp away to his study when Lily, the housekeeper, appeared on the landing above him.

'Oh! You're home, sir,' she cried, weeping. She was weeping!

Hubert took the stairs two at a time and caught her turning away.

'What's wrong? What's happening?' he cried, almost shaking her. 'My wife. Is she ill?'

Lily raised her face to him, eyes streaming. 'Please, sir, the doctor is with her. And Miss Adele.'

She stepped back, cringing against the wall as he strode away from her, certain now that Gabi was at death's door.

He was halfway down the passage when the doctor emerged from their bedroom, his face reflecting anguish as he closed the door quietly behind him.

'How is she?' Hubert begged, but the doctor held up his hands, as if to prevent him entering his own room.

'What is this?' he demanded. 'I have to see my wife.'

'Just a minute, Hubert. A word with you first. Let us sit down here.'

Suddenly feeling very vulnerable, weak at the knees, Hubert allowed himself to be led to the sofa in the alcove at the top of the stairs.

'You have to be very strong—' the doctor began, but Hubert waved that aside.

'For God's sake! My wife . . . what has happened?'

'She has had a stroke, Hubert, but she's recovering . . .'

'Oh dear God!'

'Yes, she'll recover, but the Lord is asking more of you. I cannot tell you how sorry I am to have to . . . It is my sad duty . . .' He had tears in his eyes. 'Erik and Ernst . . . they were killed in action . . . the French, at—'

'No! No. That can't be right. Not both of them. Impossible!'

'It was a cavalry charge, Hubert. They were very brave . . . their colonel said . . . proud of them. They were in the thick of it. Fighting side by side. The Colonel himself will . . .'

He was still speaking as Hubert got to his feet. 'I tried to break the news to Gabi as gently as possible, Hubert, but she won't accept it at all. Perhaps you could . . .'

But Hubert had stumbled away, too shocked to hear any more. He ran down the stairs to his study, slamming the door behind him before collapsing in tears. He had to restrain himself from shouting in rage, from screaming at himself for allowing this to happen. He should have listened to his wife. Put them on the first ship sailing to anywhere! Made them desert! Made them live! But no, he had been too proud to consider such a thing.

Later he made his weary way upstairs to sit with Gabi and Adele, to try to console them. He put his arms about them and held them close, praying with them, but his heart was broken, and with it his dreams.

Father Beitz came often, doing his best to help them through this terrible time. He prayed with them, and for them, because Mrs Hoepper, who had always been sickly, was deteriorating before his very eyes. There seemed to be nothing the doctor could do to stop the fits of vomiting that assailed her every time she swallowed any food, and then it became difficult to persuade her to eat anything. He thought it was probably a form of hysteria brought on by the loss of her sons, a suggestion which irritated the physician, who, in desperation, was in favour of force-feeding. But Mr Hoepper would not permit such a thing. Silently Father Beitz was thankful for that small mercy.

Just six weeks after the death of her sons, Gabi Hoepper suffered a heart attack and only lingered on for a few more days. Not even the love and attention of her distraught husband and daughter, and the prayers of so many friends and relations, could save her. She wanted to be with her sons, and it was their names she breathed at the last.

Father Beitz was busy, tremendously busy. Fortunately he didn't have a parish to worry about, having been 'put out to pasture', as he called his involuntary retirement, but he no longer had Hubert Hoepper to guide him, and he felt the loss quite severely.

Jakob Meissner had stepped into the breach, but it wasn't the same. After all, the priest told himself haughtily, Hoepper was a businessman and Meissner only a farmer.

There was no comparison. In fact he'd been greatly impressed that a man like Hoepper would even consider throwing in his lot with the mixture of farmers and peasants presenting themselves for this endeavour. Like a true leader, Hoepper was man enough to overlook class distinctions, and Father Beitz was grateful. He found no anomaly in his own attitude to Jakob Meissner, though. The priest was not given to self-observation; he'd been too long the lord of his parish manor. Though open to advice on occasion, he liked to be boss. This was his bailiwick, this grand mission. Meissner was a little too forward; he needed placing back a pew or two.

Jakob did know his place. He had wanted to call on Mr Hoepper and express his condolences for the loss of his sons, so he'd found the address in one of the committee's notebooks and made his way there, but he'd been intimidated by the row of tall dwellings, even before he located the Hoepper residence with its heavy carved door and shiny brass knocker. Embarrassed, hoping he hadn't been seen, Jakob retreated.

Hoepper, of course, no longer attended the meetings, and Jakob was having a hard time with Father Beitz, who seemed to think that he didn't need permission or agreement to make purchases with money from the common purse. He bought foolish things, like a supply of light summer hats, and bags of produce that had to be shared out right away since they wouldn't last until sailing time, which, as yet, had not been established. He bought several bolts of cloth to be used to clothe the natives who would come to his mission. Then he absent-mindedly left them at the door of their meeting hall and they were promptly stolen. But apart from this and other equally silly spendings, he went ahead and bought land in this town of Bundaberg without further reference to John Henderson.

Apparently the priest had been in touch by mail with a land agent in the city of Brisbane for quite a long time, and out of the blue he announced that they were the proud owners of forty acres of beautiful fertile land in the township that they'd chosen, on Henderson's advice, as their destination. Except that Henderson couldn't place the property or the road mentioned on the receipt.

Everyone else – the Kleinschmidt crowd, the Fechners, the Jenners and all the rest – was thrilled, carried away by his rhetoric, leaving Jakob and Freda Meissner to shake their heads and hope the forty acres would be suitable. It was too late to turn to Mr Hoepper for his support.

Then they heard from Father Beitz that Gabi Hoepper had died, broken-hearted over the loss of her sons, and they were devastated.

This time Jakob did visit Hubert Hoepper. He did not attend the funeral, though Father Beitz, of course, went along, representing the group. Not wishing to intrude, Jakob waited a few weeks after that before making his way to the door again.

A servant ushered him into a warm, comfortable parlour and Hoepper rose from a deep armchair to welcome him.

'Good of you to come, Mr Meissner.'

'Thank you, sir. I didn't know if you'd receive me. If you'd mind, I mean. I didn't want you to think that we'd forgotten you.' Jakob was suddenly so shy he was babbling, and he knew it, but somehow couldn't stop. 'I felt so bad about your terrible losses, I had to come here to tell you myself. I hope you're feeling all right.'

Hoepper didn't look all right. He looked terrible, very pale and drawn, and so much thinner.

'Thank you,' he said. 'I do appreciate this, Mr Meissner. Perhaps you might tell me how the travel arrangements are progressing. You understand, of course, that I won't be joining you.'

'I thought as much, sir, though you will be a great loss to us. Our main problem seems to be the numbers. Several people dropped out recently . . . fifteen, to be exact, including the Jenners.'

'Why? Cold feet?'

'Not in this case. They joined another large group of emigrants heading for a southern state in Australia, where they will be able to grow grapes and establish wineries.'

'That's interesting. How many do you think you have left?'

'I'm making the bookings this afternoon. On the *Regina*. She's two and a half thousand tons and carries about four hundred and sixty-five passengers, but this is what I wanted to ask you. My count is twenty-six, including the children, but Father says there are more. I think he wanted more, a lot more, but for my part, I think what we have is more manageable. People, I mean.'

'Do you have to book the passages today?'

'Yes. And pay for them. The last day. I have the subsidy documents, and the money, but too much money. Father Beitz insists I book for forty in case others turn up before she sails.'

'And when does she sail?'

'In three weeks.'

Hoepper sighed. 'I see your problem. But you don't have any more names. The shipping company will require names, genders, that sort of thing, to work out where to put so many people, so you won't have a choice.'

'I see. I couldn't just go along and book for forty anyway?'

'No. Your twenty-six definites will have to do for now. There may be space for more later.'

'Thank you, I am so relieved. But there is one other thing . . . Are you sure you won't change your mind and come with us? You and your daughter? We do need you.'

Jakob felt he had gone far enough in his mild criticism of Father Beitz, so he couldn't quite say why he thought this man was needed. Apart from the fact that he was a charming person.

'No, I'm sorry. I wouldn't consider going now.'

'But I heard you have sold your business, and so I hoped—'

Hoepper shook his head. 'The business was sold some time ago. I couldn't go back on my word. I had to let it go. Not that it matters. I wouldn't be interested now anyway.'

'You have retired?'

'Not exactly,' Hoepper said coldly. 'Totally lost interest, more like it. Why would I want to work now? Nothing to work for.'

'Oh, sir. I am sorry you feel that way. Is there anything I can do to help?

'No. Tell me, who are your twenty-six intrepid travellers?

Your pioneers. Because that's what you will be, you know. This place sounds like virgin territory.'

They talked for a long time. The servant brought coffee and cake and made a point of smiling and fussing over Jakob, even taking him aside before she ushered him out of the front door.

'Sir, the master asked you to call again. I hope you will have the kindness to do so. He is so broken-hearted he stays in there all the time, rarely sees people and never asks them back. I don't know what to do about him. His daughter Adele is the same. She doesn't go out anywhere, won't see people either, just stays in her room. Ah, this is a melancholy house, sir, truly too sad.'

Stunned, Jakob nodded. 'Of course. I will be back. While I can.'

And he was. On his last visit, the day before *Regina* sailed, he brought a large holy card, decorated by his wife Freda, with all their signatures on it and farewell notes to Mr Hoepper and his daughter. As he walked away after delivering it, Jakob was so very sad. He had established a rapport with Hoepper, and they'd been able to talk of many things over coffee, many things. Now he would indeed miss him.

On that last visit, also, Jakob had plucked up the courage to admonish Hoepper ever so gently.

'I saw your daughter, Miss Adele, before I came in this afternoon, Mr Hoepper. Is she well? She doesn't look well. I suppose it must be very hard for you to console her. She's so young to have suffered so much already.'

But Hoepper only nodded, making no comment.

Jakob walked down the street for the last time, admiring the symmetry of the tall, narrow houses, appreciating the small public park at the corner, with its wintering trees, its stolid benches and the brave little statue of Cupid. He was trying to set in place a remembrance of everything he could about this city of Hamburg, so *schön*, knowing he'd never see it again once the *Regina* sailed.

Shipboard life was a revelation to Jakob. It was like being in a rabbit warren, people everywhere. Folk travelling on assisted passages had berths in segregated areas, with three levels of bunks crowded together in rows, and when he saw them Jakob was appalled. He thought they were worse than a rabbit warren, more like pantry shelves long enough to place humans on. Since he had made the bookings at the shipping office, he felt responsible for their plight, and offered to make a complaint to the Captain, but Rolf Kleinschmidt, spokesman for a dozen young people who all seemed to be related by kin or marriage, wasn't concerned.

'Don't worry about it, Mr Meissner. We didn't expect any better. Only I would have liked my wife Rosie to be by my side. A sailor told me married couples might be able to make other arrangements once we get going. Once we see if there are any vacancies.'

'Are you sure, Rolf?' Jakob asked, peering into the cramped dormitory, wondering how these people could be saved if, God forbid, there was a fire or the ship was sinking.

'Yes. We're all looking forward to the voyage. It will be great fun.'

Jakob blinked. He didn't feel old at forty, but since he couldn't see much fun in their predicament, he guessed he must be getting on. He decided, then and there, that he too would find fun as well as adventure on this strange ship, no matter what.

That attitude was to serve him well over the next few months, when tempers became short thanks to overcrowding, poor rations and the ever-present seasickness. He and Freda were in married quarters below decks, separated from the first-class passengers, but there was little privacy. Their cabin was only a curtained-off space, tiny at that, one of the many along this section of the ship. The curtains were weighted canvas – remains of sails, he supposed – and could not be expected to contain sound, so he and Freda, and everyone else in the row, were reduced to whispering all the time. After a while they all gave up, until the days turned into weeks and the noise grew and voices were heard shouting for people to shut up.

The saving grace was, after all, the number of people packed into the ship, for it meant that Father Beitz's contingent was not thrown together all the time. There were plenty of other people to talk to, play games with, stroll their section of the deck with, to enjoy.

The Captain arranged a great party when they crossed the equator on the southern run down the coast of Africa, but Jakob didn't see much of it because Father Beitz, overcome by the stifling heat, was taken ill, and he was called to his side.

Jakob thought the old priest must be delirious when he clutched his hand and whispered: 'I'll be better as soon as I get off this ship. I won't take that doctor's foul brews.'

'They're not foul brews, Father. They're cooling drinks. Let me sponge you down. You are perspiring a great deal. You have to drink plenty of water.'

'The water is foul, don't touch me with it. Help me up. I want to go on deck where it's cooler.'

'Later. We can go later when the celebrations are over.'

'Ah, yes, Jakob, I heard. No wonder I'm so ill, with all that blasphemy and cavorting going on up there, and no one to speak for the Lord, to thank Him for keeping us safe.'

'I'm sure they will, Father.'

The patient sighed. 'Never mind. We'll be putting ashore in a few days and the first thing we will be doing . . . and let there be no argument on this . . . I want the whole ship's company to go down on their knees and thank God for preserving us. Before they disembark, all of them. Do you hear me?'

'You should try to sleep now, Father. Here's some medication to make you sleep.'

'I don't need that,' he wheezed. 'Pray with me, Jakob. In two days' time we'll be in Australia and we'll start our work.'

The next morning, the old gentleman who was sharing a private cabin with Father Beitz came searching for Jakob.

'Your priest is a lot better, Mr Meissner. But he is packing. He seems to think we are nearing our destination, though I've tried to tell him that the *Regina*'s first stop is Cape Town.'

In the end Jakob had to enlist the support of the Captain to explain to Father Beitz that Australia was not an African state. That it would be months before they reached their actual destination. That after the Cape they would not be calling at any more ports before they reached the east coast of Australia.

Father Beitz was shocked. Jakob wouldn't have been surprised if he'd disembarked in Cape Town and returned to Hamburg, but he did not. He stayed.

In the meantime, ship's gossip had picked up on the story, and the priest was a laughing stock. Jakob found this ridicule of the elderly man offensive, and said so very sharply, soon quashing that joke.

After that, Father Beitz took to wandering about the ship, a little distraught at the thought of the months ahead. He didn't seem to know what to do with himself. Though many tried to distract him, he leaned on Jakob a great deal, at the same time criticising him at every opportunity. He compared Jakob, as a lowly farmhand, to his good friend Mr Hoepper, a wealthy merchant, who would have, with his fine family and their servants, accompanied the priest on his mission had he not been struck down by tragedy. And in the telling, to anyone who would listen, Jakob came off badly, so much so that in the end Freda was fed up.

'Why do you jump to attention for him like that? He won't thank you. He's using you as his servant: "Get me this. Take me up top. It's too hot, take me down!" Stop it, Jakob.'

'I can't do that. He's alone, he has no one to care for him.'

But when she heard Father Beitz refer to her husband as a peasant, she attacked him.

My husband is a farmer! No less than that. Do you hear me, you old goat? If you refer to my husband as a peasant again, I'll wring your neck.'

'You're a madwoman!'

'No I'm not. You think up too many ways to belittle a very kind man, and I won't have it. You stop or you'll hear from me.'

When Jakob heard this he was mortified. 'I don't need you to fight my battles, Freda. And anyway, there are no battles here. Father Beitz is just a cranky old man. My Uncle Hans-Joachim was just the same. We shouldn't be worried about the priest, we have to look to the future. We have the most astonishing adventures ahead of us, Freda, what does it matter if I have to be the servant of a poor old man for a short while?

Look at those stars out there. We're in the southern hemisphere, we've even got a wealth of new stars to learn about! By the way, where's Karl?'

'He and his friend Michael have agreed to give up their canvas cabin to Rolf and Rosie, so he lives down in the dormitory now.'

It was a beautiful starry night, but Jakob's thoughts were still with his Uncle Hans-Joachim, who had always given a blunt response to his nephew's concerns.

'We're so poor,' Jakob would say. 'We work hard. Why is there never enough to go around? Our children are thin, the crops are weakening from overuse of the land, the women huddle over scraps . . .'

'I'll tell you then,' Hans-Joachim would reply. 'It's your grandpa who's to blame, lad. He used to boast that he'd fathered eight sons, and his sons between them had fathered more. But he never gave thought to how our little valley farms were supposed to support them. He thought we'd all go on in the old way, but that can't be, now. There are just too many Meissners.'

Just too many Meissners. And wasn't that a fact? All of them barely earning enough to exist after they'd paid their dues to the Junker, a newly rich former colonel who'd come by this valley through a deal that none of the lowly people toiling on his estates were privy to. Not that they cared. The dues still had to be paid. Farm rents. In cash in winter and in produce in the summer. No matter who got them in the end, the collectors were always the same cold, hard men who would never relent, and who showed no pity despite the distress of so many poor families.

Thinking back now, looking about at all the people who preferred to sleep on deck on these hot, sultry nights, it was hard to recall the winters they had left behind. Hard winters, miserable, freezing. Especially the nights. Jakob remembered how Freda used to tease him, claiming he'd only married her to keep warm at night.

It was Freda's brother who had come up with the idea of emigrating. For him, though, it was only a pipe dream. He brought home a box of papers that provided information on several countries and had Jakob read them to him, since he could neither read nor write himself. He enjoyed these reading sessions so much that he ended up being able to recite the information by heart, but it was Jakob who caught the urge to emigrate. Freda was all for it too, but poverty had them in its clutches, had them fearful of taking that giant step, until the day fate smiled on them and Freda came into a small inheritance! They knew this was the time. Now or never. They had to look to their son's future as well as their own. They packed up and travelled to Hamburg to make further enquiries into what point of the compass might best receive them, eventually meeting the Queensland agent, John Henderson.

'So here we are,' Jakob said now, hugging his wife to him. 'Any regrets?'

'Bit late for that,' Freda replied, with her usual candour.

Chapter Four

Father Beitz ushered all his chicks ashore in Brisbane, had them stand together on the wharf so that Theo Zimmerman could do a count, and then called them to prayer, to give thanks to the Lord for their deliverance from the great oceans over which they had travelled. At the Amen, he announced that everyone was to follow him on a walking tour of the town to stretch their legs.

'What about all our luggage?' Theo asked him. 'It has to be transferred to the coastal steamer.'

'Jakob's in charge of that. He's seeing to it. But you may go and help him if you wish.'

'No!' Eva Zimmerman cried, clutching her three children to her skirts. She looked over at the lush green town on this lazy April morn, and saw a few white colonial buildings and not much else beyond the usual riverside warehouses and bedraggled boathouses. 'Theo stays with us,' she said, turning to him. 'Don't you dare leave us, Theo Zimmerman. There are savages and wild animals in this country, you wouldn't know what dangers lurk around the corners!'

Hanni Fechner wasn't too thrilled either. 'How far do we have to walk, Father? It's a hot day. I'd prefer to sit down somewhere and have coffee and a nice cake. I can't recall when we last ate anything nice.'

'Pity about her,' Eva sniffed, but Lucas Fechner explained to them that the Captain had said that this was only a small town, and quite safe. In fact, small though it was, the town was the capital of the state.

'How can that be?' Rolf Kleinschmidt asked.

'I don't rightly know,' Lucas said, 'but we might as well have a look while we're here. Lead on, Father!'

The priest took them up the hill, right into what was obviously the main street, fussing over them like a nun leading schoolgirls, and Eva found herself laughing as passers-by, normal everyday people, stopped to stare at them. This was a very nice little town; there were no savages to be seen.

In double quick time, Father Beitz herded them up one street and down the next, so that very soon they were standing in front of a grand sandstone building, which they learned was the Parliament House, and only a few years old.

Rolf Kleinschmidt was at it again. He'd been driving Father Beitz mad all the way, asking questions. This time he wanted to know where the Parliament was before this was built, and since no one could answer, he walked right into the building and enquired, returning with a booklet and a mine of information.

'There was no Parliament before this,' he grinned. 'Now I'm even more confused.'

Eva liked him. She understood that thirst for knowledge. She used to be like that herself. Her father used to say: 'That girl would question the archangel at the gate!' But married life and a succession of misfortunes had taught her not to further complicate her days, to concentrate on the job at hand. At thirty-eight, Eva knew there was only a glimmer of that girl left in her. But it was there. By God it was.

For years now she and Theo and the children had been reduced to living in a two-roomed tenement building in the slums of Hamburg: a kitchen that at least had a stove to keep them warm when they could afford wood, and a bedroom. That was all.

Father Beitz interrupted her thoughts. 'Good. We've seen the town. Now we go back to the wharves and board the steamer *Tara*. See how it is spelled . . . T-A-R-A . . . and no, Rolf, I do not know what the word means.'

'You go on down to the steamer, Father,' Rolf said. 'We'll be all right here. It doesn't sail until four this afternoon. I think it would be good for the children to stay ashore a while.'

His wife, Rosie, laughed. 'And the big children too.'

Eva wanted to agree with Rolf Kleinschmidt, but there was the matter of food. It was midday, her children, Robie, Hans and Inge, were hungry, and she had no money. The Zimmermans had travelled on assisted passages, as had all of the Kleinschmidts and a few others in the group, and they had little cash of their own. What with one thing and another, even before they reached Brisbane, her husband Theo only had a few shillings in his purse, which Eva found hugely embarrassing, though it didn't bother Theo.

'We'd like to stay, Rolf,' she said quickly, 'but we can't. We have to go back to the ship.'

'No you don't,' Rolf said. 'It's such a lovely day and this is a pretty spot down here by the river, we ought to have a picnic. Everyone stay here, Walther and I will see to some eats!'

Walther Badke was a big fellow, a brewer by trade, who had become an ardent follower of Father Beitz. Eva had heard it said that Walther would follow him into the darkest wilderness, so great was his faith in the priest's mission. Something of a cynic, she thought they were probably doing that anyway. From what they'd seen so far, the dark green wall of this coastline could hold myriad terrors.

But still, they had a wonderful day, and the children were able to run and play after all those weeks at sea. The two men came back with a box of fresh food, including bread, meat, cheese and a heap of fruit. Eva glanced at her elder son Robie, who was ten, happy to see him looking so well. He had always suffered from serious respiratory problems, and would catch a cold if the wind blew, but now he was running around without his usual panting and wheezing. Doctors had told her that Robie wasn't long for this life, that the skinny boy didn't have the strength to fight off all those bad colds indefinitely.... Eva hoped to God they were wrong.

It was the only reason she had agreed to emigrate. To move her children to a warmer climate, hoping Theo had it right this time, and that emigrating wasn't just another of his harebrained schemes. She sighed. Her husband had tried just about everything and failed, and kept on failing even though he'd been adamant, with each new job, that this time he'd do well. He had been a street vendor, a commissionaire, a bootmaker, a circus clown, a hospital orderly, all sorts of things, and now, in the new land; he saw himself as a farmer. Probably a gentleman farmer, she thought grimly, but she had warned him that once they got to this town of Bundaberg, there would be changes.

She had decided, made a promise to herself, that she wasn't about to put up with his nonsense any longer. Or anyone else's for that matter. Her days of being pushed around were over. New land, new life, new Eva. She knew now that if she didn't make herself responsible for her family, her children, no one would. And so far, thank God, the climate was on her side. At least Theo had got that right. This was April, and it was a marvellous day, blue and sunny, not a cloud in the sky.

They were all on deck as the little steamer, PS *Tara*, sailed across Herveys Bay, making for the lighthouse at Burnett Heads, and when the pilot came aboard, Father Beitz was so excited he was close to fainting. Freda Meissner found somewhere for him to sit on deck, and left her son Karl with him while she went in search of Jakob.

She found him below decks, piling up and checking the group's luggage.

'Leave that right now,' she said. 'There's plenty of time to do it when the ship berths. We're crossing the most beautiful bay . . .'

'I know,' he smiled. 'I had a look. It's called Herveys Bay.'

'And we're entering the Burnett River,' she went on, 'and that leads us to the town of Bundaberg. This is the last part of our journey and I want the three of us to be together, Jakob. So please, come up on deck now.'

Jakob was surprised. His wife was rarely given to sentimentality, but he understood that this was an important time for the Meissners, even historic, one could say.

He nodded, kissed her on the cheek. 'Whatever you say, my darling.'

They lined up on the rails with the other passengers as the ship slid slowly upstream, looking out at banks of green forests.

'I wonder where our land is,' Karl said. 'We might even be passing it.'

'Possibly.' That land still had Jakob worried. He had heard since that many people purchased land sight unseen, on the advice of agents, but the concept still didn't sit well with him.

He looked about him. They couldn't see much beyond the forests, but there wasn't a mountain in sight. It had to be fairly flat land then, good for farming. The air was clean, crisp and sweet, and when he realised that he could identify that aroma, he reached over to Karl.

'Smell it, boy. Eucalyptus. It really is very strong. If you look into the forest, you'll see eucalypt trees everywhere.'

Jakob was pleased with himself for that small knowledge in this strange country. For it was strange, no matter how much they'd read or been told. A mindset remained of how the air should smell, how forests should look, but these woods were unusual . . . He could see palms in among the trees, and shoulder-high grasses, yellow against the dark foliage. Then there was the river itself . . . Odd to see a big river just ambling along. And you would expect distant countryside like this to be quiet and restful, but no, over the dull chug of the engine there was an excitement of bird calls and screeches emanating from the trees, and occasionally a flock of gorgeous birds would speed across the sky.

Freda turned quickly to ask a crew member what sort of birds they were.

'Only parrots,' he said, and she smiled at his nonchalance. To her they were the most exotic creatures she had ever seen.

They were headed for a bend in the river, and the Captain gave three sharp blasts on his steam whistle that sent a thrill through the ranks of the immigrants, who had now come to the end of the line and were all wondering what lay ahead for them, not just in this town but in the future. Kindly, Jakob called to the young Lutze boys to join them. They were orphans who'd been gathered up by Father Beitz, fine lads . . . Max was sixteen and Hans fifteen. They came over shyly, as always, and then Lucas and Hanni Fechner joined them too.

The Fechners had both worked on some grand estate, and it was whispered that they'd run off from their duties. Absconded to Hamburg, where they'd met Father Beitz. Jakob was quite fond of them, though Freda was inclined to dismiss the wife, Hanni, as a flibbertigibbet.

Automatically, Jakob found himself counting heads again, ducking about to get the fair-haired Kleinschmidts in sight, all twelve of them, eight men and four women. The eldest of the clan, their leader, Rolf, was himself only twenty-four. They were a handsome lot, and jolly. They'd thoroughly enjoyed the voyage, but were surprisingly disciplined, never missing an English lesson, any of them, though they'd obviously found five lessons a week heavy going.

And there, towering over everyone, was Walther, his ruddy face a picture of joy. Many of the group, as well as Father Beitz, had been stunned to learn how long the voyage was taking, but Walther was more concerned than anyone. Though they showed him maps, he could not imagine how they could possibly find their way across these oceans to a tiny little speck on a page. The delight and relief was there in his face as he lifted up little Robie Zimmerman to give him a better view.

What would they find here? Not for the first time, Jakob experienced a stab of doubt, of fear. Were they doing the right thing? Suddenly the forests crowding the river banks seemed lonely, menacing and secretive, for they showed no sign of life except for the birds, who'd disappeared anyway, warned off by those whistle blasts. Change had come for them too, he supposed.

The women had been worried about the natives they would encounter, and Jakob had kept on assuring them, on Hubert Hoepper's advice, that they were friendly and would do the settlers no harm, but in a weak moment he had approached a sailor on the *Tara* and asked the same question.

'The Abo's?' the man had replied. 'They won't bother you round Bundaberg, nor Maryborough, not in those towns. But you won't want to go too far into their territory or you'll get a spear in your back. A mate of mine was killed up at the Cape River a while back. Mad, I say. I wouldn't want to set foot near the place. But that's the gold fever for you.'

It was days before Jakob, in a fit of panic, was able to discover that the goldfields of the Cape River were indeed in this state of Queensland, but a thousand miles to the north, so it was unlikely that those wild tribes would be bothering the Bundabergians. But that knowledge brought home to him the size of this country.

'If this state is more than a thousand miles long, and God knows how wide,' he said to Freda as he pored over a map the Captain had loaned to him, 'how big is this country? This continent?'

'What does it matter? It just goes to show that's why they need so many immigrants.'

'It does matter,' he said moodily. 'I feel like an ant.'

Freda laughed. 'Don't be crazy. An ant! What next?'

Jakob felt less than an ant at his first glimpse of their future home. It was with a shock of disappointment that he surveyed the place, little more than a lonely hamlet cut into the high bank of the river. This was the first sign of habitation they'd encountered since leaving Brisbane, and he found the isolation suddenly overwhelming. He wanted to push back, to stay on the small ship and be delivered from this depressing outpost, but he was moving forward with the crowd, heading down the gangplank, too late to turn back, so he took his wife by the arm, put on a brave face and stepped ashore in Bundaberg.

They cleared the wharf and gathered on the adjacent dusty paddock, and were standing peering about them when a man shouted:

'All immigrants to the Customs House over there.'

It was just as well he pointed, because none of them, Jakob thought, would have taken the bare, single-roomed timber building for a Customs House. It looked temporary, as if a good wind would blow it away. Beyond this paddock, though, was a street of sorts, and Jakob wandered over to have a look, seeing first a dozen or more goats moving aimlessly about. The street could only boast a few more of the plain wooden buildings, all unpainted, housing a store, a telegraph office, some work sheds and, further down, a police station. The rest of the street seemed to gape with open spaces, unkempt blocks of land overgrown with dried grass and skinny trees. In contrast, heavy old trees had been left standing to shade a

67

roadway still embedded with tree stumps. He saw a couple in a gig manoeuvring their way around these obstacles, with no sign of concern. They waved.

Some of the others came over to take in the view, such as it was, and several of the goats, chomping and chewing, sidled over to gaze at the newcomers with an unmistakable air of superiority.

Karl caught up with his father. 'Where's the town, Dad?'

It was Freda who answered, lips pursed, voice cold. 'This, I believe, is it. I'm told we are looking at Quay Street, and beyond that is Bourbong Street.'

'Maybe the next street is busier,' Jakob said hopefully.

Apparently the Customs Officer was away, so they were met by a policeman who introduced himself as Constable Colley. He collected the German contingent and took them further down the street to a long, low stone building.

'These are the immigration barracks. You folk can stay here until you get yourselves sorted out. Over under the trees there, the ladies of the town have prepared afternoon tea for you, because we want you to feel welcome in our little town, and we hope you'll be happy here.'

This was a surprise, but Father Beitz, looking worn and travel-weary, was up to the occasion. He stepped forward and thanked the Constable, walking with him towards the ladies and the neatly set tables.

Karl Meissner didn't wait to hear the speeches; he slipped away to get a better look at this place, hurrying along Quay Street but finding only another store, a butcher shop, a grog shop and a small hotel. Round the corner were some tiny cottages and stables, plus the inevitable blacksmith, then he found the wide Bourbong Street, which was just more of the same, another rough, untidy street, another collection of dismal shops with ugly awnings. He saw several horses waiting listlessly by hitching rails, and there were a few people standing about, but they looked to him unreal, like figures in a tableau.

He shook his head in disbelief. This wasn't a town, it was only a settlement, a shabby little dump that gave no air of permanence. Karl was shocked. He had expected fine new

68

houses with tropical gardens and waving palms, a traditional rural village made more exotic by the climate. It was hot, but dry and dusty. Disappointment brought angry criticism as he raced back to share the tea and cakes.

'It's an awful place,' he told his father. 'They haven't even got a village square. There's just nothing here!'

Then he gaped. Standing watching them from a grove of trees were a dozen or more natives, men and women, and they weren't wearing a stitch of clothing!

Nora Stenning and her friends loved to watch the ships come in especially when they brought immigrants, who always looked so strange, so confused. A few weeks ago a group of Scots had come through, the men wearing kilts and the women with their babies bound to them with heavy shawls. And, her father had said, some of them were so poor they were carrying empty suitcases.

'Why would they do that?' she asked.

'Pride,' he'd laughed. 'They can't admit they've got nothing.'

She'd found that very sad. Not funny at all. But they'd all passed through the town quickly, taken up as station workers. The Germans, though, this lot, were said to have purchased forty acres of land somewhere around the town, so it was expected, hoped rather, that they'd stay, swell the numbers in the town, help the few shopkeepers stay afloat. That was why Jim Pimbley, who owned the Sunshine Store across the street from the barracks, had asked the ladies to put on this spread, and the newcomers seemed to be enjoying themselves. They'd come an awful long way.

Nora watched them as she refilled plates with scones. They were nearly all fair-haired, strong folk, skin fair too, and rosy-cheeked. The men's clothes were heavier, leather jackets, waistcoats, even leather trousers. The women wore shawls as big as capes, prettied with fancywork, as were their bonnets, and some of them wore fancy pinafores over their dresses, which the onlookers found odd for streetwear, but it was all very interesting.

The women around her leaned forward to listen to the deep

69

foreign voices, some eyes skimming the men with special interest.

'I'll bet some of the big fellows are timbermen,' a woman said. 'Les Jolly will be after them. He needs more loggers.'

'I heard they're all farmers. Do you see the clogs? Some are wearing real clogs.'

'Who's the old bearded bloke? He looks like Father Christmas.'

'Don't be so ignorant. He's a priest.'

Nora's friend Jenny Pimbley nudged her. 'Some of the lads are really good-looking. I like the one in the black jacket. I heard them call him Karl.'

'No, he's too young. I prefer—' Nora didn't get to finish the sentence, to say she fancied the big blond man with the rucksack on his back. He had a lovely smile and seemed to be thrilled with everything. But someone yelled, shouted. What could be causing such a disturbance?

The priest was shouting, pointing at the blacks, rushing about, making all the Germans turn away, spluttering at Clem Colley about sinfulness, demanding that the natives be removed, be clothed.

'Here is proof that I am needed here,' he shouted. 'That you should all stand by, witnessing nakedness, is blasphemy!'

Clem ran like a startled goat to chase the natives away, while some of the newcomers tried to quieten the priest, and Nora, laughing, caught the eye of that man with the lovely smile. He nodded, obviously amused too, and reached for a piece of fruit cake.

Jakob was grateful for this unexpected burst of efficiency in the form of barracks accommodation. He'd been wondering exactly how they would cope when they stepped ashore with no home to go to, thinking they'd probably have to find a boarding house or two, to take them all. Just as well that hadn't eventuated, since Karl had said there was only one small boarding house, in the next street.

He saw to it that everyone had their cabin luggage and arranged for all the rest of their possessions, located in the hold, to be transferred to a warehouse and collected when

70

they found homes. All of that completed, Jakob walked back to the barracks to find that trouble had erupted already.

They had sorted out the sleeping arrangements without any bother because the barracks were simply divided into male and female. Between the two sections was a communal kitchen, which was all very well, but as Freda told Jakob, 'We haven't any food.'

He looked at the women as if they were mad. 'There's a store across the street. Get what you need.'

'With what? Father Beitz has our money. He says we've done well enough today, we don't need anything for supper.'

Eva Zimmerman broke in. 'I don't care about myself, Jakob. But my children have to be fed.'

'Don't worry, Eva, there will be supper. I'll fetch Father Beitz.' And as an afterthought he added, 'And Walther.'

The group walked over to the store, where they were met by Jim Pimbley, who had been one of the welcoming party earlier in the afternoon.

'What can I do for you?' he asked, rubbing his hands on his apron. 'I stock everything here from sugar to saddles.'

Freda stepped forward with her list, but that was already too much for the priest. Despite Walther's attempts to stop him, he grabbed the list, read it and fumed: 'No. No! This is too much. We can't afford all this. Two dozen eggs! Bacon and oats and soap and coffee, and all the rest. No. We only want bread and milk for the children.' He tossed the piece of paper on the floor.

The shopkeeper blinked, looking from one to another, and Walther picked up the list, also uncertain of the next move.

'We will have to resolve this,' Jakob said to him quietly. 'That's why I wanted you to come along. I wouldn't even try to talk to Father Beitz about money. I'll pay this bill today, Walther, but tomorrow it will have to stop. He can't be allowed sole control of the funds.'

'But what can I do?'

Jakob called to Mr Pimbley: 'Excuse me, sir. Is there a bank in this town?'

'Yes, sir. Across in the next street.'

'Thank you.' He turned back to Walther. 'You know he

71

keeps all the money in cash in the leather purse. That won't do now. It will have to be banked tomorrow.'

Meanwhile Father Beitz was allowing that perhaps they could buy eggs as well, but nothing else.

'Don't be ridiculous,' Freda said angrily. 'The loaves and fishes story won't work here.'

The priest looked about him serenely. 'The Lord will provide. You mention fish. Well, that river is full of fish. I saw them jumping.'

Jakob took the list to the counter and handed it to Pimbley. 'I'll be paying,' he said quietly.

'If you do, it's out of your own money!' Beitz snapped.

Jakob took the priest by the arm and led him outside. 'It is your duty to attend to spiritual matters, Father, but you must allow the ladies to do their duty. It will be difficult enough for them in our primitive circumstances, so please let them get on with it.'

'They can get on with it, but I won't pay for their extravagance.'

Jakob sighed. They had at least two hundred pounds in the common fund, which wasn't a great deal for so many people, admittedly, but Beitz was being unrealistic. They would have to be careful with their funds until folk got started, but there was no need to begin by starving everyone.

'I will buy whatever is needed,' he insisted. 'And you will repay me, Father. We'll have no further argument.'

The priest shrugged, and stormed away.

Freda was furious when she saw Jakob paying from his own purse. 'It's not right. We can't afford all this. You go over and demand that he pay you right now.'

'I can't very well hit him over the head and grab it. He's old and confused, Freda. Leave him be. I'll try to have him put the funds in the bank tomorrow, if possible.'

'It will be possible. I'll make sure of it,' she said. 'I suppose we ought to thank the Lord that this place actually has a bank.'

The women had made sure there was enough food to begin to stock a larder, so breakfast the next morning was a new pleasure, standing in line on a beautiful morning for a share of this wonderfully fresh food.

Mr Pimbley had brought them a box of pineapples and bananas, which he said was free, compliments of his wife.

'Once they get this ripe we can't sell them, so you might as well have them. And the butcher sent round some steak for your breakfast.'

Steak for breakfast! The women were cooking eggs. They looked nonplussed as he took the slabs of beef out and slapped them on top of the stove one after another. Freda made a move as if to stop him, but Rolf Kleinschmidt was too quick for her. He'd sized up the situation very quickly and moved to help Mr Pimbley rather than allow the meat to be salvaged for a more appropriate meal.

'The butcher didn't have any chops this morning,' Pimbley said in apology to Rolf, as he poked at the sizzling beef.

'I see,' said Rolf, humouring him. 'Then chops are more correct for breakfast here?'

Pimbley blinked. 'Chops? I dunno. We have what's going for breakfast . . . chops, steak, bacon, sausages. With the eggs.' Then he grinned, 'A bit of the lot is best, though, isn't it?'

Rolf had a smile on his face too. If that was what these people put away first thing in the morning, then he was all for it. He hoped meat was cheap. And then dared to ask, in a roundabout way.

'Plenty of meat here, sir?'

'Any amount, son. You're in the heart of beef and sheep country.'

Jakob too was delighted by this windfall of a meal, surprised to hear the whisper that these big juicy steaks were normal fare for breakfast in these backwoods.

After his meal he walked over to Father Beitz, who was sitting on an upturned box, well apart from everyone.

'Did you enjoy your breakfast, Father?'

'I had my boiled egg.'

'Can I get you something else?'

'No.'

'What about some tea? They've made tea.'

'God gave us water. I can drink water.'

'You ate a lot better on the ship, so I know you have a good appetite.'

'The food on the ship was free.'

'No it wasn't, you paid for it in your ticket.'

'I did not. You'd better watch out, Jakob. By the time those women are finished, we'll have nothing left.'

'You worry too much, Father. Everything will be all right. We have the climate we always wanted . . . a lovely blue day, and this is autumn.'

'You believe that tale? What a fool you are, Jakob. Anyone can see it is summer.'

'Never mind. We haven't ended up in a desert, so all we have to do now is take a look at our land.'

Jakob felt a swell of pride at the thought. Their land. Their beginnings. Forty whole acres, all to themselves.

'If you get the papers, Father, I thought we could take them over to the shopkeeper, Mr Pimbley, who has been very helpful. I'm sure he won't mind directing us to our land.'

That brightened the priest. He was up in an instant, hurrying towards the barracks to bring forth the precious title deeds.

Jim Pimbley studied the papers that Father Beitz handed to him: the title deeds, the receipt from the Tom Taylor Stock and Station Agency, and the pages of area and section maps.

'I'd say the scale of this map is a bit out of whack,' he said eventually. 'By the looks of it, your land is by the river, but I'd say it's a fair way inland.'

'How far?' Jakob asked.

'About three miles, maybe more. Walking distance. He's got Ferny Creek marked here as running through your block, so we shouldn't have much trouble if we keep the creek in sight. I'll bring the buggy round and we'll go out and see if we can spot it.'

'Now?'

'Yes. The missus can mind the store. Not much doing anyway. I haven't been far down Taylor's Road, what he calls it on this here map. We call it Taylor's Track. I didn't even know there was land taken up out that way.'

Father Beitz was so excited he was shaking. 'I'll just run back and get my coat.'

'No. Stay here,' Jakob said. 'I'll get it for you, though I don't think you'll need it.'

But the priest rushed away, calling to him not to go without him.

'As if we'd dare,' Jakob grinned, but his smile froze when he realised that the priest had alerted everyone. They all came dashing out of the barracks, running across the road, the men hastily planting hats on their heads, the women grabbing at their shawls.

'Are we going out to our land?' Freda, one of the front-runners, asked him.

'No. This gentleman is just going to take Father Beitz and me to try and locate the land. The map is rather vague.'

When their new friend Jim brought the buggy to the front of the shop, Freda was the first to ask him: 'Please, may I come too?'

'Sure. Room for one more.'

And with a hop, step, Freda was in the buggy, waiting for her husband and the priest, before they realised she was aboard.

Jakob called to the company: 'Thanks to this gentleman we have transport to find our block of land. As soon as we do this, we'll come back and you'll hear all about it.'

Walther, too, was excited. His eyes shone. 'We can walk. We'll follow you.'

'Bit of a maze out there, that flat bush country,' Jim told him. 'You could easily get lost. Waste a lot of time.'

'Just stay here. Be patient,' Father Beitz said. 'We will locate the block, and tomorrow we will lead you to it. Tomorrow we move on to our own land! Praise be to the Lord!'

There was a short thrill of applause and a reluctant acceptance of his ruling, but as they stepped back Jim spoke to Jakob, who was sitting next to him, with Freda and Father Beitz in the back.

'I wouldn't be too sure about that.'

'About what?'

'Moving on to the block so soon. Some of that land is scrub country.'

'Excuse me. What does scrub mean?'

Jim slapped the reins and the horse trotted down the street and rounded the corner, heading inland.

'Scrub? Let me see. Most places, scrub is just rough timbered country with a lot of useless stuff lying around.'

'I suppose all of this land was once scrub country.'

'Not quite. The town area is river flats. Not hard to clear. Then you've got the plains further out, all taken up years ago. Good grazing land.'

'But I still do not understand this scrub you speak of.'

'That's understandable. Usually scrub is just that. What I told you, rough country. But there's some land hereabouts they call The Scrubs. Nothin' but jungle . . . I'm hoping that's not what you've bought, but I heard a Tom Taylor sold a lot of blocks out there before folk woke up to him. They ran him out of town. Two men that he duped burnt his office down.'

Jakob wasn't too concerned. He had expected that virgin land would need clearing for farming. This scrub land was obviously more timbered than the open eucalypt woodlands they were already driving through. From a distance the forests looked dark and cluttered, but as they drew closer he observed that the trees were well spaced for light and the trunks were tall and skinny, as if they'd raced for the sky from birth.

Freda screamed, and Jim pulled the horse to a halt with a jerk.

'What is it?' he cried.

'A kangaroo! Over there. Look! There are two, no, three of them! Father Beitz, have you ever seen anything so lovely?' She was clutching the priest's arm and Beitz was equally dazzled.

'They're tame, I think. Such beautiful animals. Can we pat them?' he asked.

Jim gave a noisy sigh of relief. 'Good God! She gave me such a turn. I thought she'd fallen out!'

He clicked the horse into moving on. 'No, Father, they're not tame. They'll bolt if you go near them.'

'Aaah,' was all the priest could say, lost in wonder at finding himself so close to the strange doe-eyed creatures.

Jim took pity on him. 'If you get a baby kangaroo, a joey we call them, they make good pets, Father.'

'Goodness me,' Beitz said, still charmed.

Taylor's Road *was* only a track, as Jim had warned, and a bumpy, rutted track at that, but there were markers cut into a tree, so Jim stopped to investigate. He tramped through tall grass, stared at the tree and called: 'Lot One. See this arrow? It points ahead. You're Lots Seven to Fourteen. A good way in yet, if this is the right place. I reckon you've bought half of Tom's Banjoor Estate.'

As he turned, he picked up a rough noticeboard that had fallen from the tree 'Hang on. Here we are. Banjoor Estate. This is Taylor's selection all right. He always was one for putting on airs. Doesn't look too bad from here, folks, but it leads right into The Scrubs.'

'Then we must keep going down this road,' Father Beitz said happily, not understanding the implication, and Jakob didn't feel up to explaining. Not yet, anyway. There was always hope.

'We're looking for Lot Seven,' he said. 'We have to keep a lookout for marks on trees.'

'Or roadside pegs,' Jim added.

Freda looked about her, probably hoping to see more kangaroos. 'What does Banjoor mean?' she asked Jim.

'Aborigine word. The blacks here are the Taribelang people, and their clans, or families, have their own names. One is Banjoor, so there's your name. Another one is Bunda, so you've got Bundaberg, see?'

'Yes. Thank you,' Freda said. 'Look – isn't that a sign on the tree over this side?'

'Certainly is. There's Lot Two.'

They made slow progress along the track, searching out more lots while Jim manoeuvred the buggy over bumps and rocky obstacles, until it ended abruptly. A dead end.

Without having to be shown, Jakob knew, heart sinking, that a sign blazed into a tree ahead of them read, 'Lot 7'.

It had two arrows, one pointing to the left and one to the right.

Here were their blocks. Dense, impenetrable jungle.

'This is it all right,' Jim said ruefully. 'The Scrubs. I wish I could have taken you to better country. Plenty of it around here still.'

They climbed down from the buggy and walked along in front of the block as if looking for a gate, an entrance into this wall of greenery. With a farmer's eye, Jakob examined the forest confronting him. Aged ivy-laden trees stood waist deep in wild, tangled undergrowth. Younger trees sprouting from the dense base formed their own barriers, and thick bushes crowded for space.

He shook his head and looked to Jim. 'Be a hard job to clear this.'

'Bloody hard, mate. It'd take a year just to get a foothold.'

It was very quiet, with just the breath of a wind, and Father Beitz called to them from a few feet into the wilderness.

'Listen! A stream. I can hear it. We must find it. I have to see this!'

Before they could stop him he had plunged into the scrub, only to find himself entangled in a thorny bush within minutes.

The other men soon freed him but they could not dim his enthusiasm. Father Beitz had to see the stream, noted on his map as Ferny Creek.

Jim went back to the large box he kept on a shelf under the tray of his buggy, and returned with an axe and a machete. Soon he and Jakob were slashing their way through ferns and high grass, stumbling heavily as they encountered uneven ground, rocks and fallen tree trunks hidden by the deep undergrowth. They ducked under heavy branches, cursing quietly so as not to upset the priest, who was following blithely, as if through the Red Sea, but at last they came to the stream, almost hidden by ferns, a crystal-clear creek that spilled from a rocky spring down into a shallow pool before flowing on its merry way.

Beitz was delighted. 'This is wonderful! How fortunate are we? Our own water. You must drink and give thanks to the Lord. Tomorrow everyone can move out here.'

'Move where?' Jakob asked him. 'There isn't enough room on this block to put a chair.'

'Then we sit on that road until we make the room.'

'Father, it isn't just room to sit. We need to clear for crops as soon as possible, for food. For some farm animals. The land is just not suitable.'

'You'd need an army to clear it,' Jim added.

'We have an army,' Beitz persisted. 'There are plenty of us. You have to have faith. The Lord will provide.'

Driving back towards the little town, Jim was silent, obviously not keen to become involved in their differences. Freda, entranced, was nursing a bunch of wild flowers that she'd picked alongside the track, and still looking about her with the excitation of a tourist, unwilling to miss anything. The priest had taken refuge in his missal.

'It's so bright here,' Freda said. 'The light . . .'

Jakob nodded. It was bright. Almost manic, he thought sourly, an alien place with a sky too blatantly blue, a sun so gleeful and glittery as to be irritating when a man was trying to concentrate.

A weird drawn-out hoot, like mad laughter, startled him with its suddenness, coming as it had from the quietness of the bush.

'What the hell is that?'

'I know,' Freda cried. 'It's a kookaburra, isn't it, Mr Pimbley?'

'Sure is, Mrs Meissner.'

'Wonderful! Where is he? Can you see him?'

'No. But there are plenty around. Not hard to spot.'

Jakob wished they'd stop their chatter, Jim talking over his shoulder to Freda. They should have put her in the front seat. He had to think quickly. And clearly. Like everyone else, he had intended to pitch in and build a small co-operative farm on the common land, and then gradually move on, as circumstances allowed, into the general community. But that land . . . Even if they started with one acre it would take time. First they'd have to clear and burn that terrible undergrowth, then start cutting down the small trees to make some space, then on to the aged monster trees and either plough around the massive roots or take more time dragging or burning them out. At least there was plenty of good timber. They could use it for building. Or sell it to timber mills. Some financial support there.

On the other hand, common sense told him that he ought to move into the general community straight away, not wait for that land to be any use, even for shelter. While they still had the money, they ought to buy their own land, something decent, before prices rose past their capacity to pay.

Yes, he nodded to himself. And lose your investment in the common land. Everyone who could afford it had been asked to donate towards the common purse, and Jakob had done so willingly. He didn't regret that action, because later on, one day, that would be the site of their Lutheran church and school, but it did mean a shortage of money for the three of them if they struck out on their own so soon.

And what would the others say of the Meissners? Disloyal? Selfish?

He looked back at Freda and she saw his angst. Recognised it, and frowned at him. A frugal woman, she wouldn't be keen on setting out on their own so soon, relinquishing their stake in the commune. And, he supposed, plunging into the unknown before they'd tested the waters. That had been the whole idea. The communal effort was to have provided safety, comfort and financial support in the difficult early days of their pioneering endeavours. Now, though, Jakob doubted the fiscal viability of the scheme. There had always been the worry that their land had been too cheap, and therefore, perhaps, poor country, but in his wildest dreams Jakob had never envisaged anything like that mouldering, primitive forest. In his mind's eye he could still see huge trees draped in blankets of vines, trees like wizened old men glaring from the depths, grey-bearded foliage massed about their faces. They seemed defiant, as if daring strangers to enter.

Father Beitz spoke suddenly. 'The natives. Would they enter that forest?'

'You mean your land back there? The Scrubs?' Jim asked.

'Yes.'

'I suppose so. You needn't be afraid of them. They wouldn't want to be dragging through rough country like that any more

80

than we would. They'd only go there to hunt.'

'Ha! Hunt. This is something now. They hunt for food?'

'Yes. Snakes, lizards, scrub turkeys, roots, berries, no end to the stuff they'd ferret out . . .'

The priest clapped his hands in delight. 'What do you say to that, Jakob? The Lord has already provided for us. We shall learn to hunt.'

Jakob saw the grin on Jim's face as he turned, and found himself grinning too, not so much at the priest's announcement but at Freda's face. It was chalk white.

'Aren't you well, dear?' he asked, but she turned away from him, head high, refusing to acknowledge, as yet, the shock of the proposed natural diet. Freda's profile was quite lovely, it never failed to stir his admiration. He was sorry now that he'd teased her, because judging from the circumstances presented to them, there were seriously difficult days ahead.

Difficult days on the farm back home, caused by slender means and endless family disputes, had almost cost them their marriage. Now that they were freed from family involvements and interferences, they could make up their own minds what to do, but their decisions would have to be taken very carefully. It was plain to see that they would have to talk through this first move, and, he realised with a slight start, it would be necessary to include Karl in their discussions. At eighteen, beginning a new life in a new country, he was entitled to have his say.

As they turned into the main street of the sleepy settlement, with its few ragged buildings, languid horses hitched to rails on either side of the wide street, hardly a soul in sight, Jakob shook his head in wonder.

'Must be mad,' he said to himself. 'There's nothing here and there never will be. We ought to get out altogether, while we can. Go back to that Brisbane town. At least it's civilised.'

That was the first question he posed to his wife and son, as they sat together on the river bank that balmy evening.

Freda was pleased with herself. She had persuaded the old priest to place their funds in the bank, in a tiny timber building operated by the Bank of New South Wales. He hadn't been too enthused about the plan, but she'd rallied several other ladies to help persuade him, and they'd nominated Walther Badke as joint signatory on the documents with Father Beitz. Then she had requested payment of the moneys her husband had expended on food, and Walther saw that it was done immediately.

When Jim offered to open an account at his store for the German contingent, Father Beitz was delighted, remarking that it was very generous of him. Walther turned to Freda.

'Does he understand this, Mrs Meissner?'

'I don't think he's ever had to handle money before, Walther. I'm sure he thinks the account is charitable contributions to our cause.'

'It's a responsibility being joint signatory,' Walther complained. 'I don't know I like it.'

'You'll be fine. If you want to know anything, you just ask the bank manager, Mr Rawlins. He seems very nice.'

'That is so. But it's a funny-looking bank. Do you think it's real?'

Freda was laughing when she related the story. 'Poor Walther. We didn't realise how worried he was, thinking he was aiding and abetting us to lose all our money by handing it over to a charlatan.'

'I don't blame him,' Karl said. 'It's only a shed. It doesn't look like a bank. This is a really weird place.'

'Oh dear. Don't you like it?' Freda asked, unwisely, Jakob thought, but the reply surprised him.

'Yes! It's exciting. But we'll have to have our own horses here, Father. The blacksmith told me that. He says no one walks, everything is too far away. That's why there's no one much round the town. People who live beyond only come in once in a while, and they stock up for months. A lot of horsemen came galloping in and he said they were stockmen, come to town to put their money in the pub. Really wild-looking fellows, too.'

'You're a mine of information,' his father said. 'We'll need you to keep an eye out for us. But right now I'm tired and very confused. We'll have to talk in the morning, to see how we can work out this situation.'

But in the morning, while everyone was packing up, the Meissners were still undecided.

The way Karl saw it was this: contrary to the tale the priest had told the assembly, their land wasn't worth spit. He was angry that his father hadn't stood up and contradicted Father Beitz, rather than letting everyone buzz about with the excitement of moving there the very next morning, but his mother said it was best to let people see for themselves, not be trying to influence them in any direction.

'Like what?' he asked. 'What direction?'

That had them stumped. His parents, and maybe some of the others, had the means, barely, to start again, but the rest did not. They were stuck with the priest's folly. And by the sound of things, the sooner they picked up their axes the better.

'I was thinking,' his father said eventually, 'we ought to return to Brisbane.'

Freda was appalled. 'We're farmers, not town folk. What would we do in a city?'

'It didn't look much of a city,' Karl said.

Jakob sucked on his pipe. 'I know, but we could find some farmland nearby.'

'No.' Freda was adamant. 'We're not going back to a little farm ever again. You said that the further we went from civilisation, the cheaper the land would be . . .'

'This looks like the end of the line,' Karl said, but she let that pass.

'Jakob, you said we owed it to Karl to make a new beginning. It won't help him to use up the last of our money on a small, expensive block. You said we could buy land out here as big as the estates back home for only a pittance, so get on with it. We're not taking a backward step.'

Karl listened to them arguing, finding the gist of the situation exhilarating. They really were taking his future very seriously. Maybe he would get a horse pretty soon.

His father turned to him. 'It appears we are unable to agree on our first move. If we stay with everyone else at the Banjoor Estate—'

'Where's that?'

'It's the name of our land. If we stay with the group, life will be very difficult for a very long time. But if we leave, strike out on our own, we lose our equity in the common fund. That in itself is a backward step.'

'What do you mean? Difficult?'

'Primitive,' Freda said. 'We'll be living along the road like gypsies.'

'When you buy our own land, Father, will it have a house on it?'

'No,' Jakob said thoughtfully. 'We'll also be starting from scratch. We'll have to build our own shelter, and it will be primitive because I can't be spending money on a house just yet.'

'But it will be our own shelter,' Freda added. 'We won't be sharing it with twenty-three other people.

'We brought our own tent,' Karl said. 'Father and I bought it from the military stores. We can live in that. We won't be sharing.'

'The main problem is space,' Jakob said. 'The Scrubs, as they are called, are dense jungle. I have never seen a forest like this in my life. It's obviously in an area of tremendously rich soil to cause such growth, because Jim says the rest of the country is open forests or plains. At present our common land is just not fit for habitation.'

'Then what are you worried about?' Karl asked them. 'We can't go out to that mad estate if it's as bad as that, so you just tell Father Beitz you want your money back or you'll take legal action.'

His mother was stunned. 'We wouldn't dream of doing that. Be sensible, Karl. We have our allegiance to the Church. Why would we want to do that?'

'Because you've been sold a pig in a poke. You're legally entitled to demand the return of your investment.'

'Ho! My son the lawyer,' Jakob laughed. 'Who should we sue? The priest or the invisible agent? I can't see much result either way. I suppose we'd better pack up too. We might as well go along with everyone else for the time being.'

Karl turned on them. 'This is typical of your arguments.

You go round and round in circles. I'm surprised you ever made the decision to leave home at all! Now you ask my opinion and ignore me!'

'We're not ignoring you,' Jakob said. 'We can't sue, it's not practical, but if you have any other suggestions . . .'

'I have. We need a horse. You said it's a three-mile trek to the land out there. How are we to find out what else is on offer in the neighbourhood if we can't get about? We'll be—'

Before he had finished his plea, his father agreed. 'Yes, a horse is essential.'

Freda looked about her. A horse-drawn lorry had been hired to carry all of the group's belongings to the proposed campsite at the end of Taylor's Road. People were dashing over, adding last-minute bits and pieces on to the lorry, and children were being hoisted up for a ride. Others were disappearing up the road, stepping out strongly, enthusiastically, towards their new home.

It was a beautiful day, Freda reflected, and just as well. The disappointments and discomforts ahead of them might be more easily endured under tender skies. And as for a horse . . . Very well, but not just yet. Not until they were able to assess their situation more carefully. See what everyone else decided to do. She could just imagine one horse among this crowd. There'd be never-ending requests to borrow the poor beast, and it would not be neighbourly to refuse. Jakob and Karl should take their time on that one.

By the time the Meissners came to Taylor's Road, the main group, led by Father Beitz, was not far ahead of them, all singing lustily, joyously, and Freda smiled.

'All God's children indeed! Babes in the wood, more like it. Where on earth do we start, Jakob?'

'We pitch tents and forge a path through to that stream, I'd say, water being the first essential. You can see kangaroos out here,' he told Karl. 'They look tame. At least we won't be bothered by wild animals in this country, they don't have any.'

'Except snakes,' Freda said. 'I wish you hadn't reminded me.'

'And crocodiles.' Karl laughed.

The singing had stopped. Abruptly, it seemed. Their friends were spreading out, peering into the dark woods confronting them. The driver of the lorry was standing by his horses, sucking on a pipe, and as Jakob approached he shook his head.

'This your land?'

'Yes.'

'Don't look like your mates are too happy.'

That, as Jakob had expected, was an understatement. There was rage, tears, bewilderment and aggression directed at Father Beitz, who stood his ground, arguing with the men, until Jakob and Walther stepped in to protect the old man.

'You knew about this!' Eva Zimmerman screamed at Freda. 'Why didn't you warn us?'

'You had to see for yourself and make up your own minds. You would have wanted to see anyway. We'll just have to wait now. Find out what the men can do.'

For a while, Walther and Lucas pushed wild brambles aside to make some inroads, but soon emerged from the gloom.

'Is it all like this?' Walther called to the lorry driver, a local man.

'Reckon it is, mate. The Scrubs, we call it.'

'Forty acres we have,' Walther said grimly. 'Father Beitz says the boundaries are marked by blazed trees and pegs. Me, I'm for looking all round. All the way. Maybe I'll find better ground. You'll come with me, Jakob?'

'I think I'd better stay,' he said, with a glance at Father Beitz, who was still surrounded by hostility. 'Karl will go with you.'

Walther understood. He dumped his heavy rucksack, whistled to Karl, and paced away. Reluctantly, Karl followed him, while Father Beitz, whose enthusiasm had not dimmed a scrap, began moving among the others, who were just standing, gloomily, uncertainly, along the verge of the track.

'Come on now! All hands to the wheel. You, Jakob, take some men and make a nice path in here, through to the stream. Max and Hans, you'd better unload the lorry. We need our tent houses in place before nightfall. And you ladies, don't just stand there, you have to make a kitchen.'

'What do we cook in?' Eva demanded. 'There's no stove. We're going back to the barracks.'

Paul Wagner, Rolf's brother-in-law, intervened. 'No need. Plenty of rocks hereabouts. I'll collect them up and make a good cooking pit, you'll see.'

As he took an axe from the lorry and joined the crew of men preparing to clear an entrance to their land, Jakob appreciated Paul's resourcefulness. Paul never had much to say, but it was clear he would be a very useful member of a working community. And there was plenty of work ahead of them. All of the men would have to pitch in. Nevertheless, with the first blow of his axe at the leathery vines blocking his way, something about that cooking pit bothered him, but he couldn't identify what it was. Then he was too busy to think about it.

More than an hour later, a dozen men were hacking, slashing, dragging at the stubborn scrub, sweating in the heat and humidity of their claustrophobic surrounds, while far above them patches of blue sky teased through the canopy of treetops. And yet, Jakob realised, despite the discomfort, the scratches, the mishaps, the constant tests of strength required to win this fight, they were all cheerful, they were working together for the first time, achieving something. They shouted to each other, joking, cursing, warning, challenging; they helped, hauled, shouldered each other over rafts of mangled tree roots that hid solid ground; and they marvelled at the rich red soil they discovered beneath this impossible forest.

They worked steadily, strongly all day until, at last, they had cut a narrow lane around the more difficult obstacles to the precious stream called Ferny Creek, and only then did Jakob grasp the relevance of the rocks that were strewn about the road. The same rocks were, of course, on their block. Since the path they needed at this stage was for foot traffic only, they'd detoured round boulders and cast aside the smaller rocks in their way, finding them less of a hazard than the massive foliage, but . . . Jakob shook his head miserably. Even when, or if, they managed to clear the land, those rocks littering the fields would be a nightmare for any farmer, hidden enemies of the plough.

He wondered if anyone else had noticed. This good soil was obviously volcanic, and the rocks that went along with it proved the point. They'd probably been hurled out in one great volcanic explosion aeons ago, and left here to further try the patience of this little band of pioneers. Maybe even to finish off their dream once and for all.

Nevertheless, under Paul's command, a camp was established along the track, some people housed in tents, others in makeshift shelters made of saplings and foliage. Walther and Karl had returned with nothing new to report except that Ferny Creek flowed through from some good pastureland, which they'd looked upon with envy. But Walther, hungry now, was more interested in the cooking arrangements, so he and Paul became the chefs, big hearty men holding sway over large pots of soup in the hot coals of the new campfire. Nearby the women worked quietly, doing their best with the supplies they'd brought from town, searching for plates and utensils, trying to sort out this confusion without even the basic kitchen provided back at the barracks.

The exhilaration of the day soon wore off for the workmen when they realised they were totally unprepared for this battle with nature. They had expected green fields. Land that could immediately be put to growing vegetables at least. Land that would support a few cows and chickens and pigs that they imagined they could buy locally. Land that they could mark out into small selections so that each person, or family, could have a little privacy round a central kitchen and recreation area. They could not countenance squatting on a road like this, on this track like gypsies. They were appalled. What would their neighbours think of them? God in heaven!

'What is to become of us?' Eva asked her husband. 'What have you done? Bringing your family to such shame.'

Father Beitz called them all to prayer at sunset, a glorious orange and pink sunset which did not impress his sullen congregation. He exhorted them to thank the Lord for their deliverance from the very real dangers of the great oceans, to thank Him for bringing them to this beautiful place, to thank Him for their new and beauteous land.

Few could even manage Amen.

Chapter Five

Jakob would always remember that dawn. Warm, dewy, insincere as a cat's compassion. Unhindered by the rightful protection of walls and roofs and curtains, it gushed its golden light on weary sleepers who wanted none of it. Few had found much comfort in camp mattresses or their folding canvas stretcher beds, hardly more than the men who opted for only a blanket under the stars.

Apprehension emerged with the morning, causing folk to remain within themselves as long as possible, turning away rather than voice thoughts. Silence seemed preferable, as if this intrusive dawn was, after all, entitled to some respect.

They wandered about in a daze, Jakob reflected, no better himself, as if he were in someone else's house and not sure what to do first. His muscles were already taking revenge on him for the sudden hard work he'd inflicted on them the day before, making each movement a penalty of pain. Not that he was a stranger to hard labouring work, like most of the other men in the group, but they'd lived the soft life for too long on the voyage. The blisters on his hands seemed to have blossomed overnight, and as he creaked stiffly into the bush to relieve himself, they reminded him that worse was to come. It would be days before the muscles relaxed and the blisters turned into calluses.

Walther came by, hale and hearty. 'I'll be able to help more today. First we should dig proper latrines. Bad enough for us fellows without them, but unpleasant for the ladies to have nowhere to go.'

By the time Jakob got back, Karl and Freda were up and

dressed. Both quiet. Confused. The Zimmerman children rushed down to Karl to ask if he'd take them exploring for wild animals in the forest, but he shook his head. 'Later.'

He turned to his mother with the usual question. 'What's for breakfast?'

'How the hell do I know?' Freda snapped, and charged back to her tent. Not ready for any confrontations this morning, Jakob stepped back into the gloom of the forest and took refuge at the base of a massive tree with mangled roots like logs. At least these roots made a comfortable seat for a man who did not wish to be disturbed. He was now twenty paces in from the track and in a greenhouse provided by nature. A peaceful place, away from the hostilities brewing out there.

In a moment of fright he saw a fat snake slithering towards his boot and kept very still until it flashed a blue tongue at him and he recognised a harmless lizard. Someone had shown him a picture of one of these creatures, but he'd never really expected to encounter one.

He returned to contemplating their little colony, and wondering about all these people. With their differences and complaints, were they any different from the Meissners family back home? Had they simply jumped from one fire into another? At least at home they didn't have the added problem of this jungle, this mad estate, as Karl had called it.

Jakob knew he was suffering, and encouraging, a bout of homesickness, but he had no wish to end it. To cut it short. Alone here, under this strange tree, with threads of beaded seeds hanging about him and fat pods like figs lying around on the ground, he could wallow in his unhappiness, his stupidity, before he had to report back out there, see if they could get organised, if they would even bother.

He remembered that it had been Hubert Hoepper who had shown him the picture of that lizard and other creatures of this land. Mr Hoepper. What could he say to him about this fiasco? What could he write? Nothing for the time being. His last letter, sent from Brisbane, had announced their safe arrival, and that would have to do. It was such a shame that tragedy had struck Mr Hoepper. He would have been very helpful to them all now. He would know what to do. He was a businessman, his advice would be invaluable.

As a farmer, Jakob knew that their 'promised land' was useless in the short term, and his friends would have to accept that, but he didn't want to break up the community. He wished he could figure out what they could do, in co-operative terms. What was their alternative?

He didn't know, and that was a fact. He would have to look to his own family. Do what was best for them. He'd have to keep his promise to buy land right away, but he'd need more money, even for cheap land. There'd be no common purse, the Meissners would have to support themselves.

For a minute he thought Hubert Hoepper was there with him, as he heard a rustle in the nearby trees, but it was only one of the men walking past. And then it hit him! Hoepper the businessman would have gone straight to the bank manager for advice and a loan, had he found himself floundering in this odd situation. That was what businessmen did.

A bank. The very word terrified Jakob. Farmers saw banks as the enemy. He'd never ever set foot in the tall stone portals of such an establishment. Then again, that bank in Bundaberg was no more than a wooden shed. An outhouse. Hardly daunting, a place like that. He would do it.

He scratched at his beard from habit, and forced himself to stand, to go out there, face the troubles and break the news to Freda that he intended to borrow money from a bank. But as he stood, he saw a bulky presence in the fork of a gum tree only about ten yards from him, just above his eyeline. As he stared, it took shape, dappled by light, and Jakob realised it was a koala. The animal, with its benign face and fluffy ears, simply blinked at him, making no attempt to depart. It seemed to have no opinion about him at all.

To Jakob, this furry presence was such a joy he wanted to go forward and pick it up like a puppy. He thought better of disturbing it, however, and instead rushed out of the forest to find Freda, but she was working with the other women, serving boiled oats and coffee, and judging by the grim expression on her face, this was not the right time. Contrarily, he would not invite anyone else to see his koala; he simply sighed and lined up for breakfast. The oats were burned.

* * *

Theo, red-faced, apologetic, advanced on Father Beitz to break the news that he was taking his family back to the barracks.

The priest was stunned. 'You can't do that! No! No! I won't allow it. There's work to be done here. What did you expect? A cottage built for you? Don't be foolish, Theo.'

But two of the Kleinschmidt lads stepped up. 'We're leaving too, Father. We're very sorry but this is no good here.'

'I'll come out every day,' said Theo. 'I'll work, but this is no place for my family.'

'You can't stay in those barracks too long,' Father Beitz said angrily. 'They'll move you on.'

'I know that, but we'll just take one day at a time.'

Karl nudged his father. 'We have to go too. You ought to speak up while the barracks are still available.'

'Yes. Speak up now,' Freda urged, so Jakob reluctantly joined the exodus, sooner than he'd meant to.

Stubbornly, Father Beitz refused to return to town, but at least he would have company. Walther and the two Lutze brothers were angry that everyone was giving in so soon, upset at what they called this desertion. They chose to stay.

'How can you give up so easily?' Walther demanded of Jakob. 'Have you no faith in the Lord? This will be His sacred land one day. We are working for Him. We cannot turn our backs on Him.'

'It's the time it will take,' Jakob tried to explain. 'You've seen what a tough job would be ahead of us here. It's just not good farmland.'

'But it will be . . .'

Jakob put a hand on his shoulder. 'Walther, you're a good man. But you're single. I have a family to care for . . .'

'That's a weak excuse. Your wife and your son are blessed with good health, you have a fine tent there. What more do you want?'

Within hearing of the others, Jakob couldn't bring himself to tell Walther that he didn't want to be still here when the common funds ran out, and the land was still not productive. Instead, he returned to the tent and, along with so many others, began packing up.

'I don't know why we even bothered staying here overnight,' Freda said crankily. 'We never should have come out at all.'

'It was best that we did,' he replied. 'For the best, if only to be a little help.'

Then a woman screamed and they all froze, looking about them for the cause of such terror. Some of the women ran for the safety of the bush when they saw what was happening. A band of natives, about thirty fierce-looking fellows, were coming down the track towards them. They were tall, sinewy men, very dark, most with thick lank hair and shaggy beards, and apart from adornments of beads and shells, their only attempt at dress was the presence of lap-laps or codpieces strung from bare lean hips. They carried spears, tall, menacing spears.

Jakob went to find out the reason for this visit, but Walther was ahead of him, so he held back, gratefully, it had to be said, because this mob of bushmen looked far from friendly.

Walther marched up the track to head them off, his height and bulk an advantage, Jakob thought, and he watched as a conversation seemed to be taking place with a great deal of gesticulation.

'What's going on?' people around him asked.

'Will they attack us?'

'No. Surely not.'

'How do you know they won't?'

A skinny, elderly black man stepped forward and shook hands with Walther, and everyone breathed a sigh of relief. The two men walked towards the camp but the rest of the natives remained on the track, waiting, shyly or ominously Jakob couldn't tell.

'This is the chief,' Walther called. 'His name is Tibbaling. He says I speak bad English. Wants to talk to our boss. Where's Father Beitz?'

Having herded the women and children away from the immodest scene, the priest now dashed into a tent and eventually emerged to answer the summons, his cassock carefully buttoned. His cross hung about his neck, his breviary was in his hand and his black cleric's hat was firmly planted on his head. Jakob had the impression the old fellow was nervous of

93

this first encounter with the natives he had come to save, and had donned his armoury for the occasion.

'What does he want?' Father Beitz asked tremulously as the chief thudded his spear into the ground before him and thrust out his jaw. Tibbaling's beard was grey and wispy and his ancient features were the colour of gunmetal. He too wore his badges of office: a cone-shaped headdress of dried clay daubed with fur; a short spear in his hand; and around his neck a necklace, featuring, with as much pomp as a precious pearl, a very large tooth. Maybe a shark's tooth, Jakob thought, since they weren't all that far from the coast. A shiver came to him then. Maybe this river town of Bundaberg wasn't too far inland for sharks to be inhabiting the waters washing the shores. He must ask.

He moved closer to the action and Walther turned to him. 'I messed up,' he said dismally. 'I forgot I was talking German. This fellow speaks some English. Better he talks to Father anyway.'

Father Beitz came forward, bowed, and began to bless the chief with a volley of high-sounding Latin.

'English mistah,' the Aborigine said curtly, and Jakob felt laughter rising within him at this confused confrontation. Or maybe hysteria, he mused, considering the situation at large.

'Ah yes,' the priest said in English. 'You are big chief Tibbaling? Is this not so?'

The question remained unanswered. 'What name you?'

'Father Beitz.'

'Fader Bites!' the old man grinned. He turned and called back to his mob something to that effect in his own guttural language, and to everyone's surprise they fell about laughing, slapping their foreheads and their thighs until he raised his spear for them to cease.

Abruptly he turned back to the priest. 'You whitefeller magic man, eh? Then you tellum this our place.' He pointed a bony finger into the property, stamping over to stare at the cleared path. 'What you do? Muck up everything. You get out, you Fader Bites. Take all your people wid you. Get on out!'

'No! No!' Beitz said frantically. 'This is our land. We paid for it.'

'Nebber!' The elderly native spat. 'This Banjoor country.' He waved his arms about. 'All Banjoor country. You go'way!'

Beitz was so upset he broke into his own language, explaining to Tibbaling that he came with love, in the name of Jesus, that he wished to embrace all the fine black people . . .

He reached out, arms outstretched, and Tibbaling, already confused by the strange language, leapt away from him as if from some contagion.

'English!' Walther reminded Father Beitz, whose shoulders slumped in despair as he realised he'd wasted his little sermon.

'I'm sorry,' the priest said to Tibbaling. 'You must understand, this is our land. We bought it. But you are welcome here too.'

'You like all de rest!' Tibbaling snapped. 'Banjoor doan see no buyin' money. This our home. You go home!'

As they set to, arguing again, Eva Zimmerman began packing a canvas bag. 'That does it. We're leaving. Get the kids ready, Theo!'

'We're going too,' Hanni Fechner called, and her husband nodded. 'We can't stay here.'

Tibbaling beamed on them, obviously convinced that he was the instigator of this outburst.

The priest turned away from the chief, trying to persuade people to stay, but the exodus had begun. Most of his flock were returning to the barracks, promising to send the lorry back to collect the rest of their belongings.

Freda and Karl had not made a move yet; they were too interested in the situation with the blackfellows, who no longer seemed threatening. Their chief was standing back, leaning casually on his spear, and his men made way for the Zimmermans on the narrow road, grinning happily at the children.

'We'll stay a while,' Jakob told Freda. 'We still have to sort this out with the blacks.'

Within the hour, everyone else had departed except for Walther and the two Lutze lads. The Aborigines didn't seem to be in any hurry to leave, so Jakob walked over to Father Beitz, who had taken refuge in a canvas chair plonked at the entrance to his land.

'Would you like me to talk to them?' he asked, but the priest jumped up from the chair, shoving his breviary into a deep pocket.

'Certainly not. This is my business.'

He strode over to Tibbaling. 'That's all of them. The rest of us stay now.'

'You get out!'

'No. We are your friends. What do you want? To kill us? I don't think so. We intend to live here. You can live here too if you wish, but this is our land and that's that.'

Jakob heard Freda draw in a quick breath. 'Did you hear that, Jakob? He's inviting them to live here too!'

Tibbaling frowned. He scratched his head with the point of his spear, and then turned on the priest in a sudden burst of anger.

'What right you allasame say this land belonga you?'

'God gives me the right. He wants me to bring you to Him.'

'He in there?' Tibbaling peered into the undergrowth.

'God is everywhere,' Father Beitz intoned.

The black man gave up on God and returned to the original argument. 'This huntin' place belonga my people,' he said firmly.

'Yes. Yes, chief,' said the priest, relieved. 'This your hunting place, yes. Very good. Me and my people, we live here, see. We want you to join us. Live here too.'

Tibbaling picked up a twig and snapped it as he stepped back to survey these strangers again.

'Your peoples live in dere? Plurry mad!'

His comrades out on the track were becoming unsettled, moving about, unable to interpret their role in this exchange, and Jakob wondered about their problems. Not only had white men invaded their territories, they'd had to learn a new language without the benefit of the written word. And here was this old fellow, about the same age as Father Beitz, arguing with him, both struggling with a foreign language.

'What a strange place the world is,' he said to Walther, who simply shook his head, bemused. As he watched the two old men, Jakob couldn't help comparing their backgrounds. One from the colonnaded portals of St John's Seminary in

Hamburg, an elder statesman who had earned the right to become a missionary, at his age, by dint of pressure and the refusal to be pensioned off. The other a primitive man, flung from his pristine Eden into a whitefellow world as alien as anything he could ever have imagined.

A sadness came upon Jakob. He felt guilty that he was about to abandon Father Beitz. He felt guilty that he and his family were an ongoing part of the white avalanche that was crushing a nation of innocent black people.

'We can't go,' Beitz was saying. 'We simply can't. We have no other place to go to.'

'No place?' the Aborigine said in disbelief. 'Where you whitefellers comen from? You go there.'

Jakob stepped in to try to end this. 'That's not possible, sir, but as Father Beitz here says, we are friends. We wish you no harm.'

As he spoke, Jakob felt another rush of guilt, because, come to think of it, that statement wasn't entirely true. What would be left for the Aborigines to hunt once the blocks were cleared for farmland?

But then the crack of a rifle shot split the air and they all swung about as a horseman came galloping full pelt down the track.

The Aborigine troop dived wildly for the bush lining the track and disappeared, while the rider, scowling, rode into the roadside camp.

'You part of the German mob?' he yelled at Walther, who was closest to him, but Walther, lacking confidence in his English, declined to be spokesman, edging aside and deferring, by a nod, to Jakob.

'Yes, sir,' Jakob said warily. This fellow was in uniform, a black uniform with silver buttons, but it had no insignias. He guessed he was a civil servant of some sort, but the rifle spoke of a different and more dangerous authority.

The rider dismounted and glared at Jakob, dark eyebrows beetling over cold eyes.

'What's your name?'

'Meissner, sir, and this is my wife, and my son Karl.'

Out of the corner of his eye, Jakob saw that Karl was

grinning. He'd enjoyed the gunfire that had scattered the natives. His father frowned and Karl's grin disappeared.

'Well see here, Mr Meissner, my name is Stenning. Jules Stenning. Got it?'

'Yes, sir.'

'Right! Now, for your information, I'm the Customs Officer in these parts, and I'm the government representative for most other departments as well, except the police, and that is Constable Colley. You met him?'

'Yes, sir.'

'Good. Now listen, the lot of you!'

Heads already turned to him lifted a little higher in response, but Stenning didn't continue. He'd spotted Tibbaling.

'What the hell are you doing here, Tibbs?'

Father Beitz stepped forward. 'This gentleman is our guest, sir.'

'He's no gentleman, Father. He's a bloody medicine man, as tricky as they come. Get him out of here.'

Tibbaling had remained standing, making no effort to leave, even seemingly uninterested in this conversation. His eyes met Jakob's for a second and brushed on past, but a fleeting giddiness bothered Jakob, irritating him. He wished the old fellow would go away too; he seemed to be complicating whatever was afoot with the Customs Officer. But Father Beitz didn't see it that way.

'The gentleman is doing no harm. We were having a conversation. What was it you wanted, sir?'

Stenning strode over to him, elbowing Tibbaling aside. 'I'll tell you what I want, Father. I want to know what the hell you lot are doing out here. You're not supposed to leave the immigration barracks without first reporting to me! Any of you. We can't have foreigners running about all over the countryside.'

'We were not advised of this,' Jakob said, taking over. 'You were not there to receive us.'

'Then you should have bloody waited. And the doctor has to see you too. Dr Strauss. He's one of your lot. Comes from Vienna, he reckons. Really! Germans and Danes wandering about the countryside. I don't know what the world is coming to.

'You got a table I can sit at?' he asked, and Jakob managed to provide that amenity, a folding camp table and chair, while Stenning unstrapped a leather satchel from his saddle rig.

Jakob noticed that the rifle was holstered in a pouch near the saddle now, and it looked very much in place. As if it were normal for civil servants to carry arms. Anxiously, he wondered if this country were so peaceful after all.

But now Stenning was poring over a slim ledger, adding spit to an indelible pencil.

'You will kindly line up here,' he called, 'so I can take down your details, starting with you, Father. What's your name, date of birth, nationality and so forth?'

As Father Beitz gave his answers, Stenning recorded the information with care.

'Religion?' he asked, without looking up. 'RC, I suppose.'

'Lutheran High Church. The only true voice of the Lord!'

Stenning shrugged. 'I'll mark that as L. Are you all Lutherans?'

'Our group, yes,' Jakob told him.

One after another they trooped over to be officially accepted into the country, having answered the few questions Stenning fired at them, including the name of their ship, point and date of departure and their occupations. The interviews took only a few minutes and Jakob thought it didn't seem much of an accounting. No more than ten questions made short work of their individual descriptions. Are we so inconsequential? he wondered. Did the world not care that they'd taken such a brave and bold step in coming here? Did no one here care about their heritage? Their culture? It was all so cold and impersonal, it depressed him.

'I hope these facts are correct,' Stenning said to them. 'What address can any of you produce, other than the barracks?'

'This is our address,' Beitz told him. 'This is our land.'

Jakob saw Tibbaling's head jerk up at that, but he must have decided against intruding at that stage.

'If that's your land, move on to it. This is a road, a public thoroughfare, there'll be no camping here.'

He looked about at the remnants of the overnight camp strung along the track, then spotted Tibbaling again.

'You still here? I told you to get out of here!'

Once more Father Beitz stood up in the chief's defence. 'Mr Stenning, I told you, this gentleman is our guest. He is helping us to get settled. You must not be bothering him.'

'Bother him! He's a troublemaker. He's got too many blackfellows under his thumb. It's dangerous for any of them to have that much influence, in case they get too pushy.'

'I don't think we'll have that problem, Mr Stenning. I'm opening a mission for the natives as soon as we build our church, so it is important we make them welcome.'

'A mission?' Stenning seemed to be placated. 'Then I wish you well. Something is needed to keep the blacks off our streets.'

That wasn't what the priest had in mind, as Jakob well knew, and he was relieved that Beitz chose not to argue the matter.

'One other thing,' the Customs Officer announced. 'I want you to wait here until Dr Strauss comes out and passes you as fit, so that we make certain of checking everyone.'

That made Freda nervous. 'Excuse me, sir. What happens if a person is declared by the doctor not to be healthy?'

'Quarantine!' he said. 'Immediate removal to the quarantine station. We are referring here to infectious diseases, madam, not your common cold, though I daresay that has its moments as well.'

When he had left, they regrouped.

'Does that mean we have to stay here again tonight?' Karl asked.

Jakob nodded. 'Until this Dr Strauss comes along.' He grinned. 'The German from Vienna.'

'Time to get back to work,' Walther said, but Karl wasn't so keen.

'I'm hungry, Mother. What can I eat?'

Overhearing, the priest turned. 'I wouldn't mind some bread and cheese, Mrs Meissner, and some for my friend here.'

Tibbaling was delighted. He waited eagerly for his share and ate it with relish, remarking that Stenning was no good, but that, 'Fader Bites, he one brave fella.

100

'My guest,' he added proudly, possibly unable to distinguish the difference between friend and guest, but his attitude had improved remarkably since the priest had refused to send him away.

He stayed a while longer, watching their labours, picking about the camp like an inquisitive old rooster, using the spear as a staff. Then he wandered away without bothering to take his leave of them.

Later in the day, when the latrines were dug, and fenced with foliage, and they had begun dragging out heaps of discarded brush that were impeding their progress, Tibbaling returned. He brought with him three natives, brawny young fellows, and instructed them to help the whitefellers.

Grinning broadly, they went to work with all speed until a large bonfire lay waiting for a match out on the road. The two old men, watching proceedings, nodded their approval.

Father Beitz was thrilled at this new turn of events. 'Tibbaling will be my first convert,' he told Jakob. 'And he will bring all the rest. I'll have a mission underway in no time.'

'Don't you think you ought to forget about the mission until you've got your own people settled?' Jakob said anxiously.

'No, no, no! I must be about Our Father's business. Pastor Ritter from the seminary back in Hamburg will be coming out as soon as he completes his studies. I can't have him arriving and finding no mission!'

'But we've only been here a day or so, Father. You have to look to your own congregation before inviting others.'

The priest was terse. Disappointed. 'No I don't. Here is the land. If our people wish to use it as intended, as their first temporary home, well and good. But now most of them do not wish to stay here. Though they turn their backs on me, I will still be their pastor, they are still my flock. I am here for them in spiritual matters, not simply temporal ones as you seem to think. God gave us free will. It is not for me to be demanding that anyone stay or leave. And already He has sent these heathen folk to me . . . right to my door . . .'

Jakob escaped the sermonising, shaking his head. He went in search of Walther. 'I think you're in charge now, my friend. Are you clear on what has to be done and what can be done?'

101

'Yes. It will take time, but the Lutze boys and me, we like it here. We've got the nice sunshine, work to do, food to eat. What else could a man want? Aren't you staying?'

'I think not. We'd be too much strain on the common purse. But some of the others might return.'

'They are welcome,' Walther said simply.

Dr Strauss had declared them all to be in good health, even young Robie Zimmerman, so another meeting was held at the barracks the next morning. The mood was sour, resentful. No one could agree on the best course, as a group, or even work out how they might stay together, since, after all, that had been the original plan. It was suggested that some men with reserves of funds should purchase a better block of land, where they could all live in collective housing similar to these barracks, and operate a co-operative farm, but that fell flat through lack of volunteers to provide the necessary cash, and immediate complaints from others that they might as well go back to what was now becoming known as the commune.

'I think we all had in mind to have our own little village, our own settlement here,' Jakob said. 'And it was a fine idea, but we now see that it isn't possible. Nevertheless, I hope you will all stay in this district so that we'll have our land and, eventually, the church as our focal point.'

'All very well for you,' Theo said. 'We didn't expect to be forced out like this. We'll go wherever we have to go.' He looked back at the almost deserted streets. 'Where will I find work in a place like this?'

Jim Pimbley had ambled over to listen to the proceedings, and Theo's despairing remark spurred him to intervene.

'Mind if I have a say?' he asked.

Heads nodded, so he proceeded. 'You don't want to get the wrong idea about Bundaberg, folks. It might look as if there's nothing doing here, but the town is only starting up. Most of you, from what I can make out, are country people. You must know that the main thing needed in the country is labour. And that's what we need to get this district moving. We need loggers, boatmen and camp cooks to work in the timber industry, just a ways upriver.

'Out beyond the town are big sheep stations. They need stockmen, shearers, fencers, grooms, they always need workers. And your ladies can easily find work as cooks, domestics, nursemaids. There's no shortage of jobs here; the only shortage we have is people. No one to take on all these jobs.'

Theo was stunned. 'Where do we find this work, sir?'

'They'll find you, mate, just as soon as word gets out. As a matter of fact, I'd say some jobs are on their way now. The bloke riding towards us is Les Jolly. He's the boss timberman, he's always looking for workers.'

Jim introduced Les to the group. 'They're looking for jobs. What have you got to offer?'

'Plenty,' said Les with a grin. 'I'll have a talk to some of these blokes.'

Eventually he decided on the Kleinschmidt group. 'I've got jobs for all you lads. You can bring your women with you.'

'A loggers' camp doesn't sound a proper place for our ladies,' Rolf Kleinschmidt said nervously.

'You can build log huts. That's no problem up there. You'd have your own homes to go to. Then, as the timber is taken out, you can buy the land for a song, and clear it yourselves for farming.'

'What do you think of this?' Rolf asked Jim. 'It sounds too good to be true.'

'It's hard work. And hard living in the bush, but he's right about getting the land cheap. And he's a fair man. I'd give it a go.'

Karl listened to all this and dashed back to his father. 'I want to go with them to work as a forester. Did you know they get forty pounds a year?'

'You're staying right here. I'll find enough work for you when we get going.'

That very afternoon the Kleinschmidt contingent were farewelled by their friends as they boarded a ferry to take them across the river, on the way to their new home deep in the forests, where precious cedar trees grew in profusion.

Suddenly the folk left behind seemed a wan little group, standing at the jetty after the ferry had departed, as if Les

Jolly had swooped on them and stolen their strength. And the barracks seemed so empty.

'What will we do now?' Hanni Fechner said plaintively.

'I think we go to the hotel and have something to cheer us up,' her husband replied.

'I'll come with you,' Theo said. 'What about you, Jakob?'

'Not just now.'

Jakob knew the time had come to take the plunge and make an appointment to see the bank manager, a nerve-racking task made even more difficult since he'd be asking for money. To Jakob this was begging; it was beneath a man to go cap in hand like that, even though Freda had said the bank charged for the money, the loan. If it were agreed upon.

'Do you want me to come with you?' she asked.

'No. This is men's business.'

'But I have already met him. His name is Mr Rawlins. He's a very nice man.' She smiled to encourage him. 'He doesn't even look like a bank manager. He's only about forty, no beard, just a little moustache, and he wears open shirts, no tie.'

It wasn't so much the bank manager's appearance that gave Jakob heart as he approached the bank; it was this funny little building, like an ugly doll's house, unpainted, with three steps up to the narrow door. And inside he found a high counter with a young teller presiding, and behind him the man, Rawlins, working at a table. This had to be the smallest office he'd ever seen, it didn't seem real.

'I wish to make an appointment with the manager of the bank,' he said, knowing his words sounded gruff, though he was only concentrating on his English.

'No need for an appointment,' the man at the back called out. 'The name's Rawlins. What can I do for you, sir?'

Introductions over, seated at the table, Jakob began with his rehearsed speech, explaining that he wished to borrow money so that he could build a house and stock a small farm on land that he intended to purchase. 'I will do well. I am a good farmer, hard-working as you will see, sir, and my son who works with me is a strong fellow. My wife, too, she is accustomed to farm work. We will work hard and repay you every penny, this I promise and will put it in writing. As you see, sir, this kind loan to us is important for the welfare of my family, and so how much might you give me?'

'Whoa! Hang on. You're beginning at the end, Mr Meissner.'

'Then you do not wish to give us a loan?' Jakob knew it! Stupid to come here asking rich banks, even if stuck in poor premises, to grant a stranger a loan. Mortified, he grabbed his hat and jumped to his feet.

'I am sorry. I will not take up more of your time.'

'Hang on. Sit down. I didn't say I won't lend you the money. You sound a good bet in my books, but I need to know a little more. Where is the land you intend to purchase?'

'I haven't found it yet. I thought we could live on our communal land for a while, to give us time to look about . . .'

'Ah, yes. I heard about that. You're stuck in The Scrubs.'

'Yes. Disappointing. So now we work faster, that is all.'

'It will be necessary for me to see the land first, so that I can assess what sort of a farm you can make of it. Your prospects, so to speak.'

Jakob blinked, then nodded. 'You think I make the same mistake? Buy scrub land? No, no. Not me. I will be looking most carefully.'

'Good. Any area in particular?'

'I haven't yet had the time. I had first to make sure of the loan.' He held up his hands in despair. 'I am sorry, sir. I waste your time. We talk in circles. For me the money first, then buy the land. For you, the land then loan the money.'

Unconcerned, Rawlins reached into a drawer and took out a large map. 'It isn't as bad as it sounds, Mr Meissner. Now take a look at this map. Here's Bundaberg, or rather, the area set aside for a town. Over here are The Scrubs, rain forest, actually. You can see the course of the Burnett River as it makes its way to the coast. It's an important river and hails from far inland. The big sheep and cattle stations owe their lives to rivers like the Burnett.

'Now see this section here . . .' He swept a hand over one huge section of the map, which dwarfed the area allocated to the township. 'This is Clonmel sheep station.'

'All of it?'

'Yes. More than a hundred square miles.'

Jakob was astonished. 'How can a man afford to buy a hundred square miles of land?'

'The same way that you will buy your land. All of this area here is in fact Crown land. It belongs to the government. The squatters who run the big stations only lease it. And so far that has been fine, but now the government wants some of it back for closer settlement.'

'What is that?'

'As populations expand, land is needed for settlement close to new towns like Bundaberg. The owners of Clonmel have to relinquish some of their leases; the government is resuming them.'

'What do the owners of this Clonmel estate think of that?'

'Naturally they're not happy about it, but not much they can do. Growing towns like Bundaberg need agriculture to survive, so they need more space for settlers outside of the town limits.'

'And some of this land will be available?' Jakob said, eyeing the map, which showed that Clonmel Station bordered the river.

'Yes. Good pastureland, good for farming.'

'And how much?' Jakob held his breath while Rawlins searched his brain for a figure.

'Let's see. First you select land, then the surveyors mark it out, and they'll charge a fee, depending on area. After that you register your selection and take out a lease. You have to make improvements on the land, inspectors will check, but I'm sure that won't be a problem for you. Eventually you'll be able to buy the land, but there's no rush.'

'How much will it be?'

'Right now? About three shillings an acre.'

'Three shillings an acre? And we can move on to the land as soon as we have a lease?'

'Nothing to stop you from moving there as soon as you make your selection. Others are already squatting on their selections. Best to get in early.'

Jakob was having trouble taking all this in. 'When the government tells us it's time to pay up, to make ownership of our leased land, how much an acre then?'

'About sixteen shillings, I'd say. But then you'll have had some years to start farming, earn money to buy it. That's how people get started here. It's not an easy life, too primitive for a lot of starters, but others thrive on it.'

'I ought to see this land,' Jakob said. 'How far out is it?'

'About thirty miles or so from the outskirts of town. You could hitch a ride upriver with loggers if you like. But if you're not doing anything tomorrow I could take you. Show you round. I've got other customers out that way too. I'd like to see how they're getting on.'

'Can I bring my wife and son?' Jakob asked, not used to having important matters move along at such a pace. He needed their steadying influence.

'Of course. We'll be riding, though. Does Mrs Meissner ride?'

Jakob felt a fool. 'I'm sorry. I haven't even got a horse yet. Maybe you can tell me where to buy one?'

'Yes. The stables down the far end of Quay Street. He's always got a few mounts for sale.'

'How much does he ask?'

'For a good one, I'd say about fifteen pounds. And don't scrimp on the horse, Mr Meissner. Wherever you go here, it'll be your lifeline. What about meeting me in front of the bank at six in the morning? It'll be dawn then, a beautiful time to ride and enjoy the countryside.'

Jakob resisted the temptation to call by the shanty hotel to show off his horse, a solid two-year-old called Dandy. He was no thoroughbred, but a strong fellow with good teeth and a healthy chestnut coat.

When the sale was concluded – sixteen pounds including the horse's blanket, saddle and bridle, and a bag of oats for good measure – Jakob rode proudly away, only to discover that Dandy was rather temperamental, preferring to go where he wished. But Jakob was strong too.

'You behave yourself, my lad,' he smiled, 'or you'll get no oats tonight.'

He turned towards the barracks, by this time smiling broadly. It was so good to be on a horse again, his own horse this time, and he felt on top of the world. Nothing, he felt, could go wrong now. He would find his farmlands, take Freda and Karl out there, and never have to look back again.

They came running, amazed and delighted that he'd already bought a horse, and right away both clamoured for a chance to ride Dandy. Their horse.

They saw him riding past. Jakob Meissner on a horse! Looking like a prince.

'I always knew he had money!' Theo grumbled. 'His wife is always talking about buying their own land. They shouldn't be travelling with us, taking a share of the common purse when they can afford to support themselves. It's not right.'

Lucas disagreed. 'Don't forget he made donations to the cause in the first place to help Father Beitz get us all started.'

'Yes. Paving his way to a share of the profits, like I said.'

'What difference does it make?' Hanni asked crossly. 'We've only got a few shillings to our name, we'll starve if we don't go back to the church land, Lucas. At least there's money for food there.'

'What about me?' Theo groaned. 'I had to borrow two shillings from Walther!'

They had already learned that this inn was called a hotel but more often a pub, and Lucas, grinning, had explained to the others that 'pub' probably meant it wasn't much of a hotel. Nor was it. Single-storeyed, timber, with a corrugated-iron roof, it had a bar and a saloon bar, which doubled as a dining room, though only boasting rough tables and chairs set on a split hardwood floor. Most of the drinkers, though, congregated on the veranda.

'In the hope that they might see someone come past,' Lucas, the joker, had said earlier. 'Or even find something to look at in this empty town.'

The publican, Patrick O'Malley, and his family, lived in a shanty at the rear of the hotel, and had confused the Germans when they walked in by asking if they'd be paying cash.

Offended, Theo had slammed the pennies on the counter to prove they were paying customers and not beggars, but a little later he was surprised to see a fellow come in and buy a drink with no money changing hands. The publican simply chalked it up on a slate hanging on the wall.

Just then Dr Strauss came along. He strolled past the group, now settled on the veranda, with a courteous greeting, and went into the bar. He was followed by the police constable, who stopped to make cheerful conversation with them about the good weather and the good beer. He wished them well and also marched through to the bar.

After a while, when they were wondering if they should afford themselves the luxury of a third beer, since after all they were served in half-sized glasses, the Constable came out to enquire if any of them were looking for work.

'All of us,' Lucas said.

'Well now, Mr Dixon, the boss out at Clonmel Station, is looking for a married couple.'

'What to do?' Theo asked.

'Wife, house duties; husband, fencer for a start, but if he can handle a horse good enough, there are always jobs as stockmen and boundary riders . . .'

'Good pay?'

'I suppose so. Much as everyone gets paid out there, and keep.'

'Keep?'

'Bed and board. Meals and accommodation are included in the pay.'

'Do they take children as well?' Hanni put in quickly, and Theo glared at her.

Colley shook his head. 'I wouldn't think so. Not at Clonmel. The quarters don't run to room for kids.'

'We'll take it,' Lucas said in a rush. 'We can, can't we, Hanni?'

'If they'll have us,' she said shyly, glancing at the handsome young constable.

He looked at the fair-haired girl with her big blue eyes, and nodded warm approval. 'I'm sure they will. I suppose you can cook, Mrs Fechner?'

'She's an excellent cook,' her husband enthused.

'All German women are,' Theo said caustically, but the decision had been made, all over as suddenly as that. The

109

Fechners had not only found work but somewhere to live as well. It was agreed that they should stay at the barracks until Clem could get word out to Clonmel Station, after which Mr Dixon would send a buggy to collect them.

'Are you sure he will?' Lucas asked.

'Of course. He doesn't have time to come in and interview people. He expects us to send staff we think are suitable, and I reckon you two will be just fine.'

'Thank you, sir, thank you so much,' Hanni said. 'We are so grateful to you.' She hugged Lucas. 'See how easy it is? We've been worrying over nothing. Tomorrow we'll walk out to say our goodbyes to Father Beitz and ask for his blessing.'

This was a day Freda would never forget. Jakob had slipped away from the barracks so early she could think of nothing else to do but return to bed and worry. She was sure he had it all mixed up about those leases, not for three shillings an acre anyway, and he was so impressed with the friendly bank manager that he was liable to get carried away and commit himself to some folly. Just like Father Beitz. Then again, after discussing that situation with Mr Rawlins, her husband had decided it wasn't so bad after all. The land might be useless for a good while yet, but it was freehold land, already surveyed and registered in Father Beitz's name. No one could take it away from church ownership.

'Would anyone want to?' she'd asked.

'I was simply trying to explain that when people lease land, as we intend to do, they have to be careful to abide by the rules of selection. They send round inspectors to check on properties. To make certain they are being used and not bought by speculators.'

'I don't like the sound of that. I don't want inspectors breathing down my neck. We have our money, we ought to buy our land outright.'

'We can't. Not this land. And who'd want to? I figure if we can get land for three shillings an acre, leased, we'll have enough left to get started without having to borrow a penny from the bank.'

Freda was astonished. She lay there in the narrow room

looking up at the bare iron roof, certain there was a catch here somewhere. But what if Jakob were right, and they could do that. Wouldn't that bank manager, Mr Rawlins, be offended? He was going to the trouble of taking a stranger out into the wilds, showing him about, and the man might end up not borrowing a penny from him. Wasting the poor fellow's time. Truly, she worried, it wasn't very sensible to go offending your neighbours when everything was so new and strange, when it was so very important that they be accepted by the other villagers.

She had almost managed to doze off when the commotion started. Freda hadn't heard such a racket since the screams and shouts of the food riots in the village at home five years ago, when, she was upset to recall, men from her family had fought Meissners for three whole days. But then Eva Zimmerman burst in on her.

'Where's Jakob? We need him. We've only got Theo and Lucas to defend us.'

Frantically, Eva pushed her children in to Freda. 'You protect them! We're being attacked by savages!'

'Oh my God!' Freda was up in a rush, dragging on a blouse and a skirt, shoving the children under the bunk. She pushed the flimsy door open and ran into the narrow passageway between the partitioned rooms, immediately colliding with a huge blackfellow with a bare chest, a head of woolly hair and glittering white teeth. He smelled of oil, coconut oil, she thought later, but right then she screamed, pushing him away, appalled that she had actually made contact with that smooth dark skin . . . touched him with both hands. But he seemed unconcerned. Other men were following him, terrifying men. Savages. And this fellow made for her door, as if to open it and enter.

Bravely, Freda flung herself across the doorway. 'No!' she screamed. 'Get away, you brutes! You can't hurt innocent children.'

She saw that others were opening doors, peering in, moving in, taking over their barracks, and she looked frantically about for Eva, and for Theo. Where were they? And the Fechners? Was she the last one left to protect these children? She shivered. Someone had to make a stand.

111

Freda Meissner did just that. She ducked back into her room, told the children to stay quiet and returned with the only weapon she could find. An umbrella.

Once outside the door, she defended it with gusto, banging indiscriminately at the crowds of savages that seemed to be feeding through the barracks, whacking at them, forcing them to dodge past her, some of them laughing, grinning, some whooping with delight at having to run the gauntlet without harm, others not so pleased when the umbrella banged hard heads or backs, but they all ignored her, all too busy claiming rooms, it seemed, for their own savage reasons.

Freda knew her actions would not go unnoticed. That these fearsome natives, ugly men with bones in their noses and stark white shell necklaces, would not forget her bitter resistance, but she stood her ground, fighting back tears, until her umbrella collected a white man.

'Look out, missus,' he said. 'Leave off. I'm Constable Colley. Come to see if you're all right.'

'Of course I'm all right! Get these savages out of our barracks immediately! This is an outrage! Have you saved the others?'

She was near to fainting. Babbling. No idea what she was saying, as the Zimmerman kids peered out and the Constable apologised, promising it wouldn't happen again.

Nobody cared or even noticed that Freda had put her life on the line for the Zimmerman children, and in a way, she thought, it was just as well. She'd have looked a fool. As it turned out, it was all a big mistake.

These blackfellows were not Aborigines, the Constable explained, but Kanakas. South Sea Islanders brought into this country to work on the sugar plantation across the river. Harmless. More frightened of you than you of them.

'They were sent to the wrong barracks, that's all,' Colley said. 'A seaman got it wrong. Their barracks are about a half-mile down there. Past the police station. Simple enough mistake. When the boat pulled in, the seaman saw these buildings and sent them over here.'

'Simple mistake!' Theo shouted. 'Damn barefoot savages running through our quarters, terrifying my family!'

'I wasn't frightened,' Eva put in.

'You were so,' Freda said. 'You left me to protect your kids.'

'I did not. I left them to look after you.'

'Really?'

'What about breakfast?' Theo asked. 'I'm starving. Is there anything left in the communal larder?'

'Very little,' Hanni said. 'We'll have to buy more from the store.'

'Do that,' her husband said, 'and put it on the church account. We shouldn't have to pay for ourselves yet.'

Later, Freda made a mental note not to send Hanni shopping again. The silly woman had bought basic supplies, but also a chequered tablecloth, fans for the ladies, tobacco for the men and a wide straw hat for herself with a veil attached as protection from the flies, which were admittedly numerous and sticky.

Exhausted by the morning fracas, Freda left Eva to argue with Hanni. It had always seemed to her that Lucas and Hanni were mismatched. They had beauty in common, and she supposed that was the pull of all life, the stirrings that improved the species, for Lucas was surely a handsome man. Tall, dark and handsome, as the saying went, with dark brown hair, beauteous limpid brown eyes and lovely long eyelashes. Freda remembered taking a second look herself when she'd first seen him at an early meeting. No more than thirty years old, Lucas, with his physique and good looks, was an Adonis. So it was no surprise when they met his wife. Hanni was beautiful in a Dresden-doll way ... but while Lucas was a man with some style about him, Freda thought Hanni was rather common, and flighty as well.

Still ... something else was worrying her now. In response to Theo's curiosity about those Kanakas, the Constable had explained that natives had to be employed on the sugar plantations because white men couldn't do manual labour in this climate. The heat was too much for them.

Freda looked about her, bewildered. What heat? The weather was superb, sunny and mild, a perfect day. But what would the summer bring? Could the heat be that bad? And what was the difference between plantation and farm work? Not a lot, as far as she could make out. In which case, how would it be possible for them to work their own farm? She wondered then if they would have to employ native labour, those Kanakas, in the summer. It seemed to Freda that they were making a terrible mistake even considering a farm here. Maybe they should look to the south of this country, where there had to be cooler climes. She hoped Jakob hadn't committed them to any definite purchase, or lease.

'Where was Karl when all this was going on?' Jakob asked, intrigued by her story of the native workers.

'The town was stirring when you left, so he went for a walk. Missed all the confusion. Eventually he came back to tell me he'd got a job for the day with the blacksmith. He's still there.'

'Good for him.'

Jakob walked her away from the barracks so they could talk in private, heading along the river bank towards the police station; but Freda baulked. 'No. I don't want to go that way. Those savages are down there.'

'Very well,' he shrugged. 'We'll go the other way. I want to tell you about my travels. I had a very interesting day.'

'No. Wait. I found out something more important. Did you know it gets so hot here that white men can't work in the open? They can't suffer the heat. That's why they import those Kanakas. They're used to fierce sun.'

Jakob stared at her. 'No! That can't be right. I met farmers this morning. People starting up their own farms.'

'Maybe they don't know about this.'

'Surely they do,' he said anxiously.

They saw the Constable walking towards them on the other side of Quay Street, and crossed over to have a word with him.

'Is it true it gets very hot here in the summer?' Freda asked him, and he nodded.

'Yeah. It can get pretty hot. Humid. For about six months or so, but we have a fine winter to make up for it.'

Jakob needed to check his wife's story with the Constable. 'And that's why those natives are brought in?'

'Yes. For plantation work, and other work here and there. Cheap labour, too.'

'I see.'

When Colley had walked on, Freda grabbed Jakob's arm. 'See. I told you so. We have to leave here and go south to a better climate.'

Jakob shook his head. 'We can't do that. It's too late. I selected land this morning. Applied for leases.'

'Then go back quickly and tell them you've changed your mind.'

Jakob paced on, turning a corner before coming to a sudden stop. 'No, Freda, we stay. I found good land, wonderful land, and we'll have a fine farm. If other people can work in the heat, then so can we. White people, black people, what does it matter? We're farmers, Freda, we'll manage.' But he kept in mind the availability of cheap labour. For when they could afford it.

That night Jakob had some explaining to do. Having convinced Freda and Karl of his cleverness in working out how to begin farming without having to borrow a penny, he now had to admit that he was arranging a bank loan after all, and predictably, Freda wasn't impressed.

'What an example for your son. Borrowing money when you don't even need to. What foolishness is this?'

'It isn't foolishness, it's being far-sighted. Now that Karl is here, I'll tell you all about it. I found some land with a river frontage which will be suitable. It even has an old shepherd's hut on it, so that will be the starting point for our farmhouse.'

'Does it have a stove?' Freda asked.

'It has a large brick fireplace.'

'I will need a stove.'

'We'll see about that later. Mr Rawlins and I met a gentleman who has selected farmland nearby. Ninety acres.'

'Ninety acres?' Karl repeated, stunned.

'Yes.' Jakob rushed on then. 'To cut a long story short, I selected ninety acres too. It seemed to fit the picture.'

'You took up ninety acres?' Freda cried. 'What will we do with all that land?'

115

'We'll own it. But then I thought that Karl would want his own farm one day, so I selected ninety acres for him, too. Next door to the first block. That is why I will need extra cash from the bank!' He ended with a sigh that said, there, that's done, and waited for the result.

But they were both speechless, Karl with delight, Freda with anger.

From then on the Meissners were very busy. They needed transport but there wasn't much available. All they could find in their price range was a dray that had seen better days, but the owner promised to repair it for them.

Next came a conference with Jim Pimbley on what stores, farm implements, seed and stock they would need.

'And a stove,' Freda added.

'Sorry, can't help you there, Mrs Meissner. I'd have to order one from Brisbane for you.'

'Leave that for the time being,' Jakob said. 'We've got pots and saucepans with us, they'll do. I'm more interested in getting a cow, or maybe some goats. And some chickens.'

'I'll organise them for you when you give me the nod,' Jim said. 'No point in dumping them on you until you've got somewhere to put them.'

'From what I can make out, there's hardly anywhere to put *us*,' Freda snapped as they made their way back to the barracks, but Jakob knew that under her bluster, she was as excited as he and Karl were. He decided to celebrate by taking them to the hotel for a glass of ale.

Theo Zimmerman was there. 'Heard you're moving out. Bought a farm, have you?'

'I wish I could say yes,' Jakob said. 'We've leased land, Theo. About thirty miles out in the country, near the river. Now we have to turn it into a farm.'

'Must be costing you plenty.'

'Not to lease land. You ought to look into it.'

'You mean you don't have to pay for it yet?'

'Only a nominal amount for a start.'

Theo nodded knowingly. 'I get it. You use other people's money.'

'You'd do better to listen to Jakob instead of criticising him,' Freda snapped.

'I was only asking,' he whined. 'Anyway, from what I've seen, none of the country round here looks up to much. It's either jungle, like our land, or just that dull endless bush.'

'That's true,' Jakob allowed. 'The countryside doesn't look very interesting, but it will do us. Besides, I forgot to tell you, Freda, the wildlife away from the settlement is wonderful. We saw kangaroos and dingoes and flocks of emus . . .'

'Oh no! You should have let me come with you.'

Jakob smiled. 'I guess they'll still be there when we get to look about us. Our nearest neighbour is about ten miles away, but we won't see much of him for a while.'

'Why not?'

'He's in jail,' Jakob grinned.

'Oh, dear God!' Freda said. 'That's a great example for your son.'

Karl didn't care. He was still excited that his father had seen fit to buy a second ninety-acre block in his name, and not a little disappointed that Jakob hadn't bothered to mention this to Theo. Tact, he supposed. But anyway, Karl was looking forward to writing home to tell his cousins this fantastic news. How he would crow! They'd all said emigrating was madness. Stone stupidity. And now they'd find that he, cousin Karl, had ninety acres of land of his very own! They'll all be rushing to emigrate now, but maybe there wouldn't be any good land left by then.

The shepherd's hut was on a small rise, about a mile inland from the track which formed the eastern boundary of both blocks. It was in a dilapidated state, as Freda had expected, because Jakob had warned her about that, but at least a small area around it was cleared and there was a glimpse of the river through the woodlands that surrounded them.

Jakob was almost ecstatic in his enthusiasm as he rushed them through the woods at the rear of the hut to show them a small stream almost hidden in the undergrowth.

He began pulling away the intrusive bushes. 'See! It's very pretty, and good clean water. They call it Mischief Creek, what do you think of that?'

'Very nice,' said Freda. 'But don't you think we ought to unpack before we start work?'

They worked. They toiled. Father and son. Beginning with axes and saws to cut timber to repair the hut and make shingles for the roof. Freda scrubbed her new home from top to bottom before she would allow them to unpack her linen, and said not a word to Jakob about the confines of a one-roomed house, and a very small room at that. She knew he didn't have to be told what was needed.

They built a cowshed and a chicken coop, already aware of the temptation the chickens would be to the dingoes they'd seen nosing about. The men kept on clearing, working from dawn to dusk, and Freda set to work on her vegetable garden, putting in long rows of potatoes and pumpkins and maize. The weather stayed kind to them – nights were cool, the days still fine, with occasional bouts of rain – and they hardly noticed the weeks go by, until all at once they had visitors. The surveyors came, camped down by the river and set to work. The horse-drawn lorry arrived, with the same driver, called Bert, who had delivered belongings to the church land. This time he was bringing the rest of the order from Jim's store, including the chickens, and best of all, trudging along behind, a calmly quizzical cow.

Freda threw her arms about it, hugging it for sheer joy. Never before had she tried to make meals without dairy products of any sort. For a while they'd lived on the supplies they'd brought with them: salt beef, potatoes, turnips and onions, along with hard biscuits and tinned food, which she despised. But there was plenty of game – wild fowl and fish. And the huge emu eggs, of course. A meal in themselves.

'Is there any order for me to take back?' Bert asked, and Freda nudged Jakob. 'The stove.'

'No,' he said quietly, showing her the list he had made, a long list of hardware items from nails to fencing wire, axe handles and so forth. 'We're getting close to the limit of our loan. We have to start earning soon.'

Somehow that realisation seemed to make the work harder. They were all still working long hours in their little bush camp, but there was an urgency about the labour now.

118

Occasionally they had help. An Aborigine couple wandered by, interested in this activity. They stood apart, just watching Freda as she scrubbed shirts in the creek, until she could stand it no longer.

'What do you want?' she asked, trying not to appear nervous, since her men were nowhere to be seen.

Apparently nothing. The girl grinned, shrugged, jerked her head at her companion and padded silently away.

They came back several times. Often the girl had a baby strapped to her back, and eventually Freda gathered the courage to take a peep at it. She was rewarded by joyful smiles from the proud parents when she cooed and clucked over the pretty little girl with huge dark eyes.

'Freda,' she said, pointing to herself.

The girl responded. She was Mia, the baby Wonti and the father Yarrupi, or so the names sounded to Freda, who found herself asking them to stay, to have some biscuits. They stood at the back door, munching away until the plate was empty, after which they casually wandered away. But the next day Mia was back, on her own, to present Freda with a wooden gourd full of honey.

Freda was surprised. 'This honey. You get it in the bush?' she asked, using hand gestures, and the girl nodded, pointing too.

'Bush,' she said quite clearly.

When the men came in, Freda couldn't wait to show them. 'Taste it, it's lovely. Obviously it's wild honey.'

'I suppose there's plenty more food in the bush we don't know about,' Jakob said. 'They don't have farms. We ought to encourage them to come here so that we can learn what they live on.'

A few days later, Jakob and Karl were hard at it, dragging huge tree roots, already burned, from the soil, with the help of the horse, when Yarrupi strode towards them to lend his considerable strength to their operations. After that he was a familiar sight working nearby. He wouldn't be pinned down to any particular day or job, and he seemed to prefer pitting his strength against tree roots or logs, as if this were some sort of contest, just entertainment for him.

They all began to explore the property more carefully, tying coloured scraps of cloth to trees so they wouldn't get lost. Jakob and Karl took to fishing or hunting more often to break the monotony, and although he was nervous of Jakob's rifle, Yarrupi liked to hunt with them. His prowess with the spear was more reliable than Jakob's aim, so they always came home with a bush turkey or two, and a wallaby for Yarrupi, for Freda forbade her men to kill the small animals she'd become so fond of.

When she wrote home, Freda made their life sound idyllic, but it was, in fact, very difficult. She had found that primitive living lacked the everyday conveniences found in a normal house, such as papers to start the fire, spare rags for cleaning, chimney brushes, all sorts of things that sounded trivial but were persistently irritating. And like the men, every hour of every day meant work, from the milking at first light to supper at night when they were all too tired, too exhausted, to talk much. So the time came when Freda decided they were to have a day off.

'If not for us, for Karl's sake,' she told Jakob. 'You can't keep working the boy like that. He's young, he needs a break.'

'It's for his own good. We have to start making some improvements on his block soon, to satisfy the inspectors that we're not just speculating.'

'A day off won't hurt,' Freda insisted, but then Les Jolly, the logging boss, called on them to inspect their timber.

'Rawlins said you might be interested in selling good stuff, Mr Meissner.'

'Indeed I would be. We have some stands of cedar I can show you for a start.'

The two men toured both blocks and Les marked trees as they went.

'Who has leased the blocks up from here?' he asked.

'I don't know. The surveyors said people were taking up the leases but I haven't seen anyone yet.'

Les nodded. 'Probably waiting for the better weather.'

Jakob thought that remark was amusing, since the weather was perfect. This winter was like the summer back home. Warmer even.

It was agreed that Les should send over several of his men to take out the good timber and float it downriver to the sawmill.

'But how do they get the logs from the woods all the way to the river?' Jakob asked.

'Bullock teams. They'll drag the biggest logs out, no trouble at all. Hitch on the chains and away they go. And by the way, if you want anything delivered out here, Jakob, say so now. The bullockies will haul it for you.'

He repeated the question back at the house and Freda reminded Jakob about her stove, but again he shook his head.

'Well at least get a water tank,' she said angrily. 'I'm not carting any more water from the creek.'

Jakob was about to say: 'Why bother yet, there isn't much rain about to fill a tank, when he realised what Les had meant about the better weather. As a farmer, he should have known better, instead of basking in the warmth of the sun; working at clearing and hand-ploughing, taking occasional light falls of rain for granted. Hadn't Freda complained recently that they'd have to start hand-watering their small crop soon? Surely not. He was reassured, looking out over the field . . . the maize was high and green, the pumpkins and other rows of vegetables doing well. Another month or so and they'd have enough produce to take to market. Then they'd have a day off. Nevertheless, he did order a water tank in case this dry winter turned into a drought, and Freda was delighted.

'The timber will pay for it,' he said gruffly.

Karl wasn't worried about a day off, since there wasn't much to see in Bundaberg and he was anxious to show some sort of movement on his land to please the dreaded inspector. He thought a cleared area close to the main track would be a good start, and a front fence, or part of a fence, at the entrance might help. But that seemed rather pointless, and it wouldn't fool the inspector. A better idea, he decided, would be to clear and fence a tract of land along the creek, just as his father had done on the home block.

And that would take ages, he thought dismally.

They began to worry about the weather. Day after day the sun rose into a flawless blue sky, and the fields became so dry

121

they all worked a bucket brigade at dusk to bring at least some moisture to the crops. In this task they were frustrated once again by a trivial matter. They only had two buckets. To solve this problem, Freda enlisted the help of Mia and Yarrupi whenever they appeared, rewarding them with some turnips, which they loved, and a piece of her home-made cheese, which they tasted, spat out and handed to their dog. So turnips and potatoes became their accepted fee, and they carried them away to their camp, the location of which seemed to be a secret. Freda was able to ascertain that they lived with 'fambly' – quite a few people, by the sound of things – but never where they were.

A week later the bullock team came trudging up to the house, a large water tank tied securely to the tray of the long lorry, and all three Meissners were stunned as they watched it approach.

The team consisted of sixteen bullocks, walking in pairs, a driver sitting up on the lorry and another 'bullocky', as Les Jolly had called them, walking alongside with a long whip. As if that weren't enough of a surprise, the bullocky with the whip was none other than Theo Zimmerman! The bullocky's assistant, as it turned out, and none too happy with his lot.

The owner of the bullock team, a tough, wiry fellow called Davey, jumped down from the lorry and made for Freda.

'You Mrs Meissner?'

'Yes.'

'Good. I brought extra provisions. A side of beef, corned mutton and a bag of groceries. Where do I put them?'

'I didn't order that!' she cried, but Davey grinned at her.

'You didn't need to. Les Jolly sent it. We can't expect you to feed five extra blokes, now can we?'

'Five?' she said, looking about.

'Yeah. There's me and Theo, and three blokes'll be coming across by boat from the timber camp. Loggers. They'll be here any day. Any minute, I reckon, now that I'm here. Les don't like to waste time.'

As he strode back towards the lorry, Freda called to Jakob, who was already engaged in a conversation with Theo, 'Do *I* have to cook for them?'

'Looks like it,' Jakob said, with a querying eye for Theo.

'It's usual,' he told them.

'I don't mind, but I haven't got pots big enough, Theo. And no stove!'

'Davey will lend you some, he carries his camp with him. I have to go and water the bullocks. I'll be back soon and we can have a talk.'

As they attended to the huge beasts, every one of which Davey knew by name, since he loved them all like children, Theo looked over to the Meissner house. He'd known they'd leased a lot of land, doing real well for themselves, but they didn't seem so smart after all.

'Not much of a place they're living in,' he said to Davey. 'Only an old hut.'

'Some people know to crawl before they walk,' Davey snapped. 'And don't drag Daisy's collar off like that. She's not made of wood. Have a care, man.'

Theo hated this job, hated trailing about the bush at a snail's pace, but he was stuck with it for a while. Until he could find something better. Not being well-off like these Meissners, he didn't have cash to fall back on, so he had taken the first job he was offered, working in a boiling-down works where they produced tallow from the carcasses of sheep and cattle. A disgusting job. It made him so bilious he had to quit after a couple of weeks. But Eva still wouldn't go back to the church land, so he'd been obliged to move the family from the barracks to rented rooms in the home of the manager of the sawmill. It wasn't much of a place, only a poorly constructed collage, just thrown up, like everything else here, as if things weren't meant to last.

He wondered about that too: whether this so-called town would last, hanging on the edge of a river out in the middle of nowhere. It seemed to Theo that the place could go to seed when all the loggers left, the good timber cleaned out. The graziers who owned all the surrounding land didn't need Bundaberg, they'd got along fine for years before someone had the bright idea to make this lonely spot a town. And of course that was where the good jobs were, out on the stations. If Hanni Fechner hadn't jumped in, they could be settled out at Clonmel Station by now. But no, that selfish woman had

123

put her interests before those of needy children.

So had that rotten old priest. Theo had gone out to ask him for some money to go on with, until his next job, but Beitz had refused.

'You will have no need of money if you come back here, Theo. No rent to pay. We need workers, since most of our flock has deserted us. Bring your family back and we will rejoice in the providence of the Lord.'

'I can't do that, Father. You haven't made much inroad into this jungle at all. There's nowhere to live.'

The four men had built a humpy in the bush, a shelter made of bark and brush, and they cooked over an open campfire. They seemed content with it, but it wouldn't do for a family, especially with a little girl. Theo knew Eva wouldn't allow it without even asking her.

Since then he'd taken odd jobs, digging post-holes for fences, really hard work that, back-breaking; and then helping a carpenter build a timber dwelling for the Harbour Master. He'd even worked as a yardman at the pub for a week when Patrick O'Malley was down with the fever, and had hoped to stay on there, but when the publican was on his feet again, he didn't need any help. The fencer had been difficult, wouldn't take him back, so Theo had moved to this job, for a change of scenery. A chance to see the countryside and get paid at the same time. But it was hard. They were away for weeks at a time, always on the road, and the work could be dangerous, dragging massive logs out of the forests and getting them into place on high river banks.

It was easier when they were carrying supplies – the bullocks could haul up to two tons in weight – and they went out to the stations where the moneyed folk lived. At Clonmel he saw Hanni Fechner, looking pleased with herself, working as a maid in the big Dixon homestead.

'Yes. I've been out to Clonmel Station,' he told Jakob later. 'They say this land around here is only a small part of Dixon's holding. The Fechners are out there. She's a servant. He's working as a stockman now. Don't know how he got a job like that. They say those tough little stockhorses are hell to ride, throw you as quick as look at you.'

'I suppose so,' Jakob said. 'And what news of Father Beitz?'

'They're still on the block, living like natives in primitive huts.'

'Are the Aborigines still helping?'

'Every so often. Father Beitz and Tibbaling get along fine, except on Sundays.'

'Why Sundays?'

'Because he can't get it through the chief's head that the blackfellows have to come to mass on Sundays.'

Jakob squirmed. 'That makes me feel guilty. We've almost forgotten Sundays exist.'

'That is wrong, Jakob. You must do better than that. We walk out to the church block every Sunday to attend the service. When Tibbaling turns up and sends a couple of his young bucks in to do some clearing, Father Beitz has to dash out and stop them. They have great old arguments. And by the way . . . Walther was bitten by a snake!'

'Dear God! That's always a worry out here, but it would be much worse in that dense undergrowth. Is he all right?'

'He was sick for a few days but he got over it. Strauss said if it had been one of those nasty snakes he'd have been dead in a few hours. Not much consolation, is it? Eva is trying to find out what the venomous snakes look like, but that's a waste of time, I say. If you're bit, you're bit.'

'I suppose so,' Jakob said anxiously.

'And here, I nearly forgot,' Theo said. 'Father Beitz sent you a letter.'

He produced a crumpled envelope from deep in his trouser pocket. 'What does he say?'

'I'll read it later,' Jakob said, in case the priest had something private to say, and went back to chop the side of beef for Freda.

He forgot all about the letter until just before he turned out the lamp that night.

The contents didn't surprise him, but they were a worry. Father Beitz sent his blessings to all, chastised Jakob for not bringing his family in for Sunday services, and informed him that the common purse was now seriously short of cash. Their pastor had decided to solve the problem by tithing all of the congregation who were living and working independently, and had decided on the figure of one shilling per week, per person, excluding children.

It didn't occur to Jakob to refuse to pay his dues, but it had come at an awkward time, since they hadn't yet earned one penny, let alone a shilling. He was beginning to regret his largesse in leasing that second block for Karl.

Freda was more optimistic. 'The bullock driver said they have a market day in Bundaberg on the first Sunday of every second month. It gives people from the bush the opportunity for church meetings and to sell their produce. The next one is in two weeks, in August. We'll go, Jakob. We'll sell vegetables and my cheeses. I've got some ready. We'll manage.

'Maybe we could give Father Beitz produce instead of money,' she said as an afterthought.

'I wouldn't like to do that.'

'Let's wait and see.' She grinned. 'See what's left after market day. We may not sell anything, so we will have food to give them. That's as good as money.'

Jakob went in search of Theo. 'Did you know Father Beitz is short of money?'

'Yes. I thought that's what he'd be writing about. I haven't got any to give him. Walther said Father has written to the seminary in Hamburg asking them to send money with the young curate who's coming to help him, but he's not expected until next year. Looks like Walther and the Lutze boys will just have to get jobs like the rest of us. Proper jobs.'

'And the clearing they have done will grow back into jungle. We can't let that happen. Is there any good timber on the block that Les Jolly might buy?'

'Plenty. Jolly has already been out there. But Beitz won't sell. He says he needs some of the best timber for the church, otherwise the trees stay unharmed. He won't let go of a stick of it.'

Jakob gave up; he had enough worries of his own.

Chapter Six

At first the Kleinschmidts lived in the loggers' camp deep in the forest while the men lined up for work, but since they had women with them, Rolf needed to get everyone more settled as soon as possible. He was relieved to find the other timbermen were generous with advice and assistance for the new-chum Germans, and he gladly accepted their help.

'One thing we've got plenty of,' they told him, 'is timber. Nothing to stop you building your own huts. We'll give you a hand come Sundays. Nothing else to do.'

So Rolf and his friends trekked through the bush to examine a logger's hut. It was only two small rooms but good and solid, and his wife had a little vegetable garden alongside. She seemed very happy in this lonely place and took a liking to the young 'foreigners', urging them to stay for tea.

'Get your huts built before the rainy season,' she warned them, 'or you'll all get the rheumatics from the damp. That's what one of the first surveyors died of. Too wet for him, the rheumatics finished him.'

Rolf had heard enough about the wet summers here to be stirred into action. The first log hut, two rooms with a veranda for good measure, was soon completed, and it was decided it should house Rolf and his wife Rosie, his two brothers, Hans and Thomas, and his sister Helene, with her husband Josef Wagner. The day they moved in they had a great celebration, to which they invited the volunteer loggers and their wives, who were delighted with the mouth-watering food the German girls provided. A wonderful change from their diet of stews and damper.

So word got about. When they began the second log hut, a half-mile down the track, more volunteers turned up.

The next house was allotted to Brigitte and Paul Wagner, Paul's sister Katja, who was married to Rolf's cousin Herbert Kleinschmidt, and the two other bachelors, Herbert's brothers, Alix and Dieter.

The boss himself came to the christening of the new house, declaring himself partial to Katja's beef dumplings, so she gave him some to take home to Mrs Jolly.

'How do you sort out all these lads from one another?' one of the loggers asked him.

'Easy,' laughed Les. 'Rolf came to me first so his name stuck, but after that I had to use nicknames like Snow, Big Joe, Bluey, the red-headed bloke, Blondie, Darkie, Chooka and Tiny . . . he's the big bloke with arms like tree trunks.'

Then it was back to work again, the axes echoing through the quiet of the forests, smoke curling above the tree tops from the few houses scattered along the trails, and a general air of contentment. There were accidents, though. The only bullock driver operating with his team this side of the river was badly injured in a fall of logs, his legs crushed. The men rushed with him to the nearest landing and took him downriver to the town by boat, but he was in a bad way. He died a few days later.

The funeral was held in the forest near the landing stage, where his bullocks waited for their master, and Josef Wagner felt so sorry for the weeping widow, who kept asking what was to become of her, that he stepped forward and offered to buy the bullock team and rig.

Helene wasn't very impressed when she heard her husband was now a bullock driver, but, as he pointed out, someone had to do it. 'And what's more,' he added, 'the timber has to run out eventually, but people will still need transport. I can work from the sugar plantations too. I'm betting there'll be more than one plantation soon. They say sugar grows well here. Not sugar beet, sugar cane.'

Both Helene and Josef became besotted with their bullocks, as had many a driver before them, but they needed a lot more space and stables for them, so a month or so later, after they'd built stables and sheds and fenced a small paddock for the animals further down the track, they built their own house there as well, moving out of the crowded hut. By now the pocket settlement of Germans along the River Road, as the track was now known, was taken for granted, and the women were becoming well known for their talents in making pickles and smoked sausages, causing many a traveller to detour to their door with pennies in their hands.

Quietly the families progressed. Both Katja and Rosie were expecting babies. Paul Wagner built a smokehouse. Rolf bought a horse. Hans brought home two cows. The men began to be away for days at a time as the logging operations moved on, and the women kept each other company, grateful that they'd been able to stay in touch. They made friends with Aborigines who wandered by, pleased to see them and admire their piccaninnies as a break from their everyday chores. They learned to laugh with the Aborigines, to stand up to the men, who would on occasion try to bully the white women into giving them more tucker, and to tell the difference between bush fruit and berries that could be eaten and those that should never be touched.

One day Rolf called a meeting at his house, insisting that everyone attend. When they had all arrived, he brought out a mysterious parcel and had them walk with him all the way up the road to the crossroads of River Road and a track that veered inland.

Solemnly he unwrapped the parcel. Inside was a sign, professionally printed, that gave a name to their little settlement. Their village. He nailed it high on a tree, and when he allowed them to come round and read it, they all let out a sigh of delight.

The sign read: *Obrigheim*. The name of the town in Germany that had sheltered the Kleinschmidts in their hour of need.

There were tears and handshakes, then Rolf invited them all home to enjoy the wine that Josef had brought in after his last trip. This was their first celebration, and it was tinged with awe that they were so far from home and yet managing quite well.

That night Rolf sat outside, smoking his pipe under a huge full moon. He was twenty-five, tall and rangy, and seemingly a calm, confident man, but this wasn't necessarily so. Tonight was the first time he had been able to feel settled, freed from the niggling pains that had lodged in his stomach ever since the time he decided to migrate. From the time the others, two by two, like the passengers on the Ark, had stepped up asking if they could come as well. And so they had, but he worried, felt responsible. He'd tried to dismiss the burden. Tried to brush it off. But every time something went wrong, like the bad food on the ship, the occasional frightening storms, arguments among the group, the shock at seeing the town of Bundaberg as nothing but a settlement – it didn't even rate as a village in their vocabulary – and that terrible block of land, their promised land nothing but matted jungle, his stomach pains had worsened to such an extent that he'd had to curl up in pain with his usual excuse, that he was feeling bilious.

By this they'd all accepted that Rolf Kleinschmidt had a weak stomach. Rosie too. Dear Rosie. She went out of her way to give him bland food, which he hated but ate, to please her. He couldn't bring himself to tell his wife that his stomach pains were just nerves, brought on by worry.

What a weakling he was. His father would be ashamed to think his eldest son was running around worrying about his nerves.

Oddly enough, his father had been a forester before Count von Pressler had forbidden the removal of any more trees, and Rolf was now profiting from his example. 'If I say so myself,' he nodded, in a rare moment of self-satisfaction, 'I'm as good an axeman as any of the loggers here, thanks to my dad.'

But then the Count had also banned all agricultural pursuits on his estate, having decided he wanted it returned to its natural state: 'To the virgin beauty that the Lord created,' he'd insisted.

Rolf's father had tried to explain to the Count's squire that a forester's job was not just to cut down trees but to manage a forest for its own good, but he'd have none of it. The tenant farmers were thrown off the land. Even the small farming community that worked beneath the shadow of his great house, providing food for his own kitchen, was ordered off at the whim of this foolish dreamer.

At his wife's urging, Rolf's father had retreated to Obrigheim, her family village, and many of their relations followed, but this sudden influx put a strain on local resources and fifteen years later caused another exodus: emigration.

So many people had warned them about taking such a reckless step, and folk who knew about these things had cautioned them on what they would find at the end of their imaginary rainbow... fearsome savages lurking in dark jungles, wild animals that would tear them apart as they slept... if their ship managed to get there at all.

Rolf grinned. Who would have thought the dark jungle that really did confront them on their communal acreage wasn't a scary place at all but simply a great nuisance? And a nuisance that had pushed them towards this new life, their own little village.

As for wild animals, the snakes were a problem, admittedly; and dingoes, such handsome dogs, were just another nuisance, forever menacing Rosie's chickens. The only animals or reptiles that had them all really nervous were the crocodiles, the monsters that inhabited the river. Rolf had only seen a couple of them, when they were floating logs downriver to the sawmill, and he'd been shocked at the size of them, and the malevolence of their eyes. Fortunately, now that the logging had moved further inland after the pine and cedar, they'd been using drays and bullock teams instead of the river route. For which all the men were grateful.

Rosie called to him: 'There's a horseman coming down the road, Rolf. Come see who it is. What would people be wanting at this time of night?'

Rosie had surprised him. A meticulous, houseproud woman, she hadn't turned a hair at their primitive bush camp before the house was built, coping very well with the total lack of facilities. Once in her own home, however, though only a log cabin, she had become very fussy again. She and Helene had taken up the challenge of this odd household with gusto. Though there was no glass in the two narrow windows, they were soon curtained. The women pasted strips of calico on the

131

unlined walls and made mats of reeds to cover the earthen floor. In fact, their resourcefulness was a diversion for their menfolk.

Rolf took the lantern and went up to meet the rider, who turned out to be one of Les Jolly's men with a message.

'Les says for you and your brothers to go across the river tomorrow and start logging on some blocks there. He says there's good ash, pine and cedar. He has marked some but there's plenty more. Probably take you a couple of weeks.'

'How do we get there? Across the river?'

'Go down to the landing where we used to float the logs out, and he'll have a boat there for you. You can come home nights if you want to, but Les says it'll be easier to camp on the job. He says the bloke over there who owns the land is a mate of yours anyway.'

'Who would that be?'

'Meissner. He's got two blocks there. Well timbered for a start, easing out into plains, used to be part of Clonmel Station. You got that then, Rolf? I'll be on my way.'

'No. Wait a minute. Where on the river is this land?'

'Straight across from our landing spot.'

'And how do we get the logs down to the river?'

'No need to worry about that. Les hired another bullocky. He'll be there waiting for you, so don't muck about.'

Rolf frowned. None of his folk were in the habit of 'mucking about', as this fellow put it. But local etiquette required that he offer the man something.

'We have soup on the stove. Can I get you some before you go?'

'No thanks, mate, I have to make sure they put the boat in the right place for you, then I can go on home.'

'The Meissners? Just across the river? Well for heaven's sake!' Rosie was intrigued. 'What do they do there?'

'Farming, I suppose. It will be nice to see them again. You could come if you want.'

'I would like that. Did I hear that gentleman say you could go over there daily?'

'Yes. We could do that.'

132

'No you won't. You stay there and finish the job and then come back home. No riding rowboats at night on that river, with sharks and crocodiles swimming around you. No.'

'It will be more than a couple of days.'

'Never mind. I've got the rifle. We'll be safe. You men have been away before.'

Rolf grinned. 'All right, but just don't go shooting at shadows. I'll tell Hans and Thomas in the morning.'

Jakob couldn't believe his eyes when he saw who the loggers were, and he took them up to see Freda with unabashed pride.

'Will you look at the lads now! Timber men! With a big job ahead of them. Some of the old trees here are immense, but I suppose they're just as big the other side of the river.'

'That they are, Jakob. Beautiful timber. Strange to think we're cutting wood to send to Europe.'

Wasting no time, Rolf borrowed Jakob's horse to explore the blocks, while the others spared a few moments for a talk, to catch up on the news and relate their experiences.

'You've got your own houses?' Freda said, fascinated.

'Only three,' Hans said. 'It's our turn next. Me and Thomas. We must get our own homes, then we'll look for brides.'

'Heavens above! I'm so pleased to hear you're all doing so well.'

'So are you,' Thomas said. 'All this land! You'll have a big farm one day. But you need a bigger house. Kitchen and all in the one room is hard for ladies, Jakob.'

Hans was mortified. 'Don't take any notice of him. He doesn't mean to be rude. He always says stupid things.'

'I'm not rude. Jakob's got enough timber here to build a city. We ought to give him one of our Sundays. God knows there's enough of us, what with Theo and the bullocky here as well.'

'What's one of your Sundays?' Jakob asked.

Thomas smiled at Freda, a broad, mischievous smile. 'We build log houses on our special Sundays. Would you like one, Mrs Meissner?'

Freda glanced about her. 'We're all right here, Thomas. Really we are.'

He nodded. 'Of course you are. But we might have a little talk with Rolf when he gets back. He's the boss.'

Rolf had learned a great deal about these tracts of land from Les Jolly, and from the surveyors who were fanning out from Bundaberg in all directions. These men had difficult jobs, working, or hacking more like it, through tough terrain in all sorts of weather, measuring up land for settlers. The concept fascinated Rolf. He'd never thought he'd be a witness to the transformation of virgin land to the beginnings of civilisation. Back home the farms and villages were taken for granted, as if they'd been born that way, but here he was watching history in the making.

Once out on the job, the surveyors had no care for time. They established camps, with folding tables as desks in their tents, and kept working and note-taking for a prearranged span of time. To do with their rations, Rolf thought. But anyway, Sunday to them was just another work day, so he was often up early on Sundays, cutting across country to find them and offer his labour. It was gratefully accepted. He became expert as a chainman, carrying the chain of twenty-two wire links, each a yard long and measuring out this peculiar span. He laughed when it finally dawned on him that the chain itself was a physical measurement. One chain, a basic measure. So simple it had seemed obscure to him at first.

But now he understood all the measurements, and like the surveyors, he could envisage an acre, even a square mile, in his mind's eye. And like Les Jolly, he could look into a forest and take a close estimate of the number of trees to the acre, depending on the average distance between them. Six feet apart you would find twelve hundred to the acre, and so estimates went, higher or lower.

Rosie disapproved of his working Sundays and made him put his labouring wage aside from their weekly earnings until she decided what was to become of it. The answer arrived in a letter from Father Beitz. It would be their tithe money. Rosie, a good God-fearing woman, refused to see the humour in this, so Rolf refrained from teasing her.

With all his surveying experience, Rolf soon recognised

the wooden stakes hammered into the ground with surveyors' markings, picked up on the blazed trees that pointed to beacons, spotted the recent campsites used by the surveyors. He easily found the boundaries of Jakob's blocks, which, he hoped, were far enough from the river to be above flood level. He even found, with a thrill of excitement at his latest skill, the personal signature of one of his surveyor friends, George Stilwell. For the fun of it, the surveyors often left their mark, and George's was a simple base arc, a smile cut into a tree, or more often into a rock so that there was less chance of it being removed. This one smiled at Rolf from a rocky outcrop near the boundary of Jakob's property, which, he'd been told, had been resumed from Clonmel Station. And he bet the squatter wasn't too pleased about it. This was fine grazing country, open plains, good for agriculture but not much use to loggers. Rolf turned back. He'd seen enough. The eastern section of Jakob's land would yield a good supply of fine timber, keeping them working over here for a few weeks.

He rode towards the river to find his way back to the Meissner house, only too aware that a man could get lost out here in this bush. The sameness of the trees and the landscape was worse than a maze, and the distances, taken for granted by the local people, added to the hazards of bush life.

Closer to the river he found a stock route and followed it right through the border of tall gums to the river bank to allow the horse to drink.

While he was standing there, he gazed across at the cleared remnants of old rafting grounds, where the logs were chained together to be floated downstream. Dieter had taken on that job for a while, not minding it at all, but then Dieter was a daredevil. He'd try anything. He loved the excitement, the danger of managing those heaving slippery logs. When the logs reached their destination, the loggers then had to remove the heavy chains, haul them into a dray and take them upriver to start the process all over again.

Rolf shuddered. He remembered the shouts and curses of the men the day he'd stopped by to watch them in action. He'd seen a man fall into the river, between the logs, heard him scream. They'd rescued him though, and he was soon back at

135

work. But that scream . . . In his memory it was so real, it was almost as though he could still hear it. Suddenly he jerked up to listen, and the horse, taken by surprise, snorted and pranced away from the water's edge.

There was someone calling, but from where? He looked about him. Even up into the trees, in case he'd mistaken a bird call for a human voice. He nosed the horse through the trees along the river bank, but finding no one, he turned back. Ahead was a high mound, cutting off access by horseback, so he hitched Dandy to a tree and began the climb. He was almost at the top of the pleasant green knoll when he saw a man in the river!

Rolf was almost transfixed with shock. The man had seen him and was screaming at him for help. He was clinging to a tree branch, caught on a snag out in the middle of the river.

'Help!' the man screamed again. 'I can't swim!'

Rolf wondered what he was doing there. How he'd got there if he couldn't swim. He looked about for a boat that might have floated away, but couldn't see one. He had to help this fellow, but how? It was a wide river and very deep. He didn't fancy trying to swim it. Maybe he could swim the horse out there.

He ran down and jumped on Dandy, putting him straight at the water, hoping to move along the shallows until they were opposite the marooned man. But Dandy would have none of it. He plunged and bucked, and would not go in, no matter how much Rolf whacked and kicked him. Rolf didn't blame the horse really. He was afraid the animal could smell crocodiles or their haunts . . . or his own fear. He too was terrified of the creatures that dwelled in these waters.

So. He couldn't leave the fellow there. He had to force the horse to swim or go out there himself and bring the man back. The non-swimmer. Who was shouting at him to hurry because something was breaking up. Was abusing him! Cursing him!

Rolf dragged the saddle from the horse, took off his own heavy moleskin trousers, got back on the horse and gave it an almighty wallop with the buckle of his belt, and Dandy lurched forward into the deep water. The horse fought furiously against the current, seeming to know by now exactly where he was going, as Rolf guided him in an arc to pass by the man, close enough for him to grab hold. Then they were on their way back, the two men now aboard the horse, which was unfazed by the extra weight, swimming strongly for the shore with a new burst of energy.

As soon as they hit the shallows, Dandy shook the men off and bolted up the high bank, glad to be rid of them, standing shuddering in the safety of a clump of trees.

'You took your bloody time,' the stranger said to Rolf as he followed the horse up the bank. 'I could have drowned.'

'What were you doing there in the first place?' Rolf said, ignoring the ungrateful remarks.

'I was rowing across the river upstream there, hit something in the water, got tipped over. Couldn't get hold of the dinghy, got washed down here, swallowed half the bloody river, ended up stuck on that bloody snag. You German?'

'Yes.'

'You the bloke selected this land?'

'No. I'm here for the timber.'

'The hell you are. That timber belongs to us.'

'Who's us?'

'My family. Dixons. We own Clonmel Station. This is part of our station. Or was, until the government started letting in these bloody beggars. What's your name?'

'Rolf Kleinschmidt.'

'Well take my advice, Rolf. I owe you that. Forget the timber here and get along home. You touch any of our timber, you'll be in for a pile of trouble.'

'Who are you to be saying this?'

'I'm Keith Dixon. My old man's the boss around here. J.B. Dixon. His dad opened up this area, so he don't take kindly to cocky farmers lobbing on sheep pastures.'

As Rolf retrieved his trousers and saddle, Dixon moaned about the loss of his boots. 'Nearly drowned trying to get them off,' he said, 'and keep afloat at the same time. Damned fine boots they were too. I say, could I make myself beholden to you again?'

'How?'

'Lend me the horse. I've got about ten miles to go to get home; you'd only have to walk downriver for a couple of miles from here.'

Rolf had had enough of this fellow and his irritating manner. 'Sorry. This I cannot do. It is not my horse. And I cut its rump with my belt.'

'I saw that. Bloody wretch of a thing. Listen, I'll buy it from you. I'll give you an IOU.'

'I told you. It's not my horse.'

Dixon stood up and took off his shirt, flapping it in the warm sun to dry it off a little. 'Well, no point in hanging around here dripping like a bloody clothes line if you won't give me the horse.'

With that, he turned and strode away. Unconcerned, Rolf let him go. Dixon, who looked about his own age, was a well-built, muscular sort of fellow, heavily tanned from the sun. Obviously no stranger to the bush. Rolf guessed that the ten-mile hike back to his home was not much of a problem to this fellow, or he'd have made more of a fuss about needing a horse. It seemed to Rolf that asking for the horse had been worth a try, just that, and no more.

But now he'd have to get back to Jakob's house and explain why Dandy was hurt.

'You'd better learn to swim!' he called after Dixon, who simply trudged on without a backward glance.

Horse and rider were a bedraggled sight entering the house paddock, and Freda stared.

'What happened to Dandy?' she asked angrily. 'He's covered in mud, and look, he's hurt!'

'I can explain, Mrs Meissner. If you could let me have a bucket I'll swab him down.'

'No. I'll do it. You go on up to Jakob.'

When his story was told, Rolf brought up the subject of the timber-getting.

'That fellow Dixon said you have no right to the good timber here. He says it belongs to them.'

Jakob shook his head. 'Impossible. This land was resumed by the government, specifically for agriculture, and they have leased it to selectors. There is nothing on my lease that says I don't own the timber growing on my land.'

'How could there be?' Rolf said. 'I'm only passing on Dixon's claim for what it's worth. Anyway, Les Jolly knows his business, he wouldn't have us trespassing.'

The bullocky, Davey, was standing nearby, sucking on an old briar pipe. 'I wouldn't be too sure, mate. Them Dixons aren't too keen on rules. They got the timber off Mike Quinlan's land.'

'Who's Mike Quinlan?' they asked him.

'An Irishman. He's got a block south of here, next to yours I'd say. A corner of Clonmel Station too. Got it legal all right. Leased it and all. But they still took his timber.'

'How?'

'Got their men to do the logging while Mike was away. He's a dairy farmer. Went down to Maryborough to buy a dairy herd and walk them back to his block. By the time he got back it was all over, see. They picked the eyes out of his timber.'

'And there was nothing he could do about it?'

'Oh yeah, there was. He's a wild man, Mike Quinlan. He rode on over to Clonmel Station and shot one of Dixon's prize merino rams. Shot it stone dead. He's in jail now, of course. You can't go around shooting merinos. Little gods, they are.'

Rolf looked to Jakob. It seemed neither of them knew what to make of that information.

'Reckon your best bet is to get your timber out as fast as you can. Before old Dixon thinks up trouble. Me and Theo, we'll give you a hand. Your boys are already up there, Rolf.'

When Freda came back, she thanked Davey for the use of his cookpots. 'I think some of my pumpkins will be ripe enough to pick now, and some turnips, so I'll need the bigger pots.'

'No trouble, missus. I've got a camp oven out there. I'll make you some damper later on, if you like.'

'What's a camp oven, Davey?'

'Ah . . . I'll show you. It's a little square oven that sits in the campfire, that's all.'

'And you can bake in it?'

'Sure you can.'

That sounded like heaven to Freda. To be able to bake again, instead of having to live with boiled food or meat cooked on a spit. This she would have to see. It would obviously be a lot cheaper than a real kitchen stove.

As they walked over to his lorry, a breeze raised dust and Freda flapped her apron distractedly. 'It's so dry,' she said. 'When will we get some rain?'

'Nothing much in sight,' Davey replied. 'Never much about in the winter. But I reckon it's a bit worse than usual this year. Bleeding countryside's tinder dry, and me having to push my team on harder to keep within march of lagoons or waterholes.'

The camp oven was a battered old black box and Freda reserved judgement. She was very interested to see what it could do.

A week later, Keith Dixon and two of his men came to call. Freda offered them coffee as she would any visitor, giving no hint that their arrival was worrying her. The two men accepted, but Keith declined. He went off to talk to Jakob.

Freda found the stockmen some cold pudding, knowing they would enjoy it, and stayed to make conversation with them, hoping she would hear what Dixon junior was up to. They only talked about the weather, though, and about the problem of the drying grasslands. Then she remembered that Lucas and Hanni Fechner were working at Clonmel Station.

'Do you know Lucas Fechner?' she asked.

'Yes,' the older man said. 'A good fellow. Hard worker. It took him a while to get his bearings. He got lost in the bush one time and we spent half the night searching for him, but eventually his horse brought him home. Yeah, he's getting the hang of the job real good now, I'd say.'

'He and Hanni came on the same ship as we did,' she told them. 'We migrated as a group.'

'Yeah. My folk came from Scotland like that, a whole troop of them. They did all right. You people settling in then?'

'Oh yes, thank you. I'm glad to hear Lucas is liking his work. And how is Hanni getting on?'

She saw the frown on the man's face and the angry jerk of

140

his head towards his friend before courtesy dictated his response. 'She's going along fair, as far as I know.'

'Oh good,' Freda said vaguely, very much aware that something was wrong there, but she did not enquire. Instead she glanced over to the woods between the house and the river, where logging had begun.

'That Mr Dixon, is he the only son?'

'No. The eldest son was killed in a fall from a horse, and the middle son is overseas with his wife, off travelling the world.'

'How lovely for them. And this young man, Keith, he must be a great help to his papa.'

'Yes. But old J.B. is still the boss. He don't take no interference from no one.'

'And Mr Keith, is this a neighbourly visit, or does he have business with Mr Meissner?'

They gazed about them uncomfortably. The younger stockman pushed back his hat, scratched his neck and said: 'Bit of both, I suppose. You've got a nice patch here, missus, reckon them veggies will do well in this soil.'

'With a bit more rain,' Freda said wanly.

'Yeah! Well there's always somethin',' he told her, handing back the plate. 'That was real nice pudden', thank you, missus.'

Rolf and Thomas were high on a narrow ledge, safety ropes slung round their waists, beginning to chop into the trunk of a massive cedar tree. There were so many huge trees in these forests that at first they'd been awed by the grandeur of the scenery, but they soon learned instead to be in awe of each majestic tree. Respect for the power of the tree saved lives and saved timber, they were told, and this they discovered was good advice, as the axes flew and the great beings came crashing down.

It was Thomas who saw him first. 'There's a rider coming up through the timber. Who could that be?'

Rolf glanced down. 'It's Keith Dixon from Clonmel Station. The one I pulled out of the river.'

'He's probably come over to thank you properly. He might even have a reward for you.'

'Not him. It's my bet he's after the timber. Keep going. Jakob can deal with him.'

Jakob, who had been working with Theo cleaning up scrub near a felled tree, walked down to greet the stranger.

'Jakob Meissner,' he said. 'What can I do for you, sir?'

The rider climbed down from his horse, a fine thoroughbred, and nodded without offering his hand. His name was no surprise to Jakob.

'I'm Keith Dixon. Your neighbour. Clonmel Station. You'd better call off these loggers; that timber belongs to my dad. Unless, of course,' he grinned, 'you're logging it for him. In which case he'll be mightily grateful to you.'

Jakob shook his head. 'Mr Dixon. You are mistaken. This is my land, I have an official registered lease. Your father has no claim to this timber. Would you please explain this to him?'

But Dixon had strolled past him, staring up into the heights. 'Is that Rolf up there?'

'Yes. And his brother, Thomas.'

Jakob stood watching them too. It was fascinating to be able to see these axemen at work. The two Kleinschmidt lads had become experts by now, and even Dixon was impressed.

'They're good, aren't they? But you'd better get them down. They're only wasting time.'

'We'll leave them there for the time being,' Jakob murmured. 'Is there anything else I can do for you, Mr Dixon?'

'Yes. You can read this. I guessed you wouldn't listen to me, so we've put the matter in writing for you, so that you have it clear and make way for our loggers to come in. Probably within the next few days.'

Jakob took the letter Dixon proffered but didn't bother to read it. 'If any of your people come on to my land to cause me a nuisance, Mr Dixon, I will regard such as trespassing.'

'Please yourself,' Dixon shrugged. 'But we don't regard getting our own timber as trespassing.' He walked back to his horse. 'We'll meet again. Soon.'

Not until Dixon was out of sight did Jakob give in to his curiosity and open the envelope. There were three pages, and Jakob found the writing difficult to decipher because of the unfamiliar formation of the letters, so he sat down on a stump to study them.

Written by J.B. Dixon, the first letter claimed the legal right to the timber and gave notice that loggers employed by Clonmel Station would shortly enter the two blocks leased by Meissner. Jakob didn't set much store by that; he knew he was legally entitled to the timber. But the second and third pages worried him. The stationery was headed 'Philps and Sons, Attorneys at Law and Legal Supplicants', and the letter read:

Opinion at law as to ownership of timbers growing on land occupied by J.B. Dixon of Clonmel Station and subsequently resumed by State Government for lease to agriculturalists:

It is hereby shown that aforesaid timbers are located on land resumed by Government and not sold in voluntary communion, as in normal land sale procedures. According to the Lands and Mining Act 1864, minerals found on that land remain the property of the discoverer, insomuch if said discoverer does register a claim on said minerals, that claim to be the first lodged. In the same manner be it shown that though said property was resumed by Government, and the discoverer of commercial timbers on said property did register claim of ownership and be the first to register same, then right to log belongs to the claimant, in this case J.B. Dixon of Clonmel Station.

Be therefore advised that illegal removal of commercial timbers from the two blocks described in the attached page will be met with the full force of the law.

It was signed on this day of our Lord and so forth by a Jefferson Philps.

Jakob felt weak at the knees. He was relying on the sale of the timber. They still had no other income apart from the little they might earn from sales of vegetables, which they needed now anyway, to be able to provide a decent table for the extra men. Searching for blame at finding himself in this predicament, he turned his anger on the bank manager, Rawlins. Why hadn't he told him that all this magnificent timber wasn't part of the deal? Had they discussed the timber at all? He couldn't remember. Had he just taken ownership of the timber for granted? How could he have been so stupid? Had he known this, he never would have taken up two blocks, with the extra expense the second one would incur. He was in a dark mood as he trudged back to the house rather than have to call to the loggers to cease work.

Freda read the papers he handed to her, and was shocked.

'This can't be right. It can't be.'

'It says so there, in black and white. The timber isn't ours. We're in for lean times, my dear.'

'You'll just have to borrow more from the bank.'

'Never! As I was coming down here I was remembering what old Uncle Hans-Joachim said to me before we left: "Keep your wits about you, Jakob. You'll be in a strange land, among strangers. It'll be hard to tell the sheep from the wolves."

'So I'm wondering if Rawlins was in league with Dixon. He talked me into selecting not one but two blocks, with never a word about the timber. He probably knew it wasn't ours all along. It's not in my nature to be suspicious of people, but Father Beitz got tricked and now it looks as if we have been too.'

Davey helped Freda prepare supper for seven hungry men using the camp oven, and the meal was declared a success, though depression replaced conviviality. Despairing, Jakob aired his suspicions about being tricked.

'All of us. We're the damn-fool Germans. Sitting ducks for trickery.'

Thomas nodded. 'Did you hear about Paul Wagner, Brigitte's husband? A fellow came by with samples of rum. Local rum, grown from local sugar plantations there on the other side of the river. They say sugar grows as well as corn here. I met one of the bosses, a plantation manager; they're building a sugar refinery out there somewhere, and he said we could come and look around any time we wanted—'

'Paul Wagner,' Freda interrupted. 'What about Paul?'

'Oh yes. He bought a cask of rum. They can make beautiful casks from local timber, you know.'

'So?' Freda reminded him.

'Ah yes. Paul paid a whole pound for it . . . Tasted it first, of course, said it was very good.'

'A lot he'd know about rum,' Rolf laughed, and then was quiet as Freda glowered at him for maybe getting Thomas off track again.

'Anyway,' Thomas continued, 'he also sold Brigitte some fine skeins of knitting wool. Took their money and hurried off down the road with his wheelbarrow to bring up the goods. His wheelbarrow was a sample shop, see. His boat in the river was his shop.'

'Except there were no goods,' Rolf said. 'Nothing. He just took the money. The next day at the loggers' camp they laughed at Paul. Said only us German boobies would fall for that old trick.'

'Yes. They think we're dummies,' Hans added. 'Now they've got you as well, Jakob. I suppose we'd better pack up in the morning and go home. You too, Davey. No point in hanging about with no timber to haul. Not by the looks of that order from the Dixon lawyers.'

Davey looked to Freda. 'Do you mind if I light my pipe in here, missus?'

'No, I think Jakob will be reaching for his when the coffee's hot,' she said, worrying that they were down to almost the last of her coffee, which was much dearer than the tea people seemed to prefer out here.

'Yes. Have your pipe,' Jakob said, and Davey edged about the backs of the men to get to the fireplace. He lit his pipe with a fine splinter and turned back to the company.

'I don't know if anyone's noticed, but I'm one out here. I'm not German and you blokes keep whingeing on like I am, or like I don't exist.'

Apologies flew, but Davey would have none of them.

'Don't worry about me. I can look after myself. But you lot, it's no use whining. Someone's out there to rip a man off at every corner, no matter who you are. There are a lot of smart alecs around. But let me tell you this. They won't be taking

145

advantage of you because you're Germans, or Danes, or bloody Zulus; they'll be trying to take advantage of you because they think you're dummies. Which your mate Paul was. Payment on delivery isn't a bad rule.'

Freda served them coffee, ignoring Karl's grimace when he tasted his watered-down share, the last of the dregs. As plates were passed over to her, the men stared glumly at the table, or into the fireplace, the remaining glow of hot coals a comfort on this chilly July night that had succeeded a warm day. After the meal, the hard day, crowded together in this little house, they felt rugged up, secure, but they all knew wolves were howling at Jakob's door. He was in trouble. But how to help? The Kleinschmidt men were only loggers; what could they do?

But the crafty old bullocky hadn't finished.

'Now listen to me,' he said suddenly. 'I reckon you ought to get yourself a legal man, Jakob. Get him to look into this stuff Dixon's pushing at you. You gotta go that extra yard.'

'What is this extra yard?'

'Dixon's got himself a lawyer. You gotta get yourself a better one. Worth a try.'

They drifted into another bout of silence, waiting on Jakob's response. Finally he stood up.

'I'll have to find Les Jolly. See what he says. But as for employing a solicitor, I couldn't possibly afford that, Davey.'

Rolf agreed. He was certain that Les Jolly would know the answer.

'I'll row back over the river in the morning. In the meantime, everyone keeps working. We should at least get another load for Davey.'

Rolf spent the day tramping the woods, finally tracking Les down at the number four loggers' camp.

Les was none too pleased to see him, guessing Rolf was the bearer of bad news, but when he heard of Dixon's claim he exploded. 'Bloody rot! He can't do that. You're wasting your time, Rolf, falling for that cock-and-bull story. Go back to work.'

'We thought so too,' Rolf persisted, 'but young Dixon gave these papers to Jakob. They seem to put Dixon in the right.'

Les read them, reread them, frowning. 'I don't know about this,' he said eventually. 'The lawyer fellow says he does own the timber, and he ought to know. But I never heard of it before. Though come to think of it, Dixon took the timber off Quinlan's land and no one stopped him. Then again, with Quinlan away I suppose there was no one to say him nay. Except the police, and Clem Colley wouldn't have the guts to take on Dixon.'

He handed the papers back to Rolf. 'I reckon you'd better pull out. Plenty of timber over here. Yes, get the lads back.'

'But what about Jakob? He needs the money the timber will bring him. He can't just stand by and watch Dixon's men come in and take it from under his nose.'

'Doesn't seem much else he can do.'

'Unless he gets a lawyer.'

'The nearest is in Maryborough, like this Philps and Sons. I'd like to help him, Rolf, but I can't afford the mess a charge of trespassing would get me into. I'd probably get fined and have to hand the timber over anyway. It's no go. Bring the lads back and set them up on the west block of the Jupiter Plantation. The manager there needs land cleared to plant more sugar. He's already ringbarking everything in sight.'

The house was quiet. The bullock team had left for Bundaberg with a couple of huge logs aboard. Rolf and his brothers had gone and Jakob was working with Karl once again, clearing the smaller trees and brush to enable them to utilise patches of land. But they both knew it was time to call in loggers if they wanted to attain their vision of fields of corn and potatoes and other vegetables. To have a real farm with more livestock . . . a dream that was fast receding, disappearing out of their reach.

'Why don't I ride over to Clonmel and tell the Dixons to get on with it? Take the damned timber and get it over with? At least then we'll be able to start ploughing,' Karl said.

'No!' Jakob said savagely. 'No! This is wrong. I won't let them take my timber.'

'How can you stop them?'

'I don't know, but I can find out. I'm going in to Bundaberg now. This minute. I can't go on worrying about it.'

147

The decision made, he stormed down to the house to tell Freda.

'You're right,' she said. 'Someone must be able to help us. Maybe even Mr Rawlins. I'll come with you.'

'No. The dray is too slow. I can't afford to waste any time. Get me a clean shirt, and you'd better give me a haircut and trim my beard if I'm to look smart enough to talk to town people again.'

In the months that they'd been living out on their farm, Bundaberg had changed considerably. The track along the riverside veered inland after a few miles, bypassing the bends of the river in favour of a direct route to the town, and all along this road were signs of habitation, if only cleared land and the occasional fenced paddock. Closer in, though, Jakob was surprised to see quite a few farmhouses set back from the road. He supposed the bullock drivers would come this way, but there'd been no discussion about the changes. Davey probably took it for granted that the newly established farming family was aware of this progress. Jakob smiled as he rode towards the town, thinking how easy it had been to just slip away into the countryside as they had done, too busy to regard themselves as members of any community, and yet here they were, settlers. Farmers, if they could hang on. No longer cautious immigrants staring at a forlorn hamlet with few buildings to give grace to streets littered with tree stumps.

Other roads joined this one, so Jakob knew he must be riding in the right direction. He passed families on loaded drays heading inland, and they waved merrily, no doubt on their way to begin a new life too. He wished them well.

Then, within a few miles of the town, his heart sank. Acres of land here were covered in vegetation, not bush, but carefully planted vegetable gardens. Rows and rows of flourishing cabbages and pumpkins and potato plants, all sorts of healthy-looking vegetables being tended by Chinese workers.

Jakob was stunned. He hadn't been out this way before and no one had bothered to mention that there were Chinese market gardeners established on the outskirts of the town. Chinese! He looked at them in wonder. Strange people in their pointy hats and pigtails and loose garments. He had never expected to see them here. They belonged in exotic picture books.

'Wonders will never cease,' he murmured as he went by. They didn't wave. They were working; they didn't even look up.

'I think we'll have to eat our own vegetables,' he told his horse, 'and stick to the bigger crops, like corn. And turn to dairying.'

The town itself was a surprise too. There was a new hotel, a pharmacy, a presentable and quite large shop that boasted general drapery, and, next door to the bank, a barbershop. There were other new buildings in the side streets, he noticed as he made his way along Bourbong Street, but he didn't have time for sight-seeing. He had to find Mr Rawlins.

But Rawlins was away, the young teller advised him. Gone to Brisbane on annual leave.

Dumbfounded, Jakob walked back into the glare of the midday sun, trying to figure out what to do next. He felt lost, disoriented. He wished he'd allowed Freda to come with him, even if the dray was slower. He saw Constable Colley ride past and turned away quickly, for fear of contact with this fellow, reported to be a friend of the Dixons. He ducked across the street, making for the more familiar Quay Street, passing a newspaper office on his way, vaguely surprised that the town could afford a local newspaper but too concerned with his own problems to give it much thought.

Then he ran into Eva Zimmerman.

'Heavens to be! Jakob Meissner! What are you doing here?'

'I came to see Mr Rawlins, but he's away.'

'Oh yes. Theo told me you've run into trouble with Dixon. They're powerful men, those squatters. Not a good idea to get on the wrong side of them. Not a good idea at all.'

He walked with her to a cottage set unhappily in a paddock overgrown with weeds, listening to her news of the town.

'Dr Strauss is staying here for good. He's hung out his shingle in Quay Street and is building himself a nice house, looking out over the river. The Lutze boys have got themselves jobs, odd-job men for the Harbour Master. Did you notice that the wharves that were under construction when we first arrived

149

are all finished now? And they're rebuilding that bridge across the river. Apparently it was unsafe.'

She sighed. 'Come in and have a cup of tea. I'm really upset about the Lutze boys. They sneaked in and got those jobs without a word to Theo. We see them every Sunday and not a peep out of them that any jobs were going. Not till they were well and truly settled in. Serve them right that they have to walk all the way into town every day.'

Jakob followed her through to the kitchen and sat disconsolately by the back door, only half listening to her. Who else could he seek advice from, if not the bank manager?

When she handed him a cup of sweet black tea, a drink he'd become quite fond of since he'd first encountered it on the ship, Eva was talking about Walther.

'He's still out there with Father Beitz. Him and a tribe of blackfellows. Father Beitz is talking about having a big christening day, baptising them all, but Walther doesn't think it's a good idea. He says they don't understand religion at all. Oh, and Walther, he's got a lady friend. Young Nora Stenning. I don't suppose you know her. She's the daughter of that Customs fellow, and if you ask me, she's the one doing the courting.

'They say she had her eye on Walther from the first. Chases him up all the time. Goes riding out there as if by chance, makes a great fuss of Father Beitz too, so he won't send her away . . .'

'The Customs Officer,' Jakob said. 'What was his name again?'

'Jules Stenning.'

'Ah yes. He wasn't a very pleasant man, as I recall.'

'True enough. If you want to stay here and rest you can, but I have to bring in the children, they're playing near the barracks.'

'No, no.' Jakob drained his cup. 'I have to be going. Thank you for the tea, it was very refreshing.'

He found the Customs Office near to where he'd hitched his horse. It was more like a shopfront, with a veranda that sheltered several long benches, presumably a stopgap waiting room. An ornate blackboard set by the door announced that this was the home of various government authorities, including Customs and Excise, Immigration, Lands and Survey, Agriculture, Education and several others, but Jakob thought the Lands Department would be his mark.

The place seemed deserted, so he walked in, past the open front door and along a passage with rooms on either side. He peered in the first one, then another, seeing only tables and benches overflowing with papers, and that irritated him. Jakob was a neat man, he liked everything to be in its place. He'd thought, a little guiltily as he'd drunk his tea back there, that surely Eva and Theo could have cleaned up their overgrown yard, even if they were only renting.

Suddenly Stenning himself poked his head out of a doorway.

'What do you want? I'm closed Wednesday afternoons.'

'I'm very sorry, sir, I apologise. I did not know this. But I only have a small question to put to you. It is advice I am needing.'

'You German?' Obviously Mr Stenning didn't remember him.

'Yes, sir.'

'You one of that mob living out on Taylor's Road?'

'No, sir. I have a farm. This is what I wish to talk about.'

'Ah . . . all right. Come in here.' He ushered Jakob into one of the offices and, shoving papers aside, half sat on a desk, pointing Jakob to a chair.

'My clerk is useless,' he said. 'Worse than useless. I'd fire him for leaving this mess if I had someone else to do the job. Too much responsibility, that's my problem. The government leaves everything to me as if I've got ten hands. Bloody impossible to keep up with everything. Now, what's your gripe?'

'It is regarding the timber on my land, sir. I have the lease but the previous owner claims he owns the timber.'

'He what?' Stenning boomed. 'Never heard such rot. Take no notice.'

'I would like to, but I received this correspondence, which set me to worrying.'

He handed the three pages to Stenning, who perused them

151

intently before handing them back. 'This is a different story. If those lawyers say that the timber belongs to Clonmel Station, then it must be so. I'm not a legal person. I'm here to see that rules and regulations are adhered to, but on reading that I'd have to tell you to step aside and let Dixon have his timber.'

Jakob jumped up. He was furious. He'd seen the change in Stenning's attitude the minute he'd spotted Dixon's name.

'But you said the idea was rot!'

'I thought it was, but obviously I was mistaken.'

'I don't think you were, Mr Stenning. I think you know it is not legal for them to be claiming my timber, but you changed your mind when you saw Dixon's letter.'

Stenning bristled angrily. 'What are you accusing me of?'

'This is the office of the Lands Department, and you, I note, are its representative. I believe you should know right from wrong in this matter. But you are misinforming me.'

'How dare you! Get out of here! I listened to your query and gave my opinion, though I need not have, the office being closed. And you repay me by this impertinence.'

Jakob clutched his hat, stubbornly ignoring that outburst. 'I think maybe you need more time to consider this matter. Maybe you could look in the book of rules and regulations about leasehold lands and find that you were right in your first reply to my question!'

'I'll do no such thing.'

'You could try in the name of duty. I will come back tomorrow. Tonight I will stay with Father Beitz on Taylor's Road,' he said defiantly, and immediately wished he hadn't.

'Good,' Stenning snapped. 'You get on out there, and tell that great oaf Walther Badke that if he doesn't keep away from my daughter, I'll horsewhip him. And don't bother coming back tomorrow; the answer will be the same.'

Father Beitz was delighted to see him. 'Ah, Jakob, my good fellow! How wonderful to see you again at last! By the looks of things the Lord has been kind to you. And how are Karl and Freda? Come. Sit. We have so much to talk about.'

Jakob was surprised to see how much they had managed to clear of this land. A good half-mile of road frontage lay open now, and it looked very inviting, almost park-like, with the great old trees still in place alongside a variety of colourful native bushes, some of which he could even identify from his own experience, although it was Freda who was the expert. As he walked into the old priest's domain he couldn't help admiring the lovely gardens they'd uncovered. Brilliant hibiscus, red and gold grevilleas and banksias, clumps of cabbage-tree palms, even orchids, all springing to life now as if from the pages of Freda's book of Australian flora.

And of course, with easier access to this magical forest, with its treasures of nectar and seeds and the other myriad delights, birds of all shapes and sizes were busy investigating now that the shrouds of the ages had been removed. He watched entranced as hundreds of pink and grey parrots roamed the grass, nibbling at seeds.

Father Beitz came rushing after him. 'Where did you get to? I thought you were following me. If you keep going in that direction, Jakob, you could get lost. The jungle in there, our jungle, is merciless, believe me. Swallow you in a gulp. Come back this way. We built in here for privacy and to be closer to the stream. Here we are. What do you think?'

They had a little village of thatched huts. About six of them, all quite large, all made of brush and stripped branches instead of timber. There were no doors, and in some cases only three walls. In the centre was a long table protected by a thatched canopy that hung from ropes strung from tree to tree.

Jakob gaped. They were living like natives. He was embarrassed to think that the poor remnants of their community had come to this. He would pay the tithe right away and urge everyone else to do the same.

'Did the natives build this for you?' he asked timidly, and Father Beitz burst into merry laughter.

'Goodness, no. Oh Lord, no. They think our homes are very grand. Too grand. They're not impressed at all. To them shelter is just a roof, not all this luxury. Come and see, my house is quite beautiful.'

Jakob took a deep breath. He shook his head as if shaking up his brains, As trying to grasp what was going on here. Father Beitz looked and was acting ten years younger. He still wore the cross round his neck, but the black soutane was gone. Worn out, Jakob supposed, thinking ruefully of his own dwindling supply of clothes. Now Father Beitz was wearing a rough canvas shirt and canvas trousers, held up by thin rope. But he seemed happy. Gone was the studied, pompous intonation of voice, the expected tones of the sermoniser. Instead, Jakob heard the localised English with its wry connotations, as if there were a hidden joke here somewhere. Whatever it was, Father Beitz had discovered it – he wore a smile a mile wide.

And the priest looked healthy too, the long grey hair and beard by no means lessening the liveliness of his shining brown eyes. Father Beitz, in his late seventies, had at last achieved his lifelong ambition . . . to be a missionary, to have his own mission far away in the lands of the savages, to bring them to God. Hadn't he told them that often enough?

The priest's hut was indeed comfortable, containing the essentials of home-made bunk and benches, room for his trunks in a far corner, and woven mats on the floor. His small carved hassock with its faded red velvet upholstery, brought all the way from the old world, didn't even look out of place in this tropical retreat.

But the tour was not complete. They had to go further, towards the great wall of jungle that marked the boundary of their exertions so far, to find Walther, who was clearing scrub with several Aborigines, men and women, trailing about picking up after him. They were clothed, he was relieved to see, but in oddments of shirts, ill-fitting trousers and, for the women, cotton shifts.

Walther, that great bear of a man, was thrilled to see Jakob. He hugged him to his chest and then called to the natives to come up and shake hands with his old friend. Which they did, eyes dancing with delight.

He was taken down to the creek, which had now been freed from the clutter of bush and weeds to emerge as pretty a stream as Jakob had seen anywhere, with nearby a grassy space big enough, he was informed, for their church. Which was to be the Church of St John, named after the seminary back home.

Since he had business in the town, Jakob accepted the invitation to stay overnight.

'Though exactly what business I can do,' he told them, 'I don't know.'

He went on to explain his problems with the squatter, Dixon. Father Beitz was distressed. 'I wish I could help,' he said. 'I am falling down on my pastoral duties. I thought I should be able to walk about my parish but the distances here are too great.'

'But we're buying a horse,' Walther put in. 'With both of the Lutze boys working, we'll have enough soon. Then Father can go out and visit everyone as he pleases.'

'Since they do not have enough faith to come to me,' Beitz added crossly.

'For the same reason, Father,' Jakob said gently, though he knew his family, owning a dray, had little excuse. Even so, a round trip on a Sunday would have been difficult when they were working so hard to get settled. 'I wonder, though, how you will find your way, Father – there are no signposts.'

'I have it all worked out. Mr Tibbaling will provide us with guides.'

'Oh. Excellent.'

'And my first visit will be to Clonmel Station – to see Hanni and Lucas, of course, but I will also call on this sheep man, Mr Dixon. I'll tell him he has to behave himself.'

'Thank you, Father, but you would only put the Fechners' jobs at risk.'

Walther returned to Jakob's problem. 'If Stenning won't help you . . .'

'That reminds me. Are you courting his daughter?'

'Miss Stenning is a friend,' Walther said shyly. 'I am not sure about courting.'

'She's fond of him,' the priest said enthusiastically.

'Then you'd better watch out, Walther. When I saw Stenning today he was angry about the connection between you and his daughter. In fact he threatened to horsewhip you if you don't keep away from the girl.'

Walther grinned. 'He's going to horsewhip me? A little feller like that? I don't think so. But, Jakob, you won't get any help in this town. The people here rely on the big station owners, and all their workers, to survive. It will be a long time before there are enough new settlers to support the shops without them. I notice the really busy days are when big groups of those stockmen come to town. Stockmen and shearers and all of those fellows, they like to spend their money.'

Depressed, Jakob listened to their talk of the town, its progress, its setbacks, even their shocked discovery that there were three brothels in a back street. Beitz had lodged a complaint at the police station and with the newly formed Progress Committee, but to no avail. He and Walther were truly well-informed about the little settlement, and it pleased Jakob that they were able to take such interest in the place.

'I think you'll have to go to Maryborough,' Walther said suddenly.

'Maryborough? Why?'

'To get yourself a lawyer. Otherwise you might as well go on home and let them take your timber.'

'But it's sixty, maybe seventy miles away.'

Walther shrugged. 'So? They have lawyers. More than one. I see them advertised in the newspaper.'

'I'd never find my way.'

'Let me talk to Mr Tibbaling. He might find you a guide,' Father Beitz said. 'We'll send one of the boys to fetch him.'

By the time the Lutze brothers came home from work, Walther had prepared dinner for all, with Tibbaling an honoured guest.

Jakob took Max Lutze aside. 'Can you help Theo find work down at the wharves? He's not happy working as a bullocky's offsider.'

'It's hard to help Theo, Mr Meissner. He's lazy, everyone knows he disappears from jobs if he's got any money and makes for the pub. They're behind in the rent at the cottage. Mr Cross, the manager of the sawmill, says they'll have to pay up before his wife gets here, or out they go.'

'But that's terrible. Where would they go?'

'They'd have to come back here. It's not so bad. We'd build another hut for them.'

Jakob tried to see Eva's point of view. 'I don't think Mrs Zimmerman could cope with this concept. You see, to her a house is a house, Max. And that's the end of it. Freda's a bit that way too.'

'Then I don't know what's to become of them.'

Before retiring to a bunk in the hut occupied by Walther and the Lutze boys, Jakob paid the tithe as requested by Father Beitz . . . paid it before selfishness got the better of him and he hung on to it. But he slept well.

In the morning he was awakened as usual by the cacophony of bird songs and screeches, and so familiar had their dawn choruses become that he thought for a few minutes he was back on the farm. Until Max called him to join them for morning prayers.

Tibbaling made an appearance again. His dark hair, patched with grey, hung down to his shoulders in matted frizzy curls. They looked fierce, framing the ancient leathery face, but the dark eyes were not; they were calm and composed.

'You still want someone to take you to the big town?'

'That's true. If it's possible. I have to find my way there somehow.'

Tibbaling nodded, and his eyes brushed Jakob before he looked away. 'Why you come to my country?'

Jakob sighed. 'We had to leave. Too many people. Not enough land. Not enough to eat.' He supposed that simple explanation was as good as any. Then he added, 'I wanted to give my son a better chance. More room to breathe out here.'

'Ah.'

The silence made Jakob nervous. He felt alarmed. Maybe he had said the wrong thing about there being more room out here. Out here in Tibbaling's country. Where his race was being pushed aside.

But this time Tibbaling overlooked the mistake. Instead he murmured: 'What about your other son, boss? Doan he get no land?'

Jakob almost choked. He felt as if all the air had been punched out of him. His face flushed so hotly it must have

157

been bright red. He was glad there was no one else about to notice his shock.

'How . . .' was all he could gasp as Tibbaling began to walk away.

'I find someone go walkabout with you, boss,' said the old man. Then he turned back. When he spoke again, his voice was sad, appealing. 'Plenty of room here for one more boy, boss.'

Jakob staggered to the quiet of the forest, to its shelter, needing to hide from the world awhile, to quell the panic that had suddenly seized him as he thought of Traudi, poor Traudi . . . and that day so long ago.

Jakob Meissner had been seventeen, in mortal fear of the wrath of Traudi's father, but Traudi had vowed not to tell who had fathered the child she was carrying.

'I'm in a lot of trouble when he finds out, no matter what happens,' she told Jakob. 'And he wouldn't let me marry you, because he has an arrangement with his friend, Wilf Berger.'

'But he's too old for you.'

'He's got money. That's all they care about. But Jakob, you couldn't support us anyway, you haven't got any money. And it's not as if we're real lovers. You're not madly in love with me, are you?'

'No,' he admitted. 'I like you.'

'And I'm not in love with anyone. I just have to do the best I can. If Wilf will have me now, I'd best marry him.'

So she never told a soul that Jakob was the father of her son, and weathered the storm that went on for months, until Wilf agreed to marry her and the village moved on to newer scandals.

Jakob lost touch with Traudi altogether. She and Wilf moved away and that was the end of the matter. More than twenty years ago.

Until just before Jakob and his family confirmed their plans to migrate and that became news in the district. Until Traudi came to see him, waiting patiently at the end of the lane for him to come by, rather than call at the farmhouse and draw attention to herself.

She looked tired and worn. Wilf had died years ago and she'd been left to bring up the child on her own, because her father wouldn't have her back in the house. And Wilf hadn't had much money after all . . .'

'That was a mean joke, wasn't it?' she smiled wanly. 'A joke on me. The brute was after a young wife, that was all.'

'Traudi, I'm sorry. What can I do? I'm married, we have a son ourselves and very little money, that's why we're emigrating.'

'No, no. I don't want money, Jakob. I only came here because I heard you were emigrating. Going to a country where there are big farms and everyone has plenty of money.'

'It's not going to be that easy, Traudi,' he said, troubled by her sudden presence.

'I suppose not, but I've come to ask a favour, not for me but for Eduard . . . please.'

'Who is Eduard?' he whispered, as if his full voice would give away that he already knew, guessed.

'You didn't know? You didn't even know his name? Your own son's name. Oh, Jakob, your first-born son, I thought you might have at least wondered about him.' She gave a deep sigh to pull herself together.

'Oh dear, forgive me, Jakob. I'm all nerves. I had to pluck up the courage to come here today. I was afraid you wouldn't see me, or wouldn't talk to me.'

'That's all right,' he said gently. 'What is it you want, Traudi?'

'I want you to take Eduard with you. He's twenty-one now. He was married but his wife died. He's a fine man, you'd be proud of him . . . you really would be. And he's a hard worker, you'll see. He'd work hard for you—'

He held up his hand to stop her. 'Please, please, Traudi. Stop. This isn't possible. My wife doesn't know about him. I never told—'

'Why should you? That doesn't matter. You could tell her now. She'll understand.'

Traudi was shivering, clutching a thin overcoat about her. She shoved a hand in her pocket and pulled out a folded sheet of paper. 'This is his address. He lives in Hamburg, I haven't

159

told him who his father is, but you can look him up when you go there. Ask him to come along with you. His father. I beg you, Jakob. It isn't too much to ask, surely?'

'I'm sorry, Traudi. I don't know how I can do this. I have no money. To tell you the truth, we wouldn't be going at all if my wife hadn't received a little inheritance. So you see, it's her money.'

'And he's your son!' she said fiercely. 'Your son. He's cost you nothing for twenty years; a little help now . . .'

Her voice faded, replaced by the hiss and rattle of a clump of bamboo behind him, by the sounds of morning activity in Father Beitz's commune.

How could he have sprung that on Freda after all these years? How might she have reacted? And his own son, Karl. What would he think? Would he see in his father a deceitful man? A cruel thought. Self-criticism lurked. He had been so secure within the arms of his little family that he now feared losing their respect. He'd tried to teach Karl responsibility, by good example. What price that example from a man who had refused to take responsibility for his own child? Who had never enquired as to his well-being? It was too much. All too much.

He had kept the slip of paper, an innocuous name and address, but he had never made use of it. He had not . . .

Father Beitz was calling him, and Jakob welcomed the interruption. He hurried back to the huts.

'Walther has gone to town on an errand,' the priest said. 'So would you help me here? I want to mark off a proper path in from the road so that we can line it with wood. They say this soil can turn into a mudheap when it rains.'

'When it rains,' Jakob said despondently.

'Quite so, but we don't want to be caught unawares. We're very fortunate, thanks be to God, that we arrived at the right time of year, or we'd all be in trouble. They say the rainfall is prodigious.'

'I was wondering, will Tibbaling find me a guide?'

'Of course. He has gone to get him. Pick up that hammer and those stakes, there's a good fellow, I want to get this done this morning. Walther believes we have done enough clearing of our land for the time being. What do you think?'

Jakob sighed. He was confused, thanks to the strange encounter with the old blackfellow, who had known about his other son. How had he done that? Stenning had said he was a magic man, but he had meant more of a trickster. Was Tibbaling really a mystic of some sort?

The priest was measuring stretches of the path with a length of rope, and Jakob followed obediently, tapping in stakes as instructed.

Then again, it need not have been a magic trick at all. Tibbaling might have taken it for granted that Jakob had more than one son. That was feasible. In fact, a more sensible explanation.

But the confusion remained, and Jakob was feeling so low that he had decided he would go back home, forget this wild scheme of speaking to a lawyer. How would he do that anyway? He'd never even met a lawyer. What would he say? And was his English good enough for the occasion?

'You're starting to get above your station, Jakob Meissner,' he muttered to himself. 'Just because you've got a huge farm. That isn't paid for, don't forget.'

'What did you say?' Beitz asked, straightening up.

'Nothing. Wouldn't it be faster to just run a string along here?'

'We haven't any string.' The priest's face lit up. 'Walther's back, and he's got a surprise for you.'

'What surprise?'

'Look. We bought a horse. It will be so much easier for us now, but first we are lending it to you.'

'I have a horse,' Jakob said, mystified.

'But your guide hasn't,' Walther grinned. 'Blackfellows don't have horses, and you can't expect the poor fellow to run alongside.'

Later that day a young black fellow reported in to Father Beitz. He had often worked as a stockman and would be glad to take the boss down to Maryborough.

Jakob felt trapped. 'I don't know about this,' he murmured, taking the priest aside. 'Who am I to be talking to lawyers?'

161

'A man with a question, is all. Walther is preparing some rations for you to take with you.'

'But I don't know how much lawyers cost. And how much will I have to pay the guide, the young man over there?'

'Lawyers I don't know about. The young man's English name is Billy, and he would be glad of a few pennies, I'm told, but not as payment. Goodwill it seems. He'd be happy to take you for nothing. That is their way.'

The lad came over. 'I take you first to Childers, little town, then on to Maryborough, big town on big river. This right, eh?'

'Yes, Billy, that's right. Very kind of you.'

It was very kind of all of them. Jakob and Billy were packed up and sent on their odyssey without further ado, the priest waving them off and promising to send a messenger boy out to the farm to tell Mrs Meissner her husband's whereabouts.

They went back up the road and made a few turns before striking out on to a worn track heading south. Billy, it seemed, had noticed Jakob's bewilderment. He looked to him and grinned.

'We be alri', boss. We get goin' now!'

With that he pumped bare heels into his horse's flanks and they raced away, the track ahead being long and flat. Dandy jerked into action too, taking Jakob by surprise, forcing him to hang on tight as both horses galloped towards a nonexistent winning post.

Jakob had heard about hard-riding stockmen, and now that he'd seen one, and finally managed to rein in his horse, he knew he'd have to have a chat with Billy about the pace of travel, or the boss would end up with a broken neck.

But for now, he might as well make the best of it. New countryside to see, new lands all about him. And there . . . a mob of emus flitting through the trees. Gradually, a contentment came over him, and he began to enjoy this ride.

Chapter Seven

To Hanni, this Clonmel sheep station was more of a village than a farm. The main house, or homestead as it was called, was built entirely of timber and seemed to have evolved and grown as the need arose, with rooms added on each side, turning it into a long, low house facing into the morning sun. All of the rooms opened on to verandas, so to reach them, and the rooms built behind them again, was a matter of stepping from one veranda to another or across breezy spaces where mean dogs lurked.

The furniture in the house was all rough-hewn, made from the best of timbers, she was told, but hardly what you would expect of wealthy people like the Dixons. Certainly no style about it at all, not like the beautifully appointed mansion owned by the Reinhardts they'd worked for back home. On the other hand, like the Reinhardts, these people bought well. They used the finest china, their linen press was a joy; the curtains, often roughly used in doorways, were mainly lawn and lace. Oh no, they didn't stint themselves. Hanni liked that. She particularly liked the glint and polish of the music room and the large library, which were airy and lovely, not like the musty, gloomy old rooms inhabited by the miserable Reinhardt family. In all, this was a pleasant house and the people were pleasant too.

'As long as you do your work,' Elsie the housekeeper had said when Hanni was given the job of housemaid, 'no one will bother you.' And she was right. The job itself was so easy, Hanni finished her tasks in half the time allotted. It was simple work, no more hours spent polishing floors, cleaning brass and silver and all the rest of the finicky maintenance needed in worn-out old houses. She only had to make the beds, sweep and dust . . . not that dusting did much good.

'There's always a lot of dust blowing about in the dry season,' Mrs Dixon told her. 'Sometimes it's a lot worse than this. So don't worry too much, Hanni. Just do the best you can.'

That was how they all were in this house. Do the best you can. Hanni used to giggle to herself about that. She'd been trained as a servant from the age of twelve, and she knew her second, no, *third* best would be enough here, but since they were so nice to her, she'd given of her very best. She cleaned under beds, finding heaps of dusty kapok left by the last maid; she prettied the rooms with her own extra touches of flowers or a sprig of green; she climbed up and took all the books down, dusted them and replaced them; and she always kept herself neat and clean too, checking in every mirror as she passed.

Mrs Dixon and the housekeeper were delighted with her, calling her 'a find', even paying her a little more than originally offered in the hope that she would stay. Hanni had learned by then that station people found it very hard to get servants willing to work on their lonely properties. As it was, the laundresses and the scullery maid were black girls, and the cook served the meals herself. As far as Hanni could see, the housekeeper didn't have much to do apart from ordering supplies and checking the house. She was in fact more of a companion to Mrs Dixon. The two women, both at least sixty, went riding together every so often, and Hanni was impressed that Mrs Dixon could be so casual with a servant. But that sort of thing didn't seem to worry this family at all. Hanni decided they were quite eccentric.

The father, whom they all called J.B., was a big man with a booming voice, but he wasn't about the house much during the day, and neither was the son, Mr Keith. Too much going on out there where the real business of this place was on show. Out there where Lucas worked.

The front of the house looked down on a large lagoon that was home to hundreds of waterbirds, and at the back was an orchard. On the western side a tall, fragrant hedge led to the

164

stables and on from there to the blacksmith. And that was only the beginning of the workplace. There was a dairy, a large storehouse, a saddlery and huge shearing sheds. She and Lucas had a room at the end of a guest wing, but all the other men lived further away, in long huts, and took their meals in a canteen shed attached to a big kitchen known as the cookhouse.

Lucas had taken her for walks around all these sheds, but Hanni didn't share his enthusiasm for his workplace. Not even the wool sheds, which he said were astonishing in their size. But why wouldn't they be? Hanni thought. These people had thousands of sheep, thousands; the pens past the wool sheds looked like an endless maze of fences.

It pleased her, though, that their walks drew whistles and cheers from the workmen; they all thought she was very pretty and weren't at all slow in letting her know. They often said, in front of her, that Lucas was a very lucky man, and Hanni loved the attention, but lately Lucas was getting sick of all the fuss.

'You encourage them, Hanni. You shouldn't do that. It is hard for them that there are no single women out here.'

'There are so. The Dixons often have lady visitors.'

'But they don't mix with the men. They keep to their side of the hedge.'

'I can't do that. We live down here. And I can't help it if they admire me.'

'Just don't flaunt yourself, Hanni. You've been doing that a lot lately.'

'I have not! And you're just jealous. You'd think you'd be proud of me . . .'

'Hanni, dear, I am. God knows I love you more than anyone or anything in the whole world. Haven't I shown you that? Haven't I?'

He made her turn to him, this day when they were in their room going over the same old argument. 'Look at me! Haven't I? You wanted us to be together. You said I had a choice. It was either Hilda or you. I chose you, Hanni, because I couldn't bear to lose you, and so we left, and I gave up everything for you.'

'So what?' she said, irritated. 'What's done is done. I know you love me, and I love you. But stop accusing me of making eyes at all those ugly men. I mean, there isn't a nice-looking one among them, and all they ever talk about is horses.'

'So . . . you've been looking them over?' he snapped.

'Oh, stop! You're getting on my nerves. And why were you so late coming in tonight?'

'We were mustering sheep a long way out. And by the way, we'll be going further tomorrow, the foreman said, probably a two-day muster.'

'Not again! What am I supposed to do? Just sit in this room staring at the walls when I finish work?'

They lived strange lives, she thought. He had become a stockman, riding after sheep all day, while she pottered about with this easy job, so they were both quite satisfied with the work, but they ate separately. She took all her meals in the kitchen and he ate with the men in the canteen. Hanni had afternoons off but no full days, while Lucas had Sundays off. Hanni often took a nap in the afternoons, so she was as bright as a button when Lucas came in, but he was physically exhausted most nights, still trying to adapt to strenuous days on horseback and the demands of bush work. He always managed to find the energy to make love to her, but Hanni fretted that he was no longer good company. He slept like a log and was up and out at dawn, while she didn't have to report to the house until seven. These days it was dawn at six, but the cook told her that in the summer the sun was up by four thirty.

'That hour? My husband will walk out my door sleeping.'

The cook had laughed, but Hanni wasn't amused.

On Sundays now, they took to walking by the lagoon and through the orchard, which Hanni found boring, but Lucas liked to sit under the trees and look back at the house.

'Look at that. We'll have our own station one of these days, and a really nice house. I found out the Dixons don't own all this land, they lease it.'

'What's the difference? It's still theirs.'

'Well there is a difference, darling, but the main thing is it tells me how to get started in this country. First you learn about sheep stations and how they operate, the way I'm doing, then if you want, you can go off and lease your own land. That's what we're saving for, Hanni. Our savings will soon build up.'

'Of course they will. We haven't got anything to spend our money on. No wonder they can't keep servants out here.'

Lucas worried. 'Hanni, what do you want? Just tell me. I thought you had everything you need.'

'Why would I want anything?' she sulked, unable to specify exactly what she would buy were there a decent shop within walking distance. 'I don't get to go anywhere.'

And so their days went by, Hanni becoming more and more bored with her lot and Lucas loving every minute of this wildly different lifestyle. Working on the Reinhardt estate he had progressed to chief groom, but that would have been the summit, as far as he could have advanced unless he tried for some other occupation, which would not have been approved anyway. Here, beginning as a lowly fencer, he'd soon been promoted.

Lucas smiled to himself. He'd been promoted to a mere stockman sure enough, but he had gained respect for his efforts among these hard men, and that made him feel good. Made him flex his muscles and want to achieve more. Lucas, for the first time in his life, had met up with ambition. He would work, watch and learn and he would have his own station one day. Maybe begin with a partner if it meant achieving his dream faster. But Hanni's attitude worried him. He understood the problem. She had time on her hands and she didn't know how to entertain herself, so loneliness crept in. She'd talked about the big library in the house and so he'd suggested she ask permission to borrow books, but he'd forgotten Hanni had trouble reading English. He wished he could think how to help her, but that didn't mean allowing her to take pleasure in the attentions, however innocent, of the other men. That was something else she didn't understand. That men like these should not be teased.

Or did she? She had teased him for months, coming by, flirting, calling out to him until he'd thrown caution to the winds and walked over to give her a little teasing back. And

167

look where that had led him. He had regrets, of course he did, but he'd do it all over again. He didn't just love Hanni. He adored her, she was the prettiest girl he'd ever known, and soft and sweet with it. One day she would have her own home, and friends to call, and babies to care for. Maybe that was the answer. If God were to give her a baby, that would keep her busy.

For all Lucas's warnings about the rough working men, it wasn't one of them who bothered her; it was a guest, Mr Mayhew. And he was drunk. He was the only other occupant of the guest wing; and had been at Clonmel for just a few days when he ran into Hanni on the path down from the house.

The black girls were sent off to their camp before dark, and for a good reason, Cook had told Hanni.

'Too many randy white blokes on the station, and not just the station hands,' she said, pursing her plump lips. 'Too many young blokes coming here visiting think them black girls are fair game, but Mrs Dixon, she won't have none of that. Chucks them off the station quick fast if she hears they're chasing the gins. She don't care who they are.'

That meant Hanni took over from the scullery maid of an evening, but she didn't mind. She had her dinner in the kitchen, amused that Cook would stoop to serving the family when she could have done that for her. But Cook really liked to take in the food, chatting to the Dixons about their likes and dislikes, promising specials and lapping up compliments. Hanni stayed on to help with the washing-up, tidying the dining room and setting the table for breakfast. Then she went down to her own room.

· Most nights, the family – Mr and Mrs Dixon, Mr Keith and the housekeeper – sat down to dinner at six o'clock, but they didn't linger in the dining room, preferring to move on to the parlour where they took coffee or tea. If they had guests, though, they would offer wines from the cellar during dinner, and port afterwards, and more again if they were in a party mood.

Hanni found their lifestyle fascinating. Mr Dixon and Mr Keith talked to her – in passing, she had to admit – as if she were an old friend or a cousin or something. Really weird. True, they never really listened to her answer when they asked her how she was going, but Hanni found the question strange. As if she'd dare say anything but '*Gut*. Good, sir. Thank you, sir.'

For heaven's sake!

Hanni would have loved to be able to write back to the girls who'd worked with her all those years under the iron rule of Frau Neuendorf, the Reinhardt housekeeper. Under the whip that woman had used on them, and the savage clouts when any of them were within reach of her temper. Silver had to be cleaned with fingers, raw until they bled. Meals had to be brought up the winding back steps, steep stone steps, quickly so that they wouldn't arrive cold, three floors up. A maid-servant's life had been tough back there; you worked so hard for gentry, with never a chance to lift your head, let alone have the Reinhardts ask 'How are you going?' Some day, Hanni promised herself, she had to get around to writing to them.

This night, the Dixons had only the one guest. Mr Mayhew was staying in the first room of the guest wing, down the other end from the Fechners' much smaller and plainer room. Hanni had seen him occasionally, going out with Mr Keith, riding, chasing sheep, whatever they did all day. He was a porky, ginger-haired fellow, not very tall, but he had a loud laugh. That was all.

As she walked back to their room, she was thinking about the letter. Perhaps Lucas would write it for her. She so much wanted to tell Frau Neuendorf all about the life of a house-keeper here. That would be the most marvellous revenge. Have her find out what a rotten life she had and how the other half lived out here. The housekeeper being treated as one of the family. And more.

Elsie had her own bedroom and sitting room; Neuendorf had had only an attic at the top of the back stairs, and she was never allowed to address the family, only through the master's steward. This letter, she giggled to herself, would have no end. How would that bitch like to know that a housekeeper sat at table, laughing her head off, with the wealthy squire and his family? And that servants like Hanni had a choice of meals. She could eat what she wished.

There was only one stipulation. The housekeeper had requested that Hanni take the back path around the guest wing, which would deliver her right to her door, rather than trotting along the veranda in front of the guest rooms . . . those never-ending verandas, they seemed to be law here. Every room had its own. Cook had said people slept out on them in the summer – and that was another thing Hanni wanted to put in her revenge letter: it is never cold here. It doesn't snow. They don't know anything about snow or ice. And Hanni could wear the lovely cotton embroidered blouses her *mutti* had made for her everyday wear. The ones with the puffed short sleeves. They were so pretty, and they suited her so well.

At the thought of her *mutti*, Hanni caught her breath and held it until the pain subsided.

'No good will come of this,' her mother had warned. 'Go back to work before it's too late, Hanni. Tell them you had to stay with me, that I had another bad turn. Please, Hanni . . . don't be foolish.'

Much as she loved her mother, she would not turn back. She could not.

'Good *will* come of it,' she had said. 'I'm getting away from here, no matter what else happens.'

Everyone said she looked like her mother, that Mutti had been the prettiest girl in the village. As Hanni threw her few belongings into the satchel Lucas had found for her, she'd shuddered. She'd rather die than end up looking as thin and haggard as Mutti was now. Once the female servants married, they were no longer employed at the big house, they simply went to their husbands to start turning out babies. Mutti had had nine babies, Hanni the eldest. Two had died, and on several occasions Mutti, too, had been at death's door, suffering from malnutrition and exhaustion. Each time she'd rallied, but the illnesses took their toll, and it was hard for Hanni to imagine this haggard woman, now in her forties, ever being the slightest bit good-looking. As a matter of fact, every time someone remarked that she was the spitting image of her mother, Hanni was horrified. And that made her even more determined to get away as soon as possible.

Hanni was proud of her looks, she knew she had little

trouble attracting men, but what men? Until she decided on Lucas, none of the local men had interested her at all. To begin with she was only flirting with Lucas; then, when he became serious, Hanni saw the break she needed. He had to choose between her and Hilda, and to do that, he'd said, they'd have to leave.

The very mention of leaving the village, of realising her dream, had sent Hanni into a delirium of joy. She loved Lucas. She adored him. She almost smothered him with her loving every time they met, down by the mill. From then on they were so much in love, there was no thought of turning back.

The cook had given her some ladies' magazines to look at, and Hanni collected them when she had finished in the kitchen, then turned out the lamp and set off down the back steps to the path that led to her room. The night was fine, a little crisp, with the usual sparkle of stars overhead, and Hanni wasn't hurrying. Lucas was away, so she only had the empty room to look forward to, but at least these magazines would fill in a little time. She loved looking at the pictures, especially the advertisements, to see what the rich ladies wore. Cook had said that Mrs Dixon often ordered gloves or other such items from those advertisements, and had them sent out to her, and Hanni was hugely impressed.

'What an exciting thing to do,' she said to herself, wondering if perhaps she could find something to have sent to her, but at that minute, she noticed Mr Mayhew, the house guest, stumbling along the path after her.

'Hang on, little lady,' he mumbled, arms falling on her shoulders. 'What's the hurry?'

Hanni ducked, to extricate herself, but he held fast, pulling her to him, trying to kiss her.

As she struggled with him, turning her face away to escape the wet kisses and get rid of the strong hand that was now clutching at her, Hanni was quiet. This wasn't the first time some lout had grabbed her, but that was back home, when she could lash out with a shout and a good hard kick. This man, though, was gentry, a guest in the house. She knew the hazards there too . . . . guests had a habit of blaming the servants in

171

these situations, and she'd known girls to be sacked because of the attentions of gentry lechers.

'Stop your wriggling, little girl,' he laughed. 'I won't hurt you. My, my, you're like a little soft mouse.'

He still hung on to her, and as Hanni lost her footing they staggered together into the bushes that lined the path. Still with her mouth clenched shut, to keep herself from shouting abuse at him, Hanni managed to pull back on to the path, only to crash into the arms of another man, with Mr Mayhew still hanging on to her.

'I say,' Mr Keith said, over her head. 'Break it up, old chap. What do you think you're doing?'

'Just having a little fun here,' Mayhew gasped, but he did release Hanni, who raced away from them, terrified now that she would be in trouble for upsetting the guest. That was the way it always went. The men were always right.

Keith picked up the magazines she'd dropped and dusted them off. 'You're drunk, Charlie. Come on, I'll get you back to your room. No, not that way, that's staff quarters down there. This way.'

'I'm not drunk,' Charlie said as his friend escorted him to his door. 'Just a little under the weather. Come on in and have a nightcap. Happen to have some good rum here. Home brew, you know, from my distillery. Damned good stuff, if I say so meself.'

Keith followed him in. 'We can't have you pawing the help, Charlie. It's not on, you know. Mother would have a fit.'

'My dear fellow, I wasn't pawing the little darling. As a matter of fact, I'll have you know I simply wanted to talk to her, but she was skittering about like a mouse, wouldn't stand still.'

'What did you want to talk to her about?'

Charlie burped and grinned. 'You have to ask? Have you looked at her? I'm in love, Keith my lad, madly in love with her.'

'I see. You met her on the path and love's arrow suddenly struck?'

'Not at all.' Charlie poured a tot of rum into the glasses on his dressing table and added a little water. 'I spotted her as soon as I arrived. Sorry if I frightened the mouse. Didn't mean to be so boorish. Bad show, I suppose.'

'Extremely bad show, Charlie. This rum isn't bad. As a matter of fact, it's jolly good. Did you say you made it yourself?'

Charlie, offended, drew himself up to his portly height. 'Don't make it sound as if I mixed it in a bloody bucket. I have a proper distillery now, with a chemist and all. But getting back to the lady, I can't believe you haven't noticed. The Fräulein is flawless . . .'

'Frau, Charlie. She's married.'

'That's a blow, but never mind. The lady is still flawless. I mean, she's the perfect woman. I've been studying her every chance I get . . . Think about it for a minute. The hair truly fair, the face lovely, the skin peaches and cream, the lips . . .'

Keith began to laugh. 'How have you found the time to observe the poor girl?'

'I've made the time. Sitting about the verandas admiring the view, so to speak. But have you no soul? Can you seriously refer to a blonde, blue-eyed beauty like that as a poor girl? My God, Keith . . . haven't you seen that busty bust? I tell you, I'm in love.'

'This week,' Keith laughed. 'And at the rate she took off, I don't think she feels the same way. But tell me more about this rum.'

'I've been telling your old man. Our plantation is going fine, we're growing plenty of sugar with the Kanakas on the job, but my dad and I figure that Jupiter Plantation can offer a great deal more.'

'You're expanding the plantation?'

'We're doing that anyway. But we experimented with the small distillery and we know we can make good rum, so we want to build a big distillery, a real one. We need finance, though, and the trouble is, my dad can't get your dad to come to the party. He wants J.B. to back him but it's not happening.'

Keith handed his glass back to Charlie. 'Give us another drop of your brew. Not much, just a taste, neat.'

When he sipped it, Keith nodded in appreciation. 'Did J.B. taste it?'

'I gave him a bottle but he hasn't even opened it.'

'Is that the bottle of brown stuff on the sideboard, without a label?'

'That's it,' Charlie said gloomily.

'He won't touch that. He reckons it could be rat poison for all he knows. You'll have to do better than that. Surely some labels wouldn't cost much. If you're serious, your rum should have a name, and a good-sounding one at that. You can't just go hawking it about like some home-made cough mixture.'

'Probably right, old chap. Probably right. Do you suppose I ought to trot along and apologise to the Fräulein? I mean, it would be the right thing to do, wouldn't it?'

'No, it wouldn't. You've still got your rocking boots on. Go to bed, Charlie. I'll have a talk to J.B. about the distillery. I think you're on to a good thing there.'

Charlie sank back on to his bed and stretched out sleepily. 'I know I'm on to a good thing,' he said drowsily. 'That Fräulein is a treasure. She is a Venus with arms.'

He was snoring by the time Keith closed the door behind him. He had picked up Hanni's magazines again, since they had no place in Charlie's room, and meant to drop them on the sideboard in the dining room so that she would find them, but he still had them in his hand when he went into his own room.

As he threw them down, he grinned, thinking of Charlie's latest love . . . lust.

He was still thinking of her when he undressed and climbed into bed. Hanni. When you came to think about it, Charlie could be right. He began to tick off her attributes, wondering why he hadn't noticed them before. Probably because she always kept quiet, eyes never raised, never volunteering to say anything. A mouse, true enough. What had his mother said about her?

'A treasure. Beautifully trained. She wouldn't be out of place at Government House.'

Until Charlie's ravings, this young paragon had only been background, never drawing attention to herself in any way.

'Jesus!' he whispered, as Charlie's observations took shape in his dreams, and Hanni, the flawless beauty, appeared before him, unclothed, divine. He tossed back the covers to welcome

174

her to passion, to a better man than Charlie could ever hope to be, dreaming of her most of the night, exciting, satisfying dreams that had him wake flushed with pleasure, disappointed that they had ended.

But Charlie was embarrassed. 'I can't believe I bothered the *fräulein* like that,' he whispered to Keith. 'I've been trying to offer my apologies, but she dodges away from me. I have no wish to embarrass her further, but do you suppose I could sneak back into the dining room? She's in there, on her own.'

'What for?'

'Well, I thought I'd give her this.'

'What is it?' Keith opened a black velvet bag and found a hand mirror set with jewelled rows of coloured stones.

'It's only a trinket,' Charlie said. 'I bought it for my sister because it is so very pretty, but I can get her something else. I'd like Hanni to have it.'

'Why?'

'A peace offering, dear fellow.'

'But she's married, Charlie. Can't you get that through your head?'

'I know that, and it makes my behaviour even worse. She's entitled to an apology.'

'All right. Give it to me. I'll do the approaching for you.'

'Bloody good of you, Keith. I would hate to leave here knowing I've upset such a nice girl.'

He did take the elegant hand mirror to her, that afternoon when all was quiet, tapping gently on her door.

Her hair was down, allowed to fall loose from the thick coils that had previously kept it in place, and Keith was taken aback by the splendour that confronted him. It wasn't exactly curly; more wavy, he observed, with wisps about her face that shone like silk.

'You want me, sir?' she asked nervously: 'What is it?' Her accent was sibilant, sweet.

'I brought back your magazines,' he said, handing them to her. 'You dropped them on the path.'

She took them, he thought, with about as much enthusiasm as if they were rat poison, thanked him quickly and went to close the door, but his firm hand held it open.

'About last night, Hanni . . .'

'I'm sorry, sir. Very sorry. It won't happen again.'

Keith blinked. 'You don't have to be sorry. Charlie's the one who should apologise.'

'No, sir. Me, I'm sorry. No more, please.'

He noticed she had the longest eyelashes over those fantastic blue eyes, the ones she kept casting down, giving him a chance to have a better look at her, to check out all those perfect attributes at close quarters. The fantasies of the night still lingered with him in a vague sort of way, and he leaned closer to her, rewarding himself by breathing her scent, a scrubbed, wholesome fragrance so intimate he felt a little giddy.

Keith's smile was benign, charming. 'My dear young lady. Forgive me for barging in on you like this, but I was afraid you might be upset over that incident, and you are. Aren't you?'

She nodded.

'Then don't be. It was unforgivable of Charlie to accost you like that. Quite unacceptable. I feel responsible that a guest in our house should upset you, so I've come to apologise to you.'

She raised those big blue eyes to stare at him, not understanding this at all, so he patted her arm, to reassure her.

'So don't you be worrying any more, Hanni. In fact, to make up for the incident, I've brought you a small gift.'

'For me?' She seemed stunned.

'For you. Unwrap it.'

She removed the velvet bag and looked at the mirror in wonder. 'It's beautiful! And it's mine, sir?'

'Yes indeedy. But I wouldn't mention it up at the house. I wouldn't want my mother to find out that Charlie has been making a nuisance of himself.'

Hanni heartily agreed with that. She nodded furiously as she thanked him again.

'Then we'll say no more about it, Hanni?' he asked, and she smiled at him.

'Oh no, sir. And thank you. So kind.'

* * *

When he had left, Hanni sat on the bed and stared at the gift in amazement. All day she'd been waiting for the heavy hand to fall. For the housekeeper or even Mrs Dixon to pounce on her, accuse her of flirting or bothering their guest. She was sure that Mr Mayhew would have got in first with his version of the incident, as Mr Keith called it. She'd even expected the two men to come after her last night with God knows what reaction to her escape from them, and so she'd spent the night with a chair wedged up against the doorknob.

But then Mr Keith had come up with this gift. And it was gorgeous, the mirror absolutely encrusted with rubies and emeralds and sapphires, or so they seemed, so brilliant they looked real. It was the prettiest thing she'd ever owned in all her life, and she would treasure it.

Hanni studied her face in the jewelled mirror. She truly was amazed at the reaction to Mr Mayhew's grab at her, and pleased that no one else would hear about it. Relieved. And she smiled at Mr Keith's involvement. Very kind of him to have rescued her from Charlie's paws, though given a few more minutes that drunk would have caught more than a mouse, she grinned. She was of average height, and by no means muscular, but just the same she was very strong . . . much in demand in the tug-of-war teams back home.

Ah yes, she sighed. That Charlie would have been in for a surprise had the situation become serious. But Mr Keith. He was another story.

He could have left the magazines in the kitchen. Very kind of him to go to all the trouble, the mirror and all, but Hanni had seen through him right from the start. He'd been making advances to her, no doubt about that. No mistaking those hot eyes or the caressing hand on her arm.

She hugged herself. Delicious! How flattering that Mr Keith would flirt with her. More than flirt really. She wondered how much more. He was much better-looking than his drunken friend. And Hanni certainly would be very pleased to keep quiet about the gift. Very quiet. She didn't need Lucas to see it and start asking questions. Make a fuss about nothing. Maybe nothing.

It would be interesting to see what Mr Keith would do next.

At least he'd broken the bored spell she'd been suffering. Instead of sitting stuck in her room in the afternoons, she really ought to take herself for walks. No one would mind.

So Hanni took to rambling about the place of an afternoon. The black girls gave her a sunhat made of cabbage tree leaves, and a stout stick, advising her to carry it at all times to ward off snakes.

'I couldn't kill a snake,' she said. 'I'd be too frightened.'

'Then you just run,' they laughed, but at least she had a good walking stick now, and she set out exploring past the lagoon, past the orchard and even up over the rise that gave a fine view of the winding river.

And on the third day he turned up, even sooner than she had expected, riding by her as she was walking back towards the orchard. He dismounted and walked a little way with her, talking about nothing much in particular, asking her how she was enjoying station life.

Hanni enthused. She said she adored it. So beautiful. So huge. All the things he wanted to hear. Neither of them mentioned Lucas.

Mr Keith was wooing her the same way she had wooed Lucas. Always about. Smiling at her from a distance. Coming upon her in the fields as if by accident. Or over at the jetty in the river, where she liked to stand and watch for fish. He wanted her to make the first move, Hanni knew that, but she pretended innocence. Always appreciating that he was the master and she the servant who was shy in his presence. Who obviously looked up to him, though, as a fine, important man. Keeping her distance.

After a while the chance meetings became hard for her. She desperately wanted to lift her eyes and give him the full treatment, which Mutti had said was outrageously obvious. She had warned it would get her into trouble one day. It never had, but she couldn't do that any more. She was a married woman and she didn't want to scare Mr Keith off. The game was too much fun.

Quite probably it was the fact of her being married that was keeping him down, she mused. But it wouldn't last. Since he'd begun to pay her attention, Hanni had listened to kitchen talk about him. He was self-willed, they said. Liked his own way a bit too much. Was very much a gay dog with the ladies, but then the girls round here weren't backward in setting their caps at him.

That interested Hanni, who continued to do just the opposite. Sometimes she wondered where the game might end, or how, but not often. Strangely, thinking of Mr Keith gave more impetus to her lovemaking with Lucas, somehow made it more exciting, and there were no complaints from her husband.

When it did happen it was a surprise. He didn't grab her like Mr Mayhew had. He didn't start spouting undying love and all that stuff. He just came upon her at the jetty, reached out to help her step across the mud, and then quietly kissed her hand. That was all.

That afternoon he rode off with some of his men. He was away for a week. A whole week. Hanni had no idea where he had gone and didn't dare ask. She missed him and it angered her. After all, she did love Lucas; she'd only been teasing with Mr Keith. Then why was she so agitated? Her insides in a turmoil. Dry-mouthed at the thought of him. Wanting him. Yes. Wanting him. Love? She didn't know. Lust, more like it, her *mutti* would say. But that was what she'd said when Hanni had fallen for Lucas.

Lucas was surprised to see Theo trudging down towards the camp. At first he thought he must be with the drovers who'd just brought in a mob of sheep, but Theo said he was with the bullocky, who'd spotted their camp and stopped for a yarn and a cup of tea. They had a big load of supplies for Clonmel Station.

'They buy enough to feed a town,' Theo growled.

'A lot of people work here,' Lucas told him. 'And they say the shearers will be along soon. Do you want tea?'

'Might as well. Tastes like dirty water to me, but it'll do.'

Lucas brought him back tea and a biscuit, and they squatted by a sheep pen.

'This where you live?' Theo asked, looking at the rough shelters by the campfire and a battered tent behind them.

'No. This is only a temporary camp for us stockmen when it's too far to get back to the homestead of a night. We sleep out here. There's always someone sent out to cook for us.'

'You get waited on like gentry, by the sound of it.'

'The hell we do. We work hard, Theo. I don't know about the others, but if they didn't put a feed in front of me at night, I'd be too tired to bother.'

'So you leave Hanni back there alone? She wouldn't like that. Is she in a camp too?'

'No. We have a room, quite nice it is too. You have a look when you get there.'

'We won't have much time. Davey, he's the bullocky, he says we'll get to the homestead soon, offload the stuff, and turn right around while the going's good. I think he means the weather. Though the next minute he'll be groaning about how dry the country is, praying for rain. But listen, Lucas . . . what did you say about shearers? I hear they get top money in these places.'

'The shearing starts when the weather warms up. You'd think it would be hot enough already, but apparently not.'

'Why don't the station men do their own shearing?'

Lucas shook his head. 'I don't know. It beats me. There are plenty of stockmen around all the time. I haven't even met half of them. Maybe it's because there are just too many sheep.'

'How many sheep does this farm have? I mean, if they bring all the animals in, what else would the stockmen have to do but shear the things?'

Lucas looked about him nervously. The other men were standing about the makeshift cookhouse, smoking, talking, hats pushed back from dusty faces, getting ready to move out again. This light meal with billy tea was called smoko; it wasn't a proper meal break.

'Theo,' he said, 'there's a lot I don't know. I don't like to ask too many questions and make a fool of myself. I've done that often enough, and let me tell you, these men might look an easy-going lot, but they're not. They're tough, and they compete all the time.'

'I only asked you about the shearers.'

'And I'm trying to tell you about the sheep. I don't know

180

whether they're teasing me or telling me the truth, but I think there are about twenty thousand or more on this farm.'

Theo laughed. 'They're teasing you, Lucas. And why wouldn't they? You're a groom. Do you tell them how to keep the stables neat? Do they know you're not really a stockman? You don't know anything about sheep.'

'I do now.'

'Rot. I worked as a shepherd once, when I was young. I could shear a sheep when I was sixteen. I know about sheep. Now listen, go and find out about a shearing job for me. I've got three kids, Lucas. Plodding about the country as Davey's offsider isn't any good. I don't earn enough to feed myself, let alone the kids.'

'The head stockman isn't here,' Lucas said, watching a black boy bringing buckets of water to the thirsty horses.

'Ask someone else. What about the cook?'

'All right!' Lucas said, irritated. 'I'll ask.'

He went over to the cook. 'My friend over there wants to know how to go about getting a job as a shearer, Lenny. Can you advise him?'

Lenny picked up empty cake tins. Kicked ash over the dying campfire and spat in the dust. 'Shearer? Pretty much a closed shop, that lot. Is he any good?'

'I think so.'

'How good?' He strode over to Theo. 'How many sheep can you shear in a day, mate?'

Theo looked at him, mystified. 'A day? This I don't know. I've never counted.'

'Take a stab at it!'

'I don't know. Maybe even ten.'

'Ah, get out of it, Lucas,' the cook sneered. 'And take the kiddy with you. He wouldn't get a job as a shearer's dump boy.'

He tramped out to where the stockmen were saddling up again and related the story to hoots of laughter.

Lucas sighed. He'd get ribbed mercilessly about this one, even though he had no idea how many sheep a man could shear in a day. He hated being laughed at, but he would suffer it again and again, if necessary, until he got this job right.

Until he too could laugh at the new chums. It was, he worked out, only a matter of time, and the pecking order. The ladder was there for him to climb and he would do it. One day he'd have his own station.

A shrill whistle from Davey had Theo on his feet.

'You made a fool of me,' he snarled at Lucas. 'You did that on purpose. You could have told me what to say.'

'No I could not, Theo. I don't know myself.'

'When you two stop jabbering in that lingo, we have to get going, Theo,' his bullocky boss said. 'I wouldn't mind camping here with this mob, they're set up pretty good, but we'd be wasting hours. Best we move on; the sooner out, the sooner in.'

'How are things in town?' Lucas asked Theo hurriedly as his friend responded to Davey's call.

'What do you care? Out here in the middle of nowhere, making a big fellow of yourself, pretending you know about sheep!'

Lucas was shocked. He ran after Theo and pulled him to a standstill. 'Don't talk to me like that! Have you gone mad? We're friends, remember? We came right across the world together. If there is anything I can do to help you at any time, Theo, I'll do it. Do you need money? Are things as bad as that?'

'Yes,' Theo admitted. 'I'm sorry, Lucas, I'm going under. We can't live out at Father Beitz's jungle. We've rented part of a cottage, the only place in that excuse for a village we could find, but I can't keep up the payments. I can't. I'm trying.'

He was almost in tears. 'It was a terrible mistake coming out here, I know that now. I left a good job as a commissionaire at a first-class hotel thinking this would be a better place to bring up—'

Lucas cut him short. 'You mustn't give up now. It is a good place. Not what we're used to, that's all. I can lend you a pound, but I haven't got any cash on me, and I won't be back in tonight. Hanni keeps our savings in a tin. You know how women are . . . they like to see the money growing . . .'

'I wouldn't know. Eva spends my money as soon as she gets her hands on it.'

'Then go up to Hanni when you get to the homestead. Tell her I said to lend you a pound. You can pay it back when things improve.'

'Not too many people got a pound to spare,' Theo sulked, 'but I'm in no position to refuse. I'll see Hanni about it.'

'Good. But Theo, I don't have pounds to spare. That was to be my tithe money for Father Beitz, but I think your family is more deserving.'

'Then why do I have to repay you?' Theo said angrily. 'You're just patronising me, like everyone else.'

'Theo, I have to go. Please yourself about the money.'

Lucas was relieved to get away. And embarrassed. He strode over to his horse, tested the girth strap and swung into the saddle. The saddles the stockmen used were much lighter than the European style. No wonder he'd been bumping about like a novice when he'd first mounted one of these stockhorses.

As he turned his horse to catch up with the other men, who were already riding away, he looked back to Theo to bid him farewell, but Theo was marching over to the waiting bullock team without even casting a glance in his direction.

'What a stupid thing for me to say,' Lucas muttered to himself, letting the horse break into a canter. He and Hanni had saved a huge sum. Two pounds. Five shillings of that had been won on a horse race, the day of the Clonmel Races, when people came from near and far with their best thoroughbreds to put them to the test on the Clonmel track.

That was another joy of station life, new to Lucas. Neither of them had ever been to a race meeting before, but they both knew that this bush track was a far cry from the superb race courses back home so much loved by the gentry. Nevertheless, everyone had a great time at these races, which were more like a picnic day, except that the surrounds were dry and dusty, a corrugated shed housed refreshments, and several of the ladies insisted on riding in the races as well.

Hanni had to work most of the day, unfortunately, since the crowds had to be fed, but she managed to tell Lucas that he ought to back Paddy's Dream.

'How do you know?' he asked. 'We can't be wasting our money betting. I'm surprised at you, Hanni.'

183

'I heard it in the house. I heard them talking. Please, Lucas, Mr Dixon is acting as bookmaker. Go and put on the bet.'

'How much?'

'Sixpence. They're saying it is tens.'

'Tens what?'

'I don't know. Just do it.'

So he'd won five shillings. But what had possessed him to blurt out to Theo that they would be paying Father Beitz a pound? That was what he'd asked for, but Hanni had refused to even contemplate it.

'The priest should give up that timber,' she said. 'You know what the men here told you. That the timber in there, in the church acreage, is worth a fortune. Why should we work to support him when there is no need?'

Just the same, Lucas thought, they should send something. The five shillings, maybe, but Hanni was so angry at that suggestion, she wouldn't speak to him for hours.

'You need a keeper, Lucas,' she'd railed at him. 'You say the first thing that comes into your head.'

It was true. He had that failing. Words tumbled out. They did have some relevance, but not always, he thought dismally, were they related to sense. He remembered when his mother died, when her sister came to their house, and he was fifteen, old enough to know better. She'd come to collect furniture which she claimed belonged to her. Family heirlooms, she'd said.

'Heirlooms be damned,' his father had retorted. 'But they came from her side of the family, so let her have them. They're not worth arguing about.'

His father was out in the fields. Lucas was to let her take the furniture, the table and chairs and the Indian rug, and the big armchair with the broken springs, but no more. They were stored in the hay shed.

'Not that the stupid bitch is entitled to any of it,' his father had told Lucas. 'Your Aunt Inge came out of the poorhouse. Her mum died in there and left this newborn, and they didn't know what to do with her, someone had to have her. So in the end it was your grandma who took her in, only because there was no one else. So she isn't really of your mother's family at all. No relation.'

Lucas hated to think about all the times he'd put his foot in it; this was just one he couldn't help recalling because his father had given him such a belting. But it was only because Aunt Inge kept insisting she was entitled to the inlaid sewing table, and the carved daybed, and the butter churn with the flowers painted on it, among other things.

He had tried to make her leave. The furniture Papa had said she could have was packed on the dray, the driver waiting impatiently, Aunt Inge screeching and shouting, and he not knowing what to do because she would not leave. She would not. She raced into the buttery and started dragging out what was not hers, and that was when Lucas, in desperation, told her why she shouldn't be making such a fuss. That she wasn't entitled to any of this stuff, if the truth be known.

The previous screeches were only whimpers compared to the racket she made when he blurted out the reason. Some said they could hear her in the square. To shut her up, he let her take whatever she wanted.

There were five stockmen in this group. They broke away from the track and headed west, cross-country through open bushland, where Lucas caught up with them. He hoped none of them would remember that this was where he had become lost on the thirty-mile ride over to the Dilba lagoons. He'd ridden round in circles, they'd told him afterwards, and he'd come in for a lot of ribbing, but he did appreciate the huge effort they'd all put in, searching for him through the night. Strange people, he mused.

But so was Theo. Lucas didn't know what to make of Theo now. Suddenly he was pleased that he wouldn't be able to get back tonight. At least he'd avoid the problem he'd caused about the loan to Theo.

'You're weak,' he said to himself. 'And cowardly too.'

Then he laughed, spurring the horse on as if to distance himself from them, from Theo who'd line up to ask for money, and from Hanni who would no more hand over a precious pound than fly in the air.

I meant well, Lucas shrugged. I did feel sorry for him, but Hanni won't see it that way.

* * *

She did not.

'Lucas told you to tell me to give you what? Is he mad? Got the sunstroke, maybe, both of you. You've got a job, Theo Zimmerman. Use your own money.' No matter how much he argued, she wouldn't hand over a penny, not one penny, and Theo was furious.

'Lucas promised me,' he shouted as he backed away from her door. 'He's a good man, and fair. He won't let me down. He'll send it to me,'

He held back on telling Hanni what he thought of her, for fear she'd repeat it to Lucas, who would be cross, but when he sat down with the stockmen that night, he heard an item of interest. They were gathered outside, round a campfire, smoking, yarning, filling in time before turning in. Someone asked him if he knew Lucas. As he explained the connection, he picked up a conversation from a group behind him. About Hanni. Pretending to be interested in a story some fellow was telling him, Theo strained his ears and heard something about her doing all right for herself with the boss.

'Who? Young or old?' a voice asked.

'Young, of course. Keith. I see them out walking together.'

'You do?'

'Yes. Shut up.' The voices drifted into whispers, but it was enough for Theo. He waited a while and then quietly left the group, wandering towards their quarters and then stepping sideways on to a path that led past the stables and up the track to the building that housed the Fechners.

When Hanni opened the door, she was in the process of removing a long frilly apron, and she still had a maid's mobcap on her blonde hair. Theo was reminded of how pretty she was, but her attitude was far from becoming.

'What do you want now, Theo? I'm tired. I've just finished work.'

'Are you sure it was work?' he asked slyly.

'What?'

'I get about, Hanni. I hear things. A lot of things.'

'Like what?'

'You'd be surprised.'

'No I wouldn't. Unless you've come to apologise.'

186

'Not me. You should, though. I've heard a few things about you and your goings-on behind Lucas's back.'

She stood calmly at the door. 'As I said, like what?'

'Let me have that pound. Or wait on, I'll be easy on you. If you let me have ten shillings, I won't tell Lucas.'

Hanni stepped out on to the veranda. She didn't ask him what he knew. She didn't ask him not to tell Lucas. She made no attempt to go back inside to get the money. She just stood there in front of him for a few minutes, worried, Lucas thought. I've got her rattled now. There's no way out of this except to pay me.

He didn't see it coming. She didn't just slap him. She hauled off and punched him so hard it felt like a hammer striking his face. Taken off guard, he staggered back and fell down the short staircase, landing in a heap on the ground.

As he looked up she went back into her room and slammed the door. Stupid bitch. Not that he would have told Lucas. It would be a brave man who went to Lucas Fechner with a tale like that, right or wrong.

The next day Davey only shrugged when he heard that a bit of an altercation with a stockman had produced Theo's black eye. Fights raised little interest in their all-male environment.

Her knuckles were sore, but it had been worth it. Hanni put the chair back against the door and sat down to take off her shoes. Theo could say what he liked; she had done nothing wrong.

What a delicious feeling to be really and truly innocent. For a change. She sucked on her knuckles, stifling a giggle. There was nothing wrong with being accompanied on her walks by the boss, when he happened to be going in the same direction, or when he simply came upon her outside of the house. She saw him quite often indoors and he was always polite. Genteel, he was, Mr Keith. And how thrilling to think the men were actually talking about them! Hanni felt it was a feather in her cap to have her name associated romantically with Mr Keith. It was exciting. And ever so flattering. But there was nothing Theo could say to Lucas that would cause her a minute's bother. Anyway, this had nothing to do with

Lucas, it was just a little amusement she and Mr Keith were having.

She thought of him kissing her hand, so gently, so nicely, as she undid her blouse, took it off and then unlaced her cotton vest, releasing her breasts from their restraints. It was amazing how much that kiss had affected her, still did; it aroused her every time she thought about it. Made her feel all sexy and needy. She cupped her breasts and showed them to the small mirror on the dressing table, fantasising about showing them to him. He wouldn't be able to resist them.

The next day the cook was in a bad mood because there wasn't enough wood for the stove.

'Where's the yardman?' she asked angrily.

'I haven't seen him this morning,' Hanni said, so the cook turned on Lulla, the scullery maid.

'What have you got such a long face about?'

The black girl cringed away. 'Debbil sky out dere today. Bad day dis, missus. Better I go back to camp.'

'Better you get out there and find old Tom. Tell him my wood box is empty. Go on, girl!'

The girl darted away, just as the housekeeper came into the kitchen.

'Keith is home. He got in late last night. When you're finished here, put him up his usual, steak and the works, and I'll take a tray in to him. Then he can sleep for a while, so Hanni, don't go clattering about near his room.'

Hanni almost swooned at the thought of taking a tray into his room, of waking the drowsy man and smiling down at him . . . bliss. Almost offered to take on that duty, but thought better of it.

The trouble was, Lucas was the last to hear the gossip. The knowledge had crept over him like a shadow, leaving him too chilled to absorb it properly.

At first it was the silence. The sudden change of subject when he neared a group of fellow workers. The sheepish looks. Then the digs, the grins directed at him by mean-spirited men in work parties, the few who could always find something to be sour about. Sly remarks about his wife and Keith Dixon. Stupid remarks. He and Hanni were very much in love; Hanni wouldn't look at another man.

Nevertheless, he did worry. It wasn't unknown for gentry to take advantage of pretty girls, no matter their standing. And even though it was a worry for him, how could he mention this to Hanni? How could he humiliate her by telling her she was the subject of men's dirty talk? She would be terribly upset. And fearful. This would certainly give her cause to worry about her job and the reaction in the homestead, because there was no basis for this gossip. None at all. Hanni and the boss! It was too much to consider. Her husband would have known if she was up to mischief. He supposed this situation came from her flaunting herself in front of the men, exactly what he'd warned her about. If not the young boss, the gossip would have teamed her with someone else. Lucas tried to smile. Even the old boss, J.B.

They were working hard today. Hanni seemed to think all they did was ride about the countryside like princes. He wished she could see them now, knee deep in mud. The water shortage was becoming acute, not only on this property but in most of Queensland, he was told, so they had to do all they could to keep water available for all of the sheep. So many sheep. It had become such an impossible task that drovers had been cutting out the old and the weak and taking them into the Bundaberg boiling-down works.

All of the stockmen had orders to keep a careful eye on water levels everywhere: the river, the creeks and especially the lagoons miles away from the river. J.B. Dixon was even looking for a good water diviner to find underground springs for him. In the mean time, the land was drying out, and feed for all these animals was becoming so scarce that it was pitiful to see mobs of them scratching about in the dust for a few blades of grass.

The water level in this lagoon had become so low that Sam, the foreman, had them in there digging out the caked mud to provide access to the shallow spring. They did the best they could there, and then began digging post-holes in the hard earth so that makeshift pens could be built here ready for

189

mustering. Lucas was only now beginning to understand what a big operation it would be to muster so many sheep, bring them in to the sheds for shearing, and keep them fed and watered at the same time. He began to yearn for the green pastures of home.

The original plan had been to return to base that evening, but they'd seen a herd of brumbies, wild horses, near the lagoon, and Sam decided this would be a good opportunity to capture a few of them.

'With the shortage of feed, they'll be weaker than usual,' he said. 'We might have a better chance of capturing them because with luck they won't put up such a fight.'

Lucas knew that Hanni was expecting him home, but he could hardly disagree with Sam's decision, and besides, like the others, he was looking forward to the excitement of rounding up wild horses.

'Not an easy task,' his friends had told him, 'and dangerous. Those bloody brumbies will be mad as hell if we corral them. They bite and kick and scream, so keep well away.'

In the morning, the brumbies were still there, waiting to get the water but keeping their distance, so the men set to work building tougher fences, setting up a race built of heavy saplings to withstand the weight and hooves of angry horses.

Someone remarked on the dark purplish sky out on the western horizon, such a contrast against the pearly hues of dawn, suggesting hopefully that it could be a storm.

Sam sniffed the air. 'Don't smell like rain. And look at those brumbies; if there was rain in the air, they wouldn't be getting so desperate for our water.'

'Could be a dust storm,' one of the men said, as Sam stepped out from the trees they were stripping for saplings to get a better look.

'Long ways off,' he said, squinting. 'Might be dust, dammit.'

Dust? Lucas wondered. I guess I'll find out soon enough.

'Dust!' the housekeeper shouted, dashing through the dining room. 'Shut down.'

Hanni was shining the mirrors, but it was almost time to set the table for lunch. Three today, with Mr Keith still in the house, instead of the usual two women only. His father was always out during the day. Except on Sundays.

She jerked up, mystified. 'Shut down' was all that she'd heard, but the words had come in such a rush, so unexpectedly, she failed to translate them. Something was urgent, though, so she hurried into the kitchen, only to find it empty. She peered into the pantry and went on out the back door, surprised to see the cook over by the laundry, dragging clothes from the line and shoving them at the laundress.

'What is happening?' she called.

'There's a dust storm coming, everything has to be closed up tight.'

'Oh!' Hanni ran. 'Oh, Lord! The dining room!' She got back in time to bang the French doors shut and then ran towards the parlour, but the housekeeper had already been there.

Mrs Dixon came running from the library. 'Are all the bedrooms closed down, Hanni? Windows and doors?'

'I don't know,' Hanni said, bewildered. This house had more doors and windows, more exits, than a beehive, no central plan to speak of.

Mr Keith came upon them in the parlour and his mother immediately asked if he'd shut his room down.

'Tight as I can,' he said. 'How are you going, Elsie?'

The housekeeper rushed in, banging the door behind her. 'I'm all right. I think we're all shut down, Mrs Dixon. Cook got the linen in and I've stuffed the gap under the linen press door with papers. Nothing much else we can do.'

'We'll sit it out in here, Elsie,' Mrs Dixon said. 'You go back and keep Cook company, Hanni. And don't look so worried. There's nothing to be frightened of, just a lot of dust blowing about, and a dreadful nuisance.'

'Come on then,' Keith said to Hanni. 'I'll go out through the kitchen. I'm going down to check the stables, Mother.'

In the kitchen, which was now in semi-darkness with shutters on the windows, Cook had made a fresh pot of tea, and was sitting at the table, seemingly unconcerned.

'Oh Lord,' Hanni said. 'I was airing the guest rooms this morning. You said there were visitors coming.'

191

'So?'

'So they're wide open,' Hanni wailed. 'I have to close them.'

'Let's go then,' Keith said. 'I'll give you a hand.'

Hanni was shocked as they pushed out on to the veranda. The air was thick with swirling red dust that had reduced the sunlight to an eerie glow. Together they fought against the wind all the way down the path until they reached the long veranda of the guest block.

The open rooms were already swallowing dust as they ran into them to slam the windows shut. They had closed them all when Mr Keith remembered her room at the end. 'Is that open too?' he gasped.

'Yes.'

'Come on then, be quick,' he cried, grabbing her arm and pulling her along the common veranda.

By the time they reached her door, wind was whipping thick dust round them. Hanni was choking: she could hardly breathe. He shoved the door open and as one they were inside, both falling against the wall.

Keith rushed across to the window, closed it and turned back. 'When I've gone, shove a pillow down the bottom of the door there, to stop more dust getting in. This damn dust, it blows in everywhere even when we're shut down. Are you all right?'

Her eyes were running, she had regained enough breath to break out in a succession of sneezes, and all he could do was laugh.

'Your first introduction to a dust storm, Hanni.'

She scrabbled in her apron pocket for a handkerchief, sniffing into it, apologising, as the room darkened.

He put an arm about her. 'Don't worry, Hanni. It will blow over soon. This dust from the desert can be so thick it blots out the sun, that's all.' And then he kissed her, as if this was a nice thing to do, on her cheek, all innocence. He nursed her in his arms as that terrible wind became worse, louder, battering at the walls, shaking the roof. She could hear crashing noises outside.

'This is a bit worse than usual, I have to admit,' he murmured, his lips nuzzling her ear, and Hanni almost swooned for the second time that day because he was here with her, Mr Keith, and he was so gorgeous she couldn't resist turning her lips to his and sinking into his arms for a passionate kiss that almost took her breath away again. It was heavenly! He took off her apron, still kept kissing her; he unbuttoned her blouse and her shift, and Hanni couldn't believe her fantasies were coming true. He cupped her breasts in his hands and looked at them, devouring them.

'Beautiful,' he said. 'Beautiful. I knew it.'

She swelled with pride as his lips closed on them, but at the same time he slid her down to the bed and she began to worry. This wasn't such a good idea after all. It was flattering that he was attracted to her, that Mr Keith was right here in her life making love to her breasts, but she didn't want to go all the way with him. Not now that she was a married woman. She smiled to herself. A matron now. A reformed character. Flirting was one thing, but she wouldn't let him go too far. He didn't love her. Or at least he wasn't saying so. Just burrowing down there with her, in this bed, orphans in a storm.

He was trying to undress her, trying to take off her skirt, so Hanni began to resist. 'Please, Mr Keith. Don't do that.'

'It's all right, Hanni darling. I won't touch you. I just want to see. You can't imagine what it's like for me to see you in my own house and dream about you.'

Hanni was surprised. 'You do? You dream about me?'

'I dream of the seventh veil. Of you removing that very last layer and allowing me the privilege of seeing you. Admiring you, that's all.'

Hanni had never heard of the seventh veil, but she got the idea and it sounded fun, and harmless. Why not let him see? She did have a beautiful body. Wasn't that what had enticed Lucas away from Hilda, his fiancée? Why shouldn't she?

He had her pose for him on the bed with a sheet draped delicately for a modicum of modesty.

'That's it. Let your hair fall down. Oh God, if I were an artist I would paint you. I would never have another model. Have you ever been an artist's model, Hanni?'

'No, Mr Keith,' she said, thrilled. 'Never.' But then she realised that he was undressing too.

'God!' She clutched the sheet as the flattery-induced trance gave way to reality, and the roof above her shook at her stupidity and the windows rattled their disapproval.

'No,' she said to him, as he pushed her back on the bed. 'No.' And then she reached for a lifeline, to avoid upsetting him. 'Someone might come in.'

Mr Keith laughed. 'There's timber flying everywhere out there. No one will come in.'

'We'd better get dressed, then. I think these rooms could fall down.'

'We're safe, don't worry.'

'Please, Mr Keith, I don't want to do this.'

'You don't? You've been flirting with me ever since you came here; you've been asking for it. What are you holding out for? Money? That's all right. I don't mind giving you a quid or two.'

'No.' She kept struggling. 'No. I don't think we should.'

'Of course you do. If your husband could satisfy you, my dear, you wouldn't be trying to seduce me. Would you?' He shook her, and Hanni became annoyed.

'Mr Keith, I am sorry. This is my fault.' Her English was failing her again; she knew there were German words mixed up in this, but they had to suffice. 'Please forgive me. This is true. You are a nice man, and in my foolishness I did this flirting, but I now know this was a mistake and to you I apologise for the flirting.'

Hanni deliberately took all the blame, to give him an escape route, though she knew that it had definitely not been a one-sided affair, that he'd been flirting too.

He was straddling her on the bed now. 'You stupid bitch. You take *me* on, you get to ride all the way. Don't go pulling the virgin trick on me, not a good idea. Not from a married woman especially.'

Decision time. This man would not take no for an answer. He would attempt to rape her. If she fought him off, injured him as she was very capable of doing, since he was only lolling above her, she and Lucas would be fired.

As if he knew what she was thinking, he looked down at her. 'You asked for it, Hanni. You'll get it. My pleasure. And yours too, if you do as you're told. If you don't, how sad. The Fechners will have a long walk back to Bundaberg. A bloody long walk, wouldn't you say? What with the hot weather coming on.'

Hanni didn't get a chance to make that decision, to fight him off or to surrender. His fist came down suddenly and smashed into her stomach. He rolled her over and punched her about the waist and buttocks. He pulled her to the side of the bed and bound her mouth with her stockings, and then he sodomised her until she bled.

'Did you think,' he asked her as he dressed, 'that you might seduce me into giving you a Dixon kid, heir to all our money? Not a chance, Hanni. I wouldn't fall for that.'

As he ranted on, Hanni lay on the bed trying to block out his voice, wondering if he were mad, demented, to be going on like this. But the storm had abated, and he was leaving. She prayed he was leaving.

'Next time,' he said as he walked to the door, 'it will be better.' Hanni stiffened in shock, but he went on, his voice cheerful, even soothing: 'You'll see, we'll do nice things, Hanni, just you and me. It'll be our secret. And there'll be no mentioning this to your hubby, will there? I mean, we've already talked about that long walk back to town.'

When he opened the door a rush of clean air seemed to come to her rescue, delivering her from the ugliness that had just departed, but she was to have no rest. She had to get back to work.

Wearily, painfully, she picked up the heavy jug and poured water into the china basin on the washstand so that she could sponge herself down, try to remove every whiff of that vile man, but she would not weep. She must not return to work with even a vestige of tears about her and have them ask questions. Dust might have been an excuse, but Hanni knew that once she started to weep she wouldn't be able to stop. She was already fighting off the sobs building up inside her.

Next time. She shivered in fright at the thought, realising that he'd meant there would be more and more times, that he expected her to be at his disposal. That was it. At his disposal. Whenever.

He was right. She couldn't tell Lucas about this. Impossible. Disastrous. And apart from that, Hanni was angry with herself.

'Face it,' she said, brushing the knots from her hair with furious strokes, 'you were stupid, too stupid to see you were getting into a dangerous game. I know, you thought he was a gentleman. You thought you had him wound round your little finger. Pride, that's what brought this on. Damn pride!'

She flung down the brush and dressed with extreme care. Not a hair out of place. Little bows exact. Shoes gleaming. Her second apron neatly in place. She went up to the kitchen, walking strongly despite the pain, to tell the cook she would begin by cleaning out the guest rooms. Then she strode back with her mop, broom and dusters, thinking of him. She would have to face him day in and day out as long as they lived here. And he'd be laughing at her. At what an idiot she was.

Beautiful. Have you ever been an artist's model?

She blushed scarlet from her cheeks to her fingertips, choking back another sob. But he'd hurt her, raped her, bashed her . . . bashed her so carefully in the stomach and on the buttocks, where the bruises, already purpling, would not show, which made her think this wasn't the first time he'd attacked a woman. It was too methodical, too planned.

Hanni looked at the first room. Everything was covered in a film of red dust. She began with the bedspreads, taking them outside to shake them, before realising that wouldn't work, they would have to go to the wash. She left them in a heap and went back for the mats. These she hung over a wire line, and marched around to the laundry to collect the rug beater. Then she set to, banging and beating those mats amid clouds of dust, still banging and beating when not a speck remained, and over and over saying to herself: 'He thinks he got away with it. He thinks I'll let him get away with it. Well I won't. I won't. I won't.'

As she took the mats back, Hanni hadn't worked out what she would do, but she knew she would do something. It was only a matter of time. He'd pay. Somehow he'd pay.

Chapter Eight

'He's a mongrel, that Keith Dixon.'

Jakob was startled that a lawyer should use such language. He'd been under the impression that these gentlemen were of solemn, sedate stock, not rowdy and belligerent like this Maryborough fellow, Mr Arthur Hobday. Solicitor at Law and Public Notary.

Maryborough was another river port, but much busier than Bundaberg, and the township was more advanced. Jakob had smiled as he rode into town with Billy, to see that they were in a street by the river which was named Quay Street, the same as the first street he'd come across in Bundaberg. He wondered if that was the rule for these towns or just coincidence. He thought he recalled seeing a Quay Street in Brisbane too, during their short stay. But more important matters were to hand.

They'd arrived late in the afternoon and camped by the river overnight, giving Jakob a chance to spruce up as best he could in the morning.

This time he walked down Quay Street keeping an eye out for the offices of legal gentlemen, but the first he saw was Philps and Sons and he shied away like a spooked horse. He rounded the block, still searching but also taking in the newness of this town and its residents. There were still the eyesores, the shanties and the overgrown vacant blocks, but a couple of quite splendid hotels stood out, along with sets of respectable shops, several churches and a sea of very plain but adequate houses. Jakob felt a little envious, wishing they had come here first, making a mental note not to mention this to Freda and upset her.

But then, he mused, the land all round here is under cultivation or well stocked, and you'd have had to go even further into the backblocks to find cheap land in this area, so be satisfied with your lot.

Eventually he found the office of another lawyer, Mr Hobday, back in Quay Street, right across from the office of Philps and Sons but upstairs, overlooking the street.

Mr Hobday was a tall man with a balding head and a large moustache. Standing at his door in his shirtsleeves and waistcoat, with a gold watch planted across a generous paunch, he was bellowing at an escaping clerk as Jakob approached the staircase, standing back to allow the fellow to fly on past him.

Hobday laughed, beckoning to Jakob. 'You looking for me? Come on up. Clerks! They'd forget their heads if they weren't screwed on!'

'You're from Bundaberg?' Hobday commented after the introductions. 'Good spot, that, it will do well.'

Jakob wasn't so sure now. 'I was surprised to see how this town is flourishing. It makes me wonder if Bundaberg can survive.'

'Don't worry about that. All these towns are gateways to huge country out there, all of these ports will prosper . . . But tell me, Mr Meissner, how did you come to set sail for this part of the world?'

He was interested in everything about Jakob and his friends and their homeland, and Jakob was wondering if they'd ever get to his problem, but eventually the clerk returned, made tea for them, and Hobday got down to business.

Jakob began to relate his situation, and it was when he came to the confrontation with Keith Dixon that the lawyer gave his uncomplimentary opinion of the fellow.

'You know him, sir?'

'Know them all. The father, J.B. Dixon, is bad enough, but that Keith is worse. Nearly got himself jailed for belting one of their stockmen with an iron bar.'

'Nearly?'

'The stockman backed off at the last minute. Wouldn't prefer charges. Obviously they bought him off. So you've taken up land resumed from the Clonmel Station holdings? Can't say you've got the best neighbours there, but what's the trouble?'

'We have loggers ready to cut the good timber on our land, but Mr Dixon won't allow it. Says the timber is his.'

'Rot and rubbish!'

'That's what we thought until we received these papers.' He handed them to the lawyer. 'This official letter says we have no legal right to the timber, even though our ownership of the land is not in dispute. I thought you might advise us on what we can do.'

Hobday's eyes widened as he read the Dixon claim.

'Well I'll be damned!' he said. 'The bloody cheek of them! I reckon they were counting on you to be too intimidated to query this.'

'I beg your pardon, sir?'

'I'm saying they thought you'd be stupid enough to fall for it. But good on you, Mr Meissner. You stand up for your rights and you'll do well here. You tell your mates that. Don't let people con you.'

Jakob didn't know the word 'con' but he got the gist of Hobday's reaction. Which was all very well, but was he saying that the Philps opinion was incorrect?

'I'll tell you what I'll do, Mr Meissner. I'll trot across the street and have a word with our mate Jefferson Philps, and the son, if he's around. You have another cup of tea. I shouldn't be long.'

Philps senior was stunned when Hobday came pounding into his office, waving some letters about.

'What's the meaning of this?' he roared. 'Are you stupid, or are you in the pay of J.B. Dixon? The legal advice you've given – in writing, Philps – is damned tripe and you know it.'

'I don't know what you're talking about.'

'This! This, sir! Your stationery. Your signature to the worst bit of skulduggery I've seen in a long time. You deliberately misled a landowner as to his rights.'

Philps read the pages nervously. 'Someone must have got hold of our stationery. That's not my signature.'

'Yes it is. I'd know it underwater, Philps. Who owns the timber on duly leased and registered land? The lessee or the previous owner?'

'The previous owner could if it's only a lease,' Philps whined. 'I'm sure he could.' He took off his glasses and wiped them with a large handkerchief, as if to draw attention away from his predicament.

'Could? Could not!'

'I may have made an error then, let me see . . .'

'More than one error! Who would the previous owner be anyway?'

'The Dixons, of course.'

'Wrong again. The government resumed the land. Mr Meissner is leasing it from the government, the previous owner, not from the Dixons. You're so far out of line here, Philps, I'll have to report this to the Law Board. You could be in serious trouble.'

Hobday listened to Philps's excuses, knowing that this wasn't the first and wouldn't be the last time this shady character bent the rules in favour of his wealthy clients. It was one of the reasons why the Philps family had a fine residence overlooking the river and the Hobdays still lived in their modest cottage next door to the Bluebird Café. He'd be wasting his time trying to pin a charge on a man who would shamelessly admit error to the Law Board, thereby leaving no basis for censure beyond a mild caution, but he couldn't allow Philps to get away with it. Besides, his client, Mr Meissner, was a sensible fellow. How would it help him to have one lawyer give an opinion, and another refute it? Obviously the man could not afford and did not need to be faced with court procedures.

He picked up the letters. 'It is plain to see that you are in error, Philps, to say the least. There's no getting away from that fact. If you would rather I did not report this to the Law Board, then write a rebuttal for me to take to Mr Meissner. That will do.'

Philps had recovered a little confidence by this.

'Don't waste my time, Hobday. If you disagree with me, you write your opinion for your client.'

'Ah, no. That would be doing our profession a disservice, showing us up as mere squabblers. Then again, if I took your opinion down the street to the local newspaper and asked the editor to print it . . .' He stopped to straighten his waistcoat with firm, decisive movements. 'I think the public outcry would be heard in Brisbane. Folk here know the rules, they're not new chums like you've got up there in Bundaberg.'

'Very well. What do you want?'

'Simple. A note to Mr Meissner, who is waiting patiently over there, informing him that you've made a mistake. Say what you like, but make it clear and plain that as lessee of this land, he is entitled to ownership of the flora on that land in its entirety.'

'You can't publish my letter. It is private correspondence.'

'Wrong again. It is owned by Mr Meissner, just like that timber. Now write the note, I can't stand here all day.'

'He's coming.' The clerk stood by the window, peering down. 'Crossing the road now. Looks to be in a good mood. I hope he didn't wallop Philps.'

'Wallop?' Another new word for Jakob.

'Yes, last time he had a run-in with them he boxed the son's ears.'

Then the lawyer bounded up the wooden staircase and burst in on Jakob. 'Here you are, Mr Meissner. You don't have to rely on my opinion. Our friend over the road has retracted his statement to you and now freely admits that the flora – that means all the plant life – on your property is owned by you. Including the timber, of course. You can call the loggers back in now, and take no notice of Dixon's babblings. Another thing to keep in mind, Mr Meissner. You bought the land from the government, not the Dixons, so don't give them a thought.'

Jakob sat back in the chair, almost overcome with relief. He was suddenly tired, as if he'd come to the end of a long journey and was able to set down a burden at last.

He stood. 'I'm very grateful to you, Mr Hobday. I didn't think this could be worked out so quickly.'

'Lawyers known to be long-winded?' Hobday grinned.

'No, sir. Not at all. I did not mean to be rude. Coming here to Maryborough was for me maybe a gamble, that someone could help us. It is so far from our farm, you understand. Then suddenly it is over. The worry. I'm sorry, I am getting mixed up now. But I must thank you.'

'My pleasure, Mr Meissner.'

Jakob took out his purse. 'Could I pay you now?'

'Certainly. That'll be two bob. Two shillings.'

The clerk raised his eyebrows at that figure, and Jakob had the impression that he was being undercharged.

'I can pay my way,' he told Hobday. 'Is this all, the two shillings?' He placed the money on the lawyer's desk.

'Plenty, my friend. I had a bit of fun with Philps into the bargain. Now let me buy you a drink before you hit the track again.'

Before he knew it, Jakob was being whisked down the street with this formidable man, across the road and into one of the fine hotels he'd noticed previously. It was impressive inside also, with red plush carpet runners over polished floors, lace curtains at the tall windows and shining brass lamps and fittings on the walls. Glass doors ahead of them led to a dining room, but Mr Hobday turned to a passage that led from the foyer to a large bar, also very well appointed.

'What about an ale?' Hobday asked, and Jakob nodded.

They stood at the bar, talking; or rather, Jakob smiled to himself, with Mr Hobday the questioner and he responding with the answers, because the man still wanted to know everything about him, his family, the voyage, his homeland. Eventually Jakob realised that the lawyer was genuinely interested in people and places, so he lost his shyness and insisted on buying a second drink, since Mr Hobday had bought the first.

Jakob Meissner was enjoying himself. He felt human again. A man in control, looking forward to going home triumphant.

'Call me Arthur,' the lawyer was saying. 'We don't stand on ceremony here. I hope you don't mind all my quizzing, Jakob, but we're a long way from Europe, I don't suppose I'll ever see it, so the next best thing is to ask.'

A dark-haired fellow standing behind Arthur turned about with a mischievous grin.

'Ask and you shall receive,' he announced.

For a second Arthur looked at him in surprise, and then he gasped: 'God speed the plough! Mike! When did you get out?'

'Not a minute too soon, me dear. Got time off for good behaviour and for curing the Governor's horse of the belly sickness.'

'I'm glad to see you. You don't look any the worse for wear.'

'No fault of the bastards that took me in,' he growled.

Arthur nodded. 'I'm sorry.'

His high spirits seemed to have deserted him as he introduced Jakob to this man, Mike Quinlan.

'I failed Mike,' he said to Jakob. 'I couldn't keep him out of prison after he and J.B. Dixon engaged in a private war.'

'The bastard!' Quinlan added.

It was beginning to dawn on Jakob who this fellow was. Hadn't Davey mentioned him? Or someone with a similar name . . .

'Have a drink on me,' Arthur was saying, 'because Jakob here fell out with the Dixons too, but this time we won.'

He called to the bartender, who obliged with three more pots of beer, and Jakob began to worry about Billy out there waiting for him.

'How did that come about?' Quinlan asked the lawyer, but Jakob cut in. 'Excuse me, Mr Quinlan, but I think you're my neighbour. On my eastern boundary.'

'On Clonmel land?'

'Yes.'

'Well I'll be buggered!'

'They took your timber?'

'That they did, the bastards.'

'Come on now, Mike, you hit them where they hurt too,' Arthur said, but Quinlan obviously still held a grudge.

'They didn't have to do time, though, did they?' he asked bitterly.

'Don't go getting your Irish up again,' Arthur said, and that interested Jakob, who, having finally got his tongue around the English language most of the time without the fumble of translation, was now beginning to recognise accents. Of which, he reminded himself, there were far more than he'd expected. But this one, that he'd heard before and noted as pleasing, could now be identified as Irish. He'd also identified the Scottish accents, but that was some time back, on the *Tara*, when they were sailing from Brisbane to Bundaberg. To be truthful, he hadn't understood a word those Scottish folk had said, even though he'd been assured they were speaking English. Now he put that down to his inexperience, blaming himself. As for the local people, born in this country, Jakob had discussed their voices with Freda. Some seemed to be more clipped, use rounder vowels than others, but they were not as hard to understand as the Scots.

The lawyer seemed to think he was responsible for not being able to keep Quinlan out of jail; the sign of a dedicated man, Jakob thought. On the other hand, he was thrilled that Jakob could thumb his nose at that obnoxious family.

'We'll all go back to my place for lunch,' he announced. 'Stella will be pleased to see you again, Mike.'

'I'm sorry,' Jakob said. 'I do not wish to be ungrateful, but my guide, a young Aborigine lad, is waiting for me.'

'Then we'll collect him on the way,' Arthur said.

'We don't get a lot to celebrate, Jakob,' his neighbour said. 'Grasp it when it comes, me lad.'

Jakob had to laugh. This well-known rascal was at least ten years younger than him, even-featured, normal height, but his eyes . . . Normally Jakob didn't take a lot of interest in men's eyes, though ladies' had entranced him many a time, but this fellow, this Mike . . . his eyes were dark, glittery, they danced. They spoke of fun and mischief and, at the same time, of iron resolve. Jakob found himself wondering what Tibbaling would make of the man.

Mrs Hobday gave them a hearty meal of chops and sweet potato pie, followed by generous servings of bread pudding, while Mike outlined his new plans.

'Forget the dairy herd, they're long sold, Arthur. I'm going in for sugar. You should too, Jakob. It's the up-and-coming thing. Our red soil is perfect for it. I kept thinking about it when I was in that place, seeing the lovely green of cane fields swaying in the breeze.'

'I don't know anything about sugar,' Jakob said.

'Neither do I. We can learn.'

'I'll think about it,' Jakob said, rather than be the cause of disagreement in this pleasant company, but soon it was time to leave. He thanked the Hobdays, promising to keep in touch.

'If you come to Bundaberg I hope you'll find the time to visit us. We're not so far out of town.' Jakob realised that he too was starting to take distances for granted, like everyone else up here.

'The day is almost over,' Mrs Hobday said. 'You can stay the night here if you wish, Jakob.'

'Thank you, but we'll get a start this afternoon. We can get a long way before dark.'

'Don't worry about them,' Mike grinned. 'I'll look after them.'

Jakob swung about, questioning, but Mike reminded him, 'I'm your neighbour, remember? I'm coming with you. Wait until I get my swag from the pub, and we'll be off.'

As the three men rode out of the town, Mike called to Billy: 'Which way did you come down?'

'Come through Childers, boss.'

'Good. Then you won't mind going back the other way, Jakob. Get to know the countryside.'

'I didn't know there was another route. Do you know it, Billy?' He saw Billy frown, but Mike laughed.

'Nothing to know. A blind man couldn't get lost this way. Matter of fact, if you'd taken the coast road you wouldn't have needed a guide. It's simple, Jakob. We follow the river to the coast, that being Herveys Bay. Then we head north, follow the coast to the mouth of the Burnett River. Our river. Turn inland, follow that river, and lo and behold, we're home! That's right, isn't it, Billy?'

'Right enough,' Billy allowed.

This seemed to Jakob a splendid idea. His mission to Maryborough had succeeded, and at the same time he'd been given the opportunity to acquaint himself with a little more of the countryside. He looked back to the blue of the mountains as they turned the horses on to a road that bordered the Mary River, remembering that Davey had talked about those mountains inland from Maryborough.

'Is it true there's gold up there?' he asked Mike.

'Buckets of it, mate. That's where I'm going to find the shekels to bankroll my sugar plantation.'

'Then why are you going home?' He'd called it home, for want of a better word, but in fact the Quinlan land was just that. Land. There was no house, nothing to see but scrub, almost overgrown with high grass now, and a proliferation of stumps of valuable trees, trees that had been stolen by the Dixons.

'I have to, mate. The bloody inspectors don't take jail for an excuse. You know right well that the leases are plain and clear. We have to make improvements on our land, housing and fencing and the like, or get kicked out. I haven't had a chance to lift a finger yet. I have to get to it.'

'Would logging be regarded as improvements?'

'No. The whole idea of improvements is to stop speculators. The government needs to populate the place, see. They can't have smart alecs getting cheap leases and sitting on them until they get a good offer, at which time they pay off the lease, sell at a profit, and bolt. Wasting years with no contribution to agriculture. I not only have to make improvements, I have to prove I live there. So I reckon my best move is to build a house, wouldn't you say?'

'I suppose so.'

'Well, there's no use fencing paddocks when I've got no livestock to put in them.'

'That is true.'

'Hey, Billy! Why don't you come and work for me?'

'I'm a stockman,' Billy grinned. 'You got no stock.'

'No stock on this run either, so what you doing carting Jakob about?'

'Tibbaling send me.'

Mike sat back, slowed his horse. 'Oho! You're in high-falutin' company, Jakob. Tibbaling no less. What kin are you, Billy?'

'He my father's father.'

'Right. So I'll pay you to work for me. Owe you for a start, but I'll put it in writing if you help me build my house.'

'Promise good enough.'

Jakob was to find that travelling with Mike Quinlan was never dull. He was a man full of enthusiasm and surprises, not all of them welcome. Jakob rode along, half listening to the other two arguing about the size of the house Mike proposed to build, the Irishman proposing a decent farm-house, and his 'apprentice' pointing out that that would take too long, without pay. Mostly Jakob's mind was on his own little farmhouse, which could be extended depending on the return from the sale of timber. Their timber, he chortled to himself. Wait until they heard *that* good news. He'd send a message to Les Jolly as soon as they reached Bundaberg. And while he was there, he ought to buy Freda a present, to celebrate.

Before they reached the mouth of the river, Billy suggested they ought to turn north, but Mike disagreed.

'We can't do that, Billy. We're exploring. We want to see it all, and not from the deck of a ship.'

'Take days longer that way,' Billy said. 'And hard riding. Not much tracks, only blackfella foot tracks.'

'But we want to follow the coast.'

'Coast bulge out here like a belly. This track longer than the Childers track already. Best we cut across here.'

Jakob had been immersed in his own thoughts, but he heard that. His head jerked up. 'Billy! Did you say this route is longer than the way we came?'

Billy grinned. 'Take my track, only two days longer, maybe more. Take his track you might got seven-, ten-day trek, and you fellas ain't got enough tucker.'

'What? I thought this route was quicker.'

Quinlan stared at him. 'Haven't you seen a map of this coastline?'

'Of course not!' Jakob despaired. 'I can't be wasting time out here. I have to get home.'

'Ah, but you wouldn't be wasting your time, for they say this coast, following the lovely beach round the bay, is truly scenic. God's own country. I tell you what. We'll compromise. We'll take Billy's track from here, if it gets us right on to Herveys Bay, then we can see our way home.'

Jakob looked back. He'd wasted half a day getting this far. Another half-day to return to the Childers route, then set off again.

'How long from here, Billy, if we go on? Exactly.'

'Depend on the river, suppose two, three days.'

'God help us! What river? The Burnett? That's our river.'

'No. River crossing in between.'

Jakob looked at Quinlan. 'How are you crossing rivers without a boat?'

'Not too well, I'm sorry to say. I reckon we ought to camp here by the river. Do a spot of fishing for our supper and turn back in the morning, great is the shame. You sure you wouldn't like to go that much further to swim in the sea?'

'No!' Jakob said emphatically.

Jefferson Philps was not bothered that Hobday had caught him out on that little 'error', since he was assured the letter to Dixon containing his legal advice would not be published. That was Hobday's weak spot. Having given his word, Philps would be willing to bet a hundred to one that Arthur would not renege, so that just left J.B. Dixon, who should be warned that the German had called their bluff. That he could be had up for trespassing if he or any of his men entered Meissner's land without permission. Not that he needed to explain that bit to J.B.

He took a pencil and note pad and prepared to compose a telegram to J.B. that would say neither too much nor too little to the telegraphers and their curious friends in Bundaberg.

After a half-hour of cross-outs and erasings, with an eye to cost, his telegram was finished and handed to his clerk to run with it to the telegraph office. It read:

Regarding timber claims on two non-British leases urgently advise and regret rights of lessee held up under law this day Philps.

The telegraph operator in Bundaberg didn't find it interesting; about as dull a message as you could get, but . . . it was addressed to J.B. Dixon, and that meant money. Normally telegrams for outlying camps, farms and stations went with the mailman in his wagon, on rounds that could take weeks. Not for J.B. Dixon, though. His telegrams were handed to riders with fast horses, who were paid a pound on delivery. A whole quid, split between the telegrapher and the rider he chose. If there was no time-wasting.

He hotfooted it down to the pub to take a good look at the horses hitched to the rails under the big red gum tree, and then marched to the bar.

'Who owns the grey?'

Late that night a rider on a grey horse galloped up to Clonmel homestead, ran up the steps to the veranda, peered in the open front door, put two fingers to his teeth and gave a shrill whistle.

A woman came from the darkened interior, holding a lantern. 'What do you want?'

'Telegram for Mr J.B. Dixon, ma'am.'

'Oh, I see. Good. Hold on a minute.'

He did hold on. He waited as she took the telegram, placed it on a table and went to a drawer, whence she took a cash box. While she went about her routine he looked into the room, interested. This front entrance wasn't a hall or a lobby or anything, it was a sitting room. It was what he'd heard many times, that this house had started as a log cabin with a veranda and all the other rooms had been tacked on like extra pens, for people instead of sheep. He nodded to himself, interested. Now he'd be able to say for himself that the great Clonmel homestead wasn't all that grand. Not like the place his own boss, Charlie Mayhew, was building. Charlie might be only a plantation owner, but one of these days, the rider was sure, he would outrun all these squatters in the money stakes. You bet your life he would.

'Thank you, ma'am,' he said as she counted out the pound in shillings.

'That's all right. Go round the back, the cook's still up. She'll give you a feed. You can sleep over in the men's quarters. Goodnight, and thank you.'

He stuck his hat on his head and jingled the coins into his pocket as he retraced his steps back to his horse. Not a bad night's work, plus a free bed and feed, though he couldn't see what was so urgent in the telegram, which he had, of course, read. Just a folded sheet, why not? He made sure his horse got a good feed too that night. After all, Bluey, his pride and joy, the smartest and prettiest colt this side of the equator, had earned him ten bob for a ride he would have done for nothing, had anyone asked. But there you go, he grinned. These folks out here – more money than sense.

They were in the library, sitting at the long table, poring over newspapers, and stock and station magazines, when Elsie poked her head round the door.

'What's up?' J.B. asked, setting aside his pipe.

'Telegram,' she said, handing it over. 'Can I get you anything before I go to bed, J.B.?'

Keith turned to her. 'We could do with some more port. This decanter's nearly dry.'

'You've had enough already,' J.B. grunted as he opened the telegram.

'No I haven't. It's a particularly good vintage. Who died?'

'No one.' J.B. waited until Elsie had left. 'That bloody German's been and tested our ruling about the logging.' He tossed the telegram across the table.

'What German?'

'For Christ's sake, Keith. The Meissner fellow. At least I think that's what this bloody telegram is about. Don't know why Philps can't write sense.'

Keith nodded, studying the page. 'Yes. It would have to be him.'

'Get into town first thing in the morning, telegraph Philps and wait for the reply. I want this verfied in plain English, and I want to know how he found out.'

Elsie returned with a bottle of port. 'Shall I decant it for you, Keith?'

'No, I'll do it. And what about a couple of sandwiches? Any of that roast beef left over from dinner?'

'Yes, of course. What about you, J.B.? Can I make one for you too?'

'No. I'm going to bed.' He stood, stretching, and peered over his glasses at his son. 'That timber's mine. It's on Clonmel land. I don't care what they say. But by Christ, if that idiot Philps has let them get under his guard, invoking the bloody law, then they're up against me. If I can't have the timber then no one gets it, especially them bloody migrants. Do you get my meaning?'

'Sure do,' Keith grinned as he rummaged in a drawer for a corkscrew.

'But don't go off half-cocked. Check with Philps, get the story straight first.'

Philps was back at the telegraph office in Maryborough to respond to a curt message from Keith Dixon. His reply read:

The subject of my correspondence regarding timber on former Clonmel land sought legal advice here yesterday. He engaged Hobday. Philps.

'Bloody hell!' Keith reread the second telegram, astonished. It had never occurred to him that these people – anyone, for that matter – would question official advice from a lawyer. What was the world coming to? When his father had shown him the letter, instructing him to shove it in the face of that Meissner bloke, he had believed the advice to be correct. Well, why wouldn't he? So what made him really mad now was the fact that the German hadn't believed it. Making a fool of him. Then the cheek of him to actually go to Maryborough and – what was that word? – *engage* a solicitor of his own. Hobday. That holier-than-thou character had shown Philps was wrong. Obviously, J.B. had known that all along, and taken it for granted that his son had known as well. Keith was relieved that he hadn't commented. Made a fool of himself. Because if

Philps really had been right, J.B. wouldn't have accepted Hobday's 'advice' so readily.

Keith realised then that it had been a put-up job. That his father had instructed Philps to write the damn letter, giving J.B.'s version of the rights and wrongs of it. No doubt about it, J.B. was a cunning old bugger. But he didn't like being upstaged. No, sir, not one bit. And the German had won the argument, pulled in his own lawyer to set Philps back on his tail. Not hard to imagine that would have been a surprise and a sock in the eye for Philps, but he was the least of the Dixons' concerns. The timber was the problem. They couldn't let Meissner and all those loggers, including Les Jolly, have it now, have everyone crowing that the German had beaten the Dixons. That was not on. Couldn't be allowed. People had to be shown that the squatters still held the reins out here; they were still the big bosses.

He was riding back across Clonmel land when he met up with three of their stockmen on their way home. He joined them but was in no mood for conversation, too busy thinking of Meissner, having passed within a couple of miles of the German's property, where the timber still stood. If Meissner were in Maryborough yesterday, he could probably be home some time tomorrow. Keith doubted he'd be back yet. And he thought about that.

Suddenly he wheeled his horse about and called to the men to follow, which they did without question. Maybe among themselves they were asking where they were going, but on the Dixon station they learned to jump first, question later.

Keith was excited now, riding fast across open country, challenging the stockmen to put the pace on. They spurred their horses and came after him, but eventually he beat them to Hangman's Point, a rocky outcrop with an obvious history, that was also a warning to riders of rougher country ahead. He slackened his pace then, taking more care as he led them through open woodlands, making for Quinlan's block. He and his father had studied the maps. They knew that the first of the Meissner blocks was on the riverfront, adjacent to

Quinlan's, and the second was inland from there. The cheek of the bastard, taking up two blocks!

They were riding single file now, still moving swiftly, though, dodging trees, taking the horses over fallen logs and gullies, and Keith laughed, calling over his shoulder:

'Keep up, boys!'

He was an expert rider, a star equestrian. His horse was a thoroughbred, maybe lacking the bush skills of their stock horses, but it did as it was told, beautifully, perfectly, so there was no risk to him as his mount shot through the dappled forest of gums, crunching across the forest floor feet deep in dry leaves.

It didn't bother him that in challenging them he was putting his men at risk of a fall; he was too intent on locating the Irishman's land. That would be his starting point.

An hour later, his objective was achieved. He slowed as they rode through the land that had already been logged, where high dry grasses were beginning to hide the stumps.

Sam, one of the Clonmel foremen, moved up to ride beside him.

'Isn't this Quinlan's place, Keith?'

'Top of the class, Sam. This is indeed Quinlan's, to enjoy when he gets out of prison.'

'That bastard,' said Sam. 'To shoot the ram in cold blood, it fair near broke me heart. Lovely animal it was.'

'You can say that again,' Keith said, with genuine regret. 'Duke was almost human. More like a pet.'

'Jesus, yes. And the wool! Christ almighty, did you ever see the like?'

'Irreplaceable. I don't care how many of his lambs the ewes drop, there'll never be another Duke. But I tell you, Sam, we've got another threat to our merinos now.'

'How come?'

'It's happening,' Keith said mysteriously. 'Threats and all. So we're about to hand out a little lesson, warning them to back off.'

'Who?' Sam said, belligerence in his voice. 'You just let me at them, mate.'

They followed the boundary of Quinlan's block, but Keith

213

made no attempt to enter the neighbouring property. Instead he continued, watching for the surveyors' stakes until he found the second block, still an unfenced wilderness. This time he led them boldly past the markers and turned to Sam.

'You reckon you know Clonmel like the back of your hand. Whose property are we on now?'

'This lot's leased by Meissner, the German.'

'Well done. You're good, Sam. I thought I'd trick you. Now – it's this German that's been giving us the threats . . .'

'Why?'

'That's between him and J.B. Our job is to give him a bit of a fright.'

He dismounted, and as the others drew up they did the same, looking to Sam, who, with a wave of his hand, told them to hang on a minute.

Keith began kicking leaves and dry branches into a heap.

'Got a match?' he asked Sam, who handed over his wax matches. Keith lit one and threw it into the heap, watching as it quickly burst into flame.

'Jesus! Look out!' Sam cried, grabbing his arm. 'You'll start a bloody bush fire. The place is as dry as a chip.'

'Meissner thinks he can pull the same stunt as Quinlan, without getting caught. Our merino rams are precious, Sam, we can't stand guard over them indefinitely. Haven't you noticed they've been guarded day and night lately?'

'Jesus! Can't say I have, Keith.'

'You probably get in too tired of a night.'

'That'd be right.'

'So. We have to show we're not as vulnerable as these foreigners think. The wind's blowing that way. Exactly right for us. Don't be worrying, Sam. They've got the river on their side, it's a fair fight.'

Keith's fire was crackling away merrily, but the other men were just standing staring at it, confused.

Sam took Keith aside, lowering his voice. 'We better be careful here. That bloke over there in the leather waistcoat, don't you know who he is?'

'No.'

214

'It's Fechner. The German. He probably knows this Meissner bloke.'

Keith turned slowly, deliberately, so as not to register any surprise or irritation. He tipped his hat back, already feeling the heat from the fired grasses.

'So it is,' he drawled. Jesus! Hanni's husband! What a bloody nuisance. But then, what could *he* do? He was a dumb bastard anyway, bringing a woman like that on to a sheep station. There wasn't a man alive who wouldn't want to root her.

'Hey, Lucas!' he called. 'We're burning off. Take this branch, light it up and fire the scrub across there, and the rest of you go that way in a straight line. Watch the wind. We can't have it blowing back on us. Sam, get the horses out of the way. Come on, everyone, move it. I'm thirsting for a beer, we'll have a half-dozen bottles all to ourselves when we get home.'

Lucas was irritated by this stroke of bad luck. If they hadn't come across Keith they'd be home by now. He would have had a chance to spend a rare afternoon with his wife. Poor Hanni, she was so lonely. Bad enough that talk about her and this Keith fellow; lately she'd been so withdrawn that Lucas had become terrified that the stories might be true.

He'd put it to her very carefully. Very mildly. 'Hanni, dear, I worry that you don't love me any more. You barely let me touch you lately.'

'I'm just tired,' she snapped.

'And irritable,' he told her. 'There are so many men here, I worry sometimes you might find someone more interesting than your Lucas.'

'Oh for God's sake! I suppose Theo told you that one.'

'What's it got to do with Theo?'

Hanni burst into tears. 'He was rude to me. He accused me of flirting with other men, and now you are doing the same thing. I hate you. I hate you all.'

It took days to overcome the damage that conversation had caused. She was furious with him and barely spoke to him, and even when she'd calmed down, she was still cool with him. No longer the loving wife.

'What is wrong now?' he'd asked, only to be told she was unhappy, she hated living on the station. She wanted to leave.

'Get a move on, Lucas!' Sam yelled at him now, as he stood staring into the grass fire.

'Yes. Sorry!' He picked up a dry branch, lit it from the burning grass and, using it as a torch, set fire to the grasses in front of him.

Still unsure of what they were about, he turned to Pike, the other stockman. 'What is this burning off?'

'We burn off dry grasses so they don't flare up on their own and start real bush fires. Cleans the rubbish out.'

Lucas nodded, and at Sam's direction lit more small fires until these were fairly blazing along, helped by a westerly wind. He stood back then, wondering how long this would take, and Pike sidled over to him. 'The silly bugger, he's lighting so many fires over there on his side he'll have a real bush fire on his hands after all.'

'Who? Keith?'

'Yeah. Not overloaded with brains, he ain't. Burning off is a controlled fire, mate. You're watching one that is fast getting out of hand.'

'Shouldn't we warn him?'

'Sam's over there. He'll slow him down.'

Lucas could hardly see the others now for the smoke, so he began backing away from the grass fires. Suddenly there was a roar, and the low-level fire seemed to burst into life all around them as trees went up like torches. It happened so fast he tripped trying to escape the heat, and by the time he was back on his feet, the furnace was all around him. Lucas ran! He tore back from the flames and battled through the smoke to emerge right beside Sam, who was arguing with Pike.

'It's nothing to do with you,' Sam said. 'The horses are safe. Keith's taken them further out. Now we just get out of here.'

'What sort of bloody idiot would start a bloody fire like that on his own land?' Pike spat angrily.

'It's not his land,' Sam grinned. 'It's Meissner's.'

'That's bloody criminal!'

'Shut your mouth, Pike. We're goin' home.'

Lucas stumbled past them, searching for the horses, the smoke clearing now as the fire raced across a wide line of bush. He caught up with Keith, who was still leading them away, and grabbed his arm.

'Whose land is this?'

'Get your hands off me. It's Clonmel property.'

'No it's not. It's Meissner's. You're burning Meissner's land!'

'We're not burning anything. Grass fires start up all over the place in this dry weather.' His grin was a leer.

Lucas saw more than the bare-faced lies in that man's face; he saw the contempt that Keith Dixon held him in as he shrugged and moved on, and he knew by that gloating leer that the contempt had something to do with Hanni. With her husband's weakness, even now. His inability to do anything about these situations.

But Keith was wrong. Slow to anger, Lucas was now in a rage. He lashed out, pulling Keith back with one hand and punching him with the other. The horses bumped and plunged to get away from them as Keith barrelled into Lucas, punching and kicking. Lucas knew he had no time to waste. He clasped both hands together over his left shoulder and brought them down on Keith with all his strength, poleaxing the man as he was about to stand again. Then he ran for his horse.

Sam was back, pulling Keith to his feet. Pike grabbed the other horses.

'Which way is the river?' Lucas gasped.

'That way! What the hell are you doing, Lucas?'

'You're fired!' Keith was screaming. 'I own that bloody animal. Get back here with my stock horse. Sam, get my rifle . . .'

But Lucas was on his way. What a fool he was! He was almost sobbing at his own stupidity. He should have known these were Jakob's blocks. They'd been pointed out to him before by other stockmen, but this time they'd come towards them from a different direction, from a large logged area which he'd taken to be still part of Clonmel, and then they'd trailed back towards home territory from there. Stupid!

He had to warn Jakob. Nothing much he could do about this end of the land, which was still blazing furiously, but he

217

had heard that Jakob had the beginnings of a farm near to the river, which was several miles away yet. He had to try to help. Maybe they'd have time to burn the grasses back towards the fire to create a break. The air was so full of smoke, his horse was spluttering as they cantered towards the inferno ahead of them, letting Lucas know that this was not a good idea.

True enough, he thought: we can't ride into it, we have to get round it somehow. As he watched, he was appalled at the speed of this fire, and terrified of it. Looking up, he could see it leaping from treetop to treetop like a fiery trapeze act. What if the wind changed and it turned on him? Trees were blazing all around him. All the beautiful timber that people were always talking about up here. He pulled the horse to a standstill, or tried to. It danced about angrily, as if urging him to make up his mind what to do. What had possessed him to attack Keith Dixon? He'd only made matters worse. He couldn't stop this fire, and he doubted if Jakob could either. It would probably burn itself out before it even got near the river, anyway.

He heard a roar as another huge tree was torched. And maybe it wouldn't. But what about Hanni? At least she'd get her way. He'd lost his job. What would happen now?

Lucas was becoming confused and disoriented. The sun was blotted out now and he was just walking the horse through the devastation, a blackened graveyard. There was no way round it; this fire had arms miles wide, and furnaces for feet, and the blazing head of a Gorgon. It would beat him to the river. Why was he bothering? Would he get there in time to tell Jakob he'd helped to light the fire? Why not just go back, collect Hanni and leave that place? He'd tripped himself up as usual by leading with his lip instead of his head. What had he accused Keith of? Oh God! What if this was all just a mistake? Who could tell in this endless damn country, where everything looked alike, where thousands of identical gum trees stood before thousands and thousands more? It was not unusual for people to get lost, and no wonder, with no landmarks like at home for guidance. Even the stars were different. He would have to learn about these stars. They would help.

There was a green patch in front of him. It reminded Lucas

of the backdrop of the stage at the Lutheran Hall back home, so fake as to be outlandish, but there it was. A corridor of that waist-high grass like skirts of wheat, of trees with bark hanging from them like paper, begging to be burned, of green gumtips drooping languidly in long threads towards the forest bed, for all the world a condescending presence, unfazed by the furore around it, as if to say that it had seen it all before.

Lucas went for it. He leapt on to the horse, dug in his heels and went through the gap at full gallop. The horse, though, was a brumby, a wild one, caught and tamed, not bred to the paddocks, and these horses came with a kitbag full of tricks. Its eyes flared in fear at the walls of fire on each side of them, and its ears flattened down to cut out the noise, the clamour of this terrifying fire that seemed to be closing in on it. High in the treetops the fire was creating its own wind now, hurling sparks about in a flurry of smoke and ash. Had the dust storm not put an end to the stockmen's attempts to capture brumbies, Lucas might have had a chance to learn more about their habits, but that was an opportunity missed.

The horse began to pull back, fighting its rider's urging, but Lucas would not allow a retreat. He hadn't noticed that the gap was narrowing; he was too intent on forcing the horse to keep going. But then, through the smoke and the haze, the horse saw the gully ahead of them, knew it would be too wide to jump and too deep to take at this pace, so reached for a trick well known to experienced stockmen. It came to a halt, at the same time dropping its forelegs almost to a kneeling position, and Lucas had no chance. He went straight over the horse's head and crashed into the gully, where weedy growth was already smouldering.

For a minute the horse stared down, but the man was very still, so it swerved away and bolted, not forward into that furnace, but back to safety, picking its way across the blackened countryside, bridle trailing, until it came to clean land, where it nosed about for some nourishment in the scattered thickets.

This smoke, from a distant fire somewhere in the countryside, had a distinctive aroma of eucalypts, Freda noted, but more strongly charged than that of fresh leaves. She took particular notice of all these things to do with the bush, for reference, to help herself in dealing with their new surrounds. Her journal was already filled with descriptions of birds and plants, most still waiting for someone who might be able to give them a name.

She finished watering the vegetable garden, having allowed it barely enough to survive, and sat on the back step, exhausted. Karl was carrying on clearing bush where the loggers had left off, and Freda promised herself she'd take him up a billy of tea in a minute, because he did work so hard. But not just now, it had taken hours to water this garden. She wondered why she kept on planting, but rains had to come soon.

They both missed Jakob. They hadn't seen a soul since he left, except for the Aborigine messenger boy who'd come out to tell them that Jakob had gone on to Maryborough.

Freda sighed. That only meant one thing. That he'd failed to get any support in Bundaberg.

'What good can he do in Maryborough?' Karl had asked.

'I don't know. How far away is that place?'

'About seventy miles, I think. Or more.'

'God in heaven, seventy miles of wilderness! He could get lost or attacked. He'll be away for days. Where will he sleep? I tell you, if I'd had any say in this, he wouldn't be going off on a wild-goose chase. Wasting time, I'd say. Those awful station people, wouldn't you think they'd let poor people like us have the timber? They've got plenty of money. They don't need it.'

Now she took off her hat and mopped her forehead with a cloth, glancing up to see a few scraps of ash floating on the breeze, and that had her worrying about the fire. How close was it? Hard to tell. The bush surrounding the house was quiet and serene. The birds were especially quiet, though that wasn't unusual on these warm afternoons.

'Missus! Missus!'

Freda spun around to see Mia running towards her. She had the child in its sling on her back but that didn't stop her grabbing at Freda, pulling her away.

'Fire, missus. Come quick.'

'Where to? Where's the fire?'

The black girl was pointing frantically and still trying to drag Freda in the other direction.

'Just a minute,' Freda was saying to her, showing that there was no need to panic. 'I can smell the fire. But it's a long way away. You stay here, I'll take a look. I could walk up the creek and see if anything's happening in our direction.'

But then Karl came running, and with him Mia's husband, Yarrupi.

'Mum, he says the fire is very close. I climbed a tree with him. It's huge. Stretches for miles across and coming this way fast. We have to get down to the river.'

'The creek is just here,' she told them. 'We'll be all right there.'

'No, missus. No,' Yarrupi said. 'Go now.'

The enormity of it suddenly hit Freda. 'What are they saying? That we won't be safe here, Karl? That we won't be safe in our home? Our house! All our things! No . . . this can't be right.'

'I'm sure everything will be all right,' Karl said to her. 'But that wind is hot. We'll be cooler down at the river.'

'Don't be absurd! We can shelter in the house.'

'No, missus!' Mia cried. 'House allasame burn up. Go now! Quick, please.'

Freda turned to Karl and screamed: 'What did she say? That the house will burn? No! I won't believe that. If Jakob was here they wouldn't be frightening us like this. Tell them to go away.'

'Lissen, missus,' Yarrupi said, and as she stood back, bewildered, Freda heard the sound of an approaching bush fire for the first time. To her ears the sound was like a chimney on fire, but it was unreal, because there was no fire to be seen and right here, her own chimney, the brick stack against a wall of greying logs, was cold. It was still difficult to believe a fire threatened.

More minutes were wasted when she ran into the house to escape their panic, looking about at what she might take with her should it be necessary to evacuate. The old family bible, with its memorabilia, the worn valise that held Jakob's business papers – they caught her eye so she picked them up. Then she grabbed their money tin and stood there, too confused to make any more decisions. This could not be happening.

But the sky had turned into a canopy of sparks and flying leaves and she was running with them then, running down the wagon track to the river, hearing that monster behind them bearing down like a tidal wave. The noise was real and terrifying now, but they couldn't look back to the house, to their vegetable garden, as the track twisted and turned through the bush.

They were safe in the river, grateful for the ancient mangrove swamps that effectively barred the fire from invading the shelter they shared with forest animals. Dingoes lay panting in the mud, ignoring the koalas and kangaroos that sought safety in the shallows in front of the humans, who stood waist-deep in the water, crocodiles forgotten in this crisis. Yarrupi had brought the cow to safety, but there was no hope for the chickens.

Freda wept. She watched their farmland, their farm, succumb to the roar and blaze of the huge bush fire. Saw the evil glow reflected in the river, on this, the worst day of her life. Their ship of dreams burned to the waterline. They were ruined. What would Jakob say? What use his defiance of the Clonmel people now? She looked about her at the animals as they watched the burned shores nervously, and felt a surge of pity. How many of the forest folk had died in that furnace? Trees gone, birds' nests with them; the lizard community, so shy and harmless. And what about all the rest of the animals, with so few representatives left here now? The devastation was so awful that when Mia said they could come out now, Freda was sick. She vomited right there in the water and it was all round her, but Mia walked her forward and splashed her clean. Always meticulous, Freda determined that as soon as they got back to the house, the very first thing she would do was wash off this mud, tidy herself up, put on a fresh blouse and skirt and only then see what damage the fire had caused.

Afterwards she couldn't imagine what she could have been thinking of, to have that plan in mind as they tramped up the banks, because there was no house. There was only the chimney, standing blackened against a nightmare of scorched earth.

The old man watched them ride in. He took a short cut through the stables to the sheds adjacent to the horse paddock, waited until they'd released their horses and stowed their saddles and bridles under cover, then gave a light whistle.

His son looked up, nodded and walked over to him.

'Grass fires over near our east boundary,' Keith said, with mock gravity. 'Bad luck, eh?'

'Did Philps confirm that the German got a new ruling?'

'Yes. He engaged the other solicitor, Hobday, who must have pointed him in the right direction. Obviously let him know we don't have a claim on the timber now. But it was a worth a try, J.B. The German could have saved himself a lot of trouble if he'd settled for Philps' instructions, not gone haring off to complicate things.'

J.B. grunted agreement. 'Sam and Pike, they were with you?'

'Yes, but they're on side,' he grinned. 'Sam got it in his head that the German was out to shoot more of our stud merinos, so he was all for teaching him a lesson. Pike's all right. He's been around too long to stick his nose in our business.'

'See he doesn't.'

'I'm just about to shout them a few beers. Thirsty work today!'

Several hours later, when he was inspecting the work of carpenters who were repairing the raised sheep runs in preparation for the shearing season, one of the carpenters drew his attention to a lone horse, still saddled and trailing a bridle, that was ambling across the plain.

J.B. climbed up on a rail to get a better look.

'What the hell's that horse doing out there?' He jerked his head at a passing stockman. 'Bring him in.'

When the errant stock horse was brought to him, J. B. was curious.

'Easy now, feller,' he said as he examined the animal for injuries. 'You're all right. You're a good boy for coming on home, aren't you?'

He removed the saddle and dumped it on the ground, still talking soothingly to the horse, then he turned to the stockman.

'Who was riding this feller today?'

'I don't know.'

'Then bloody well find out! His rider could be out there hurt. He could have had a fall.'

Word came back that the rider had been Lucas Fechner, the German, and immediately J.B. heard warning bells in his head. He went in search of Sam.

'How come Fechner's horse came wandering in but no Fechner?'

Sam guessed immediately that Keith hadn't told the old man about his run-in with Fechner, and he worried that J.B. might not know about the fire either. The last thing he needed was to get caught in the centre of an argument between father and his son. He shoved his hat back and scratched his head, trying to think of a suitable reply, but J.B. cut in.

'Was he with you over there at the boundary?'

'Who, Fechner?'

'No, the man in the moon! Of course Fechner. Was he with you?'

'Yes. He helped us with the burning off.'

'He helped you? Even though the land belonged to one of his mates? Don't lie to me, Sam, or you'll be booted off Clonmel double quick.'

Sam sucked in his breath. 'Look . . . he didn't know at the time. We were going all right when he must have got his bearings. He got a bit nasty with Keith once the place was alight, so Keith fired him.'

'Lovely! Bloody lovely! So where is he now? And what's the horse doing wandering about the countryside on its own?'

'I don't know where he is now, but when Keith sacked him, he reminded him that his horse belonged to Clonmel. He

224

might have sent it home from out there, somewhere close, rather than come in.'

'And he might have joined the circus, you pack of bloody idiots,' J.B. said, storming away.

He found his son on the veranda outside his room, snoozing in a canvas chair, and brought him awake by kicking the chair and causing it to collapse in a heap.

'What the hell do you think you're doing?' Keith shouted at him. 'That's not funny.'

J.B. grabbed his son by the shirt and snarled at him: 'There's nothing funny in taking a German along to help you burn out a German's timber. Are you out of your bloody mind?'

Keith shook himself loose. 'He was just trailing along behind Sam and Pike. It could have been any one of our blokes.'

'But it wasn't, was it? It was Fechner. And now that we're getting down to it, what's that bruise on your face?'

'He caught me from behind when I wasn't looking; we had a bit of a punch-up, so I sacked him. What else did you expect me to do?'

'I didn't expect you to get us in this bloody mess in the first place.'

'It was your idea to fire Meissner's land.'

'But not to take along a hostile witness. Where's Fechner now?'

'How do I know?'

'His horse came in.'

'Good. I warned him it wasn't his.'

'Good? So you and Sam Stupid out there think he took being sacked like a man and somehow returned the horse?'

'Sounds like it.'

'You don't think he went off to warn Meissner?'

'He could have.'

'So, he goes off to warn Meissner, returns the horse and leaves his wife here. You're a bloody maniac! You never get anything right! Now you listen to me. When Fechner comes back, if he hasn't fallen off his horse and broken his bloody neck, don't you talk to him. I will. I'll sort this out.'

Keith lowered his voice. 'What if he has had a fall?'

225

J.B. thought about that for a few minutes. 'Get Sam and Pike and go looking for him.'

'Now? It's late. It's dinner time!'

'The riderless horse came in. Everyone will know about it. We have to react. Go looking for him to the east, but don't cross into Meissner's land, even if it is burned to a crisp. I'll send another gang somewhere out in that direction too, but not as far; they can go more to the north.'

'And if we find him?'

'Then you bring him in, and don't you lay a bloody hand on him.'

Elsie came into the kitchen just as Cook was about to serve the soup.

'Mr Dixon wanted me to have a word with you, Hanni. It seems there's been a mishap. Nothing for you to get upset about really. These things happen . . .'

'What happened?' Cook asked sharply.

'Lucas's horse has come in without him.'

'You mean he got throwed?'

'He could have; not necessarily, though. He might have just dismounted and the horse got away on him. Wandered off, one might say.'

'So where is Lucas?' Hanni asked them.

'Probably walking home,' Elsie said. 'He might have to cover some distance, so he'll be late.'

'Have they sent anyone out to look for him?' Cook asked.

'Yes, of course. Mr Dixon sent two search parties out, they'll find him. So don't you be worrying, Hanni.'

Strangely, she wasn't worried. Not as much as the last time, anyway. She thought he was probably lost again, only this time without a horse, but he knew the station a lot better now, he'd find his way home. She hoped he would hurry up. She didn't like being in that room on her own at night now.

'He'll be all right,' Cook said, to comfort her. 'But the men's cookhouse will probably have shut down by the time he gets in. I'll put up a plate of tucker for him and you can take it down to your room, Hanni. Have it waiting for him.'

'Thank you.'

Then Elsie remembered that Keith had gone out with the search party, so she passed on that information to Cook. 'Only three of us for dinner then. Give me that tray, Hanni, I'll take in the soup.'

Hanni shuddered as she passed over the large tray. She was suddenly frightened at the thought of Mr Keith searching for Lucas, wanting to help him.

'I don't think so,' she muttered to herself, finding an excuse to retreat to the pantry. 'Oh, Lucas, be careful.'

In the morning there was talk of an extensive bush fire near the eastern boundary of Clonmel, with only minor damage to station land, but there was no sign of Lucas.

J.B. sent out fresh search parties, instructing one group to ride further on to land owned by Mr Meissner, to see what sort of damage the fire had caused him, if any, and ask if he'd seen Fechner.

'While you're there, see if they need a hand with anything. They might be foreigners but they're still neighbours. We're here to help if we can.'

'Good on you J.B.,' the men said, and set out on their tasks. They scanned the countryside, watching for a man on foot, and kept on going until they came to the burned-out boundaries, shaking their heads at the destruction that confronted them.

'No grass fire here, mates,' one man said. 'She's a full-scale bush fire took hold, I'd say.'

They headed into the smoky ruins of the woodlands, dismounting every now and then to investigate and stamp out the smouldering residue, for fear the wind would gather the sparks and give life to another fire. They tied kerchiefs around their faces to ward off the stench of stale smoke and ash and the all-pervading stink of death, for too many native animals and reptiles had had no chance against the fire. In fact, they could see stark burned trees that held the blackened shapes of little koalas still clinging to their branches.

This was a melancholy duty. They forgot Lucas, passing right by the gully where he lay, and pushed on, making for the river, where they hoped this mayhem must have ended, eventually coming upon a burned-out homestead.

That gave them a fright. They searched about, but there were no bodies, so that was a relief. They kicked around the devastated farm clearing for a while, wondering what had become of the folk who lived there, but there was no sign of life at all, so they rode glumly on for a half-hour or so until someone noticed they were on the Irishman's land.

'Just as well the boss got the timber out of here in time. A lot of good it would have been to Quinlan now.'

'Who's Quinlan?' one of the stockmen asked.

'He's the bugger that shot Duke. Our prize merino.'

'Jesus! Well, this'll give him his comeuppance!'

'When he hears about it. He's in the clink. We'd better turn back. We'll follow the river past the burnt-out country, then fan out inland looking for Lucas. I don't know where the hell he's got to.'

'Probably home by now.'

'That'd be right, and us riding about like we got nothin' better to do.'

'I heard there was some competition between Keith and Lucas for the wife's favours. Maybe Keith don't want him found.'

'And maybe you ought to mention that to J.B. Get your face shoved in.'

They were very kind to her; Cook, Elsie, even Mrs Dixon. They let her off work. They let her sit in the sun with a stack of magazines and some tea and cake. But Hanni was scared. Really scared now.

'Something has happened to Lucas, I know it,' she said to Cook, who hushed her and talked to her about how big this station was.

'That's why they're away for days on end, even with their fast horses, dear. Walking, a man would be doing it hard.'

'With no food too.'

'There's food. You'd be surprised. You ask Lulla – she'll tell you. Her mob, the Aborigines, they never had no sheep and no veggie gardens, and they didn't starve. I'll send her round to talk to you.'

Lulla, the scullery maid, came, bringing an offering of a string bag she'd made of reeds for Hanni.

She listened to Hanni's worries, her fears for Lucas, without comment, letting her talk on, and then eventually she looked squarely at Hanni, her dark eyes suffused with sorrow.

'You bloody good scared of the boss, missy.'

'No.' Hanni was startled. 'Which boss? What is this you say?'

'Mr Keith. He frighten you, missy?'

'Why would you say that, Lulla? That's silly.'

'How silly I see you jump frighten whenever they speak his name. You bloody scared alri'. He get at you too?'

'What?'

Lulla, all of seventeen years old, now seemed to Hanni to be as old as Methuselah. She had the face of ages in her dark lined skin, and from her eyes shone a wisdom that Hanni both pitied and envied. But she could not admit her humiliation, the shocking, shocking shame, to anyone, let alone this black girl.

'I don't know what you're talking about,' she managed to say with huff in her voice, but Lulla took her hand.

'You never tell your husban', girl?' she said sorrowfully. 'Course you didna. What he say? What he say? You bad girl! How he say? Boss spit on him. Git out then nobody person.'

'Please, Lulla. Haven't I got enough trouble? Lucas is missing. He's lost somewhere out there. He may have fallen from his horse. Hurt himself.'

Lulla didn't press the issue, but Hanni now knew that she was only one of Keith's victims. Aborigine girls would be as helpless as she was . . . seduced by his phoney charm. His vicious charm.

Later on, when there was still no word of Lucas and the afternoon was fading, Lulla came down to her again.

'You want me come stay in your room tonight, missy?'

Hanni was about to turn her away, but she realised that the chair under the doorknob wouldn't be much protection from that man if he decided to visit her.

'Would you? Please?' she said, and then she was crying, trying to stop, crying and crying. From fear. From panic.

From terrible remorse. She was no longer frightened of Keith Dixon. Hanni was weeping for her dear Lucas. What had happened to him? What had they done to him? She blamed herself. She was convinced that somehow, to suit his purpose, Keith Dixon had done away with Lucas.

That night, in the waiting for news of Lucas, she talked to Lulla. She learned that Keith considered Aborigine women fair game for his sexual gratification, and that the Aborigines guessed that she would also be a target.

'Just like the last white girl,' Lulla said, 'but that girl no married. So doan you go tellin' me he didna get at you, Hanni.'

Hanni digested this information, stunned to find that his attentions had nothing to do with her prettiness, her good looks. She was just another female; young, more or less available. It infuriated her. Humiliated her even more.

She didn't actually admit he had 'got at her', as Lulla put it, because she could never tell anyone in the whole wide world what he'd done to her, but she stopped denying it, so now Lulla knew.

'They know about him up there at the house,' Lulla said.

'About me?' Hanni almost yelled in fright.

'No. About him and our girls. He comes down to our camp some nights. Grabs a girl. Pays men for us. Nuttin' we can do. Old boss, he doan care. Missus Dixon, she care. She scream and yell. I reckon, you go to Missus Dixon, she woan let him touch you no more.'

'And have my husband find out? No! And you keep quiet too, Lulla. As soon as Lucas comes back, we're getting out of here.'

Late that night there was a knock at the door and the two girls were instantly awake. Lulla, lying across the bottom of the double bed, was the first to react.

'Who's there?' she shouted in a voice loud enough to wake the dead, but there was no answer. And there were no more knocks at Hanni's door that night.

In the morning, with still no word of Lucas, Hanni was so terribly upset, she wouldn't talk to anyone but Lulla, so Elsie assigned the Aborigine girl to take care of her until this crisis was resolved.

The search party reported to J.B. Dixon as soon as they returned. He dismissed them without comment and went back to his study to mull this over. He wasn't concerned that the Meissner farmhouse had been burned down. 'It was only a log cabin anyway,' he muttered to himself. 'The remains of our old shepherd's hut. Not worth a bean.' But he would like to know where Fechner had got to. Obviously the Meissners had fled from the fire, taken refuge somewhere, but was Fechner with them? The wife was still here, that should bring him back, plus his wage payout, so where was he? If he had suffered an accident there'd be further complications, real difficulties, and all because his fool of a son hadn't noticed the third stockman. He supposed he'd have to send another search party out now, to keep up appearances, and since the last lot had checked out the Meissner property, he'd send these men to search all the countryside between the homestead and Meissner's. There was every chance that Fechner had let the horse get away on him and was wandering about, lost again.

He tapped his fingers on the windowsill as he stood, deep in thought, looking out at the wild ducks that were sailing serenely on the lagoon. J.B. had always found this view very pleasant and restful, especially since he'd planted the row of willows that now stood gracefully to the left of it, leading the eye across the Clonmel countryside. It was by no means restful today, though. If they couldn't find Fechner soon, he'd have no choice but to report him missing . . . to the police, dammit! His men would take that for granted.

That night he collared his son again. 'Three days tomorrow! Fechner will have been missing for three days. I can't hold out from reporting him missing for more than another day or so. Word will filter back through the stockmen in their dealings with neighbouring stations. So. I want you to get out there tomorrow, on your own, and find him. Dead or alive. He could be sheltering with the Meissners, hurt or something, that's why he hasn't come back yet. But someone would have sent word to his wife. You go and search, ask about, find the bastard.'

J.B. sighed. At least the weather was warming up now, the temperature rising fast, scarcely bothering with spring. It would be kind to the shorn sheep. He would be forever grateful, J.B. mused, that his father had pioneered this Burnett River district, far enough north to escape bad winters and far enough south to avoid the tropical hazards. But now that perfect climate looked like spelling the end of the great sheep and cattle stations round here, by enticing settlers to that port of Bundaberg.

'Bloody settlers!' he snorted. 'Worse than grasshoppers.'

Chapter Nine

Between them Rolf and Rosie were building a fence around their cottage. A sort of picket fence, but they had no neatly sawn timber for such a project so they were using sticks; solid, chest-high sticks, lashed together with rawhide. Thomas could only sit and laugh. He thought it was the worst fence he'd ever seen. Skinny and knobbly. Uneven. Wouldn't keep out a kitten. But they persevered. It wasn't meant to keep out kittens; its duty was to give dignity to their cottage, to give it a finished look instead of leaving it undefended, stuck in a wretched landscape on a hillside laid bare by clearing, except for those inevitable stumps, gross reminders of magical forests.

Rosie understood this had to be. That ugly as her surrounds might be now, the greenery would grow back, if not the aged trees, and cover the graveyard of stumps. She also knew that when Rolf found time, he would take on the massive job of burning out or hauling away those stumps so she wouldn't have them looking at her as if she were part of their ruination. She wouldn't dream of mentioning this, but she found their dismal surrounds rather sad.

'One day,' Rolf told her, 'this land of ours will be worth a lot of money, just across from the town.'

'If the town lasts,' Thomas put in. 'Once the loggers go it won't be worth much. Except for the squatters, and they can go back to overlanding.'

'It'll stay,' Rolf said firmly, his chin jutting, the way it did when he wanted to be right.

They were on the side section of the fence when Rosie sniffed the air. 'I can smell fire.'

'Someone's burning off,' Thomas said. 'I heard Les Jolly say folk ought to go easy on burning off these days. He says the country is too dry. He even said you shouldn't go burning stumps unless you stand and watch.'

'You'd be good at that,' Rolf said. 'We need a new post-hole there, Thomas; go and dig it for us or Rosie will take the whip to you.'

'All right.' Thomas walked over and picked up a shovel, but then became more aware of the fire, searching the skies for smoke.

'Over there,' he told them, pointing.

Rolf looked up too. 'Yes. The other side of the river; I think.'

The fence forgotten for a while, they tramped through the scrub for ten minutes until they came to the river. By then they could see a bush fire in all its force, flames dancing above the trees and gusts of wind blowing ash in all directions.

'It's a terrible fire,' Rosie said nervously, grateful for the river and the distance that separated them from it, but Rolf was worried.

'I think it's near Jakob's land. Let's go up further and see.'

'No it's not,' Thomas said. 'Jakob's farm is much closer.'

'Oh dear, I hope so,' Rosie worried. 'Wasn't their farm almost opposite the landing?'

Other folk were coming down to the river bank to see the fire, and they were all headed for the landing. Rolf broke into a run! It *was* Jakob's land, he was sure, and quite probably the blocks either side too.

The smoke made it difficult to work out what was happening across the river, but Rolf saw some people emerge from the bush, Freda among them, and crossed himself in relief. Then a man struggled through, dragging a cow. He tied it to a half-submerged log at the water's edge and ran, urging the others into the river, for safety. Rolf thought he could see Karl, but there was no sign of Jakob.

'Where's the boat?' he cried to the people who were also standing there, agonising at their inability to assist neighbours in peril.

'Never around when you want it,' a man groaned. 'Could we make a raft?'

'And do what with it?' a woman snapped. 'They're safe in the water so far. Are you thinking to drown them as well? Better you men look to them sparks floating overhead, before we lose our homes too.'

Rosie took her arm. 'Do you think their house has been burned down, Mrs Croft?'

'Had to be, Mrs Kleinschmidt. Can't see it surviving that fire. But don't be upsetting yourself. Looks as if your friends are clear.'

'But they're not. I can't see Jakob anywhere.'

Mrs Croft turned to Rolf. 'There's a new boathouse upriver. They say it belongs to Charlie Mayhew. Don't know if he's got a boat in there yet, but it's worth a look. It's about a mile up that way, beyond the bend.'

Rolf kissed Rosie. 'Nothing you can do here but fret; you go on home with Thomas, I'll see if there's a boat. We have to find one somewhere, so we can bring them across here.'

There was talk in the town of a grass fire out on the river flats. Nothing of any great interest; no reports of stock losses, or crops. Even small crops. The sawmills were all accounted for. Just a bush fire, they said, triggered by this dry weather. A self-starter that must have fizzled out at the banks of the Burnett.

Then the Welshman, Llew Edwards, rode into town to tell of a fire that had burnt out half of his neighbour's property.

'Got halfway across Mike Quinlan's land, it did, and me standing there with but a few buckets to defend my farm from the monster when the wind changed, blew it back on itself, until it had the river to face and it was all over. I tell you, mates, I went down on my knees and thanked the Lord for my salvation, for my maize crop was right in line. Acres and acres of maize, the biggest crop I ever planted in all my born days, and it'll be a bumper. I never want a fright like that again.'

Jules Stenning carried the story home to his wife.

'I thought there had to be bush fires somewhere,' she said. 'It would have started as a grass fire, the land being tinder-dry now, but then burst into a bush fire, frightening the daylights out of Llew Edwards. It died before it got to his maize crop.'

'Was it on Clonmel land?'

'No, thank God. It was on Quinlan's block, and Meissner's, by the sound of things. Do you know, that damn German came into my office the other day, even though I was closed, giving cheek.'

'What about?'

'Trying to pitch some hard-luck story about J.B. Dixon. I sent him off with a flea in his ear.'

Nora Stenning heard this conversation. She was furious that her father could be so unfeeling. She ran down the back yard to the stables, saddled her horse and headed out to what had become known in the town as the German commune, a name neither complimentary nor critical, for most of the folk here in Bundaberg understood and accepted the influx of Danes and Germans, along with the British, as necessary to the economy of the area. As her father had often said, 'All we need to get Bundaberg going is muscle.'

The immigrants had plenty of that, Nora mused, and they weren't afraid of hard work. Language didn't seem to be a barrier either. Somehow people got along, they figured things out . . . just as she and Walther had. She smiled at that thought, as her horse cantered out on to Taylor's Road.

'It's really sad that Walther's poor as well,' she said, needing to hear her sentiments spoken aloud, as if rehearsing what she might say to her parents one of these days. 'But I have faith in him, I know he'll do well eventually. And as for the religion . . .'

Words failed her there. She had no idea how to overcome that impasse. Her parents were Church of England. High Church, they said, and that amused Nora, since the little wooden church in Bourbong Street was hardly a cathedral. In fact it was much the same as the church Father Beitz was building on their property. He was using the same builders, so Nora supposed that was why the plan looked so similar. She wondered mischievously if there was a High Lutheran Church.

One thing's for sure, she added to her cogitations as she neared the German settlement: they can stop trying to throw me at Keith Dixon. I don't care how much money he's got, I wouldn't marry that wretch in a fit.

Walther was overjoyed to see her. He always was, and that was such a thrill for her. No one else had ever made such a fuss over her before. No one had ever told her she was beautiful before either, not that Nora expected such compliments, because she knew she was a plain girl. Hadn't she heard her parents remark on that often enough? Sometimes Nora studied herself in the mirror to try to disprove that claim, and on occasion she could convince herself that though she was plain, with straight mousy hair, a rather large mouth for a lady, and nondescript eyes, she wasn't ugly. She really wasn't. She just couldn't compete with her mother's good looks, that was all. Jayne Stenning had glorious black hair, big brown eyes and the creamiest skin. She was known to all as a great beauty . . .

'Today you are so *schön*, so beautiful,' Walther was saying, and Nora sighed, melting. She began to tell him what she had heard in town, but he was so excited by his own news, she decided hers could wait a few minutes.

He hurried her along the path to the clearing they'd made near the creek, telling her that the builders had come at last to build the church. They'd arrived only yesterday, with the timber, and they were all working so hard the church would be finished in no time.

'See!' he said, standing back, and Nora shared his delight. The skeleton of a church was already in place, a tiny building, even smaller than the Church of England one in town, but true to the plan.

'It's wonderful!' she said, truly impressed, because it was the prettiest setting, in among the trees with the light filtering down upon it as if beaming on their endeavours.

Father Beitz came over to join them, and Nora found herself caught up in their excitement, until she remembered her mission.

'Father, I have sad news for you. Please, just a minute . . . listen to me.' She had to take his arm to stop him dashing

237

away to oversee the carpenters. 'There was a bush fire out along the river. Quite a big one.'

'Yes. The black boys told us.'

'But the fire burned out Mr Meissner's land, Father.'

Walther was shocked. 'Are you sure?'

'Yes. I'm sorry.'

'Were they hurt?'

'Not as far as I know. No one said.'

'Jakob Meissner is in Maryborough. He's not back yet,' Walther said. 'Oh mercy, what can we do?'

'Mrs Meissner and Karl were out there on their own,' Father Beitz cried. 'We have to find out what happened. Oh Lord, where is Jakob?'

'Maybe he went straight on home,' Walther suggested, but Beitz shook his head.

'Billy would have come here. I'll send for Tibbaling. He'll find out for us.'

'I hope they're all right,' Nora said. 'I have to get back now.'

'Thank you, my dear,' Beitz said. 'God bless you. Walther, you take Miss Stenning out to her horse.'

Nora smiled. Walther didn't have to be told. He took her arm as they walked out to the road, and for a second there Nora thought the shy man might kiss her. She hoped he would. But then, Walther was very proper, very respectful, so they parted with only a wave. She supposed it was just as well. It was possible that for Walther a kiss might be akin to an engagement, and though she was hugely fond of him, maybe even in love with him, if their little romance were able to blossom, she wasn't sure that she had the courage to defy her parents in this regard. They were both very strong, overbearing people, and Nora felt quite proud of herself for disobeying them thus far, but to move on . . . She didn't know.

This time Jakob didn't mind allowing Mike to take charge. At least they were back on track, heading home, and he had recovered his good humour.

They'd camped overnight by the river, where Billy had

caught a fine fish for their breakfast, and Jakob was feeling on top of the world. The timber was theirs, he reminded himself. The first business trip he'd ever made was a success. He decided to write to Hubert Hoepper when he got home and tell him about this happening. Something different to relate for a change, beyond his rather dull farm news. He could even tell him about visiting another town, Maryborough, which Hoepper could mark on his map.

'I still say we should have taken the scenic route,' Quinlan said. 'You've got no soul, Meissner.'

'Some other time.'

But thanks to the detour, they didn't reach Childers until late afternoon, and then were surprised to find the lonely bush inn crowded.

'What's going on here?' Quinlan said. 'I never saw more than seven men and a dog in this sleepy hollow.'

As it turned out, the locals were celebrating. One of their citizens had just returned from the Gympie gold mines with his swag packed with money.

The man himself staggered out to greet them. Though still in worn and battered clothes from the hard work at the diggings, the miner sported a top hat and a large diamond ring.

'Welcome!' he shouted to them. 'It's on for young and old. Drinks and tucker on the house. He ain't got no champagne, but the whisky's good!'

'See,' Quinlan was saying to Jakob. 'Gold-mining. That's the ticket. I'll be out in them Gympie hills as soon as I've secured me land.'

That was quite a night. They ended up sleeping in the stables at the rear of the inn. Or rather, Billy and Jakob did. Quinlan had disappeared with a lady. He further delayed them the next morning by insisting on having a talk with their host, who was almost sober, to learn all he could from an obvious expert on the correct methods and pitfalls involved in the art of successful gold digging, and Jakob had to admit, he found the conversation very interesting too.

Eventually they were on their way again, arriving in Bundaberg as the sun was setting. Jakob would have preferred to keep going out to the farm, but courtesy brought him in to give thanks to Father Beitz for allowing Billy to accompany him, and, of course, to tell his friends the good news. They were met by such a furore of alarm, however, that he was stunned.

They had all run out to meet him, Father Beitz, Walther, the Lutze boys and some strangers, all babbling at once, or so it seemed to Jakob, because for a few minutes he could not take in what they were saying.

'A bush fire?' Quinlan yelled. 'Where? On Jakob's block. When was this? Yesterday? How bad?'

He turned to Jakob. 'They don't know. We better get out there.'

Billy had dismounted. 'You want I put the horse somewhere?' he asked Walther.

'No. I'll go with them.'

'Yes,' Father Beitz said. 'Do what you can. We'll pray for the Lord's mercy.'

Walther was introduced to the stranger who had ridden in with Jakob and Billy, then he mounted the horse and together they set off up the road after Jakob, who was already hurtling away in a panic. Only then did Walther remember the telegram Father Beitz had received that morning.

Now that was good news. It was from the Dean of St John's Seminary, advising Father Beitz that Pastor Friedrich Ritter, who was to be his curate, was sailing on the ship *Clovis* from Hamburg, bound for Bundaberg, on 3 November, with God's blessing, and had been entrusted with funds as requested. Letter following.

'Why didn't he put all that in a letter to start with?' Father Beitz had asked crankily. 'Wasting all that money on a telegram.'

'Because the letter would probably be on the same ship, Father. It would arrive with Pastor Ritter. The Dean thought you should know in advance.'

'That's true. Then he should be here any day. Just as well we've got the church started. I'd hate him to report to the Dean that I'm not serving the congregation.'

'Not any day, Father. That was the telegram. It came fast.

The ship has already sailed, though. It will probably be here in February.'

The priest shook his head. 'That long? The mail is very confusing. I don't know why anyone bothers. When did we leave Germany, Walther?'

'Early January, Father.'

'Strange. Very strange. Where has the time gone? The months are slipping away . . .'

So they might be, Walther thought, but the old priest was certainly sparking along, as Jakob had noticed. Full of beans he was. Enthusiasm, new surrounds, and the presence of his much-loved Aborigine friends had more than compensated for his initial disappointments. His companions, Walther and the Lutze boys, reckoned between themselves that he'd dropped ten years. He was no longer an octogenarian but a very sprightly septuagenarian, and they hoped this land would be as kind to them in their old age.

Then again, the Harbour Master, Mr Drewett, had teased Hans Lutze when he'd praised this magnificent climate, these lovely so-called winter days. 'Wait for it, mate. Comin' from your cold countries, you might not be so in love with our summers.'

They'd laughed that off. Max often had talks with Drewett, who had never experienced a northern winter, never seen snow, let alone a blizzard, and could not even imagine temperatures falling anywhere near zero. But the Harbour Master, born and bred in Brisbane, where his father had been a police magistrate and had met the famous German explorer Ludwig Leichhardt, was so interested in how people and livestock lived in cold climates that they'd become firm friends, and Max had taken a chance and invited the boss to join them for a meal one Sunday.

And so Mr Drewett had come along. He'd enjoyed their company, for he was a lonely single man. But not only that. He was not inclined to any religion in particular, but he liked to listen to Father Beitz sermonising. It was thought that Mr Drewett might be the first convert from the white community. On the other hand, Tibbaling had so many of his tribal people lining up to be initiated into 'Fader Bites's' flock that Walther was relieved the mass christenings had been postponed until the church was completed.

'Ah God, give us hope,' he prayed as the two lead riders took the road out of Bundaberg, past the Chinese market gardens and a group of horsemen heading for town.

In all this time, remaining loyal to his priest, Walther had been no further than the town. He could be excused for feeling a little guilty delight in this wild ride at breakneck speed, to keep up with Jakob and his friend, though the sun was dropping like a stone, as if it could not get out of the sky fast enough. As if something far more interesting awaited it below the horizon.

Sometimes Walther tried to envisage what that same sun would behold on the other side, when it rose to perform a day for his people in their village back home.

The horse pounded down the road and Walther's mood darkened. Trees rushed at him from either side, but the could only see one tree, a ghost from the past.

He'd been a wild fellow in his day. Mad with the girls and the drinking from the day the urge came upon him. A hard worker, give him that, but just as hard a roisterer once the sun went down, with never a thought . . .

His father had tried to talk to him, about his behaviour, he'd assumed, but Walther had cut him short.

'You don't have to worry about me, Father. I won't let you down. I know I'm a bit stupid in the beer at times. I know I get drunk too often, yes, I know that. But don't nag me, all right? You're worse than Mother.'

Even now, still, he could hear his father telling him that he needed to talk to him, but not here, 'with all your pals about'.

'We . . . I want to have a quiet talk with you, Walther. You're a grown man now, you're nineteen. I can't talk to anyone else. I need . . .'

Well, what else would you think? Walther had asked himself a thousand times. A thousand times. He swallowed a familiar sob at the memory and urged the horse on down that dark road, because he couldn't afford to lose his way.

He'd thought his father was overly concerned by his son's behaviour. By the normal roistering of young men who were

242

only following in the footsteps of their elders. He'd thought his father's concern foolish, and hadn't listened to the poor man. The son had selfishly believed that parents did not have problems. That the only reason this man had come to him for a private, maybe intimate conversation was to preach to him about better behaviour, about being in a position to give a good example to the folk who worked for them.

He was so wrong. When his father had needed him, Walther wasn't there for him, and he'd never forgive himself for that failure.

It was the early workers who found Walt Badke hanging by the neck from the tall tree by the shed.

Walther was shocked. Unable to accept such a thing. He would not believe that his father had taken his own life. In fact he cried murder to anyone who would listen, until the priest spoke kindly but firmly to him.

No one could give him an explanation for this. No one. Walther was hurt and shamed to think his father would desert them for no obvious reason. His brewery, Badke Fine Ales, was famous, and it was prospering. They had a big house in the village. Family and friends. So what was wrong?

When the family and those friends began to gather round the bereaved, and raised voices disturbed the solemn occasion, Walther was confused. He heard his mother and his aunt arguing in the kitchen. He had to intervene when Grandpa Badke refused to address his mother, shunning her in her own home. But gradually it came out; the sordid story that his mother had a lover.

'Is that a reason to kill yourself?' Walther demanded of the priest. 'Couldn't he have thrown her out? Or gone off and killed the man, got him out of the way?'

'I'm afraid your father was not aggressive in that manner. People make mistakes. You must not judge your mother, Walther.'

But he did judge, the day he discovered, after a great deal of questioning, the identity of the lover. His uncle. His father's brother. Father of his cousins, his best friends. Husband of the woman who had nursed his mother through a serious bout of measles.

243

They had betrayed them all. She, his mother, had betrayed him too. Walther was devastated, more so by the knowledge that if he retaliated he would be injuring his friends even more.

The will was read. Walt Badke left all his goods and chattels to Walther, his only living heir. He made no provision for his wife whatsoever. Neither did Walther. He sold the brewery, and despite his mother's desperate pleas, he was in the process of selling the house when the priest came by again.

'You can't do this, Walther. You can't turn your mother out into the street. She will be destitute.'

'Let my uncle keep her. He caused all this.'

He went for long walks with the priest until he was finally persuaded to relent. Or maybe I was just weary of it all, Walther thought, as the lead riders turned off the main road.

'Watch out,' Quinlan called back to him. 'This is a rough track. It don't get much traffic.'

Walther nodded. He could smell stale smoke, but there was still no sign of a bush fire.

'How far now?' he asked.

'About ten miles, Jakob reckons, to his first block.'

His first block. That reminded Walther. There had been lovely pastureland on a rise north of their village, and Walt Badke had always wanted it.

'One of these days,' he told his son, 'I'll have saved enough to buy that land, and we'll build a fine house upon it. Let's hope someone else doesn't get the same idea first.'

Walther had the money, from the sale of the brewery. Plenty of money. He bought that land, invested the rest, packed a few meagre belongings in his rucksack and left quietly, bidding farewell to only a few friends. He took to wandering after that, taking jobs as a farmhand here and there until he found himself working on a farm outside Hamburg. Then he heard about groups of people emigrating and his enquiries led him to Father Beitz.

He was entranced with the whole idea. A devout Lutheran, he considered he couldn't find himself in better company and left all the arrangements to the priest and his committee, after insisting that he pay his own way.

But it was time now to worry about Jakob. They had their first glimpse of burned fields by moonlight, and they were horrified. Charred trees, cold and motionless, suddenly reared up before them, and Jakob cried out in shock.

'Steady,' Walther called out to him. 'This may not be your land.'

Quinlan shook his head. 'By my reckoning I'd say this *is* his land, sad to say. Looks like the fire started up here.'

They rode silently down the narrow track that cut through the gloom, and to Walther it was like riding through a cemetery; everything left standing in the blackened forest either side of them was so still. It was eerie and chilling, and he was glad to be following them because he dared not speak of his own fears for Freda and Karl, left out here alone.

He could hear Jakob and Quinlan talking now. Though their voices were low, they carried in the stillness of the night.

'This'd be your first block here,' the Irishman was saying.

'Yes.'

'You took up two blocks?'

'One for my son.'

'Good move. If you're worrying about your wife and son, Jakob, don't be now. You said your house was within sight of the river. Water don't burn, you know. Anyway, maybe the fire ran out of puff before it got anywhere near your home block. And mine, I'm thinking.'

So for a while, and at short intervals, there was only the voice of the Irishman, trying to keep Jakob's spirits up.

Eventually they came to a division in the road, with one track leading off to the left, and here the Irishman reined in his horse.

'Well, mates, with my luck, how would I expect to get off light?'

'This is your land?' Walther asked him.

'That it is. And that'd be Jakob's territory on that side. The bush fire's been right through here, nothing to stop it but the river. We've both been burned out.'

Unable to keep to the slower pace any longer, Jakob took off, galloping down the track, throwing caution to the winds.

He'd never known such terror. This nightmare landscape with its scarecrow trees had conjured up the most fearful images. It all seemed alien to him. He kept telling himself this wasn't his land. It couldn't be. He must have taken a wrong turning somewhere along the road. Easy enough to get lost out here in daylight. Hopeless now.

His horse swerved to avoid yet another obstacle on this road of ruins, and Jakob realised he wasn't guiding the animal any more; it knew the way, it was going home. A deep sigh escaped him as he braced himself for whatever lay ahead.

Too soon he was upon the turn, the track to the house. There was no gate. Nor was there a fence. There was nothing to flag a visitor in the direction of the Meissner household. There never had been, but everyone managed. The few people who did call, come to think of it. No one much really. The bullocky and his team, with Theo. The gentlemen from Clonmel. What was that argument about again? Jakob was becoming disoriented. The horse had stopped. And why? He didn't know this place. Just more blackened forest with a brick chimney standing stupidly in the clearing.

Quinlan and Walther were prowling about. What for? He wanted to call to them, but his throat had constricted, his voice failed him. They were talking but he shut his ears to them. He sat the horse, stayed on his horse. Dandy understood. He was frozen to the spot too, no longer wanting to take the lead. But the poor beast had had a long day, it must be thirsty. Slowly Jakob turned it away from that ghastly lunatic chimney, out here in the middle of nowhere, and let it tread carefully through the brush, the burned brush, headed for the river.

The iron bars that bound his chest were crushing him, crushing the life out of him, Jakob felt, as he struggled for breath. Freda and Karl would be safe in the river, Quinlan had said, but were they?

Had they escaped the fire at all? The darkness could be in cahoots with the lingering presence of that fire, hiding the truth from him. Jakob rushed his mind back to the river, to the safety of the river. He could hear it now, the quiet rush of waters in the distance. The only sound he could hear in the bush that he'd known so well, where nights used to be alive

246

with the squeaks and grunts and shuffles of nocturnal animals and the resentful screech of birds, disturbed in their slumber.

But what sort of safety was the river? For God's sake! Jakob gagged on bile, grasped the horse's mane to keep himself from falling, and sat straight in the saddle, trying to regain some confidence, with the other two men trailing along behind him.

The track was dropping down to a lower level, so he held the reins tightly to prevent the horse from slipping on the ash-covered earth. Suddenly it shied, lurching into the trunk of a huge tree now scorched black. Jakob had to push it away to prevent injury to his leg, but then he saw the cause of the fright. Standing sadly before them was a cow, Freda's cow. It gazed at him but made no effort to move as a voice came out of the gloom behind it.

'That you, Mr Jakob? We bin mind your cow.'

It was Mia, their Aborigine neighbour.

He was down from that horse in a second. He threw his arms about her. 'Mia! Oh, dear girl. Where are they? My wife. My son.'

She pointed. 'Gone. Over de river in a boat. Allasame friend Rolf come get 'em. I say I mind the cow.'

'Thank you. Thank you. But what about Yarrupi and your baby? Are they all right?'

'Yes, boss. They gone upriver to fambly camp. They good.' She sighed. 'Too bad fire burn up your lubberly house.'

Jakob found himself smiling, to please her. 'Never mind.' But he did mind. The smile turned bitter. Not only was the house gone, but everything they owned. They were destitute.

'All's well then,' Quinlan said, patting him on the shoulder. 'I told you they'd be safe. We might as well camp here for the night. I'll see what sort of mess my place is in tomorrow.'

Watchers on the other side of the river saw their campfire and called out their halloos, and in reply Jakob shouted his name and they acknowledged him.

They sent a runner down to Rolf Kleinschmidt's house to let the woman know her husband had returned, and that sent Freda off into another storm of weeping. She could only imagine how shocked Jakob would be, to come home and find that devastation.

'What will we do now?' Karl asked Rolf. 'Do we go back there or will Dad come over here? There's nothing there any more, nothing to go back to.'

'It's still your land. It will green up again.'

'When?' he said angrily. 'And what do we live on in the mean time? It's all been a terrible waste of time. Could you get me a job as a timber cutter, Rolf?'

'We'll see,' Rolf said cautiously, knowing that Freda was listening.

The pain brought Lucas back to consciousness, but he could not think through it. Could not determine where he was. What was he doing lying here in a ditch? It was a ditch, that much he knew, from his earthy surrounds. Or was it a grave? A place in a nightmare. Somewhere out in the open, he thought as he reached for a piece of foliage, hoping to ease himself up a little, but it disintegrated in his hand, dissolved right in front of him! Lucas closed his eyes again, cringing. How could that be? That was not real. He let his face drop into the dirt again.

Daylight now, and he was very stiff. Damn cold, too, yet he had a near memory of heat. His head ached, and his hand found a lump over his right temple. He must have fallen and hit his head some time last night. But then he recalled the ditch. Last night he'd been lying here in this ditch too dazed to get up. He must have passed out again.

'Dammit!' He pressed both hands into the ground to push himself up, grimacing at the texture of this dirt, soft and spongy, clinging to his hands like mud. The slight delay caused by his surprise at the murky soil saved him from the agony a sudden movement would have afforded him, because already stabs of pain were attacking his right leg.

'Oh God,' he puffed, as he waited for that warning pain to subside. 'Something's wrong with my leg.'

The effort took time and was agonising, even though he was trying to be careful as he examined the leg. Broken! Smashed. Lucas felt nauseous. He manoeuvred himself into a sitting position so that he could rest his back against the side of the ditch, and thought about concussion, but the exertions had taken their toll and he passed out again.

Now there was heat. The sun was high and glaring down on him. There was no shade. Peculiar, that. He tried to move his leg, thinking that he might have imagined it was broken.

'No,' he groaned as the pain flared up again. 'You didn't imagine it.'

Then he noticed that his hands were black. From what? The soil around here was reddish-brown. His shirt too was black; his clothes were filthy, as if covered in soot, like a chimney sweep.

Soot! His eyes widened as he took in his surroundings. No shade. Of course there was no shade. The trees were all stripped bare. Blackened. The fire! Oh, Lord God! The fire. It had come through here. He'd been riding down to warn Jakob, hadn't he? Lucas still wasn't too sure. So where was his horse?

'There's no hurry,' he told himself, as yet not competent to gauge the seriousness of the situation. 'I'll just sit here until I work this out. Now how did I get here?'

Gradually, muddled memories of the bush fire began to tumble into some logical order. He thought the horse must have tripped and thrown him, and he hoped it wasn't injured. This was Jakob's property, that was why he'd been riding to warn him. And he must have been overtaken by the fire. But how could that have happened? And what was he doing out here on his own? But he hadn't been on his own. Where were Keith Dixon, and Sam and Pike?

'And the horse didn't trip!' he said suddenly. Indignantly. As if explaining to an audience. 'It threw me! Bucked me off. That's how I landed in the ditch. The fire must have passed right over me. Oh, Lord God, thank you.'

But where were the others? He worried about them until the argument with Keith filtered back, then he was suddenly afraid, knowing that that conversation reeked of danger that he could not define. Had they left him here to die? But why would they do that?

Confronting these questions only served to confuse him now, because he believed that the row he'd had with Keith must have been about Hanni. About all that talk, that gossip, surfacing at last. Keith had been savage about it and so had he. No wonder there'd been trouble. He'd ridden away to escape them because Keith, that powerful man, was now his enemy. And when he recalled that in fact he'd been riding to warn Jakob about the fire, it did not relate to his fight – and it was an actual fight – with Keith Dixon. There was no reason to be fighting with Keith over riding to warn Jakob of an approaching bush fire. No . . . it had something to do with Hanni . . .

And there lay his conclusion. Without a shadow of a doubt Lucas knew he was in danger from his boss's son. And when two riders from Clonmel came through the scorched forest it wasn't difficult to hide from them. To lie low in the soot and ash that had initially astonished him. It was far worse than mud, he thought, as he listened to them riding by; dirtier, filthier, awful. He must look a mess. Hanni would have a fit when she saw him. She'd have to take the hose to him to clean some of this muck off, before she'd allow him in the door.

Lucas let them go by. He knew where he was, it wasn't as if he was lost. He was on Jakob's land. He had only to make his way down to Jakob's house and all his problems would be solved. They would leave Clonmel. Hanni would be delighted, she'd been wanting to leave anyway. They'd go back into Bundaberg, they had some cash now. Get jobs there. They could even go back to Father Beitz for a while. That would be nice. See everyone again. His forehead was hot. Very hot. Probably been sunburned again. Gosh, that first day that he'd ridden out on the range with the other stockmen, out there from dawn to sunset . . . he'd been so sunburned, and windburned. 'Winter burned.' He sniggered. In the past he'd been sunburned in winter snow, never as bad as that, but winters were cold . . . That line of thought petered out for want of a link to whatever he was trying to work out. And whatever it was it could not compete in importance with his latest achievement. Those men had missed him. Gone on by.

Lucas Fechner nodded his head in benign satisfaction. First mission achieved. Now he had to find some sticks and put a splint on his leg the way doctors did, so that he could walk down to Jakob's house. He started to haul himself out of the ditch, groaning in agony, spitting filthy ash and soot, and once over the top he lay exhausted, staring out at the mayhem before him. Then he wept. Not for himself, that hadn't occurred to him. No, Lucas wept for Jakob Meissner. For the devastation of his beautiful lands. The tears added grime to his face. The grime reminded him that once he got to his feet he would have to be very careful trying to walk through miles of deep ash.

He blinked. Miles? Could that be right? No! Jakob, he'd heard, had bought acres, not miles. He was learning about these measures from Sam. Learning to acquaint himself with distance so that he could say, one of these days, with the right amount of insouciance, 'Not far. Just up the road. Only about fifty miles.'

The insouciance, the devil-may-care attitude, had hold of him now. He set off on his rear, bumping along, dragging the leg. Only for a start, of course. There were huge trees standing around the forest like silent black widows. In the morning he would use one of them to pull himself up, then it would be easy, lurching from one to the other. And all the while he was doing sums in his head. Sums about acres and miles and square miles, trying to work out how ninety acres translated into miles, into real distance.

That was what they'd said back at Clonmel. That these farm blocks were all measured at ninety acres. Though the men on the sheep station didn't actually call them farm blocks; they resented them, they called them piggeries, such was their contempt for small-time farms. Even ninety-acre farms, Lucas had marvelled. And they called the farmers 'cockies' . . . after cockatoos, birds which swooped in and lodged in great numbers where they weren't wanted. To his present shame, Lucas had not pursued his enquiries about the farmland acquired by his friend Jakob Meissner once he realised that he'd taken up residence in the opposing camp.

He'd even found himself on the side of the Dixon family. What a cruel world it was that an estate that these people had forged from the wilderness only a generation ago was being scissored by the government, block by block. The Dixons had pioneered the country, they'd endured immense hardship far from civilisation, they'd battled the black tribes, and they'd overlanded their sheep hundreds and hundreds of miles, to and fro, to and from the only markets available.

And yet, men like Jakob knew no better. They bought land offered in legal transactions. Lucas wondered if he would have the same problem when he had his own sheep station. Would cockies come along, pressing in on him, until there was too little room for his sheep to graze? For one day he would have his own station. He remembered the bitter words of his boss back home, the stablemaster, and the father of his fiancée.

'You go off with her, you bloody fool, and you're ruined. Don't come creeping back here again. You're not wanted in these parts if you do this to my daughter, with the wedding only a week away. You're a waster, Fechner. You'll never make anything of yourself.'

A waster, he thought drowsily. I don't think so.

Then it was night again, but he pushed on. Determined to reach Jakob's house. But his course was haphazard, each obstacle requiring a detour that became a direction. By now he knew that standing and hopping was too difficult, that the fire had robbed him of sturdy saplings that might have aided him as crutches, so he pushed and dragged himself until his hands bled and his left thigh was grazed raw through torn fabric.

Being sent to search for Fechner suited Keith. He would simply have the day off, riding about. Better still, he could find a quiet reach of river, catch some yabbies, his favourite food, and boil them up in his billy. Take a nap for a while. Who needed to find Fechner after all? By this time he'd have caught up with the Meissners somewhere and be blabbing his tale of how the fire had started.

'While three of us call him a bloody liar,' Keith said to himself as he rode away from the homestead.

But if Fechner was hurt, had been thrown by the horse, then he could stay right there. Why would Keith bring him in? It'd be smarter to put a bullet in him. Shut him up for good. Keith believed his father was over-reacting. They should just get rid of Hanni Fechner, send her back to Bundaberg, and forget about the pair of them. One thing was for sure, he wasn't going anywhere near Meissner's property in case the Germans came gunning for him.

Come to think of it, he decided, what was to stop him from going in to Bundaberg? Have a few drinks in the pub and ask around about the fire. He was dead curious to know where the Meissners were now. And he ought to ask after Fechner. Yes. Ask if anyone had seen him. Sound worried.

He went to the new pub, the Royal. It had a wide veranda overlooking the river, and it was already very popular. Friends called to him to join them, pointing out that the new publican was engendering goodwill by serving free lunches all this week.

'I wondered why there was such a mob here,' he said to them. 'He's taking a risk. You lot eat like vultures. You'll send him broke before he gets a go on.'

A few beers later he managed to turn the conversation to the fire out along the river, and everyone had something to say there, so he leaned against the bar and listened to the talk. Apparently the Meissners had taken refuge across the river with some loggers, Germans too, who worked for Les Jolly. Their house had been burned down and their small crops burned too. Poor buggers. Damned if a fire wasn't the worst thing . . .

'I dunno,' someone said. 'You get a big flood, it comes fast. People get drowned.'

'Don't we know it,' Keith said. 'There was a huge flood here years ago. My old man told me about it. His outstation manager was drowned. By the way, the Meissners, they didn't get hurt?'

'No. They're all right. Mother and son went across the river. Then Jakob Meissner got home, he'd been away someplace, so he had to go over there too.'

'I thought there were four of them.' Keith said, fishing for news of Fechner.

'No, only the three. The couple and their son.'

So that sorted that out. Lucas wasn't with them. Later he asked in an offhand way if anyone had seen Lucas Fechner, a

253

Clonmel stockman, anywhere over the last few days, but no one even knew him. In any case, he hadn't been seen.

The beer was flowing by this time and somehow the conversation came round to the fire again; not that it interested Keith, until he heard two men arguing about Jakob Meissner.

'He wasn't on his own,' one man said. 'I was there. I saw the lads bring them across the river in Charlie Mayhew's boat. They brought Jakob and another bloke over from where the farmhouse was burned down.'

'What's Charlie Mayhew doing with a boat?'

'It's a longboat. He bought it from a ship's captain. Uses it to take Kanakas out to his plantation. He says it's quicker than hauling them cross-country. And easier on them.'

But Keith wasn't interested in Charlie's boat. He could feel a nervous tic at work at the side of his mouth, and tried to control it by jutting his chin forward. So Fechner was with them? He had to know.

'Who was the other fellow with Meissner, then? If it wasn't one of the family like I said.'

'It was me.' A deep voice beside him gave the answer, and Keith turned to find Quinlan glaring at him.

'Who let you out?' he snapped, and without waiting for an answer turned to his mates. 'I thought this was a respectable pub.'

'So did I,' the Irishman said. 'But you got in, you dirty little crook. Now get out of me way, and give me room at the counter.'

Too many drinks had given Keith rare courage. 'Here's a jailbird calling me names. You go someplace else and buy your booze, Quinlan. If you've got any money.'

Suddenly he was no longer at the bar. He was being heaved away by Quinlan and sent sprawling across the floor, crashing into other customers and causing them to stumble clear, spilling their drinks, mostly on him. No one came to his aid. Instead there were enthusiastic grins all round, as men stepped back to allow them space if, as was hoped, a fight developed.

But the new publican was having none of it. He stood back against the mirror-lined shelves behind the counter, as if defending his considerable stock of bottles on display, and produced a rifle, which had them all very quiet, very still, in a second.

'Now, lads,' he said. 'I tell you this but once only. I want no fighting in my pub. I've had pubs on the goldfields. I've seen more bloody fights than you lot have had feeds. This pub cost me and my partner a lot of money. But it's ours. If anything gets broke, you pay double for it. If you fight, you're barred. And this rifle is always loaded, so don't no one get smart with me.'

He looked to Quinlan. 'You toss my customers about again and you're barred. You got it?'

'Yes, sir,' Quinlan grinned.

'And you, smartmouth on the floor, I say who drinks in my pub, not you. Now get up and shut up.'

Keith struggled to his feet. Now there were helpers, the fun over. He shook them off and strode over to the publican, who was carefully placing the rifle under the counter.

'Excuse me. You don't appear to know who I am. That's understandable, you being new to the town, but—'

The burly publican leaned across the counter. 'Then we're quits, mate. I don't know you and you don't know me. These things work themselves out. I wouldn't worry about it. Now what's your poison?'

On principle, Keith stayed, though he'd much rather have gone back to O'Malley's pub, where he could expect respect. But all was not lost. It was definite now that Lucas had not gone to Meissner. That no one knew the fire had been deliberately started, let alone who might have done the deed. Keith laughed, pleased with himself. Quinlan would burst a boiler if he knew he'd been standing next to the man who'd fired his land too. But he didn't know. And obviously, by what Keith had heard in town today, he never would.

He stayed for the free lunch, and when he was served a large plate of shepherd's pie, he tasted it, found it delicious, pushed it aside and pronounced it inedible.

'I'm going back to O'Malley's for a decent meal,' he said.

Chapter Ten

Quinlan was on the veranda with his mates. He watched Dixon leave without comment. He had other things to think about. There was nothing much he could do to help Jakob, except to volunteer as an unpaid farmhand to help him clean up the mess, and he wasn't about to bother doing that on his *own* land. You can't rake up the ash on ninety acres, he'd tried to explain to Jakob, who had double that amount of land.

'You're better to let nature take its course. In this climate the trees and grass will be greening in no time. You'll see. 'Tis sad about your house and your things, but then again, you're alive and healthy. You could have been drowned at sea like so many hopeful emigrants from the auld countries . . .'

'Shut up, Quinlan,' his new friend had said, and he supposed Jakob was right. A man needed time to kick at the witches of misfortune before picking himself up and starting again. Hadn't he done that himself? Nearly broke his kickin' foot when the witches turned into prison walls. Stupid it was of him to shoot that ram. But it got them where it hurt, it sure bloody did.

He'd talked to Billy. No job any more. No point in building even a hut right now, but the rules of leasing could not be ignored. He'd called on Clem Colley with his dilemma and the policeman had told him to hotfoot it over to O'Malley's pub, where the inspectors were staying.

The so-called luck-of-the-Irish had never featured in Quinlan's life. He had told his mum he must have been behind the door when it was handed out, and visiting him in jail, she'd agreed with him. He'd found that a mite disconcerting, but then she'd gone off and bent the ear of Walter Scott, the

Member of State Parliament for the electorate of Mulgrave, about his incarceration.

' 'Twas a mad thing to do,' Quinlan told his fellow inmates, 'but I hadn't reckoned on me dear old mum being a born snoop. She worked in Maryborough as a cook for a high-falutin' family that turned out to be the home of one John Douglas, who was, God help us, Premier of our great and glorious State of Queensland.

'This is a true story I'm tellin' you, lads. So her employer comes up in the world to the high seat of Premier, but it didn't help her poor benighted son at all until she got the lowdown on a visitor, this Walter Scott. She heard he had sworn enemies called the Dixons, big-time graziers no less. It was then, with this little gem of knowledge in her purse, that me dear old mum, hands wringing, the blarney flowing, made representings to her representative on behalf of her poor son. And when Scott heard the word "Dixon" and the story of it all, I was as good as free.'

So Quinlan had taken himself off to see the land inspectors. 'It's relieved I am to find you in town, dear sirs, since I was about to go in search of my good friend Walter Scott.'

'Who?'

'Mr Scott, our Member of Parliament. About an extension to my leasing contract. I've come here to begin the necessary improvements to my land – house, fences, sheds and all – but fate has struck me a severe blow. You heard about the fierce bush fire out there?'

They were seated at a long table in one of the rooms across from the office of Jules Stenning, who Quinlan had no wish to meet. The table was covered in ledgers and papers and other paraphernalia of office, necessary window-dressing of the bureaucrat, he thought, as they nodded in unison.

'Then God help me, 'twas my place. Burned me out. So I can't get started on the improvements now. And the poor fellows I'd employed to assist me in the work, I had to let them go. I'd be obliged then, sirs, if you'd sign me a time extension of another year and I'll be on my way.'

The younger of the two inspectors blinked, as if not quite taking in this intelligence, and searched among the folders in front of him for the Quinlan file. He studied the single page closely, leaning forward to read the small print, and then turned to his superior.

'I see nothing here that allows setbacks due to bush fires to be taken into consideration, sir. Nothing. And that means he has breached the obligations of his lease and must forfeit his land.'

Quinlan's smile and the twinkle in his eye didn't falter as he rifled in a pocket for his own papers and accidentally dropped a wad of notes on the floor. 'Nevertheless,' he said, 'gentlemen in your profession do have the power of discretion, like any magistrate. Like Mr Scott would. The understanding being that such measures should be taken for the good of the district, for never let it be said otherwise.'

'He has a point,' the elder man said.

'I fear not, sir, the regulations state—'

'The regulations and the courts would allow compassion, Sykes. Have a bit of sense. Stamp his papers, extended. One year.'

The Irishman beamed. 'Good of you, sir. Now while I'm here, would you see your way clear to extending the time on Mr Meissner's two blocks that were also burned out? He can prove with many a witness that he did make wondrous improvements on his land, house and all, only to have them burned down. This is but a matter of course, your approval of that extension, to keep things neat.'

'Where are his papers?' Sykes asked suspiciously.

'In the bank, thank the Lord. He'll bring them in when he recovers from the shock of it all.'

'Damn shame, that,' the senior inspector said, standing and stretching. 'I think I'll take a walk.'

At the front door, Quinlan slipped him a pound, grateful that he hadn't asked for double on account of the Meissner contract, because that pound note had been wrapped around a wad of newspaper to give the impression of affluence.

'How long have you been out?' the inspector asked, letting Quinlan know he was aware of his background.

'Long enough.'

'I was thinking. You being friendly with Scott, you might put a word in for me. I've got my name down for the next magistrate's appointment. It should be soon.'

'Consider it done, but then your name, sir?'

'Pinnow. Laurence Pinnow.'

'Of the Pinnow family, sawmills?'

'Yes.'

'Ah, good for you! I'll be runnin' along then.'

He was still at the Royal Hotel, looking over the river and contemplating his future, when he thought of Pinnow again. Put in a good word for him? Not a hope in hell. That was Mrs Dixon's family. Old J.B.'s wife was a Pinnow.

Then he began to laugh. For a minute there he had had himself convinced that Walter Scott, MLA, really was his friend.

'You're looking pleased with yourself.' It was Davey, the bullocky.

'Why not, on such a fine day as this and barely a bean in my pocket?'

'Then I'll shout you a pint if you join us. This is Theo Zimmerman, my offsider.'

'How do you do, Theo.'

He spent time with them, mostly discussing the fire and the effect on the Meissners, and then his own plan to make for the goldfields.

Theo was fascinated. 'You mean they really are digging up gold? Near here? Real gold?'

'Sure they are.'

Quinlan remembered he had to get to the bank to ask Rawlins to have Jakob's leasehold papers registered as extended, while the iron was hot. That was about all he had left to do in the town, then he was off on the big adventure.

Theo took him aside. 'Are you going on your own, Mike?'

'I sure am.'

'Could you do with a partner?'

'Why? Are you thinking of joining me?'

'If that is permissible.'

'Why not? The more the merrier.'

'I have to buy a horse,' Theo told Eva.

'Why? You can ride on the lorry when you're not walking with the bullocks.'

260

'One of us has to have a horse. If there's an accident we've got no way of going for help. And we often need extra things.'

'Funny, Davey got along without one until now.'

'Risky, more like it.'

Eva understood, though. It certainly made sense for them to have a horse, travelling to the outback all the time. And after all, Theo's wages had them more settled once she'd insisted that Davey pay the money directly to her. It had surprised her that Davey had agreed to this arrangement, but he was a wily old fellow and probably knew it was for the best. As for Theo, apparently he'd been furious when Davey broke that news to him, but what could he do? Abuse his boss? Instead he shouted at Eva for heaping such humiliation on him, but she simply ignored that, telling him to speak to his boss about it, not to her.

Anyway, it was working. The rent was up to date and she'd saved money. And why not get a horse? It was hard living in a country town without one. It would make a difference to their Sundays if Theo happened to be home from the job. They could take turns to ride out to Father Beitz's services. The more she thought about it, the happier she felt, and she even smiled benignly when her husband rushed away like a kid to see if they had an animal available at the stables.

They did. A nice horse, a grey, not too flash, but lovable, called Belle. When he brought Belle home the children were ecstatic. They fell in love with her. They could hardly eat their dinner that night for all the excitement, and Eva was hard put to get them to bed; they wanted to stay up and mind Belle, who was all alone out there in the dark.

A few days later Davey went to the house to tell Theo they had another job, carting a load of furniture and fittings from the wharves to a new house out on Burrum Street. He was in a good mood; shearing had started on some of the stations so there would be plenty of work ahead, hauling those huge bales of wool to the port. The graziers paid well for their precious bales to be transported with all care.

Theo wasn't home. The wife was a picture of misery.

'What's up, Mrs Z.?' he asked.

'Did you know about the horse?'

'What horse?'

'I thought so. I've been had.'

'How's that?'

'He talked me into buying a horse. He said you and him needed a horse, and now he's gone.'

'Gone where?'

'To the goldfields. He left this note. Wouldn't even face me.'

She thrust it at him, but it was written in German. Davey shook his head. 'What does it say?'

'That he's gone to the goldfields in Gympie, wherever that is, and he'll be back soon with a fortune. A fortune! Theo?' she laughed bitterly. 'Never. He's as much chance of making his fortune as flying to the moon.'

'Who did he go with?' Davey asked.

'He says a fellow called Mike Quinlan. Isn't he the jailbird? I hear talk of him.'

Davey nodded. 'Quinlan's all right, Mrs Zimmerman. Theo's in safe hands with him. I'm sorry. I meant, if he had to go at all.'

Later he worried about her and the kids. Quinlan knew his way around all right, but he wasn't known for his luck. In fact, poor Mike was a loser. Too hot-headed for his own good.

'What a pair,' he muttered as he made for the pub to find a replacement for Theo, who might have had the manners to give him a warning. 'Quinlan and Theo. Gold-diggers! Jesus! The gold would have to fall on their bloody heads.'

In the mean time, Keith Dixon had taken himself home after a night spent cavorting in the fancy Black and White bordello that had opened in a lane off Bourbong Street only a few days ago.

'Bundaberg is really looking up,' he told his mates back at the station, 'to have a flash place like that. It's clean, and it's all done out in black and white, sheets and covers, curtains, the lot. And you take your pick of the women, black or white or both.'

He also told them that he'd seen Fechner in town. Actually, that had just slipped out. He'd been laughing, telling them about the sassy bawds, when someone put the question to him.

'Have you seen Lucas Fechner?'

'Yeah, saw him in town,' he said, irritated by the interruption. 'I sacked him, remember. Where else would he be?'

'What about the missus? Is she staying on?'

Keith almost froze at that. He'd just opened his mouth to tell them that the place had a Chinese whore too, high-priced. Now he forced back a gulp. He'd forgotten about the wife for a minute. Only for a minute, but the damage was done . . .

'Hanni? Ah, yes. We'll have to take her into town for him. With his wages, no less.

Stop, he told himself. Don't enlarge on that or you'll get in deeper. He waved them off, telling them to save their shillings if they ever expected to get in the door of the Black and White. 'They're pricey gals.' He grinned, unable to resist the boast that he could afford them.

'Why don't I believe you?' J.B. sneered, swivelling round in his chair. 'Where exactly did you see Fechner?'

'In town, I told you. He was walking past O'Malley's.'

'So you gave him a bit of a wave and asked him what you should do about his wife? The one he's forgotten out here, along with his luggage?'

'Something like that.'

'Florence!' J.B. shot out of his chair and shoved his head out of the door to shout for his wife. 'Florence, get in here!'

She came running, tucking wisps of fair hair behind her ear. 'What is it?'

'It's your brilliant son again. Guess what? He saw Lucas Fechner in town!'

'Oh, thank goodness. Did you ask him what he's doing? His wife's worried sick about him.'

'We have to send her to town.'

'Where to in town?'

'Yes,' J.B. said silkily. 'Where to in town?'

'Out to the Germans' block, I suppose. He didn't actually say.'

'See, Florence. Isn't he a marvel? The last time he sees Fechner they have a punch-up. But now, only a few days later, they have a nice little chat outside O'Malley's pub.'

His mother looked to Keith nervously. 'At least we know where the man is.'

'I wasn't the only one to see him,' Keith said defensively.

'Is that so?' his father roared. 'Like who?'

'Some of the blokes.'

'What blokes?'

'I dunno. I just heard them saying—'

J.B. lashed out and clouted him across the face. 'Start again, and I'll have the truth this time. No, you stay, Florence. Sit over there and shut up. Now, genius . . . where's Fechner?'

Keith sank into an armchair, nursing his cheek. 'I don't know.'

'Who saw him in town?'

'No one.'

'Right. But you told some of our men you did.'

'They caught me off guard. I didn't mean to say it. I didn't know what else to say.'

J.B. turned to his wife. 'Do you see what we've got now? A right mess. This idiot says he saw Fechner, and Fechner wants his wife sent to town. This leaves me with no choice. I have to send the bloody woman to town.'

'Couldn't Keith just tell them he was mistaken?'

'Jesus! You're as stupid as he is. The whole bloody Pinnow family are as dumb as oxen, and he's a prize specimen. How can he say he was mistaken, for Christ's sake? Like he talked to the bloke but now it wasn't him after all. Stockmen aren't stupid. They'll smell a rat. We have to go along with it now. Send that wife of his packing.'

She sighed. 'That would be a pity. She's the best maid we've ever had.'

'So what? Get another one, but move her out fast.'

'All right. She can go in the morning. In the wagon. Keith can take her . . .'

'Let him take her? Are you mad? He can't keep his hands off the black gins, let alone a pretty white girl. If he hasn't had a go at her already.'

'That's quite enough,' Mrs Dixon said. 'I won't listen to talk like that.'

Keith took courage from her stand. 'He forgets what this is all about, Mother. He told me to get rid of the Meissners on the resumed eastern blocks. He was pleased I burned them out, because they wouldn't hand over their timber.'

'That's business,' J.B. growled.

'Sure it is. Burned their house down with all their belongings. And their timber and their small crops. I made a good job of it for him. He'd look bloody stupid if I told the police how that fire started . . .'

J.B. shook his head as he turned away. 'Go on and tell them, you dummy. You'll look bloody stupid in jail. I'll deny it. Then again, jail might be good for you. You might learn something there. Get out of my sight, the both of you.'

Hanni was confused. No one seemed to know what had happened to Lucas. Then Elsie told her that he was in town.

'He had a falling-out with Mr Keith,' she said. 'And got sacked.'

'Why didn't someone tell me that before?'

'Because we expected him to come in, and when he didn't everyone was worried. Especially when he had just let his horse go. But now that we know where he is, everything will be all right. Mrs Dixon is really sorry you're leaving. She put a bonus of ten shillings in your pay, and of course there's Lucas's pay too. You can take it to him.'

Hanni thought it must have been a bad row Lucas had with Mr Keith, that pig, not to want to set foot here again. That sounded like Lucas. It also sounded like Keith, who was vicious enough not to allow him back on the station. She hoped they hadn't been fighting over her, because Keith was capable of telling Lucas all sorts of lies. She shuddered as she packed their bags. What had Keith said to him? Had Lucas left as a result? He could have.

Night brought yet another fear. They'd said someone would take her to town in the wagon. But who? Hanni decided that if her driver was to be Keith Dixon, she would flatly refuse to go with him. They couldn't make her. And since she was at last to leave this horrible place, she didn't have to worry about offending any of them.

265

It wasn't the same wagon that she and Lucas had come out in; this one was much finer, with leather seats and a hood. Almost like a coach with no sides. Hanni had never seen the likes of it but it did shade them from the sun. Her and the housekeeper and Dan the driver, who was a stockman.

They stopped halfway to town, and Dan boiled a billy to make tea while Elsie unpacked cakes and scones from a hamper. Hanni resented the delay. She was finding it hard to make conversation with a woman she didn't know very well; dragging out the hours was simply another chore for her. But then Elsie, this ever-so-strict housekeeper, produced a bottle of gin.

'Would you like a shot?' she asked Hanni 'Since you aren't working for us any more, it's all right for me to ask you.'

'I don't think so. I've never tasted gin.'

'It's quite foul, but you get used to it. Do have a nip. I don't care to drink alone, and we've got hours of this boring trip ahead of us.'

They drank the gin from cups, which were not repacked in the hamper, and neither was the gin.

Elsie was right, Hanni thought. It was a bit foul, but she'd tasted worse alcohol on the ship, and once they were on their way again, the second cup, drunk with a giggle as they bounced along, wasn't so bad at all.

It turned out that Elsie was Mrs Dixon's cousin. She'd suffered 'severely', she said, at the hands of a wretch of a man who had run off with a hussy only one and a half weeks before their wedding day.

Hanni felt her ears tingle as she heard this, and made no comment as Elsie told her tale of woe. It involved her wedding dress, made for her by Grandma Pinnow, and the subsequent confusion, with guests already in transit from afar and the reception at a Maryborough hotel cancelled, and the brides-maids weeping as if it were they who had been jilted. It was a long story, but it filled in time until they stopped for lunch and a change of horses at a large farmhouse. Their hostess here, a kindly woman, turned out to be another of Elsie's relatives.

As they were leaving, this woman plied them with cakes for Elsie to take in to Grandma Pinnow, and some bottles of her own special lemonade, and once out on the road again, Elsie produced the cups.

'Would you like some lemonade? She really makes a good lemon drink.'

'Yes please.'

'And it goes beautifully with gin,' Elsie added.

So it did. The lemonade turned the foul drink into a cool and delightful nectar, and Hanni settled back for the last leg of their journey into town, thinking how much more pleasant this was than the long ride she and Lucas had endured when they were driven out to Clonmel. That wagon had been old and hard, and they'd only had one stop, for billy tea and biscuits by the river, where the driver could let the horses drink.

But then, she sighed, they'd been so happy to have jobs waiting for them, and so enthusiastic about this strange landscape, as well as the excitement of seeing so many native animals. Neither of them had ever seen animals like kangaroos or great birds like emus, even in cages, let alone wandering about the countryside unhindered. A long, bumpy, dusty ride that had been, but fun.

Elsie was still chatting on, something about a gentleman who owned a great station in the far west, and Hanni, though barely listening, did wonder vaguely about that. Clonmel was a long way inland, to the west they called it. How much further away was the far west, for God's sake? The gentleman's name was Henderson, and she thought that was vaguely familiar, but her thoughts were with Lucas as Elsie poured them another lemonade. She did so long to see him again, dear Lucas. It had been horrible, worrying all that time, days feeling like months, wondering if something awful had happened to him. Never in all her life would she flirt with another man again. She'd even tell Lucas that. Never again. So he needn't ever worry that she was being silly, foolish . . .

The gin bottle was finished. Elsie let it slide into the soft red soil by the side of the road so that the driver wouldn't notice its passing, and not long after that they approached the outskirts of town, finally pulling into the driveway of a house next door to a sawmill.

'This is where I get off,' Elsie said. 'It's Grandma Pinnow's house. Dan will take you the rest of the way, Hanni. I'm really sorry you're leaving Clonmel, but never mind. You look after yourself now, and say hello to Lucas for me.'

They went through the town and out along Taylor's Road, and finally stopped.

'Where are we?' Hanni asked, staring at a swath of cleared bush.

'The German place,' Dan said. He jumped down, hitched the horses to a rail and began unloading their boxes.

Hanni remained seated. 'Where's Lucas?' she asked, surprised that the words came out with a whoosh, like 'Whersh Lucash?'

'Around here someplace, I suppose.'

Then Father Beitz was coming out, walking towards them, and Hanni was so pleased to see him. So relieved. He looked like an angel, all in white, with his white hair and beard, much nicer than when he used to wear that black cassock thing.

He reached up to her, obviously delighted to see her, and that was so nice, so lovely after all she'd endured.

'Hanni, my dear. What a lovely surprise . . .'

She stepped down, wobbling a bit. 'Father Beitz. You're so beautiful, absolutely jus' beautiful . . .' But before she could reach him, the ground gave way under her.

The priest stared as Hanni fell flat on her face at his feet.

She awoke in a hut with the sun streaming in on her through a hole in the roof where the thatching had collapsed. She found herself on a low-slung bunk only inches from the floor, so she lay there watching skinks dart across the room. She was accustomed to all manner of lizards now, after having met them at Clonmel Station, along with an alarming collection of insects and spiders. She rather liked these little lizards and the sweet-faced geckos that had stared down from the ceiling of their room. But this room didn't have a ceiling. It was thatched. And there was no door, simply an open wall looking straight into the bush.

'Where am I?' Hanni sat up with a jolt, sending streaks of pain through her head. She didn't know this place, though her

268

boxes were there, her cloak and bonnet sitting on top.

With a rising sense of panic, Hanni realised she'd slept fully dressed, and in her best skirt too, with its embroidered bib. She stumbled across the earthen floor in her stockinged feet to peer outside. The birds were making a racket but there was no one about, and suddenly Hanni remembered she'd come to town to meet Lucas, so he must be here somewhere. Though why he'd let her sleep in her clothes like that, she had no idea.

'Lucas!' she shouted. 'Lucas! Where are you?'

But it wasn't Lucas who answered her call. It was Walther Badke!

'What are you doing here?' she asked him.

'I live here, Hanni. Are you well this morning?'

'Yes thank you. Where's my husband?'

'Lucas? I don't know.'

Hanni's hair was hanging loose from its plait on one side. She pushed it back. 'I'm sorry. I must look a fright. I don't know this place. Where are we?'

'This is our commune, Hanni. On Taylor's Road. Don't you remember?'

'Oh. Yes, of course. Did you build this hut?'

'This and other huts. The Lutze boys, Father Beitz and me,' he said proudly. 'And the church is now being built.'

'Oh.' Hanni sighed, finding it an effort to take this in. 'I had to meet Lucas here,' she said at length. 'Hasn't he arrived yet?'

'No.'

'So you put me up? That was kind of you. I remember now, I came in the wagon from Clonmel Station. I was very tired. It was a long way.'

'Yes.' Walther nodded solemnly. 'Would you like some breakfast?'

'Please. I'm really hungry. Could I just tidy up first?'

'Hanni's waiting for Lucas,' Walther told Father Beitz.

'Glory be! See, I told you. They'll all come back here eventually and we'll have our congregation living and working here. I'll be able to get started on my mission school very soon.'

But Walther was thinking they'd need to build another hut, a more private one, now that a lady would be joining them. And they would have to take more care with their attire. It may not be proper for the men to wander about here now wearing only cut-off trousers. And he wondered why the Fechners had left the sheep station. Last he heard they were doing well there. Also, he worried, if more people came back, though most welcome of course, food would be in short supply. He'd have to clear and clean more land for small crops, and extend the chicken coop, a huge job in itself. That didn't leave much time for fishing, the mainstay of their food supply. The days were just not long enough, that was the trouble.

Tibbaling was fascinated by the young woman with the incredible white hair. Actually he was fascinated by all of these people, who were of a different tribe from the local white folk. They had a different language and built different houses. In that regard, their houses were more after the fashion of the dwellings preferred by the South Sea Islanders. The Kanakas had told Tibbaling's people that their folk back home lived in large and elaborate thatched huts. They were interested to hear that the German tribe did likewise. In fact, one of Tibbaling's Kanaka friends had come by to inspect the German houses but hadn't been impressed at all. He'd said they were primitive.

'Still better than the humpies your folk live in,' he'd teased.

Tibbaling had laughed. 'We know how to keep warm and dry, but when the stars are out we like to see them. We don't want to hide from them; all our babies and ancestors are up there.'

The young woman, called Hanni, had been there all day. Walther had gone into town on the horse looking for her husband and had returned without him, and without any news of him. They were a strange lot. Only yesterday he and Fader Bites had been consoling another lady, whose husband, Theo, had run off. Usually she came with Theo and the children for their weekly ceremonies, but this time she was without him and distraught.

Fader Bites didn't seem too concerned about the one called

270

Theo, saying he'd be back, but he was worried about the other husband, Lucas.

Tibbaling did not intrude on their conversations with the pretty white-haired lady; he squatted by the side of the hut, saddened by the miseries that beset her. He couldn't recall the husband they spoke of – there had been so many of these people in the first days – so he looked at the man called Lucas through her eyes. Then he nodded. Ah, yes. He could see him now, a tall, dark-haired man. Absently, he flicked pestering ants from his legs.

Tibbaling appeared to be slumbering there, sitting cross-legged by the hut, his old bones soaking up the waning warmth of the afternoon sun, and maybe he was. But another part of him was thinking itself into that void, a place of nothingness where even contemplation was unknown. He fingered the shark's teeth that hung round his neck, symbol of his high office as a spirit man, and sought out Warrichatta, the great and fearless shark who had come from the skies in the Dreaming to represent all the fish in the sea, and protect them from Gongora.

Through Warrichatta's eyes he searched the river depths, from its headwaters to the mouth by the white sands of the bay, in case the missing man had fallen into the deep waters. When that proved fruitless, with not a little fear, he then sought Gongora, for if the white men could not find one of their own, with all their cleverness, then it seemed fairly obvious to Tibbaling that the man had drowned in the river. Or worse.

The world through Gongora's eyes was awesome. It was tinged an ugly yellow and smelled of rotten eggs, and you went at it with a hammer, fast and furious, flicking and twitching the monstrous tail in sickening plunges. Not like Warrichatta, who was elegant, smooth, a pleasure to accompany. But Tibbaling endured the crocodile view of the river and the mudflats for as long as was necessary, until he was certain that the man, Lucas, had not drowned, had not been taken by a shark or chewed up by a crocodile. After that experience he was sweating badly, and the ants that kept pestering him were now biting.

He brushed them off impatiently, removed himself to the bush and took up a better position in a mossy grove by a clump of bamboo. But then the rattling of the canes bothered him and the birds with their shrieks and cackles were making his task impossible.

He stood up, broke off a cane and heaved it into the air as if he were throwing a spear. It soared above the trees and stayed there, suspended . . .

'What's that?' Father Beitz asked Walther.

'What?'

'Everything has gone quiet. There's not a sound anywhere.'

'Must be a hawk. I've noticed that they frighten the birds off.'

'But I can't even hear the creek.'

Walther didn't notice. He was too busy trying to make excuses to Hanni about where her husband might be. Walther thought he must be visiting someone in town. In some place he hadn't thought to look. And maybe Lucas hadn't realised that she, Hanni, could get to town so soon. More interested in their conversation, Father Beitz allowed the phenomenon of silence to pass, while Tibbaling resumed his position, mollified. The cane dropped gently to the ground, and the birds, reproved, were quieter.

He let his mind drift to that empty place again, but after the unsettling journey with Gongora, he kept one hand firmly clenched round the root of a nearby tree to keep himself well anchored, for Gongora was capable of conjuring up minor evil spirits who could, and would, cause terrible trouble. Gongora had offered these evil spirits and their capabilities to Tibbaling on many occasions in an effort to form a bond of friendship, but Tibbaling knew better than to ever align himself with Gongora, who could never be trusted. Sometimes he thought that he might take revenge on the white invaders by releasing Gongora's cruelty on any of them if they came close to the river, but Warrichatta in his wisdom advised him against it.

'I have seen them the earth over,' he said. 'There are too many. Gongora can't help. They spit on him.'

'On Gongora? They must be powerful.'

'I will talk to your warrigal people for you, Tibbaling. Your dingo people are very clever. I will have them meet with the powerful shark spirits of all the seas to find out what you must do about the white invaders.'

Tibbaling had settled into a beautiful state of contentment as he recalled the advice that Warrichatta eventually brought back to him, so it didn't upset him as much as it had so long ago.

'They are mournful,' he was told. 'They have searched through the memories of our tribes for a thousand generations, but there is no precedent for this problem. Others have come to our shores and have either been fought off or assimilated by our people. As witnessed in several of our northern tribes.

'They wring their hands in shame, for they cannot provide a solution. These are spirits,' Warrichatta wept, 'who can turn back tidal waves. They can hurl down lightning. They can cause the land to dry up. But they cannot counter the weight and fury of the white men.'

'Why not?' Tibbaling was weeping too.

'Because they are of our mother earth. They can only call up earthly powers. There are too many of our enemies, and our spirits have to acknowledge that they have spirits too. Their spirits demand the right to walk our earth unhindered.'

Tibbaling was shocked. He had no idea the invaders might have their own spirits.

'So all is lost?' he asked Warrichatta, and the shark's grey eyes managed a glint.

'They don't think so. They think a new Dreaming era is to hand. More contemplation is required to find a way through this evil fog.'

'That's a big help.'

'Some help is offered, though. Some wise men like yourself . . .'

'Please don't say that, Warrichatta. I'm not a wise man. I've done all that the spirits required of me. I've fasted, I've listened to the wise men, I've suffered the nine fiends of the north, fought in their caves and on their mountains, done all these things. But wisdom is denied me.'

'They say it is a wise man who knows he has much to learn.'

273

'True, and I have few years left, my friend. I can't help my people. Time has beaten me.'

'No. Our spirits have beaten time, Tibbaling. You and many more wise men like you have been given another lifetime to learn.'

'What is this?'

'The great spirits understand that if they cannot find solutions, what hope has mere man with one lifetime? So they've granted you another.'

'Another?'

'Yes.' Warrichatta, his sleek greyness, was disappearing into the silvery sea. 'Another lifetime,' he whispered, 'to learn more, Tibbaling. You've been granted another lifetime.'

'So,' Tibbaling wheezed now. 'So.' Then the wheezing ceased as he drifted away again and the dingo came closer to him, the warrigal spirit, not only his totem but his friend. Always loyal. This warrigal was rarely seen, but he was always nearby. Together they scanned the land, from the distant hills, across the plains, over the dried-up creeks and billabongs, past the great trees that had known them even in the Dreaming, on and on . . .

Tibbaling came out of the reverie with a screech. His body was covered in ants, the giant biting ants. Frantically he slapped and whacked at them, but when he tried to stand, he could not. His right leg, a furnace of pain, would not support him.

The dingo leapt back, surprised by this interruption, but then his eyes widened and he lowered his head, watching the ants, listening to them . . . After a while he turned quietly and padded away into the bush.

Lucas realised he must have been travelling in circles. He was still on burned land. He should have either left it or met the river by now. At times, though, he was in so much pain that he'd lapse into dark shadowy dreams that would eventually toss him back to consciousness, sweating with fear. After that he'd have to rest, too tired to move on.

He rested against a tree, trying to decide on a plan, some way of marking trees as he progressed, but his mouth was so dry, thirst agonising now, that it was a relief to doze, to escape.

He knew he shouldn't sleep in daylight hours, that they should be used to find a way out of this maze, but the temptation was too strong. He was almost asleep when the discomfort began, the itch, the vague scratching, the irritation inside his shirt that had him drowsily rubbing his chest, and then he was fully awake, frantically dragging himself away, cursing as the heat of hundreds of insect bites seared his skin. Lucas was lying on an ants' nest.

'Bull ants,' he spat, rolling away from the vicious beasts that were swarming all over him. Stockmen had pointed them out to him in the camps, warning that they could serve up a very nasty bite, and here he was, stupid enough to be lying on a nest. And they weren't just bites, they stung like bees! Lucas was weeping tears of pain and rage as he fought them off without the aid of a shower of water or a friendly stream. He tore off his shirt, flapping it about, but he couldn't remove his trousers over that broken leg, so the battle continued until the ants decided they'd delivered their punishment and recalled their warriors. Lucas was left panting, exhausted again, lying on an open stretch of ground.

At first he thought it was just the sun, but the hot breath had to be something else. He opened his eyes to find a large fierce dingo staring down at him.

'Oh no,' he groaned, feeling like Job. As if the Lord were thinking up more and more cruelties to inflict on him. He couldn't even react to the dingo. Let the thing bite! He didn't have the strength to chase it away. To shoo it off.

It didn't bite. It backed away, sat down and stared at him.

Good dog, Lucas thought, but he couldn't say it. His tongue was too large for his mouth. He wondered how long he'd been in this place.

The dog stayed, almost as if it were keeping guard, but Lucas lost interest. He had to move on, somehow.

The ants had gone but something else was disturbing Tibbaling. He called to the warrigal, but it too had gone. He scratched his head and looked about him. The bush had lost its colour. It was stark black and white. A fire had been through here. He began walking through the scorched land, trudging on, for there was the warrigal up ahead. Sitting, minding something. A form in the ashes. A man.

'There you are!' Tibbaling said to him, distressed to see the man was in pain and in urgent need of help.

That place was cold and silent, a miserable place, and he was pleased that the familiar gurgling of the creek brought him back from that dream to the bush near Fader Bite's camp.

He went in search of Billy, his protégé, who, Tibbaling had told the spirits, would need three lives to be able to achieve the understanding of these times, where so much was happening, so fast. It was difficult for his people to hold on to their Dreaming, even though in this area most of the murderings had ceased, because white men were tramping everywhere. And newer tribes, who spoke other languages, as well as the Chinese and the Kanakas. He had never seen such a cultural mix in all his born days. It would take a man a lifetime to learn the ways of each one.

'I want you to go to the warrigal,' he told Billy.

'Where will I find him?'

'He will find you. I think he must be in the burned country, where the fire went through recently. Take a canoe upstream. The warrigal will show you where you must go after that.'

All night the dingo stayed with him, keeping him warm, comforting him. In the morning it was gone and an Aborigine stockman was standing over him. Lucas heard him call over his shoulder:

'He doesn't look too good, Yarrupi. Gonna be a job gettin' him outta here.'

Lucas reached up to him, tried to speak, but there was that tongue again, like having a hard lump of fur in your mouth. When it moved, though, he tasted blood; his lips, cracked and bleeding. Sound croaked from his parched throat but they understood. They brought him water, dribbling it into his mouth, on to his face. Time passed. They carried him somewhere . . . to running water . . . a creek, and they cared for him with infinite patience, as if they had all the time in the world, and Lucas worried that darkness might fall again and they might leave him. They had swabbed dirt and ash from his face, he knew that. And done something about his leg, bound it, for it was still painful but it felt secure.

He thought he recalled them rubbing him down with a potion that felt like sap, something to do with bull-ant bites, and he didn't know why that was necessary. Had he been bitten by a bull ant? Why that bothered him he had no idea. He had a broken leg. Why didn't they do something about that? And he was hungry. Starving. Lucas grabbed the arm of the one called Billy and asked him to get his horse.

'I have to get going,' he said, and Billy nodded.

'What did he say?' Yarrupi asked, in their language.

'No idea. He's out to it. We'll have to carry him down to the river. I reckon he's been here for days, poor feller.'

'We take him to our camp?'

'No. Better we hand him over to white folk as soon as possible. You help me get him into the canoe and I'll take him downriver.'

'You be careful on that river, Billy. Not much feed about this old season. Gongora people hungry.'

Billy was too shy to tell his friend Yarrupi about what was happening in his life, even about the little allowable things that Tibbaling was teaching him. They all knew that Tibbaling was a magic man with great powers, but no one, absolutely no one, had any idea of the extent of those powers. Not obvious things, but mind work, as Tibbaling put it, mind work that required long, long hours of intense concentration . . . too much to even think about now. But the warrigal had brought him here. How could he explain to Yarrupi that he'd seen the way through the warrigal's eyes until he came upon him sitting by the man Lucas? And as soon as he and Yarrupi had arrived, the warrigal had slid into the shadows.

But Billy also knew he'd be safe in the canoe. Tibbaling had sent Warrichatta to accompany him and stand guard against that monster Gongora and his tribe, none of whom could be trusted. Even the white men with their guns feared the crocodiles, as they called them, and well they might.

At the river, Mia, who had been minding Jakob's cow, brought milk for Lucas, refusing to allow them to give him solid food yet.

'Poor man,' she said. 'He's very sick. Looking that bad yellow. Take him quick, Billy. And come back to see us soon.'

Billy put his arm around his sister. 'I come home when I can. You people look out for Jakob. He's my friend too. Tibbaling arranged that.'

'He arranges too much,' she said testily. 'He should let you come home and be family.'

With Lucas cocooned in the bottom of the canoe, Billy manoeuvred it out into the current and set off downstream. He looked back to Mia and Yarrupi with not a little envy. How much simpler his life would be, he thought sadly, if he could throw off this stockman shell he was required to wear, to learn more about the white folk. If he could throw off the chains of learning that had him bound, and at the same time enthralled, as his mentor took him from level to level. How much happier he would be.

Then again, maybe not. The world beyond the world was there to be discovered by anyone with the patience to listen and the courage to explore. One mystery, of many, kept eluding him. How was it Tibbaling knew so much, in intricate detail, of things that had happened long before he was born?

Lucas cried out in delirium. Cried out for Hanni.

'Won't be long now, mate,' Billy said, swishing along. 'Won't be long.' The words made a song that Billy sang to keep Lucas awake, and soon Lucas joined in the monotonous chant: 'Won't be long now.'

Neither realised that they were making a chant in their own languages, not English, worlds apart, but Tibbaling heard, and he smiled.

He watched as the good Lutze boys lifted Lucas from the canoe with a shout, and Billy was thanked and made a great fuss of before the jinker was brought over and Lucas was whisked away to the sick house they called a hospital. Then Tibbaling went back to camp for a meal; for he was very hungry and he didn't much like the food Fader Bites, in his kindness, gave him.

Chapter Eleven

Les Jolly and Charlie Mayhew were passengers on the coastal
steamer *Tara* when it left Brisbane. Both men had business
interests in the capital: Les with timber exports and Charlie at
Parliament House, where he had talks with the Premier and
his own representative, Walter Scott, MLA, on the subject of
Kanaka labourers. They found that *Tara* had only a few
passengers on the last leg of the voyage, from Maryborough
to Bundaberg.

'They all piled ashore at Maryborough like stampeding
cattle,' the Captain said, and Charlie laughed.

'Yes, I saw them. Looked like a race to see who could get
off first. How do they get to the goldfields from there?'

'Hoof it,' Les said. 'Unless they can afford to buy horses,
and they're in short supply now. A man should rustle up a
team and go catching brumbies. Money to be made there.'

'Will you listen to him?' Charlie said. 'He's a money-
making machine as it is. I heard you bought the sawmill.'

'And he owns the new pub,' the Captain said.

'The Royal? You own it, Les?'

'Half-share with Baldy Grigg, the licensee. It's solid-built
too, best timber and best carpenters in sight. But what about
you, Charlie? You're always talking about building a good
house on your plantation. Why not let me have a go while I've
got the tradesmen here?'

'A wonder they haven't bolted on you by this,' the Captain
put in. 'Gold's a powerful temptress.'

'They'd better not. I left them to renovate that cottage near
the Royal. It was home to the manager of the sawmill but he

279

had to quit because his wife refused to live in Bundaberg.'

The Captain's laugh rumbled round his small cabin as he poured his friends a farewell whisky. 'I had her aboard! She took one look at Quay Street and refused to disembark. Wouldn't set foot ashore, no matter how he entreated. And didn't she give him the rounds of the kitchen!

' "I'm not a country bumpkin!" she screeched. "How dare you bring me to a place like this!"'

'Yes, that's her.' Les grinned. 'There's a German family renting it temporarily, but they'll have to move on when the renovations are completed.'

Charlie felt a twinge of embarrassment at the mention of the German family, hoping that Keith Dixon had delivered sufficient apologies with that little gift to Mrs Fechner.

'So what about your house, Charlie?' Les was asking. 'Didn't you say you already had an architect's plan drawn up?'

'Yes, I have.' Charlie dragged his thoughts back to them and brightened up at the possibility of building his dream house.

'I want it in the true colonial style, two-storeyed with verandas all about to defeat the rain and the heat, but elegant . . .'

'My lads'll make it as elegant as you want.' Les grinned, but Charlie wasn't so sure.

'With all due respect, Les, I don't want just any builder, I want the best. You've got the carpenters, but can they interpret my plans? Find me the builder and we're in business.'

As would be expected, when *Tara* was safely docked, the two men accompanied Les over to the Royal Hotel, where the licensee was happy to serve Mr Jolly and his friends in a private room and acquaint them with the local news and happenings in their absence.

They heard of the bush fire at the Meissner property. 'There, and the land adjoining, they say.'

'Not Quinlan's place?' Charlie said.

'Yes, that's the name.'

'Did the fire get to the Meissner house?' Les asked.

'Yes. They got burned out. And another fellow got caught

in the fire. Lucky to be alive. The blacks found him and brought him in to the hospital.'

'Who was it?'

'A German. Lucas Fechner.'

'Doesn't he work at Clonmel?' Charlie asked, recognising the name instantly.

'Did. Got the sack.'

'Where are the Meissners now?' Les asked.

'Over the river, staying with loggers, I'm told.'

Les Jolly rarely spared the time to socialise. After two drinks he took his leave and made his way down to the manager's house, pleased to see the renovations were almost complete. The carpenters had transformed the old timber cottage into a neat suburban house with a porch, and now, as well as the bare two bedrooms and kitchen, it was graced with a parlour and a bathroom.

He hadn't meant to disturb anyone by going in just yet, but Mrs Zimmerman came running down to the gate.

'Oh, Mr Jolly, please forgive me. I know I'm behind in the rent but I haven't any money. I told the clerk in your office what had happened, but he says it doesn't make any difference. If you'll just give me a little more time, I'll find the money . . .'

'What's happened, Mrs Zimmerman?' he asked kindly.

'Theo's gone!'

'What? He's left you and the children?'

'Not really,' she said, fighting back tears. 'He's gone off to the gold-diggings.'

Les gave a jerk of impatience. 'Oh well, let's hope he gets back soon. You do know I'll be bringing in a new manager, Mrs Zimmerman. You'll have to vacate then.'

'But I don't have anywhere to go, Mr Jolly. I've put the children in school. It's free. I'm so lucky to have a school start up, I can't move from here!'

'Can't you go out to Taylor's Road? Father Beitz and the others will look after you.'

'No, no! I can't do that. Father Beitz won't let my children go to school here. He disapproves. He says we must wait until he builds the mission school and they can go there.'

It was too much for Les. 'All right, don't worry. We'll work something out.'

'The house is so lovely now,' she said. 'You can see inside, Mr Jolly. I don't let the children touch anything . . .'

'Yes,' he said absently. He was thinking about Theo. Bloody fool. He'd had a steady job with Davey. He may never find gold – he probably won't find gold – so what was his family supposed to live on? Les had had experience with gold miners before this. Once they got the fever, it took a lot to kill their hopes. Almost impossible to prise a miner away from the diggings while there was still a chance of colour . . . They'd drop in their tracks first.

'Mr Jolly,' she asked, 'do you know where I could find a job? I have to get some money from somewhere.'

'You want a job?'

'I must.'

He pushed his hat back and shoved at his thatch of fair hair. 'Well. I don't know. There might be work at the hotel. The Royal. You could go there. Kitchen work, maybe. Tell the publican's wife I sent you. Mrs Grigg.'

'Oh, thank you. I'll go right away.'

'Just a minute. I believe the Meissners' house was burned down?'

'Yes! It's shocking. They've not got a stick nor a stitch left. I don't know what's to become of them. And then there's Lucas Fechner, nearly killed in the fire . . .'

He made his way to his office to attend to a backlog of work, but he couldn't help thinking about that fire, cautiously exploring the timing. Had the German set fire to it himself to prevent the Dixons from getting their hands on that timber? Madder things had happened in these backblocks. Especially when Quinlan was involved.

'I don't suppose they'd risk burning down their own house,' he told himself. 'Though burning off all the undergrowth would make clearing a lot easier. The fire could have got out of hand . . .'

Later, his clerk mentioned not the fire, but Jakob Meissner. 'He beat the Dixons, you know.'

'What do you mean? Beat?'

'Remember you took your men off the Meissner job because the Dixons claimed they were entitled to the timber?'

'Yes.'

'Well . . . it's quite a joke in town. Meissner got legal advice from Arthur Hobday. Called their bluff. Meissner owns the timber.'

'You don't say? That puts a different light on the matter.'

'It sure does.'

But Les was thinking about the fire again. The timing. With spite in the air, the Dixons would be front runners. They'd be ropeable to have the Germans beat them. He didn't want to become involved in local disputes, but this was interesting. It was worth attention. The fire might not be the end of the argument. He decided to ride out and take a look when he could find the time.

'When is the new manager coming, Les?' his clerk asked. 'The manager of the sawmill.'

'He's not. Changed his mind at the last minute, the rat. It's hard to get workers to come here. This town is lagging far behind Maryborough.'

'That's where all the government money goes. They won't spend anything here. Someone should give Walter Scott a shake-up.'

'Like who?' Les asked.

'Keith Dixon is talking about throwing his hat in the ring. His father's got enough cash and push to put him there.'

'God help us.' Les shrugged. He was thinking again about a manager for the sawmill, and had someone in mind.

'How is he?' Eva met Hanni Fechner outside the hospital. 'I've been so worried about him.'

She had never seen Hanni so miserable. She seemed to have aged ten years since the voyage. Her eyes had lost their sparkle, her whole body seemed to droop and her clothes, usually so neat, could have done with a press. That, of course, wouldn't be her fault. Those primitive huts out at the commune were no place for ladies. She'd said it before and she'd say it again.

'He's improving. His back was burnt by the fire,' Hanni was saying.

'Oh my God! I didn't know that. What agony for him! And the leg?'

'It will be in plaster for a long while. Everything is wrong, Eva,' she cried. 'Even his poor hands are all bandaged up. He wore the skin off them trying to drag himself out to safety.' She was weeping. 'It's all too terrible. I don't know what to do. We're both out of work now. I just don't know where to turn . . .'

'At least you've got Father Beitz to fall back on, Hanni. He won't see you starve. So please don't cry. It'll work out.'

'How can you say that, Eva! I hate it out there. You won't stay there yourself.'

'I may have to. I can't stay at the cottage, the new manager is moving in. But Hanni, I've got a job . . .'

'You have? Where?'

'At the new hotel. The Royal. I'm a kitchenmaid, but the cook is nice, she says when I get to know the routine I can fill in for her on her day off. I never thought I'd end up a damn kitchenmaid, but what can you do?'

'Are there any more jobs at the hotel?' Hanni asked eagerly.

'No. They've got a waitress, and men clean the bars. I brought some cake for Lucas, I'd better go in. Are you coming?'

'I can't. I'm too upset. I'm going to walk the town and knock on every door, trying to find some work and somewhere to live, even if I have to leave Lucas with Father Beitz for a while. He'll be out of the hospital in a few days.' She stopped to take Eva's arm. 'I'm sorry. Loading you with my troubles when you've enough of your own. How are the children?'

'They're well. And so happy here. They're going to school; it's a new school, only been open a few weeks, so everything would be fine if I could just find somewhere to live. And by the way, Hanni, please don't mention to Father Beitz that the children are still in the government school. He forbade it.'

Hanni stiffened. 'You leave them there! Don't let him give you orders. And you speak to your landlord! I think it is cruel of him to throw a mother and children out in the street.'

'Oh no. It isn't Mr Jolly's fault. He's a very kind young man. We were only supposed to be there a little while. Another of Theo's half-baked arrangements.'

Hanni didn't bother to ask how Theo was getting on as a gold miner. Obviously no good news there. Yet. It occurred to Hanni that if Lucas were only able to work, as a last resort they could have gone gold mining. Apparently women went too. Anyone could go. But Lucas could not work, and if she couldn't find a job they'd end up charity cases.

'You go in,' she said to Eva. 'And thank you for bringing the cake. I'm sure it's lovely.'

She watched Eva stride across the veranda of the small hospital, wishing she could be as lively and sensible as her. Recent experiences seemed to have knocked the life out of her. And she was still smarting from the lecture Father Beitz had inflicted on her about the evils of drink, demanding she repent and do penance for her sins.

Sins, she thought angrily. What does he know about sins? I could give him an earful. On principle, she never did say any of the extra prayers he'd ordered for her penance.

She wished she could have a piece of that cake Eva was taking in to Lucas, and heaving a sigh, as if shouldering a burden, she set off on her search for accommodation and a job.

Heat was tingling in the air, shimmering on sharp gumtips, spreading a silvery mirage across the road. Walther looked about him, interested. The day was hot. Suddenly very hot. Easily eighty degrees, he estimated. He'd heard someone say, 'Looks like winter's over, thank God.' As if the preceding warm months had been a severe trial. As if they'd at last stumbled into summer.

'So what happened to spring?' he asked himself as he pushed up his sleeves. But he saw Nora sitting under the trees by the river and the weather was, immediately, the least of his concerns.

He hurried over to her, took her hand and brushed his lips over it. 'Have you been waiting long, my dear? I had to take Hanni to the hospital.'

285

'Not long. How is your friend Mr Fechner?'

'Improving, but very unhappy.'

'That'd be an understatement,' she smiled. 'I heard a rumour that someone deliberately lit that fire at Meissner's farm.'

'Oh no. That wouldn't happen. Who would do such a thing?'

She shrugged. 'It's just talk, I suppose. Nothing much happens round here, so they have to invent a few tales.'

Walther sat by her. 'Our church is finished. We only have to do the inside now. We've started making pews . . .' He turned to face her. 'I was hoping we could be married in our little church.'

'Married?' Nora jerked back. 'Are you proposing to me, Walther Badke?'

He nodded. 'I am wishing you would do me the honour.'

When she didn't reply, he rushed on, nervous now. 'You know I love you most sincerely and I think maybe you care for me, but if you don't, then I will understand, and if you do . . .'

Nora looked about her, and seeing no one in sight, kissed him. A signal for him to take her in his arms, a wonderful relief. Overjoyed, he kissed her passionately, in no hurry to conclude the most marvellous moment of his life.

When Nora drew back, he gazed down at her in sheer delight. His dream girl, with her shiny brown hair and that broad smiling mouth and, most of all, her eyes. He could not define their colour, but he'd seen something else right from the start. Intelligence. She was a good, steady, sensible girl, and nobody's fool. Walther liked that about her. Loved her.

'So you accept?' he breathed, sure of himself now.

'I can't. My father won't approve of it. I would marry you if I could, Walther, you know that. But . . .'

'Don't worry. I'll speak to him myself. It will be all right. You'll see.'

'No it won't. And you mustn't go to him, Walther. Definitely not. He'd bundle me off to Sydney on the next boat. Please, Walther, don't you understand? You haven't even got a job, let alone a house. How could you support me?'

'We can live at the commune for the time being . . .'

'In the first place, my father wouldn't have that, and more importantly, I don't want to live there. But for now, and for heaven's sake, Walther, why don't you get a job, a proper job?'

'I have a job, Nora. There's plenty of work to do at the commune.'

'I mean a paid job. With wages. I don't believe you intend to become a missionary, so why are you doing this? Why do you stay there?'

'Because I promised Father Beitz. He has this dream of a mission, to convert natives as well as establishing our own Lutheran settlement. I want to stay until he has it organised, or at least until the new priest arrives to assist him.'

'When will that be?'

'Early next year.'

She sighed. 'Then I think we should wait until then. Wait until you can go to my father armed with your own proposals of how you will support me, and where we will live. I know my father can be very nasty, but when it comes to marriage arrangements, Walther, I don't think he's any different from other fathers. You tell me I'm wrong.'

Walther shuddered, his day ruined. He realised that he'd been kidding himself, thinking love would overcome all obstacles. That Nora would appreciate spiritual life at the commune over and above material needs. He'd been kidding himself because he so enjoyed living there. He really did. It was simple, carefree, idyllic.

'You wouldn't like to live at the commune?' he asked her. 'You always seem to enjoy your visits.'

'Visits, love. Visits. I wouldn't mind it for a week or so. Like a holiday, funning about. But life is serious, Walther, and that is not serious living, no matter what Father Beitz and his dreams tell you.'

He smiled at her. 'Do you suppose I've been playing truant? Hiding away there?'

'Yes, I do. And I'd like to know why. I don't think you're hiding any dark secrets, not you, love, but you've never told me why you left Germany. About your family. If we're to be married one day, I think it would be nice to talk about these things.'

'I didn't think you'd be interested,' he said, recognising part truth and part excuse in that response.

'Of course I am. Your country, Germany . . . I mean, it's so exotic, with all those fascinating cities we read about, and the really old buildings, and all those kings and queens . . . it must be marvellous!'

Walther nodded ruefully. 'We have a saying: the grass is always greener on the other side.'

'So do we.' She kissed him on the cheek. 'I really have to go. I have to do some errands for my mother before lunch. So tell me you're not upset. I'd hate that.'

'I'm not exactly pleased,' he allowed. 'But we'll see . . .'

Nora wasn't exactly pleased with her own response either; Walther's courting had become more intense lately. They'd had deliciously fond meetings in the lovely rainforest glades surrounding the commune, so she'd known he was of a mind to propose to her, and she'd given the situation much thought.

One day she'd tell him how much it hurt to have to speak to him like that, being so critical, but hers was the softest rendition she could muster of the fierce answer he could have expected from her father. If he deigned to receive Walther at all.

And there was another matter she hadn't even dared mention. By this, Father Beitz had told all who would listen about the mission he was founding to bring the Aborigines to God. He boasted that he had already gained the confidence of many of them, and that was certainly true, but as for bringing them to God . . . that ambition had become a joke in the town.

'He'd have more luck with the Kanakas,' people said. 'A different race, more dreamy-eyed, and they've had missionaries swanning about their Solomon Islands for years. But the Aborigines? Fat chance!'

Nora felt they were right. The Aborigines had their own religion. It was the earth and all of nature, which somehow also meant their Dreaming and spirit world. Their religion wasn't learned; it *was* them, as far as white people understood it, and the introduction of Christian rules and regulations made no sense to them. Generally, missions failed. Aborigines were enticed out of curiosity or by food handouts, but they usually wandered away when it suited them, or on more serious occasions reacted violently to insults, real or imagined.

Whether Walther realised this, she didn't know. But at least the Lutheran church and its expected congregation was real, and that had to be considered also.

She sighed and hurried down to Pimbley's store. Lutheran! Her father was against them too. And her mother. She wished she and Walther could elope, go to Germany. Now that would be exciting!

The Stennings had a visitor. Keith Dixon. When Nora walked in he jumped up, took her basket and insisted on carrying it out to the kitchen for her.

Nora accepted with bad grace and, having no choice, returned to the front room to sit with them while her mother apologised to him about this wretched cottage they were forced to inhabit.

'We've been thinking of getting a piece of land on the Hummock,' she informed him, and that caught Nora by surprise.

'That's a good idea, but it's miles out of town, Mother. Would you want to live out there?'

Her father poured two whiskies from the tray on the sideboard and handed one to Keith. 'Who'd want to live in this town?' he laughed. 'It's a crude place. The Hummock is closer to the sea, and it's the only elevated land for fifty miles around.'

'Have you seen the view from up there, Keith?' Mrs Stenning asked, and he nodded.

'Fabulous. It never occurred to me that one could build up there, but of course! I'll have to look into it myself. Would you care to ride up there and explore, Nora? We could go this afternoon.'

'I'm sure she'd love to,' her mother enthused.

'I can't,' she said. 'I have to visit a friend in hospital.'

'Who would that be, dear?'

'Mr Fechner.'

Her father glanced over, his frown not unexpected, but Keith's expression was shifty, furtive.

289

'Who's he?' he asked in that stupid, rude way of his, as if the person he was enquiring about was a nonentity.

'You know perfectly well who he is,' Nora snapped. 'He worked for you.'

'Oh yes, the fellow we had to sack,' he said airily, but Nora had known Keith all her life, and she saw his wary, almost fearful flinch. The Stennings were station people too; their family property was over towards Mount Perry, further west than Clonmel. Her grandparents and uncle were still there, but Jules Stenning had brought his family first to Maryborough, and then to Bundaberg, when he took up various appointments in the civil service. Station people mostly kept to themselves, the élite of the districts, so she'd grown up, as she'd often said, 'with Keith breathing down my neck'.

Jayne Stenning was constantly surprised, and pleased, whenever Keith arrived on their doorstep to renew this odd affection he had for Nora. Which was not reciprocated. And that infuriated her. Was the girl mad? All Nora would ever say was that Keith was the mad one. That he only chased after her because she wouldn't have anything to do with him.

'He's an idiot, Mother! You don't know him like I do. He might be heir to Clonmel and the spoils, he might be good-looking in a dumb sort of way, but he really is a fool. He totally lacks common sense.'

'And I suppose you have bags of it!'

While the Stennings entertained a more eligible suitor, from their point of view, Walther walked over to the pub, bought himself a pint of ale and stood stolidly at the far end of the bar, meditating. No one bothered him. Few in this rough crowd would deem it advisable to intrude on Badke, who, they all agreed, was built like a brick chimney. Not that he was ever hostile. Not at all. He just liked to come in, have his pint and go on his way. Nothing wrong with that, was there? A man was entitled to a bit of peace.

So Walther was left to his thoughts. His worries, more like it. He would have to do something about the commune finances, or Father Beitz's creditors would be sending in the bailiffs. On the other hand, if he were to make a decent showing as Nora's suitor, he would have to prove to Jules Stenning that he wasn't necessarily a poor man. He couldn't do both. As it was, every penny he'd brought with him had gone into the common purse by now. Not that he minded. He rather enjoyed the common cause, but it wasn't working and it never would. That was plain to see.

Walther had already arranged to begin work on the morrow as a chainman for two surveyors, helping them to map roads. He'd been warned it was hard work, but well paid, which was his priority at present. His wages would help to pay the tradesmen working on the stained-glass windows for the church, but this extravagance had to stop. Father Beitz could not go on spending money that was needed for basic living. It was all very well to be saying 'the Lord will provide'. The Lord was doing that. They did have food and shelter, but not enough for a building fund, especially when the priest was airily handing out their precious stores to Aborigines, to entice them to prayers and Bible readings.

Walther Badke ordered another pint, unaware of the surprised glances all around him. He still had his investments, and his land, back in Germany. Obviously it was time to sell up. To settle for this country. A big decision.

He'd emigrated more in anger than as a result of careful thought, and finding compatible people to travel with had been a bonus. Also, he'd been totally enamoured of this idea of a German commune in a faraway land. A Utopia that he could be a part of . . .

The beer was watery. He could make better beer than this in his sleep.

Nora wanted a house. A fine house. He could give her that. Strangely, he had no regrets about handing the family home back to his mother. With all the contents. His animosity had fizzled out, become obsolete.

But now, to spend a lot of money on a fine house would mean deserting the commune in its time of need. It seemed to Walther that the money had to be put to better use, placed where it would do the most good. Though Father Beitz was relying on the funds to be delivered to them by the new pastor, that would only be a stopgap. That money wouldn't last long, and there'd be another mouth to feed.

Walther heaved a sigh. Of disappointment, really. He'd hoped to make his own way here, without having to fall back on his inheritance, but he'd failed. No point in blaming anyone else; he'd made his choice, now he'd have to stand by it. Selling that prime land back home would be a wrench; somehow he'd envisaged building there at a future date, but that pleasant dream would have to be foregone. He decided he'd better make a move before he changed his mind.

He went round to Pimbley's store, bought some writing paper and an envelope, borrowed pen and ink, and stood at the counter by the gauze-covered cheese to compose his letter. A letter to his cousin and best friend Kurt, asking him to sell the land on his behalf. He went on to invite his cousin to come to Australia, to bring the proceeds in person, because there was work for him here. Kurt was a brewer, and also a qualified chemist.

The explanation was dashed off in a few lines. There was a distillery here for rum, and there would be more as sugar crops extended, but there was no brewery. Ales were imported from Brisbane. Walther intended to transplant the famous Badke beer to Bundaberg.

Signed and sealed, the letter was handed to Jim Pimbley, who, in his role as postmaster, demonstrated his expertise by quoting the price of stamps at fourpence. He also showed Walther his latest acquisition, a box of postcards, which he said worked out much cheaper for next time.

From there Walther went to call on Mr Rawlins, the bank manager, who was pleased to see him.

'The church account is overdrawn, Mr Badke.'

'I thought it might be,' Walther said wearily. 'Don't worry about it. I'll see to it. I'm here on another matter . . .'

Rawlins was surprised that this fellow, whom he had taken for another poor German farmer, was in fact quite well off.

'You could have knocked me down with a feather,' he told his clerk, 'when he handed me a list of his German shares and bonds, substantial holdings I can tell you. He wants to convert them to cash, but needs advice. I'll write to a stockbroker in Brisbane and see what's best to do about them. In any event, he has gone off to search for some farmland. By the sound of things he's deserting the commune too. I'll have to keep a tight hand on that overdraft if he does.'

'What does he want the land for?'

'Farming. They're all farmers at heart.'

Not exactly. Walther was looking for agricultural land, but he intended to grow crops for his lager. Barley and hops. He should have told Kurt to bring some seeds with him. He would write a longer letter as soon as he had the time. Maybe Kurt would bring some of the workmen from the brewery with him, especially a cooper to make their casks. Walther had seen some superb timber here, very suitable for the cooper's trade.

So, he mused, as he made his way to the hospital to visit Lucas, cousin Kurt has been thinking about coming to Australia; now he'd better get on with it.

The matron of the Cottage Hospital had given up trying to enforce set visiting hours, because no one in this unruly town took the slightest notice. Folk simply wandered in when it suited them, entering through the front or side doors, even the kitchen. They appeared from all directions and were a constant source of annoyance for her. Especially in the men's ward, where visitors tramped about in dusty clothes, propped themselves on the beds, commandeered chairs or stood about filling the air with pipe smoke, which, of course, was also banned.

Today was no exception. Two nurses were trying to serve meals to the patients, with cheeky visitors teasing, examining the food, bumping out of their way, offering to help and generally causing a nuisance. One look at the scene was enough for Matron. It was one of those days when everything went wrong. They were already nearly an hour late in serving lunch.

'All right!' she exploded. 'Everyone out. Outside!'

A woman, with her family crowded about the second bed, looked up, surprised. 'We won't get in your way, Matron.'

'I said everyone, Mrs Court. My girls haven't got room to move. Now out!'

'You don't have to be so snappy about it,' the woman huffed, apologising to her husband, the patient. 'I'm sorry, love. We won't be long. Now you eat up. If it's edible!'

Lucas watched them all trooping out, among them Hanni and Walther, and he was distressed when Walther called back: 'I'll come again tomorrow.'

He had wanted to talk to Walther privately. He could have found an excuse to send Hanni on an errand. She spent most of the day here, or marching about the town searching for a job, and that upset him, on top of everything else.

He'd been here a week now. His back and his skinned hands and knees were healing, but the leg was in a cast; he wouldn't be able to get about without crutches for ages. No work. No pay. In all his life, Lucas had never been so depressed. It pained him to have people feeling sorry for him, praising him for lasting so long out there in the wilds, asking questions.

The questions. So far he'd kept quiet. He knew he had a propensity to talk too much, say the wrong thing, so he was presently sheltering behind memory loss. 'Can't rightly remember much,' he'd been allowing, so far.

Somewhere along the line he recalled saying that the horse had thrown him, and even that was a mistake. The obvious question then was, 'What were you doing there?'

And he didn't know how to answer. Yet. Couldn't decide.

Father Beitz certainly didn't believe him. That was obvious. 'Why can't you remember?' he'd asked point blank. 'There's nothing wrong with your head.'

Eva Zimmerman had come to his rescue. 'It's the shock, Father. And exposure to the elements for days! It's a wonder he didn't die of his injuries, let alone thirst. People in town are saying he's a hero, is Lucas, to have the courage and the stamina to hold on that long.'

Beitz hadn't been impressed. 'Heroes come cheap here, then. He didn't have much choice!'

At least while they bickered they were leaving him alone, he mused, wishing he could scratch his leg. Hanni, too, had been on at him to explain why he'd been sacked. How come his horse was wandering about loose? The trouble with lies was they were hard to control. Easier to keep dodging the questions. Headaches, faintness, dizziness aided him awhile, but they couldn't last, and anyway, now Matron was on at him too.

'What's this I hear about you having severe headaches?'

Lies again. They stuck like flies.

Flies. He had never known so many flies existed. They buzzed about even in here, with fine wire on the doors and windows, and sticky strips hanging from the ceilings to trap them. It occurred to him, in passing, that he must be assimilating to slip into a local expression like that. About the flies.

He was hungry. He finished off the watery soup and the tasteless stuff they called potato pie, and pushed aside a concoction known as sago custard, waiting for his visitors to return. Hoping that Walther would have changed his mind.

What was he to do? They'd said that tomorrow Rolf was bringing the Meissners in to see him.

God! How could he look them in the eye? It hadn't occurred to anyone that the bush fire might have been deliberately lit. Should he tell them? What a row that would cause. Uproar! But what would it achieve? Dixon would deny it. Yet he had been there. Lucas Fechner. He saw. And in his stupidity he had helped to fire the dry grass. There were two other witnesses as well, Sam and Pike, though they might be too scared to speak up. Anyway, when all was said and done, he pondered, regretting the missed chance to talk this over with Walther, who was a sensible fellow and would keep his mouth shut if asked, you got back to the same question. What would telling the story achieve? It was over. The forest was burned. The Meissners had been burned out. They had nothing left and nothing would bring back their belongings, their clothes and the precious family mementos.

Father Beitz had told him how Jakob had gone to Maryborough to fight off the claim by the Dixons for the timber on his land, and he'd won. Now Lucas understood what Keith Dixon had been up to. Spite. Sheer spite. He wished he could cheer, as he would have at the time, at hearing that Jakob had beaten them, but again it was too late. It was all too late.

Hanni was back. 'You look sad,' she was saying to him.

'Don't be. It's good for us to be back in civilisation again . . .'

'Is that what you call it?' Lucas said bitterly. 'Last night I dreamed we were back home and we had our own little house, and it was snowing and we had this huge feast all set up on a round table outside the front door . . .'

'Just goes to show how stupid dreams are,' she said. 'What was the feast made of? Ice? Now, Matron says you can go home in a day or two . . .'

'Home? That's why my dream was stupid. We don't have a home.'

'We didn't have one before you broke your leg, Lucas. So cut that out. I told you Eva has a job at the Royal Hotel, didn't I?'

'Yes, and she seems happy there.'

'I know. But when I asked her if there were any other jobs going there, she said no. This morning, though, I was staring at that new hotel and thought she must have been fibbing. It's two-storeyed, Lucas. There are rooms, guest rooms, they must need housemaids.'

'Hanni, Eva wouldn't lie to you.'

'I had to make sure. I went to the back door and asked if they needed housemaids. And the woman said no, the guest rooms aren't furnished yet. All of the furnishings have to be brought up here from Brisbane . . .'

Lucas remembered punching Keith Dixon. He remembered the leer that had something to do with his wife. With Hanni . . .

'. . . so they didn't need anyone. Eva was right. But Lucas, she was coming down the back stairs outside the hotel and she nearly saw me come out of the kitchen. I had to duck back and go out the side door.

'Good,' he said, absently.

'What do you mean, "good"? She would have been furious with me for doubting her.'

'Has Walther gone home?'

'Yes, he had work to do. You're not listening to me.'

'Yes I am, Hanni. I was worried about you, that's all. How will you get back to the commune?'

'The same as I do every day. I walk back out there with the Lutze boys.'

'It's a long walk.'

'Only a few miles. You get used to it.'

'And the Meissners are coming tomorrow?'

'Yes. It will be so nice to see them again. It looks like we're all in the same boat now. Except for the Kleinschmidts. They're doing well. Building their own houses.'

'I know . . . I wish I could get out of here, Hanni. It's a crazy thing to say, but I really don't feel up to seeing them, any of them.'

'But you must, Lucas. They're very concerned about you.'

He groaned, feeling trapped.

They came in with Rolf, on their way to take up temporary residence at the commune, so they weren't the most cheerful of visitors. Jakob was planning on rebuilding their house with the help of the Kleinschmidts as soon as he'd had a discussion with his bank manager, and Freda was fretting over the ill-fitting charity clothing they'd been forced to accept. Karl stood silently in the background, looking thoroughly dejected, and Lucas's heart went out to him. Bad enough for his parents and their friends to have to face these crises, but here was a lad, obviously wondering what had happened to all the grand dreams he'd been expecting in this new land. When Karl did speak, it was to engage in an irritated exchange with his mother and earn a rebuke from his father. No doubt the strain was taking its toll on the family. On everyone, for that matter.

And it shouldn't be happening, Lucas thought angrily. This shouldn't be happening at all. If it weren't for Keith Dixon and his attack on Jakob's land, they wouldn't be here in this miserable situation. Any of them.

The more Lucas thought about that, the more outraged he became. They had resorted to talking about the weather and about the sameness of the bush in contrast with the amazing diversity of wildlife, especially in the world of birds . . .

'Freda is becoming quite an expert on the local birds,' Jakob said proudly. 'She's been cataloguing them and sketching them; she sketches very well too. You should see her book, it's—'

'Burnt,' Freda said, despair in her voice. 'Burnt, like everything else.' She dissolved into tears and Jakob put an arm about her. 'Now, now, dear. Bear up.'

Rolf looked to Lucas. 'I have to get going. Les Jolly wants to see me.' Then to Freda: 'I know you're unhappy about going to live at the commune, Freda. You can come back to my place if you want to. You're very welcome.'

'Thank you, Rolf,' Jakob said. 'You've done enough for us. We couldn't be crowding in on you any longer. But please let me know when you've got a free Sunday.'

'It'll be soon, don't you worry. We'll have a house for you in no time. You look after that leg, Lucas.'

The town was busy. Market day brought folk in from near and far. Vendors with their goods took up positions along the river bank from the wharves over to the Immigration Barracks and on past the Kanaka depot. The Chinese with their coolie hats and singsong voices were the main attraction; their crisply fresh vegetables laid out neatly on barrows were haggled over until the last green bean or monster pumpkin left the field. Not to be outdone, the Kanaka women, plump and seductive in their colourful sarongs, murmured their own little songs as they held up luscious tropical fruit and sat hacking the green casing from coconuts with heavy knives. Their sisters offered raffia hats and dilly bags and strings of beads and wondrous artificial flowers, all of which earned them a few pennies to augment the meagre wages of their husbands working in the canefields.

There were also whittlers and leather workers, and old men more than proficient in the art of making whips, demonstrating their prowess in cracking stockwhips with no care for life or limb, as startled passers-by fell back into the crowds to dodge the vicious leather whips.

Children ran helter-skelter, begging farthings from their elders so that they could buy coconut ice or toffees or homemade lemonade from the German lady by the Moreton Bay fig tree.

Eva was flustered, trying to keep her table upright and sell her produce at the same time, what with folk jostling and those awful goats allowed to run loose, sniffing and attempting to chew her tablecloth. But her enterprise was proving successful. Within the first hour she'd sold out, handing over the last of the melting coconut in its square of newspaper wrapping, and dropping pennies into her apron pocket with a satisfying jingle.

That was just as well, because she was due at the hotel later in the morning, but at least she had time to look about now and see how the children were doing. It had taken arguments, but since market day was a Saturday, she felt they should work too, so she'd brought them the wherewithal and instructed them to set up their shoeshine shop with nothing more than a tree stump as their premises. Her elder son, Robie, thought she was mad, and said so, then fell back in fright at the fierceness of her response.

She berated him about responsibility. About work. About the necessity to work. 'Nothing's free,' she shouted at them. 'Not in Germany and not here. You work or you starve, get that through your heads right now. Don't go dreaming of easy ways, they don't happen. So you three better get used to it! What did I say?'

'Work or starve,' they echoed.

'But no one cleans boots here; a lot of them don't even wear any,' Robie rightfully argued.

Eva nodded. 'True. But what wears boots out faster than anything? Neglect, that's what.'

They found a large piece of cardboard and printed on it: 'NEGLECT RUINS BOOTS. SAVE THEM HIER.' No one noticed the spelling. Grinning men, and even some ladies, placed their boots on the old tree stump to have them shined, and saved, for a penny by the enthusiastic Zimmerman kids. The boot-savers were the novelty of the day; few, if any, of the locals had ever heard of anyone paying to have their boots cleaned, and the primitive stall was more fun for the folk than a merry-go-round would have been, if one ever found its way to this lonely hamlet.

That night, the triumphant children were treated to another lecture by their mother.

299

'You see what work did? You made money. Each one of you can keep a penny. The rest goes into this tin for school books. But now I'll tell you this. You're lucky to be going to school, to a proper government school. You like it, don't you?'

'Yes.'

'So you get in there and learn. Listen to every word to get your English right. They have tests all the time. If you fail, I'll pull you out and make you work somewhere, but the others can stay. If you don't want to be the only one in the family not to go to school, be the dunce and stay home.'

As she enlarged on the necessity to pay attention at school, Eva was hard put not to throw in her footloose, lazy, stupid, selfish husband as a prime example of what happened to people who didn't work. But the kids loved their daddy. They couldn't see his shortcomings. All very frustrating, but for now, apart from her job, she had found a way to earn a little money on the side. Next time she'd make a lot more sweets.

She would have been shocked to know that the brown-skinned Kanaka women, making their way back to the camps, were thinking the same thing. They'd sold out too. They would bring more next time. And the Chinese women noticed that the South Sea Islander women did a roaring trade in the sale of pawpaws, so they instructed their husbands to bring them pawpaw shoots. Afterwards, as the market was packing up, Aborigine girls sashayed through the grounds collecting the odd piece of bunting or discarded half-coconuts, ignoring a box of Chinese vegetables that had been lost and forgotten because they had no idea that the foreign plants were even edible, let alone how to cook them. But they liked the tail end of the excitement, an innocent day's fun before darkness set in and more sophisticated possibilities beckoned.

'We have to go,' one girl warned her friends. 'It's getting dark. We have to be back in camp by sunset.'

'Not me,' an older girl said. 'My father says I can stay in town, and if the white men pay me, then good.'

'We can't stay,' the others cried fearfully. 'And you mustn't stay either. It is Tibbaling's rule and the rule of Fader Bites. Their medicine is too strong.'

'Tibbaling says if we dally with white men we will turn

300

ourselves into hags.'

'Fader Bites is worse. He says he has powerful magic and if we dally with white men he will turn us into termite mounds, forever out there, staring into the sunset.'

'White men magic is powerful . . .'

Constable Clem Colley, soon to be made sergeant, according to the latest report received in his office, shook his head in bewilderment as he saw groups of Aborigine women heading out of town. He couldn't believe his eyes. He was here for the express purpose of shooing the lubras out of the township, it being Saturday night, with the lads on the prowl. Not that he was ever successful; they simply dodged away from him and slunk back over vacant blocks and shadowy lanes, looking for the coveted flattery of the whitefellas.

But now look at them! They were leaving. En masse! About forty of them. He wondered if this was a ploy and followed them aways, but they soon disappeared into the bush at the end of Quay Street. With luck, he mused, he could have a quiet night.

Rolf had been trailing about with his boss, Les Jolly, for a couple of hours, still not too sure if this was a social or business arrangement. They'd been down at the wharves watching timber being loaded on to a coastal steamer, then over at the sawmill for more than an hour while Les checked various things and called on Rolf to have a go at identifying sawn timbers. They seemed to drift into the office, where Bob, the manager of the place, dug out a bottle of rum and they sat about downing several nips apiece and discussing the financial state of the mill, which sounded in good order as far as Rolf could make out. He thought that Les must simply have been in the mood for company, showing off his sawmill, taking a break from work . . .

'So what do you think of the mill?' Les asked him.

'Very good,' Rolf said, gathering his thoughts in a hurry. 'Yes. Looks very good, though I am not knowledgeable in this matter.'

'Who is? I didn't know anything about logging,' Les grinned, 'until I hired some axemen and sent them over the river.'

'Is that so?' Rolf said, surprised.

'Too true, my friend. Same goes for the sawmill. Just because I own it doesn't say I'm an expert, if you get my meaning.'

'Yes,' Rolf agreed, though he had no idea why these meanderings were being foisted on him.

'So I'd like you to work here in the sawmill.'

'Me? Why?'

'Because when Bob here ups and leaves because his missus took one look at our town and bolted, I'll need a sawmill manager. Isn't that right, Bob?'

'Yes,' said Bob.

'And you're going to train Rolf before you go, eh?'

'Of course.'

'Train me to do what?'

'Run the bloody sawmill, Rolf. What else? You'll be manager and you'll earn double what you're pulling in as a logger.'

'Me?'

'Yes. If you want the job.'

'At the sawmill?'

Rolf was completely taken by surprise. Thinking quickly, he supposed he could learn how to manage a sawmill. And cope with the paperwork. He'd always been good at numbers. He and Rosie would have to move to town, but that would ease the situation in their little house. Hans and Thomas were planning to build their own place, but that could wait now, and they could turn their hands to the more pressing job of rebuilding the Meissner farmhouse.

'Well?' Les asked.

'Ah! Yes. I'd be honoured, sir. Honoured. I thank you.'

'You do a good job and I'll be thanking you, mate. But you have to be on hand all the time, so I want you to bring your wife and move into the manager's cottage. Bob will be there for a week or so with you, but after that you'll have it to yourselves. Rent comes out of your pay. That all right with you?'

'Yes,' Rolf stuttered. 'Yes, sir.'

'The name's Les.'

After Rolf had left, Bob had to remind his boss: 'What about the other tenants? The Zimmermans?'

'Dammit! I forgot about them. Theo's gone bush and Mrs Zimmerman can't keep up her end of the rent. I really wanted that to be the manager's place, not a boarding house. Rolf's got potential, he's entitled to respect . . .'

'Yes. I'm sorry I can't stay, Les. I saw this as a good steady job, but there you are. Man proposes, wife disposes.'

Les laughed. 'Then do me a favour. It's hard, I know, but will you tell Mrs Zimmerman that they have to vacate? That new people are coming in? I want her out before Rolf comes back to town, so he can't be blamed. They're probably friends, so I don't want him embroiled in her problems. It would be a nice mess if I have to evict the Zimmermans *after* Rolf and his wife move in.'

'I'll make it a clean break,' Bob said. 'It isn't as if she's got nowhere to go. The Lutheran priest called by, nice old chap, he said their commune is progressing and he'd like to see the children back there by the time he opens his mission school.'

'Well there you are,' Les agreed. 'You fix it, Bob.'

Chapter Twelve

'You what?' Constable Clem Colley gasped. 'What sort of charges?'

'Criminal charges, I suppose,' Lucas said. 'That is what we would call them back home.'

'Yeah? Well, things are a damn sight different out here, mate. You can't go round casting aspersions on people like this. And let me tell you, certainly not on good folk like the Dixons.'

'I didn't say the Dixons,' Lucas told him calmly. 'I said Keith Dixon. It is against the law here to deliberately start bush fires, isn't it?'

'Might be,' Colley allowed.

'Bush fires deliberately meant to burn out a neighbour's property and possessions?'

'Depends on what you say is deliberate. Burning off ain't no crime, mister. If a man's burning off to protect his land and it gets out of hand, it's no crime either, so you better watch yourself. What we got here is backburn. Burn back land so that a bush fire has no place to go. That's what you would have seen.'

'No it wasn't. I saw him deliberately light fires with the wind in the right direction to bear down on that property, and he had us help him. Pike, Sam and me . . .'

He knew Colley would pick up on that, but it couldn't be helped. Lucas felt the exact truth was essential to get the story straight. But as expected, Colley laughed.

'There you go again, telling me you helped to light a bloody fire, and at the same time accusing a gentleman of arson –

that's the word – but it don't go down with me, mister. Not in this case. Seems to me you've got a set on young Keith because he sacked you, and this is your way of payback.'

'And it seems to me that you are refusing to do your job. I want charges laid against Keith Dixon and it is your duty to do this.'

'You can't just shout that stuff. You have to sign papers.'

'I understand that. You draw up whatever papers have to be prepared and bring them to me, and I'll sign them.'

'Nice way of thanking people,' Colley growled. 'I help to get you and your missus a good job out there at Clonmel, and what do you do? Bite the hand that feeds you. I bet Keith had a damn good reason for sacking you.' He turned to leave. 'I'll think about it.'

'No you won't,' Lucas shouted after him. 'You'll do it!'

'What was that about?' Matron stuck her head out on to the veranda where Lucas was sitting, waiting to be taken home.

'Nothing much,' he said.

She shrugged. 'If you say so. But Lucas, you watch out. You don't want to get off side with the likes of him.'

A nurse drew her attention away and she returned to the ward; the same nurse who had kindly dropped by the police station early this morning to tell Constable Colley that Mr Fechner would like to see him. And that had worked out well. He'd managed that audience just in time. Since he was temporarily crippled, Jim Pimbley was due any minute to take him out to the commune in his wagon.

Lucas fumed. He felt so helpless. So horribly dependent on people. It was driving him crazy. Possibly, he admitted, this had a bearing on his decision to bring Keith Dixon to justice. Dixon had brought disaster on two families and he shouldn't be allowed to get away with it. That damned policeman had better draw up those papers or Lucas would want to know why.

Weeks had passed and Theo was still away. He'd only written twice, each time to tell her that they were on the verge of a big strike, but so far the strike had not eventuated, Eva assumed. She'd never forgive him for leaving her in the lurch like this.

And she'd never forgive Rolf and Rosie for pushing her out of the cottage. It was unbelievably selfish of them, no matter what they said. Throwing little children on to the street! Turning on friends like that! Theo would have something to say about it when he got home. She didn't believe for one minute that a nice man like Les Jolly would refuse to allow them to share the house. Just because Rolf was the manager of the sawmill now, he and Rosie were bunging on airs, that's all it was.

Then there was Father Beitz, refusing to allow her to 'shelter under our wing', as he put it, unless she took the children out of that 'heathen' school. She tried to convince him that it was a good school, a government school with trained teachers.

'Trained in what?' he snapped. 'Counting to ten? I won't have our children contaminated by those heathens. What prayers do they teach? What religion?'

Eva was careful not to admit that the religious instruction at the school was Church of England, though the prayers sounded much the same. Instead she retaliated with praise for the teacher who was kindly helping the children with their English.

'Mr Hackett understands how difficult it is for children to learn their lessons when they're also learning the language. He gives them private lessons after school.'

Father Beitz wasn't impressed. 'Mrs Zimmerman, let me remind you of the whole point of our communal emigration. You seem to have forgotten that part of my mission is to protect our religion, our traditions and our language. Did you hear that, madam? Our language. Would you have your children forget their heritage? I am shocked by your attitude. This wouldn't be happening if Theo was in town. Does he know his children are being led astray?'

Eva couldn't stand any more. He'd established enough guilt in her to have her seriously concerned about the state of her soul, but even that would not shake her determination to have her children properly educated, and not by a priest, but by a real registered Australian teacher like Mr Hackett. So that they could do the tests that were acceptable in the eyes of

307

important people. Neither she nor Theo had had any formal education. In Theo's case the family was too poor; he had been a chimney sweep at the age of eight, and a fish-gutter at ten, working at the Hamburg fish markets, then he had run away to make his fortune on his own.

'And he's still running,' she sighed.

She day-dreamed about her children's future. Nothing would be allowed to stand in their way. Robie would be a doctor. Hans, who was more of an outdoors type, would be an architect. Or sometimes a veterinarian, because he loved animals. Inge, dear little Inge, now in first grade, would be a teacher. But not an ordinary teacher, with all due respect to Mr Hackett, who was highly intelligent; she would be a professor. Something like that. One of those people in universities who *taught* teachers. Oh yes. Eva Zimmerman was aiming high for her children, and for that she made no apologies.

Having refused to accept Father Beitz's conditions, Eva went back to town, bought a canvas tent and set up camp on the river bank off Quay Street. Taking pity, Bob, the vacating manager of the sawmill, helped them move their belongings and promised to have another word with Les Jolly.

But Jolly only repeated: 'I told you, Bob, it has to be my manager's place, not a boarding house. If a decent boarding house is needed in the damn town, then I'll build one when I get a few quid together. Now you clear the way for Rolf, so he doesn't walk into a situation that we'll be stuck with for ever. Theo's useless. The Theos of this world are dedicated non-payers of rent and bills, believe me. He could pick up a mint at the diggings and he'd still come home broke. They have a pattern about them, Bob. I ought to know, my father was one of them. Bloody useless bastard!'

Bob helped them move into their tent. And he gave Eva sheets and blankets that he'd bought, that he wouldn't be needing now.

'Thank you, Bob.' Eva stood tall, stoical, refusing to admit in front of them – the kids, Bob, and two strange men who'd offered assistance setting up the tent – that she cared, though inside she was dying of embarrassment.

Their tent was hidden under a huge tree and it looked out over the river with its sandy banks. The children loved it. Even while she was unpacking necessities, they were paddling in the warm shallows, and children from another family living in a nearby tent had come to join them.

Apparently, she thought sadly, we're not the only homeless people in Bundaberg, and when she put the question to the visiting children, they appeared surprised that she would ask.

'We come up from the goldfields. Our pa's flat broke. He's gonna start here somewhere, get a proper job.'

Eva wished them well. And herself, remembering that she'd been ashamed at the thought of living the gypsy life out at the commune, and yet here she was, in a worse spot.

'Ah well, never mind,' she told herself. 'Your pride can stand a few dents in a good cause. And the children don't know any better. They think camping out is fun.'

She had just put the children to bed one night when she had a visitor. Her boss, Mr Grigg.

He looked about him, frowning, and Eva quaked. He was a tough character at the best of times, with his bald head, broken nose and large jaw.

'How long you been livin' here?' he asked with a growl.

'Only a week or so,' she said, rather than admit to several weeks.

'It's not right, Eva. Not right for a woman to be on her own in a camp. Too many strange types about. Your husband down at the diggings, is he?'

'Yes.'

'Not much in these raw towns in the way of spare rooms, I suppose?'

'No.'

He walked over to stare at the wide river, flecked by moonlight, and everything was so quiet that Eva could hear fish plopping in the water. She wondered where she would go if he ordered her to leave here. She would have to obey him; her job in his kitchen was at stake.

'Lucky for you it's the dry season,' he remarked. 'You'll be washed out of here in the first good rains.'

'Oh. I didn't know that.'

'Yeah. Well, this won't do, Eva. My missus was telling me about you and the kids down here, so I thought I'd take a look for myself. Now listen here. You know that big shed beside the stables down the end of the hotel yard?'

'Yes.'

'It was full of carpenter's junk and stuff left by the builders. I got some blokes to clear it out so you can move in there with the kids.'

'Move in? Me?'

'Yes. It's only a shed, but it beats a tent, wouldn't you say? You ladies can tidy it up, make it fit for living. Better get on to it tomorrer.'

She stared. Gasped. 'Thank you, Mr Grigg, I'll do that. We'll move in there tomorrow. But please, how much rent will we be paying?'

'Rent? For a shed? Nothing. You can make arrangements with Mrs Grigg to pay for your meals, you and the kids. I better get back, a big mob of lairs in the bar tonight.'

With that he walked away, his step so light he hardly made a sound as he covered the apron of dry grass before reaching the street, and Eva sat down in her only chair with a thump. He was right. That shed had a corrugated iron roof. It would be much better than a tent. What a nice man!

'Be thankful for small mercies,' she reminded herself, deciding she would save every penny she could, because she would never rent again if at all possible. Her next aim was to buy a place, no matter how small; it was the land here that was worth money. People talked about it all the time. Pioneer town, cheap land, until the population started to expand. Eva hoped they were right. Some folk said this would be a ghost town one day, but it didn't feel like it. Newcomers were appearing all the time.

Freda Meissner, too, had refused to stay more than a few days at the commune, but only because there was work to do. Jakob had managed to extend the loan so that he could purchase a new wagon and farm implements to begin clearing up the area around where the farmhouse had stood. He and Karl were preparing to leave, to go out to their property and start over

310

again, expecting Freda to remain in town awhile, but she couldn't bear the inactivity.

'I'm a pair of hands,' she told them. 'I'm needed as much as ever. Every camp has a cook.'

They too were living in a tent by the river, but a long way upstream from Eva's camp, and with each passing day a small piece of land was retrieved from the blackened landscape.

Freda did find camping difficult but she didn't complain, except to say she'd be glad to get back into a house again to escape the heat.

'It's much hotter living in a tent,' she said.

'It's much hotter anyway,' Karl told her. 'It's summer here now.'

'Surely not. It's too early. By my calculations this is spring.'

'Call it what you like. I figure the day temperatures now hang at around ninety degrees, and that's summer for me.'

That night, light rain fell, adding to their discomfort, but when the same falls came, night after night, leaving the days clear, Jakob took note.

'I think this is the end of the dry season, thank God. October. We must remember that.'

To their astonishment and delight, green grass peeped through the scarred ground and shoots began to appear on the blackened eucalypt trees, as if the land had decided to throw off all traces of the fire as quickly as possible.

That was when Les Jolly came to visit them, with apologies for not having called on them earlier. Freda ran for her shawl and hugged it about her in an attempt to cover her worn and ill-fitting dress, found in a box of second-hand clothes that Father Beitz had collected for them.

The men were talking about the weather, as usual, and Jakob remarked on the convenience of the night rain.

Les grinned. 'Yes, that often happens at this time of the year; later, the rain man isn't so helpful. I suppose you know Rolf is running the sawmill now?'

'Yes. We heard.'

'Is that why the lads haven't time to help us rebuild?' Karl asked crossly. 'They promised, but talk's cheap.'

'Karl!' Freda snapped. 'That's enough! People are

311

busy. They can't just turn up when it suits you!' She turned back to Les. 'Actually, Jakob and Karl are progressing well; they have already cleared suitable land ready to use for building.'

'That's what I wanted to talk to you about,' Les said. 'The lads haven't been over to help you because I asked them to hang on a while, until I found time to look about here.'

Freda thought it was rather high-handed of Les, wanting to look about their place, since it was none of his business, but fortunately she held her tongue.

'I've been examining the trees on your property on the way down here,' he told them, 'checking them with my trusty old axe, and do you know, Jakob, all is not lost.'

'What do you mean?'

'I mean a lot of your big old trees have survived. They're so old and so big they've probably been through dozens of bush fires. It was their age that made me think of it. Bush fires are a way of life in this country. Good rains speed up growth, the undergrowth gets too thick for its own good, dries out fast in the dry season, then lightning or a spark comes along and, whoosh! You've got a fire.'

'Yes,' Jakob said politely, wondering where this lecture was leading.

'So. Don't you see?' Les plunged his axe into a nearby tree. 'The timber's still in good shape. We can still use it. A lot of your trees have huge girths; we don't use the outer rims anyway, the sawmill will strip those off. That leaves good strong timber. You've got ironbark, ash, cedar . . . we're in business.'

Jakob was dumbfounded. Karl too found it hard to believe. 'Are you sure?'

'My word, I am. You've still got stands of beautiful timber here, you'll see once we clean it up. I was thinking of starting my loggers here next week, Jakob. What do you think? Do you still want to sell?'

Jakob gulped, nodded. 'Yes.'

Les smiled at Freda. 'I'll give you a fair price. And I wouldn't rush it for the log house, Mrs Meissner. You can have good sawn timber now. Build a decent farmhouse—' He stopped short. 'I'm sorry, I didn't mean to be telling you your business. I just meant—'

But Freda threw her arms about him. 'Les, you're a wonder! Thank you! How can we ever thank you enough?'

Les stayed a little while, very pleased that he'd been able to bring them good news, for they surely needed it. They were living so poorly, struggling along in that wretched camp with only the bare essentials to keep life and limb together.

'Real battlers,' he said to himself as he rode off. 'They deserve a break. Especially since . . .' since, he mused, 'I'm pretty damn sure that fire was deliberately lit.'

He'd come in from the outer boundary of Jakob's second block, which he'd looked over for the timber months ago, and had seen the first signs of the fire, the sharp, burned edge that was presently allowing green shoots to appear. But there wasn't just one burned edge a few yards wide, from where the grass fire had taken off. There were several. More than a hundred yards apart, and yet almost, you could say, in a straight line. What sort of lightning pulls a stunt like that? he wondered. Or sparks? Sun on a stone could reflect enough heat to start a grass fire, but not a series of blazes. He dismounted, walked about. The wind had taken the fire east; it wouldn't have jumped sideways and started individual fires over here, he noticed, as he strode along, and here. No, sir.

Then he picked up an empty matchbox. A discarded matchbox. Anyone could have tossed it there. It didn't prove a thing. It just made Les Jolly very suspicious. Not that he'd be asking about; he had a damned good idea who the culprit was, or whose men had done the job, and he'd be keeping it to himself. The damage was done; everyone had to move on.

It seemed to the folk in Bundaberg that a shipload of madmen had come ashore from the *Loch Nevis*. They were coal miners from Scotland who had been persuaded to emigrate to Australia with assisted passages and report to the mines in Newcastle, a port north of Sydney. Apparently they'd been happy with this arrangement until they reached Newcastle and heard there was gold galore in north Queensland. Then they'd discovered that the *Loch Nevis* was due to proceed to the port of Bundaberg, and en masse, the miners decided to stay put, to head north with their ship.

They tried to talk or even bribe the Captain into sailing further north than Bundaberg, but he had his commitments and insisted that this was impossible. The *Loch Nevis* took on timber in Bundaberg and would be commencing the return voyage from that port.

He did, however, charge the fifty miners twelve shillings each, after hours of haggling, to carry them on to Bundaberg, which was, he assured them, much closer to the newly famous Palmer River goldfields, where the river itself glittered with gold.

Several hours later, the *Loch Nevis* turned about with the tide and headed down the Burnett River for Wide Bay and all ports south. Only the bosun, himself a Scot, felt a stab of regret for what they'd done to the poor ignorant fools.

The miners, wildly happy to be on solid ground at last, spread out into the little town, feeling their oats. They filled in only a few of the forms as requested by the Customs Officer, Stenning, then dumped their gear at the Immigration Barracks; they ran mad across the grassy verges between the wharves and Quay Street for the sheer joy of stretching their legs. A few of them plunged into the river, leaping and splashing like schoolboys, for some weren't all that much older than that anyway.

While some were kicking a ball in the street, others looked for a café or a fish shop, somewhere they could buy a bit of grub, but this no-account flat-as-a-tack apology for a village had nothing to offer growing lads, so they were directed to the pubs, where their canny mates had already discovered that the cheapest drink on offer was a local rum, and a rare sweet dram at that.

No one was ever sure how long it took before the awful truth confronted this invasion of Scots. Before they realised exactly where they were. Exactly.

'We're off to the goldfields,' they told Grigg at the Royal, once they got to talking.

'Ah, yes, Gympie.'

'What's Gympie?'

'Goldfield near here. Been paying for years.'

'No, mon, we're for the Palmer. We bed here this night and we march up to the Palmer tomorrer. We'd no be wastin' time on the leftovers. Not us, mate.'

'The Palmer?' Grigg stared at their eager faces. At their fair, freckled faces and gingery looks. 'You'd never make it, lads, give it away.'

'What's this?' he was asked by a spokesman for the miners. 'What's this about the Palmer goldfields being a distance from here?'

'More than a distance,' said Grigg. 'How are you lads figuring to get there?'

'Shanks's pony,' they laughed. 'We're hoofin' it.'

Grigg shook his head. 'You better have a rethink on that. The Palmer's a thousand miles from here, I'd reckon.'

'Come on now. It canna be that far. We'd fall off land's end.'

There were angry rumbles as the Scots, disinclined to believe the publican, asked other locals, but few were able to express a definite opinion about the location of the river and its gold since it was somewhere up there beyond the bounds of civilisation, as they understood the situation.

Walther came in but he was unable to help, never having heard of the place, and soon after, Constable Clem Colley appeared.

'Will you tell them where the Palmer diggings are?' Grigg asked him. 'Settle the argument.'

Colley turned to address the Scots. 'A bloody long way, lads,' he announced. 'More than a thousand miles, they say, and overrun with cannibals.'

'But there's gold?'

'Tons of it,' Clem laughed. 'I reckon you blokes have made a wrong turning. Don't seem to me you know where you are.'

Now, the Scots were already getting the message that they'd been dumped in this lonely port and left like shags on a rock, a world away from their destination. They were not amused by the Constable, and they certainly didn't appreciate being the butt of his humour. Angry rumblings and mutterings were starting to be heard when, as luck would have it, Jules Stenning, in his capacity as Customs Officer, bowled in, waving a clipboard and shouting angrily. Apparently only half of the Scots had obeyed his instructions to report to his office, and he was in the middle of giving them a good telling-off when one man shoved forward through the crowd and grabbed the clipboard.

'Bugger your rules,' he snarled, then cracked the clipboard in half and sent it flying over the veranda rails, papers fluttering behind it.

With that, the Constable sprang to Stenning's side, telling a now very nasty body of men that if they wished to stay in this town they had to behave themselves.

Walther thought it was a stupid thing to do, considering the mood of the crowd, and he looked to Grigg, but the publican had disappeared out the back door, obviously to replenish supplies.

As if on cue, chairs were cast aside and thrown about, and the mob surged towards Colley. They picked him up bodily and handed him back to the fury of the men at the rear, who threw him after the clipboard, out over the veranda, with hoots of laughter.

Glasses were smashed, tables overturned as some stockmen attacked the strangers, and what had started as a small riot turned into a full-scale brawl. Stenning, left in the firing line, was punched and kicked to the floor, and Walther, with a sigh, ploughed forward into the mob, shouldering men aside as he dragged the battered Customs Officer from being trampled underfoot. He hauled him back towards the safety of the kitchen, fending off punches as he went, until suddenly a gunshot rang out and everything came to a dead stop.

'I'm out of booze and out of tucker,' Grigg shouted. 'The pub's closed.'

Walther handed Stenning over to Mrs Grigg and left the hotel. He saw some men carrying Clem Colley by the shoulders and legs.

'Is he hurt?' he asked.

'Silly bugger. Got himself plenty of dents and bruises for his trouble! We'll cart him over to the hospital.'

By now the mob of Scots were in the street, tramping angrily about. Some headed for the Immigrant Barracks, where Walther hoped they would settle down and let their anger subside, but there was still a nervousness, an unease in the town. Shops were closed and the streets deserted, except for the miners and a few curious Aborigines.

That evening some of the local businessmen slipped into the rear of Pimbley's store to see what could be done about the miners, who were still prowling about the town, causing damage to fences and shop windows. Keith Dixon arrived in town and immediately saw an opportunity to take advantage of the situation. He was still shaky over the debacle with Fechner, hardly able to believe his luck that nothing had come of it. His father had been convinced that Fechner would be bleating all over town, but he was wrong. The fool was in hospital and there hadn't been a peep out of him.

'Anyway,' Keith had told his father, 'he can say what he likes. No one will listen to him.' But that had been bravado, Fechner's German mates would have listened.

'You better pray that's right. We've got work to do in Bundaberg, drumming up support for your run for parliament, and I don't want any problems. And listen, see that you're seen about more with Nora. She's very popular, good family and all, an asset. I don't know why you two aren't engaged by this. You've known each other long enough.'

Keith squirmed. He'd never told his parents . . . he'd never told anyone . . . that twice he'd asked Nora to marry him and twice had been turned down. In fact, though she didn't actually avoid him at dances and social functions, she was distant these days. Sometimes even snippy. Friends said she'd taken up with some German lout, which infuriated him, but he hadn't mentioned this to his parents. He'd never hear the end of it from J.B. Her parents always made him welcome, and that was comforting so he made a point of calling every time he was in town.

'You never know,' he sighed. 'She might come to her senses one of these days.'

He had ridden in too late to witness the fight at the Royal

Hotel, and though he now castigated those louts in a very loud voice for their disgraceful and criminal behaviour, he was sorry he'd missed it. He'd have chucked a chair or two at Grigg himself. Keith hadn't forgotten that new publican's insults. But for now, this was a great opportunity to further his political ambitions, to take the floor here, take the lead while these other fools pussyfooted around.

'They're well and truly marooned here,' Pimbley said. 'No ships due to call for days. That I know of. So how do we get rid of them?'

'We can't,' said Dr Strauss. 'And I suggest we disperse this meeting . . . leave them be.'

'What are you here for?' Keith snapped at him. 'What sort of a goat comes to a meeting to call it off?'

That raised a laugh, so he continued: 'I reckon you earned more today patching blokes up than you would in a year. Are you hoping for another brawl tomorrow?'

'I'm hoping you will understand their predicament. I talked to some of them before I came here. They know they were out of order, and they're sorry about that. They do appreciate that they have accommodation at the barracks . . .'

'Sure they do,' someone shouted. 'That's why they bashed up Stenning, who was only doing his job.'

'Stenning?' Keith asked. 'What happened to Jules?'

'Just a few cuts and bruises,' the doctor said curtly. 'He'll survive. What I am saying is we should just leave them be for now—'

'And let them pillage our town? They're out there now; who knows what they'll attack next?'

Les Jolly stepped forward. 'The doctor's right . . .' But Keith howled him down, demanding they call for police reinforcements from Maryborough immediately.

'Don't you understand?' he shouted. 'Those blokes aren't going anyplace, and our womenfolk are in peril. Will this be the first town in the country's history to admit that ladies are not safe in our streets? Because we're too sissy to stand up for ourselves? I say we telegraph for troopers right away and we use the night to arm every able-bodied man in the town. When the dawn comes those foreign jokers will be in for a shock . . .'

318

'Ye'll never be callin' Scotsmen foreign!' Jock McAvoy, a new arrival who had opened a ship's chandlery in Quay Street, was outraged, and that gave Les the opportunity to step in.

'We haven't met before,' he said, extending his hand. 'But sir, I think you're just the man we want. What about coming with me and we'll have a sit-down with those blokes. See what can be done.'

'We know what's to be done,' Keith said, eyeing the waverers. 'We get our guns, our horses and our whips ready, and first thing in the morning we run them out of town, into the arms of the Maryborough police.'

That brought on a cheer, a muted cheer for fear that the enemy in the street might overhear. They were all fired up, looking forward to this scrap of excitement, even Jim Pimbley, who was heard to say he was quite a sharpshooter in his day.

Les Jolly grabbed his arm. 'What are you saying? You want to shoot them? Christ almighty, Jim, pull yourself together. We've had fights in the pubs before . . .'

'But we haven't had fifty roughnecks take over our town,' Keith fired back. 'What if they decide to stay? We're outnumbered, near enough. Someone said they're marooned here. They've got feet, they can walk. North, south, west or into the sea, I don't care. They're not doing any more damage in this town. I'm going to the telegraph office right now.'

It was Mr Hackett, the school teacher, who reminded him that not just anyone could call for reinforcements. It had to be the local police, and their only representative was in the hospital.

'Never mind. Leave it to me,' Keith said. 'I'll attend to that. You blokes be up and ready at dawn. We'll meet on the back road by the sale yards. And be careful going home. Don't show yourselves. Let them think they've got us bluffed!'

Les shook his head as Dixon disappeared out the back door, leaving him with a nervous Jim Pimbley, who now didn't know which way to jump, the Austrian doctor, and Jock the chandler, who couldn't bring himself to turn on his countrymen.

'How would you feel,' Les asked Pimbley, 'if you were headed for Sydney and you got dumped in Tasmania?'

'I think I'd be pretty cranky,' Jim admitted.

'Then give them a go. You stay home and shut up. And set the example by opening your store as usual.'

'They're miners,' Jock said. 'They say the Palmer goldfields are tough goin'. A mon would have to be desperate to try that hell, and these blokes are new chums. We ought to help them get to the Gympie goldfields, they're bad enough.' He grinned. 'They couldna be worse than the coal mines, though . . .'

Les clapped him on the shoulder. 'Why not, Jock? Let's see what we can do. You coming, Doc?'

Constable Colley was in serious pain. It was no mean feat to be thrown off a high veranda and survive, without breaking one's neck. He was still appalled that such a thing could have happened. He'd never heard of such a shocking thing. To find yourself flying through the air with only seconds to glimpse the rock-hard ground before it sped up to meet you, and bang! Bang! That was what it had felt like. Bang, crash! Breaking every bone in his body, he was sure. Even though that stupid German doctor said nothing was broken, he did not believe it. Would not. If not broken, then they all had to be jolted out of their sockets, because he was in agony. Bruised, battered and bleeding he was, when they brought him in. Sore and scratched. Knees and hands grazed too, stinging like hell. Those bloody Scotchmen, he'd jail the whole bloody lot of them when he got out. The whole bloody lot! If he could think where to put them. His own bloody lockup was only three yards by six, with a high barred window. Bastards! He could chain them to trees, that was legal when a lockup wasn't available.

He chewed on a hard piece of toffee Matron had brought him and thought about that until Keith Dixon came barging in without so much as a 'how are ya'.

'We're calling for reinforcements, Clem. Those bruisers can't be allowed to bail up a whole town. They could ransack the place. Rob us blind, if we don't get help. This just goes to show how stupid it is having only one policeman here. I'll be taking a complaint on that right to the top, you mark my words. Now, since you're stuck here, the best thing is for you

320

to write out your urgent request for more police here immediately, and I'll run it round to the telegraph office.'

'What for?'

'What for? To send the bloody thing. Why do you think?'

'Matron says I can leave tomorrow. After the Doc does his rounds. I'll do it then.'

'Are you mad? The town could be burned down by then!'

'Can't be helped. The telegraph office is closed.'

'Jesus! I know that. I'll get him up.'

'But the office at the other end will be closed. He don't open until nine o'clock.'

'Oh, Christ!' Keith hadn't thought of that. He was reminded of the posse he'd organised for the early morn, the posse he was to lead into action against the Scots. Without the expected police backup. They could round them up, he supposed, but what would they do with them then? And who would guard them until the police from Maryborough did turn up? If they agreed to come at all. Keith was starting to feel sick to his stomach, wondering too what would happen if the Scots took umbrage and put up a strong resistance. His own men would likely run a mile, rather than actually use firearms . . .

'I wanted a word with you anyway,' Clem was saying, 'about that bloke who used to work for you.'

'What bloke?' Keith snapped, marvelling that this apology for a copper seemed to have moved on from the problem at hand without a backward glance.

'The German stockman. You sacked him.'

'Yeah. Fechner. So what?'

'He reckons you set fire to the Meissner property.'

Keith controlled a sharp reaction by bending down to tighten the laces on his boots. 'Where'd he get that idea from?'

'He reckons he was there, seen you do it. Wanted to lay charges.'

'When was this?'

'When he came out of hospital. He got caught in the fire, remember. It was in the paper.'

'That was ages ago. You put him straight, I hope. I don't go round starting bush fires. Spend more time putting them out, Clem, as you well know.'

'Course I do. I just let it pass, Keith. Didn't do nothing. Thought he'd forget about it. Then he wrote me a couple of letters, from the German settlement out there on Taylor's Road. Couldn't come in because of the broken leg . . .'

'Just as well. The man's an idiot. Got a set on me for sacking him, that's all. Trying a bit of payback with his lies.'

'Looks like it, but he turned up at the police station a couple of days ago, wobbling in using a crutch and putting the pressure on. I was figuring on coming out to tell you. He insisted on laying the charges, watching me write it up and signing it himself. I'll have to have a word with Sam and Pike too. The bugger claims they witnessed the crime.'

'Witnessed the crime!' Keith hissed. 'There wasn't any crime.'

'I know that. I just have to go through the motions, so don't take it out on me. Next time Sam and Pike are in town, have them come to see me and we'll shut this down.'

'You'll be waiting for Sam and Pike. They don't work for us any more. I think they joined the Palmer gold rush.'

'Oh well, there you go. That's the end of it.'

But Keith was furious that this mess should have surfaced again. No doubt Meissner himself was behind it, getting his mate Fechner to prefer charges. They really had him in the gun now. Even without witnesses, Fechner could cause a real fuss if he kept on with this complaint. He wouldn't win, but stirring up more trouble would bring J.B. down on Keith's neck again. His father had hit the roof when he was told that the two stockmen had been paid off, Pike a few days before Sam, who had been offered a better job down on Armidale Station in New South Wales. The station was owned by Seth Dixon, who was happy to do a favour for his nephew.

J.B. had ranted and raved about losing two good men, blaming Keith; had argued that it looked suspicious getting rid of that particular pair, but eventually the fuss had died down. Now Keith felt quite smug. It had been a good move getting shot of the witnesses. Nevertheless, he had to somehow shut Fechner up once and for all.

'No matter how good you are to them,' he said to Clem Colley, 'people let you down. I don't blame you for recommending those Fechners, Clem, they seemed all right, but they were trouble right from the start. He never got the hang of the job at all. Knew nothing about sheep, got lost. I'd say that's what happened after I gave him notice . . . he got lost again, forgot to hobble his horse once too often. The horse made its own way home while he stumbled into burned-out country, fell down a gully or something and broke his leg. Simple as that.'

As he was relating all this, his mind was turning to Hanni. Ah yes, Mrs Fechner.

'Then there was his missus. A hussy, that one, making eyes at all the men, strutting around in front of them, lapping up their ogling, I can tell you. And she was a thief. One of my mother's favourite possessions went missing. A hand mirror, beautifully decorated, encrusted really, with gorgeous stones in a gilt setting. It was a work of art, expensive, truly it was. She loved it. Any woman would. Now we couldn't accuse Mrs Fechner outright, we still can't, but it was a relief when she left.'

'Did the mirror ever turn up again?'

'Of course not. My mother has forgotten about it now, and we don't remind her. But I'm betting I know where it is. Next time Fechner turns up, ask him if his wife has a jewelled hand mirror . . .'

Clem sighed. 'I suppose I could do that. God, I'm sore. This bloody bed is made of concrete. I'll get a message to the telegraph operator first thing, Keith, but I think they'll want to know more of what's going on before they send more men.'

'By that time the damage'll be done.'

'You can't blame me. I did my best and got busted up for my trouble. I reckon they'll send a replacement for me, though. I could get a holiday out of this. Jesus, I'm thirsty. Could you get me a cup of tea from the kitchen, Keith?'

The visitor stuck his hat on his head. 'Ask the nurse. I'll see you later.'

* * *

323

They were beginning to gather by the stand of bamboo at the entrance to the sale yards, walking their horses quietly along the high fence, but the bamboo clattered in the early morning breeze as if determined to give the game away.

'Keith's late,' someone whispered.

Jules Stenning's horse was well trained. It waited patiently while the other nags edged and sidled about. He patted its neck in appreciation and gave his rifle holster a pat too. He hadn't attended the meeting, too groggy to rise from his sick bed after the pounding he'd taken from those bastards, but he was glad they'd thought to let him know. Bruised though he was, with a gash on his arm and a monster of a headache, he wouldn't have missed this for the world. Those blokes would get their money's worth this morning. They'd find out they couldn't rampage in a town like this and beat up government officials, high-ranking government officials.

'They might get away with this sort of behaviour in the slums they come from, but not here. They're in for a shock this morning, I tell you,' he announced.

'Too right, Jules,' a voice agreed. 'I wish the rest of the blokes would get a move on, or we'll lose the element of surprise.'

There were eight horsemen so far, all mounted, all armed.

'Where are the rest?' Jules asked angrily. 'I was told there'd be at least twenty of us, and more when they got to hear what was going down. Like I did.'

'Jim Pimbley was supposed to be coming.'

'Well, where is he? It's sun-up.'

As if they needed to be sure, heads turned to the east, to a long, low bank of harmless clouds streaked with gold, and the sky beyond, which was fast fading from warm pink to blue. Birds were already chattering and magpies singing solos from high trees, and a huge flock of parrots screamed over them before wheeling back towards the river.

'Oh, Jesus!' one of the men complained. 'Those bloody birds could wake the dead.'

'It's going to be a hot day,' someone said. 'I reckon we're in for a blazing summer.'

'They say this is going to be a real wet season too. We

should get a bumper crop of mangoes and pawpaws. My missus planted thirty pawpaw trees down our back yard, and she says—'

'Will you shut up!' Stenning fumed. 'Those rogues will be up and out by this, we can't wait any longer. We have to have them corralled before the troopers get here, otherwise they could disappear into the countryside.'

One of the men wanted to know about that. 'What does it matter as long as they get out of Bundaberg? Who cares where they disappear to?'

'Because they're illegal immigrants, that's why.'

Stenning knew that wasn't strictly true. Not all were illegal. Only the ones who hadn't filled in the forms, or who had proffered nothing more than an X, accepted for people who couldn't write if they'd given their names and relevant information to the attending officer. Which these ones hadn't bothered to do, and that had infuriated Jules right from the start.

'They don't give a dud penny about us,' he added. 'They think that because they come from the Old Country they're better than us. They wouldn't even deign to fill in my forms properly. Made a joke of it. But this town is no pushover, we'll teach them how to behave. We'll teach them to wreck our pubs and bash up our folk. If it hadn't been for Grigg pulling me out of that mêlée yesterday, they could have killed me. It's disgraceful! And this in a peaceful little town like Bundaberg, where we've always been hospitable to immigrants! But no more, no bloody more . . .'

'I heard it was Walther who pulled you clear,' one of the horseman called to him, but Stenning saw Keith coming at last.

He wasn't impressed with the attendance. 'This won't do. There aren't enough of us.'

'Yes it will,' Stenning said angrily. 'We've got the jump on them.' What he really meant was that he would be dragging out ringleaders and holding his own court before the police arrived. Those louts had to pay for the beating he'd endured. He'd see to that. Flogging was too good for them, but it would do. In the absence of Constable Colley, he was next in line in the power stakes, and he meant to use his position. His heart was pounding now, excitement building.

He rode to the head of his small troop, shouting, 'For the honour of Bundaberg! Charge!'

It was often said, in all seriousness, that they did look impressive, those few brave men, charging down Bourbong Street (the long way, some said), around the corner and into Quay Street to take on the fifty thugs who threatened their peaceful little town.

'It was early,' a woman said. 'We were just up and about as they came thundering past our front fence. It was truly a sight to see. And we were bloody proud of them. Our menfolk. I don't care what people say.'

What the papers said the next day was that Stenning and Keith Dixon had led this ridiculous charge against Scottish immigrants who had already written a letter of apology to the townsfolk for their behaviour on the previous evening. A letter that was published in the paper the very day of the charge.

Stenning led the advance, placing his men at corner points around the Immigration Barracks and shouting to the men inside:

'I demand you surrender forthwith. Stand to, out here, in the name of the law.'

Some of the Scots wandered out, more curious than concerned at the sight of firearms at this hour, but several ladies came bustling out too.

'What are you silly men doing?' the doctor's wife demanded. 'We have come to give these gentlemen breakfast before they leave, since no one thought to offer them a welcome yesterday. Now get away with you!'

'You're feeding them?' Keith Dixon shouted as he rode over to Stenning. 'They're about to be charged with rioting, damage to property, and assault.'

Then Les Jolly appeared and told them that he and Grigg owned the Royal Hotel, and although there was some damage, no charges would be laid.

'What about me?' Stenning shouted. 'I am charging them with assault on my person.'

326

'You can't charge them all,' Les said. 'You make your charges to the police, not here. Now put those firearms away before you shoot one another.'

'You think you're smart,' Keith yelled at him. 'We want all of those tramps out of there. Stenning here says most of them are illegal immigrants. They're not entitled to shelter . . .'

Les Jolly strode over to him. 'How will you get them out, Dixon? Set fire to the place? That's your deal, isn't it? But let me tell you, people here are awake to your tricks. It's time you pulled your head in.'

The flush seemed to come up from his neck. Keith was mortified that he couldn't stop it. Some of the horsemen had heard the exchange and it was their turn to be curious.

'I don't know what you're talking about,' he muttered, wishing he dared point his rifle at Les Jolly, give him a fright.

'Oh yes you do,' Jolly said. 'If you are stupid enough to think you can win a seat in Parliament, try it. You'll be lucky to get a second vote after your own. And especially after this episode. You're a bloody fool, Dixon. Go home.'

Stenning noticed that most of the vigilante group were quietly retreating, backing their horses away and turning to the street. He wondered what the clash between Les and Keith was all about, but this was no time to be worrying about Dixon. He was a fool of a man really; Nora had his measure.

'You don't seem to understand,' Stenning told Les. '*I* am here on legitimate business.' The implication being that he had had no part in Keith Dixon's escapades. His rifle was still in its holster by his saddle, where it was always kept.

'All of these men must register correctly as immigrants or face arrest. That's the law and you know it.'

'Then we'll get them all registered. As soon as they're fed I'll send them over to your office to get that out of the way, because they're all leaving town. That's why we're up and about so early.'

Stenning was bewildered. 'There are no ships. Where are they going?'

'Down to the Gympie goldfields. If you hurry along the paperwork, they'll be on the march before the shops open.'

'But I was assaulted. I could have been killed!'

Les shook his head. 'No point telling me, Jules. Go see Clem Colley.'

Nora Stenning and her mother were reading about 'The Charge of the Vigilantes" in the kitchen and were doubled up with laughter.

'Just don't talk about it in front of your father,' Mrs Stenning warned. 'He is not amused.'

'But he was one of them,' Nora giggled.

'He says not. He wasn't even at the meeting the night before. It was all Keith Dixon's bright idea. Your father only went over there to complete the registrations.'

'I bet he did!' Nora laughed. 'And did he tell you that it was Walther who rescued him from the mob?'

'Nonsense.'

'It's true. I haven't seen Walther to ask him, but everyone's talking about it.'

'Whether he did or not, it makes no difference. You keep away from that German fellow. He is simply not suitable.'

Nora sighed. 'Yes. I told him that.'

Her mother blinked as Nora headed for the pantry. 'Good Lord,' she said. She knew it would be pointless to ask her daughter to explain that, so she merely shrugged and turned back to the chops. Jules liked them well done, almost charred.

'I had another talk to the Constable today,' Lucas said, but Hanni was tired of the subject.

'Why do you waste your time? He doesn't believe you, he won't lift a finger, and what does it matter now? Did you get me the stockings I ordered at Pimbley's store?'

'You don't need stockings here. Father Beitz says it's healthier not to enclose our feet. The open-weave sandals are sufficient.'

'Tell the truth, Lucas. We haven't any money left. You've handed it all over to him!' Hanni stormed back into the small hut they now occupied, just another native hut with a thatched roof, hidden among the trees on the other side of Walther's kitchen, such as it was.

Lucas followed her angrily. 'What else could I do? I still can't walk without the crutch, I haven't a hope of getting a job until my leg is strong again; we have to pay for our keep.'

'You call this keep?' she cried. 'Living like animals in stables? The horses you had in your care back home lived better than this. I can't bear to think about them in their lovely secure brick buildings, with real floors and beautiful rugs and men like you paid to pet and pamper them and—'

'Shut up! Do you hear me? Shut up!'

Hanni sat down on their bed with a jolt, shocked that he would shout at her like that. Lucas had never even raised his voice to her before.

'I'm sick of your complaints,' he said. 'I'm not here by choice either. It's humiliating for me to have to spend my days like an old pensioner. So shut up!'

Hanni didn't dare say a word. Father Beitz had Lucas filling his days making pews for the church from offcuts of fine timber that Rolf Kleinschmidt had donated. Lucas was no carpenter, he'd freely admitted that, but he was learning. Trial and error, he'd told his wife, and in the end she'd envied him having something to do that he was beginning to enjoy. She'd been relegated to the vegetable garden, where she didn't know weeds from prized plants and didn't want to know. Everything here grew to monster size, there were no tiny little flowers peeping from delicate leaves; blooms exploded into colour and then fell away, they didn't seem to last. Certainly not the kind of flowers one could gather up and take into a house.

Lucas was standing, leaning against a doorpost saying nothing, just staring out at the bush. Not that there was anything to see, except for that bunch of green bananas hanging high above them. They'd been watching them for ages, waiting for them to ripen. It would be a thrill to eat bananas straight from a tree.

Eventually Lucas turned to her. 'I have to ask you something, Hanni.'

'What?'

'Where did you get that pretty mirror?'

'What pretty mirror?'

Lucas groaned. 'The one in the bottom of the trunk.'

'Oh, that! My mother gave it to me.'

He hobbled over and sat beside her. 'Hanni, this is import-ant. I know your mother didn't give it to you. You didn't bring it with you or I would have noticed it long before this.'

'She did so give it to me.'

'Please don't lie. That's not true, Hanni. Just tell me where you got it from.'

'What does it matter where it came from? I have to go, I've got to do the vegetables for supper.'

She moved to get up but he pulled her back. 'I asked you a question. Now you stay right there until you answer me. Truthfully.'

'You're being obnoxious, Lucas. I hate you when you're in these nasty moods. It's bad enough having to live here without putting up with your moods . . .'

'Where?' he insisted.

She bridled. 'I found it, if you want to know. I found it.'

'Where?'

'I can't remember now. Forget the stupid mirror. Actually, I was thinking of selling it on market day. See what I have to do? Selling my pretty things . . .'

Hanni wondered what on earth had brought this on. Even if he'd had some sort of conversation with the policeman today, they would have been talking about the fire, not about the mirror. His questions seemed pointless, but Hanni knew they were not, and she was frightened. She sat, looking down at her feet, hoping this would all go away, whatever it was.

Lucas, too, was upset, she could see that, but it was his own fault for nagging at her.

'So. You found the mirror. You don't know where you found it.' He heaved a sigh. 'Then let me tell you what Constable Colley has to say. He has been informed that the mirror was much prized. It belonged to Mrs Dixon, and you stole it.'

Hanni was shocked. This was the last thing she'd expected. Her answer came blurting out. 'Stole it! I did not! How dare they say that! He gave it to me.'

The silence was startling as Hanni realised what she'd said. Lucas received the response like an unexpected blow. When he did speak, his voice was a croak.

330

'He? Who is he?'

'What does it matter? I didn't steal it. I'm not a thief, you know that, Lucas. Don't let them accuse me of stealing. Please, Lucas. You tell the policeman it was a gift.' She was crying, clinging to him. 'I worked hard out there. They said I was very good at my work. They gave it to me.'

Gently, firmly, he drew back and faced her. 'You said "he". Who was he?'

'I didn't mean it. I meant they. Mrs Dixon, or the house-keeper, I can't remember. One of them.'

Through floods of tears, Hanni stuck to her story, and they parried back and forth until Lucas could stand it no longer.

'It was Keith Dixon, wasn't it? Keith Dixon. And now he's using you to make me withdraw the charges of arson. If I do that, he won't charge you with theft. Colley made that very plain.'

'Then you must drop those charges. I told you it was a waste of time anyway. Don't let them drag me into it. They might put me in jail.' Hanni was almost hysterical by now, and she flung herself on the bed, sobbing into the pillow, lifting her head only to insist he make peace with the policeman. Put a stop to all this trouble.

'Very well,' he said at length. 'I'll withdraw the arson charge, so you won't have to worry, but I would like to know when and why Keith Dixon gave you that gift.'

Her weeping stopped abruptly. 'I never said he did,' she sniffed.

'You don't have to. I know that much. So now I want you to tell me why he gave you such a splendid gift, and when it was.'

When she refused to answer him, Lucas was furious. 'I was warned by the men I worked with that something was happening between you and Dixon – not so much in words, but they were letting me know – and I wouldn't believe them. I was a fool. You were laughing at me. He certainly was . . . and you . . .'

He seemed to have run out of words. He grabbed the crutch and climbed to his feet, rushing to get out of there.

'You don't understand,' Hanni cried.

Lucas turned back. 'Oh yes I do. You betrayed me. You made a fool of me out there at the station, and now you're doing it again. I have to go cap in hand to Constable Colley, he'll report to Dixon that he's off the hook, so who gets the last laugh? Your lover, Keith Dixon. So . . . you can do what you please from now on. Stay here, leave, jump in the creek. I don't want to know you any more.'

This time Hanni didn't even attempt to reply. She managed to stop crying but inside she could still feel deep, miserable sobs that looked like remaining with her for ever. She sat up, fished in her apron pocket for a handkerchief and blew her nose.

'Keith Dixon had the last laugh ages ago,' she said bitterly as she heard Lucas tramping along the leafy bush track.

'What's this about Jakob Meissner's property being deliberately fired?' Father Beitz asked.

'I've no idea,' Lucas replied.

'Hanni says that is why you two are having difficulties. Have you mentioned this to Jakob?'

'Of course not.'

'That's a relief. I shouldn't want gossip like that to cause trouble. I'll speak to Hanni again. In fact, I should like to have a few words with both of you. This evening, if you please. After prayers.'

'There's nothing to be said, Father.'

'My dear fellow, whatever your problems, don't shut out the Lord.'

'Then I'll have a private talk to Him, Father, if you don't mind.'

Father Beitz did mind. He kept trying to discover what ailed this marriage. Surely they wouldn't be so seriously at odds simply because Hanni was unhappy living at the commune. Neither of them would discuss the problem, not even with Walther, so it remained a mystery and a disruption to the harmony of the small settlement, and it distressed their priest. He felt he had failed in his pastoral duties with only three of their Lutheran group content to live the communal life. And a marriage falling apart right under his nose.

But he had another problem. Before they left Hamburg he had ordered a beautiful church bell to go in the belfry of the church he proposed to build here in Bundaberg. His church was almost ready. St John's Church it would be named, at the blessing ceremonies. Walther and Lucas were making the pews and the altar rails, and some gentlemen were putting the two lovely stained-glass windows in the wall behind the altar.

He'd received a shipping notice advising him that the bell had been landed in Brisbane and would be forwarded to Bundaberg upon payment to the manufacturer's agent the sum of £22 7s. 6d. Further shipping costs of seventeen shillings would be payable on collection, plus customs duty.

Father Beitz would have despaired had his faith not supported him. His church didn't have a belfry. He couldn't afford to add one yet. He couldn't even afford to pay the gentlemen who were working on the stained-glass windows, let alone send that outrageous amount to Brisbane for his bell. Walther had tried to postpone work on the windows, but that could not be allowed. And now Tibbaling and his people seemed to have become captivated by them. They had never seen anything so beautiful. They came from far and wide, bringing their little darkie piccaninnies to gaze at them as they neared completion, to rush inside and view the gorgeous colours reflected by the sunshine on the fine cedar flooring, and to look up at Jesus himself, on one side, with little children in beauteous colour; and, not to be outdone, the Holy Trinity on the other side.

Father Beitz himself was so thrilled by the joy his almost completed stained-glass windows were bringing to the natives that he had tears in his eyes when he saw them drop to their knees. They were obviously convinced that his God had finally arrived. The God he'd been talking about all this time. Now they could see Him in living colour. Though the natives, including Tibbaling, kept referring to Him as the white man's gods. Gods! Only now did Father Beitz realise that his choice of subject for the second window was, perhaps, a mistake. Or rather, a little premature.

It was difficult to explain the Trinity, particularly to Tibbaling, who could be irritating at times, with so many questions. But after much discussion the old Aborigine seemed to have grasped the concept, and Father Beitz was delighted. 'You understand now?'

'Yes, Fader. Allasame bloody simple,' Tibbaling chortled. 'You talk too much hard stuff, Fader. Get all mixed up in your own self. Now you say you got one God. Only one. No more. Good I like to meet your God one day.'

'You will, my dear fellow, it is my fondest dream.'

'Because we people got no God, only spirits, and that's orright. Meet your'n. Pretty good, eh? Make bloody sure,' he laughed, punching the priest in the arm. 'More good spirit is the better, eh?'

'Yes,' the priest allowed.

'And you call them three fellers Trinity?'

'Yes.'

'And the young one with the beard, he came to earth?'

'Yes.'

'And them other two you say are spirits?'

'Well, there's the Holy Spirit, yes, and the Father . . .'

'That's what I say too. Up there you got three men walking. One shows himself to the earth people, them others walk with him allatime, eh? But we doan see them.'

'You could say that,' Beitz said, bemused.

Tibbaling looked earnestly at the priest. 'Even you? You don't see them other two fellers in real? Only on the glass?'

'No, they do not show themselves. But we know they are there.'

Tibbaling accepted this as a matter of course. He nodded, understanding. 'Is good, your Trinity. Three-Men-Walking. Good.'

Returning now to his worldly problems, Father Beitz contemplated Walther's assessment of the situation. They had no money left in the bank. Their only income was the meagre wage the Lutze boys brought home. They couldn't pay the men who had been sent here specifically to put in those windows, at the priest's request. They would have to be asked to wait for their money. And Walther didn't even know about the bell. Father Beitz dared not mention it.

He decided that all he could do was pray more and eat less.

334

Tibbaling gave a great deal of thought to his friend Fader Bites. A great deal. You only had to look into his interesting blue eyes to see this was a good man, a holy man.

Tibbaling spent a lot of time stripped of the trousers and shirt his friend had provided, for modesty, walking through the thick and lonely jungles that surrounded the German camp. This was not a sacred site, it was too overrun with greedy plants, all fighting for space because the boom-boom soil overfed them. Vines like pythons curled and foiled around trees that had no place in there, any more than the sinuous succulents did. It was a madhouse of a forest, dry and spiky in the dry season and a swamp in the wet, but it was a source of food and must be respected. When he looked at what the white men had done, along this river, he was pleased that he'd allowed Fader Bites and his people to make camp here. Not that he would have been able to stop them, troopers with guns would have seen to it . . . But Fader Bites didn't seem to know that and was grateful, so much so that he was preparing to introduce Tibbaling's people to his God. A great honour.

There was only one problem, which caused Tibbaling some sadness. Though Fader Bites was indeed the leader of his people, and well respected, it didn't seem that his god, or His accompanying pair of invisible gods, gave much in return. Here was their holy man beset with worries about material things when he should be given more time for contemplation. Fader Bites had said so himself. He said he missed the life in his previous home, where much time was given over to meditation, and Tibbaling agreed that this was of great importance for a holy man, so that he could look into the mysteries of nature. He even offered to arrange a private retreat for Fader Bites, in a holy place where food would be brought to him but his solitude would be uninterrupted.

But no. Fader Bites could not do this, he was too busy. Tibbaling thought it rather mean of his Gods that they didn't step in to assist such a faithful servant. And worst of all, they allowed him to come to a place where his magic wouldn't work. Poor Fader Bites, he had no Warrichatta, no Gongora, not even a warrigal to help him connect with what was happening all about.

Fader Bites said that this god and the two spirits lived in heaven above the stars, and yet he didn't know any of the stars. Tibbaling didn't know how *he* would cope without the Harah spirits of the moon and the star babies. He knew all the stars in the earth's roof; how would he not? That was why he'd tried to teach them to Fader Bites, so that the magic might come more easily to him. But Fader Bites only fell asleep, without even a woman to soften his nights.

In all, Tibbaling wasn't impressed with the way the gods treated their holy man, and he intended to say so when one of them decided to manifest himself, as Fader Bites had said would happen.

'You will see the face of God if you have faith, Tibbaling,' he had said. 'You will see Him.'

Tibbaling didn't doubt for a moment that he would. Connecting with spirits wasn't a matter of faith, as in believing, because of course he believed in spirits. Who on this earth did not? They were everywhere. Meeting them could happen to anyone. Knowing them required a higher plane. Ahead were the mysteries.

He was looking forward to meeting God Jesus, his father and the spirit known as Holy.

Chapter Thirteen

Though he had yet to meet him, Pastor Ritter had already become a veritable saint to Father Beitz, who daily asked someone where that ship *Clovis* might be by now. He couldn't believe it was taking so long to cross the oceans, having forgotten, or blotted out, the tedium of their own interminable journey, and he grew more and more impatient for the arrival of his curate. The money he was bringing would be helpful, but the pastor himself was desperately needed by the old priest, who felt he was failing in his endeavours. Ritter was young, he had volunteered for missionary work. That in itself was a brave and blessed deed, Father Beitz told Walther.

'Too many young priests seek upper-class parishes these days, pandering to the gentry in order to feather their own nests. But here we have a godly fellow, ready to fight the good fight the minute he walks out of the seminary.'

Father Beitz was disappointed that he wouldn't be able to introduce Pastor Ritter to a Lutheran village inhabited by happy German migrants, and a flourishing mission school attended by native children as well as their own, but that couldn't be helped. His grand plan was simply taking longer than expected. He had no doubt that it would succeed, that other German migrants would join them. In fact, lately, he had had a great idea . . . to establish their own press, their own newspaper. What a boon that would be! A sure way to overcome the great problem of distance here, and to keep in touch with the congregation. He'd have the new pastor look into that. It could be his project.

But there was the other matter, the reason why he looked

forward to Ritter's arrival with such fondness. His own days were numbered, that was obvious, and now in these twilight years Father Beitz missed having his own pastor. At times he became quite emotional about this, in the privacy of his hut, rather like enduring a bout of homesickness, he sighed. He needed to be able to talk to one of his own, as he used to do back home. To spend evenings with friends in the priesthood, discussing philosophy, theology and history, and the changing world as it applied to their circumstances . . . and, he smiled sadly, every little thing . . .

'Today, though,' he told himself, 'I can't be indulging in self-pity. Not today, the anniversary of the birth of our Lord and Saviour.'

Christmas Day. Father Beitz had discarded his tropical clothes for this important festival, and was resplendent in his best vestments, including his good white surplice, ready to welcome his flock to morning mass, to be followed by a midday feast.

He was disappointed that only the occupants of the commune had attended his Christmas Eve service, but he supposed it could not be helped, considering the distance some of his people had to travel. But he'd brook no excuse for today.

At his request, Lucas had built an archway at the entrance to the commune, and in recognition of the special day, Aborigine women had garlanded it with hundreds of gorgeous tropical blooms.

So the old priest was up early, looking his best. He hurried out front to peer down the long road for the first-comers, and when he saw the lovely archway he was delighted.

'What a wonderful surprise, ladies. Just beautiful. Thank you.'

The women, relieved that he was pleased with their efforts, giggled and grinned in their usual shy manner and then settled on the grass verge to watch for his expected visitors.

When at last one of the women dashed into the commune, calling, 'Wagon comen!' Father Beitz sprinted down the path to greet it.

By the time the wagon grew close, the other men were

waiting with him. The priest prayed that Hanni Fechner would be on board. Some weeks back she had found employment at the Royal Hotel as a housemaid and had left Lucas, and the commune. Since she was also working at the hotel, the publican had permitted her to share that big shed with Eva Zimmerman and her children, which was a pity. Her place was here with her husband. Father Beitz was appalled that Lucas would permit such wicked behaviour, but he flatly refused to make any effort to bring her back.

'But she's your wife, Lucas! It's bad enough for Eva to be there, though she has an excuse of sorts, without her husband to guide her. You're allowing your wife to come too close to occasions of sin, especially around a tavern . . .'

'I don't care, she can please herself what she does.'

No matter how hard he tried, pleaded, Father Beitz could not unearth the reason for the animosity between the couple, and no one else seemed to know either . . .

But there she was, sitting beside Jakob Meissner, along with Eva. Thanks be to God. Maybe today they would reunite, put away their differences.

The children jumped down and sped off to explore, only to be called back by Eva to greet Father Beitz in a proper manner.

'Bless you,' he said to them when they dashed over to him, patting each one on the head. They were growing, these children. It was another disappointment to his cause, that their father should still be at the goldfields. Theo should know what a bad example he was to his children and other young people.

The Meissners seemed very happy, and so they should be. Walther said they'd earned a lot of money form the sale of their timber.

'Welcome,' Father Beitz said to them. 'Happy Christmas. Tell me, Jakob, is your new house finished yet?'

'Not yet, Father, but we have a roof now.'

'Thank heavens,' Freda added.

'You always had a roof here,' the priest sniffed, but Karl missed that.

'This house is big and roomy,' he enthused. 'A real farmhouse. You'll have to come and visit, Father, and I'll take

339

you to see my block. I'm building a barn there first . . .'

'Who is this coming?' The priest walked away to greet another wagonload of callers.

'That's Rolf and his clan,' Karl said to his mother. 'He could see that.'

'I don't think he wants to hear about your block,' she laughed. 'Did you bring his Christmas present?'

'Yes. If he hates it he can always sell it.'

'He won't,' Jakob said, though it had also occurred to him that Beitz might sell the good strong walking stick they'd bought for him. 'Let's go on in.'

Walther was happy to see them all assembling in their Sunday best, a proud day for everyone. There were even visitors: the schoolteacher, Mr Hackett; the Harbour Master, Mr Drewett; and Davey, the bullocky, Theo's former boss. Walther wished Nora could have joined them too, and even lingered out front for a while after the others had gone on to gather outside the church, in the faint hope that she might come riding down the road. Not possible, of course. The Stennings would be attending their own church and enjoying their own Christmas dinner.

He wondered what his reaction would have been if they . . . remote chance . . . had invited him to join them on this festive day. Would he have accepted? Attended the Anglican church? Forsaken his friends on this very special Christmas Day?

No. So how could he have expected Nora to accept his invitation? He'd been unreasonable over this, he now knew, but at the time he'd been so excited at the prospect of the first Christmas at their church, and the first full gathering of the congregation since they landed, that he'd been hurt when she refused without giving the question a second thought. And besides, there was the misunderstanding over his land.

He should have known that news travelled speedily in these little towns, but he'd been busy working for Father Beitz and earning extra money as chainman for the surveyors three days a week. Then all of a sudden she'd confronted him.

'Walther! You bought land! You actually did it! Right in

town. And overlooking the river! A house there would be so lovely. Why didn't you tell me?'

She clutched his arm, hugging herself to him in her excitement. 'My father is flabbergasted. He heard it first, of course. He was surprised you could afford it. So was I, but I didn't let on to him. Was this meant to be a surprise?'

'No.' He was embarrassed. 'No. I mean, it is business, Nora. The land. Not for a house.'

'What for, then?' she asked, confused. 'Why else would you want land at Sailor's Point?'

'For a brewery. I will have a brewery there.' He smiled. 'That is my trade. My family, all brewers. This is better than a house, Nora. This is earnings, security for our future.'

'A long way in the future before there are any earnings,' she said acidly, and he was surprised.

'That can't be helped.'

'If you say so,' she'd muttered, and he didn't know what to make of that, because she wouldn't discuss it any further.

He feared that he was losing her. That the gap between them was widening. Sadly he realised that if he did build the house she wanted at Sailor's Point, the situation would be different, but he could not bring himself to settle for such a short-term plan. He only had so much money and it was imperative that he spend it wisely. In time, Father Beitz might come to understand that he was not disloyal; he was just trying to do his best for everyone concerned.

He turned to follow the others down the path but, just in time, his eye caught a rider in the distance. He gulped, his heart beating a little harder, thinking, hoping, it might be Nora, until the horseman came into view. Of all people! The Irishman, Mike Quinlan!

'Thought I'd find you here,' Quinlan said. 'Anyone object if I join you today?'

'No. I'm happy to see you. Is Theo with you?'

'Afraid not, Walther. But he gave me two pounds to give to you for his wife.'

'Where is he?'

341

'Gone out to Charters Towers goldfields. Still chasing his luck.'

Walther frowned. 'This is so wrong. He should have come home. His family is living in a shed, the wife working.'

'I'm sorry,' Mike shrugged. 'Theo's not doing well. It took a big effort for him to raise this money. There's a letter too, wishing them all a happy Christmas. I'm glad I got here in time.'

'He should have come himself.'

'Oh, you know how it is,' Mike said. 'Theo wants to come home the big man. You could say he's a dreamer.'

'Or a malcontent!'

The Irishman laughed. 'Whichever way you want to look at it.'

'And did *you* find gold?' Walther was burning with curiosity about these strange exploits.

'In the end, yes, I did all right. To begin with, me and Theo worked the claims and found not a speck of stuff. Then he took up with another bloke who reckoned he was on to a good thing, and I was all for giving it away. Miserable bloody business, Walther, when you're doing no good. Like losing at cards in a marathon game, especially when other people make the grade and go whooping off to the banks.'

'It must be depressing,' Walther breathed.

'You can say that again. I was leaving, riding through the hills on my way home, when I met up with a mate of mine who needed a hand. His mine had caved in, his partner had done a bunk. I stayed to help him dig it out so he could get to his tunnel again, and lo and behold, I spotted the gold on the second day. The cave-in revealed a pretty little vein if ever there was one.'

'You don't say!' Walther was astounded. 'So you're a rich man now?'

'Not rich, Walther, but poor no more, me lad. We got about five hundred pounds each out of the darlin' little mine, and that's all I need for starters. I hear you've a church here now?'

'Oh, yes,' Walther had to drag his mind back to the matters in hand. He hoped he would have a chance to hear more about

342

the intriguing gold mining. 'Yes. A fine church, Mike, we're very proud of it. The Church of St John.'

'Good on you. I don't suppose St John would mind a Catholic comin' on into his church to say a few words of thanks to the Boss?'

Walther grinned. He liked this man. 'You put it well. We do have the same boss up there in the heavens. Come along and enjoy Christmas with us.'

Mike was charmed by St John's Church. He had seen many a small-framed church like this in remote areas. They were all constructed of local timber, and reflected the dreams and best efforts of their pioneering congregations in the addition of at least one stained-glass window and lovingly crafted pews. These buildings could rarely accommodate more than fifty people, but that was fine. They sufficed. Most of the tiny churches he'd seen were to be found high on lonely hills, district landmarks, or in lonely, deserted paddocks miles from anywhere, guarding a half-dozen windswept graves, but not St John's. Oh no, he smiled. His Lutheran mates had done themselves proud here. This church was set in exotic gardens, with clumps of palms either side of the front door. Spreading out from there were banks of flowering shrubs that sent pink and red blooms cascading to a wide carpet of lawn, sheltered by more vigorous tropical plants.

The natural amphitheatre of lawn had its uses, he observed. Groups of Aborigines were settling there this morning, all facing the side windows of the church in eager anticipation, as the white folk filed inside.

' 'Tis a picture of serenity, is it not?' he said to Walther, who nodded. 'Yes, I think God's in His heaven today.'

Mike's peace and serenity lasted until after the service, when Mrs Zimmerman rushed up to him waving Theo's letter, and the two pounds.

'Are you Mr Quinlan?'

'I am. And you'd be Mrs Zimmerman?'

'Yes. Where's my husband? And what's this money he's sent me? Where's the rest of it? He's been away for months,

343

there has to be more. What have you done with it?'

'I'm sorry, ma'am, that was the all of it. He had no more.'

'Of course he did! Even the meanest of wages would bring in more!'

'But the gold mining doesn't work like that, dear lady. Not at all. No gold, no money. And Theo only found a few scraps before he left for Charters Towers.'

'This is all your fault,' she screamed, wept. 'You put these fancy ideas in his head. You took him down there. Why didn't you bring him back?'

Ladies rushed to quieten her. Jakob took Mike by the arm and walked him away.

'Don't take any notice of her. It's been a shock. All along she's been saying he'll probably turn up today, to surprise the children. Hard to believe he hasn't. But how are you, Mike? It's good to see you again. Did you make your fortune on the goldfields?'

'I didn't do too bad, and there's why I had a mind to talk to you today. I've got a proposition for you. That we pool our resources, us being neighbours and all.'

He could see that Jakob was far from impressed by that idea.

'Now don't go closing the door before you've heard me out. We can't talk business today, but I'll be around.'

As he spoke he saw Tibbaling, the old magic man, standing on a rocky incline at the other side of the church, done up in his finery of beads and shark's teeth and his conical headdress. Mike thought it was a pity the poor fellow had to spoil his image with the mandatory waistcoat and battered trousers, but even so, from this distance Tibbs, as the locals called him, looked imposing. Younger than his years.

The Irishman was surprised to see a grave marked with a white tombstone near where Tibbs was standing, the commencement of St John's cemetery, he thought sadly. But before he could enquire about it, Jakob was introducing him to various people, the priest was making announcements about a feast, and Mrs Zimmerman came over to apologise to him for her outburst. By the time he was free of the crowd, and able to look back, Tibbs was gone. But Mike could no longer make out the grave.

Feigning interest in the building itself, the fine new church, Mike walked over to that side and scrutinised the area carefully. There was no grave, nor was there anything that even faintly resembled a tombstone. He was glad he hadn't mentioned it now; not the sort of subject to introduce on a festive day. Asking who had died would have been a spoiler. They'd have thought him mad.

But Mike knew he was not mad. He also knew that he hadn't imagined that tombstone. Having been brought up with the folklore of the Druids, the people who knew things, just as did old Tibbs, he did not doubt the mysterious tales and events that surrounded the Aborigine ancient. Obviously, Tibbs had something to do with that apparition, so a man should ask him straight up what it was all about. Mike was quite excited at the prospect of looking into a mystery.

The tables were set in the open air, under a roof thatched with palms, and though buffet-style to cater for so many people, it was as fine a Christmas dinner as Mike had ever enjoyed, prayers and all.

'This time last year I was sweating it out in a prison cell,' he told Mrs Meissner.

'Oh dear. How awful. But don't you have any family, Mike?'

'Only me mum, and she's finally found the chance to visit the auld country. She has always wanted to see Ireland.'

'That's nice. How did that come about?'

' 'Twas a Christmas present from the goldfields.' He grinned. He noticed that the Aborigines were having their own picnic in among the trees, and went in search of Tibbaling.

'He not here today,' the women said. 'He gone to his home camp.'

'He wasn't here at all?'

'No. He allasame go home camp.'

'Where would that be?'

The answer came in their own language, place names beyond his comprehension, so one of the women drew him a map in the dirt.

'Ah. At the mouth of the river, by the sea?'

They nodded. 'Good fishin' dat place. Good sea swimmin'.'

'Why don't you go too?' he laughed, but they looked shocked.

'Nebber! Dat taboo. Men's business. Our place long way ups.'

Though their responses were honest, he took his quest back to Walther. 'Have you come across an Aborigine called Tibbaling?'

'Ah, yes. He is often here. Talks to Father Beitz. They are friends.' Walther smiled. 'More like, what you say? Good mates. Yes, good mates those two, an odd pair.'

'I thought he might be about. Is he here today?'

'No. I haven't seen him for many days. Is he a friend of yours?'

'No. My young mate Billy is related to him. I'll be looking for Billy to do some work for me, but it can wait.'

So, you're not here, Tibbaling, the Irishman mused. And neither is that tombstone I saw. One hallucination I might be able to accept, but not two. Apparently no one else saw you, so what do you want with me? He shivered. 'I sure as hell want no part in your shenanigans,' he said aloud. 'Leave me out of them.'

He travelled out to his block in a buggy with the Meissners that night, letting Karl ride his horse while he put his proposition to Jakob.

The farmer was mildly interested but Freda, his wife, threw in her opinions before Mike had hardly begun.

'A rum distillery, Mr Quinlan? No, definitely not. What sort of folk will people think we Germans are? What will the new priest have to say when he arrives on the scene to find his parishioners are building not only a brewery, but a rum distillery? God help us, we couldn't even consider it. We're respectable people.'

In the darkness as the horse plodded along, Mike had a feeling that her husband was amused by her reaction. He thought he heard a chuckle, but maybe it was only a cluck to keep the sleepy horse on the move. It was late. Near midnight. There'd been partying and singing for hours after the feast, and Walther had played his flute, and the beer and wine had flowed, and his German friends had really kicked up their heels, revelling in their national dances. Mike had even done a jig for them, fast and furious, to the rhythm of Walther's flying fingers, and of course it was Walther who had been the star of the day. He surely could play that instrument. Though the priest hadn't been impressed. It seemed the gentle giant was in the bad books for some reason.

'Keep talking, or I'll fall asleep,' Jakob said. 'Tell me again about growing sugar cane.'

But Mike was wary now. Many a slip 'twixt the cup and the lip. Between the boss and the missus. He had to get the wife on side or she'd ruin his grand plan.

'Are you comfortable there now, missus?' he asked of the woman sitting in front of him on the hard wooden seat. She had been bumping about on that seat for the last hour.

'As much as it is possible,' she replied stiffly, hanging on to the elbow rail.

'Ah now, they're hard on ladies, these rough old wagons. I suppose where you come from, people don't ride in such farm contraptions.'

'The roads are better,' she allowed.

'So they would be! Now I never thought of that. All of our roads being a shovel away from scrub tracks. But then in the cities here I've seen wondrous vehicles, well sprung for the worst of roads, and cushioned inside and waterproofed against the weather. Can you believe that?'

'We have them at home. Any amount of them in Germany, from the everyday to the most luxurious,' she told him. 'But I've not seen one here.'

'I suppose not. We should make a pact, Jakob. Your missus, livin' right out here, should be the first to—'

Freda interrupted him. 'The Dixons have comfortable vehicles, I'm told. Though I haven't seen them.'

'Then they don't count. When we bring in our sugar cane crops we'll outstrip them.'

'What sugar cane crops?'

'You must have been dozing,' Jakob said. 'Mike told us about meeting with government agriculturalists.'

'I was not. Who are these people?'

'They're gentlemen who go about the countryside advising farmers on what to plant and what not to plant.'

'I never heard of such a thing. If farmers don't know, then who does?'

'Ah, but us new chums to these districts, we don't know the soil and we're taking pot luck on the climate. These fellers, they head us off from going in the wrong direction.'

Jakob turned to her. 'Walther's a careful man, he talked to them.'

'I'd say Walther's more than careful. He's got more layers than a bear in a blizzard. I didn't know he was a moneyed man, I thought he was just a brewery worker.'

'It was Walther who called in the government men. Mike talked to them too, in Maryborough on his way home, and they told him that this rich brown soil is perfect for sugar cane.'

'Who says they're right? What do they know? They don't live here, do they? We're farmers, Jakob, we grow what we know and never mind these fellows with their book learning. We ought to have a bigger dairy herd; the cows we've got are doing marvellously.'

Why would they not? Mike asked himself as he slumped back on the tray of the wagon. They're eating grass worth bloody gold.

The night was hot and humid, myriad stars in a sweep overhead, but a damn sight cooler than the frazzled heat of Christmas Day that they had all tried manfully to ignore. He'd noticed that the two pregnant women were finding it trying, as was the fellow with the limp, Lucas. A nice fellow. Someone said he was a stockman, but Mike doubted that, he looked too pale. Underfed, even.

He let the matter lie. In the morning he'd be up with the kookaburras to help the Meissners with the milking. In a more sober state, he could not fail to warn them, to warn her, that these hot days were not just little heat waves. This was their first summer in Bundaberg, and this Queensland coast was deceptive. By all accounts immigrants were taken in by the balmy winters, unable to foresee the tropical season ahead. There was no such thing as a cool change, and shortly,

348

intermittent rains would transform to the well-known wet season. This wasn't Borneo or Equador, but sometimes Mike felt it might as well be.

The Meissners kindly put him up for the night, in their partly built house, a disappointment for their neighbour. He'd heard they'd managed to sell a fair amount of their timber, but to find they'd spent the proceeds on a farmhouse distressed him. Injuring his great plan.

Come the morn, though, he was able to put his project to Jakob without interruption, and that night, after he had departed, Jakob outlined the plan to Freda and Karl.

'Apparently the planter gentleman across the river, Mr Charlie Mayhew, wants to build a co-operative rum distillery, a large concern. He needs partners in this concern, sugar cane growers to make the distillery viable.'

'I told you, we're farmers, not planters,' Freda said, but Karl disagreed.

'What's the difference? If sugar cane grows well here, then that's what we should be growing, especially if we have the market for our crop right here . . .'

She shook her head. 'You don't understand. Walther is building a brewery, we can't all go in for alcohol.'

'Freda dear, sugar cane is just that. Sugar. It's as much a staple as wheat, for heaven's sake. And sugar refineries keep jam factories in business. Please be reasonable.'

'Who cares what Walther is doing?' Karl said angrily. 'This is our business and I say we switch to sugar cane. Is that what Mike Quinlan is about?'

'Yes,' his father said. 'He wants us to plant sugar on all three blocks so that we can pool our labour and resources.'

'Labour?' Freda cried. 'We'll have those islanders here? The Kanakas?'

Karl was delighted. 'All our land, and Quinlan's, growing cane. Imagine that! We'll have a sea of crops, it'll be huge!'

The sticking point was the islanders. Freda was nervous of having them actually living on their property, especially when she heard they'd need at least thirty of these labourers. They argued well into the night, until Jakob made a decision.

'We'll finish the house as cheaply as possible. Then I'll go

349

in to see Mr Rawlins again, because we'll start clearing and planting on Karl's block first, to satisfy the inspectors. I will need a new loan to get started on accommodations for the Kanaka workers.'

'I told you—' Freda began.

'So you did. But the Kanakas are cheap labour and essential to our enterprise. If you are unhappy with so many black-fellows, then I understand your feelings, and I will arrange for you to live in town. But once and for all I intend to grow sugar cane.'

'You think you can dump me back there with Father Beitz?' she asked angrily.

'No,' he said calmly. 'I shall find you lodgings in town where you will feel much safer.'

'Perhaps you should send me all the way! Find me lodgings back in Germany, then you won't have to bother about me at all!'

'If you wish,' he said sternly.

As Jakob had expected, there was a great deal to be discussed in meetings between Mayhew, Rawlins, Quinlan and himself, and further talks with Charlie Mayhew that were essential to their understanding of the business.

They visited Charlie's plantation, where they heard that New Guinea canes were the best to plant, and spent a day learning about the management of such a huge concern. It was important to Charlie that they succeed, so that the co-operative distillery could flourish. He did his best to answer all their questions and offer as much help as he could, and he invited Karl to stay on at his plantation, working and observing, until such a time as their own Kanakas were landed and their planting began.

In the meantime, to appease Freda, the two men decided to commence building accommodations, kitchens and storerooms on Mike's land, near the river. Taking the advice of Charlie Mayhew at every step, Jakob and Mike worked hard, and when they'd completed the Kanakas' compound they turned their hands to barns, stables and storerooms at various other sites. Then the backbreaking toil of fencing areas that needed securing. Sometimes Jakob was away for days on end, camping out or living in the sheds they were building, because Mike still didn't have a house of his own. Nor did he care. All his energies were directed at making a go of this plantation.

Freda didn't really mind being on her own. The two carpenters finished their work on the house and left, and then Davey and his bullock team arrived with the furniture.

He was too polite to comment on the paucity of the load, for which she was grateful, because it was taking an effort of will to fight back her tears. Jakob had warned that he would be cutting back on the furniture and fittings needed in the new house, and Freda had taken great care in listing her exact requirements. She might have known that the happy hours she'd spent compiling that list were too good to be true. The house itself was exactly as she'd envisaged it: two bedrooms, with a parlour and a dining room, a separate kitchen, bathroom and laundry, connected by a walkway, and a wraparound veranda across the front of the house and along the sides.

They had planned it so carefully, the separate kitchen to protect the house from the risk of fire, well warned on that score now. They had noticed that wide verandas were put to good use here, as sleepouts and sitting rooms. Furnished, her house would have been lovely, she thought miserably. But Davey had delivered only the bare essentials: beds, kitchen table and chairs, the bath, a few other odds and ends including some household linen, towels and blankets . . . and the stove.

That made her angry. It was just as well Jakob was away. She was sure he'd allowed the stove as a sop to her, a buffer against the anger the meanness of this delivery would cause.

Between them, Davey and his teamster set up the beds, and as they tramped through the empty dining room, their boots clanging on the timber floor, Freda finally broke down. She couldn't resist complaining to Davey as the tears welled up.

'He could at least have let me have a dressing table for the bedroom, and the sideboard for in here. The place is so bare and ugly, I haven't even got any curtains.'

'Ah there, missus. Don't go on so. Ain't no use cryin'.

You've seen worse, now haven't you? Only a while back you had nothin' but your tent.'

She nodded, a little comforted, until she realised that Davey was grinning at her, his pipe stuck in the side of his mouth.

'I can't see anything to laugh at,' she said bitterly.

'I suppose not, missus. But it just seems a bit comic to be wanting the sideboard and that, right away, when you got nothin' to put in them, like.'

Freda stared at him, insulted. How dare he criticise her? Laugh at her!

'I mean, you got burned out, missus,' he said, still grinning. 'What's the rush? First catch your chicken before you make the soup, they say, or somethin' like that.'

He looked out the window. 'This'll be a nice spot to sit of an afternoon, beat that western sun.' Then he turned back to her. 'If you don't mind me to say, missus . . . you don't want to take things too serious. Too many things can go wrong in the bush, as you've seen, to be worrying about small matters . . . I'm not saying all your nice furniture isn't important to you, but it's not life and death, is it? It's just a little disappointment that it'll be late. Nothin' to get upset about.'

'It doesn't matter anyway,' she retorted. 'I'll be moving into the town when those Kanakas come out here.'

'Why? They're nice people, the Kanakas. Don't you think they're human? You ought to meet a few of them before you make a move like that. Now the Kanakas and their ladies . . . they like a laugh. They don't take life too serious, they work hard but they enjoy themselves, given the chance . . . Wait a minute. I nearly forgot! I've got a letter here for Jakob.'

He winked at her. 'Shall I place it on the sideboard, madam?' he asked with a flourish.

'I think on the master's desk over in the corner,' Freda laughed, 'after I have dusted it.'

'There you go!' Davey said, approving. He handed her the letter and she tucked it into her apron pocket.

When Jakob came home, bursting with news of their progress, he was accompanied by Mike and two Kanakas. They were dark fellows, skin bronzed rather than the metallic darkness of the Aborigines, and they were both shabbily dressed, as if their clothes were second-hand. As they probably were, Freda thought, wondering if they minded, as she had, that humbling experience.

'This is Henry,' Jakob said, 'and his son Herbert. They're both experienced workmen, and we were lucky to get them to come work for us, Freda.' His voice was loaded with expectation that she be nice to them, and she surprised him by stepping forward and extending her hand to them.

'How do you do,' she said to Henry, who responded with a broad smile, shaking her hand enthusiastically. Not to be outdone, Herbert, a handsome young man, she noticed, grabbed her hand. 'How do you do, missus!'

Mike Quinlan laughed. 'You've got mates for life there, Freda. Not often they get to shake a hand.

'She's a nice lady, isn't she?' he asked them, and they nodded furiously, smiles bubbling into life.

Finally they went on their way with Mike, and Freda followed Jakob into the kitchen. 'I'll make you some coffee,' she said. 'And there's a letter here for you. Who is Eduard Berger?'

She saw him drop into the heavy kitchen chair with a thud, his mouth open, speechless!

'I didn't realise it was private,' she said, though that wasn't exactly true. Home alone for days, with that letter on the kitchen table curiosity had got the better of her. Normally it wasn't her practice to open her husband's mail, but then he'd always been nearby . . .

By now, she almost knew it by heart. She watched as Jakob scanned it.

Dear Mr Meissner,
It is my sad duty to inform you that my mother Traudi Berger passed away last week. She died here at my home, so thanks be to God I was able to be with her in her last days. She died peacefully after a severe bout of pneumonia and asked me to write and let you know of her passing. She also asked that I remind you of her request.

353

The nature of that request she did not explain, so I am led to think that you are aware and hopefully recalling.

Go with God, dear sir,
Eduard Berger

'So who is Traudi Berger?' Freda urged.

'A friend of mine. She was a good friend,' he said sadly.

'What did she want? This request.'

'I'll have to think about it!' He pushed aside his chair and stormed out of the house, but Freda was angry. Haven't I tried to help him by addressing the Kanakas? she thought crossly. And gone out of my way not to complain about no decent furniture? Now I have to put up with this rudeness. This sudden secrecy!

'I just won't,' she said, and marched out after him.

'It seems to me you've had plenty of time to think about it, Jakob. And I haven't had anyone to talk to for days, except that big old goanna who now lives under the veranda. I would appreciate some conversation. What did she ask of you?'

'She wanted me to bring her son to Australia with us.'

'Bring? She asked you about this before we left?'

'Yes.'

'When was that?'

'For God's sake, Freda, before we left! What does it matter exactly when? I told her it was impossible and that was all there was to it.' He sat on the kitchen step and took off his boots 'How do you like your new stove?'

'It's beautiful. Davey and his new teamster set it in for me and lit it to make sure the flue was working properly. How old is this Eduard?'

'I don't know. About twenty-one or -two, I think. I've never met him.'

'You didn't even try to do your old friend a favour?' she asked, aware of the suspicion in her voice. 'He's writing from Hamburg; obviously he lives there. You must have known that. Why didn't you refer him to Father Beitz? He'd have helped him to emigrate. He'd have jumped at the chance for another starter . . .'

354

'It's none of your business, Freda. Nothing to do with you.'

'I think it is, otherwise you wouldn't be so secretive. So defensive. What is it you don't want me to know about this?'

'Leave it, will you? I'll dig those rocks out of the bottom of your vegetable garden while there's still light.'

Being new, the heavy iron stove still produced fumes that made the kitchen uncomfortable, and Freda considered serving their dinner outside on the donated folding table they'd used in their tent days, but decided he could eat in here and put up with it.

She sniffed at the fumes. 'We have a dining room but no table.'

'I could move this table in there.'

'Brilliant! What would I use in here?'

They ate in silence. The kitchen was hot and steamy, making the fumes even worse. Jakob looked over his shoulder. The window was open but there wasn't even a breath of a breeze. Freda removed the soup plates and used them to serve the beef and dumplings, then placed the boiled vegetables in a dish in front of him.

'I'm sorry about the furniture,' he said suddenly. 'I didn't realise how bare the house would look. Are there any of Eva's pickles left?'

She went to the larder for the jar and stopped to look about her. It was well served with provisions. Jakob had replenished the meat safe. And there were six bottles of wine on the shelf.

'Where did the wine come from?' she asked him, incredulous.

'The pub!' Jakob laughed; he loved using that word. It amused him. 'The pub! I was wondering when you'd notice. I thought we might have a little spree, just the two of us, what with Karl away, but I didn't realise how depressing this empty house was for you.'

'I never said that.'

'And you never offered to show Quinlan about our fine new home either.'

Freda blinked. 'You're very discerning in your old age.'

'Not really. We met Davey on the road. He said you were rattling about here like dice in a box.'

'So I was. So we are.' Freda thought about that larder, about the abundance of good food here, about the delicious fruit and honey and nuts that grew wild, free for the taking, and she remembered Davey's remarks about treating life too seriously.

It was hard to back down for the second time in one day, so this effort wasn't as spirited as her handshakes with the Kanakas. 'A glass of wine would go well with our meal,' she allowed.

She watched as Jakob uncorked the bottle and reached into the box that served as their kitchen dresser. It was a hotchpotch of donated china, mugs and kitchen implements that as yet had no decent home, and his face fell.

'We haven't any glasses!'

Men! she thought. It had only just occurred to him!

'Don't take things so seriously, Jakob. The mugs will do, they're clean.'

'Oh! Good!' He was back at the table in seconds with their wine, on his best behaviour like a naughty boy. As if he'd committed a crime by depriving her of that furniture and needed to buy his way out of this situation.

'A toast,' he said. 'To us, Freda. And to better times.'

'Thank you. But I think this is our best of times, Jakob. We have more land than we ever dreamed of owning, an amazing house with windows we don't need to close, and we're all safe and well.'

'Amen to that,' he said, relieved.

The wine, they agreed, was rich and plummy, probably better suited to cooler climates, but for Australian-grown it was excellent, almost as good as their own local wines. And not having their furniture yet, they agreed, was not so bad after all. And the Kanakas, to be housed on Quinlan's land, weren't so bad either.

'So you'll stay?' he asked.

'Yes. I'll have to get out of the habit of wondering what the neighbours think, when our nearest neighbour is ten miles away and nobody cares anyway.'

Jakob refilled their mugs, emptying the bottle. 'Don't say that, dear. I care. I want you to be happy.'

'So name me one person here who would criticise if we had to furnish our house with home-made stuff, instead of store-bought. No one, Jakob. I've been foolish, wanting everything at once.'

'I would do more if I could,' he said, 'but we need every penny as well as the new loan to get the plantation under way.'

'You're not listening to me, Jakob. I said it's all right. It doesn't matter. Davey said we're too serious about things.'

He looked up, surprised. 'So does Mike Quinlan! And Charlie Mayhew. They say I worry too much. I'll get ulcers. They say everything is just fine, but I don't know whether it is or not, or whether I'm making the most awful mistakes.'

Freda was laughing. 'I think I'm getting the joke at last.'

'What joke?'

'What's worse? Having no glasses or nowhere to put them?'

'I don't know. I think you're tipsy, Freda.'

'I am. I'm happy. That's what I like about wine.'

'Then you'll have to explain that joke to me.'

'No I don't. It'll come to you. It's the attitude of these people. The humour is exquisite. And quite awful. Davey laughed at me. Now I can laugh at you, my darling. What is it that you have done that you have to keep it a secret from me?'

'I haven't done a thing.'

'Be careful now. We are alone here, in our own Eden. No son to look askance. We could take our mattress outside and make love out there under the stars, if only you would confide in me.'

'Oh God, Freda, not that again.'

She came around the table and sat on his knee. 'Put it this way. If you don't explain, I'll have to come to the conclusion that this young man, Eduard someone, is your son.'

Freda almost ended up on the floor. She had to clutch at him to regain her balance and footing.

'I think I'll make some coffee while we discuss this, Jakob.'

* * *

'I like her style,' Freda said. 'On her deathbed she has put it to you again. And you know you can't refuse this time. What a wretch you are! Your own son!'

'It was your money, Freda. Your inheritance. How could I have asked you to include a stranger?'

'You couldn't,' she said, surprising him. 'Anyway, I would have objected. Truly. Because we were headed for the unknown, into the jaws of dragons for all we knew. I wouldn't have brought my own mother along. But now that we're here, things are different.'

They sat outside on the front step of their home and talked about this young man Eduard, Jakob's son, whom neither of them had met, and eventually they decided to invite him to join them.

'What will Karl say if we do this?' Jakob worried. 'What will he think of me? He may not appreciate or welcome Eduard into the family.'

'We'll see. What he thinks of you fathering a child and ignoring its existence is your problem. As for not welcoming his own brother into the family, I'll deal with that. I couldn't give him a brother or a sister. Now he has one. It'll be good for him. He won't be alone in the world, our darling boy, when we go . . .'

'Now you're getting morbid.'

'You're quite right,' she said sleepily.

Hanni plodded through the rain on the way back to the hotel. It was teeming, but like everyone else she'd learned to cope with what the locals called the 'wet season'. And it was surely that, she sniffed, leaning into her umbrella, but at least it was warm. Steamy. She had good news for Eva; she'd been in time to secure a cottage, having learned only last night that the owner, a Mr Gibson was moving with his family to Maryborough.

It had been awkward at first. He'd known that Eva's husband was still away and was not inclined to let his house to two women and three children, so Hanni had rushed in to explain.

'No, no. My husband, Mr Lucas Fechner, will be in charge.'

'Then where is he?'

'At work, sir. It is left to me to make these arrangements.'

'And he will be able to pay the rent for all of you? For the Zimmermans as well? A tall order, Mrs Fechner.'

'Oh no. That is not a problem. Mrs Zimmerman is now cook at the Royal Hotel, and I work there as a housemaid. We all have wages.'

'Very well. I expect you to keep my house in good order and to tend the garden; my wife would be very upset if you let her plants wither.'

'We'll take care of the garden, sir.'

'Very well. Rent to be paid to Mr Pimbley at the store. Do you know him?'

'Yes, sir. He is a friend.' Hanni prayed that Mr Gibson didn't find out from Jim Pimbley that she and Lucas were still separated. She hadn't seen Lucas since Christmas, but Eva, who still went out to church on Sundays, had said he was working for Walther, building the foundations for the brewery.

At least he was working now and had a good future, Eva had said, getting in with Walther at this early stage.

'The two of them, they'll do well, Hanni. You want to watch out, you'll get left behind. I don't know why you don't make it up with Lucas. Too much pride, that's all. Believe me, you have to swallow your pride to get on these days . . .'

What pride? Hanni wondered. After what happened to me! After my husband blamed me for everything. She was glad to be moving out of that shed at last. Looking forward to having her own room, such luxury. It had been chaotic sharing with Eva and the kids, but it had been kind of Eva to take her in, so she shouldn't complain.

She stopped under the awning of the new draper's shop in Bourbong Street and watched riders herding a mob of horses on to a vacant block. It bothered her to see horsemen coming into town now, frightened her, in case Keith Dixon was among them, in case he might abuse her, call her names or something, in front of people. Hanni had changed. She had been thoroughly intimidated by the cruel happenings, and being called a thief on top of everything else . . . Sometimes she thought she ought to speak to Father Beitz, confess all so that she could go back to church in good conscience, but she doubted he would understand. He was just as likely to make things worse by pointing the finger of shame at her, solely at her. God knows how he'd react, she told herself, but you can be sure you'll come off the worst, so leave things be.

'I wish I could go home,' she muttered as she left the shelter and pushed on, sloshing through deep puddles in her bare feet. Now that the interview was over, she had her shoes strung round her neck by their laces. No point in letting them get ruined altogether.

'That's what I'll do,' she said suddenly. 'I'll save the money and go home. Back to Hamburg, anyway.'

Charlie Mayhew was walking towards the pub with Constable Colley. He saw Hanni turn the corner, making for the rear of the building.

'I say, Clem. Wasn't that the German lass who works out at Clonmel?'

'Worked, Charlie. She hasn't been there for ages. They sacked her.'

'Good Lord! Why? She seemed such a nice person, and very efficient.'

'Just goes to show you never can pick 'em. She's a thief.'

'Surely not!'

'It's true. They sacked her for thievin'.'

Charlie frowned at him. 'I find that hard to believe.'

Just then a stockman sauntered down the steps of the pub. 'Hey, Colley. A bloke has been looking for you. Six of his stockhorses have gone missing.'

'Where is he?'

'Headed for the police station again.'

'Bugger!' Colley said, and tramped away without so much as a nod to Charlie, who was relieved to be rid of him. He didn't like Colley, but the fellow had fastened on to him as he'd walked up the street.

Jules Stenning was waiting for him in the bar. 'Charles, old chap! What kept you? I'm two whiskies up on you already.'

'Meetings and more meetings! I'll have a beer, I'm dying of thirst.'

Stenning ordered him a pint while Charlie continued: 'I had no idea there would be so much red tape involved in starting up a distillery. You'll have to sort it out for me, Jules.'

'It's complicated. Importing of spirits is well regulated, but you're breaking new ground, producing your own rum, wanting to sell it here and export it. Do you really think it'll be good enough, Charlie?'

'It'll be the sweetest rum you've ever tasted, Jules, and it'll be the making of Bundaberg. There are more farmers looking to sugarcane these days, if they know what's good for them. More crushing mills will be established, and probably bigger and better distilleries than mine, but you mark my words, one day these plains will have canefields as far as the eye can see.'

He picked up the pint of beer the bartender had placed in front of him and swallowed half almost in one gulp.

Jules laughed. 'No point in speechifying at me. I'm only a civil servant, old chap. But now, don't forget your venture depends on getting a new set of regulations entered into the licensing laws. You can't set up a rum sly-grog shop. You must have the State Parliament amend the regulations to allow you to operate.'

'I know that. And you will word the amendments for me, won't you, Jules? You know the lingo.'

'Of course I will, but surely it hasn't escaped you that our parliamentary representative is a teetotaller.'

'No. And that's why he has to go. We have to campaign, get him out. We should start a campaign fund for Keith. I know the Dixons have enough to pay for a dozen campaigns, but a support fund gives people the impression of him being an everyday chap, in need of a quid. It also involves people, gets them fired up, if they've put up their two bob's worth. Then we have to make sure people here are on the roll; half of them aren't, as you would know, Jules . . .'

'Hang on! I have to keep out of this. I'm supposed to be neutral. You set up a committee, Charles. Get them working. Leave me out of it. I'm on your side of course, but not publicly. Nevertheless, at this stage I'd say you're your own worst enemy. I've been talking to Keith. You may be a friend, but he's not inclined to back your distillery.'

'What? Why not? I know old J.B. thought it was a lost cause. He would, he only sees sheep. But Keith . . . he will.'

'No he won't. He's got a set on all the Germans turning up here. Taking over, he says.'

'They're not taking over. Any more than the Danes. Cripes, Jules . . . fifty Danes came through here recently. What's he on about?'

'It seems the Danes have disappeared into the countryside, but your Germans are up front, taking over.'

Charlie was astonished. 'You can't believe that. They're no different from the rest of us. We're all new, none of us born here. The bloody place didn't exist a couple of years ago. What makes them any different?'

His friend sighed. 'There it is. If you think your distillery will be big business some day, we're all very pleased. But not if you've got German partners. You see what Keith is saying, Charles. They're taking over by stealth. You'll find yourself pushed out by their avarice one day. They'll ease you out.'

'But I've only got the Meissners as partners, and Mike Quinlan!'

Jules shrugged and ordered two whiskies. 'Hardly the best choice if you need Keith's help. And then there's the matter of the other German who is busy trying to establish a brewery. I mean to say, Charlie, with their own church and commune out there, where they get up to God knows what, trying to indoctrinate the blacks, and then that fellow Kleinschmidt—'

'Who's he?'

'Another one of the German mob. He manages the sawmill now. So he says who works there and who doesn't. More German infiltration of our society. Not to mention all his kin, running the logging camps up there . . .'

Charlie was livid. 'There are about a thousand people living in and around this town now, Jules. As far as I know there are only about a score of Germans. About twenty, do you hear me?'

'I think the roll, when it's drawn up, will prove otherwise, Charlie. But in the mean time, if you want your distillery you'd better give the foreigners the shove.'

'How can I do that? They're the only ones prepared to take

the financial risk with me. I told you J.B. Dixon wouldn't . . .'

'Ah, yes, but he can't bear to see factories and grubby villages shooting up in this lovely countryside.'

'In his sheep country,' Charlie said angrily. 'Is that why he's pushing Keith?'

'Not at all. A parliamentarian in the family is an honour.'

Charlie left the bar thoroughly confused. He'd heard that Stenning had shifted allegiance from Keith after the débâcle of the Scottish miners, and was often heard to refer to Dixon junior as a fool of a man. He'd decided to meet with Jules to persuade him to stick with Keith, because the parliamentary incumbent was a teetotaller. But now the positions were reversed. It was possible that Jules, a devious fellow, had some sort of agenda of his own here, but that didn't explain the Dixons' attitude.

Thunder rumbled in the distance and heavy storm clouds were gathering to inflict more rough weather on the already beleaguered port, and Charlie glanced up, frowning. His Kanakas had cut all of his cane in the nick of time, had it all to the mill before the rains started, and that was a blessing, but the Aborigines were forecasting that this build-up of tropical storms they were experiencing could be a forerunner to what they called a 'big-feller rain'.

He hoped they were wrong. He was already trying to cope with minor flooding on his property, and it was only January. It was said this wet season could last well into April. But this other problem nagged at him now. Charlie resented being told what to do, especially by people who claimed to be friends. 'How dare they attempt to dictate who I might and might not do business with?' he muttered, diving for shelter as a bolt of lightning delivered a deafening clap of thunder and the rain began in earnest.

He set off again, hurrying towards the stables. 'I've a mind to look about for another candidate,' he said to himself. 'To be truthful, the town doesn't need Keith or our present Member, if they won't encourage the rum industry. But who? There's not a lot of time, the elections are in March.'

Charlie did accept that Keith wasn't exactly against the rum industry, only against Charlie's choice of partners, but it made no difference to him. He was a stubborn man, well educated. Brought up in Sydney, he'd studied chemistry for a while, but then the wanderlust took him travelling. He ended up in Jamaica, staying with friends on their sugar cane plantation, and thus, as he'd told his father, the seed was sown. He would be a grower too, and produce his own rum.

Charlie had no doubt that he would succeed, thanks to the initial investment supplied by his father, owner of several jewellery stores in Sydney and Brisbane. He would not let his father down, nor would he allow backwoods cowboys like the Dixons to interfere.

'I'll do some interfering of my own,' he said as he dodged across the road to run down the muddy track to the stables.

A week later Charlie was back in town, calling on his friends, pointing out that they needed a good strong representative in Parliament, and that this ruled out Keith Dixon. Some worried that the struggling town could not afford to offend the Dixons, though Keith, as it turned out, was not popular.

'Who cares?' Charlie asked. 'It's a secret ballot. No one will ever know who voted for who . . .'

The following Friday there he was again, searching for a consensus of opinion in naming a popular candidate, only to find that the name handed about was his own.

'No! No! Much as I appreciate the support,' he told Jim Pimbley and the Harbour Master, 'I can't leave the plantation for that length of time. I've got eighty Kanakas working out there, and only four white men. I manage that property myself.'

Jim nodded. 'Some folk said that. Said you couldn't get down to Brisbane for months on end, so we did have a second choice. Les Jolly. And what's more, he's interested. He could be a goer.'

Jules Stenning was astonished to have so many men calling at his office to register on the electoral roll, and to verify that voting was indeed a secret ballot. It wasn't too long before he ferreted out the reason for this sudden interest in political affairs. A new candidate was about to enter the fray. Les Jolly! And he had a great deal of local support, by all accounts.

Stenning smiled. He was in the fortunate position of having two bob each way. If Keith won, he wouldn't give the Germans an inch, and that meant Romeo Walther's plans of a brewery wouldn't happen. The building he and his mates were working on would end up a white elephant.

And then there was Les Jolly. A nice fellow. Enterprising. Busy. Fingers in pies everywhere. Logging, sawmill, hotel, land . . . All land sales had to be registered in Stenning's office, and he had watched Les Jolly buying vacant blocks, one after another, wondering where the money was coming from.

He'd asked Rawlins.

'Every penny he earns he ploughs back in again, Jules. He raises loans, pays them off on the knocker, repeats the process. I'd say Les Jolly is on his way to his first million without having to leave his office.'

Jules sighed. He wished he could be like that. He'd thought of buying a few blocks of land in town, land that was a quarter of the price of Maryborough commercial property, but had always baulked. No one could guarantee that this town would last. It was still only an outlet for wool from the big stations. He agreed with J.B. Dixon, though he hadn't admitted this to Charlie . . . his dream of huge sugarcane plantations and rum distilleries was all hot air. Too far-fetched for this one-horse town.

But, he chortled to himself, who is Nora's latest suitor? None other than Les Jolly. In a way, Jules hoped he would make it to Parliament; that might impress Nora as Keith never could. Not that it was likely. This was a big electorate. Bundaberg was only a speck on the map. Squatters like the Dixons had the game sewn up. The big station owners would back their own; and their strongest base was Maryborough, a town big enough to hold the key to the prize. For Keith Dixon.

'Sorry, Les.' He shrugged. 'It would have been pleasant to have a son-in-law in the Parliament.'

Part Three

Chapter Fourteen

Despite the turbulent clouds that rumbled overhead, despite the deep green forests that lined the shores, refusing to reveal what lay beyond, the Pastor was overwhelmed with relief when *Clovis* dropped anchor in Moreton Bay. The long, appalling voyage was over at last; Brisbane was nigh.

'I could fall to the deck in a weep,' he said to Freddy, crossing himself expertly. Habit, these days.

'I was beginning to think this was all a cruel hoax. A penance. That we were doomed to sail on for ever and ever . . . into the cold and heavy mist . . .' He giggled, lightheaded. Relief making way for triumph that he had actually made it to another world. Where respectability was assured. Where the good life awaited.

A barge carrying several uniformed men pulled alongside the ship, and Friedrich jerked away from his vantage point on the rails as they were assisted on board.

What if they were after him? Come for him? To pull him off and drag him to their prison? People on the ship had said that the prisons in this country were the most ferocious in the world. Felons were flogged mercilessly. Murderers were thrown to the sharks. He *was* ready to weep now. Now . . . after he'd come so far, endured so much, surely they wouldn't do this to him? He ran, pushing and shoving, down to his cabin, shaking, sweating, until they came, calling out:

'Father Ritter! Father Ritter. Are you in there?'

He wouldn't answer. Couldn't. His mouth was dry, his face dripping with sweat. He fell to his knees. They couldn't arrest a priest at prayer, could they? Terror had him actually praying.

'Please God, spare me. Have pity on a poor sinner . . .'

'Father?' The frail door was opening. They were coming in. Uninvited. To get him.

'Father? Oh! I'm sorry to interrupt your prayers . . .'

Through half-closed eyes he saw it was only the steward.

'The mail is aboard, Father. I have a letter for you.'

What letter? Who would be writing to him? It was a trick. He ignored the intruder, muttering unintelligible prayers, play-acting for all he was worth, casting his eyes heavenwards.

'I'll just leave it here then, will I?'

The Pastor lowered his voice to a resonant mumble, irritation in the tone, and the steward took the hint.

'Sorry, Father.'

He was gone. Friedrich waited. No one could be writing to him. To Freddy. Any letter would have to follow on the next ship. He turned and eyed the thing. It had been left on his trunk. Sitting there as innocent as a rat trap.

Up top the excitement was reaching fever pitch, voices shrill against the thump of heavy objects being dumped and lumped around, prior to the arrival of boats of some sort to transport passengers and their effects upriver to the city of Brisbane.

Friedrich gulped. 'Don't tell me you know people in Brisbane, Freddy? You haven't got people meeting you here? Christ! Did I miss something in your papers? I ought to do a bunk right here. Slip ashore as soon as my longboat hits land. God knows who this might be, dammit! And I had myself so well rehearsed to take up my cushy job in Bundaberg! Well, we'd better see . . .'

He pounced on the letter and tore it open.

'Oh Christ! Praise the Lord and pass the plate! It's from your boss, Freddy. My boss. The old priest. Writing to welcome *Clovis* and my good self to this new and blessed land, blah, blah . . . He wants me to collect his church bell at the Customs Office. That's all. God! Did your Father Beitz give me a start? He says they have a beautiful church and a happy and holy congregation awaiting us. Me. So let's get moving. Heigh ho, as the sailors say. We're off ashore.'

* * *

370

The relief at being off that ship brought Friedrich an unexpected rush of sentiment as he wobbled across the wharf. Despite the appalling sentence of months at sea, suffering the hardships of the damned, he now recalled sweet occasions, when, through the parent, he'd been able to spend time with the beautiful Miss Adele. She'd blossomed as the weeks passed. Her fair hair had grown longer, silky curls often free to tangle with the breeze, her facial expression had become sunnier and dainty freckles dappled her cheeks. Those precious occasions had been far too few but all the more enchanting for their sparsity.

He'd learned a lot about the Hoeppers from stewards, including the fact that the old man was a wealthy merchant . . . important . . . and that Miss Adele was an only child. The rest of the family had been lost in some disaster. This information enabled him to offer Miss Adele compassion, the first chance he got . . .

'My dear girl. I can see you have been touched by tragedy,' he said and she'd looked at him, surprised.

'You can?'

'Ah yes. The eyes are windows of the soul. It is all there. I also see your courage in keeping cheerful for the benefit of your father. I shall pray that sorrow does not become a burden.'

'Thank you, Pastor. You're very kind.' Tears welled in the lovely blue eyes. 'It's hard to cope sometimes. I often wonder if I'll ever get over it.'

'You will Miss Hoepper. You will. And if you feel like lightening the load of the cross you bear, you can always talk to me.'

That formed the basis of their rare and precious conversations that were able to take place when Hoepper insisted the Lutheran Pastor be permitted to come into first class, on occasion, to minister to members of that persuasion on the upper deck. They always invited him to have coffee and cake with them after the service, never dinner, expecting him to be grateful, he supposed. Were it not for that dear girl, they'd be inventing their own church services. Just as he was doing.

But Friedrich saw his own tragedy in the situation, comparing it to Romeo and Juliet. Miss Adele was up there on her

371

balcony . . . in first class . . . out of reach, and he, the poor Romeo, was doomed to stay below. The lovers separated by forces beyond their control. He was certain that given a chance to court her, instead of having to play Pastor on these flying visits, she would succumb to his charms. She did like to talk to him, if only about the value of prayer.

He'd fantasised that scenario so often on the ship, it seemed a wrench to have to let it go now. Dazed, he stared about him as scores of passengers from the lower classes piled ashore, clinging to each other in initial bewilderment, like flotsam thrown up by the tide.

With an effort he gathered his thoughts and moved on. The first class passengers would have disembarked earlier. And he had no interest at all in any of the others. Glad to shake them off, in fact.

Friedrich supposed he ought to pick up this damn bell and get it over with, then he could enjoy the day in his own fashion.

His enquiries took him from the Customs House to a series of warehouses. When the bell was finally located, he stood and gaped.

'What is this?' he demanded. He was confronted by an enormous crate, weighing a ton. And a bill of lading. A huge bill.

'Let me see,' said the clerk who'd located it. 'First you've got the bill from the makers of this bell; it has to be paid before we can hand it over. Then there's the import duty on it, and then there are the surcharges for late payment, and—'

'No! No. This damn thing. What's in this crate?'

'The bell, Father. A church bell, for a steeple I suppose.'

'But . . . but . . . I was expecting a small bell. A Sanctus bell. One I can carry.'

'What? Are you saying they sent you the wrong thing? Crikey, that's a mistake and a half!' He started to laugh. 'A whopper of a mistake, if you don't mind me saying, Father.'

'Yes,' Friedrich agreed. He wasn't about to part with his money to pay for that monstrosity. 'Yes, you are right. A whopper of a mistake.' Whopper was a new word to him, but the use flattered his companion. 'We have to send it back.'

'Who pays then, Father?'

'The manufacturers pay. They made the mistake.'

'So they did. Right you are, Father, just sign here.'

He noticed the account was addressed to Father Beitz, so he signed that name, and the clerk was none the wiser. The whopping bill was on its way back to Hamburg with its charge.

Having sorted that out, Friedrich trekked up to a busy street and began his own explorations.

'I must know a little about this town in case I have to beat a hasty retreat from our parish,' he told Freddy, but then he saw himself in a shop window and stood back, amazed.

'Unbelievable,' he said. 'I really look the part. In this getup, with the long hair and the beard, I wouldn't have recognised myself. I make a fine figure of a priest, even if I do say so myself.'

He preened, straightened his hat and moved on with steady, measured steps, finding an unexpected newness about the shops and offices, as if they'd only recently sprung into being. 'Which is quite possible, for all I know,' he murmured.

Then he came across two theatres, and almost did a little jig, such was his delight, for they were of a high standard, judging by the large and plushy foyers. *Othello*, one of his favourite Shakespeares, was playing at the Victoria, and across the road at the Playhouse a comedy was running. *Dash the Duke*, it was called. Friedrich almost threw in the towel there and then, tempted to dash for a barber to shear the beard from his handsome face . . . to clip his locks back to the soft brown nape-of-the-neck curls that ladies found so entrancing. He would adore to have a part in *Dash the Duke*. It sounded such fun.

'How would you go on the stage, Freddy?' he asked. 'We'd shine. There couldn't possibly be any decent actors in this outlandish place. Then again, I wouldn't be Friedrich any more if I did that. I'd be someone else, someone with a name like, say, Percy Buckingham . . . that'd be English enough, I think. And my German accent would help; after all, their royalty are ours. And . . . you'd have to go, Freddy.'

He laughed, and continued down the street without even

373

searching for brothels. They'd be here. He was now too close to home to be skulking about; he had a reputation to protect for as long as it suited him.

The street was as wide as a river, with flash horses and even flashier vehicles darting past lumbering wagons, and the pedestrians were as gaudy and gay as any you'd find in Hamburg gardens at midsummer. The gentlemen cut a dash – dukes maybe, he giggled – in light suits . . . envied all the way to hell by the Pastor in his awful cassock and deadly black velour canonical hat.

The ladies were a frolic, a confetti of colour resting in swishy hats and reams of muslin and gingham and voile with bold sashes that would do justice to the King's dragoons. Miss Adele would have to watch her step, he thought. He noticed, however, with an eye to the rumpled sky, that they wore frumpy black boots on their presumably dainty feet. With summer gowns! No doubt they knew a thing or two about their climate or this sin of style could hardly be tolerated. Even here.

For luncheon, he chose the Britannia, a moderately expensive hotel. He was escorted to an unobtrusive table with a view of the river, and was apologised to that the fish was 'off'. Not knowing whether the waiter meant that it was off the menu, rotted, or not recommended, Friedrich gave a great sigh.

'This is a pity. I was recommended your fish . . .'

The chef, a Chinaman of all people, dived out from the kitchen to render heartfelt apologies to His Worship, stating in a high-pitched scream that it was true, his fish was the best, but not today. He bent double with his apologies while a dowager in a black dress with a large diamond brooch stood nearby, assessing the worth of his sentiments. Then she stepped forward.

'I'm sorry, Father, are you from St John's?'

'I am indeed,' he said, impressed by his ability to recall that the Bundaberg parish was St John's, but apparently that was just a slice of serendipity. He soon learned, as she chatted and he was delivered of a claret rich enough to knock his (damp) socks off, compliments of the house, that St John's was the name of the proposed Church of England cathedral in this

374

town. One fine day... he told Freddy. Anything for a quiet life and free wine.

The Chinaman himself shuffled out with the fish replacement, a rack of lamb. Delicious, superb, marvellous lamb to die for, with a lemony taste and rich gravy and a tureen of baked vegetables. It all came with more apologies and the Pastor accepted them ever so graciously.

They could have served him tripe. They could have served him pig hocks or oxtail and he would have slavered. Anything was better than the stinking slime that had passed for food on that ship, down in the lower classes anyway. He thanked the cook before he left. Made a point of it. Almost choking with laughter as he pressed a folded Lutheran pamphlet into the eager hand of the Chinaman.

By the time the Hoeppers boarded *Tara*, the Pastor had installed himself in a first-class cabin, tucked in his luggage and was trying not to lounge about in the very small well-appointed salon that doubled as a dining room. He decided to keep Brisbane in mind for a rainy day, for the so-far fictitious Percy Buckingham, famed actor, because he liked the place. But ahead, he reminded himself, was a permanent role and myriad opportunities to drag in money, so Brisbane had to be no more than an interesting backdrop for now.

He sat at table with the Captain, the Hoeppers and two couples who, he learned, owned large sheep farms. They were charming people and invited the three German travellers to visit them so that they might see more of the countryside. Friedrich had no interest in countryside, let alone farms, but they were obviously wealthy folk, so he promised he would take them up on their invitation at a convenient time, as did Hoepper.

That evening he managed to stroll the deck with Adele, as if by accident, and it was sheer joy. Though he did not touch her, he managed to make love to the little virgin, in his fashion.

'I didn't put a finger on her,' he told Freddy. 'Not so much as a brush of fingertips. I simply chatted with her about everyday nothings, keeping my voice low and intimate. I practically swallowed her with the sweetness of my attentions, and once I managed to look into her eyes so deeply she almost swooned. So did I. Her lips nearly drew me to her, but I knew that I would have to court her slowly, the little pet. And thank God for your cassock, Freddy, or she might have spotted my manly reaction to her. Not that you'd know about that.'

He laughed as he undressed. 'Or would you? I bet you and your fellow saints know plenty about it!'

As the coastal steamer ploughed north, the rain increased, so Friedrich retreated to his cabin rather than allow his companions to spend too much time with him. Idle conversations led to questions about family, the home and hearth, connections that had to be avoided. He had become adept at keeping people at arm's length without offending them, but he missed very little about *them*. Reward for being forced to listen instead of speak, he supposed.

But now, as he stared at the rain-misted sea, he realised it was time for a serious approach to this role as a curate amid a flock of God-fearing simpletons. He had prepared his opening address, a masterpiece of loving greetings, thanks to God, humility and flattery. No matter what they looked like or what they'd done, he'd praise them for their faith, forbearance and hard work . . . their shining example . . . whatever. Folk loved to hear nice things about themselves, rare in sermons. No, unheard of. They would love his sermons.

After a couple of days at sea, *Tara* bucketed across a bay, took on a pilot, and continued through driving rain across the mouth of a wide river. The rain increased, so there was nothing to see, nothing to do but hang about in his cabin peering at some ladies' journals he'd found in the salon. Along with an attractive brass lamp which was now resting deep in his trunk.

When at last the ship's hooter blared their approach to civilisation, Friedrich donned his hat and cloak and made his way up top, excited now as if for a first night.

They hauled to port, to the usual dreary wharves and warehouses, with shadowy figures huddled in the rain as welcomers, and labourers splashing about with mooring ropes and gangways, and then the rush was on. As if there were a prize for first off again, he mused, taking his time as a gentleman and a priest should, reaching out to assist an old lady with her umbrella, turning to find the Hoeppers bidding him a temporary farewell.

'A steward is taking us over to a hotel, Pastor,' Mr Hoepper said. 'The Royal, I believe. But I'm sure we'll see you soon. It certainly is a very damp beginning,' he added, as they hurried away, set deep under their umbrellas.

Friedrich couldn't see any point in hanging about, waiting for his luggage, so he had it sent to St John's Lutheran parsonage and dashed up the rise to find a horse cab, but he was intercepted by a young man.

'Excuse me,' he said excitedly. 'Are you Father Ritter?'

'Yes.'

'Oh! I'm sorry, Father. You should have let us know you were coming.'

This was without enlightening the priest on how this could have been accomplished, though he discovered later that a telegram could have been sent.

'But never mind. I'm Hans Lutze, and here ... coming now is my brother Max. We work here so it was fortunate that I saw you disembarking. Max!' he called. 'This is Father Ritter. Our Father Ritter!'

Max was just as effusive in his greetings, and when he could get a word in, Friedrich asked them to address him as Pastor, in deference to Father Beitz. They nodded in agreement, more concerned about taking him 'home'.

'I'll find some transport and get the luggage,' Max said to his brother. 'You look after Pastor Ritter.'

'Yes, perhaps you could come with me?' Hans asked him.

Friedrich nodded. Neither of them, in their work clothes, seemed to have noticed the steady rain. He wondered if he were imagining that his black velour hat was dripping, probably ruined. His face was streaming, while his heavy cloak, heavier with rain, had turned into a Turkish bath from which his steaming body had, at present, no escape.

He was given shelter in the maw of a leaking warehouse, where Hans, now over the spontaneity of the meeting, lapsed into shy silence, so Friedrich plied him with thanks for

377

his kindness in delivering him from the confusion of his unheralded arrival. Then he asked about the job, and what work others had found, in order to begin an assay of his congregation. By the time Max came back, Friedrich had learned a great deal about these people and made a friend of Hans. He was surprised, though, at the size of the Lutheran group. He'd imagined there'd be at least a hundred, but twenty or so, with a couple of newborns, was much better. Less chance of dissenters and meddlers. Much better.

'I'm sorry,' Max said, 'I couldn't do better for you, Pastor, not just now, but Davey here will take you out to the commune.'

He'd already learned that Max and Hans and a few others lived proudly on the beautiful church land, in an idyllic communal arrangement. Hence commune. Obviously near to the church and the parsonage. Having often survived for months within a tight theatrical company, sharing funds and pleasures, Friedrich approved of this arrangement, and congratulated Hans on his loyalty to the church. Another plus in his initial project, his first priority, to win over all of the group, to have them love and trust him.

Davey was a wiry little local fellow with a strange English accent which the Pastor could barely understand, and worse, he was the driver of an enormous lorry packed with furniture and hauled by a team of large bullocks.

'Good God!' Friedrich cried, appalled that this should be his transport, as if he'd cadged a ride along a byway, but then he saw their faces crumple. Max and Hans had taken fright, fearing they were treating the holy father with disrespect. As they were. But Friedrich, at all times aware of the popularity stakes, saved the day. Quick as a flash he rushed forward to admire the bullocks.

'Good God!' he said again. 'What magnificent beasts! Marvellous animals, and gentle. Just look at them!'

Davey's rugged face creased into an expression of pure joy as he hurried over to introduce the young priest, the sainted young priest, to each of the beasts by name, and proudly expound on their personalities . . . this one a leader, her too, this one a tease, another a bit on the lazy side, another very strong and knew it . . . and so it went on, with Max and Hans all smiles again.

And that was how Friedrich set off for his long-awaited new home, sitting up front with Davey, an oilskin cloak over his shoulders. Behind him, stuck in a cage made from an upturned table and a fence of wire, chickens cackled and complained. Behind them again, in the mountain of furniture, was his luggage.

He had missed seeing the town of Bundaberg, had glimpsed only the outskirts, he presumed, since they'd trundled away from the wharf along a street full of potholes and old tree stumps, which turned out to be the norm, he now realised.

The rain kept up its soaking pace, but in any case there wasn't anything except forest to see along the roads.

'A dead end,' Davey said eventually. 'Your place is right at the end of Taylor's Road. I'll have to turn about then and head off. I'm taking this furniture out to a station.'

'Oh, you have a railway?'

'No, Pastor. That's our name for the big sheep farms. Here you are.'

'Where?' They were still looking at forest.

'See that archway over there? That's the path in. It's getting a bit overgrown; the weather, you see, stuff grows faster than you can cut it back. I'll go and give them a hoy.'

The priest was as old as Methuselah, and mad as a hatter. He came dashing up a path that was almost hidden by thick jungle, barefoot, his frail frame rattling about in a loose shirt and baggy trousers made of rough cotton. Friedrich doubted the flowing grey beard had been cut for a decade . . . but these observations, though important, had to be filed away for now.

Father Beitz hugged him, kissed him on both cheeks, called on the Lord to hear his heartfelt thanks, called on a weird group of natives standing grinning beside him to witness this glorious day, hugged him again, kissed him again, and burst into a set of hallelujahs. When Friedrich broke loose, he fell to his knees and spoke with all the humility he could muster.

'Father Beitz, I beg your blessing on this unworthy soul and seek your guidance in this our mission.'

379

Brought to heel, Father Beitz took a deep breath and went to work, tears of happiness glistening in the rheumy blue eyes. He made the sign of the Cross over his curate, cleared the decks with the Our Father, as Friedrich told Freddy later, and then went into songs of praise to the Lord '. . . for sending us this upright and true young priest. For sending us, Lord, a good strong fellow, for this is a physical circumstance in which we find ourselves. Muscles of the body as well as the mind are needed here, Lord, as you well know . . .'

What the hell is he talking about? Friedrich wondered, his knees soaking up moisture from the wet planks, but at least the rain had stopped, and a crease of blue sky suddenly gave way to a sun whose force almost had him staggering sideways into the jungle. That first glimpse of tropical sunshine was so unexpected it hit him like an axe blow, and he dropped his head.

Father Beitz, still droning on about the preservation of the newcomer from the demons of the sea, delivered to this shore only by an act of faith, now grabbed his hand and jerked him up.

'Stand, Pastor Ritter! On your feet, my dear fellow. Welcome to our happy home. I can't tell you how wonderful it is to receive you, how much I have looked forward to your coming. We will have happy times together, dear boy, happy times! Now let me introduce you to some of our native friends, then I'll take you to see our church.'

'My luggage, Father . . .'

'Don't worry about that. The natives will bring it in.'

The natives were a motley lot, some old, some young, with a couple of nubile girls thrown in, he noticed, but they were all dressed in the most outlandish tattered clothes he'd ever seen. The clothes made them look like loonies but Friedrich's sharp eye saw intelligence behind the dark faces, and that made him feel a little better. He didn't feel like being surrounded by loony savages.

They proceeded to the Church of St John. He'd never seen such a small church! It was built of bare wood, unpainted, with home-made pews and altar, and two small stained-glass windows beaming down at them. Ridiculous. What would the plate take here? Next to nothing. These were things to think about as the priest led him to the altar and fell to his knees beside him, lost in prayer.

They stayed there so long the bare board on which they were kneeling turned into rock, knobbly rock. Or maybe he had knobbly knees. Whatever, Friedrich couldn't allow this old fellow to outlast him; he had to win him over, prove that he was stout of mind and body, if that was what he required.

An age later, he was trying not to hobble as he accompanied Father from the church vigil. The old priest turned to him.

'Did you bring the bell?'

'What bell? Oh . . . the bell! Father, I'm sorry. I received your letter and went immediately in search of it, which took me many hours, because the Customs people were unable to locate it, but I knew it had to be there somewhere and I pursued the matter through offices and warehouses in Brisbane, like a gundog, but finally I learned its fate. Rather, I saw its fate.'

'What happened to it?'

'They sent it back, Father. The heartless fools sent it back to Hamburg because no one had collected it and the fines for late payment for the delivery had become too extravagant.'

'Extravagant?'

He leaned down to whisper. 'Overdue, Father. Long overdue.'

'They sent back my bell! What a dreadful thing to do!'

'Yes, disgraceful. I dashed about hoping to retrieve it before it had actually sailed, but I was too late. Only two days too late, Father. I was so disappointed. I feel I have let you down already.'

'No, no, dear boy. It's sad, but it's not your fault. Might I call you Friedrich? Between us.'

'Of course, Father.'

The afternoon was grumbling to a close, those clouds not seeming to make up their minds whether to go or stay in wait for darkness, only a measure away. Friedrich looked back to the church.

'There's no bell tower or steeple. No place *for* a bell, Father.'

'I know. I was saving up for that. It's in the plan. I just

couldn't afford it yet. These things take time. I want you to write to Hamburg, Friedrich, and order another bell.'

The hell I will, he thought. The days of the useless belltower are numbered too!

'As you wish,' he said. 'I am already seeing what a load you carry here, Father, so please feel free to call on me at any time. I am at your service. And I hope you don't mind, but I would very much appreciate a cup of coffee. I'm rather parched. This weather, you know...'

'Of course, dear Friedrich. Come with me. Our quarters are this way, along this track. We own forty acres of land here, did you know? Forty acres... an estate in itself. Isn't that wonderful?'

He didn't know what one acre, let alone forty, would constitute, nor did he care. An acre could be the size of a dance hall for all he knew. Looking at the gloomy surrounds and listening to a sudden chorus of frogs and insects, and the deafening commotion of birds arguing over nesting rights, the curate came to the conclusion that this section of the commune was deposited in a swamp, and he hurried behind his leader to get out, to get to the sanctuary of their parsonage.

There were thatched huts. A confusion of thatched huts set in a maze of slippery paths. The jungle noisiness had not retreated; if anything, it was louder. The plants that he had to shove aside to keep to any path were gigantic, their leaves platters, almost indecent. A bunch of green bananas swung overhead but Friedrich would not spare them a glance. Props, that was what they were in this sultry, surreal world. And he still hadn't plumbed the depths.

'Here we are,' the cheery old soul said, stepping into a thatched hut where, sure enough, the Pastor's luggage was sitting grandly in an unfurnished, miserable dwelling. Except for some bunks lying a few inches above the earthen floor, and several other travelling trunks over in a dim corner in an apologetic heap.

'Tomorrow we'll build you your own hut,' he told Friedrich. 'As a priest, you are entitled to that respect and the solitude required to fulfil your obligations to the Lord. Had I known

382

you were coming, I would never have billeted you with our workers, but you have to sleep somewhere . . .'

Friedrich still hadn't sighted the coffee. He was near to fainting at this revelation. It didn't take a genius to work out that this idiot had no house, let alone a fine parsonage. He lived like a native in this dump. He was so stupid that he thought having your own goddamned hut was a mark of respectability, compared with his 'workers', who shared this shabby accommodation, if such was worth the word.

Stark raving mad, that was Beitz. Stark raving mad.

'Father,' he said, 'excuse me. But could I have this coffee?'

'The kitchen is along this path, my boy. Don't get lost, the bush is full of ticks, horrible things. I'll get you some water. We don't have coffee, it is too expensive. Extravagant, dear boy.'

So. No parsonage. Only these awful huts, hemmed in by a steaming jungle, far out of town with not a neighbour in sight. And the church, of course, their pathetic little church!

Four men lived here with the priest, Friedrich was soon to discover, and their earnings, along with the tithes contributed by the other members of the Lutheran community, supported Beitz and his building programme.

At dusk, after the Lutze brothers came in, Friedrich made the acquaintance of the other two workers, Walther and Lucas, both of whom were thrilled to see him and promised a special dinner to celebrate. The curate could hardly wait, having been informed by Beitz that he fasted during the day. 'Breakfast and dinner are enough for any man.

'I suppose,' he added, 'even that is largesse for you after four years in the seminary. I remember my days there . . . we had bread and dripping for most meals and mutton stew on Sundays. Quite sufficient it was too.'

Already Friedrich had had enough of Beitz. He'd spent the last hours of the afternoon dragging about the jungle with him, fighting off stinging insects and listening to the great plans of the megalomaniac.

'In this section we'll be able to build the mission school, because there aren't so many trees. It will be easier to clear.

And up here – look out for snakes – will be the refectory, and further on the dormitories for the native children. Keep your hat on, Friedrich, it protects you from the ticks that fall from the trees.'

'What are ticks, Father?'

'Dreadful little insects, they burrow into your skin and suck your blood.'

Friedrich jammed his battered velour hat hard down over his ears as they pushed through slimy bushes and emerged at a large vegetable garden.

'I'm disappointed in Walther and Lucas. They only work in the garden on Sundays, which I have to allow because they've taken up their own enterprises outside the commune. Very disappointing. But at least now that you're here, we can look after it ourselves. We could plant a lot more vegetables and sell them. Things grow ever so well here, thanks be to God.'

Now, settled in their dining room, another thatched hut, Friedrich began to rebel.

'Oh no, Father. Times have changed. Food at the seminary was always plentiful, and of good quality. We were losing too many novices from starvation rations,' he said meanly. 'They died, or got consumption and rickets and became such a drain on the community that the Bishop decreed it was cheaper to feed people properly.'

'Good heavens. Times *have* changed! Ah, here's our repast. We will stand for the blessing.'

Walther and his helpers provided a reasonable meal of soup and a good thick beef stew, ignoring – Friedrich noted with interest – the priest's admonition that two courses were unnecessary, and then brought out the pièce de résistance, a platter of peeled and sliced fruits so sweet and delicious that Friedrich almost slavered over them. Learning the names of these fruits, none of which he recognised apart from bananas, made a good conversation piece, and the four workers were able to enjoy the company of their new priest. He asked to say grace after the meal and loaded the prayer with praise for the cooks.

'I haven't had a meal as good as that since I left the

seminary,' he said, with an innocent smile on his face. 'Two of my travelling companions have gone to a hotel in the town. I'm sure not even they are doing as well as I am.'

'Who would that be?' Beitz asked.

'Mr Hoepper and his daughter. Charming people. They are from Hamburg, come to see how your little community is progressing.'

'Mr Hoepper!' The priest leapt up from the table. 'Why didn't you say so before? We must go in and welcome them! Walther, quickly! Get the horse hitched up to the wagon while I change. Oh, what great and good fortune has brought all three of you to us, Friedrich. No, don't get up. You stay here. Walther will take me into town . . .'

Within minutes, it seemed, they had rushed away and he was left with the other three, who fortunately all had chores to do. Rather than become involved in domesticity, Friedrich asked them to point the way to the church so that he could pay a visit before retiring, there being nothing else to do.

Armed with a lantern, he managed to find the church and stood by the front step to do some thinking.

'He could have asked me to come to town,' he said to Freddy. 'I'm better acquainted with Mr Hoepper and Miss Adele than they are. He needn't think I'm going to be stuck here weeding gardens while they socialise. I have to find out more about their finances. The size of the congregation could be a problem financially. I'm not about to stick around here if there aren't decent pickings. I ought to get myself moving to meet the rest of the flock and see how they're placed.'

For something to do, he took a turn around the outside of the church, seeing nothing of interest except two large kangaroos grazing on the lawn. He walked over to get a better look at the strange animals, but they bounced away from him, and then he noticed an elderly native standing nearby.

'Who are you?' he demanded, but the old fellow ambled away and disappeared into the overgrown forest that infested this area.

Friedrich shrugged and forgot him; he had more important matters to contemplate.

While Adele was busy unpacking, Hubert retreated to the small sitting room at the top of the staircase, delighted that they'd arrived at last. It seemed they'd been travelling for years. He was still in awe at the realisation that they had voyaged over the three great oceans. He'd done it after all! And here he was in Bundaberg.

The hotel was reasonable, and quite new, much better than anything he had expected to find practically on the edge of civilisation. The rooms were airy, opening on to a wide veranda, and the meal, their first meal, had been excellent. He lit his pipe, pleased to see the rain had ceased, and considered taking a walk now that he had his bearings. What a joy it was to be on firm ground again and to be able to stride out at will. His legs really needed a good stretch, he told himself, and decided he'd better take that walk now, before the sun went down. He'd already noticed there were no streetlights, nor any footpaths for that matter. It wouldn't do to fall in a ditch on his first night.

Now in great humour, Hubert took the liberty of removing his jacket, having observed that most men hereabouts resorted to shirtsleeves in deference to the hot and muggy weather. It felt quite jolly to be so informal in public, he found, as he made his way down to the front entrance and stood uncertainly by the steps.

There was a great deal of noise coming from the public bars and he saw that as a good sign; business must be brisk, all the better for his friends already settled here. It occurred to him that some of his compatriots could be in there right now, but he felt he would look too inquisitive to be peering in. Perhaps later he might pluck up the courage to walk in and buy a drink; certainly the climate lent encouragement to such a bold step.

He had decided to walk to his right, to see where this street led, when he heard someone calling to him, and turned to see Father Beitz dashing across the road, arms outstretched in welcome, and Mr Badke hurrying after him.

'Mr Hoepper!' the priest cried as he embraced his friend. 'How wonderful to see you! You must forgive us for not meeting you. Oh good heavens, I am mortified that you should be treated so! My dear fellow, I couldn't believe my ears when Father Ritter said you were here. Impossible, I thought. But you are! God bless you. You changed your mind! How wonderful . . .'

Hubert managed to break through the old man's enthusiasm to allow Mr Badke his word of greeting, and then sugested they retire to the upstairs sitting room where they could have a good talk.

'I'm so pleased to see you gentlemen,' he said. 'I had planned to visit you tomorrow, but this is a most pleasant surprise. I must call Adele to join us.'

At the priest's request, all four kneeled in prayer to thank the Lord for delivering them in safety to these far shores, and then Father Beitz expressed his concern:

'And how are you, my dears? I have prayed for you all the time, to help you over your sad loss.'

'Time heals a little, Father, as you said then. We are both feelling much better. It was a dreadful time, but I have Adele to thank for us being here today.'

'Oh no. Not really, Daddy . . .' she began, but he smiled sadly at her.

'It's true. I'm not proud of the selfish misery I wallowed in for months, to the exclusion of my dear daughter, who was suffering as much as I. It seemed to me that my life had ended with the death of my darling wife and the boys . . .' His voice shook, but he carried on. 'I turned my face from God, I would not be consoled. I could not bring myself to talk to anyone until my sister, Mrs Muller, stepped in, shocked me, really, into seeing the sinfulness of my—'

'Surely not sinful,' Mr Badke, whom Hubert now knew as Walther, put in. 'You were tormented beyond reason.'

Father Beitz frowned. 'No torment can excuse turning from the Lord. I'm surprised at you, Mr Hoepper.'

'Which is why I feel the need to confess this openly, Father. You were so kind to us then, so much of a solid support in our grief, I feel I let you down.'

'A pity I couldn't have stayed longer.'

'Ah, well. I got the rounds of the kitchen from Mrs Muller,

who showed me how cruel I had been to Adele, giving her no thought at all.'

'Please, Daddy,' she said. 'Don't upset yourself. What he is trying to say is that we were both lonely and miserable in that big empty house, when Daddy received such an interesting letter from Mr Meissner, about your travels. You'd all just arrived in Brisbane then.'

'So Adele said why didn't I go out there to Australia and see how you were all getting on, since I was still so interested in your endeavours. And obviously I had nothing else to do because I'd sold my business. And she agreed to accompany her old papa, so here we are. We can't ever stop mourning the beloveds that God saw fit to take from us . . .'

'Amen,' said Father Beitz. 'But you have to do the best you can, that's all He asks. We will pray for the repose of their souls and then we have so much to tell you. Everyone, I am pleased to be able to report, is well and healthy, for which we owe much to the Lord.'

By the time they'd compared notes on their voyages and their introductions to this small spot on the world map, the hour was late so Walther persuaded Father Beitz it was time to set off for home.

'Of course,' the priest said, not a little disappointed. 'Mr Hoepper and Miss Adele must be tired, I'm sure. But why don't I come by for you tomorrow? I can drive the wagon. I'll take Walther and Lucas to work and then come for you. I shall be your tour master and show you all about the town.'

'Excellent idea,' Hubert said. He was tired, and was looking forward to sinking into the very large and inviting bed in his room, that would be heaven after hard ships' bunks.

He and Adele saw their guests to the front door of the hotel and then walked back up to their rooms, thereby losing their chance to inspect Father Beitz's transport.

Had he known they would be bouncing around in a rickety old wagon in the clutches of a far from proficient driver, Hubert would have made enquiries about hiring a more appropriate conveyance and driver. But there was Father Beitz the next morning, ready with the wagon outside the hotel, his white-bearded face a picture of delight.

388

'My word, you do look well, Father,' Hubert said. 'Seeing you here, in the light of day, I truly think you look ten years younger.'

Adele agreed. 'You really do, Father. You look extremely well.'

'Ah, it's the natural life one leads here. No overcivilised fripperies.'

Hubert didn't know what to make of that, but let it pass as they set off up and down the few streets of the little town and along the river bank, from the wharves to a ferry and then to a bridge under construction.

He was surprised that they didn't go straight to the German settlement, but supposed that would come later. Instead their driver turned the horse away from the town and soon they were bumping along a country track bordered by forest.

'The forest is very strange,' said Adele. 'Really dense and overgrown. I don't recognise any of the trees.'

'No. They call it bush,' their guide said. 'The trees are very old. I'm taking you out to the ocean front; they say it's very picturesque.'

'Wonderful,' she replied happily.

They passed blocks of cleared land and many in the process of being cleared. They saw established farms with flourishing crops, and they had to pull off the road to make room for a huge flock of sheep to pass, accepting the cheerful waves of the drovers on horseback. They saw, to their utter delight, kangaroos, emus, large lizards that didn't disturb the horse one whit, and a huge array of brilliant birds. But no ocean.

A few times Father Beitz turned the wagon about, following different tracks.

'I'll find the right one in a minute,' he told them. 'It's just hereabouts.'

The wagon seat was hard. Hubert climbed back to sit on the tray, to give the other two more room on the only seat. The sun was high; it was very hot and humid, with not a breath of breeze, and around them the forest seemed to come alive with the zinging of insects, a perpetual hiss assailing their ears. At last they came to the end of a long track. A dead end.

Turning back, Father Beitz again seemed uncertain which

track to follow, so Hubert suggested, gently, that they return to town.

'We've had a very interesting tour so far, Father. Perhaps you would like to join us for lunch in the hotel?'

'Very well,' their driver allowed. 'We might just trot back to town.'

Easier said than done. A half-hour later it dawned on Hubert that they were lost, but he was afraid of offending their host by remarking on it, until Adele turned back to him, looking decidedly flushed and cross.

'Perhaps we could ask someone the way?' she offered.

'No, no!' the priest said. 'We go east just down here somewhere.'

'East?' Hubert echoed, certain that neither he nor their driver could ascertain east on this flat scape, and sat wistfully quiet as they passed a farmhouse nestled among trees far back from the track. There were no roads as such, only these tracks over strange soil almost the colour of chocolate. He had remarked on this earlier and Father Beitz had told them the commune was blessed with the same rich soil.

'We can grow anything,' he'd told them, leaving Hubert, and probably Adele, wondering why they were searching for the ocean instead of visiting the all-important commune.

It was Adele, a good hour later, who refused to put up with their discomfort any longer.

'I am so thirsty, Daddy. I don't feel well. If you don't enquire the way the next chance we get, I will!'

She also took over the directions, insisting that their driver not go back again into what she recognised as another dead end, and when a horseman approached, turned to glare at her father until he spoke up.

'Excuse me, sir. Could you please direct us to Bundaberg?'

'Certainly,' he grinned, raising a battered hat to the priest. 'It's Father Beitz, isn't it? Thought I recognised you there, Father. I'm Les Jolly. A lot of your boys work for me. Good workers too, you must be proud of them.'

For some reason Father Beitz only grunted at that compliment, but Mr Jolly didn't seem to mind.

'Well now. Back to town, Father. You're heading in the

wrong direction. Another mile and you'd be at the beach. Never mind, though, turn about and I'll take you to within striking distance of town.'

He looked to Hubert, and, obviously recognising him as a newcomer, though he hadn't been introduced, explained: 'The roads, or rather bush tracks, out here are a bit of a maze, new settlers making their own way over old stock routes. One day we'll have a proper road, but these things take time.'

Hubert appreciated that Mr Jolly was generous with his time, riding slowly ahead of them to allow the creaking wagon to keep him in sight as they made their way towards the town, and only turning off with a wave when they reached the long main street.

Finally, they came to rest back at the hotel, but Father Beitz declined to come in, claiming he had to water the horse.

'But surely the hotel grooms will do that for you, Father?' Hubert said.

'No! No! You go on in. I have things to do. I hope I shall see you at Sunday service tomorrow. Sharp at eight. And after that we shall have a feast in your honour.'

'How very kind of you,' Hubert said, bemused. He watched the wagon trundle down the street and turned to his daughter.

'I presume the service is at the good Father's new church, St John's,' he said.

'If we can find it.'

'Oh yes. After lunch I shall see about hiring a light vehicle.'

'With padded seats and a hood, please.'

'Very well,' he laughed.

Thoroughly upset and embarrassed, as well as suffering from the heat in the heavy soutane he rarely wore these days, Father Beitz did take the horse down to the next corner, where it could drink its fill at a horse trough, and then dragged himself across the road to a shop, where he asked for a drink of water.

The woman was very kind, insisting that he sit awhile. 'You look mighty overheated, Father. You stay awhile in that cane chair until you cool off or you'll be dropping in your tracks out there. 'Tis a horrible day for us cold-country people.'

He was grateful for the respite and almost dozed off before he remembered his invitation to the Hoeppers. He had meant it, of course, but he'd forgotten that a private feast would not be possible. All his parishoners could be expected to attend tomorrow, especially with the Hoeppers and the new priest in town. The meal would have to include everyone. Which would be very nice, except there wasn't much food in the larder. He worried that he should have taken Mr Hoepper out to the commune today after all, but he was feeling a little guilty that he hadn't made more progress.

In fact, he thought sadly, he had deliberately postponed inviting the Hoeppers to the commune because of his concern that on a working day, with the men away, it would appear a failure. Nothing like the co-operative community Mr Hoepper would be expecting. Just deserted huts with two priests and some blacks in attendance. He'd thought that Sunday, with everyone about, would give a much better impression, especially when he could offer them Walther's best fare.

'Oh dear,' he worried. 'A feast for all it will have to be.'

His decision surprised Walther, who had thought it might be appropriate to serve a buffet lunch this Sunday, in honour of Pastor Ritter, Mr Hoepper and his daughter, but hadn't mentioned it because the old priest had made such a fuss about the expenditure for the Christmas Day buffet. It really had been a simple affair, just plain food with plenty of fruit and vegetables, most of which were in abundance here, but Father Beitz had called it a feast . . . and now he was declaring they would have another one tomorrow!

'That's short notice, Father. There isn't much in the larder.'

'Then come along. We have to gather up supplies.'

Walther whistled to Lucas, who came tramping over. 'What's up?'

'Looks like we're having a party tomorrow. Big day for all our visitors. So that's the end of work for today. We have to go shopping.'

Friedrich had slept heavily despite the humid night and the snores of his companions, and their cheerfulness when they woke him for prayers around dawn aroused nothing short of rage in him, but the enforced silence of their long morning meditations gave him a chance to doze and begin to recover. Then the porridge and more fruit helped him to regain his usual affable temperament, for he liked to think of himself as a courtly person, well fitted for this gentle role.

His affability was hard pressed, though, when the priest brought him a set of the ghastly peasant's attire he seemed to prefer: a loose cotton shirt, and trousers that tied at the waist like a sack.

'You'll be more comfortable in these clothes, Friedrich. The temperature gets to a hundred here some days, and as you've seen, the rain doesn't seem to help to cool things down. Keep your other clothes for good, and for outings. Now there's a lot to do in the vegetable gardens these days, and keep an eye on the church. Open the windows but, dear chap, do rush to close them if it rains. Should you want to wash any of your smalls, the laundry is out back by the water tank.'

Walther overheard the instructions and came back to offer some advice on the quiet. 'But if you ask any of the natives who wander about here at will, they'll help,' he grinned. 'They'll also help themselves to the food in our larder; that's why it has a door on it and a lock. But the key is under the mat, and you will find cold meat and bread and cheese in there for your lunch.'

'Father says we don't eat lunch.'

'He won't know.' Walther laughed.

Why won't he know? Friedrich wondered, until he saw them all departing for work, the old priest with them.

'I'm taking Mr Hoepper and his delightful daughter on a little tour of the district today,' he called back to Friedrich, who stood gaping, realising he was being left alone in this jungle outpost. Appalled.

He spent the morning learning about the commune by examining the contents of Beitz's sea chest, with special attention to private papers and journals, pleased to see that the priest kept meticulous records. Not too pleased though to discover that his eminence was in debt to the bank. Daily expenditures, mainly on food, were itemised with care in a separate ledger, and balanced precariously by weekly deposits of three trifling amounts. Wages, of course, but why only three?

'Who isn't paying their way, Freddy? Can't have this. Beitz and the curate are the only ones allowed free rides in this Eden.'

From the priest's quarters he moved to the communal hut, where he searched through his companions' belongings, interested to discover that Lucas, a rather handsome fellow, was married. So where was the wife? The tickets were still here, souvenirs of passage, in the names of Lucas and Hanni Fechner. But in a smaller sea chest he found Walther's story. He too had a bank overdraft! What was with these people? Walther owed even more than the priest, who, come to think of it, didn't actually owe anything personally. That debt was in the name of the Lutheran Church Building Fund, which gave rise to a possibility of some sport, he mused. What bank would sue a church?

Among Walther's papers he found his father's death certificate; unimportant, until he saw that a careful clerk had inscribed: 'By his own hand'. Good God! What a scandal!

'Walther, who looks rather a blockhead, is a great one for keeping every tiny bit of paper in good order,' he told Freddy. 'It seems he has a little mine of money on paper as well as this bank money, and he's building a brewery. What a damn good idea. You see, Walther and his daddy were brewers, so Walther is about to carry on the family tradition out here. But what I don't understand is why his daddy did himself in when he could have just drunk himself to death and gone out with a smile.'

Everything was put back in order. It occurred to Friedrich to go back and have another look at Beitz's list of people who had come with him from Hamburg, because he'd entered personal notes about them, but he decided he'd make up his own mind. And besides, he was hungry. After a visit to the larder – amused by the fact that there was a sturdy lock on a frail door of bamboo and straw – he took his lunch of cheese and bread and pickles, and sat under a tree like a ploughman in the fields. Pleasant enough, except for large blackbirds with white tails that nagged him for a share, marching along the wooden table as if they owned the place.

'They can have it,' he said to Freddy.

A walk then. A stroll through the jungle. Why not? Effort, he mused, finds rewards. He found a busy stream almost hidden by greenery, the clear crystal waters too enticing to a man already suffering from the heat. He stripped off, tripped across the sandy bank and waded in to sink, enthralled, into the wonderful coolness, thinking he might never leave here, wallowing in the arms of sheer luxury.

Friedrich lingered and lingered. Floating, dreaming, plotting, wearing away an afternoon. He heard giggling and saw three young native girls watching him, and became his debonair self again. Never let it be said that sea voyages are not good for one, he smiled, as he raised himself up in the shallows so that they could admire the physique of a white man now come to his prime, the hungry, bony years left behind. Though he was said to make an excellent Cassius.

'Ho, ladies,' he called in English, 'would you care to join me?'

They ventured out shyly, and dear God, in the natural state! Friedrich reached out to assist the dark bodies with their full breasts into his sparkling, splashing pool, and they were coming towards him from their side, stepping over rocks, when they hesitated. Stopped. Frozen thère, it seemed, these nymphs, the sheen of their nakedness highlighted by the soft spray of a nearby waterfall, their nipples burning red in the sunlight, their smiles so bright, friendly, welcoming, suddenly shattered by screams as they looked past him. They turned and they ran, slipping, sliding in their haste, deliciously firm bottoms scrambling into that jungle.

He turned to see what it was that had frightened them but saw only a dog. And a sweet-looking, handsome dog at that. He bypassed the animal and studied the banks on his side, but there was no one. Whoever had given them the scare had taken off too. Probably a mother or a father, watching over their girls' virginity, he supposed. And with daughters like that, there'd be good reason. Somehow he'd have to acquire one of these beauties for himself. He wondered what the other men did for sex; that was something to find out as soon as possible. The confessional would be the place. Friedrich fell back into the pool, laughing at the very thought, and then he saw the dog. It was still there. He liked dogs.

'Good doggie,' he called. 'Come on down here.'

It looked at him quizzically, the way dogs did, head tipped to one side, then it rose and slowly padded away.

Ah well, he thought, disappointed. Another day. It would be nice to have a dog like that for my own. Unless there's some damned rule about that. He supposed he ought to leave, to march back into the furnace that Beitz called 'rather warm'.

His body dried as quickly as a hard-boiled egg, but as he stepped into his clothes he saw a huge lizard, as big as a man, tramping towards him, flat paws slapping on the rocks like paddles. His first thought was: was that thing in the water with me? He clutched his genitals in an understandable reaction even as he was pulling on those – thankfully – easy to manipulate cotton trousers, and sped away, hopping and jumping until he was properly clothed, and lost in Beitz's forest.

By the time they all returned home, the new curate was lying on his bunk. Sulking. Biding his time.

Chapter Fifteen

Eva and the children had no trouble persuading Hanni to come to church this particular Sunday. Despite her estrangement from Lucas, she, like all the others, was bursting with curiosity about the new curate, who, she prayed, wouldn't be as narrow-minded as Father Beitz. It had been kind of Eva to go to the old priest with the explanation of that incident on her arrival at the commune, insisting that her friend Hanni should not be labelled as a drunkard; she'd been plied with drinks by another woman.

'I saw what I saw,' he'd said. 'Mrs Fechner was intoxicated. I'm surprised at you, encouraging a woman like her to work at a hotel, an occasion of sin for weak women inclined to the bottle.'

She wished Eva hadn't told her his reaction; it only made her angrier. But anyway, today she was on her best behaviour and had promised Eva she would even be nice to Lucas. If he spoke to her.

Which, of course, he did, charging over to her when they first arrived at the church.

'So you haven't given up your religion as well,' he said. 'Or are you just here out of curiosity?'

'I can please myself what I do,' she snapped. 'I hear you're working for Walther now. And being paid. Pity you wouldn't pay your wife some support.'

'You have a home here. Think about that first.'

'Some home!'

Hanni was suddenly aware that Father Ritter was standing nearby, listening to them, and she blushed, turning away, pulling her bonnet down to hide her confusion. Not daring to look back, she joined the women walking down the path to the kitchen, where another of Father Beitz's feasts was being prepared in honour of three new arrivals.

Hubert was very happy to attend the service with Adele in the sweet little church, and extremely touched that the congregation stood to sing his favourite hymn, 'Shine O Heavenly Light' in fond memory of their dear departed loved ones, his wife and sons.

Concerned that he might find this reminder too painful, Adele took his hand, but though he appreciated the gesture, he was surprised to realise there was no need. He wondered whether time or distance had played the larger part in leading him from the deepest depths of mourning, but whichever it was, he kneeled in St John's Church to plead forgiveness for his lack of faith. He hardly dared to admit to himself that had it not been for the responsibility of a daughter, he would gladly have died by his own hand, back there in Hamburg.

This morning he'd woken with a sense of exhilaration that he hadn't known for a very long time, even before he'd lost his darlings. And the amusing part was, he had no reason for it at all, except for the newness of his surrounds and his interest in exploring not only the town but also its pioneering inhabitants. He smiled. Friedrich Ritter had been granted the honour of delivering the sermon on this his first Sunday, and though he felt the young pastor had rather overdone his fulsome praise at the way his compatriots had adjusted to life in this odd environment, he meant well and his sermon was well received.

The accommodation here at the commune was certainly odd too, but Father Beitz was satisfied and obviously was thriving . . . But here they all were now, hurrying from the church to welcome him, and it was quite wonderful to see them.

Jakob was overjoyed to see Mr Hoepper again, and looked forward to a conversation with him. He certainly had plenty to tell him about his ups and downs and would be most interested to hear how Hoepper's voyage had gone.

'You two aren't doing so well,' Freda remarked with a laugh.

'What do you mean?' he asked.

'You are busting to speak with Mr Hoepper, but Father Beitz isn't about to let you get a word in, and poor Karl is mooning after Adele Hoepper, but the young preacher has him blocked. He is rather dashing, isn't he? Tall and handsome. With that long hair and soft beard, he bears a resemblance to Jesus Christ, if you look at him.'

'What a thing to say!' Jakob was scandalised. 'Father Ritter is the only person here that Miss Hoepper really knows, outside of her father. She met him on the ship. It is natural that she feels comfortable with him.'

'Have you no care for your poor son? He's been pining over Adele ever since he met her in Hamburg. All his Christmases have come at once to have her arrive here.'

'I think you have a vivid imagination, my dear.'

'Of course I do. Now I want you to invite them, the Hoeppers, to visit us . . . Oh my God! We can't ask them to stay. We haven't any furniture!'

There has to be some way out of this, Freda worried as she went in search of her son.

'Am I imagining it, or do you have eyes for Miss Hoepper?'

'Why wouldn't I?' he said defensively. 'She's lovely, she's German, and all the lads have eyes for her. So what hope have I got? Max Lutze says she's got her cap set at Pastor Ritter. Do you think that's right?'

Freda lied without a qualm. 'No. It's not right. In fact I saw her looking your way quite a few times.'

'You did?'

Freda sighed as he rushed away. 'If nothing else, I've made my son happy,' she thought.

She took her basket of provisions through to the kitchen, where Rosie Kleinschmidt was nursing her new baby girl.

'What a little darling,' Freda said. 'When is the christening?'

'I don't know. Father Beitz hasn't said.'

'Then you go right out and have him set the date and put it in his book, Rosie. With the excitement of his visitors he's likely to forget. Get Rolf to go with you, so he doesn't put it off. Your baby should be baptised as soon as possible.'

She smiled, watching Rolf and Rosie drag Father Beitz away from Mr Hoepper, and shot forward to fill the breach. In no time she'd issued the invitation to the Hoeppers to visit their farm, apologising for her forwardness by explaining that her husband could hardly wait for an opportunity to enjoy a quiet conversation.

'My dear Mrs Meissner, we should be delighted. Jakob's letters helped me through a very bad time, I am honoured that you should think so kindly of us.'

She smiled as she walked away. No Father Beitz. No Pastor Ritter. No beds, but we can overcome that. Mr Hoepper can have our bed. Adele can have Karl's. We'll have to doss down on the veranda.

Jakob was appalled. He rushed to warn Mr Hoepper that their house was unfinished, it lacked suitable furnishings, but Hubert – 'Call me Hubert, for heaven's sake, Jakob' – wasn't concerned at all. Nor was Adele.

Pastor Ritter was moving among them quietly, reverentially you could say, listening to them, assessing them, with Miss Adele trailing along and all the single fellows, except Walther, panting after her. By all accounts, none of the settlers had made a fortune yet, though some had high hopes, and Mrs Zimmerman's husband had gone to dig for gold, taking a short cut to Easy Street, which Friedrich found commendable.

'Very resourceful of him, Mrs Zimmerman.'

'Not really, Father. He left me, and the children, destitute.'

'You don't appear to be destitute.'

'Oh no, I have a job now and we share a cottage in town with Hanni Fechner . . .'

'Then all's well. The Lord will provide. How true that is.'

She frowned uncertainly while he guessed that the pretty blonde girl walking towards them was Hanni Fechner.

'You're Lucas's wife?' he asked softly, and she nodded.

'But you stay in town? I gather you're not on the best of terms with Lucas. Is there anything I can do to help?'

She surprised him, moving closer, almost clutching his arm, or so it felt, and there was desperation in her voice.

'Could I speak to you about that, Pastor? In private. Please?'

'Certainly, Mrs Fechner. Would you care to walk with me awhile?'

'Oh yes. I don't want to take up too much of your time, Pastor, but . . .'

'My time is yours, Sister.'

The gathering had begun to bore him anyway. He might as well listen to the tale of woe she'd serve up about her cruel husband, as they all did, although Lucas seemed harmless. Oh well, here goes, more trivia to add to the collection.

They walked but she didn't have much to say after all, she was too nervous.

'I've had great difficulties since coming here, Pastor. It has been very hard for me. Please don't think badly of me for not living here with Lucas . . .'

'Now why would I do that?'

'Well, Father Beitz is cross with me, but he doesn't understand, and there are things I can't discuss with him.'

He smiled. 'That I can imagine.'

'You can?' Her big blue eyes widened, amazed. Friedrich was enjoying himself. No time like the present to start undermining the old goat.

'Yes, but he's old. He's out of touch with our generation, no idea really. Would you like me to speak with Lucas on your behalf, begin the mending process?'

'No, Pastor, it's not that. There are other things, terrible things, that I can't tell him.' Then she panicked – 'No. I can't tell anyone!' – and turned to walk back.

'Not even a good listener who'd never tell another soul?' he urged, but she shook her head, tears in her eyes.

'Another time, perhaps, when you're feeling stronger?'

'Yes,' she whispered to him. 'I hope so. It's hard for me even to go into the church.'

The Pastor was intrigued. What mischief was afoot here? But then Father Beitz came tramping towards them, spoiling everything. He gave Mrs Fechner a cold nod and spoke to his curate.

'I hope you're counselling this woman on the paths of righteousness!'

401

'Father, I am indeed. Sister Fechner was just saying how much she and all the others rely on your guidance.'

'Humph! When it suits them! Could I have a word with you?'

At that, Mrs Fechner fled.

'Friedrich,' Father Beitz said, geniality restored, 'in all the excitement lately, I forgot about the donations. I believe it was quite a sum, and I can do with it, I assure you.'

'Donations? Whose donations?'

'From the Hamburg parishioners. The Dean informed me that he was forwarding financial assistance, that you would deliver it to me. You have the money with you, surely?'

'Father, would that I did. The Dean had not even a penny for me. I was fortunate that an uncle was able to give me a purse with a small amount to see me on my way.'

'But you must have it! I need this money. I'm relying on it!'

So you can buy a ridiculous bell that no one will ever hear, to put in a nonexistent bell tower? Spare me your troubles, Friedrich thought, but he said:

'Did you know there was a fire at the seminary? The chapel caught fire. Burned to the ground, Father.'

'Oh no! Not our beautiful chapel! Oh, what a tragedy! Oh dear God, how dreadful!'

'Yes. The Dean was broken-hearted. He had to start a fund to rebuild it. I believe it will cost thousands. We were all sent out – this was the week before I left – to beg in the streets because he didn't even have enough money to pay the architects. I'm sorry, Father. It seems to me the donations you speak of would have had to go to the chapel fund. A shame . . .'

The priest staggered away, his face ashen.

The feast was a success, especially for the three newcomers, who had not yet taken for granted the abundance of exotic local fare. The table was piled with pineapples, bananas and coconuts and several other fruits that Hubert did not recognise. He was pleased to see Pastor Ritter had a healthy appetite, tucking into the cold cuts of meat and the boiled potatoes, and following up with the fish that Walther was serving on another table, but he could not be persuaded to try the oysters, brought in by two native lads.

'They're excellent quality,' Hubert told him, to no avail.

'Never mind, all the more for us,' Lucas Fechner laughed.

After lunch they gathered together and sang songs, reminiscent of their homeland, and Hubert told Father Beitz that he couldn't remember when he'd last had such a pleasant day. The relief on the old man's face was soon replaced by a beaming smile.

'I'm so pleased you enjoyed yourselves, my dears. I was afraid you'd find our poor little community rather pathetic after the grandeur of Hamburg. But now feel free to visit us any time, visit the church whenever you please; after all, you have been part of our community from the beginning.'

'It is all very strange, though,' Adele said to her father when Rolf Kleinschmidt had deposited them back at the hotel. 'The church is sweet, but how many of them live in those huts?'

'I'm not sure. I think we'll learn more about the setup from Jakob Meissner.'

Their visit to the Meissner farm was another eye-opener. Jakob himself came in to collect them, driving a cushioned buggy, warning that it was a long journey. It would take several hours to reach the property.

'For heaven's sake, man. What time did you leave this morning to come in here?'

'Early,' Jakob grinned. 'But it's my pleasure.'

They broke the journey several times, for Jakob to have his horse re-shod at a roadside blacksmith's, and later to visit a large Chinese market garden, where they were given refreshing tea and small pastries while Jakob discussed the merits of various crops with the owner.

Neither Hubert nor Adele had ever met Chinese people before and they were fascinated by the merriment of their host, who seemed to find everything they said very jolly. Hubert bought some produce in return for the tea, and as a gift for Freda, and was amazed at the tomatoes and vegetables that were heaped on the tray of the buggy.

'Did I buy all that?' he asked bewildered.

'I don't know,' Jakob laughed. 'I never know what I'm buying when I call in here, I just hand over coins and wait. Anyway, Freda will be pleased. She's trying hard to grow all our own produce.'

The next stop was at the home of Jakob's partner and neighbour, the Irishman Mike Quinlan. They found him a charming man but were shocked at his primitive residence, which was only an iron hut set apart from a long shed that housed his Kanaka labourers.

In an aside to her father, Adele worried, 'Mrs Meissner said that conditions on their farm were primitive. Like this, do you think?'

'I couldn't say. But don't forget your manners, whatever happens. We are guests.'

As it turned out, they were pleasantly surprised. The Meissner farmhouse was a long, low timber building with a shingle roof and a wide veranda across the front. A new house. Hubert remembered then, that Father Beitz had said their first dwelling had been burned down in a forest fire. Thoughtless of him to forget such a dreadful event but he'd been bombarded with so much information since they arrived – including Jakob's disclosure, on the way out, that the commune was in financial distress – that he was becoming a little confused.

As he walked inside, Hubert looked about him, thinking that one could hardly call it primitive. It shone with new timbers and had a sweet aroma from the fine cedar flooring, especially in the rooms as yet unfurnished. The lack of furniture didn't bother the guests at all. It seemed to give their visit a sort of picnic atmosphere, since they enjoyed the informality of sitting on the edge of the front veranda to take the air. However, the surrounds presented a different tale . . . new growth barely concealing the aftermath of the bush fire, which must have been devastating for them.

But further away from the homestead, Hubert saw the real task that Jakob and his son had before them, and was stunned. With the help of some coloured labourers, they had taken on the back-breaking job of clearing their land, work that would

404

take years of toil, though they planned to operate in sections so they could begin ploughing, and eventually planting their cane. They were, of course, enthusiastic about their future, but could not disguise the frugality such work would demand, since it left little time for actual farm work, the basis of this hopefully self-sufficient home. Not by the men anyway. Yet Mrs Meissner seemed unfazed by the prospect of being the farmer in the family.

'I've discovered I can grow all sorts of interesting vegetables here,' she said, 'and I'm trying to persuade some Aborigines to camp here permanently, to help me with the chores. It isn't too hard . . . Our hens are good layers and there are plenty of fish in the river. We will have to buy meat from a neighbour, but mutton is cheap and there is always game, when the men have time to go shooting.'

'It isn't too hard . . .' On their return from their visit to the Meissners', Hubert remembered Freda's words as he took time to relax back at the hotel.

Not hard! They must all be working incredibly hard. Their faces were already wind-bitten, their clothes showing wear. He was mightily impressed by their determination, and touched by the fact that all three had taken time off from work to entertain their guests, and one of their precious chickens had been sacrificed for a fine dinner. And that was why he had decided not to accept their invitation to stay longer, despite Adele's entreaties. Hubert had no wish to impose on their good friends.

Now, when he looked back on the daydreams he'd had for his family, of a beautiful farmhouse presiding over attractive fields of green, of gentle rolling countryside, he had to admit his dreams were far off the mark. This wasn't gentle country; it was hard country, ancient, and by no means welcoming. Every step in the taming of the wilderness would be fraught with problems and setbacks. Guiltily he wondered if his sons, city bred, would have appreciated such a challenge, and quickly turned his thoughts to other matters, rather than find an uncomfortable response.

Father Beitz, for instance. Hubert had learned more of the rather strange commune from Jakob. While their priest was content to live 'naturally', as he called it, of the four men who remained with him, only the Lutze boys were happy with the status quo.

'Walther is still there from loyalty,' Jakob said, 'and Lucas has nowhere else to go.'

'But I thought you were all planning to form a community there on your own land.'

'Too tough to clear, it was going to take too long. And we were all short of money. Basically, lack of funds beat it, I think.'

'Or lack of commitment?'

'Maybe. But we all hope the commune will survive somehow.'

Hubert thought about that conversation. He and Jakob had gone over it several times without coming to a conclusion as to what could be done to improve the situation. Freda was adamant that none of the women would have lived there unless sensible buildings were erected, and now it was too late. They'd all moved on.

'Maybe I should talk to some of the others,' he said to himself. 'Tomorrow. I'll start with the ladies right here in the hotel, and then find Rolf's people.'

Seated in the unfamiliar surrounds of a hotel kitchen, Hubert heard how Mrs Zimmerman had progressed quickly from part-time cook, a stand-in, to taking over the position full time because the previous cook had run off with a bachelor grazier . . . 'Where she'll be the lady of the house, and the cook.' Mrs Zimmerman laughed. 'A lucky day for me.'

He also heard that Mr Zimmerman was away digging for his fortune on one of the many goldfields that littered this continent, and since the wife didn't sound at all pleased about these arrangements, Hubert soon changed the subject, interested to hear this woman's opinion of the commune as it now stood.

'Not suitable at all,' she said firmly. 'I can't live there even if I wanted to. Father Beitz disapproves of me sending my children to the local school. He insists that he will teach them when his school opens.'

'But in the mean time, you want to keep them at the local school?'

'Yes, of course.'

'Tell me, Mrs Zimmerman, what did you expect to find here, or to happen when you arrived?'

'Here?' She stood back, put her hands on her hips and thought about this. 'Let me see. Well, I tell you, Mr Hoepper, there's good and there's bad has come of this. I thought we'd be on a big farm, fenced off to keep the blackfellows out, and we'd all work the farm together, see, and be happy ever after.'

'And the schooling?'

'Yes. We'd have our own school and the priest would teach us.'

'And yet you've changed your mind on that score.'

'Because I didn't know there'd be free schools here, and I hadn't thought about the language. I expected Father to be teaching in German, which he intends to do, but Mr Hoepper, you've got to talk to him about that. It won't do at all. Our children have to learn English as fast as possible, I know that now, but I didn't know before.'

'If you had the Lutheran school with an English-speaking teacher,' Hubert asked, thinking of Pastor Ritter, 'would you consider bringing the children back to the commune?'

'Ah, no, you see, there's that other thing . . .'

'What other thing, Mrs Zimmerman?'

'The mission school. Father Beitz keeps talking about a mission school. I never thought about it much before we left, to be honest. I was too keen to get going. But what's going to happen there? Will he have two schools?'

'I don't know, that's hardly feasible.'

'Anyway, Mr Hoepper, it's all beside the point. I've got my freedom now. I won't be going back there, except for church. And I doubt Mrs Fechner will either.'

'Who's taking my name in vain?' The young woman who was employed as a housemaid came in cheerfully, bearing several water jugs from the bedrooms, but when she saw Hubert she jumped nervously.

'Oh, Mr Hoepper, I'm so sorry. Am I interrupting?'

'Not at all,' Mrs Zimmerman said proudly. 'Mr Hoepper

407

just dropped in for a chat. To see how we're getting on, like, and I've talked him into a cup of tea.'

'Oh, I won't stay. I only wanted to wash these jugs . . .'

'If you could spare a minute,' Hubert said. 'We were discussing how the commune is turning out.'

'Oh, that!' she retorted. 'Who cares?'

Hubert spoke very quietly. 'I take it you're disappointed, Mrs Fechner.'

'Very much. I thought we were coming to our own village, and with all that land and only a few families, we thought we'd have farmland of our own. We were ready to work hard, we really were, so that we could make a lot of money.'

'And what then? When you'd made your money?'

'We could go home. Back to Germany to buy a nice farm.'

Pastor Ritter called, as he often did, usually at mealtimes so that he could join them, but today he too had a gripe about the commune, and a request for Hubert to put to Father Beitz.

'He doesn't seem to understand, Mr Hoepper, that we should be treating the Aborigines the same as the Kanakas who work in the canefields. They should be working our fields at set times and set rates of pay. That way we can clear and expand land at a much faster rate, we could be self-sufficient and begin to make a profit. Thirty or so natives working for us would turn our finances around very quickly. You do know that the church bank account is in debt?'

'Yes. I did. It is unfortunate. I have been trying to think of a way to help . . .'

'Thank you. Donations would be much appreciated.'

'I doubt they'd be much help in the long run. What does Father say to the employment of natives?'

'Definitely not! He believes that when they are converted to Christianity they'll be happy to work for a few handouts and the love of God. He lives in a dream world.'

'Maybe so,' Hubert said, wondering what could be done to preserve that dream.

He talked to the lads across the road at the wharves, Max and Hans, for their opinions, and was amused to discover that though they were quite content with the status quo, they had faced initial disappointment. Simple fellows, they'd taken Father Beitz's words at face value. As soldiers of Christ, they'd expected great adventures in the wild far-away land, where they'd be fighting off the bloodthirsty heathens who would be menacing their village.

'What did we find?' Hans said. 'Them natives, they're good fellows. They laugh at how hard we work. Not much adventure at all, but it's all right. We're never cold any more and we like our jungle camp.'

'I'm happy to hear that. You said the Aborigines laugh at you working, but at what? At manual labour?'

'No. They say there's plenty of food to be had for free – fish, game and other stuff that grows wild – so why pull down trees and plant our food, that birds and wallabies pull up and eat anyway?'

'So you don't think they'd like to work in the fields like the Kanakas?'

'No fear. Neither would we. Those poor fellows are worked hard.' Max shuddered. 'You wouldn't want their life, far from home. A lot of them were kidnapped from their islands and brought here. They'll be lucky if they ever get home.'

'Who told you this?'

'It's common knowledge. The blacks aren't dummies they keep well out of the way in case they get bashed into working like that. They like Father Beitz; he's kind to them. He lets them be.'

'Except he wants to bring them to the Lord,' Hans said. 'And that's a good thing. We're going to have a school for all their children, about forty for a start. We'll be clearing more land soon, to build the school. And that will be a great day.'

Hubert worried about that as he walked down to collect Adele from the Kleinschmidt house. She and Rosie had become good friends, and of course baby Louise was the centre of attention.

He had coffee this time, much more to his liking than tea, and found himself quizzing Rosie, since he was now engrossed in the subject of the commune.

'So many people had different ideas on what to expect here,' he said, 'compared to the reality.'

Rosie laughed. 'Helene Wagner and I were shocked when we first arrived, what with natives standing around stark naked, a derelict-looking town without even proper streets, not that they're much better now . . .'

'But what about the commune?'

'Oh, heavens! That was the greatest shock. I thought we were going to a tropical island with a white sandy beach and waving palms and balmy weather, and instead we came to that jungle down the end of a long, dusty road.'

'What did you think your men could do to earn a living on a tropical island?'

She smiled. 'I didn't think that far along. I never even told Rolf about my island, I felt such a fool.'

'But then you ended up in log huts,' Adele said. 'That must have been terrible.'

'Actually, it was quite fun. I didn't mind it at all. I believe Rolf is taking you over that side of the river tomorrow, to visit the rest of the family.'

'And have a look at a sugar cane plantation,' Adele added. 'Looks like a busy day. Mr Meissner and Karl are coming over too; they are anxious to be shown over a plantation and a distillery, since they're going into that business as well.'

They spent the next few days touring. First across the river as planned, and then on an unexpected day trip out to the ocean at the invitation of Mr and Mrs Wheatley, the graziers they'd met on the coastal steamer. And this time, in a large, comfortable vehicle, they did make it to the ocean, or rather to a very large and beautiful bay, the same bay they'd crossed on their way to the mouth of the Burnett River.

It seemed that several of these people, owners of large inland sheep stations, had decided to build beach houses out here to escape the fierce summer heat, so they had an enjoyable morning searching along the seafront for the best positions, after which they sat under a shady tree to share an excellent picnic lunch.

'You should stake a claim too, Mr Hoepper,' his hosts told him. 'This really is a delightful spot, as you can see, and acreages can be bought for a song.'

'What would a song be?' Hubert asked with a smile.

'Only a few shillings at this stage. It's hardly good grazing land and too far from town to be much use commercially.'

Hubert was astonished. 'Count me in,' he said after further discussion. 'This seaside looks very enticing, and look . . .' He pointed to a ship crossing the bay. 'We can watch ships go by from here as well.'

When they returned to the hotel, Rolf was waiting to have a quiet word with Hubert.

'Is anything wrong?' Hubert asked anxiously.

'Not yet. But I wonder if you could speak to Father Beitz for us?'

'About the church finances?'

'Yes.'

Hubert sighed. 'I don't know. Pastor Ritter came to me about these matters, but I really don't like to interfere. It's up to you people to sort it out. It's a great pity that the original plan to have a co-operative community living on the forty acres of church land couldn't work out, but—'

'Excuse me, Mr Hoepper, but I think now that it is the best thing that could have happened. It is forcing us into the mainstream community where otherwise we'd have been isolated; not a healthy way of life to be too dependent on each other, and it would have made the locals suspicious of us. What's happening now is for the best, but Father Beitz has to accept limitations.'

'Such as?'

'Mr Hoepper, this is a very small town. Everyone knows everyone else's business. I just heard that Father Beitz has applied to the bank to extend the loan so that he can build a school.'

'Who for?' Hubert asked nervously.

'A mission school, for the black children. Now I don't have any objections to this, except that the money is not there. We are already tithed to support the clergy and the church, and

411

that's hard enough on a congregation struggling to get started in a new country. So if he digs us even deeper into debt, most of us will wash our hands of the whole thing. He'll be left with no support at all.'

'I wish you people would discuss this with Father Beitz yourselves . . . a delegation, perhaps?'

'Mr Hoepper, you have to understand. Father Beitz has been a parish priest for a very long time. Where he comes from, parishioners do not chide or disagree with their priest. He simply will not listen to any of us. He just won't. Now you may be able to get him to listen to reason. I hope you can. If not, the priests are on their own.'

Father Beitz greatly valued the healing capacity of prayer, and once again, the Lord did not let him down. He had been upset, truly upset, to hear of the destruction of the beautiful chapel at the Hamburg seminary, and, wrongly, even more upset over the loss of those donations. Devastated, in fact. For which he had to beg forgiveness, when he came to his senses. He had forgotten his own rule . . . the Lord will provide. So, to make up for his failings, he prescribed hard work.

With the help of Friedrich and a dozen or so natives, he instigated daily working bees clearing more land and carrying away the infernal rocks scattered everywhere. He was using them for a fence along the entrance to their block and it was beginning to look very smart. In fact, he was standing admiring the way the native lads were grading and placing the rocks when Tibbaling came along.

'It looks very good, doesn't it?' he said to his friend.

'What for?' Tibbaling asked. 'Why you need your fence?'

He tried to explain that it was really only for effect, since at hip height it could not be expected to keep anyone in or out, but gave up on that.

'By the way, have you met Pastor Ritter, our new priest?'

Tibbaling nodded sagely. 'Ah yes. I have seen him, Two-Men-Walking.'

'What?'

'Two-Men-Walking. Your new feller. Holy man.'

'Why do you say that?'

'Why you ask? He a holy man, he walk with the Holy Spirit, yes?'

The priest blinked, trying to follow the reasoning. 'Yes, of course. Indeed yes. He is a holy man. You're quite right. He does walk with the Holy Spirit.'

Tibbaling wandered off to watch the toilers, guessing that the Father intended to have them plant more food, which he supposed was a more reliable source than bush provisions, but not as tasty. Especially the leaves they ate. He could see Two-Men-Walking near Tom-Big-Toe and Jumping Jim, two of his lads, all three heaving at a large rock with iron sticks.

The new holy man was a lusty fellow. Tibbaling had admired his fine body shape when he'd seen him bathing in the creek, and was pleased to see his manly reaction to those naughty girls. He was fond of all the whitefellows who lived at this camp, but until Two-Men-Walking had shown up, none of them had taken women to their beds, and that was a mystery. Not that he had, the new holy man, but he had surely shown that he was willing. It would be interesting to watch what happened now. And a good time to keep the naughty girls away from the commune. Tibbaling did not approve of tribal women copulating with white men; it weakened the strong family strains. A man wouldn't know what sort of families the whitefellows came from.

Fader Bites stamped out, shaking his cane at the three of them like a cranky old woman, telling them to get on with it, not be standing about, and Tibbaling doubled up laughing. They'd only stopped for a rest! He was sure that Tom-Big-Toe and Jumping Jim wouldn't be volunteering for this work again, even for a plate of Walther's stew, and Two-Men-Walking glared knives at his boss. He didn't seem to be enjoying the toil either. Tibbaling could feel the smouldering resentment even from here, and the Holy Spirit who walked with Father Friedrich all the time misted a little against the background of low clouds.

Tibbaling smelled the air. This was a bad time of the year for storms, too much rain, and heat, and winds made for confusion, causing everything to blow up, like brooding family

413

rows. He hoped the spirits were paying attention. Which reminded him. Why was the Holy Spirit walking with Father Friedrich instead of Fader Bites? Surely *he* had seniority. And the great wisdom of an elder. The new priest must be supremely important, there could be no other explanation. He would like to ask Fader Bites about this but thought it might not be nice. Not polite. Who was he to guess the ways of the white men's spirits?

Take the man they called Mike, he of another clan from these people, with a different-sounding voice. A good man. Billy was fond of him. That was why he'd tried to warn him that seabirds were wailing his mother's name. Mike's spirits must be powerful, he mused, to break through to his own and manifest in the voices of seabirds. Then again, it could simply be a mother's love. Saying farewell to a beloved son. It happened.

He sighed. Billy said Mike didn't even know that his mother had drowned, yet. Lost at sea with so many weeping souls from a big ship. So be it.

He walked along the rows of the food patch, heading for the gate, and turned back for no particular reason. A wave, a smile, maybe? But what he saw caused him to recoil in shock.

Fader Bites was bending over his garden, examining the growth, and across from him was Two-Men-Walking, right away on the other side. There was no one else in the picture. Not a soul. They all seemed to have disappeared; the workers, even the Holy Spirit was no longer present. Only the two men. He saw the new priest stand tall, stand tall and proud, and then there was this flash. Tibbaling could hardly believe his eyes! The new man was pointing the bone at Fader Bites. Pointing the bone! Calling down death on him. On poor Fader Bites.

Then it was gone. There was only that flash of a happening. Now they were all back, working away. Women following Fader Bites, carrying baskets to collect his food. Tom-Big-Toe groaning, looking to escape from the field, Two-Men-Walking raking over the soil that had contained the rock, calmly, quietly, his Holy Spirit beside him again like a shadow as usual, and Jumping-Jim dragging the rock away with ropes.

Tibbaling pushed on into the bush and settled in a hutch of

thick leaves to digest this. He was no novice in these matters. He was no Mike Quinlan, who, sadly, could not interpret the signs. He was just a sad old man who didn't need to scratch his head, or to make fires and smoke to think on these happenings. He was also too terribly sad, all of a sudden, to want to look.

How could this be? Why would someone want to point the bone at a good man, an elder? Who had lived a blameless life, that was easy to see. Why would they wish him ill?

Tibbaling had no doubts about what he had seen. None at all. And he knew he had no right to interfere. This was tribal business. White tribal stuff. And what he'd seen was the real thing. Many a blackfellow had tried the trick of pointing the bone at enemies while lacking the knowledge to perform the ceremony so it meant nothing at all . . . and why should it? he mused. We couldn't have these people running about pointing bones at everyone and anyone. There'd be chaos in the camps.

And, surely, the new priest wouldn't have any idea how to perform the ceremony either, not correctly anyway, so think on that, old man.

He did. He chewed tobacco and thought on that.

It came to him in the end that a white spirit had broken through to him again. Was he getting too close to them? Too involved? Was it time to pull back before he became confused?

This was very worrying. He sat for hours in that same place, looking over the field, long after the workers had left, long after the contrary clouds subsided into darkness, but he dared not leave until his sad, sad heart had grappled with the meaning. His old muscles cramped. His bones ached. But he would not let go. A bone-pointing ceremony had taken place and he would not deny it, though voices tried to muffle him, to turn him away, evil voices, while others, softer, sweeter, told him of imaginings, but he battled on knowing that something was wrong with that ceremony. He'd seen it often enough over his tumultuous years; he should know, the voices told him, that this was only a trick. Badly performed. A novice could do it better.

The voices were a tumult in themselves, some trying to convince him he saw nothing real, others trying to show him

415

where it was all wrong, but he didn't want to listen to them; he wanted to go deeper, to find out the whyness of all this, but the waters were deep. And dark. And fearsome. He wept, forsaken by his own spirits in his attempts to pierce the mysteries of the white world.

'Leave it,' they said. 'Don't bother us with them.'

But he couldn't do that. Fader Bites was his friend. Fader Bites, he insisted, was a good man with the evil eye upon him. Someone should care.

The dingo came and curled up with him, warming him, encouraging him, and together they watched the fiery dawn light up the sky until the dreary clouds shut down their display.

Tibbaling nodded. He patted the dog. There had been a flaw in the scene he had witnessed. In that flash. When a competent man points the bone, it is very real. No one knows better than the victim. He knows from that instant. And from that instant, no matter what is said and done, no matter what pleas and sacrifices are offered, no matter what abject apologies come forth, the victim is dying. From that instant.

That was it. He climbed slowly to his feet, testing each creaking bone, and walked out into Fader Bites's food field, to stand looking about him, by no means released from his melancholy.

He knew now that what he had seen was the whitefellow equivalent of pointing the bone. But that ceremony was flawed, as if performed by a novice, because something had been overlooked.

The victim had to know! To realise the threat. So . . . until he knew, he was safe.

Fader Bites did not know the spell had been cast. Tibbaling had no trouble conjuring up his friend now, rising from his sleep, talking to his men, pottering about in his way, no sense of fear. No sense of the fear that should be frightening the life out of him! But Tibbaling himself froze at the very thought. The minute, the second that he told Fader Bites, went to him and warned him that he was the target, the victim of this evil, the invisible spear would start working. His life would begin its slow ebb to its close. The priest's only safeguard was his

416

ignorance of the impending doom. There was no way that his friend could possibly warn him.

But why? Why was it happening at all?

Tibbaling used all the power in his lungs to shout at the heavens, at the spirits, the birds, the animals, the denizens of the waters . . . *WHY?* But no one answered. No one knew. And that was a fact. No one did know.

Two-Men-Walking and his Holy Spirit were too strong. Too remote. They had their own reasons.

But as Tibbaling walked away from this awful dilemma, padding down the whitefellow track towards his own camp, a small bird tweaked at his ear, a little honey-eater, saying to him, 'No, no.' Such a little voice, he hardly heard it. And yet it disturbed him so much, it added to his worries.

Chapter Sixteen

An advertisement in the four-page local newspaper informed Hubert that the lawyer Jakob had mentioned, a Mr Arthur Hobday of Maryborough, would be available at Progress Hall on this very day, for the convenience of clients, so he took himself around there, content to wait his turn outside with other gentlemen who chatted amiably with him. By now, Hubert had overcome enough of his shyness and aversion to informality to be able to join in conversations with complete strangers, since this appeared to be expected here. Probably born of distance and loneliness, he had decided, since he'd noticed the empty roads and the sparse population of Bundaberg and its surrounds.

'Sorry to keep you waiting,' Mr Hobday said cheerily after the introductions.

'Quite all right. I had nothing else to do.'

'Well, there's a sad admission, sir. Surely you've got something to do?'

Yes, Hubert thought, I've got to beard the priest in his den, but he said, 'Not a lot. I'm retired. Just here on a visit.'

'A man of your age retired? Come now, you don't look the type. Too many brains peering out of those eyes. They won't stay shut down for long. But here, enough of my talk, what can I do for you, Mr Hoepper? Would you be a friend of Jakob Meissner? Ah yes, I thought so. Fine fellow. So what's the problem?'

Hubert found that the voluble Mr Hobday was also a good listener, and they soon came to an arrangement for the solicitor to purchase the seaside acreage on behalf of his client, since, as Hubert explained, he was not familiar with the checks and procedures involved, and had no set address in this country.

'And what was it you retired from?' Hobday asked. 'I have an insatiable curiosity about travellers from the other hemisphere.'

'I was a merchant, sir,' Hubert said grudgingly. 'Importing, exporting, that sort of thing. In Hamburg.'

The solicitor took the hint. 'Sorry, Mr Hoepper. I didn't wish to pry. Before you go on your way, don't forget to leave me an address. Here's my card. You ought to have a look at Maryborough too. I'd be happy to show you around.'

He stood, and walked Hubert to the door. Then he grinned and slapped him on the shoulder. 'Poor little Bundaberg could do with a real merchant with plenty of savvy, you know.'

'I'm going out to the commune this morning,' he told Adele. 'Do you want to come?'

'No thanks. I thought I would do some sketching by the river.'

'Don't go too far away.'

'No. I'll only be across the road.'

The stables in the next street had a presentable gig that he and Adele had hired a couple of times, and on this occasion Hubert rather hoped it would be in service to someone else, but it was available now.

'Better you take the gig than ride, sir,' the groom said. 'It looks like rain.'

'It always looks like rain here,' Hubert smiled. 'And what's more, when it looks like rain here, it does.'

There was a downpour just as he left the town, but by the time he reached the commune the sun was out again as if that squall had never happened. As usual, Father Beitz was forewarned by his native lookouts so was there to greet Hubert.

'How pleasant to see you, Mr Hoepper. Come along in. I have such good news.'

The good news saved Hubert from the problem of how to broach the subject of church finances that he'd been worrying about all the way. Father Beitz hurried him along the paths, past the living quarters, past the church and on to where several

420

natives were beginning to clear dense bush.

'See there? We've started clearing; I want a good flat field here so that we can start building the mission school as soon as possible. A proper school, built of sawn timber like the church. Matching, you see.'

Hubert gulped. 'The mission school,' he echoed. 'I was under the impression that you were short of funds.'

'We might be, but the bank isn't. They'll give me the money.'

'I thought you already owed them money.'

'Yes, but I can extend the loan with collateral.'

'What collateral?'

'Why, the land, of course.'

'But Father, you will have to repay the loan. How will you do that? Apart from the building and equipping costs, the school will need maintaining, and the native children won't be able to pay.'

'Goodness me, you are a worrier. The school won't cost much to build. Only timber, you know . . . and a few desks after that, and slates and things.'

'Father, doesn't it strike you as odd that you're building a timber school, yet you and the others live in huts?'

'Not at all. My mission school will be a model school. People will want to come and see it. Important people. It has to be just right. I've drawn up the plans. There'll be two classrooms, of course. One for boys, another for girls . . .'

He talked enthusiastically about his plans while he gave Hubert a drink of water as they sat in the shaded dining area, and eventually Hubert took a deep breath to continue his line of questioning.

'Can you tell me, Father, how this loan will be repaid?'

'Walther will look into it,' the priest said testily. 'And I was thinking of taking up a special collection on Sundays, earmarked for the school.'

Hubert sipped on the tepid water, wishing it were something stronger. 'I'm afraid that won't work, Father. To be honest, I think it would be unwise of you to take out a new loan at this stage.'

'But I have to . . . the mission school.'

'Can't you teach the children just as easily in a hut? But Father, even more to the point, are you sure you're not overstretching yourself starting up as a schoolteacher when you've got so much else to do here? I mean, shouldn't you be working towards a more permanent accommodation here, as a priority?'

The priest sat up sharply. 'You're the one with the priorities wrong, Mr Hoepper. I am about the Lord's work, sir. I am here to convert heathens, to bring them to God.'

'And what about your parishioners? Don't they have a say here? They are, after all, tied in to this commune. This land, might I remind you.'

Father Beitz looked squarely at Hubert. 'Are you criticising me?'

'Not really, Father. I'm just trying to tell you that if you go ahead with this loan, your people will be upset, you'll have a revolt on your hands.'

'Rubbish! Where do you get such strange ideas? What sort of revolt?'

'I am given to understand that they will no longer support this commune at all. The tithes will cease. You can't rely on the men who live here to finance the commune and pay off the loan from their wages. I'm very sorry to have to tell you this, Father, but perhaps the mission school plans could be postponed?'

'You disappoint me, Mr Hoepper. I thought you understood my vision for a fine German community here, with educational facilities for our own and the black children, a model society, self-sufficient unto ourselves, but I see you are a doubter too.' He shrugged. 'I can't give an answer right now for you to take back to the other doubters. I will pray on it.'

'Thank you, Father. I appreciate your wisdom.'

'Oh yes, I'm sure. Now will you excuse me? I must get back to work.'

As Hubert was able to report to Rolf later, 'I really hurt the poor man's feelings. It's such a shame.'

'Better you than the bank manager rejecting him; he'd find that much more embarrassing.'

Hubert couldn't bring himself to tell Rolf that the bank

might not reject a loan for fifty pounds when the collateral was forty acres of land containing fine timber and very rich soil. Nor did he mention that he was in the process of purchasing seaside land here. And, after his talk to Mr Hobday, and that dig about retirement and so forth, he might see what the going rate was for land in the town centre. Land suitable for an importing business. The town would soon outgrow the little retail shops; a merchant buying in bulk could service them as well. Make goods cheaper for all concerned. A thought.

Father Beitz was offended. Mightily offended that his friend, *his* friend, not theirs, should take their side against him. How dare he! Didn't he understand how much had been achieved already, 'And through my efforts,' he muttered. 'Mine alone.' Who had gathered them all together, helped and advised them, shepherded them across the world and brought them to this paradise? They'd been mollycoddled all the way, that was their trouble. They didn't have to stumble ashore, lost and bewildered like so many other immigrants they'd seen, lonely souls with no one to turn to. Oh no. Not these fortunate travellers from Hamburg; everything was laid out for them . . . their own land, their church and their priest. Not to mention the consolation of language, their own German language. Why, he himself had been called to the Immigration Barracks to translate for some newcomers but found they were not German, and thought perhaps they were Polish or Hungarian. Anyway, he couldn't help. No one could make sense of them, of any members of the young family. He'd heard later that they thought they were in Brisbane. Disembarked at the wrong port.

Now, of course, having taken all he had to offer, the ungrateful wretches were turning on him, and hiding behind the good graces of Mr Hoepper, who should have had more sense than to listen to them. Revolt? We'll see about that! On Sunday they'll get a sermon about ingratitude. About the work of the Lord, in which we are all engaged. Did they think the Lord had brought them all here safely just to allow them to turn their backs on him?

The core of a good sermon was building, so he climbed out of his bunk and went down on his knees where he did his best thinking, only to find he was very giddy; the walls seemed to be swinging around. At the same time he was struck with a splitting headache, so he had no choice but to drag back on to the bed and wait for Walther to come in with his morning glass of milk.

'You don't look very well,' Walther said, feeling his brow. 'And you're very hot. I think you'd better stay in bed awhile.'

'I'm all right. I'll get up in a minute,' he grunted, but the giddiness returned when he tried to rise, and he had to clutch the side of the bunk to steady himself.

'There's no need for you to get up, Father, if you're not well.'

'Oh yes, you'd like that, wouldn't you? You'd all like it if I stayed abed for good. Kept out of your way.'

'No we wouldn't. You look tired, you could do with more sleep.'

When Friedrich heard that Father Beitz was laid low with a mild fever, he feigned concern. 'I'm so sorry. Is there anything I can do?'

'No, this happens every so often,' Walther said. 'Don't be alarmed. The poor old fellow wears himself out, running about too much; he just needs a day or two of rest and he'll be up ordering us about again.'

Friedrich smiled. 'Yes, he does keep busy for a man his age. I had hoped to go into town today, but I suppose I'd better stay.' He couldn't bring himself to say 'stay home'. This jungle camp wasn't his home.

'No need. If you have business in town you can ride in with us. Father will be all right. There's nothing you can do. He doesn't need to be eating with a fever, and I've left him a bottle of fresh water. He just needs rest.'

They rumbled into town on the old wagon, dropped Max and Hans at the wharves, then went on to the sawmill to collect some timber, loaded that on and headed back through the town towards Walther's building site.

'It's a very small village,' Friedrich remarked dismally, but Lucas laughed. 'You should have seen it when we first arrived.

It was only half this size, and so dry and windswept we thought we'd come to the end of the world.'

'Dry? I can't imagine it dry, it has been so wet ever since I got here. But it's still a peculiar place. I mean, there are vacant blocks everywhere. Wouldn't you think people would have put their shops and businesses all together instead of scattering them all over the place? It's hard to tell which is supposed to be the main street.'

'It's to do with the surveying,' Walther told them. 'They only surveyed this wilderness a year or so back. They marked out a town, advertised the land and people bought it. Very cheap, of course, with nothing here but kangaroos. Some buyers have no intention of building anything, they're only speculators, waiting to make money on the resale.'

'And do they?'

'Oh yes, Pastor. New towns like this are a good investment, they say. Eventually our common land will be worth a lot of money, so it is fortunate that we got in early.'

'Our timber is worth plenty of money too,' Lucas said.

'What timber?'

'All the big trees growing on our land . . . There's cedar and ash and ironbark, a lot . . .'

'And that's good?'

'Yes. They are very valuable timbers.'

'But who would buy a tree?' City bred, their pastor had trouble making sense of this conversation, but when it was finally explained to him, he wondered why the commune was so poor.

'Forgive me,' he asked, when Walther brought the wagon to a halt at the building site near the river, 'but Father Beitz tells me the commune is short of money.'

They nodded in unison, a little embarrassed, he thought.

'Just as well the bell got sent back then.'

'What bell?'

'The one Father Beitz ordered. A huge bell, for the church bell tower.'

As he thought, they knew nothing about it.

'He asked me to collect it from the Brisbane Customs store and have it shipped up here, but it had already been sent back to Hamburg. Returned.' He shrugged apologetically. 'I'm sorry. For non-payment of the accompanying bills and fines.'

He saw their irritation and plunged on. 'What I don't understand, though, is why you don't sell the trees. I mean, it seems to me the forty acres are never going to be worth a penny covered in forest. What use could anyone make of it, except for the few patches wide enough to build a little church or two?'

'Father Beitz has decided not to sell the trees,' Walther explained, in a voice that said the decision was final, and Friedrich didn't press the matter. He had his own opinion.

Then came the good news. Walther handed him the horse's reins and asked the Pastor if he could come back and collect them after work, and Friedrich was delighted. He'd thought he'd have to walk back to the commune.

'If you need the wagon any time,' said Walther, 'just come into town with us and you can take it. If you or Father don't need it, then it might as well stay here and take us home.'

He was free! Free of them all! With his own transport! He felt like a king, so great was his relief. And even better, he realised, it was still very early, so he headed for the Royal Hotel, arriving just in time to join father and daughter for breakfast in the pleasant little dining room.

Mr Hoepper was beginning to bore him with his enthusiasm about the newness of everything, how interesting it was to see all these enterprises starting up. And worse. Miss Adele was disgustingly animated about their visit to the Meissner farm, and even more gushing about the son . . .

'Karl took me fishing. Can you imagine that? And I actually caught a fish. And we went bird-watching along the river bank, so many pretty birds . . . unbelievable . . . and a native, a friend, showed us where to find wild honey, and Karl got some for me. Did you know, Pastor, that Karl has his own farm? Or rather, it will be a plantation, they say, in a year or so. Isn't that marvellous?'

Obviously Karl had turned her head. That adolescent! Typical of silly little virgins like her to get all of a flutter over someone else, so quickly. He turned to her father.

'Miss Adele seems to be rather taken with young Karl. Does he reciprocate?'

She blushed scarlet and dabbed at her face with a handkerchief. 'Oh no. I didn't mean . . . oh, goodness!'

Mr Hoepper frowned. 'He is a fine young man. Hardworking. I hardly think he'd have time for romantic notions at this stage.'

'No, Father, of course not,' she breathed. 'Isn't it time we left?'

Friedrich thought he might have made a mistake there, because her glance at him flashed with anger. He'd only meant to tease. 'Might I take you for a drive to the commune?' he asked.

'Thank you but we have other arrangements,' she said huffily.

Her father explained. 'Yes. The Wheatleys are taking us out to the saleyards to watch horses and sheep being auctioned.'

'Then I mustn't keep you.'

As he left the hotel, he saw a four-wheeled vehicle drawn by two fine horses pull in. It was well equipped with padded seats and a fringed roof, quite smart for this village. The driver waved to him: 'Good morning, Father!' and he recognised one of the wealthy passengers from the coastal voyage.

Friedrich raised his hat and responded, but kept walking, angry that they hadn't invited him.

With nothing better to do, he wandered about the town, examining it with care, discovering bars and brothels that he could not venture into, not in this guise. He peered into shops and workshops, finding nothing of any interest at all. He was sweating for a drink as he passed another bar but resisted, bravely, he thought, and pressed on, walking into a store where he was welcomed by a friendly fellow called Jim, who called him by name.

'Heard all about you, Father Ritter. Your friends sure are happy that you made it all the way from the northern world. Can I get you anything?'

'Thank you. I would appreciate some water.'

'Ah yes, it's thirsty weather. I see the sun's coming out for a change. Would you rather have a cup of coffee? My wife makes lovely coffee.'

Jim immediately became Friedrich's best friend. He was given a glass of water while he waited for his coffee and shown the two brands of coffee beans in stock: one American, one from Jamaica. The Pastor had never been offered a choice of coffee before, so he chose the Jamaican, which sounded exotic, and bought a pound. A pound in weight, he was relieved to discover, not a pound in currency.

There were no other customers, so he perched on a high stool in front of Jim's scrubbed counter and listened to this oracle who seemed to know everything about everyone in this town and was pleased to have found a patient ear. Friedrich was in no hurry. After listening to Jim's opinions on the weather and the economy and the local politicians with some election looming, he managed to slip in a few questions about the viability of Walther's little brewery and the Meissners' grand plantation plans.

'Can't wait to taste Walther's brew,' Jim said. 'And Jakob Meissner, he can't lose, what with Charlie Mayhew backing him and Irish Mike as a partner. They'll do good, Father. Don't you worry about them. They'll make it.'

His wife brought in the coffee and two small cakes. They were plain, but pleasant, and the coffee . . . He nearly choked. The coffee was awful. Vile. He was swiftly regretting his purchase of a whole pound of these tasteless beans when he realised she'd cooked them in milk. All he had was hot milk with a mild, almost negligible whiff of coffee.

He managed to drink the slop and thank them both, so that he could resume his conversation with Jim, steering him round to the intriguing matter of selling trees. And Jim knew all about that, too. Like the timber was so valuable there were feuds over the ownership. And a sheep had got shot. A sheep? Who'd care? Jim had already told him that they bred sheep round here by the millions, or some outrageous figure, but the Pastor's main thing was money. Money for trees. Better than digging hoping to find gold.

Forty acres of money trees! Was Beitz even madder than he thought, and his disciples weaker than water? It was obvious that they weren't pleased at the way Beitz ran things, but he was their priest, and they were too browbeaten by the mighty Church to oppose him.

'Well, I'm a priest too,' Friedrich muttered to himself as he stepped out into the blazing sunlight, hanging on to his bag of coffee. 'Where to now?' He was determined not to go back to the dismal commune yet, so he called back to his friend Jim. 'Could you kindly direct me to the sawmill, please? To Mr Kleinschmidt. Rolf.'

'Certainly, Father.' Jim came out into the street, pointing to the river and back to the wharves, with a rush of directions.

'Is it near Walther's brewery?'

'No, Father. On the other side of the river. Go down to the wharves, you can get a boat across.'

Friedrich set off, but caution turned him away. Don't discuss this with Rolf. What if he's like all the others? Locked into Beitz's opinions? He recalled that he had passed a workshed that had borne a sign . . . BLOCKS CLEARED. TIMBERS BOUGHT. Might it be better to talk to independent trades-people? Or first, discuss this with Beitz. He might be pushed enough to sell. Pity he couldn't get him to sell the whole damn forty acres as well. After they'd cashed in on the timber . . .

By now he was just walking. Tramping along, lost in thought. He passed a school, remembering Mrs Zimmerman, she of the missing husband and the three kids who, Beitz said, were doomed for attending that heathen place, a state-run school.

He laughed. 'How do you reckon Beitz would go teaching these kids their sums, Freddy? He can't add up himself!'

Someone came dashing up behind him and he turned, fully expecting that one of Mrs Zimmerman's children, from among the little group playing in the yard, had come rushing to say good morning to their very own pastor. His heart warmed a little at this tinge of famousness, at being recognised and sought after, if only by children.

But it wasn't a child, it was pretty little Mrs Fechner. He'd forgotten about her and her troubles.

'Oh, Pastor Ritter,' she cried. 'Fancy seeing you this

morning. You walked right past our house. We live back there.'

'How very nice. And how are you, Sister Fechner? Keeping well?'

'Yes, Pastor, I am. I have a few hours off work. I have to go back later. I wonder if you have time . . . for me. To talk.'

And listen to your nonsense? I don't think so. He was about to make an excuse and dodge away from her when he remembered his coffee.

'Can you brew coffee?' he asked, and she looked up at him, surprised.

'Yes. Of course.'

'Right.' He plonked the bag of coffee beans in her hands. 'I'll come back with you if you make me a cup of coffee.'

The coffee was delicious. This was his third cup. For the sake of propriety, he guessed, she'd drawn up two chairs on the porch and waited patiently for her cue. Which in the end he had to deliver.

'Now, my dear. What's the trouble?'

She was a very attractive girl . . . woman . . . with flawless skin and a magnificent bosom which she kept carefully guarded by a swath of shawl. But he'd noticed her figure the first time he'd seen her and could dream up the beauty within. She was far sexier than Miss Adele could ever be, and he was wondering why, apart from a man's normal admiration for the female form at its best, he did not feel any sexual stimulation in her company. Maybe this priest role is sapping my urges, he thought.

'Pastor, I am in such shame,' she whispered. 'I cannot tell you how awful it is for me to have to mention these matters, but I simply can't bear it any longer . . .'

'Speak, Sister,' he murmured, bored already.

'First I have to ask your forgiveness for burdening you with my trouble . . .'

'Very well.'

'And apologise to you for what I have to say.'

'My dear woman, there's nothing new in the world. Nothing you could tell me would shock me, if that's what you're worrying about. I think I've seen and heard everything.' And

430

that's a fact, he thought, being careful not to allow himself a grin.

'You won't be shocked?' she pleaded.

'No. Do you want me to hear your confession?'

'I don't think so. You be the judge. I didn't deserve . . .' She began to weep, and he sighed. And waited. He should go back and cool off in that stream before lunch, and then he could have a nap . . .

She began: 'Lucas – my husband, you've met him – and me, we went to work on a sheep station way out west. We had good jobs, good pay, he was a stockman . . . they ride about looking after the sheep . . . and I was a housemaid, in a nice house, working for the family that owned the station. The Dixon family . . .'

She droned on. And on. And Friedrich was near to dozing off when she mentioned the son of the house. One Keith Dixon, whom she had found very nice and very handsome. He sat up at that, guessing adultery was about to step on stage, and sure enough . . .

Her eyes were glued to the floor. 'I want to tell you exactly what happened, Pastor. The truth, as you are my witness, so that I won't ever have to think about it again. I flirted with Keith Dixon, I will admit. I walked with him. I was lonely, stuck in our room, with no one to talk to when Lucas was away for days.'

He asked questions about the house, the people, her situation, savouring the adulterous climax to this little tragedy, guessing that Lucas must have caught them in the act.

There was the incident with Charlie Mayhew, whose name he'd heard somewhere, who had groped her in passing, then her story took a new turn. He heard all about the Meissner farm being deliberately burned down by Keith Dixon because Meissner had beaten him to the timber.

'What's this got to do with you, Sister Fechner?'

'Because Lucas saw Keith and his men set fire to Jakob's land, and he went to the police but the police wouldn't believe him. Lucas demanded that Keith Dixon be charged with arson, because the fire not only burned out Jakob's land, they lost their house and every stitch they owned.'

431

'Dear God. They play tough here.'

She gave a half-sob and nodded. 'That's only part of it. We both got sacked from our jobs, of course, but when Constable Colley told Keith Dixon about the charges, Keith claimed I was a thief. That's why I was sacked.'

'It wasn't true?'

'No, Pastor. This is the hard part for me, but I will tell you. Someone should know what happened to me. There's nothing to be done about it but it will make me feel better. And I know that you won't say a word to anyone.'

'Upon my soul, no.'

'Very well.' Her voice was firm now. Determined. She took him out to that farm, to the dust storm, to the lonely staff room she shared with her husband, who was away at this time, to a true rendition of the cavortings with the boss's son, which by this time Friedrich really didn't want to hear. He liked her. He could see how this fellow had shut Lucas up very smartly. And how Lucas had rightly guessed something was going on . . . but so was her story.

Friedrich *was* shocked. The cavortings had turned vicious. He was listening, listening to every word, half voyeur, half a fellow German, a friend even, because she had chosen to confide in him, and no one else. She told him every bitter detail, everything that pig had done to her, the things he had said to her, all of it, and when she had finished they both sat in silence for a long time.

He mulled over this, over the sorts of things priests must hear in confession, wondering how they reacted. Whether they enjoyed the tales or were offended. Weird, it was. And rare for him not to be able to think what to say.

In the end she asked her question. 'Will I have to confess my sins, Pastor? My part in it?'

'You are absolved,' he said grandly. 'Absolved, Sister, in the name of the Lord. Evil men prey on good women; you are not the first nor the last. But listen, you can't dwell on this any more. Just forget it.' He realised he'd changed his voice in the middle there, from preacher to plain man, but what the hell? 'Anyone who can make coffee as well as you do can't be bad.' He smiled. 'Now, I'd better be on my way.'

She was taken aback. She remembered to run inside for his coffee, which she brought back in a tin. 'Is that all, Pastor?'

'You mean the coffee?' he smiled.

'No,' she said nervously. 'I mean about what I told you.'

'It has to be all,' he said seriously. 'You've suffered enough. Unless you want me to speak to Lucas. But you'll have to tell me what to say. You obviously haven't told him that that villain raped you.'

The word startled her. She pushed damp hair back from her face. 'No. I couldn't. Every step seems to cause more trouble. Lucas said the same thing. He never told Jakob Meissner that he saw Keith Dixon fire his land. You can imagine what a row that would cause.'

'But he told the police.'

'He thought Keith Dixon would be taken into custody. But of course he got off scot-free for all of it. They're the bosses here, those people. We're just dirt. As soon as I can save the money I'm going home. I hate this place.'

'This Dixon fellow. Does he bother you now?'

'No. But he still frightens me. I saw him this morning . . .'

'I thought you said he lives way out in the country?'

'Yes, but he comes to town a lot, he and his men. But it's all right, Pastor. Don't worry about me. I can't thank you enough for your kindness. I'll come to church every Sunday now. That will please Father Beitz . . .'

He was walking along the street, still dazed by her testimony. He turned on Freddy. 'By Christ, the poor thing is bloody lucky I'm not a real priest. You lot would have had her burned at the stake. And stupid Lucas. I'll tell the bastard he let his wife get raped.' He didn't give another thought to his promise not to mention any of it to a soul. She was just a scared rabbit, she didn't know what was best for her.

Back he went to Jim's store. 'I bought the coffee, forgot to buy a coffee pot.'

'You don't really need one,' Jim said. 'My wife just heats it in a saucepan.'

'They may not have a spare saucepan in our kitchen. I'd better get a coffee pot, if you have one.'

He did, and it was handed over.

'Tell me, Jim. Do you know a fellow named Keith Dixon?'

'Ah, yes. Everyone knows Keith.'

'I have a message for him, but I don't know where to find him. I heard he was in town somewhere.'

Jim consulted the wall clock. 'He'd be at the Progress Hall by this time. Setting it up for a campaign fête. He's standing for Parliament, you know.'

'I didn't, but that's very interesting. He must be an important man, yes?'

He stowed his coffee and the pot in the wagon and sat nearby to think what he might be able to gain from all this, as against forgetting about it, but nothing came to mind. He thought about Father Beitz, sickabed, and what a relief it was to be free of him. He hoped he'd stay in his sickbed a few more days.

'I might be able to help him along,' he laughed. 'But what am I to do about this wealthy son of a bitch? The great lover and firestarter. And, take note, Freddy, budding parliamentarian. Is it that easy to get into government here? Oh well, we might as well trot around to this Progress Hall and take a look at the gentleman.'

He combed his hair and his beard, brushed down his cassock, and set his hat on straight. He'd come to hate this hat, it didn't suit him at all, and no matter what a soaking it got, it refused to die. He considered hurling it into the river, but it was costume, so it was safe for a while yet.

The Progress Hall was a twin for Beitz's church but without the stained glass, and only a few feet larger in length and width. Its surrounds were the exact opposite. Lacking the greenery, it looked rather forlorn stuck in the middle of a paddock, as if it should be thankful for the small mercy of being permitted there at all.

He peered inside at a glowing polished cedar floor; just like St John's, except this one held display tables and beribboned booths, and aproned ladies were scuttling about setting things up and carrying trays into the hall from the back door. The hall had a heady smell of new timber, sawdust and freshly baked cakes.

More people were following him to the door, so he stood back to allow them to pass, accepting their 'Morning, Father' with good grace.

He wandered round to the side door, where women were unloading a heavy box of groceries from a wagon. He stepped forward to assist, accepting their beaming thanks.

'They're for the grand raffle, Father,' a woman told him.

There were three men on a small stage, taking no notice of the activity below. They looked important, as did the velvet-covered table in front of them that was accompanied by three plush chairs.

'The leads,' he said to himself with a grin. 'And I'm betting the younger one is our lover.'

He turned to a white-haired, pink-faced lady, who looked no different from all the other white-haired, pink-faced ladies back home, and, forgetting, spoke to her in German.

'I'm sorry, Father,' she said politely. 'I don't understand Danish.'

Where did that come from? He tried again. In English.

'Am I right in supposing that the young gentleman up there on the stage is this gentleman?'

He held up a pamphlet he'd collected at the door. They carried photos of Keith Dixon, with his name and a flurry of printed words which didn't interest him at all.

'Yes, Father. That's him. Isn't he marvellous? He's just the sort of person we need to represent us. His mother is a great friend of mine. Would you like to meet him?'

Not necessarily, he thought. I only wanted to get a look at him. He realised he could do with an excuse for loitering here, and proffered the first thing that came into his head.

'Oh no. I would not intrude. I wish only to offer my donation.'

Politicians and priests, he thought, they're all the same. Donations ring their bells.

The woman slipped back inside and he turned to leave. Politician or priest, try to get a donation out of me, he chortled. But a hand tapped him on the shoulder as he walked away from the hall.

'You were looking for me, Father? I am Keith Dixon. I

understand you wish to make a donation to our cause?'

Friedrich was more than a match for this puppy. He smiled. Watch this, Freddy.

'Oh, dear sir. I did not wish to take up your time. I am Father Ritter of the Lutheran community.'

'Is that so? Well, I'm pleased to meet you. That's German, isn't it?'

'Yes, sir, our humble community.'

'I'm sorry. I was told you were Danish.'

'Danish?'

'Yes. We have a strong Danish community here.'

'Ah. I did not know this.'

'Are you new here?' Friedrich was aware the respect had dropped a notch.

'Yes. A short time. I am to take over from Father Beitz.'

'Your people are not too popular here.'

'I am sorry to hear that. Could you walk with me and tell me how this could have happened? We are all God's children.'

He deliberately began to walk away from the hall and away from the track that was leading people in from the street.

'No. I haven't got time,' Dixon said. 'They just have to learn to behave themselves, that's all.' But then he remembered the mention of a donation, so he found the time to walk a few paces.

'I am given to believe you want to support my candidacy,' he said. 'Why is that? I have had no prior support from the Germans.'

Friedrich extended his arms in surrender, but kept walking towards the far fence, well away from interruption.

'Mr Dixon. I am only the messenger. We are, as you know, a wealthy community, supported in our endeavours not only by the Archbishops of Hamburg and Cologne, but by Prussian merchants who are following this emigration experiment with great interest. We would of course offer financial support to stable government people . . .' Friedrich left it there. Imagination and language were failing him. After all, he hadn't rehearsed the part. But he had Dixon reeled in by now. They were plodding on, close to the far fence. On the other side was a large piggery that in Friedrich's mind didn't seem to sit well with the hall, especially when travelling artistes came to town to put on plays. Hardly the most acceptable neighbour.

'You mentioned a donation,' Dixon said. 'For myself, I have no need of such charity, as I perceive it, but my supporters require public investment so that they have the armoury to get in touch with the people in far-flung districts as well as the folk in Maryborough. Apparently this is all a costly exercise. I am only now learning about it. How much did you have in mind?'

Friedrich sighed. 'This is why I am honoured for the opportunity to discuss this with you man to man. How much is, what would you say, correct? We wish to do the right thing, you understand.'

The lover and farm-burner smiled easily. 'A couple of hundred pounds would do, Father. Unless you can match the real people of this district, who wouldn't flinch at four hundred.'

'How much is this? Are you saying pounds, sir? It is difficult for me. Four hundred pounds, yes?'

Dixon glowed. He arched his back and relaxed the muscles in his arms as if wearied from a day's work.

'Yes,' he said smartly. 'Four hundred pounds, Father. Jolly good.'

'Excellent,' said the Pastor. 'And when can I expect to be paid?'

Dixon jerked back as if he'd been bitten on the bum. Friedrich laughed. Bitten on the bum he truly was.

'What are you talking about?'

Friedrich leaned against the fence, a primitive arrangement of stones like the fences Beitz was building back at the commune. He took a cheroot from a small tin. He only had four left. He did not offer one to the candidate.

'Your donation, Mr Dixon,' he said as he flicked the cheroot into sweet-smelling life. 'Four hundred pounds.'

Dixon snorted. Irritated. Time-wasting! Idiocy! 'You stupid bastard! Get out of here. Are you raving mad? Why the hell—?'

'Good question.' Friedrich stopped him sharply. 'Why should you pay me? No, *donate* to our community four

437

hundred pounds? I'll tell you why, Mr Dixon. For the rape of Mrs Hanni Fechner at your house. For setting fire to the property belonging to Jakob Meissner. For—'

'You lunatic! You bloody lunatic. Get out of here.' He swung about, but Friedrich knew that move was only stage business. Dixon wasn't ready to go yet; he could not. So Friedrich obliged him.

'I do not like being called a lunatic, sir. Your donation is now five hundred.'

He stood quietly as Keith shrieked at him, even considering blessing him a good move, but decided against it. The man was ripe for the blackmail that he'd stumbled upon by accident. And it could work. This scenario could work!

'For defaming an innocent woman by charging her with theft,' he said. 'Mr Dixon, you are in trouble if I leave town today without five hundred pounds. Big trouble.'

'Get out of here, you bastard, before I break your neck. Call yourself a man of the cloth? You're nothing but—'

Friedrich held up his hand. 'Enough. There is a crowd gathering over there. Either you pay the price for your crimes, or I step up to that stage, and with God as my witness shout them to the four winds.'

'They won't believe you . . . you charlatan.'

'Oh yes they will. Count on that. By the time I'm finished pointing the finger of shame at you, they will believe. Your denials will count for nothing.' He moved closer to whisper: 'And they'll lap up every word, my friend, especially when I give them a description of that scene with the girl. What you did to her. Remember?'

Dixon was stunned. White-faced, he looked over to the hall, as if hoping for an escape, and his voice shook as he spoke.

'Who are you?'

'I am your conscience, sir. And your guide to the path of righteousness. Your donation to our cause will guarantee forgiveness.'

'The hell it will.'

The Pastor knew now that he had won; he just had to keep the pressure up.

'Come and see me tomorrow,' Dixon said, 'and we'll talk about this.'

'Nothing to talk about. I want your donation now or I take that stage and deliver my sermon.'

'I haven't got any money on me. I'll give you an IOU for fifty pounds and no more.'

Friderich shook his head. 'There is a bank in the next street. It will only take a few minutes to walk over there.' He switched his tone to menace. 'You'll pay up, Dixon, and you'll pay up now. This isn't an idle threat. Start walking.'

The two men crossed the road, walking quickly.

Keith Dixon was appalled. How could this be happening? He tried to bargain with this madman. Fifty pounds? One hundred? Nothing would turn him aside. All the way to the bank he tried to figure a way out of this. Five hundred pounds! That was a bloody fortune! He'd said all along these Germans were no good, and now he'd been proved right. A pack of crooks. But who could he tell? Imagine what old J.B. would say if he found out that he'd been tricked out of five hundred pounds. Even now, Keith couldn't bring himself to say the word 'blackmail' in case he spilled it in front of his father. But what would J.B. have done in this situation? Paid up, that's what. There was no way out of it.

He'd take the money out of the Clonmel bank account, put it down as fencing posts and such. With all these settlers pushing on Clonmel boundaries, fencing had become necessary on the eastern side of the property and it was costing a fortune. J.B. wouldn't miss five hundred.

'Listen here,' he said when he reached the door of the bank with this evil preacher standing over him. 'None of those things you said are true. I don't know where you got those tales, being new to the town. I'm only paying you for the sake of peace.'

'Of course you are.'

'Well, why don't I give you fifty pounds for yourself? Forget the donation. And we won't mention this again.'

Friedrich blinked. What was he talking about? Why would he take fifty instead of five hundred? Then he realised that

Dixon was trying to buy him off. He'd actually believed that stuff about the donations, he was in such a funk. What an idiot!

'The donation in full, please. Don't try to corrupt me.'

It was all he could do to keep a straight face as Dixon stormed into the wooden shed that passed for a bank. The teller in there jumped to attention, and soon the money had changed hands.

Friedrich slid around the corner, out of sight, and remained there, giving Dixon a faint whistle as he came out of the bank. Then, in the shade of the building, he accepted five crisp notes from Dixon, and raised his hand in blessing.

'Go with God, Mr Dixon.'

Five hundred pounds. Five crackling new notes. He waited until he was rid of Dixon, not caring that his victim had spat at his feet and called him a scoundrel before heading back to his supporters, then he folded the precious notes with great care and placed them in his purse. How easy was that? He looked up and down the dismal street; there were only a few pedestrians up the other end, and some old gentlemen sitting quietly in the shade of a huge tree on the other side of the road.

Friedrich began to walk, with no actual destination in mind; he didn't want to draw attention to himself by standing about, loitering perhaps. Gloating more like it, he grinned, and crossed the road.

'We could leave now,' he told Freddy. 'Get the hell out of this dump. We don't need to stay here any more. I can throw off this damned priest's costume and bolt.'

He came to another street and found himself facing the wharves. 'I don't have to make any excuses to anyone. We'll just go over there and hop on a boat.'

Then it dawned on him that there were no boats at the wharves. He stopped a workman. 'When does the next boat leave?'

'It can't leave till it gets here, mate. And that'd be *Tara*. She won't be back until next week, weather holding.'

'Damn!' With money burning a hole in his pocket. Friedrich

wandered away, cursing that he was stuck in a town that had nothing to offer. Then again, there was always the timber. He kept returning to that and reminding himself that he could earn a lot more than five hundred if he hung on a bit longer.

He was hungry. What about lunch at the Royal Hotel? Why not?

'Because lunch is served between twelve and one and not a minute later,' he told Freddy, back outside the hotel once more. 'The bastards. How was I to know it's half past one? What a pathetic place this is.'

Denied of lunch, he strode out, looking purposeful. Came to a jeweller's store, the window decked out in red velvet to show off gold brooches and rings and lumps of real gold. Friedrich was fascinated. He wandered in, only to pass the time, but the jeweller wouldn't have that. He convinced Friedrich, and rightly so, that he needed a gold fob watch, there being no town clocks and few clocks of any sort in Bundaberg.

The jeweller was a good talker. He knew all about the goldfields, had been there several times, to the Gympie mines, buying gold direct. No middleman, he said, and Friedrich was impressed. Gold! It struck a chord that made his heart sing. Was there no end to the opportunities for a man seeking riches in this country? Miserable though it was. The population was composed of geese, and his pathetic compatriots, the farming brigade, fitted in well. He still considered that, of the Lutheran flock, the only one with any brains was the fellow called Theo. Who cared how long it took to dig up gold? The others with their farms and their little brewery were looking at years before they turned a shilling.

'I'm sure you'll be happy with that watch. Father. It's Swiss. It will last a lifetime. Can I offer you a glass of wine? Just a wee glass.'

Friedrich could have kissed him. Make it a pint. 'Thank you. I wouldn't mind. I'm not accustomed to this heat.'

The glass was crystal, the wine excellent. The jeweller, who was from a city somewhere, told him tales of wild and woolly customers he had come across, here and on the goldfields, and Friedrich listened. Some day he might be able to make use of this information.

'I've been paid in gold,' the jeweller said, 'and in wool fleece; even with a block of land – that won't go astray – but the latest gent who bought a diamond ring for his lady couldn't pay and wouldn't dare ask for it back, so I have his horse. And a beautiful filly she is too. What they do for their ladies! I suppose you wouldn't need a mount, Father?'

Well he did, to be truthful. He did. And he had money to burn.

The horse was jet black, superb, gallant, fit for a prince, for any grand parade. Friedrich was so excited; this day of firsts, his first real money, his first watch . . . and now . . . His breath was coming in short gasps. He'd never owned anything like this animal, he was in love with her. And he could afford her! He could afford *Queenie*, for that was her name. Queenie. Sixty pounds they were asking, and the jeweller and the groom at the stables, located behind the jewellery store, felt sorry for him. He could see the pity in their eyes. One thing to show the poor priest this magnificent beast. Another to expect him to be able to find the money.

'For ten quid more we'll throw in a bloody fine rig, Father,' the groom had said, and the jeweller translated:

'He has a good saddle and bridle that he could let you have for ten pounds, Father, but you don't have to think about it now.'

'I'll take the horse *and* the rig,' he said, feeling grand, feeling important. But then he remembered that damned wagon. Why should he stoop to that chore now, when he had his own magnificent mount?

They solved the problem. One of the stable boys would deliver the wagon to Walther's block. Apparently everyone knew where they were working, on the foundations of the brewery.

'He'll do well,' the jeweller said of Walther's enterprise. 'It costs a lot to ship ales up here.'

'Eventually, I suppose,' Friedrich said as he peeled off a hundred. Nonchalantly.

* * *

442

Before he took Queenie out to the commune, Friedrich couldn't resist calling on Jim, the only available person known to him, so that he could show her off.

'You've done well,' Jim said sagely. 'One thing here, Father, there's no mucking about with horseflesh. No one would be game to sell you a crock. We have distances to travel. Our lives depend on good mounts. Breaking the rules on horses, or horse-stealing, could get you shot. But I have to say, they got you on that rig. I've got better here for a fiver. Do you want to take that saddle back?'

Friedrich couldn't be bothered. He had plenty of money.

'Oh no, Jim. I think the poor fellow must need that five pounds more than me if he has to cheat to get it. God bless him.'

'You're a good man, Father. I hope you'll be very happy here.'

'I would be if I could find something to eat,' the Pastor laughed. 'I'm too late for the hotel.'

'Would bread and cheese do, Father? I'll get some for you. No charge. Someone should open a café here, if only for light meals . . .'

Friedrich hitched Queenie to the rail outside Jim's store. 'See,' he said to her. 'There's no end to the money-making businesses lacking in this place. I could end up a millionaire, Queenie. If I can stand suffocating in Bundaberg.'

He managed to find his way out to the commune, after a few wrong turns, and place Queenie, with some oats, in the horse paddock reserved for the refugee from the knackers that hauled the wagon. It was just as well that the horse paddock was away to the right of the entrance to the commune, and not within sight of the living quarters, because Father Beitz was up and about and as cranky as a turkey without toes.

'Where have you been, Friedrich? Don't you know we have work to do?'

Friedrich listened, nodded, made some lame excuses, surprised that the old priest had managed to rise out of his sickbed.

'You don't look well, Father. You should be resting.'

'How can I rest when you've gone wandering off and there's no one to keep the work party going? You have to realise, Friedrich, our natives are sweet and charming, but they don't understand agriculture. Unless we are there in the vegetable garden, they won't know what to do.'

'Ah. Isn't that interesting? I had no idea, Father. Well, of course I will watch them tomorrow. Why don't you lie down? You are looking flushed. I will bring you some coffee.'

'We haven't got any coffee. We have learned to do without luxuries.'

'So I see, but Mr Hoepper bought it for you. A donation, one could say.'

'Did he? How kind. Put it away for a special day.'

'Not before you try some. Now you rest and I'll bring it to you.'

Father Beitz enjoyed the coffee. 'Quite the best I've ever tasted,' he said.

Either he's forgotten what good coffee tastes like, or the opium powders I got from the Cape Town whores aren't as bitter as I thought they were. Friedrich mused.

He'd only given the priest a couple, but they'd done the trick and he was now stretched out on his bunk, snoring his head off, leaving his curate free to relax in the cool waters of the stream and think about his future.

When the workmen came home, they found the Pastor at his prayers outside Father Beitz's hut. As soon as he was free to talk to them, he told them about his horse. They had already seen it, of course, and were as impressed with Queenie as the new owner, but bemused. Wondering about such extravagance. But Friedrich knew they were all too polite to comment.

'Once I understood how scattered our folk are, I realised I would have to buy myself a horse if I am to get about on my pastoral duties,' he told them. 'And I can't get over how fortunate I was to find a good horse like Queenie so soon.'

And that was that. End of subject.

'How is Father Beitz?' they wanted to know.

'He was up earlier, walking about, but he was coughing quite a bit and rather feverish, I thought, so he went back to bed. Best place for him, I'd say. Rest being the only cure for these fevers.'

Walther peered into the hut. 'He's sleeping.'

'What's for dinner?' the curate asked.

Hubert Hoepper was restless, and disappointed in himself. Having thrown off that dreadful depression that had kept him idle for so long, he had returned to normalcy, to the man who liked and needed to be busy. Unfortunately, he was far from busy in this little town. He had envisaged a close-knit German community, a co-operative, farming their land, with the church and the clergy at the centre. He had envisaged being welcomed among them, walking in the small fields with them, enjoying rural life for an extended carefree visit.

The welcome had been real – they were all delighted to see him, and Adele – but all the rest was a foolish pipedream on his part. The idyllic rural scene did not exist. Could not exist here. The scale of everything was too large, distances too great.

His friends were all hard at work, and that was a good thing. They understood now that there'd be no co-operative community, they went where their work took them and, he thanked the Lord, they had all settled in well considering that everything was so different here. But it hadn't taken Hubert long to feel ... well, extraneous, and he couldn't blame his friends for this. They had their work and their families to attend to. Even his new friends, the Wheatleys, were on their way home now. They had no choice but to endure the difficult journey out to their property, coping with the heat, bogs and floods; they had to return to work after the summer break.

'We're told,' they explained, 'that most of the tracks are passable now, if we take roundabout routes to our station, but we wouldn't wish such a trek on you. The best time to visit is in the winter, when it's cooler and the tracks are set hard. But do remember, you and Adele are most welcome.'

So ... that expedition was out of the question for a few months yet, even though he would have been interested to see a real outback sheep station. Their property, they said, was about two hundred miles inland, on the Leichhardt River, named after a famous German, Ludwig Leichhardt, who had explored huge areas in the west. Hubert had been surprised to hear of this man, and very pleased to learn that he was so well thought of in this country.

He looked out of the hotel window at the wide river and the few buildings on the other side of the road, and sighed, admitting to himself that he was bored. He had nothing to do and that did not sit well with him, either in Hamburg or here. Had the Lord permitted him his original intentions, he would have had his family installed here by now, with everyone busily engaged in making new lives and careers, but that was not to be. No use dwelling on the past.

Over lunch he discussed his restlessness with Adele. She wasn't surprised to hear how he felt. 'I thought you were looking a bit lost.'

'Yes, I'm not accustomed to too much leisure. I've bought the seaside land, and the two town blocks, so as not to burn our bridges here, but I thought we should go home now. We are fortunate that we don't have to decide on the spot whether to give it a go here, or settle for the old country. What do you think?'

'I'm not sure, Father. It's a difficult decision. But since we are looking homeward, could we go back via America? I can still see the big globe in your study, and the blue Pacific which is just out there . . .'

'Why not? A wonderful idea. We can visit Hawaii and Tahiti en route. But I do hope you haven't been bored here.'

'Oh no. I'll be able to say to my grandchildren that I knew Bundaberg when it was only a settlement.'

'Goodness me. Do you have such faith in the place?'

'Karl Meissner does. He says it will be a city one day, surrounded by great fields of cane as far as the eye can see. I have promised I'll come back to see that one day. Oh, God, here comes that awful Pastor Ritter.'

'Awful? I thought you liked him.'

'I did at first, but not any more. Something about him irritates me.'

She slipped out of her seat and fled before Ritter appeared.

Hubert stood politely. 'Do sit down, Pastor. We have just finished lunch, but you order if you wish.'

'That's a shame, I was looking forward to seeing Miss Adele. Perhaps later.'

'Yes, of course. How is Father Beitz?'

'Actually, he is not well. I put it down to the dreadful housing arrangements. He is such a saint, he won't spend money on himself, and insists on living in those leaking huts.'

Hubert was troubled. 'I must say, I was rather shocked to find him living in such primitive conditions, but he seemed happy.'

'I'm afraid not. He put on a brave face for your benefit, Herr Hoepper, but as he told me later, he has never been so shamed. He had hoped to have built a decent parsonage by now. He had expected to be able to invite important visitors like yourself to stay with him.'

Hubert nodded, though he did not admit that this was what he, too, had expected. Part of his pipedream. Good conversation with the priest over a glass of port. In front of a log fire . . . He nearly choked at the thought, running his finger around his stiff collar to release the perspiration gathering there.

'And Father is not well, you say?'

'Not well at all. I am afeared he will develop pneumonia, though the other gentlemen living there think not. They're young men, healthy fellows. It's hard for me to make them understand that he's too old for that sort of living.'

'Oh dear. What can we do?'

'I had a talk with him. He has financial concerns.'

'Yes . . .' Hubert began, but the Pastor continued:

'I'd heard that he could sell the timber on the land, but he has refused to do this, so I brought the subject up again. You know, Mr Hoepper, elderly people can be the very devil . . .' Pastor Ritter smiled. 'He tells me that he wants to sell the timber now, but doesn't want to back down, since he was so adamant before. He thinks it will show him up to be a fool. Someone who can't make up his mind. He is very aware of what his congregation might think of him.'

The Pastor didn't seem to know about the opposition to

expenditure on a mission school, so Hubert avoided the subject. 'Please reassure Father Beitz that his people have a high regard for him. He has had some upsets lately, but they'll be overcome.'

'Oh yes,' Pastor Ritter said quickly. 'But he does get confused. Anyway, as a result of our talk he wants me to go ahead and arrange the sale of the timber so that he can start work on the mission school.'

'I wouldn't encourage that,' Hubert said quietly. 'The man should have his priorities straight. He must have a decent house first. It doesn't have to be a mansion, but surely he's entitled to accommodation befitting his status.'

'Yes, that too . . . the sale of the timber . . .'

'I'd hold back on that, Pastor. There's no rush. I've been wondering how I might contribute to the community, and I've decided to donate the funds to build a decent parsonage. That will be my farewell gift.'

Ritter frowned. When the waitress came to take his lunch order, he waved her away absently. 'You're leaving? So soon?'

'I'm afraid so. Time to go. We intend to visit the other east coast capital cities and then take a ship home via America.'

'But what about Miss Adele? She'll be disappointed, won't she?'

'She's happy to move on. First I must speak to a builder, though. Get some plans drawn up to put to Father Beitz.'

'About the parsonage? Such a building will be costly. And there is no need. I mean, we can't impose on your generosity to that extent. I could have loggers into that huge estate within days. We'll be able to pay for these buildings ourselves.'

Friedrich was furious with Hoepper. The money for the timber was his. It was to be his fare to a life of luxury. It was said those massive trees were worth hundreds of pounds.

'Good of you, Pastor, but I'm inclined to agree with Father Beitz that those old trees are too magnificent to be destroyed unless absolutely necessary, and you'll find that quite a few of your parishioners concur.'

'That may be so, but as I was just saying, Mr Hoepper, it is Father Beitz himself who now recommends logging.'

'The poor man. He must be at his wits' end. But don't

worry, Pastor, he shall have a decent house, and I'll establish a trust to make sure he is financially independent for the rest of his days. Now I really must go. It has been rewarding talking to you. I'm excited about this plan. I'll go over to the sawmill and have a chat with Rolf. He'll get everything underway for us.'

He gathered up his hat and cane and left the dining room, while Friedrich glowered after him.

'Damn fool,' he muttered to Freddy. 'Interfering fool. Did you see him dance out of here, brimming with good works?'

'Did you want something now, Father?' the waitress asked.

'Yes. I'm ready for lunch. See that it goes on Mr Hoepper's bill.'

When he left the hotel, he was thrilled to see Miss Adele setting up her easel across by the river and settling down to do some drawing. He watched her for a while, still entranced by her general good looks and the smooth loveliness of her features, and wished he could sketch her.

She glanced up as the Pastor approached, and he saw a little frown at the interruption, which was understandable, but he pressed on.

'Don't let me stay your hand, my dear,' he said. 'Keep on, it is a joy to watch an artist at work. I myself enjoy sketching, though these days I have little time, and there's little of beauty round here to sketch except, may I be so bold to say, our own Miss Adele.'

She made no comment, so he drew closer, looking about him, hoping there was something he could bring over to perch upon, so that he could sit with her in a more intimate manner. This was the first time he'd had her to himself since they'd arrived in Bundaberg, and God forbid, it could be the last if he didn't make a move now. There was nothing, though, not even a box or a crate. He had no choice but to remain standing.

'You sketch so well,' he said. 'You've got the river and that hut on the other side exactly. I can see you're well taught.'

'Thank you,' she said quietly, concentrating on her work.

'I believe your father is preparing to leave here. I shall be very sad, myself, to see you go. I'll miss you. There'll be no grace and culture left here if you leave.'

'The people here are very nice,' she said over her shoulder, her voice tight.

'But, my dear, you must know that you stand out among them, a swan among the ugly ducklings.

'Oh, I am sure not.'

He smiled down at her. So naïve, so innocent. 'But it is true. It was the same on the ship. Everyone adored you.'

He fingered a curl at the nape of her neck, twining it around a finger, then he slid it into place, his fingers continuing on, so naturally, to stroke that lovely neck and on deeper, towards her bosom, his hand tingling with the excitement of this first touch of her, because she made no move to repulse him. She seemed frozen, probably too shy to be seen to encourage him, but Friedrich didn't need any encouragement now. Months of frustration had him gushing his love for her as he clutched at her, his Juliet, breathing in the delicate perfume of her, lifting her to her feet, embracing her, holding her to him.

'Oh, my dear, how I've longed for this moment. Let me love and protect you. Don't cry now. Don't weep . . .'

She *was* weeping. Sweet, shy girl. The innocent. Finding love, first love, an emotional experience.

'I have to leave,' she was saying. 'I have to leave.'

'No you don't. You can stay.' Let your father leave, he thought.

'Pastor. Please. Let me go.' She was pushing, roughly. Pushing. 'Get away from me. Get away!'

He didn't understand. 'It's all right, Adele. Don't be upset. We haven't done anything wrong.'

But she was shouting, though in a whisper, lest anyone hear, hissing at him: 'Get your filthy hands off me. Get away, you awful man.' And she was gathering up her sketch pads and the folio and easel, and dropping them, so he leaned down to help her.

'Adele, listen. I don't have to stay a priest. I can leave. I know that life wouldn't suit you. I've known that all along, but I can look after you. I'm a wealthy man really. I am, I've got plenty of money. My father is rich, we have this beautiful mansion on the Rhine . . .'

She clasped the folio and the easel to her bosom as if to create a barrier between them.

'I don't care how rich you are!' she threw at him, a real little spitfire now. Friedrich liked that.

'You keep away from me. How dare you misuse me in that manner! Stand back. Keep away from me.'

Friedrich was appalled. In a rare moment of reality, even honesty, he apologised: 'I'm so sorry, Adele. I got carried away. I should never have imposed on you like that, forgive me. But I have been enamoured of you ever since the first day we met on that island. You see . . .'

But she wasn't listening. She was in a rage. 'How dare you! You dreadful man. My father will hear about this. He'll have you run out of town!'

Friedrich blinked. 'Don't be like that, Adele. I didn't mean any harm. How can you find compliments objectionable? I ask you that. You must have led a protected life.'

She hesitated, confused. 'You had no right to . . . to do what you did. That is more than compliments.'

'Born out of compliments, though,' he debated. But his cause was lost and he knew it. 'Let me carry the easel for you.'

'I don't want you to carry anything. I want you to go away and leave me alone. My father will find your behaviour more than compliments.'

Who gave a damn about her father? He did, for a few more days, while there was still hope of grabbing that timber contract. The difference between leaving with a tidy sum, or doubling it. As a matter of fact, maybe he ought to have the loggers give him money up front for the right to take the timber out, and forgo the rest. Then get the hell out of this place. In a few days the steamer would be back, and farewell Bundaberg.

He accompanied her towards Quay Street, his anger building.

He turned to Freddy. 'Who does she think she is? Threatening me? The uppity little bitch.'

To her he said: 'And what will you tell your father, my dear? How you flirted with me? Encouraged me, arching that little neck of yours like a cat, wanting more, and then taking umbrage when I drew the line at public displays—'

'I did no such thing!' she cried, horrified, tripping on the rough ground.

He put a hand out to support her and held it there, grasping her elbow, tightly . . . walking her along the opposite side of the street from the hotel. On past it. As if they were a loving couple, perhaps, out for a stroll. And Friedrich gloried in the situation. He preened, giving a bow to a passer-by. She squirmed but he had her arm, hard. He was supporting her now, she'd become so weak, but he allowed her to cross the road and delivered her to the hotel entrance.

'Adieu, my love,' he whispered with a smile. Then he leaned down and licked her ear, licked it good and wet, and let her go.

Adele twisted away and fled. Into the arms of Hanni, who was walking towards them, and who had witnessed, she thought, Pastor Ritter and Miss Hoepper embracing, right there on the street. That in itself was enough . . . such a spectacle . . . to make her head spin, but then she realised that Miss Hoepper was crying hysterically, hanging on to her as if she were being chased by demons. And maybe she is, Hanni thought, suspicion growing as she glared at Father Ritter.

He raised his hat, gave a little bow and hurried off in the other direction.

Two women coming out of the hotel stopped on the steps to stare at them, so Hanni grabbed the easel and sketch materials that Miss Hoepper was juggling and turned her away, taking the sobbing girl down the lane and into the kitchen.

Eva was there, 'Good heavens! What's this? Miss Hoepper, what's wrong? Here, sit down. Hanni, get the smelling salts.'

They waved the salts under her nose, but she choked, pushing them away, sobbing uncontrollably.

'Shall I send for your father?' Eva asked, but Adele shrieked: 'No! No! I'll be all right.'

'What happened?' Hanni asked. 'What happened with Pastor Ritter?'

'Nothing,' Adele wept. 'Nothing.'

'It didn't look like nothing to me,' Hanni said to Eva. 'He had an arm around her, he was nuzzling her . . .'

'No! Pastor Ritter? Never!'

'He was, I tell you. I thought they were canoodling at first . . .'

'In the street? My God!'

'It wasn't like that,' Adele cried. 'I was trying to get away from him.'

'What?' Eva was appalled.

In between sobs and gulps, Adele struggled to explain. 'I was over by the river doing some sketches and he came by and he was bothering me. I tried to be polite, hoping he would go away, but he began telling me all these flattering things . . .'

'Well, of course. It's his manner. You misunderstood the poor man, I'm sure.'

'No she didn't,' Hanni said harshly. 'I might have known he's no better than the rest of them.'

'I didn't misunderstand him touching me, Mrs Zimmerman, truly I didn't. He put his hand on my chest, so I packed up. I told him to go away and he was horrible. He said awful things to me all the way back to the hotel, and right out front . . .' Adele sobbed. '. . . he was disgusting.' She clapped her hand to her ear and shook her head. 'He misused me again.'

Eva was confused. 'Surely not. There has to be an explanation.'

'No there doesn't,' Hanni said. 'He's a pig. All men are pigs. Especially the ones hiding behind respectability. They're pigs.'

Adele was looking up at her, maybe even a little comforted as Hanni raged: 'You're lucky that's all he did to you, Miss Hoepper. Given a quieter place, God knows what might have happened. I know what they're like, believe me. Take that Keith Dixon, he's the worst of the lot.'

'That's enough, Hanni,' Eva warned. 'Don't be upsetting Miss Hoepper any more. You don't know these things, goodness me . . .'

'Don't I? Keith Dixon bashed me and he misused me something awful—' She realised what she was saying and

453

stopped suddenly. 'I'll make Miss Hoepper some coffee.' She hurried over to the stove, but Eva spun her about.

'What did you say?'

'Nothing.'

'Yes you did. You never mentioned this before. What did Keith Dixon do to you?'

'Nothing, I said!'

'I see. Then set up a tray for Miss Hoepper. Make her a nice hot coffee, and there's some teacake in the pantry. I only made it this morning.'

The two girls were very quiet now, so Eva went back to making seasoning for two chickens she had just plucked.

'Can you cook?' she asked Adele.

'No, Mrs Zimmerman. I never learned.'

'Then you should, my dear. It's a very satisfying occupation, and a cheery one. Everyone appreciates a good cook.'

'I suppose they do.'

The tray was ready. 'Best you have it in your room, Miss Hoepper,' Eva said. 'Hanni will carry it up for you, and stay with you until you feel better. And lock your door.'

They left, both a pair of miseries, she thought, and that was sad. Young girls shouldn't have to contend with this abuse. She tapped her fingers on the scrubbed kitchen table. Neither of them wanted their men to know, not the father and, it was obvious, not Lucas. Ashamed they were. It was not right.

Chapter Seventeen

So what if she bawled to her father? What could he do? Friedrich laughed. Not that she would. Lightning would strike her dead before she'd have the guts to mention an embarrassing sexual interlude to him.

He wondered how old Beitz was faring. He'd given him the last of the opium powders in one hit, and it wouldn't have surprised him if they'd knocked him off his wobbly perch once and for all, instead of just keeping him groggy. Anyway, despite Hoepper's interference, he could get on with his own plans now, so he headed round to Bundaberg's other firm of timber-getters; no sense in alerting Les Jolly and his German loggers.

George Macken, the boss, was only too happy to oblige. And yes, he had the men to get on to it right away.

'I'd welcome the work, Father. So close to town. But aren't a lot of your lads loggers?'

'Yes, but it behoves me to see that the church earns as much as possible for the sale of our timber. I am not ashamed to admit that we are in financial difficulties. Jesus himself was a poor man. So I have to take the best offer. You understand?'

'How much is Les Jolly offering?'

'I'm not at liberty to disclose that.'

'Fair enough. I'll up his offer by five pounds. But first I'd have to get a good look at the land. Have you got the title deeds with you, Father?'

'No. What do you need them for?'

Macken grinned. 'So I don't go chopping down timber on

someone else's block. If you could get them to me this evening, I'll take a foreman out and we'll see what you've got there.'

'We have plenty of good timber.'

'I don't doubt it, but we need to do a thorough check to see they're all healthy, worth the work. See what I mean?'

'Yes, of course. I'll bring the deeds to you later.'

'Or we could look them over with you and Father Beitz tomorrow.'

'No. He's not well.'

The deeds to forty acres. Several blocks. He'd seen them somewhere, probably in the priest's cabin box with all his other papers.

Friedrich congratulated himself on buying the horse. He couldn't imagine what it would have been like having to rely on that wagon and provide transport for the workers. He knew they all envied him such a beautiful mount, but what he did was his own business. Keeping in mind that nothing had been mentioned about his pay.

'Not a word, Freddy,' he said as he rode back to the commune. 'How do you like that? You'd have been slave labour, worse off than any of them. I'll ask Walther tonight why he isn't making a weekly contribution, just for fun. I'm not supposed to know he is topping up the grocery bill every so often, according to Pimbley. Then I'll ask when I can expect to receive my weekly stipend. And how much. That will put the cat among the pigeons.'

The ancient native with the ding-a-ling name was sitting cross-legged by the side of the road, doing nothing in particular it seemed, and Friedrich rode on past him. He hoped none of the natives had been wandering loose about the place in his absence. This morning, after the workers had left, he'd chased off any natives he could find, claiming that Father Beitz was ill and didn't want to be disturbed. Certainly Friedrich himself hoped he wouldn't be disturbing the old priest in his quest for the deeds to the land. He was relying on the powders to keep him quiet.

He hitched the horse and hurried into the commune. All was quiet except for the occasional unnerving shriek of birds,

456

so he made straight for Father Beitz's hut, pleased to see the old man still asleep. His face was red and puffy, and he was tossing about, his breathing a series of rasps and grunts, as if he were trying to wake up but not making much of a fist of it.

Friedrich stared down at him. 'That's a good lad. You stay bye-byes and you'll be all right.'

He went over to the corner of the hut, pulled out the cabin trunk and started rifling through the papers, searching for the deeds, with their exact description of the blocks.

'I'm sure they were here somewhere,' he muttered, pushing aside winter vests and jumpers and feeling about for documents, but at that moment Father Beitz stirred and called out.

'What are you doing there? Who is that?'

He was sitting groggily on the side of the bunk, trying to pull himself up. Friedrich's first reaction was to leap to his feet.

'It's all right. It's only me, Father.'

'What are you doing there?' He sounded drunk, slurring his words.

'Just tidying up. I'll get you some coffee.' Friedrich dashed out of the hut, his heart pounding, annoyed that he had been caught in the act. But then even more annoyed at his own stupid reaction.

Why did he have to run away from the old boy? Beitz was too doped to know what was going on. He should have shoved him back on to the bunk. He dug into his trouser pocket, reassured that his fat roll of English pounds was still safe. He felt better then, calmer. He lit a cheroot and sat on a nearby bench to think this through.

He had to have those deeds now. He couldn't have the loggers coming out here in the morning; Beitz, any of the others, could still be about, by mischance.

His plan back on course, Friedrich marched into the hut, ignoring the priest, who was now lying on the bed, eyes open but breathing heavily, as if he'd just run a mile uphill. He went straight to the trunk and started shovelling out the contents.

'Friedrich, what are you doing?' Beitz gasped, but his curate was too intent on his search to bother with him.

The voice was stronger now. 'They are my belongings. I

would prefer you didn't . . . Please, Friedrich. Are you looking for something?'

When Friedrich didn't respond, Father Beitz became alarmed. 'What are you doing there? Get away from my private papers! They are no concern of yours.'

But Friedrich had found what he wanted, found the documents tied with pink string. He shovelled everything back into the cabin trunk, slammed it shut and jumped to his feet, but Beitz confronted him.

'What's that you're taking? What is it? I demand to know!'

Friedrich grabbed his arm, ran him backwards the few steps to the bunk and gave him a light shove. It didn't take much. Suddenly the cranky old priest was flat on his back on the bunk, wheezing like leaky bellows. The trouble with these old characters was they didn't know when to quit. Beitz couldn't get up now if the place were on fire.

It was probably only a few minutes, Friedrich reflected, but it seemed like an age as he stood there, trying to think how he would explain this later. He could confuse Beitz. Tell him it was his idea. Don't you remember? You gave me the deeds. That sort of stuff.

But why bother? What the hell! Why not bypass the arguments altogether? Put him to sleep once and for all. He was only a nuisance anyway. Who needed him? No one.

Quietly he slipped the pillow from under the priest's head. He saw Beitz look at him. No fear there. Why would there be? His curate was only moving to make him more comfortable.

Then Beitz turned his head. He was looking to the other side of his bunk, and Friedrich automatically glanced over there too.

He shrieked. He didn't recognise his own voice. In fact, the actor in him took note that he was capable of shrieking like that. But the dog was coming for him. More like a wolf; its jaws gaping, teeth bared in a ferocious growl. It was leaping at him from the other corner of the hut; the darkness of the cloudy afternoon must have been harbouring that thing all the time. He dropped the pillow and ran, raced out of the hut.

But he still had the documents he'd come for.

Safe in the kitchen, he felt like Beitz, huffing and puffing at his exertion. But the dog hadn't come after him. Maybe Beitz was its prey after all, and he had interrupted an attack. Lucky to escape with his life. By now Beitz could be good and dead. Friedrich was still panting as he crept through the bush on a short cut to the horse paddock, where he saddled up Queenie again. If anything had happened to Beitz, it wasn't his fault. He knew nothing about it.

Full of confidence now, Friedrich rode through the town and presented George Macken with the deeds to the land.

'I want all the trees costed and accounted for,' he said. 'There'll be no putting a few aside for yourself.'

'That won't happen,' Macken growled.

'Good. And I'll expect a substantial deposit when we sign the contract.'

'A deposit?' Macken spluttered. 'Never done that before.'

'I may be a man of the cloth but I am also a businessman, sir. A deposit of fifty pounds will establish your good faith.'

Macken nodded. 'Righto,' he said, accepting the terms so promptly that Friedrich was cross with himself for not asking for a hundred.

'Give me a day or so, Father. I'll be able to give you an estimate then.'

He opened up the title deeds and nodded. As he thought, this land was in The Scrubs. Valuable old timber there. How did that fool think he could keep tabs on every tree? He wasn't selling kitchen tables.

They'd pegged out the foundations of Walther's brewery at last, a much easier job than clearing the block of rocks and tree stumps, and to Walther's delight, the timber he had ordered arrived right on schedule. But enthusiasm and dedication couldn't make up for lack of experience. When the timber frame of the first section of their building fell down for the third time, it was Lucas who had to admit they needed help.

'No fear!' Walther said. 'We'll get it right. Maybe we're supposed to reinforce the corners. Help me hoist this frame up again and we'll see what else is needed.'

'I'll tell you what's needed. A carpenter. Neither of us

knows what we're doing. I thought it would be simple work, but it's not. We're wasting time and money. Every time we break a board I hear money falling away.'

'We can't afford a carpenter,' Walther said stubbornly.

'Then I quit.'

'What? You can't quit. You said you'd help me.'

'I thought I could.' Lucas laughed. 'I thought you knew about carpentering. Between us we couldn't build a doll's house, Walther, let alone a blasted brewery. We're totally out of our depth here. So: I quit, you don't have to pay me, and now you can hire a carpenter. And that's that. Time to pack up for the day. Let's go.'

Father Beitz stumbled out of his hut, calling to Friedrich, but there was no sign of him He was still very drowsy, and he wondered if he might have the sleeping sickness that was known to attack people in the tropics. He'd been sleeping far too much lately. But where is Friedrich? he puzzled. Only a little while ago he was looking for something, and then he came over to my bunk, picked up my pillow . . . it must have fallen on the floor . . . was about to hand it to me, when he let out this yell, threw the pillow up in the air and took off like a racer. The fellow really is quite eccentric. I'll have to have a word with him. But where is everyone?

He lifted the lid on the large beer barrel they used as a tank and ladled some water out, drinking a few mouthfuls and pouring the rest over his head, but the barrel reminded him of Walther's enterprise, and that irritated him. Why did they need beer, or even the rum they were all talking about, when God provided crystal-clear water like this? Muttering about their foolishness, he marched down the path and out to the vegetable garden.

It looked like a menagerie. Several species of large birds, including crows, were scratching happily about, a goanna raised its head to gaze at him then resumed chomping on his vegetables, and at least a dozen wallabies were feeding blissfully among the cabbages.

'Get out with you,' he shouted, and the birds lifted, fluttering and squawking, only to resume their scavenging further away.

'God in heaven!' Father Beitz slumped down on a mound of soil and left them to it. He felt a failure. He had his church, a handful of parishioners, and no mission school, let alone a school for their own children, who wouldn't attend even if he were able to build one which he couldn't do, there being no money left, and no extra help forthcoming from the bank. Maybe Mr Hoepper was right, he'd asked too much of the Lord. Perhaps his destiny was to attend to his flock, be content shepherding his own community and leave the mission work to younger men like Friedrich. Possibly that was the answer. He would discuss the matter with Friedrich as soon as he could. The poor fellow had received no guidance at all so far. It might serve them both well to go on retreat for a week, so that they might fully understand the Lord's wishes.

Yes. That was the way. He turned back towards the kitchen, pleased to hear Walther's voice. They were home. Already he felt better.

The Pastor took a few turns about the town on his horse, showing off, pretending nonchalance. He passed the pub, envious of the men gathered on the veranda, feet up, drink in hand, not a care in the world. Watching the goings-on.

Lamps were being lit now, shops closing, darkness descending. No street lights here. He decided he'd better head back to the commune; the lads should have dinner ready by now. But what about Beitz? He might start pointing the finger. Nah. Smile. Ignore. Be indulgent. Kind to the old fellow in his dotage.

He was whistling as he headed on to Taylor's Road, his mind made up. SS *Tara* would come chugging upriver soon, decant cargo and passengers, take on cargo and passengers, and the Reverend Friedrich Ritter would be among them. Enough was enough.

'No more dithering,' he told Freddy. 'I'll take my nice little haul and get the hell out. I haven't done badly really.' He sighed. 'I know you'd have liked me to carry on as curate, fulfilling your obligations, old chap, but even you have to admit that this place is just not up to standard. I mean, living

461

like a native, no pay, and for that matter no town . . . you can't call that dump a town, Freddy . . .'

'Who are you talking to, mate?'

The voice came out of the darkness, startling him. Two horsemen riding his way had caught up with him.

'No one.' He smiled. 'Just meditating.' He looked from one to the other. 'Where are you gentlemen off to?'

'Maryborough,' one said, his voice cheerful.

'Is that so? It's a long way from here, isn't it?'

'Not all that far if you've got a good horse.'

This was interesting. Friedrich had imagined the only way to get out of this town was by ship, but of course . . . 'I suppose I could ride all the way down to Brisbane,' he said. 'With a good horse.'

'Plenty do it. You could say the horse opened up this country, Father.'

'True.' He nodded. 'Yes.'

'And where are you off to, Father?'

'Home. To the commune down the road.' Too late Friedrich remembered that Taylor's Road was a dead end. These men couldn't be riding to Maryborough on this road, and they didn't sound as if they could make a mistake like that.

'I'd better get moving,' he said, hoping to shake them off, but the man on his right clouted him so hard, so suddenly, with his arm that Friedrich crashed down from the horse, rolling into muddy grass by the roadside.

'What the hell?' he shouted. 'I'll have the law on you.'

But then he tried to change tactics. It wasn't the first time he'd been attacked. In fact, he'd done a bit of mugging himself.

'What do you want of me? I'm a poor man. A priest. I've only got the horse. Take the horse if you must . . .'

They weren't listening. They advanced on him, beat him thoroughly with fists of iron. They kicked him, their hobnail boots showing no mercy, ignoring his screams.

For muggers, they were well prepared. Once they had him battered into a groaning heap, one of them lit a small lantern.

'Now let's see what we've got here,' the lead man said. 'Roll him over and search him, mate.'

Friedrich gritted his teeth, trying to fight them off, but he

462

didn't have a chance. They ripped the clerical cloth aside without a qualm, searching him thoroughly. Though he wept, bit, cursed them, they found his money, and they laughed as they held up the roll of notes.

'Only a poor priest, are you? What have we got here? Hundred-pound notes. Hate to think what a rich priest carries about!'

Friedrich tried to snatch his money, but the more he screamed, hurling abuse at them, the more they teased him with it.

'Will you listen to the filth of him, and him a holy man!'

'You wonder where he learned such talk.'

'This is a nice watch. I'll toss you for it.'

'No, we'll flog it and I'll go you halves. The boss just wants his five hundred back.'

'He's a bit short of the five. Got some coin, though.'

The heavier man sat back on his haunches, a menacing silhouette against the starry sky.

'Now you listen here, mate. You don't go round swindling money out of anyone here, least of all Keith Dixon. You got that? Now you'd better remember what I said, because next time you won't just get a little hiding, you'll get dead. Get your logging mates to show you the crocs in our river. People can disappear off the face of the earth, you know. Go without a trace. Isn't that right?'

His mate agreed. 'He goes slandering Keith again and he's dead meat.'

'Right. You got that, priest? We'll give Keith back his money; you shut your face, and the party's over. I reckon you got too smart for your own good, mate.'

They lumbered away, mounted their horses and left. Friedrich lay very still until the hoofbeats faded, then pushed himself up painfully until he could at least sit, and get his breath, and weep with rage and frustration. It had all been for nothing. The bastards! He was amazed. The last thing he'd expected was for Dixon to fight back. He thought he'd had him.

He heard movement and froze. Had they only been playing with him? Had they come back to kill him, finish him off?

Shut him up so that their boss, Dixon, could go on his unblemished way into the Parliament? The rapist. The arsonist. The goddamned double-crosser!

To Friedrich, that was the worst crime. He'd been double-crossed. Tricked. And by God, he'd get even.

There it was again, movement in the darkness, a tread on the road. A step. It was his horse! It had wandered back to stand looking down at him, unaffected by his woes.

For God's sake! They'd left the horse. He'd been certain they'd steal it too. They must have known this was a fine mount.

Friedrich sighed bitterly. Ah yes. He remembered. A horse thief was worse than a murderer here. They'd half killed him. They'd threatened to kill him, but they let him keep a valuable horse.

He sat awhile checking his injuries, still groaning and griping, his nose still dripping blood. He was sure that he had broken ribs. He could taste blood, and mud, and rage.

Dixon wouldn't get away with this.

Tibbaling watched the incident dispassionately. Those fellows were giving Two-Men-Walking a real bashing, but the interesting thing about this episode was the attitude of the Holy Spirit who accompanied him all the time. He didn't make any attempt to help the victim, and what was more, he didn't appear to be concerned.

That Holy Spirit, he was a powerful god, he could have struck the attackers with a bolt of lightning. Or caused the earth to open up and swallow them. But he did nothing. He just stood there, a sad-looking god if ever there was one.

No doubt this Christian religion was strange. Come to think of it, though, the two gods, the Holy Spirit and the Father God, had stood by and done nothing when the enemies nailed the son Jesus to a cross. A true happening, according to Father Beitz. So . . . their tradition must include non-interference when it came to attacks by enemies. Father Beitz had told him something about turning the other cheek for more pain instead of fighting back.

464

He gave a small smile. If Two-Men-Walking was turning the other cheek here, he was making a lot of noise about it, shrieking and wailing, even cursing. No, he wasn't observing their law correctly. And what about that business back in the hut? He'd had murder in his eyes. He was a bad fellow, he would have killed Father Beitz, suffocated him with the bag-for-resting-the-head. And yet this was the man Father Beitz liked, called a friend. The man who had pointed the bone at the good priest, and had become impatient, attempting to do away with Father Beitz with his hands.

The bashing was over. Tibbaling hoped they had killed Two-Men-Walking; it would save a lot of trouble and allow that useless Holy Spirit to go back home, wherever that was. His mission, simply as companion to the young priest, seemed pointless. Tibbaling took courage and moved closer. Shadowy though the spirit was most times, he seemed clearer on this night. He was wearing clothes exactly the same as Two-Men-Walking, and he looked very much like him, come to think of it.

But as the attackers mounted their horses and rode off, and the victim staggered to his feet, the Holy Spirit turned to Tibbaling, reaching out to him with the saddest expression, and the old man was overwhelmed with sadness too. He saw the deep gash on the side of the spirit's head, saw the blood on his shoulders and heard him speak in their German language. He didn't understand the words, but he knew. He knew what had happened.

A wind was stirring and the spirit looked back to the commune; he began moving in that direction, leaving Two-Men-Walking, leaving him, and Tibbaling nodded. There had been a mission after all. Now it was done, the spirit could go to his rest. Tibbaling had heard the message. It was too late for that spirit; not the Holy Spirit, but a gentle good fellow, murdered by the bad priest. But not too late to save Father Beitz.

Clouds were hustling across the dark skies, blotting out the stars, and the wind grew stronger. Large splotches of rain fell to the hot earth, creating a wispy ground fog. Friedrich

465

managed to stumble over to the horse and after several attempts got himself into the saddle.

'Dixon will be sorry he was ever born,' he said to Freddy, his words forced out painfully from his swollen jaw. He looked about him. His voice had sounded hollow, as if he'd been on a large empty stage. He twisted about in the saddle and gave a yelp of pain. Careful. Be very still. It took time for that burning pain to subside. He had a feeling that Freddy might have gone, run off like the coward he was, and Friedrich felt bereft. Nervous. Unprotected.

He wished he could turn about and go after Dixon, but he was too battered to think about that yet. He'd have to get back to the commune, clean up, have a rest and then start trying to get his life back into shape again. If Dixon only knew what a heavy blow he had really struck, rendering the Pastor penniless and imprisoned in this rotten town, he'd laugh himself sick.

With the squall building up around him, Friedrich, now close to fainting from his injuries, clung on to the horse, relying on it to take him to a safe haven.

'Keith Dixon is in the dining room,' the waitress told Eva, her eyes shining with excitement. She didn't even hear the cook's answering growl. 'He's got a big rally in the hall tonight,' she added. 'Me and my boyfriend, we're going. It's for voters, you know. And he's giving out free drinks and supper and he's got a band to play for dancing. A band from Brisbane . . .'

'Stop your chatter,' the cook said. She needed to think.

Despite her loyalty to Hanni and her anger over her friend's experience at the hands of Keith Dixon, she hadn't been able to do a thing in the way of revenge. She hadn't said a word to Lucas, fearing he would turn the blame back on his wife. Sometimes the truth could cause even more trouble. And Hanni wouldn't thank her, any more than that silly girl upstairs. Miss Adele still refused to tell her father about Ritter's advances.

Eva took the large shepherd's pie out of the oven and dumped it on the table. Behind her, pork chops and steaks were sizzling on the stove.

The waitress leaned over and scooped a little mashed potato

466

from atop the pie with her finger, but Eva was faster. She slapped the girl's hand with the egg slice she was using to mark out portions on the pie.

'How many times have I told you not to do that?' she snapped. 'Now, what are the orders?'

'J.B. Dixon is in there with Keith. He's having the shepherd's pie and Keith wants pork chops. Three, he said.'

'I don't need to know their names. Have they all finished their soup?'

'Yes, I think so. The commercial travellers are all having steak, and both Mr Hoepper and Miss Hoepper are having the pie.'

'Oh my God, girl, you're getting me all mixed up with the names. You say three steaks, three pies, four pork chops, I am not wanting to know who has what.'

'But you're wrong. It isn't three steaks, it's six. The commercial travellers—'

'Serve the vegetables,' Eva spluttered. This girl drove her mad. Hanni was a much better waitress, but she wouldn't do it, she preferred to work upstairs so she could avoid men like Keith Dixon and his father. Eva wished her friend had told her about that trouble before now, instead of bottling it up inside her. As it was, Eva still didn't know the full sordid story but she could guess the rest. Hanni had changed; she was so sad lately, miserable really, and Eva blamed this on Keith Dixon and of course Lucas.

She served up the meals, for once pleased that she did know where everything was going. It gave her the opportunity to serve the Dixons last.

Bonnie, the waitress, was upset. 'Eva, really! The Dixons are waiting. We don't keep people like them waiting. Where is their order?'

'Take these steaks in. I'll have it ready when you get back.'

Eva dished up old Dixon's pie, and piled three big pork chops on to a generous serving of mashed potatoes and peas. She wished she had some poison for Keith, but dismissed that idea. Too dangerous. Something, just a little irritant, would be nice. Like excessive pepper or Chinese chilli, but he'd only send the meal back. Then she remembered the children's medicine in the pantry, and came back with cod liver oil with which to doctor the thick tasty gravy.

'Enjoy your night,' she said as she gave Keith a generous ladleful of gravy.

Both meals were waiting in the open oven when Bonnie returned. 'About time,' she said, using a floured serving cloth to claim them without burning her fingers, and rushed away with them. Eva tossed out the oiled gravy and cleaned the saucepan.

This was a very strange night. Walther was boiling up a stew of lamb chops, carrots, onions and potatoes when Mike Quinlan called in. And immediately claimed they were eating Irish food. But that wasn't the real reason for his visit. He wanted them to come to town and back up Les Jolly, who was determined to beat Keith Dixon in these elections.

'You've got to vote, you fellers,' Mike said. 'I've come to ask you to stand up for Les.'

'Yes, we'll do that,' Lucas said. No argument there, and Mike was delighted. This had been easy. They would all come with him. All four men. But not Father Beitz. That was understandable. The old fellow looked a bit worn out.

'Are we voting tonight?' Max Lutze asked.

'No. This is just a rally. To get people listening. Keith's people will be at the Progress Hall to hear him. Les Jolly will be speaking in Quay Street.'

Walther was concerned. Father Beitz was very quiet. And he didn't look well. 'Perhaps I should stay home,' he said.

'No. It is a good thing to attend to your civic duties,' Father Beitz told him. 'We have to learn about these matters. Give unto Caesar . . . you know. Mr Quinlan, you will dine with us?'

'Thank you, Father. I'd have wept tears to miss Walther's Irish dish. Where's Pastor Ritter?'

Silence. Max dug into his stew.

'He was in town today,' Hans said. 'Riding about on his fine horse.'

'What horse?' Father Beitz asked, and Max frowned at Hans.

'More stew, Father?' Lucas said.

'Yes please.'

Walther looked at him, astonished. Father Beitz never had seconds.

The old priest smiled. 'I'm feeling much better, Walther. Really I am. Got my appetite back, you see. You lads go with Mr Quinlan. I'll stay here and wait for Pastor Ritter. We have much to discuss.'

'Not like him to miss dinner,' Hans said sourly. 'Anyway, what does he do all day?'

Mike Quinlan saw the void and jumped in. 'Did you know that Mr Hoepper has decided to invest in our plantation company? Now there's a sad story. He says it is a small part of the investments he had in mind for his dear departed sons, God bless their souls.'

Hans looked up. 'Why would he bother now? The lads are dead.'

'Because he wanted his family to be part of this community,' Father Beitz said sadly.

But Hans persisted. 'He's not staying, though, Father. Everyone knows he and his daughter are continuing their travels.'

Father Beitz dunked a lump of bread in the stew and sucked on it, licking his lips with a relish the others hadn't noticed in this frugal man before.

'It's to do with a dream, Hans,' he said. 'Mr Hoepper had a dream. It isn't working out exactly the way he would have liked it, and maybe it never will, but it was a good dream. A good dream is a magnificent obsession if you believe in it. Worth nothing if you lack the faith to hang on.'

He looked up as wind rattled the bamboo and a shower of rain swept in. A cockatoo screeched at the inconvenience of the sudden rain and dived under their shelter, settling himself on the priest's shoulder.

Normally Father Beitz wasn't comfortable with these aggressive birds, but this evening he didn't mind it all. In fact he was rather pleased that the bird had chosen his shoulder.

'It likes me,' he smiled, nervously offering it a nibble of bread. 'You people had better finish up and run along. There's a storm coming. Lucas, you put on your big coat, you're looking pale. Is anything wrong?'

'No, Father. I'm quite well.'

'That's good. You're well enough to do the right thing and see your wife. Bring her home where she belongs. You look to your obligations, sir.'

'Yes, Father.'

It was like a carnival night in the little town. Squally rain couldn't dampen the enthusiasm for the first political rallies ever held hereabouts. Most of the folk stepping out this night weren't the slightest bit interested in politics, they didn't care which parties the two contenders were representing, they were only attending for the fun of it. Speechmakers were better than nothing in backwoods Bundaberg, starved for entertainment.

Friedrich blinked, stared, rubbed his eyes when he found himself confronted with the dim lights of a town house.

'I must have got turned about,' he muttered. 'I'm sure I was headed for the commune. Dammit! Now what?'

Perplexed, he allowed his horse to plod on through the rain. The pain in his side was worse, his head ached and he knew he looked a sight. He needed help, but who? The obvious person to turn to was Hoepper, at the hotel, but he couldn't very well march in there in this bedraggled state.

He noticed people hurrying about and he found that surprising for a second or two, but he had just remembered the hospital. He'd passed it several times, disbelieving, contemptuous of a community that would have the cheek to call a mere cottage a hospital. But it would have to do. Friedrich leaned over and spat, the taste of blood still foul, and felt a loose front tooth, which upset him even more than his other injuries. An actor could not afford to lose a front tooth; it would mean demotion to the comedy or the fool. Miserably he turned the horse in the direction of the hospital, seeking help, seeking comfort. This had to be the worst day of his life.

'The very worst,' he said to Freddy with a tremor in his voice. 'I'm ruined. The bastards have ruined me.'

But the night seemed empty, even though the street was busy, gigs and buggies hurrying into the town centre. There was a void, a hollowness that made his voice echo when he spoke to Freddy, and it made him nervous.

'Freddy?' There it was again, only an echo, and then he realised that this had happened earlier. A while back. And he'd had the feeling then that Freddy wasn't there. That he'd run away when those thugs had attacked. But why would he? For God's sake, why would he?

'Freddy?' he called, louder now, and a gust of wind tore down the street.

From habit he clutched at his hat, but it had gone. He wasn't even wearing a hat, it was back there in the ditch along Taylor's Road. Was Freddy back there too? Or was he no longer? Friedrich began to blubber, calling to Freddy not to leave him. Overwhelmed with pain, anger and self-pity, he dragged himself from his horse and fell fainting by the front entrance to the hospital.

People came running. Strong hands grasped him. Tenderly. He needed that. The respect. The attention. For truly he had been foully done by . . . It wasn't fair. And Freddy had deserted him in his hour of need . . .

'What has happened here?'

'It's a priest.'

'The Lutheran priest, the young one.'

'He looks as if he's been trampled by a mob of cattle.'

'Poor fellow. Bring him in.'

A woman's voice. Strong, authoritative. 'Who's this?'

'It's a priest, Matron. He's in a bad way.'

'Ladies, stand aside, please. You men bring him in here to the infirmary. Nurse, get some hot water and soap, we'll have to clean him up. A priest, did you say? What's your name, Father?'

'Ritter,' he gasped.

'Well, Father Ritter, you're a right mess. Dear me, this outfit of yours has had it.'

A whisper. 'It's sort of a vestment, Matron.'

'I know that. Put him in here. Bit wobbly on the pins, are you, Father? That's right, sit up here on this bench. Toby, get his vestment and his shirt off so I can get a look at him. Thanks, Mr Tucker, we'll be right now. You look after yourself, no more lifting those huge rocks or you'll throw your back out again. Let me see what we've got here. Now, Father, what happened to you?'

He lay back on the hard infirmary bench, feeling safer now, relieved that he would not die of a heart attack or a pierced lung or whatever injuries those brutes might have inflicted on him, safe in the hands of this good woman. And braver. Much braver.

'Where am I?' he gasped as a red-headed girl unbuttoned his cassock and divested him of it, along with his shirt, clucking about the muddy, torn state of his vestment.

'I think it's past mending, Matron.'

'Never mind that. Wash his face and hands. Get the boots off. Now, what happened to you, Father?'

'I was attacked,' he gasped. 'Attacked by two men.'

'Good God! What's the world coming to that thugs should attack a man of the cloth? And you a foreigner. I'm real sorry about that. Now let me look at you. Does this hurt?'

Bravery deserted him. Friedrich screeched as she leaned on his ribs.

'Thought so. You took a bashing, eh, Father? Thought by the way you were stumbling along there that the ribs were giving you trouble.'

They swabbed him down. They even had to wash his hair, to get the mud off. They brought him cloudy water with a hideous taste to wash out his mouth. The Matron pushed and jabbed at him, she doused the cuts on his body with a brown liquid that stung like a family of wasps, all the while chatting to him as if they were in a parlour.

'Where were you attacked?'

'Taylor's Road.'

'Odd place for bushrangers to operate. I mean, that road doesn't go anyplace, except to the German camp.'

'Bushrangers?' he asked. 'What is this?'

'Oh, thieves. Outlaws. Robbers.'

'Yes. This is right. They robbed me. I was robbed of every penny I had.'

472

'How much did they get?'

Careful now. 'Six pounds,' he said sadly. 'It was community money. For the poor.'

'Bastards,' she said. 'They must be getting desperate. Now hang on, Father, I'm going to strap these ribs. You've got two broken and I wouldn't be surprised by the way you flinch if a couple of the higher ones are cracked just a bit. But considering all the bruising, you got off fairly lightly, though more through God's good grace than their efforts.'

'They gave me a kicking even when I was down,' he said. 'Even after they'd dragged me from the horse, ripping my clothes, slamming me into the mud, and I kept asking them why. I mean, what have I done to them? I'm new here, madam. I thought this was a good town. I was told the people here would be most kind.'

'We are, Father,' the red-headed nurse with the freckled face was anxious to assure him.

'Was it daylight?' the matron asked him, frowning.

'Yes, madam. Just on dusk.'

'I don't suppose you can give us a description? Our Constable Colley will need to know, Father.'

'I can do more than that,' he said, wincing as she plastered his ribs worse than a woman's corset. 'I recognised one of them.'

'You did?' Conversation and ministration were suspended mid-air. 'Who?'

He lay there thinking. The nurse put a little pillow under his head. 'One of them was heavily bearded, face hardly showing but the other one. I saw him plain as day . . .'

'Who was it?'

'A fellow called Keith. I remember now. Yes, Keith it was. Keith Dixon. The other fellow called him by name – a big fair-haired fellow was this Keith – and then when they were attacking me, when I was on the ground, I heard the bearded one say something about "you Dixons", so it wasn't too hard even for me in my battered state to make sense of it. Yes. That was his name. Keith Dixon. I'd swear to it. *And* I could pick him out in a crowd. I'll never forget his insolent face, laughing at me down there, under his feet,

473

in the mud. Would you know him, madam?'

'Oh Lord,' she said.

The schoolteacher, Mr Hackett, came to escort the two ladies and the children and Hanni smiled. He was around so often these days it seemed he was courting Mrs Zimmerman. Who, of course, denied such a suggestion . . . with a blush. It was Eva who decided they would go to the hall first, to see what Keith Dixon had to offer. The children were all for it, leaping about excitedly – they'd heard that free sweets and cordial would be on offer, and they were determined not to miss out – but Hanni wouldn't hear of it.

'How could you?' she accused Eva angrily. 'I wouldn't go within a mile of that man.'

'He might be worth watching, though,' Eva said with a grin.

'We have to go!' Robie called. 'Hurry up, Mother, we'll be late. Come along, Hanni. You like sweets, I'll get some for you.'

The other children joined in, hoping to persuade her, fearing their mother might change her mind, but Hanni was adamant.

'You do what you like,' she said angrily, and stormed out through the gate and away in the other direction.'

'You shouldn't be out walking on your own, Mrs Fechner,' Mr Hackett called, but Eva told him to let her go.

'She'll be all right. She'll find the others at Les Jolly's meeting.'

As they set out, she let the children run on so that she could whisper to Hackett.

'Hanni's got a set on the Dixon fellow, with good reason. He gave her a bad time.'

'What do you mean, a bad time?'

'Well, he hurt her.'

'He what? What did he do?'

'I shouldn't say. She doesn't like anyone knowing. I only heard the half of it, but enough . . .'

'The fellow hurt her?' Hackett insisted. 'How? Physically? Did he manhandle her?'

'Yes. And more.'

474

'Eva! What is more? This is disgraceful!'

She glanced about her as if afraid someone might overhear. 'Hanni was working at their station. He attacked her. Beat her, and raped her. But she doesn't want anyone to know. She's too ashamed.'

'My God. This is shocking. What does her husband say about it?'

'Oh please, he doesn't know. Hanni wouldn't tell him. I thought I should, but I didn't want to cause any more trouble between them.'

'Trouble be damned,' he snorted, coming to an abrupt halt in the street. 'I can well understand Hanni's refusal to attend his rally. I don't know why you want to go. This is wrong. Come back, children, we're not going that way after all.'

They groaned and complained, almost weeping, until he told them he'd take them past the Sunshine Store and buy treats for them all.

As they turned about, Eva was disappointed. She'd wanted to see how Keith was faring, but she didn't dare tell Mr Hackett about her efforts at sabotage. He might not approve. But then the horse-drawn hearse went rattling by, bells ringing, and they all stopped to stare.

'Did someone die?' Robie asked.

'No,' his mother said. 'When the bells ring for people to get out of the way, the hearse is being used as an ambulance. Someone must have had an accident.'

Possibly, Eva would have split her sides laughing if she'd been there to see Keith sprint from the stage just as the Master of Ceremonies was calling everyone to order. Unfortunately, having stepped to the front of the stage, he didn't notice Keith's retreat, and having achieved quiet, he went ahead with his prepared speech, singing the praises of this young man, a hand sweeping behind him to an empty chair. His audience, at first bemused, began to grin, to nudge, to laugh as their MC blustered on in full voice, until he came to a red-faced stop, gazing astonished at a crowd of people hysterical with laughter.

Doubling up in merriment, they pointed, called out to him,

until he realised what they were trying to tell him, and looked behind him at an empty stage.

He gaped, turned back to his audience and appealed to them.

'Where's the bugger?' he asked, stunned, sending them off into more peals of laughter.

But Keith was trapped way down the back, in the outhouse. Every time he tried to leave he'd only get a few steps away and the urge would be upon him again. So there he stayed. Hot, flushed and panicking.

It was his mother who came looking for him.

'Are you in there, Keith?'

'Yes.'

'You'd better hurry up, dear. Your MC is very cross. He says you made a fool of him. He's threatening to leave.'

'I can't hurry up, Mother. I've got the trots real bad.'

'Oh dear.'

'It's nerves,' she told J.B., back in the hall. 'I'm sure that's what it is, the poor boy.'

'Poor boy! Bloody sook, I say. What sort of politician will he make if he gets the trots every time he has to make a speech? I knew this wouldn't work. You tell him he's got two minutes to get in here before I get the hell out of here myself.'

The ambulance driver was in a hurry to rid himself of this patient, diagnosed with cholera.

The steamer *Fayette* had pulled in quietly this afternoon to put a passenger ashore, though the Captain's excuse was that he needed supplies. No one else was permitted to disembark from the ship, en route from Cooktown in the far north to Brisbane. It was carrying diggers from the northern goldfields, winners living it up in first class, losers suffering in steerage. This fellow had been handed up from steerage, and the Captain had advised the port officials of the presence of a man, name unknown, with an infectious disease. Jules Stenning tried to prevent the landing, on the grounds that Bundaberg had no quarantine station, but the Captain knew his rights. He could not endanger the lives of the other passengers and his crew.

476

They argued for some time, until an officer produced ship's records to prove that in any case this passenger had been bound for Bundaberg. This heavily bearded bushman with an accent of some sort, who, like many of his ilk, was a loner, and a surly one at that. He'd kept to himself on the voyage down the coast, spending most of the time in his bunk, so much so that it was quite a while before anyone realised he was ill.

Stenning brought Dr Strauss to confer with the ship's doctor in the hopes that the diagnosis was incorrect, and Strauss managed to solve the impasse by suggesting that they wait until dark to remove the patient, when all the curious labourers and others with business at the wharves had departed.

'I suggest you tell your passengers the gentleman has a liver ailment, that being prevalent on the goldfields,' Strauss said.

'I already have,' the ship's doctor said.

They had the fellow, barely conscious, in a tiny storeroom, and Dr Strauss decided to take another look at him. He picked up the patient's hand to take his pulse again, but the patient pulled away, as he had done before, with something still clutched firmly in his fist.

'What is it?' Strauss asked the ship's doctor.

'Only a bit of rock.'

'Worth anything?' It was a jagged blue stone, bright blue, and it sat comfortably in the palm of this fellow's hand.

'No. Not a bean. Probably a memento or something.'

'Oh. All right. I'll have the ambulance here at six o'clock. We'll take him off your hands.'

'I hope he can recover. He'll be much better off here.'

'We'll do our best.'

It was a busy night for Dr Strauss. Later on he was called to the Kleinschmidt house, where Rolf, the manager of the sawmill, had been taken ill.

He was lying on the bed, in a great deal of pain.

'Have you had this before?' Strauss asked.

'Yes. It's only nerves. Only a bit worse this time.'

'Can you give him something for it?' Mrs Kleinschmidt asked nervously.

'We'll see.'

Eventually he dosed Rolf with laudanum and went out to speak with his wife.

'It's not nerves,' he said. 'More like appendicitis. He's probably had what we call a rumbling appendix for a long time. He's lucky he hasn't had trouble before this. I'll send the ambulance for him.'

'Why? What can you do?'

'We'll have to operate, Mrs Kleinschmidt.'

'Oh no! You can't do that. No!'

'Now sit down, my dear. Don't be upsetting yourself. I must operate, his appendix might burst and that is dangerous. He has to go to the hospital right away.'

The ladies of this establishment made up for its lamentable unsuitability as a hospital by their tender ministrations, and Friedrich was somewhat soothed by their attentions. He was resting now. They had washed and scrubbed him, even his fingernails. They'd cleaned his wounds, adding gentle salves, and before he could stop them, they had dabbed the cuts on his face with that fiery liniment, assuring him it was a first-rate germ-killer.

They had groaned again over his torn and bloodied cassock – 'Not worth mending, I'm afraid, Father' – but he didn't care. He was tired of it, fed up with it.

'Throw it away,' he said.

So now he felt normal again in a shirt and trousers. He sat up to try out his new persona, but the sticking plaster round his ribs pinched and tweaked so much he gave a yelp.

The matron came running. 'What is it, Father?'

'Do I have to wear this corset?'

She grinned. 'You'll feel a lot worse without it. Just be patient for a few days to give those ribs a chance to heal. You're looking much better now. How are you feeling?'

'Not too bad.' In fact he was feeling not bad at all. Time to get out of here.

'That's good. We have a patient in the end room, Father.

He's very ill. A stranger. Danish, I think. Would you say a few prayers with him before you go? I'm sure he would be comforted.'

Friedrich's clerical days were over, he hoped, but he remembered that he didn't have a bean, thanks to Keith Dixon, so he would have to hang on a bit longer.

'Very well,' he allowed with a return to solemnity. 'What is wrong with the poor fellow?'

She came close, took his arm, whispered in his ear. 'Cholera. But we don't want that to get out. People panic.'

'Oh yes, I see,' he said sadly. Panicking! How dare she send him into a disease-ridden room!

'Down here, Father,' she said, indicating a closed door. 'In there. It's very kind of you.'

Kind? Hell! But he had no choice. She shoved him into the room, where a bearded old fellow with hair like a birch broom lay muttering and babbling. He obviously had a raging fever. Friedrich could feel the heat right across the room, and equated that with the distance germs could travel.

The French windows were closed. They opened on to a veranda, and as he peered out he could see the stables on past some outhouses. Without a qualm or a glance at the patient, he got the hell out of there, shutting the French doors behind him.

He found Queenie. Climbed aboard with more pain than he'd expected, and that infuriated him.

Where to go now?

To the police, of course. Everyone at the hospital now knew he'd been mugged and robbed. Where else would a good priest go but to the police? He was carrying evidence of the attack. Indisputable. Rehearsing his complaint, Friedrich felt weak, the shock of the assault returning, but he battled on, head into the wind, making for the police station in Quay Street.

The Stennings were lying low. Jules had decided not to attend either of the rallies, for the sake of harmony, although his wife was disappointed.

'We can go to both. Keith's rally is at seven o'clock and

Les Jolly isn't putting in an appearance in Quay Street until eight.'

'That would still require explanations,' he said. 'Best to keep clear.'

'I'm not keeping clear,' Nora said. 'I'm going to Les Jolly's rally.'

'If he wanted you there, dear, he'd come and get you,' her mother said sweetly.

Jules frowned. 'You're not going anywhere, Nora. I know you're just using it as an excuse to chase after that German labourer.'

'I am not!' she cried, and ran out of the room.

'What the hell is that all about?' he asked, and Jayne glared at him.

'You never listen to me, Jules. You know Les Jolly is sweet on her.'

'Yes, and he'd make a much better match.'

'That's just it. Nora's in a very emotional state these days. I think she's ready to give up the German, but she's a very loyal girl. She doesn't want to hurt his feelings.'

'That's life.'

'She also doesn't want to appear to be choosing Les just because he's more affluent.'

'Rich, you mean. That's life too.'

They were interrupted by an urgent knocking on their door.

Jules was amazed to find a frantic woman on his doorstep. Florence Dixon!

'Good heavens, Florence. What's the matter?'

She pushed him aside and dashed through to Jayne, clutching at her. 'My dear. You have to help me . . . quickly. I need some of Dr Moreton's Mixture. You know, the white stuff.'

'Why? Have you got the . . .?'

'No, Keith has,' she whispered frantically. 'Give me the bottle. And some water.'

The two women rushed into the kitchen.

'Why did this have to happen now?' Florence wept. 'We had everything organised so beautifully.'

Nora was at the door. 'I think you're wasting your time,

Mrs Dixon. Les Jolly is streets ahead.'

She turned angrily. 'He is not, you silly girl. Folk don't run with Johnny-come-latelies, not in these parts. Never! He might have all the ladies dashing about, but *they* don't get to vote, remember?'

'Then why are you bothering with a rally?'

'Because it's expected, my dear. Because the squatter families come to town in a show of strength. And they bring their stockmen and managers and outriders, who spend. We let the shopkeepers know where their bread is buttered. Have you got that stuff, Jayne? I have to rush . . .'

Within minutes she had fled, the large blue bottle wrapped in a tea towel. Jules was bewildered. 'What was that all about? Did she run over here from the hall?'

'Yes.'

'Why?'

'Because Keith is unwell,' said his wife. 'He needed the white stuff . . .'

'Why? Has he got the trots?'

Jayne laughed. 'Don't be indelicate. Do you think she's right, Jules? That Keith will win?'

He nodded. 'I think so. We see Les Jolly about here all the time. He's popular, that's obvious. But it's easy to forget all those wealthy station people out there in the backblocks with all their troops, because we don't see them much. They're all about now . . . the town is packed. I can't see how Les can win.'

'I don't believe you!' Nora said.

He shrugged. 'I don't care one way or the other. Les might have our town's support, but this is a big electorate. Don't forget Maryborough, and the grip the squatters have got on that town.'

Just then they heard a knock at their open front door. Jayne dashed past them. 'It must be Florence Dixon again.'

But no. This time it was Les Jolly. 'I've come to escort Nora to the rally.'

'We're not attending!' Jules Stenning called out.

There was silence. Les stood awkwardly at the door, facing Mrs Stenning.

'It's a windy night,' he said, and she nodded.

'Are you coming, Nora?' he called. 'I mustn't be late.'

She took her shawl and settled it on her shoulders. 'Goodnight, Father.'

'He can't beat Keith!' Jules warned.

'I know,' she smiled. Now it might be easier to explain things to Walther. She was still fond of Walther, but there were too many adjustments to be made. And, she mused as she walked out of the house, I think I'm in love with Les. As much as I am in love with Walther. Trouble is, I've no real experience of love. How do I know about these things?

She had a sad smile for Les as she took his arm, knowing she was now embarking on the path to marriage. She remembered her grandmother saying: 'Marriage, my love. It can be a frolic or a fiasco. Hard to tell at the starting post.'

'And that's true,' Nora sighed.

'What is?' Les asked her.

'I don't know,' she said. 'Les, they're saying you can't win.'

'That's right,' he said, hugging her arm to him. 'Not a hope. But I'm making inroads, you know, like starting a track into the wilderness. Leaving it. Coming back to probe a bit further. Hard work, but bit by bit the country is opened up to more exploration, surveyors, settlers . . . That's what I'm doing. I'm staking a claim, Nora. I'm saying, "You lot won't have it all your way for ever. I'm breathing down your necks." '

'So this rally isn't real.'

'Real? It's dead serious, my love. And Dixon knows it. He'll probably get in this time, but I'll take him out next time.'

'Good heavens,' she said, and then she saw Walther walking towards them. Maybe he'd even been on his way to her house.

She called out to him, but he turned quickly and disappeared into the gloom of this damp night.

Walther was sorry that he'd turned away, snubbing them. He hadn't meant to do that: it had only been a reaction, a panic that he couldn't think what to say, in English. He'd known for some time that Les Jolly was interested in Nora. He'd even seen them together, although he made no comment to Nora

482

when she found time for him. It was best, he'd thought, to let their love affair run its course, and it had. They had both moved on to quieter waters, to a friendship that would last. He'd wanted to explain that to her, to make it plain to Les that he held no ill feelings towards him. Les was, in fact, better suited as a husband for Miss Stenning . . .

Max Lutze caught up with him. 'Look at all the people coming to hear Mr Jolly. That's a good sign, isn't it?'

'Maybe. But I think they've been to hear Mr Dixon first, so it's hard to tell.'

He saw Eva and the children ahead and hurried to join them, swooping to pick up little Inge and hoist her in the air.

'Who would like a bonbon?' he asked as they neared the store, and of course all three children would, so he produced pennies and sent them to make their own choice.

'You spoil them,' Eva said, and Walther laughed.

'Why not? They're such good children.' He looked to Mr Hackett. 'How are they getting along in school?'

'Very well, Mr Badke. I'm very pleased with them.'

They all drifted across the road to where Les had erected a platform under the big Moreton Bay fig tree, renewing acquaintances with other friends as the crowd assembled.

Soon Les Jolly was up there, gathering them all in closer to hear him. 'Ladies and gentlemen . . . This is a very important occasion . . .'

Walther was only half listening. He could hear children romping at the back of the crowd, and it occurred to him that he would love to have children of his own. What a joy that would be.

You have to find a wife first, he reminded himself. But there were few single girls in this community. Few that weren't already spoken for. He wondered if he ought to cast his mind back to his own village, to girlfriends back home. Life would be a lot less complicated if he could marry a German girl.

The more he thought about the idea, the better it seemed. He ought to do something about it right away.

There was Matti Gunthner for a start. He'd always been sweet on her . . . if she'd come here. That thought upset him.

Not only would a young lady have to be willing to travel to the other side of the world, her parents would have to approve.

More complications!

I can only try, he decided. Let my cousin Kurt know I'm seeking a wife. Perhaps he could escort some eligible young ladies when he sails. Walther had heard of Irish bride ships that came to Australia. What about a contingent of German ladies? After all, he wasn't the only one hoping to find a wife and raise a family. Some of Rolf's kin, logging out there in the bush, were doing well, but they complained at the shortage of girls. Come to think of it, where *was* Rolf? Mr Jolly was his boss. Surely he'd expect Rolf to turn out and support him?

When Keith's Master of Ceremonies deserted in a huff, Charlie Mayhew was prevailed upon to take his place, and after a long delay, Keith finally appeared. He looked very green about the gills, Charlie thought, and he suggested to J.B. that the rally be postponed, but the old man wouldn't hear of it.

'Dixons don't quit!' he said, glaring at his son.

'Are you sure you're all right?' Charlie asked, and Keith nodded.

'Yes. I'll be fine now. Mother has filled me up with some binding stuff that tastes like poisoned starch. Let's get it over with.'

And that was about all they did, Charlie mused, as he strode away after the event. He'd introduced Keith, making the expected flattering remarks, then Keith had made a lacklustre speech and the audience had clapped, and J.B. had jumped up on to the stage to deliver a rousing call to arms, ordering them all to stick together, to vote for their own people and so forth, and that had brought a great cheer.

Now Charlie was looking for Constable Colley. He'd passed by the big crowd listening to Les Jolly say his piece, raised his hat to some ladies, and kept an eye out for Colley.

Charlie had donated to both campaigns. Normally politics didn't interest him at all, but when he heard that the third candidate was an avowed teetotaller, he was spurred into action. His rum distillery would be first class. He didn't need financial assistance from the Dixons now, not since Jakob's friend Mr Hoepper had surprised them by taking an interest in their endeavours, and then investing.

What good fortune that was. What great good fortune!

The lamps were lit in the police station, so he hurried down there to catch Colley before he closed down for the night. Two of Charlie's Kanakas had run off and he had to report them missing within the required forty-eight hours, which were almost up.

'Where did they go?' Colley asked him.

'If I knew that I'd go and get them.'

'They've probably gone bush. That won't last long,' Colley grinned. 'They'll come creeping back starved. They're not Abos, they won't know where to find a feed.'

'I thought you'd have a posse search for them.'

'No point. They're not armed, are they?'

'No.'

'Then don't worry. They'll turn up.'

'Why the hell did I have to get here and register them as missing if you don't have to do anything about it?' Charlie growled, but Clem shrugged.

'I dunno. I don't make the rules. Who's this coming?'

He watched a horseman ride into the yard and dismount.

'It's the German priest, I think. What's his name? Ritter.'

Charlie nodded. 'That reminds me. You said Mrs Fechner was accused of stealing from Mrs Dixon. That surprised me. She seemed such a nice girl. What did she take? Money?'

'No.' Clem was more curious about the newcomer, who seemed to be having trouble hitching up his frisky horse. 'She took a hairbrush, or was it a hand mirror? Something like that. Valuable by the sound of things, covered in jewels.'

'A hand mirror? I gave her a hand mirror. It was prettily decorated. Is that what they're going on about?'

'I dunno. They dropped the whole thing.' He stepped over to the door. 'You all right, Father?'

'No I'm not. I've just come from the hospital. I need your assistance.'

Colley dashed out to help. 'Yes! Right! Of course! What's the trouble, Father?'

485

Friedrich appreciated the poetic justice in taking his complaint to the police. He had nothing left to lose, and outrage at the cowardly attack was guiding his moves now.

While he was in the hospital he'd heard all the talk about the big night in town, everyone excited about political rallies, but eventually he realised that only meant a few speeches. He decided, loftily, that these country bumpkins must be hard up for entertainment. At least that explained why there'd been people out in the streets. And later he heard the name again . . . Keith Dixon was out on the hustings, on this very night.

Beyond her raised eyebrows and her 'Oh Lord!' Matron hadn't asked any more about the assault. Obviously she didn't want to be involved.

Not that it mattered now. There was no chance of getting his money back, but what a wonderful opportunity to get back at Dixon. Legally. He almost laughed as he lurched forward to lean heavily on the constable and allow himself, the victim, to be helped up the steps into the police station.

Another fellow was there, plainly interested in this little drama, and that pleased Friedrich. He worked better with an audience, and besides, he wanted what he had to say heard by the whole town. Another ear meant another mouth to spread the word.

They sat him down on a bench . . . Friedrich knew those benches well. The world over, police stations never featured anything else. They were designed to intimidate, but on this wet and windy night, Friedrich didn't mind at all. He sat awkwardly, painfully, legs splayed, shoulders sprawled, like a frog with his throat cut, he thought, and thanked the policeman for his kindness. And he thanked the gentleman who had sprung forward to offer him assistance to the bench.

'I have been assaulted,' he announced. 'Beaten, robbed and assaulted. What sort of country is this that priests are not safe on your roads?' He groaned, bending almost double, giving them a fright by threatening to vomit, but he had their sympathy and their full attention as he delivered a blow-by-blow description of the attack. And his injuries.

And the name of the attacker: Keith Dixon, in company

with another fellow. A very large bearded bushman.

Troubled, the Constable took notes. He was really worried about the story, nagging Friedrich with endless questions, because, quite clearly, he would not accept that the perpetrator, or one of them, was the town darling, Keith Dixon. Neither would the other fellow, by name Charlie, who butted in with his own questions.

'It couldn't have been Keith,' Charlie said. 'He's been at the hall most of the day and he had the rally this evening. You must be mistaken, Father.'

'I am not!' Friedrich strung out the scene, batting the argument back and forth, pretending that he was becoming angry and frustrated trying to get his story believed . . . as if a priest would lie . . . and then he let fly. No need to pretend anger any more. After what Dixon had done to him, ruined his life, blind rage was a better description, providing the excuse a priest would need to crash through his vow of silence from sheer frustration, from a cry for justice . . .

'How dare you disbelieve me!' he shouted. 'How dare you make light of my injuries to protect a criminal! Is this fellow your friend? Am I to be cast aside, just another victim of this man's abuse?'

'No, Father, certainly not,' Charlie cried, trying to soothe him. 'But I doubt that it would be physically possible for Mr Dixon to have been out at Taylor's Road at the time you specify.'

'He's right,' the policeman called Clem offered. 'It has to have been someone who looked like Keith.'

'And who has the same name,' Friedrich raged, jumping to his feet. 'I can see what is happening here. You people don't care that this criminal set fire to Jakob Meissner's land. Burned his home and his belongings to the ground . . . Oh yes, you know about that, Mr Policeman, you know and you did nothing.'

'Is this true?' Charlie asked, shocked.

'Of course it's true. Look at him. Where is the law here?'

Colley was shaking. 'No, he's got it all wrong, Charlie. He's mixed up, poor fellow. Sit down, Father. Take it easy. I'll get you a cup of tea.'

Friedrich was almost speechless. Had Charlie not been there he would have attacked that patronising policeman, bashed him to death the way he'd bashed that unsuspecting, patronising priest, Ritter. They were refusing to believe him, treating him like an idiot because he was a priest, a naïve cleric who could be tricked, conned by these more worldly personages.

Well, he had an answer for them. Once and for all he threw off the priest role. He was Otto Haupt. He smiled meanly. The villain entering. No one trifled with Otto. Especially not these hillbilly bastards.

'So you don't believe me,' he sneered. 'I'm glad you're here, Charlie, whoever you are. That bastard knows Dixon burned the Meissner land deliberately, because Lucas Fechner was a witness. He came in here to prefer charges and that piece of cow dung, in Dixon's pay, wouldn't lift a finger.'

'Surely not,' Charlie said, looking to Colley, who had backed away behind his desk, shaking his head.

'It was a lie, wasn't it?' Charlie challenged. 'The hand mirror. Mrs Fechner didn't steal it. I gave it to her in the form of an apology. And they claimed she stole it. They used it as an excuse to sack her. Why, Clem? Is the rest of this true?'

Otto pushed forward, slamming a fist on the Constable's desk, putting a stop to their conversation. He wasn't interested in their talk. They had to listen to him! He was in charge here. He could see a revolver hanging lazily in a holster from a nail on the wall. He ought to reach for it. But Colley was closer. He mightn't make it. But anyway, he wasn't finished.

'You bastard,' he sneered at the policeman. 'You have a lot to answer for. It is a wonder the Lord doesn't strike you dead.' He realised he was getting his roles mixed up but he didn't care. A flash of lightning and a deafening clap of thunder added to the threatening ambience.

He turned to Charlie. 'If he had arrested Dixon for firing the Meissner lands, a worse crime might have been prevented.'

He had listened carefully to Hanni's story and he knew his rendition of the timing was out of plumb, but why should he care? His hatred of Keith Dixon was growing with every word of his narrative.

'He could have saved Hanni Fechner, Mrs Fechner, the

young lady you obviously know, from a fate worse than death.'
He spat that at them. 'Your friend and leading citizen raped
Mrs Fechner while she was in his clutches as a servant at his
home. You ought to be charged with collusion, Colley. Were
you in on it? Did you rape her too?'

'Surely not?' Charlie cried, but Otto pushed him aside.

'I have witnesses! Plenty of them. You tell me Dixon did
not attack me? I say he did. And robbed me too, with one of
his henchmen. Lucas Fechner knows the true story of the
Meissner fires, and so do many other people. Hanni Fechner
will point the finger of shame at that same criminal. I tell you
people, do not think you can flout God's laws any longer. And
you . . .' He pointed a long bony finger at Constable Colley.
'You are cursed to your dying day if you do not do your duty.
God's will be done!'

With that, Otto Haupt flung out of the door, off stage, in a
most dramatic exit. But something else was driving him now.
He had lost interest in the two men left behind to gape at his
fury, to begin the recriminations.

'You knew all about this and you did nothing!' Charlie
shouted, his ears still ringing from Otto's screamed accusations.

'No! No! I didn't. Not all of it anyway.'

'And what about the hand mirror I gave her? I told you she
didn't steal it. Was that part of your cover-up for your mates?
I tell you, Colley, you're in real bloody trouble here if you
don't get moving.'

'I didn't know! Fechner came here with the cock-and-bull
story about seeing Keith set fire to Meissner's place. I mean,
Keith wouldn't do that. Why would he?'

'You didn't enquire? You didn't investigate? Jesus, you're
an idiot, Colley. I could have told you why . . .'

They were busy arguing, so shocked by the accusations of
rape, by the force of the priest's charges, that they failed to
notice that the wind was growing stronger by the minute, not
until the storm hit. They grabbed at the walls for support
when the first blast of wind battered the police station,
followed by another crack of thunder.

By that time, the tornado was upon them, tearing strips of

489

corrugated iron from the roof and threatening to wreck the building. The noise, the violence of the powerful wind screaming round them sent Colley under the desk, shaking in fright, convinced the curses of that foreign priest would be the death of him.

Chapter Eighteen

The weather was certainly damp and windy, maybe even building into a storm, but at this time of year storms were so frequent no one took much notice. People were still milling about the clearing by the river where Jolly's campaign assembly had taken place, talking, catching up on gossip.

'Where's Hanni?' Walther asked.

'She went home,' Eva said, and they both looked over to Lucas, who was standing with a group of people engaged in further debate with Les Jolly.

'I was hoping she would be here. We might have been able to get them together,' Walther said, but Eva shook her head.

'No hope of that, Lucas is too stubborn.'

'You can't just blame Lucas,' Walther said. 'There are faults on both sides.'

Eva reacted angrily. 'What would you know? You men love to blame us, don't you? You're all so damned holy!'

'Now, now,' Mr Hackett said. 'Gently does it, Eva.'

'You too?' she stormed. 'None of you give a damn about poor Hanni.'

Walther disagreed. 'You're being unfair, Eva. Of course we care about Hanni, but we really can't interfere, can we?'

Mr Hackett looked at him strangely. 'You know, Mr Badke, that may not be the correct course to take. I am not sure that we should all sit on our hands for fear of interfering in other people's business. Would you excuse me?'

With that, he strode away across the slippery grass, making for Les Jolly, it seemed, but instead tapping Lucas Fechner on the shoulder.

'Mr Fechner. Could I have a word with you?'

Lucas nodded, and turned. 'Yes, Mr Hackett? What is it?'

'It's your wife, Mr Fechner.'

'Oh yes?'

'It is your duty to care for her.'

Lucas stiffened. 'I tried to do that, but she let me down. And anyway, I don't think it's any of your business!'

'Do you not? That's too bad, because I consider you have failed in your duty to your wife. While she was under your protection you allowed your employer to beat and rape her—'

'I *what*?' Lucas shouted.

'You ought to be ashamed of yourself, Mr Fechner. Your wife has suffered shockingly and you reject her. Have you no pity, or are you too wrapped up in your own—'

But by then Lucas had gone, running over to Quay Street, jumping over the small fence that bordered the area set aside for a park, dashing across the road. But no one had time to contemplate this, because the first blasts of wind were sweeping over the town. A tree snapped and crashed to the ground. The campaign platform blew away like a matchbox. Then they were all running, fleeing across the road to take shelter where they could find it, in shops, hotels, cottages, as the wind roared about them.

Lucas battled on, head down, trying to avoid flying tree branches, keeping close to buildings where possible, racing across vacant blocks. He was only too aware of the danger, but he couldn't turn back. He had to see Hanni.

Was it true? That sickening stuff Hackett had said? Who had raped Hanni? Lucas knew he didn't have to ask that question. He knew. He could see the leer on Dixon's face now. And this time he read more into it. Was Hackett right? Was Lucas himself to blame?

Lucas was sobbing when he reached the door of the cottage. The front fence was flattened, and two palm trees, snapped in half, flailed about in the wind. He hammered on the door and burst into the small sitting room, shouting for her, feeling about in the darkness, falling over furniture, until he heard her call.

'Who is it? Is that you, Lucas?'

She was huddled in a corner, terrified.

So was Lucas. He was terrified that she would never forgive him.

He huddled in the darkness with her, holding her to him, waiting out the storm.

After the rally, the ladies cleaned up the hall while Keith and J.B. held a meeting of their cronies to plan the much more important functions to be held in Maryborough over the next week.

'They should all go well,' J.B. said, 'if we can keep my son out of the dunny.'

'Very amusing,' said Keith, taking the ribbing about that misfortune very well, which surprised them. The other four men at the bare table were J.B.'s vintage, all of them wealthy squatters determined to protect their huge sheep stations against the inroads of cheap settlers. These men couldn't understand why they were being forced to cut down the size of their holdings, which would mean cutting down on the number of sheep they could carry, for surely everyone knew that Australia rode to wealth on the sheep's back. Their wool clip was gold. When the first bale of Australian merino wool had gone on sale in London, in all its purity and perfection, there was a riot. Chaos. Woolclassers, buyers had gone berserk trying to pin down the sellers, turning their backs on other offerings, and crowds had pressed forward to witness this exciting event.

J.B. and his friends had a point. They had kept up the standard. Their wool was still a thing of beauty. Even better, for they'd nursed their precious stud rams like babies. Their sheep were walking bales of perfect wool. And the money rolled in. And the country prospered. But it prospered so well that the settlers came. And the farmers to feed them. Leading to the demise of these big properties too close to the coast.

But they could still wield the whip for a while yet. Members of Parliament, judges, high-ranking public servants, police commissioners still needed them. Most of these gentlemen came from squatter families, and now it was even more important for the families to stick together. None of them was impressed by Keith, whom they'd known since his birth, but none of them would criticise him. It was immaterial to them that Keith Dixon could be a dolt at times; they didn't need a genius in their Parliament, just a fellow who would look the part and who would vote as he was told.

As J.B. told him to vote, they meant, their angular, weatherbeaten countenances impassive, calculating.

Henderson, boss of a far west station, was disappointed that his son John was still in Europe working on an emigration program for the government. He'd have run rings around Keith Dixon, but he wouldn't be home in time, so they were stuck with J.B.'s lad.

And like the others, he was surprised at how Keith, who was known to be a humourless brat, was taking the teasing over his attack of the trots. Not like him at all. The bugger was a sulker of the first order, Henderson mused, but there you go.

'Wonders will never cease,' he said.

'What wonders?' J.B. asked.

'That bloody weather out there,' Henderson drawled. 'I can smell a nasty storm. I gotta fetch my missus and get going.'

Soon they were all heading for the door, pulling on wide-brimmed leather hats and oilskin coats. There was a buggy outside, the driver impatiently whistling to the Hendersons to get a move on.

Keith helped Mrs Henderson into her coat; it seemed to drown her, reaching the floor, and she laughed.

'When will they make these things for ladies?'

The others took off, sprinting away, husbands assisting ladies down the path.

'Close up the hall,' his mother called to Keith as they fled, so he slammed the front door and pushed the bolt. The ladies had already shut all the windows.

He strode across the deserted hall, taking time to appreciate the superb timber flooring, donated by his dad, and headed for the back door behind the stage. Keith was in a happy mood. Admittedly, he'd been embarrassed by the trots earlier on, but that could happen to anyone. It had been a shocking attack. The worst he'd ever had. The pain had been excruciating. But do you think J.B. cared? He'd come down and banged on the door, telling him to get the hell on his feet.

The bastard. Jesus! When he kicks the bucket things will be different.

But then, when that liquid concrete his mother shoved down his neck had begun to work, there'd been the good news. The lads had come to tell him they'd found the crooked priest and given him a working-over. 'And here you are, boss. Your money back.'

Safe and sound in his pocket. The notes that bastard priest had blackmailed out of him. How did that idiot think he could rob Keith Dixon and get away with it? There was one born every day.

This hall boasted stables. Rare. The land had once been occupied by brickworks, a failed enterprise, but the owners had allowed themselves excellent brick stables which were now the pride of the Progress Association, proprietor of the hall.

Keith slammed the back door shut and ran for the stables. The other horses had gone and his own mount was upset, spooked.

'Steady on, old dear,' he said as it pranced and plunged in its stall. 'Did you think I'd left you? Never let it be said that I'd leave you. Now settle down. There's a bit of wind and a bit of rain and we're headed for the pub. I'm sick to death of those bloody old fogies thinking they're going to be telling me what to do when I get into Parliament. I need a couple of whiskies to cheer me up.'

He slipped the bridle and the saddle on to his horse, took his hat and sheepskin jacket from a nearby hook, and swung into the saddle.

He walked the horse down to the exit and urged it at the archway that led to a paddock, just as the massive wind barrelled into the town. The horse reared but Keith held his seat, trying to turn the animal back to shelter. Then he realised that a man had grabbed the reins and was pulling the horse outside.

'Get out of the way, you bloody idiot,' he shouted, thinking this fool was trying to help, but when he looked down he saw it was that preacher again. The crook.

The horse was prancing about, frightened by the noise of the storm and the antics of the stranger, and since they were now out in the teeming rain, Keith was afraid the animal would slip.

The preacher was yelling at him, abusing him, trying to drag him down from the saddle, so Keith lashed out, kicking him until he could bring the horse around to help him fight off the attacker.

It was the preacher who slipped in the mud, and Keith, furious, put the horse at him, laughing as the fool scrambled frantically to escape the hoofs. In control now, Keith made a game of it. He allowed the preacher to get to his feet and run away, making little headway in the wind, then he ran him down, kicking him in the head as he went past.

Keith wheeled the horse to make another run at the preacher, who was up again, stumbling away, but then he saw tree branches flying and heard the crash of glass as something smashed into the side of the hall.

'What the hell . . .?'

He raced the horse back into the stables as soon as he realised this was no everyday storm. He wouldn't be venturing out in that weather; the preacher could have it.

And he was still out there, screaming abuse, shouting like a madman, a stark figure, spotlit every so often by lightning.

Keith hoped flying debris would cut him down, that the strong wind would flatten him, but he seemed to have a charmed life. He decided to ignore him for the time being, but fragments of the abuse came through to him, and when he heard Ritter shouting about the police, he had to react.

'Police!' he yelled. 'You won't do that. I'll have you for blackmail. I'll have you locked up!'

But Ritter wouldn't stop. It was hard to make out what he was raving about with all the racket out there, but he did keep on about the police, and that frightened Keith. What if he did go to Colley? However he had found out, the bastard knew plenty. A preacher backing up Fechner's claims could cause a lot of trouble. A bloody lot. And that bastard knew it. He was out there taunting him. This time he wasn't after money. Keith wished he'd left the clown alone now. Let him keep the cash. Now there was no shutting him up.

Keith was grateful for this storm. No one around to hear Ritter. He shivered as if someone had walked over his grave. If anyone heard half of what the preacher was shouting . . . about the fire, about Hanni Fechner . . . he'd be ruined. He could deny it, but it would trigger questions, and talk, and you wouldn't want that damned Les Jolly to get wind of any of it.

The storm had passed. The blacks called these things willy-willys, and this one had been the daddy of them all. A small tornado, he supposed, tearing across the land like some mad animal. Had it been daylight, they'd have seen it coming. He'd seen them before, massive funnels from sky to ground, coming out of blackened storm clouds as if sent like advance troops to attack and then vanish swiftly as they had appeared. He was relieved that it had struck this town, too far from Clonmel to have caused any damage back home.

Standing out there like a drenched scarecrow, Ritter shook his fist at him. He was finally giving up. Turning away. But was he going to the police?

By the sound of him, he'd be mad enough to do that.

Quietly, Keith took his rifle from the saddle holster.

Loaded it.

He had Ritter in his sights. The fool. Pushing into the wind. Arms wide, white shirt billowing. He lifted the rifle. It was an easy shot. Surprising himself, he fired. Before he could give himself a chance to think about this, his trigger finger had done the trick. He'd had to stop him! No choice. Too simple. He should have had the lads bump him off on Taylor's Road and be done with it.

Ritter fell. He went down like a sack of potatoes. Face down in the mud. Out there in the paddock. Everything was eerily quiet now. Not a peep out of Ritter. Keith grinned. Not so bloody smart now, are we?

Rain was still falling. Softly, mistily. Who needed maniacs like that around anyway? Religious maniacs. Crooks. Keith didn't go over to him. He had it in his head that footprints, or even hoofprints, near the body would be a dead giveaway.

Would lead the police to him. So he rode away, sticking to the track that ran past the hall and on out the gate.

Mr Drewett, the Harbour Master, was honorary caretaker of the hall, because he lived nearby. Over the back fence, to be exact. He'd heard the glass shatter and as soon as he could, in safety, he came out to investigate the damage.

His vegetable garden was ruined and the roof of his shed had flown, otherwise his property was intact, but not so the hall. He tramped around to the huge branch that had slammed into it, realising he'd need help to drag this away before they could repair the broken windows, and that was when he heard a shot. Or thought he did.

He looked about him. Not a soul in sight. Listened. Waiting in case there was another shot. Hardly a sound. He tramped round the back of the hall, noticing that the water tank was dislodged. Came out between the hall and the stables in time to see a man riding out the gate. Riding quietly away. Unconcerned. Obviously he hadn't heard a shot.

'The storm. Must have bunged up my eardrums,' Drewett muttered, turning away. But a movement over there in the paddock caught his eye, and he walked in that direction.

He was to tell the story many times. How Pastor Ritter died in his arms. Shot in the back.

'Funny thing, though. He kept calling me Otto. Must have thought I was someone else. But he died peaceful. As you'd expect of a priest. Wouldn't you?'

'Who was it riding out the gate?' Clem Colley asked him.
'Why, Keith Dixon, of course.'
'Why didn't you say so before?'
'I thought I did. You couldn't have been listening.'

Once out on the road, Keith breathed a sigh of relief. It was over. Done. Nothing to tie him to the body. They'd take ages to find it anyway. Everyone was too busy gaping at the aftermath of the storm. Coming out of their houses like little mice, sniffing the air, peering about, gathering in quaking groups to chew over events. He looked down on them from his lofty height as he rode past, experiencing a euphoria born of a tremendous sense of power. Almost glee. As if he were saying to the world: 'Don't mess with me. Do you know who I am?'

Other riders were out and about now, assessing the damage, and Keith rode with them, comfortable in that role, giving his opinions on what should be done to clear the streets and help the citizens. He felt as if he were already the Member of Parliament for the electorate of Maryborough, with this hamlet his home base.

They rode over to the wharf, where a coastal ship, *Fayette*, was berthed and fortunately had suffered no damage. These tornadoes being fickle characters, a nearby warehouse had been blasted apart and wreckage was strewn about the wharves.

'The river swallowed most of the wreckage, Mr Dixon,' a wharf labourer told him respectfully. 'And about forty bales of wool that were in there waiting for loading. They're probably washed downriver by now. Was anyone hurt?'

'Not as far as I know.'

He heard a voice shout at him: 'You lie!' And twisted about in shock. But there was no one.

The wharf labourer had picked up his long wheelbarrow and was continuing to collect debris. He looked up. 'Keep away from that ship, Mr Dixon,' he muttered with a sly wink. 'Cholera. They got cholera aboard, I hear say.'

Keith nodded. Who cared? He climbed down from his horse, feeling giddy. He needed that drink. Those whiskies. He walked the horse across to the stables behind O'Malley's pub, left it there and joined the throng of men congregating in the back bar, since, they told him, O'Malley's veranda was no more.

'The whole caboodle,' O'Malley laughed. 'It shot loose and went skywards, tossed up like a pram. If anyone finds me veranda in the morning, I'd appreciate its return.'

'It's probably in Brisbane by now,' someone laughed.

Keith downed a whisky, pushed through to the bar for another and saw his face in the mirror backing the shelves on the other side. But there were two faces. His and the preacher's.

He stood there, terrified, unable to tear his eyes away, waiting for that face to disappear, but it stayed. With his second drink Keith stayed too . . . within sight of that apparition. Curious. Disbelieving. Thinking their features were not unalike, though he was fair and the preacher had ugly carroty-brown hair. Thinking he was a mile better-looking than that scoundrel. Had to be.

The third drink had him worried. The ghost was still there. The drinkers talked of the storm, the damage, arguing as to its wind velocity. Reminiscing, boasting of worse storms encountered, and Keith was one of them and yet not, because of that thing over his shoulder, back there in the mirror.

Bells jangled. The ambulance again, clattering down the street.

'Someone musta got hurt. No surprise, that.'

'I nearly got killed meself. Tree missed me by inches.'

'You already told us that three times, Lofty.'

'Well, it's true . . .'

Two horses, running loose, added to the hazards the ambulance driver had to contend with as he raced the victim to the hospital, with Constable Colley sitting up beside him. He'd wanted to take the body straight to the mortuary, but Colley would have none of that.

'Hospital it is. I'm not taking the responsibility of declaring him dead. That's Strauss's job.'

'If he's here.'

'Sure to be. I'm betting there are a few broken bones around this night.'

Drewett, the witness, was following on Colley's horse, in company with Charlie Mayhew, who'd been appointed to bring him along.

Charlie and Clem had only just emerged from the precarious shelter of the small police station, which had threatened to overturn several times during the storm, and were standing shakily outside, glad to have survived without injuries.

'I thought it would go,' Charlie said. 'I couldn't decide whether we'd be better off inside or out.'

'It's only an oversized outhouse anyway,' Clem grumbled.

'Pity it didn't get wrecked. I might have been given a decent office.'

They walked over to examine a huge tree that had fallen across the mouth of Sandy Creek, and were still there when Billy, the black stockman, came looking for them.

'Hey, Clem. You'd better get over to the paddock by the hall. A bloke got shot.'

'Who says so?'

'Mr Drewett. I was riding past when he yells at me to come and fetch you.'

'In the paddock by the hall, you say? Right. I'll see to it. You go get the ambulance, Billy.'

'I'm coming too,' Charlie said. He wondered if that mad priest had taken the law into his own hands and shot Keith Dixon. He hadn't been carrying a gun, though. Hardly standard dress for a priest. Then again, guns were easy to come by in this town. But not with everything shut down, fending off the storm. No, it couldn't have been the priest. But after this, he decided, I'm not letting up on Clem. He can bloody well investigate those charges properly. Charlie knew it was only a minor matter, but for the Dixons to be blaming Mrs Fechner for the theft of a gift . . . his gift . . . was a fair indication that something was seriously wrong here.

At the hospital, Clem was in a panic, not knowing what to do first, so, true to form, he did nothing.

'You have to arrest Keith,' Charlie said.

'Not unless Strauss has seen the body and declared that bloke dead. We have to wait until he finishes the operation. Someone's got appendicitis, Matron said.'

'She would have told you that Ritter is stone dead, surely?'

'Yes, she did. But Strauss has to sign the death certificate and state exactly what he died of.'

'A bullet, Clem. He died of a bullet. Even I can tell you that.'

'But you ain't a doctor.'

The hospital was busy, as Clem had predicted. Sore heads, two cases of broken bones, a lad with burns, a baby screaming. The corridor was blocked with patients and their minders, and several overheard this conversation, ears pricked in excitement as the word went round . . . a murder in the town . . .

'God help us,' a woman moaned. 'What next?'

J.B. Dixon was relaxing with his mates on the balcony of the Royal Hotel, which had withstood the storm without any problems. Their conversation centred on storms and reminiscences of the real big ones, the cyclones they'd experienced, hurricanes that could wipe towns like this off the map.

'You and your hurricanes,' J.B. snapped. 'You're worse than bloody fishermen and their talk of the big ones that got away. I want to know who's going to chair the big public meeting in Maryborough, and if you can get the Mayor up on stage with us. I know he's on side, but it's time he stood up to be counted . . .'

He turned to find a barman standing in the doorway, beckoning to him.

'What is it?' he asked impatiently.

'One of your stockmen, downstairs, wants to see you, Mr Dixon.'

'Tell him to come round in the morning.'

'He says it's important.'

'Ah, Christ. All right. Send him up.'

'He won't come up. Says he has to see you. He's at the back door. A bit agitated, I'd say.'

Eventually Dixon tramped downstairs and on to the back door, ready to give this bloke an earful for disturbing him, but when he heard the news, he grabbed the door jamb in shock.

'He did what? Shot a man? A priest! Get out of here, you bloody fool! Are you drunk?'

'No, boss. It's the God's truth.'

'The hell it is. Where is he?'

'In the pub. O'Malley's pub, they say.'

'Who says?' J.B. bellowed. 'Where'd you get this bloody tale?'

'At the hospital, boss. I was there with Lenny. The lightning spooked his horse and he got thrown. Broke somethin' in his shoulder. But I heard all right. They got the body there. The body of the priest, and they reckon Keith shot him . . .'

While J.B. didn't believe this story, it was obvious that Keith had managed to get himself into some sort of trouble. He had to think quickly.

'Go down to O'Malley's and get him. Get a mate to help you if need be . . .'

'What if he won't come with us?'

'Belt him one. Bring him . . . No, don't bring him here. Take him over to the wharves. I'll meet you there. And listen. Try to get him out on the quiet. Tell him I have to see him urgent.'

'Righto, boss.'

J.B. went through to the bar, took time for a double whisky to calm his nerves, and walked outside, crossing over the road, making for the river.

There was a ship at anchor. *Fayette*. The gangplank was up and some of the passengers were on deck. He wondered if it were preparing to sail, since there was no shore traffic, but other matters pressed in on him. What the hell had that son of his got up to this time?

'If he blows this opportunity, this fast track to Parliament, I'll disown the bastard,' he muttered, standing by the ruins of a warehouse. He lit a cheroot, looking up to see that stars were emerging again, and felt better.

'A storm in a teacup, I bet. Shot a priest! Jesus! Les Jolly should be able to do better than lies like that.'

Walther was worried about Father Beitz, left at the commune on his own while they sheltered from the storm at Jim Pimbley's store. But Max reminded him that Pastor Ritter would have been home well before the wind hit, so that eased his mind.

When they emerged, quite a crowd, including Eva and her children, Max and Hans Lutze, Mr Hackett and a few others, they were dazed by the sudden quiet.

It seemed lighter outside after the dark store, where they'd dared not light a lamp, and Jim looked about with a grin.

'At least the town's still standing.'

'Your storeroom's not,' his wife called, and the men were soon working to move bags of sugar and flour and various

503

boxes of provisions to dry quarters on Mrs Pimbley's instructions. But eventually having done their duty, as Max said, it was time to go home.

'Where's Lucas?' Walther asked.

'Mr Hackett said he went to see Hanni,' Max said with a grin. 'I don't think we should disturb him. Let's just get on home.'

Billy was riding out on Taylor's Road well ahead of them. He had to see Father Beitz to tell him about this terrible murder. About the killing of the other holy man. A frightful crime! Everyone at the hospital was shocked. Clem Colley himself was all of a dither. And Billy didn't blame him. You'd have to think twice before you arrested a Dixon for shooting a priest. By God, you would.

Father Beitz was in the church when that wind descended upon it, battering the walls, stamping on the roof, bashing at the beautiful stained-glass windows, but the House of the Lord had stood fast. Yet he remained on his knees, calling to the Lord to forgive him for his failure to confront the evil that could yet destroy this church.

He could not recall how he had come to be in the church at an hour when he should have been abed, but placed no importance on that detail. He did remember, however, that he had seen Friedrich here, standing in the doorway, barring his exit. And the remembrance filled him with dread. Friedrich, his good and holy pastor, had frightened him beyond normal fear. His eyes had taken him for a blazing instant into horrors no man should ever have to see, and Father Beitz, in his terror, had clung fast to the altar rails, incapable even now of letting go. He felt as if his whole world would collapse if he did so, but was wholly unable to define the collapse of his world. He saw himself as a novice, an ignoramus, a bungler with no real knowledge of anything, no actual association with proven saintliness or proven evil. Until now. When he had seen evil. His hands would not release their grip on the polished cedar altar rails, and so there he stayed.

'*Mea culpa*,' he cried to the Lord.

It was an odd thing to see a dog wander into a church, but Father Beitz was comforted. He'd always cherished his love of the Lord, but at times he missed human love which, as an orphan and a bachelor, had been denied him. Yet he did love animals. Oh, how he loved them. All God's creatures. Another reason why this commune had become so precious to him. The wondrously tame animals and birds and reptiles here had brought him to his very own Eden. A joy that he had never anticipated.

Now here was the dog, a dingo he thought was its proper name, padding up to sit by him. Such a beautiful animal, with gleaming fur and the softest brown eyes. He reached out to stroke its head and fondle its ears, and the dog, the dingo, rested by him, its head placed humbly on its paws.

Then he realised that he had patted the dog. He had stroked its fur. His hands had freed themselves. He was free. But of what? That dread remained, and he was afraid to leave the church until he heard someone calling him, someone out there in the darkness, where evil still lurked.

All along the road Billy saw signs of the big wind's progress, so it was no surprise to see it had cut a swath through The Scrubs, taking with it the Father's dwelling houses. The stone cooking pit was still standing, but bits of the frail huts were scattered about like straw, and with them, personal belongings. It was a sad sight, he thought, picking up soggy coats and shirts, but he'd better find Father Beitz. He could be hurt, lying somewhere in desperate need.

When he called out to him, it wasn't Father Beitz who came along the track, but Tibbaling.

'He is in the church,' the elder said.

'Oh good. I'll go and get him.'

'No. I want you to call him again.'

Billy did so, and they waited. 'Why can't I go and get him?' he asked.

'Because he has to face the demons.'

'I can't see any demons.'

* * *

The priest heard the second call.

'I can't stay here for ever,' he said to the dog, but the dog had vanished, and that made him even more fearful.

Nevertheless he stood, and as he walked away from the altar the building shook and he heard a scream of rage, a frightful scream that seemed to envelop the church. All around him the walls resounded with noise, as if someone were battering, pounding at them in a fury, but he walked resolutely on. Fire lit the darkness, flames threatened, daring him to walk into the furnace but the old man blessed himself, took a deep breath and plunged out of the door, past the furies, his cross held high.

Then there was only quiet, and a dark sky alight with stars. He looked back at the little church, safe in its grotto of trees, and blessed himself again.

'Glory be to God.'

Tibbaling was walking towards him, and he hurried over. 'I have a question for you. Do you believe in evil?'

'Who does not?' Tibbaling responded.

'Ah.'

'Evil is abroad this night,' Tibbaling added. 'Your man is dead, but his stench lingers.'

'What man?'

'Two-Men-Walking.'

Father Beitz leaned against a tree to steady himself. 'I don't believe he was a priest.'

Tibbaling nodded. 'The priest Ritter is dead too. He never came here, Father. Never.'

'Then who was this fellow?'

'I do not know.'

The priest clapped his hands to his face as if he'd suddenly come from a trance. 'What is this? What am I saying? Friedrich is dead? God Almighty! What happened to him? Was it the storm?'

'A gun, Father. Feller shot him quick dead. Too fast see. He still roaming about. You heard him there.'

'Where?'

'Back at your church. He the evil, Father.'

'What? What is this? No. This can't be.'

506

He ran up the path to the huts and for a few minutes thought he had lost his way, taken the wrong track, but there was no mistake. Here was the clearing, the bamboo trees and the cooking pit, Walther's stove, but no huts. He was still standing there, shocked, when Max Lutze appeared, with his brother and Walther trailing behind.

Their first thought was for him, but he assured them he was fine; he'd taken refuge in the church, which hadn't suffered any damage as far as he could recall.

'A miracle,' Walther said. Looking at their own dismal surrounds. 'Looks like we sleep in the church tonight, if that's all right with you, Father?'

The priest appeared distracted. 'Are you well? You're sure you're not hurt?'

'Yes, I'm sure. I'm sorry, Father, but we have some very bad news. Pastor Ritter is dead.'

'Where did you hear this?'

'From me.' Billy had joined them. 'He's dead all right. Shot in the back.'

'Who shot him? Why would anyone want to shoot Pastor Ritter?' The priest seemed, strangely, more interested than concerned.

'I don't know why, but they're saying Keith Dixon did it.'

'Dixon? No. That can't be right. Dixon didn't even know him.'

They were all bombarding Billy with questions until Father Beitz intervened. 'I have to go in to town and see about this. Will you take me, Walther?'

'We'll all go,' Max said.

'I would prefer not, Max. You lads stay here with Billy. You can shelter in the church.'

The priest had been quiet all the way into town, and Walther didn't disturb his thoughts. He understood what a shock it must be for Father Beitz to have Friedrich shot down like that . . . shot down by a madman, for what else could you call that Dixon fellow?

He drove the wagon through the dark streets and turned to go

507

on down to the hospital, but Father Beitz tapped him on the arm.

'First to the wharves, Walther, if you please.'

'But they'll have the body at the hospital, or the morgue, which is in a nearby lane.'

'The wharves,' Father Beitz said firmly, so Walther turned the horse towards Quay Street.

'Stay here,' the priest instructed, as he climbed down from the wagon and began walking towards the river and the Immigration Barracks. Walther thought that the old man, sorrowing, must be indulging in nostalgia, this being their first home in Bundaberg.

But Father Beitz went a little way past the barracks and stood in the shadows for a while, waiting. A warehouse had been blown down by the storm so he had a clear view of the wharves, and the lights of a ship. He could see a tall man pacing along the river bank and make out a few people in the camping ground further down, but otherwise the area seemed deserted.

Whatever Keith had got up to, his father worried, it had to be bad this time for rumours of murder to be voiced about. He stared at the ship. Might it not be a good idea to sneak the fool out of town until he had a chance to discover what this was all about?

He walked out to the end of the wharf and whistled to an officer on watch.

'When do you sail?' he called, not interested in where the ship was bound at this point.

'On the early tide, sir.'

'I have a passenger for you.'

'We're not taking on passengers.'

'I'll make it worth your while,' J.B. said quietly.

He saw the man hesitate, and added: 'Handsomely,'

The officer leaned over the rail. 'What's handsome?'

'Fifty quid.'

The officer caught his breath. 'You the passenger?'

'No. My son.'

'Bring him here within half an hour. No later. I go off duty then.'

That done, J.B. felt better. Get him out of the way, then talk. He lit another cheroot and marched off the wharf to wait for his son.

When Keith did come, he was in an arrogant mood. And on horseback. He didn't bother to ride down to the entrance to the area, which wasn't even graced with a gate; instead, he took his horse over the low fence and trotted over to where his father was standing.

'You wanted to see me? What's up? Why are you lurking over here?'

'Because I want to know what's going on.'

'Nothing's going on. Is that all? I was playing cards. Is that a crime?'

'I heard the Lutheran priest, Ritter, got shot.'

'Yeah. Someone plugged him. So what?'

'They're saying it was you. Now get off that bloody horse and talk to me. Who did shoot the priest then?'

Keith dismounted, reluctantly. 'How do I know?'

'You've been in the pub. You must have heard something.'

'Ah . . . there's a lot of whispering but I don't take any notice. It's nothing to do with me.'

'There's a lot of whispering about who shot the man and you're not interested? Bloody nonsense! Why then is all the talk in the hospital that you shot him? Clem Colley's there. If he's in on that talk he'll be looking for you. If only to ask what you know. There has to be a tie-up somewhere.'

'Why? I didn't even know the bugger.'

'Wait a minute,' J.B. said. 'Didn't I see you talking to a priest at the hall the other day? I'm sure I did. Over by the fence.'

'I reckon you've had one too many. I don't know any bloody priest, I tell you. As a matter of fact,' he said, looking up at the calm, now cloudless skies, 'I might ride on home now.'

'Why would you want to do that?' J.B. said suspiciously.

'Why not? It'll be a long, hot ride tomorrow. They're saying the temperature will be in the hundreds again with that storm clearing the air.'

His father ground the cheroot under his boot. 'You listen to their talk of the weather but not of a murder? Don't give me

509

that. I'm betting that if you leave town Clem will have a posse after you in minutes. Don't kid yourself that he wouldn't be expecting you to do that.'

'I can outride them.'

'But why would you want to, Keith? Why would you want to? You have to tell me what happened. I'm trying to help you. Can't you understand that?'

Keith sulked: 'You're not trying to help me. You don't care about me. You just wait until I get into Parliament. I'll have the whip hand then. You won't be the big boss, you'll join the has-beens, the dodderers, you and your mates . . .'

J.B. was taken aback. 'For Christ's sake. What the hell are you on about? The slightest breath of scandal and you'll never make it to Parliament! That's why I think it's best if you lie low for a while . . .'

'You said if I try to go home they'll have a posse after me. Make up your mind. I haven't got anything to worry about anyway.'

J.B. wasn't so sure. 'Good. But to take the heat off, I've got you on this ship. Take a trip. Hop on board and leave the talking to me. I'll fob Clem Colley off until the morning, by which time she'll have sailed.'

Keith turned on him in such a rage, his father had to grab on to a post to keep himself from falling.

'You bastard! You want to get me out of the way all right,' he screamed. 'That's just the bloody devious way you'd go about it. You want to see me dead. Put me on that ship, would you?'

He grabbed his rifle, fumbling to load it as his father, shocked, cried out to him: 'Keith! What are you doing? The gun! You don't need a gun . . .'

'You wouldn't board the thing yourself, would you?' Keith snarled. 'Oh no, shove me on there. Let me get cholera. That's a bloody death ship and you know it.'

He raised the rifle and aimed it at his father.

Father Beitz saw Keith ride over to the wharf and heard the raised voices. Just then Charlie Mayhew walked over to join him.

'Father and son having a real barney,' he commented, wondering at the same time what the old bloke was doing just standing there in the dark.

'I'm sorry about Father Ritter,' he added. 'Bad show that. A witness said he saw Keith Dixon, the young bloke over there, riding away from the scene of the crime, and it seems he may have been the shooter. Although the witness says that before he died the priest said the name "Otto" several times. Would you know anyone called Otto, Father? We thought *he* might have been the murderer.'

A murderer, the priest thought. Possibly a murderer, but not this time.

He was still shaky. Tibbaling was right. The stench of evil was still about. Until this minute he couldn't have said why he was there, by the river, he just was; and when the voices grew louder and the young man started to scream at his father, the priest ran. He covered the ground so swiftly, both men were taken aback when he suddenly appeared.

'Put the gun down,' he ordered, stepping forward to stand beside Mr Dixon.

'He's gone mad,' the terrified man muttered, too shocked to move.

'You're the one that's mad,' Keith screamed. 'I'll get you, Mr Moneybags. You think you run the world but you don't. I won't let you. I can do what I like, can't I, priest? I know all the secrets round here, the fires, the rape, I know them all. We get told plenty, don't we, priest?'

Father Beitz stood very straight. 'Put the gun down, Otto. Put it down!'

Keith gaped. He looked from the priest to his father in bewilderment, and slowly lowered the rifle, but then his hands tightened, the gun came up again jerkily, as if it had a mind of its own, and he fired.

The priest had been watching his eyes; he knew this young man would never shoot his father, and he was ready for Otto's cunning. He pushed Mr Dixon aside, but he hadn't reckoned on the size or the strength of the country man, so he had to push harder, and in those seconds he couldn't get himself out of the firing line quickly enough.

As he went down he made a feeble sign of the Cross at his attacker, and Keith fell on his knees beside him, weeping.

'I'm so sorry. I never meant to do this. I wouldn't have . . .' He looked up at his father, pleading. 'I'm so sorry, J.B. It was an accident. It was an accident . . .'

Charlie Mayhew came running.

'Get the ambulance!' J.B. shouted at him as he shoved his son away, dragging a handkerchief from his pocket to try to stem the bleeding from the priest's shoulder. 'You can shoot me now if you want to,' he snarled at Keith. 'I'm still unarmed. Have a go, you bloody coward!'

'No,' Father Beitz cried. 'Not you – me! He was trying to shoot me. It was Otto!'

Keith flung the gun away and sat dazed, a few yards away from his father and the priest, and that was where Constable Colley found him and arrested him on suspicion of murder.

'That'll do for the minute,' he said to Charlie Mayhew.

Weak and wearied, the mortician struggled out yet again, complaining bitterly of the unlit streets and threatening to withdraw his services of nights if streetlamps were not provided. Nevertheless, he had become an excellent source of information for the reporter from the *Bundaberg Guardian*, who rushed into the street and chased him across town, alerted by the jangling bells.

'What now?' he shouted as the patient was being handed over to Matron, who asked the same question.

'A priest. Keith Dixon shot another priest!'

'Lord-a-mercy!'

'Is he still alive?' the reporter asked.

'Yes. Give me a hand here.'

Together they carried the victim in to Dr Strauss.

'I reckon,' the mortician said, 'Keith Dixon's got a religious bee in his bonnet to be running around shooting priests.'

The newsman nodded. 'Could be. He was acting strange at the rally this afternoon. The politicking might have been too much for him. He never was all that bright.'

'Then why is your paper supporting him for high office?'

'Was, my friend. Was. I've got to find Clem Colley. If

he'd arrested Dixon earlier we wouldn't have had a second shooting.'

The mortician peered over his spectacles. 'Colley was playing the same game as you, mate, supporting the Dixons. Backing the strength. Charlie Mayhew told him to get on with it, but no, Colley hung back, saying there were no actual witnesses. So you both came a thud.'

A door flew open and J.B. Dixon barged through.

'Did you get Father Beitz here in one piece?' he asked the mortician.

'Yes. They've got him in the operating room now. Dr Strauss was still here, luckily.'

'We have to get a proper ambulance,' J.B. said 'You can't be running sick people about in that hearse thing—'

The reporter intervened. 'Can I ask you, Mr Dixon, has your son got some sort of antipathy towards the clergy? I mean, in light of events—'

'Get out of here!' J.B. thundered, and both men made themselves scarce as Matron came out.

'Who's making all this noise? Mr Dixon! You should know better.'

'I'm sorry. I am worried about Father Beitz. How is he?'

'He'll survive. Shot in the shoulder. Dr Strauss is attending him. It will take time.'

'Good. Now, Matron, I want him to have the best. Spare no expense. Will you see to that?'

She shrugged. 'Expense doesn't help when we're short of beds. He'll have to sleep in the operating theatre tonight.'

Walther rushed into the hospital, hard on the heels of Mr Dixon. He was shattered, hardly able to believe that he had allowed such a thing to happen to Father. He'd waited patiently by the wagon for the priest to complete his meditations, thinking, as it happened, not about Father Beitz but of their wrecked huts. This was a terrible blow. They'd have to set aside the work on the brewery and rebuild and refurnish their accommodation, since even their basics of bedding and mats would be ruined by the rain. He thought he should have had more sympathy for the Meissners when they were burned out,

513

now that he found himself, along with the others, in the same position. With nothing.

Then again, he wondered if they should bother to rebuild at all. The huts were so frail they couldn't withstand storms like this, storms that Jim had said could be much worse. After all, there wasn't much structural damage in the town as far as he could make out, only extensions like verandas and outhouses failing to resist, and a lot of trees. What hope would their huts have in a worse storm?

None.

He would have to talk to Father Beitz and the other lads. They had to build more solid homes this time, but with what? All of his finances were invested in a brewery that he hoped would, in the long term, ably support a base for Father Beitz and the Lutheran community, which meant he didn't have a penny to spare. Nor did Max and Hans, and certainly not poor Lucas, who was now out of work. Sacked by his best friend.

That's something to be proud of, he sighed.

On the other hand, he could give up this dream of a brewery, a Badke brewery, sell the land and plunge every penny he could muster into building a decent communal settlement, housing that was structurally sound, so that they didn't have to go through this again. They couldn't afford to keep rebuilding and replenishing their few possessions.

He nodded, watching a half-dozen wallabies hopping across the clearing towards the trees, and then he saw a horseman come down the road, casually jump the fence and ride over towards the wharf, where there was a ship in port.

He heard raised voices in the distance, angry voices that could have nothing to do with Father Beitz; probably sailors involved in some disagreement.

Walther did not see Charlie Mayhew come across the road behind him and go towards the Immigration Barracks, but even had he done so, he would not have thought it amiss. This area between Quay Street and the wharves could almost be spoken of as a public park. There should be naught strange about a man going over to the wharves.

That was what he told himself later, but it didn't help. He

felt he should have known there was trouble; he should have taken Father Beitz out of there when he first heard the raised voices. It could have been leading to a drunken brawl at the wharves . . . except that it had led to far worse.

He heard the shot. At first he thought someone was shooting at the wallabies, but alarm bells rang when he equated it with the row in progress over near the ship.

He leapt out of the wagon and ran to get Father Beitz and take him out of the danger area, but he wasn't anywhere near the Immigration Barracks where Walther had expected him to be. He ran round it, all the way round, searching. Looked inside, but it was in total darkness. No one in residence.

Then a man ran past him, towards the road. Walther grabbed him. 'What . . .?'

'He shot Father Beitz,' Charlie Mayhew gulped. 'I have to get the ambulance.'

'The what?' Walther asked, unfamiliar with that word, but he didn't wait to find out. He ran towards the wharf. Lamps were beginning to light up the ship. People were moving out on to the decks. Voices calling, questioning. A loudspeaker boomed.

'No one leaves the ship. This is an order by law. The gangway stays up. No one leaves the ship.'

And then there was dear Father Beitz, lying stricken on the ground, shot, blood gushing, Mr Dixon trying to stay the blood and shouting God knows what.

The son. The famous one, who they'd been urged to vote against, was slumped in a heap nearby. Wasn't he the one who had shot Pastor Ritter? Hadn't Billy said that earlier? An age earlier.

Walther was confused. He dropped to his knees by Father Beitz, almost afraid to touch him when he saw the black stain on that cloth over the wound, and saw Mr Dixon's hands. Blood in this light was black. Father Beitz's blood. Dear God.

'He's living?' he asked, and Father himself breathed a yes.

'He saved my life,' the older Mr Dixon said, and Walther stared about him. Over there on the ship, people were watching from the rails, trying to make out this drama in the night light, but there was no one else about. Had Charlie Mayhew done this and run off? Charlie, friend and partner of Jakob Meissner. Surely not.

He turned towards the other man. 'You Keith Dixon?'

'I'm sorry, I didn't mean it,' Keith wept. 'Believe me, I didn't.'

Appalled, Walther climbed to his feet and walked over to this drivelling wretch, even more confused.

'You didn't mean to what?' he asked.

'He meant to shoot me,' Dixon senior said, and Walther looked from one to the other. Father and son.

He squatted beside Keith, who cringed. 'That's my horse over there. You can have it. Just give me a hand up. I'm a bit wobbly. I have to go. That ship behind us. I'm supposed to be on board. Give me a hand, mate. I have to go.'

Walther helped him to his feet. 'This was an accident?'

'Yes. I told you. My father's talking rot. I wouldn't shoot the silly old bugger. Christ, no! It has all been a terrible mistake. Charlie's gone for the ambulance. Everything will be all right. I have to go now. I have to board that ship.'

'Is it sailing?' Walther asked.

'Soon enough. Mister, that horse of mine is a Thoroughbred. Worth a heap. It's yours. Now let me go. Once I get on that ship they can't take me off.'

Walther stared at him, even more bewildered. Dixon kept asking to be let go, but no one had a hand on him. Certainly not Walther.

'Just a minute,' Walther said. 'Pastor Ritter is dead. Someone shot him. Do you know about that?'

'Father Ritter? Don't ask me about that bastard.'

'Who are you, calling a priest a bastard?'

'Listen, mate, if that bloke was a priest, I'm the Pope. He was a lowdown blackmailer. I don't know where you Germans get your ministers from, but you'd have to improve on the present crop.'

He was sure of his ground now, patronising Walther, who was still in a state of shock, a part of this tableau yet not a part of it. Walther's voice came out in a croak.

'Sir. Do you speak to me? You may not defile this good man.'

Keith laughed. 'Who's defiling? We've got an accident here, that's all.'

'An accident?' Walther shouted. 'An accident!' He grabbed Keith and lifted him into the air. 'So this too you can call an accident!'

He ran over to the bank and hurled him into the river.

But then the father was shouting: 'No! No! He can't swim. He's always been afraid of the water. Please, don't let him drown. Please!'

Walther was so incensed he would have left the brute to drown, but Father Beitz raised himself up to call to him: 'Save him, Walther. Never take a life.'

A sailor from the ship dived in too when he heard Keith's calls for help, and between them he and Walther brought him ashore.

The ambulance took Father Beitz to the hospital. The police came for Keith Dixon. Walther was too embarrassed to go to the hospital soaking wet, so he went to Eva Zimmerman's cottage for aid.

Lucas was there, all lovey-dovey with his wife, but Walther had no time for questions; he was the bearer of bad news about Father Beitz. The rest of the bad news, about the devastation of their huts, could wait until later. He just needed towels to dry himself down so he could look presentable at the hospital.

Eva tried. 'If you won't stay, your clothes will have to dry on you, Walther. Should I go instead?'

'No. I must go. I don't know how I let him get mixed up in a family fight. That's all it was. I'll come back later, if you don't mind.'

He walked in just as Matron was saying that Father Beitz would have to sleep in the operating theatre. By now Walther was tired and depressed. His home had been devastated and his best friend in the world was in there, wounded, shot.

'Might as well,' he said miserably. 'He hasn't got a home to go to. The storm took care of that.'

'Matron,' J.B. Dixon said. 'Do you think we could have a cup of tea for this gentleman? He's had a difficult night too.'

* * *

They discovered that Friedrich, if that were his name, had nothing that would actually identify him as Pastor Ritter or anyone else. No photographs. Father Beitz decided to write to the Dean of St John's Seminary and request a photograph or description so they could settle the matter.

'I will have to bury the poor fellow,' he told Hubert Hoepper, 'so I can't stay here. Could you please speak to the Matron? I am quite well really.'

She couldn't agree. 'He's an old man. He lost a lot of blood. See how pale he is, Mr Hoepper? The bullet did more tissue damage than usual because it was such close range, but he was lucky it went straight through . . .'

'No broken bones?'

'His collarbone is cracked and his shoulder is dislocated, which is causing him quite a bit of pain. I don't think I can release him. Besides, where will he go? The other gentleman said his house was demolished in the storm.'

'That's true. I was thinking of taking him to the hotel where I'm staying. He'll be most comfortable there.'

She smiled. 'I'm sure he will, but I want to keep him here one more day.'

Hubert agreed to the compromise and Father Beitz acquiesced. He seemed too tired to argue about that. However, he sent Hubert off to the mortician to arrange the burial in the little town cemetery for the following day, though he insisted that it was to be a private ceremony. No date or time to be issued, no notice in the newspaper, and Father Beitz himself would conduct the service.

Chapter Nineteen

During all this time, Rosie Kleinschmidt had her own troubles. With her baby in her arms, she'd sat up front as the strange ambulance raced her husband to the hospital. She'd waited in the hall for hours, refusing to move until Dr Strauss brought her some coffee and the good news that Rolf's operation was over and he was doing well.

'Can I see him?'

'Yes, they're bringing him out now, taking him down to the ward.'

Rosie was so relieved to see him, even though he still hadn't regained consciousness, that she hung on to him and wept until Matron prised her loose.

'You should take your baby and go home now, dear. There's nothing you can do. He has to sleep it off. He'll have to stay here for quite a few days so we can keep an eye on his wound. Why don't you come back tomorrow?'

She trudged home, fed the baby, and started to scrub the kitchen floor and then the stove; scrubbing she found was soothing, something to do when she was worried. She'd only just finished those chores when she realised the wind was gaining force, so she rushed about closing doors and windows.

But something told her this storm could get worse, so she wrapped the baby in a thick blanket and slid under the bed with her. While the winds raged and battered round her house, Rosie Kleinschmidt clung to her daughter and sang hymns, confident that the Lord would protect them.

In the morning she found her garden, with its homemade

picket fences, had been demolished, but the sturdy little cottage hadn't suffered any damage.

Ashamed that she'd been at the hospital the night before in her working dress, Rosie wore her Sunday best this time, and the new bonnet Rolf had bought for her at the Sunshine Store.

She walked to the hospital through the untidy streets, amazed that the storm could have caused such havoc, deposited the pram, picked up her baby daughter and marched inside, but everything seemed different in the light of day, and there was hardly anyone about. As she walked down the passage she thought she heard her husband's voice and opened a door, only to shut it quickly, embarrassed to have glimpsed a strange man.

'Don't go in there,' a nurse called harshly. 'Keep away from that room. Who are you looking for?'

'Mr Kleinschmidt,' she said shyly.

'Men's ward. Down the back. Don't be tiring him now.'

She was on her way home from the hospital with something nagging at her. Something she should have done. But she couldn't think what. Rolf was fine. Sore down in the belly, but fine. Saying he wouldn't have to eat bland food any more. That he no longer had a weak stomach. He was still rather groggy, though, and didn't even seem to have heard the storm, so she hadn't worried him with that subject, but the man in the next bed, the man with the broken leg, he never stopped talking. He knew everything that had happened on the previous night, terrible things that had no bearing on the storm.

'Both of your German priests shot! As true as I sit here.'

'No,' she breathed. 'No, that can't be!'

'It's true. The young one shot dead. The old one, he's right here in the hospital.'

'This cannot be so.'

'It is. The old priest, they had a bed for him in the operating room, but they moved someone out this morning and shifted him to a room down there. You go and have a look. He's there all right.'

'You hold the baby,' she said to Rolf, tucking their daughter in beside him. 'I'll be back in a minute.'

'Second door to the right,' the fellow said, so Rosie sneaked away. She was so sure that this was a lot of nonsense that she didn't dare ask any of the staff for fear they'd laugh at her. That man might be just teasing; they did that a lot in this town, always laughing, teasing people.

Then she couldn't recall whether the door was to the left or the right, and she came to one door, heard the German voice and was just about to open it when Matron stopped her.

'Your husband is in the male ward, Mrs Kleinschmidt.'

Guiltily, Rosie tried to explain. 'I was wondering. Is Father Beitz here? Is he in the hospital?'

'Yes, dear. He's in that room over there but he's sleeping. We've just settled him down.'

Rosie was shocked. 'It's true then. Someone shot him. Oh my God! What is happening?'

'Don't distress yourself. It is all over now.'

'But that man said Pastor Ritter is dead!'

'I'm afraid so, Mrs Kleinschmidt. You'll hear all about it soon enough. Is that your baby I can hear?'

They didn't encourage people to visit for long, so Rosie was on her way not long after that, pushing the pram up to the Royal Hotel to find Eva Zimmerman. She'd know what was going on.

Rosie had only just arrived at the kitchen door when it hit her.

Eva came to the door, pleased to see her, swooping to fuss over the baby, but Rosie gasped:

'I'm sorry, I can't stay. Can you mind the baby for a minute? I won't be long.'

'Yes . . .' Eva stepped outside and took hold of the pram, but before she could ask what this was about, Rosie was running across the back yard of the hotel and into the street.

Parties of men were cleaning up, large brooms and rakes pushing heavy foliage aside; others with saws were lopping off branches and piling them into heaps, but Rosie darted around them and hurried on down the road to the hospital.

Puffing, she found the matron. 'What is it this time, Mrs Kleinschmidt?' she sighed.

'The man in the other room. Not Father Beitz's room. Who is that?'

He's a stranger. Came off a ship. A Dane, it seems. A Danish fellow from the goldfields.'

'He's not a Dane. He's German,' Rosie said. 'I heard him.'

'That's good. Perhaps your husband can talk to him later. Find out who he is. He's not well.'

'But Matron, I know who he is, I think . . .' Suddenly she was uncertain. She hadn't actually recognised the man. How could she? His face was buried beneath a beard and long hair.

'Then let's see. We thought he had cholera, but Dr Strauss thinks not now, so we've just cleaned him up.' She laughed. 'Those miners let themselves go, forget what barbers and baths look like, so we don't spare them. He's proper shorn now. My ladies don't listen to their complaints, they get the scrub of their lives here.'

She opened the door, and Rosie found herself looking down at Theo Zimmerman.

'You wouldn't recognise him, now would you?' Matron said.

'But I do. Without the beard. His name is Theo Zimmerman, and his wife and children live right here in Bundaberg.'

'Good God. Would you kindly let his wife know?' Matron said quietly, ushering Rosie out the door. 'He's still very ill. I think we've stopped the vomiting but he's still got a fever and stomach pains, and he's half starved.'

She shook her head. 'People don't seem to realise how many of these fanatical goldminers die of disease and malnutrition on the goldfields.'

'But he'll be all right, won't he?'

'Can't promise. It depends on how much damage he has done to himself. His wife can see him, but no children. And I wouldn't advise you to visit either, with your baby so young. There are too many tropical diseases we don't know about.'

Another of the German ladies came running down the street. This one, the cook from the Royal Hotel, still in her apron. And a damn good cook too, the street cleaner remarked as she dashed past them. They watched as she ran on down towards the hospital, their curiosity roused, but then there'd been enough happenings in the lonely little town in the last twenty-four hours to keep the volunteer brigade comparing notes for days.

Matron told her nurse, the only trained nurse beside herself the hospital could afford; the other ladies were simply known as hospital servants.

'Turns out he lives here,' she said. 'Obviously one of the mob of immigrants that landed here last year.'

'Poor bugger. He wouldn't have known where he was when he got put ashore here. How's he doing?'

'He looks a sight better since you cleaned him up, and I think that makes him feel better, but he's a sick man.'

'He's still hanging on to that blue stone.'

'What blue stone?'

'I told you when we first brought him in, he had a rough old stone in his hand and he wouldn't let go. A totally useless bit of rock, practically embedded in the palm of his hand, and no way would he let go of it.'

'It might be a memento or something.'

'Or more likely he's convinced himself it's gold. You know how they get, these miners . . . half mad with the gold fever.'

'Did I tell you my brother found more than a thousand pounds in gold in the early Gympie days?'

'Goodness me, no! He's done well then?'

'Who knows? He ran off to New Zealand with a floozy. Left his wife and kid . . .'

Matron looked out of the window at a woman puffing up to the front door, untying an apron as she ran.

'This could be Mrs Zimmerman.'

'I know her. She's the cook at the Royal.'

Eva sat in the chair by Theo's bed, trying to remember the last time they'd talked, but she couldn't get past his lies about the horse, and his disappearance. His cowardly desertion of his family for the goldfields. No one had mentioned a horse now. Obviously that was gone too. He'd arrived back penniless. He didn't even have trousers to stand up in. Matron had ordered his clothes burned. Infection, she said. And lice. He was so ill, he had been covered in lice.

His wife was mortified. She wished Rosie had shut up. Had come to her first. But it wouldn't have made any difference, she supposed; she still would have run up here to see who it was, to confirm that her stupid husband had landed home at last, to embarrass her even further.

He didn't seem to know where he was. He was babbling about all sorts of things, sometimes in English, sometimes in German, and he looked crazy, with his hair shaved bald, leaving a white cap on his heavily tanned skin.

Eva sighed. She supposed she had better get back to work. Someone had to keep the family fed. She stood to leave but he grabbed her arm suddenly, so she spoke to him.

'Don't worry. I'll be back later. The nurse will look after you. You go to sleep.'

He still hung on to her, though, and with an effort dragged his other arm across to press something into her hand, then he fell back, exhausted.

'What's this?' she asked, staring at the heavy blue stone, but Theo was already drifting into sleep again.

Eva looked at it carefully, hoping she might find it valuable, but it was only a trinket, blue-painted and obviously varnished over that. Probably a talisman, a lucky stone, she thought, a stone that hadn't brought him any luck. She dropped it in her pocket and thought no more of it.

'Mr Zimmerman is back,' Eva told Mr Hackett.

'Oh, how lovely for you.' His voice was sincere but she could see his disappointment, and Eva was sustained by that, flattered. She had become fond of Mr Hackett over the last few months, and grateful to him for the care and attention he gave the children, but with Theo home she didn't suppose she'd see so much of him any more. That was a great pity, really sad, she mused as she stood at the gate to the school yard . . . Under other circumstances Mr Hackett and I would have been a good match. Hanni had said several times that she thought Mr Hackett was actually courting her.

'He is, Eva. It's obvious.'

'A gentleman can't court a married woman.'

'Not as you'd notice,' Hanni had laughed.

Neither of them had said that maybe Mr Hackett had been laying the groundwork in case Eva's husband did not return, but they'd thought it. Now that pleasant interlude was over, and once again she had Theo to deal with. One thing was for sure, she vowed, he wasn't getting a penny of her wages.

'What are you doing here?' Robie called to his mother.

She blushed. She never needed to come to the school, Robie always took Hans and Inge in and brought them home. Eva had put in an appearance on this occasion so that she could speak to Mr Hackett.

'I came to tell you that your father is back.'

All three children were ecstatic, dancing about, demanding to see him, but Eva told them they would have to wait a few days because he was not well, he was resting in the hospital. That was even more interesting to them, the hospital being a mysterious cottage that they viewed with awe, so their walk home brought a barrage of questions. Not that Eva didn't have a few of her own, and all concerning her errant husband.

Father Beitz was brought up to the Royal Hotel and established in a bedroom, despite his claims that a missionary should not be living in the lap of luxury.

'What about the others?' he demanded of Hubert.

'Don't worry about them. You'll be pleased to know that Lucas and Hanni are reunited; he has moved in with her. Turns out their problems were all a misunderstanding.'

'Of course they had to be. And if they had confided in me, I would have seen to it, but they had to go on their own way. But what about Max and Hans and Walther? Where are they living?'

'They prefer to stay at the commune.'

'Ah. Good fellows.'

'They've erected a tent, and are quite well organised.'

He did not tell Father Beitz that it was fortunate they had stayed there, since two men had arrived to arrange logging of their communal land.

Walther had been shocked. 'There must be some mistake. No logging here. We only take out a few of the big trees when we have to clear some land for our use. We may never clear the rest of the property, we hope to keep it in a pristine state to show future generations how beautiful it is.'

Then the loggers' spokesman, George Macken, had produced the title deeds to the property, and Walther had stared at them.

'Where did you get those documents?'

'Your priest brought them to me, so this shows we are entitled to log here. It's just a matter of working out where to start now, and I'll leave him our quote.'

'I think you mean Father Ritter, do you?'

'Yes.' It was Macken's turn to stare. 'Oh, God! Was he the one got shot?'

'I'm afraid so. And we would like those deeds back, please, Mr Macken. The parish priest, Father Beitz, is not in favour of any logging.'

Walther took charge of the precious documents and the loggers retreated.

'Why would Pastor Ritter do a thing like that?' Max asked, bewildered by these events.

'He wasn't a priest, remember?' his brother said. 'Least we don't think so. He was probably after the money for the trees. Lucky he didn't get away with it.'

'At least our title deeds are intact,' Walther said. 'I can put them back in Father's cabin box now; he'll never know they were missing.'

Mr Hoepper and Mr Dixon, both staying at the hotel, became firm friends, especially when Hubert was able to tell him that Father Beitz had declined to prefer charges against Keith for shooting him. He endorsed Keith's claim that it was an accident.

'Thank you, Father,' Dixon said. 'It was kind of you to say so.'

'Do not think I am tampering with the truth, sir. Keith did not intend to pull the trigger, of that I am certain,' Father Beitz told him, but did not enlarge. He was looking forward to discussing events with Tibbaling when time permitted. He truly believed that the evil spirit had been still at large, and that he had been the target, Otto's last spiteful act. And Tibbaling's opinion would be most interesting.

Nevertheless Dixon was grateful; the murder charge against Keith was hard enough to bear. He had engaged a leading Brisbane barrister to defend his son, and the lawyer was preparing to send a man to Hamburg to investigate the background of the victim, who, it appeared, might not have been a priest, and might even have been a criminal. This information was crucial to the defence and Dixon appreciated any help he could get. Hubert himself was able to supply a little information, at least somewhere for the investigation to start: the name of the Dean at the Seminary of St John in Hamburg, and details of Ritter's travel schedule from that city. He also recalled the possibility that the man's first name may actually have been Otto.

Hoepper and Dixon began to formulate a plan to help the commune. Hubert had mentioned that he intended to underwrite the building of a parsonage on the Lutheran estate and see what could be done about constructing permanent dwellings to house members who chose to live in a communal environment. J.B. Dixon was enthusiastic about such an endeavour. He wanted to help too.

'It's the least I can do,' he said. 'I'll donate a thousand pounds to your building fund. What do you say to that?'

'My word! It's wonderful! You are very generous, Mr Dixon.'

'Think nothing of it. But I would expect your Father Beitz to give evidence at Keith's trial. On his behalf, of course.'

'He would always do his civic duty,' Hubert said.

Though Father Beitz had insisted this was to be a private funeral, a very low-key service, the Meissners soon heard of all the drama from Rolf's relations across the river, and headed for town, unsure of what to expect. The rumours that had travelled fast to their doors were too confused to be taken seriously, and the first proof that something was amiss came when they were informed that the funeral service would be held in the local cemetery and not in their own church. Soon enough, they were to hear that Pastor Ritter really was dead, and, later, from Charlie Mayhew, an entirely different story about Keith Dixon. That he had actually fired their land. Deliberately.

In the end no one knew what to think, but they all gathered dutifully beside an open grave in the Bundaberg cemetery. All of the German community, that is, except for Rolf and Theo.

The Zimmerman children stood by their mother, Robie fascinated by the unfolding tale of shootings, and the spectacle of Father Beitz, with his shoulder bandaged and his arm in a sling, speaking to them from a large cane chair instead of standing to sermonise. This was exactly the wild adventure stuff eleven-year-old Robie had expected to find in this country, but until lately things had been disappointingly tame. Not any more, he mused, thrilled.

He looked at his younger brother, who wasn't paying any attention to the service, scratching instead at a nearby boulder with a lump of blue stone.

'Where did you get that?' he hissed.

'On the shelf in the kitchen. It's mine. Mum said I can have it.'

'Show it to me.'

Reluctantly, Hans handed it over.

Robie examined it. 'It's heavy as lead,' he whispered.

The stone was jagged, almost fish-shaped, and a good four inches long, a useless thing. Or maybe it could be used as a paperweight. Robie had seen a glass paperweight once, with snow in it, and had been most impressed, but this was an ugly thing. Nothing nice about it, not even the colour, a murky, milky blue.

He too began scraping at the boulder, deciding to scratch his name there as Father Beitz droned on and the pine coffin sat beside the open grave. Hans nudged him to give it back but he persisted, and then, curiously, the glazed blue paint started to chip off. Underneath the heavy camouflage, the stone was golden-coloured. Urgently Robie tugged at his mother's arm, but she kept shaking him off, eventually threatening to clout him.

Robie could stand it no longer. He slid slowly round the boulder and sped away. No one noticed except Hans and his mother, and both fumed. Hans contemplated running after him, but by now Eva had him by the collar, forcing him to face the front.

The sermon was based on the theme of the power of good over evil, but the old priest had little to say about the man he was burying. For the life of him, caught in this dreadful situation, he could not think of anything appropriate, though he did believe every man was entitled to a decent burial, so he simply waffled on to the assembly of bowed heads until he could reasonably conclude the service.

He was still rather weak, so Walther and Jakob took him back to the hotel in the wagon. On the way they passed young Robie Zimmerman, who was running back towards his mother.

'I saw that little wretch sneak off from the service. I'll have a word to his mother about that,' Father Beitz told Jakob. 'Just shows what sort of education those children are receiving in that heathen place. Who's that funny-looking fellow running after him?'

'I think he's the jeweller,' Jakob said, looking back at the little man in a black frock coat, who was hanging on to his top hat as he tried to keep up with Robie. 'I wonder what that's about?'

The wagon turned the corner, so they didn't see Robie fling himself into his mother's arms:

'Look! Gold, Mum, gold! The stone, it's gold. It's worth a lot of money.'

'You wait till I get you home, disgracing me like . . . What did you say?'

'Gold! This is gold,' he shouted, pushing the stone at her.

'That thing? Never!'

The man in the top hat puffed up to her and a crowd of mourners gathered to see what the fuss was about.

'It is gold indeed, madam. A very nice specimen too . . .'

'But look at it. Blue?'

'Ah. That's a very common ruse used by miners to avoid theft, and apparently successful in your husband's case. A very sensible gentleman, I would say, to use house-paint and varnish for camouflage.'

Eva raised her eyebrows. It was the first time anyone had called Theo sensible.

'It really is gold?' she spluttered.

'Oh my word it is.'

'Oh, God, and I nearly threw it away!' Eva turned deathly pale and fainted, but Lucas managed to catch her before she did herself any damage.

The jeweller handed his card to Lucas. 'Please inform the lady I should be delighted to do business with her, and I can guarantee the best price she would receive for that nugget, should she wish to sell.

'A nugget,' Robie breathed reverentially. 'A gold nugget!'

Coda

Bundaberg, 15 January 1878

My Dear Hubert,

What a pleasure it was to hear from you and to learn all about your travels through South Africa. That must have been a fascinating journey and we did receive three of your postcards, but I fear numbers one, four and six must still be wending their way in our direction, hopefully. I can quite understand how you must be happy to be home in Hamburg at last, to be able to sit by the fire and look out at the snow, but I daresay you'll be off somewhere exotic again next year. I must say I envy you that cold weather; last month, 16 December to be exact, the temperature rose to 106 Deg. F. and we nearly expired. By midday we'd decided to give up and seek refuge in the river for coolness. Freda's latest fad is swimming; our native friends have been teaching her and she is now quite good at it, and of course requiring that Karl and I learn. Fortunately Adele has escaped the regime so far. She is very well, I am happy to tell you, now, as she says, an old married woman of one year, but to Freda and me the joy of our lives. We are still counting our blessings that Karl should have been so fortunate as to wed your lovely daughter, and I promise you, Hubert, I will guard them with my life. Which reminds me that local scientists claim that mosquitoes are the cause of disturbing fevers and that we should avoid mosquito bites at all times. We are trying to do this anyway because they are miserable stingers, by use of nets, but if you could secure further information on this matter on which I am ignorant, I might then be able to assess what is an essential precaution for the family. We do have bed nets, but not the wirescreen doors, a popular innovation. I know the question is in your mind, and you are too polite to ask, so I am giving you a mind-rest: no, your daughter is not yet with child. No hurry, Freda says. Their house is looking smart compared to our farmhouse because Adele is so clever with the sewing of the prettiest curtains and things, while Freda would rather cook. I tell Karl we have the best of both worlds. And true enough, we had what they call a bumper crop last year. I never dreamed I'd end up growing sugar cane and be a partner with you, my dear friend, and others in the distillery, which is a huge place, to my mind. And so complicated you can't believe, but it begins working late this year and I hold my breath. Walther Badke's brewery is already turning out the best lager. You may have known the brand in Germany. I did not. But I recommend it. Lucas Fechner works for him; he is called floor manager, I think, and liking his job. I'm not sure of that title, but he now has a son called Jürgen, after his father, and they have bought the cottage that Eva Zimmerman was previously renting. You know that Theo brought home a nugget of great value. Well Eva sold it and promptly bought a house in Bourbong Street, in her name, and constructed a café in front. All this while Theo was recovering from his serious illness, which took months. When Theo discovered who actually owned the premises there were great ructions and it took Father Beitz all of his pastoral zeal to quiet them down. Theo is still cranky about it, never stops complaining, when he's around that is. Because he spends most of his time on the goldfields. Rolf says that it's in Theo's blood now; he'll be a gold miner for the rest of his days. Anyway, the café is going well, like the rest of us, pushing along.

Freda's pride and joy these days is our orchard, thriving it is, even with pineapples. Mr Jolly, who seems to be suited all right to being Member of the Parliament, says he'll start building the summer house on your seaside block soon, and Adele is all excited about that. Her project, she calls it. Rolf is interested to buy your blocks in town, but Adele says no, she hopes you'll settle here eventually, so you might need that good land. Worth a fair price now, it is.

There is an official Post Office in Bundaberg now, and public gardens, a soap factory and even a coach service to Maryborough, so it is becoming a settled town. No turning back now. When I first came here I wondered if it would survive, but here we are, new things every day. Thanks to you, Father Beitz has a nice house, and we raised enough to build two cottages and a communal centre, forming a very nice village square with a water fountain in the middle. Many German immigrants landing in this port have been staying there temporarily, which is a good thing for our little congregation. We are proud to be able to welcome them and give them shelter. Walther and Max Lutze still live there, as do two of Walther's cousins, both working at the brewery. Adele says Walther's fiancée is due from Germany soon, and so is my other son Eduard, who is to learn the workings of the rum distillery. I don't know if you heard that Keith Dixon was sentenced to life for the murder of Otto Haupt, but it has been cut back to twenty years because of all the confusion, and I think the fact that Haupt himself was a murderer. When you have time I would like to hear exactly how the police in Hamburg managed to identify him. Every Sunday we say a prayer for the repose of the soul of poor Father Ritter, who was foully murdered, and someone suggested a nice cross in his memory, but Father Beitz is not too keen on seeing that name about again. It bothers him. The new curate has an open-air school for the black children and loves teaching them; they are great singers, by the way.

With these many words I send my best wishes from all here, and just remembered in time to answer your question. No, J.B. Dixon did not keep his promise of donations to our community. Not a penny. I suppose he forgot with all the legal tangles.

Yours very truly,

Jakob Meissner

A Dream of Her Own

Benita Brown

It's a cold winter's night in 1906 but nothing can dampen the high spirits of Constance Bannerman and her fellow skivvy and best friend, Nella. For tomorrow, Constance can at last escape her life of drudgery at Doctor Sowerby's home in Newcastle by marrying her handsome sweetheart, the prosperous John Edington.

But Constance's last night of servitude is to end in terror. As a final act of spite, Mrs Sowerby throws her out of the house late that evening where she is met by the doctor's dissolute son, Gerald. In the front yard, surrounded by freezing fog, Gerald attacks and rapes her. Distraught and unsure of what to do, Constance marries John the next day with a heavy heart. She cannot tell John what has happened, for his is a respectable family, and shame will not allow her to reveal the truth to Nella. But the worst is yet to come, for John Edington himself has a shocking secret that will make Constance feel more alone than ever . . .

0 7472 6618 2

headline

After The Dance Is Over

Joan Jonker

There's never a dull moment when best mates Nellie McDonough and Molly Bennett get together. And there's always something to keep them busy in their Liverpool backstreet, like becoming private detectives to help a loved one – the results of which are funny, warm and wonderfully satisfying.

Then Nellie is walking on air when her daughter Lily hints that she will soon be setting a date for her wedding to Archie. But when news comes that will affect both the families, Molly sheds tears of happiness while her mate Nellie lifts her skirts and breaks into an Irish jig . . .

After The Dance Is Over continues the lively adventures of two of the most entertaining families you'll ever meet.

Don't miss Joan Jonker's previous Liverpool sagas:

'Hilarity and pathos in equal measure' *Liverpool Echo*

'Packed with believable, heartwarming characters' *Coventry Evening Telegraph*

'Touching, full of incident and tears and laughter' *Reading Chronicle*

0 7472 6614 X

headline

Rainbow Days

Josephine Cox

'You're everything to me. I would have to lose my life before I'd lose you.'

This is the vow Silas makes to Cathleen on the day he asks her to marry him. Throughout their childhood, their love for each other has grown stronger and now, in 1900, they start to plan a life together. But a jealous woman is determined to ruin their happiness and uses Silas's father – a good and honest man – to do so, forcing him to make a terrible sacrifice. As a dutiful son, Silas has no choice but to obey his father, and Cathleen must pay the bitter price. Separated, each is swept along to a place where it seems there is no love or peace and no way back . . .

Rainbow Days is the dramatic new tale of courage and heartbreak from the *Sunday Times* bestselling story-teller who has touched the hearts of millions.

'Impossible to resist' *Woman's Realm*

'Driven and passionate' *The Sunday Times*

'A Cookson by any other name' *Birmingham Post*

0 7472 5758 2

headline

Now you can buy any of these other bestselling books from your bookshop or *direct from the publisher*.

FREE P&P AND UK DELIVERY
(Overseas and Ireland £3.50 per book)

TO ORDER SIMPLY CALL THIS NUMBER

01235 400 414

or e-mail <u>orders@bookpoint.co.uk</u>

Prices and availability subject to change without notice.